THE TELEMACHIA:
A History
by Antimenes of Argos

Michael Barnes Selvin
2006

ISBN: 978-0-6151-3716-2

www.telemachia.com

www.lulu.com

a b o f - e

To Johnny

Ancient Greece

**IONIAN
SEA**
(The Large-Wide)

Boreas
Skiron   Kaikias
Zephyrus   ✴   Apeliotes
Lips   Euros
Notus

600 stadia
(68 miles)
(113 km)

ITALIA

ILLYRIA

EPIRUS

THESPROTIA

Cephallenia
(Samos)

Zacynthus

Ithaca

ACARNANIA

AETOLIA

Pindus Range

MACEDONIA

CHALCIDICE

THESSALY

Mt.
Olympus

PHTHIA
TRACHIS
DORIS
LOCRIS
PHOCIS
LOCRIS

ACHAEA

ELIS

ARCADIA

MESSENIA

LACONIA

ARGOLIS

BOEOTIA

ATTICA

EUBOEA

PELOPONNESE

THRACE

Propontis

CHERSONESES

Ilium/Troy

TROAS

PHRYGIA

MYSIA

Empire of
the Hittites

AEOLIS

LYDIA

IONIA

LYCIA

CARIA

Lemnos

Lesbos

Chios

Sporades

Delos

Cyclades

AEGEAN
SEA

Rhodes

Crete

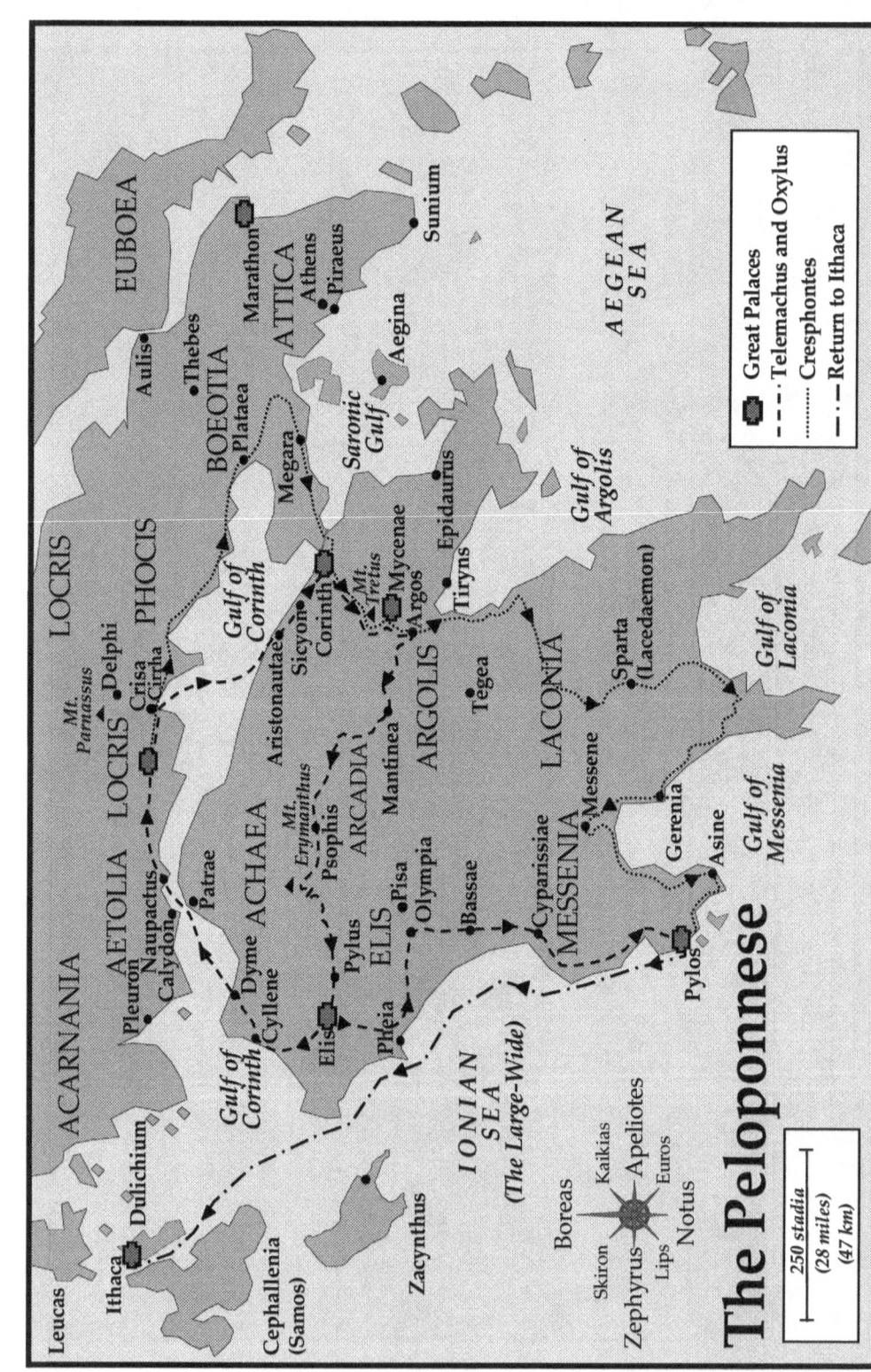

The Peloponnese

Legend
- Great Palaces
- – – – Telemachus and Oxylus
- ········· Cresphontes
- – · – · Return to Ithaca

Scale: 250 stadia / (28 miles) / (47 km)

Wind Rose: Boreas, Kaikias, Apeliotes, Euros, Notus, Lips, Zephyrus, Skiron

Labeled places and regions

ACARNANIA · AETOLIA · LOCRIS · PHOCIS · LOCRIS · EUBOEA · BOEOTIA · ATTICA · ACHAEA · ELIS · ARCADIA · ARGOLIS · LACONIA · MESSENIA

Leucas · Dulichium · Cephallenia (Samos) · Ithaca · Zacynthus

Pleuron · Calydon · Naupactus · Patrae · Dyme · Cyllene · Elis · Phleia · Pylus · Olympia · Pisa · Bassae · Cyparissiae · Messene · Gerenia · Asine · Pylos

Mt. Parnassus · Delphi · Crisa · Cirrha · Aristonautae · Sicyon · Corinth · Mt. Erymanthus · Psophis · Mantinea · Mt. Tretus · Mycenae · Argos · Tiryns · Epidaurus · Tegea · Sparta (Lacedaemon)

Aulis · Thebes · Plataea · Megara · Marathon · Athens · Piraeus · Sunium · Aegina

Seas and gulfs:
- AEGEAN SEA
- IONIAN SEA (The Large–Wide)
- Gulf of Corinth
- Gulf of Corinth
- Gulf of Argolis
- Gulf of Laconia
- Gulf of Messenia
- Saronic Gulf

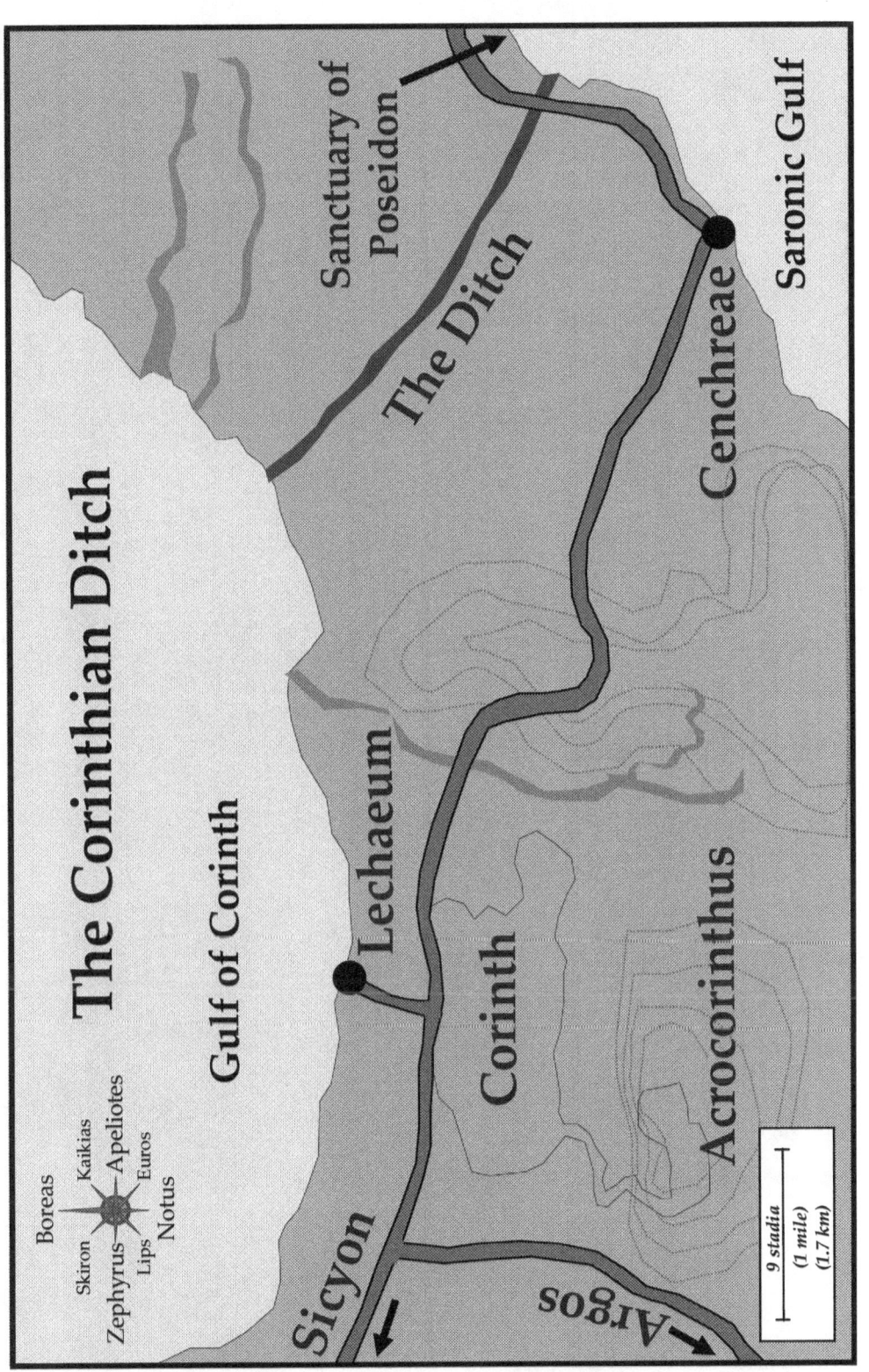

The Corinthian Ditch

Boreas
Kaikias
Skiron   Apeliotes
Zephyrus   Euros
Lips   Notus

Gulf of Corinth

Sanctuary of Poseidon

The Ditch

Saronic Gulf

Cenchreae

Lechaeum

Corinth

Sicyon

Acrocorinthus

Argos

9 stadia
(1 mile)
(1.7 km)

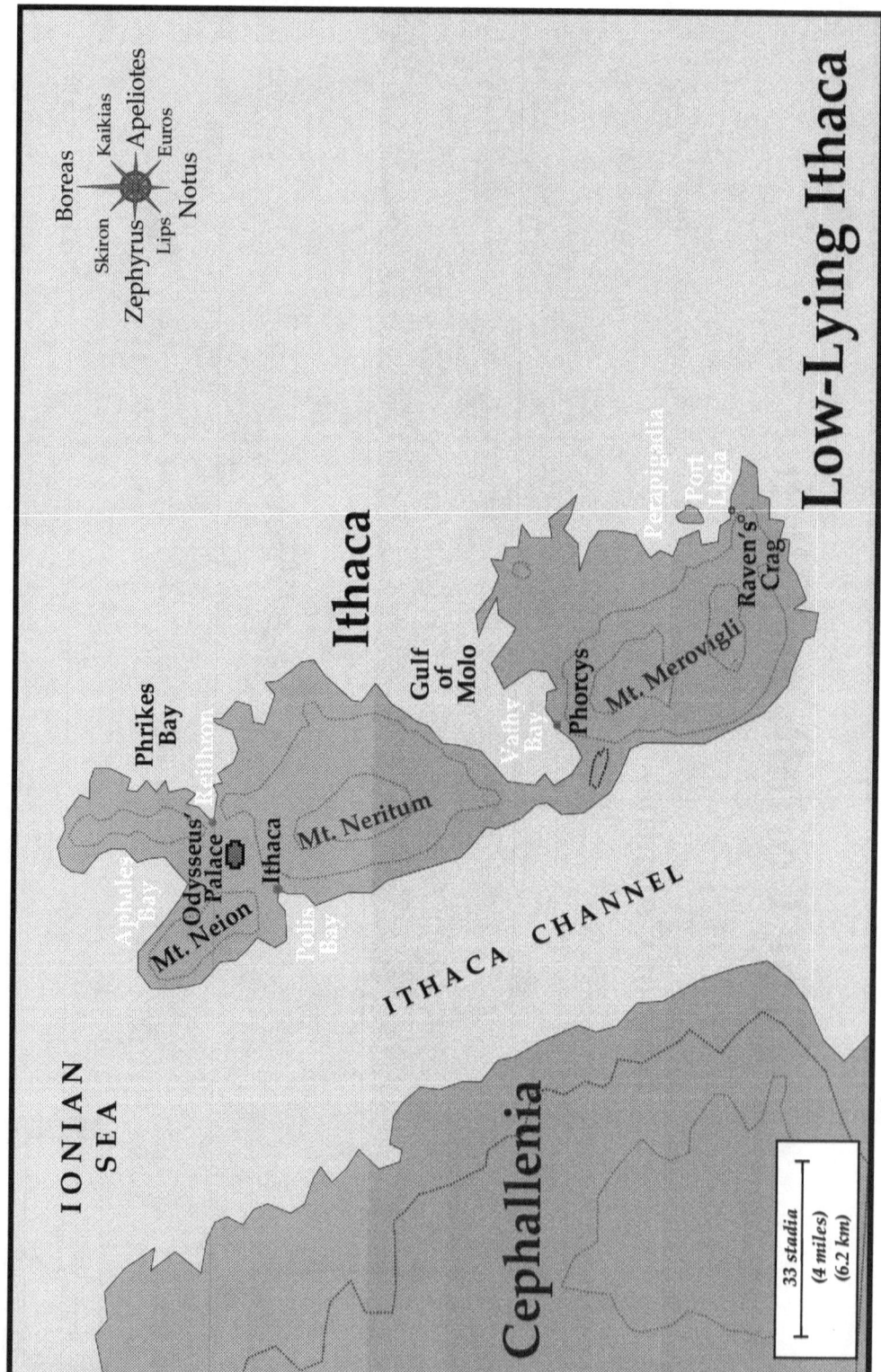

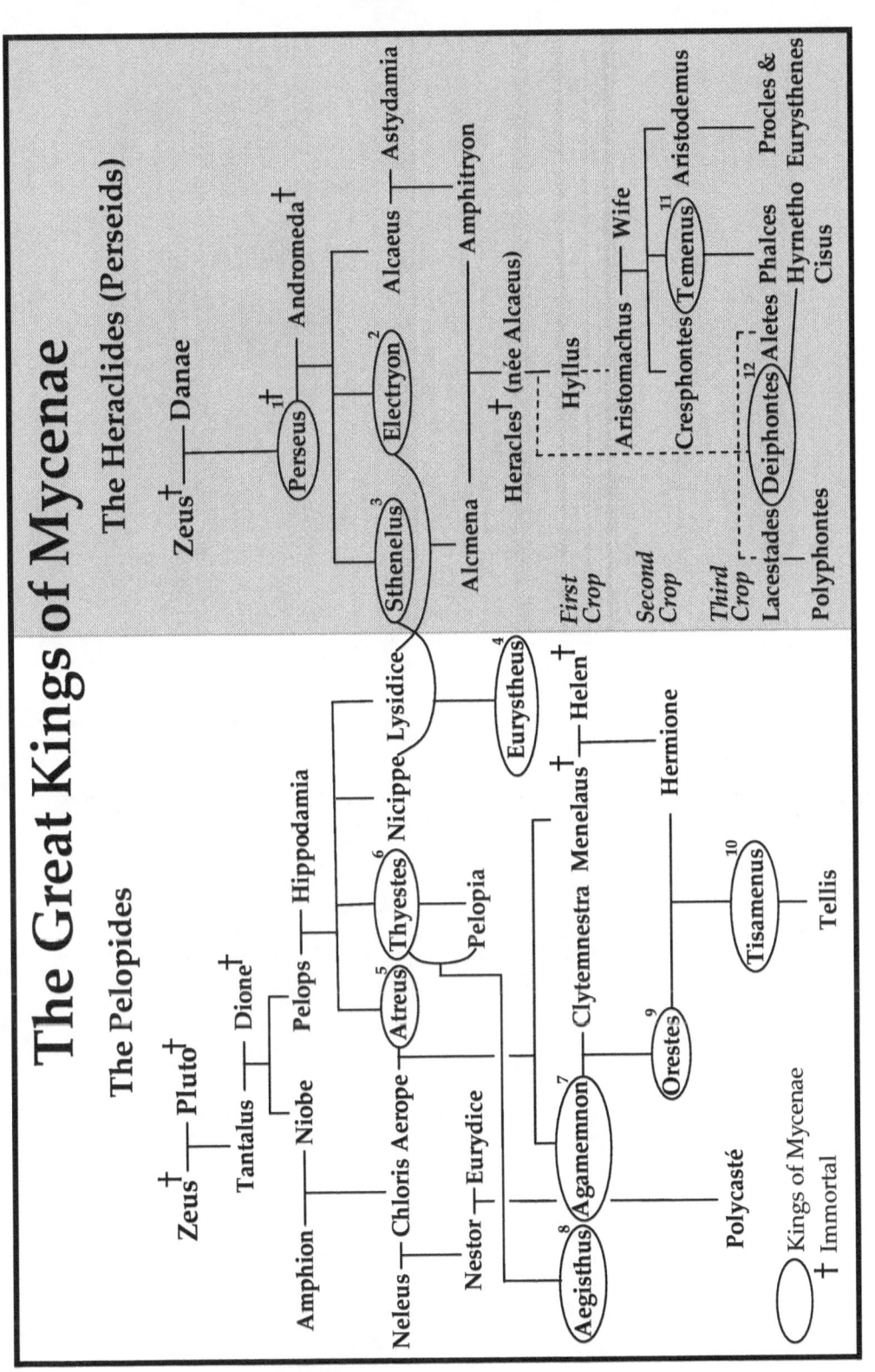

The Great Kings of Mycenae

The Pelopides

The Heraclides (Perseids)

Hesiod posed the question:
> "Come, Muse; sing not to me of things that are, or that shall be, or that were of old, but think of another song."

Homer replied:
> "Never shall horses with clattering hooves break chariots, striving for victory about the tomb of Zeus."

Hesiod, "The Contest of Homer and Hesiod"

I wish all strife could stop, among gods and among men, and anger too – it sends sensible men into fits of temper, it drips down our throats sweeter than honey and mushrooms up in our bellies like smoke. [Achilles]

Homer, *Iliad*, Book XVIII, lines 112-116 (Lombardo)

Invocation

Legends tell of aegis-bearing Zeus in the form of Cygnus the swan consorting with Leda in a mountain pool in Aetolia. That evening, her husband Tyndareus, King of Lacedaemon, had his way with her equally. She bore four children from a single egg: Helen and Pollux by Zeus and Clytemnestra and Castor by Tyndareus. Of course, the offspring of the lord of gods were immortal, and the offspring of the king, mortal. Castor and Pollux, the Dioscuri, the so-called striplings of Zeus, twin brothers, though differing in base nature, remained always faithful to each other in body and spirit. In truth, they refused to be separated even in the face of death and stood together against the will of Zeus. As a result, Zeus made Castor the evening star sinking into its earthly bed and Pollux became the morning star rising to the light of heaven: two brothers sharing one immortality.

Let us praise the Dioscuri for their indomitable love for each other: the twin deities of horse taming, boxing, waves and winds, and brotherhood.

All Hail Dioscuri, earthly sons of Tyndareus, immortal brothers of Helen, riders of swift horses!

I

I, Antimenes have entered the year 65 AD – the century only a few years older than myself. A time like so many others: when muddy Ares had the upper hand over fair-scented Apollo. A time when the Roman plague visited our cities, though the damage wrought by man was far worse. We attempt to coerce others by force of arms, by dint of argument or public brief, or by omens and prodigies to our own beliefs, rather than leading our own lives in virtue and respecting others to do so in their own fashion. As an historian, I see an era of division and separation, like the ever-expanding rings from a rock thrown into a still pond.

My wife came to my study this morning to tell me she was leaving with nary a word to the wise. That the gods reveal on occasion shockingly should be of no surprise to man. Alcathöe is joining an order of women propagating the Mysteries of Hera here in Argos as though she were a widow: my life, my love, my shared heart, the only moorage for my soul.

"You no longer have need of me," she explained. "Our children are grown and on their own. And you sit all day in your study with your followers and discuss events of no significance."

"What shall you go and do?" I asked her in my astonishment, ignoring her aspersion of my vocation."

"Attend to the Mysteries at the Sanctuary of Flowers."

The Mysteries is the common word for a number of new movements among people away from what they call "the distant gods," and it takes many forms. In Argos, it is a group of older women dedicated to aiding other women and to taking on a more spiritual and contemplative life. All over, people are seeking more personal and meaningful gods for their lives. These Mysteries eschew the time-honored gods and offer eternal life in wondrous surroundings. I would never have believed my thoughtful wife would be taken in by these charlatans.

"And what will I do without you?" I demanded, the anger and hurt welling within me.

"You can hire a serving person," she replied, misunderstanding my intent, most likely on purpose for she is nothing if not an intelligent woman. And then she challenged me as though I must defend myself, for women most often dispute by assault. "Give me one reason I should remain here."

O my foolish Alcathöe. How can I answer such a question in a moment's time? You stand at the door of my study, stamping your feet in indignation, demanding an immediate response, while I see your mind is fixed upon its course. My thoughts probe deeply within my heart to find the appropriate palliative to administer to your wounds, for I cannot claim ignorance of your grievances. Marriage is a storehouse of memories. A good marriage is one where the bonds of these memories have been carefully preserved and shared. Our marriage drifted during the years, particularly when the children departed the hearth, but also lately. I did not know to what extent, or at least, being honest with myself, did not choose to recognize how far it had strayed.

Though my mind is active, my hair has turned white and my ardor has waned, that is true. I enjoy my wine and meats more now and spend time in my garden. Where I was once lean, I have become fleshy, though not excessively so. My large hands have become soft and smooth from lack of physical labor. I have reached an age when one must contemplate the gods at closer view, just as a wave must consider the finality of breaking upon the beach. I must come to terms with my feelings, for, worst of all, Alcathöe, you give me no alternative.

As a consequence, I chronicle this history, the quintessence of my studies, and I dedicate it to you, Alcathöe, so that perhaps you may come to understand the feelings within my heart. I set out to tell my story, though not poetically as Homer might. Our modern Greek language is not attuned to the meter and rhyme of the ancient songs, though the Romans attempt such folly. I have spent my life in study of the ancients. They have much to offer us today in their outlook, and we have much to gain from understanding their struggles and failings. I have dined out on my studies, entertaining on trivia, which, though captivating at the moment, most often remained abandoned at the table. So for once in my life, I embark on this venture with a high seriousness to give thoughtful and heartfelt response to your demand: "Give me one reason I should remain here." I am a careful man, and my life is a delicate construction. You, Alcathöe, provide the underpinnings of all that I have assembled. I fear without you the entire edifice will crumble like the columns of our ancestors, leaving only hints of a past as rich and hopeful as a well watered meadow on an Elaphebolion* spring day.

That you are following the guidance of Hera, Queen of Heaven, gives me some encouragement. For behind most stories is the guilty, adolescent boy-god, Eros, the limb-loosener. But marriage is far more than Aphrodite's son would have us believe, or his mother, for that matter. Hera understands marriage and love better than any immortal and fought mightily for her husband Zeus. By recounting the romance of golden Telemachus, son of wily Odysseus, and his soft-eyed Polycasté, I hope you can glimpse into my heart, which I once shared so lovingly with your own. Hera, beloved by all the gods, shall lead us in the noble form of Penelope, wife of Odysseus and mother to Telemachus.

My studies of history and appreciation of its significance shall guide my endeavor. I am convinced that in staging life's dramas, the roles remain the same, while only the actors change. The Heroes of Hellas have come down to us dressed in shining armour, feathery helmets, and cloaks of brilliant hues. In fact, their lives were much like our own: full of seemingly unimportant decisions, mundane details, and humdrum trials. Only through the loss or faulty accounting of the past can we lose our course into the future.

My story begins with the death and apotheosis of Heracles – the defender of men and gods. His earthly spirit of good and evil, his craving for justice, his desperate search for the approval of his heavenly father, and his life-long yearning to return to his home in the Peloponnese pervade this history – and, yes, his anger. Of all Greek heroes, I believe Heracles is the greatest. His life encompassed great exploits and great madness as befits the son of god. Heracles' life and temperament for good and evil like a colossal pharos shall mark our way through these tumultuous waters.

---

* Elaphebolion is the Athenian equivalent to Roman March.

My goal though is to tell the life of Telemachus, son of Odysseus, his antagonisms, his resentments, and his labors to return to the island of his childhood and the ancestral throne of his father, namely, Ithaca. I tell the story of Telemachus, his wife Polycasté, daughter of wise King Nestor, and their sons as one might relate one's own life. For me, they are a noble family whose lives command retelling and in so doing bear on our own lives. Telemachus' return to Ithaca was a voyage on high seas, much like his father's, whose own return to Ithaca required as much as any mortal has ever ventured. Odysseus lost his kingdom, his country of birth, and, at the end of the day, his family. Telemachus' odyssey took a different path, but at the end of the day brought all of Heroic Greece to her knees. However, I tell the story of Telemachus, the Telemachia, confidently with the understanding that after any catastrophic conflagration, new plants and trees grow back rapidly in far greater profusion and soon fill the forests of time. I do so, Alcathöe, with a hopeful heart.

II

"Poisoned," Heracles called out in pain, feeling the end of life nearing. "Poisoned by the cloak of my faithless wife." His sons gathered closely about him as the once glorious man lay on his death bed in the throws of misery. He spoke resentfully and angrily:

"Even before my birth, jealous, cow-eyed Hera cursed me. From her fiery spite, my woeful future was cast. I was bathed in the icy waters of revenge and suckled on poisonous hatred.

"And now Deianira, my own wife, has poisoned me with the blood and spume of Nessus, the centaur. And the curses of the gods come to roost heavily, bitterly, and eternally. And you, arrogant Zeus, if truly that be your name, tested me through your neglect. Why did you forsake me, your own son? You failed as a father with your empty promises, and you failed as a god with your neglect.

"And women. I had countless and married three of them. But they were like hungry wolves and only added to my woes. Of issue, they made me wealthy, for of my offspring I count sixty-five with testicles. Women. Faithless beings all, so quick to jealousy, so full of themselves, so eager to please to obtain what they desire most: the mortal soul of their prey. I know them well. I can smell them. But now it is too late.

"Wait O Death. The anger consumes me and burns my flesh like a slashing sword. Odious Hades awaits my presence. Hera, Zeus' whore! I struggled mightily against your evil and labored for the defense of all mankind. What more could I do?

"And now I say to you, my sons, I have no more time. My will has lost its power to take me from this bed. Listen carefully. Hyllus, you must marry Iole, for I earned her properly by slaying her father and brothers. I charge you, Hyllus, to lead your brothers to take what is rightfully mine: the Peloponnese. This precious earthly jewel is mine, and it is ruled by imposters. Hera stole it from me before my birth. And then when I earned it back by dint of my labors, the land of my ancestors was again taken from me. The Peloponnese is a flowered land of songs and dances, fresh salty breezes, and unhurried, sunny days: a land of fishes, grapes, olives, and citrus fruits. I charge you to take back what is yours by hook or crook and not rest until you have done so. I cannot go to the other world until you grant me this."

Heracles' sons hesitated, for they barely knew this man lying before them and greatly feared him. They nodded, their faces full of impotence and terror. Hyllus, the only son brave enough to look his father in the eyes, finally agreed for them all:

"Yes, father, we will not rest until the Peloponnese is ours."

"Carry me to Mount Oeta," Heracles continued, his anger mounting, for he knew well his sons' failings, "and build a great pyre, so that Zeus may view my descent to Hades, and though a tear has never fallen from my eyes, perhaps now as I face an eternity of darkness it is a time for tears. Pity me, for the gods have never seen fit to aid me and have treated me only with vast contempt. But tears offer cold comfort. My bequest to you, my sons, is the bountiful Peloponnese. To my lovers, I give not a fig."

And so his sons carried Heracles, still clinging to life, to Mount Oeta, and placed him on a pyre of fresh cut pine boughs covered in dry needles. His sons could not bring themselves to light the conflagration, standing with their heads fixed firmly to their chests like the cowering children they were. From his bier, Heracles screamed at them to stop their cowardice and to take on manly courage. In the end, the frustrated and dying Heracles had to barter his bow and arrows to a stranger passing by with his flock of sheep. Poeas, son of Thaumacus, warily regarding the young men attending their father, set fire to the dry kindling. The flames rose into the sky, and the smoke wafted into the heavens with a thunderous peal of lightning. The mighty hero Heracles passed from this world...but not to where he expected.

Some three generations and more after his death, the progeny of Heracles, now known throughout Hellas as the Heraclides, had failed to return to the Peloponnese. The war in Troy had been fought and won, and those Achaean veterans who would return had done so, and their sons and grandsons had taken office. Apollo's Oracle of Delphi again repeated the same message of success to the Heraclides' popular leader, Cresphontes:

"You will triumph over the Peloponnese, but only with the counsel of the three-eyed one, and not until the third crop bears fruit."

III

On the prow deck of a merchant galley, Telemachus, son of Odysseus, huddled against the freezing wind and sleety sea spray washing against the high bow. He wrapped himself in his heavy woolen cloak, pulling it over his head and around his bare legs held tightly against his chest. One hand tightly gripped a carved wooden stay to hold himself in place on the heaving deck. Still his body shook with cold. He had to laugh: "thick weft on thin warp," his mother Penelope always said, as though the solution to all miseries lay with a well woven cloak.

The twenty-oar merchantman had departed from Pheia on the coast of Elis with the first golden rays of Eos, the goddess Dawn, heading to the island of Zacynthus, just off the coast of the Peloponnese. The rough and tumble seas lifted the ship on watery crests and dashed it into deep troughs. It was nearly impossible for the sailors to keep their long ash oars in the frothy sea and still maintain the cadence of the *keulestes'* drumbeat. The sail luffed and pulled at the *kaloi* and *podes*ˑ lines, and the ship pitched and rolled at Poseidon's behest. What was ordinarily a half-day sail would take considerably longer this day.

On the whole, merchant ships stayed close to the Gulf of Corinth, where they could scuttle ashore to avoid bad weather. Ships did not venture far off the coasts or did so only with the knowledge they were then in the hands of the capricious gods. This day, the merchant ship had no option but to leave the sheltered gulf and brave the earth-shaker Poseidon's wrath, since the ship's two passengers had been summoned to a meeting with Cresphontes, son of Aristomachus, archon of the Heraclides, and one of the most powerful men in all of Hellas.

"This was a mistake," Oxylus admitted.

ˑ Ropes controlling the declination and setting of both mast and sail.

For next to Telemachus huddled another man, the smaller of the two by far. Both men rode horses for a living: one for pleasure and one for pain, for the latter was a military man, a freebooter, whose small size belied his achievements on the bloody fields. In fact, Oxylus, son of Haemon, was about the size of a well-fed twelve-year-old. His curly, dark hair and beard merged without a single spot of gray, and his eyes sparkled from an olive complexion – second pressing.

"Mistake?" Telemachus asked. He was known as the greatest horse tamer in all the Peloponnese. In fair weather, his long golden ringlets fell about his neck, encircling salty gray eyes, as gray as Athene's, and a trim flaxen beard. Whereas his father Odysseus was short and thick and ugly as a giant woolly ram, as Agamemnon had called him, Telemachus was tall, light boned, and quietly strong-willed, taking after his mother's side of the family.

The third man on the prow deck was the white-haired captain, standing upright against the force of the irate winds and waves, his long braided beard sweeping out behind him, his multihued cloak flying in the gusts, and his bare legs as knobby and nimble as a young goat. He shouted orders to the helmsman. Both Telemachus and Oxylus scrutinized his face for signs of alarm, for they imagined a chilly and inhospitable grave in the depths.

"All works in their season, in particular, sailing," the captain shouted to his passengers. "We should have hauled this crate of bones out by now and packed him with stones to keep off the raging winds."

"Now he tells us," Oxylus said. "This was all a mistake. We should be before the warmth of our hearth enjoying the fruits of Dionysus."

"For this to work, we must confront Cresphontes," Telemachus said seriously, ignoring the captain and continuing their on and off discussion over the last few days. "He looks on us as servants."

"I have been treated as a servant by many men. That is not so terrible. The difficulty with Cresphontes is not knowing what thoughts lie beneath the charm."

"Underneath his charm, he is deviously plotting our demise, put aside only by our usefulness," Telemachus replied. "We can trust him as far as you would a hard stallion with a blinking mare."

9

Cresphontes, son of Aristomachus, was the elder statesman of the Heraclide family. The demands by Heracles on his funeral pyre had fallen on his shoulders. The legacy of his ancestor was Cresphontes' sole ambition and had been his entire life: to return to rule over the Peloponnese. The Oracle of Delphi foretold once again that without the necessary counselors-at-war the third attempt to return to the Peloponnese would fail, just as the other two had failed. Cresphontes was not yet convinced that Telemachus and Oxylus were the necessary counselors, but he had requested their presence just the same at the meeting on Zacynthus.

I, Antimenes trust the description of Cresphontes by Euripides, the great writer of epic plays: "an unimaginative man who understood the inner-fears of his peers and subjects and could manipulate them with facility." Alas, only fragments of Euripides' drama "Kresphontes" have been preserved. Nevertheless, we know as leader of the Heraclides, Cresphontes presented the family's case on many occasions before the king and assembly in Athens. Though lacking oratorical skills, his views were taken seriously based on his fame in the Peloponnese and the resources of the family in Attica. Unskilled in formal speeches, Cresphontes often caught himself in foolish statements, yet he could converse with common people with ease and gain their fealty. This flair gained him vast popularity and the moniker "defender of the people," just as Heracles before him had been so-named. As is the wont of Greeks, it was never quite clear whether this name was respectful or mocking.

Telemachus and Oxylus were making their first appearance before the Heraclide leaders. On the island of Zacynthus, the Heraclides could meet in secrecy from the rulers of the Peloponnese. Zacynthus guarded the Gulf of Corinth and, along with the islands of Cephallenia, Ithaca, Dulichium, and Leucas, had once constituted the kingdom of Odysseus, Telemachus' father.

They shared much in common, Telemachus and Oxylus. Both were sons of kings and had been born to rule. Both were raised in uncommon circumstances. Both lived in exile from their homelands. Both knew horses and war. And both harbored the same smoldering ambition: to return to rule.

Telemachus came from Elis, a small Peloponnesian town, with more cattle than people. He lived there in exile from Ithaca with his mother, his father, his soft-eyed wife, Polycasté, and their twin sons verging on manhood. Oxylus, too, had been exiled from his home at a young age. As the son of Haemon, King of Aetolia, he had been raised in Pleuron and high Calydon. As a young man, competing at games using quoits, he had missed the mark, striking and killing his brother, Thermius. His father would have killed him on the spot, if clearer heads had not prevailed, and, instead of death, he was banished for life.

The Heraclides wanted Telemachus to act as their hipparch, or cavalry general, and ambassador. He was considering their offer not because he believed in their cause, nor because he trusted them as leaders. Far from that. The Heraclides offered him a way of fulfilling his lifelong ambition of returning to rule over his homeland in Ithaca. As a young man, his father Odysseus had ruled over Ithaca and the offshore islands and had led twelve long ships from Ithaca and its sister islands to join the coalition at Troy. In Troy, Odysseus won fame, but he failed to return to Ithaca for nineteen long years. As his son Telemachus verged on manhood, suitors for the hand of Odysseus' wife Penelope gathered. These men hoped to win the throne of the king by marrying the queen. When Odysseus returned from Troy belatedly, all changed. He sent all one hundred and eight suitors to Hades. Fair Penelope, no longer in widow's robes, suddenly had a husband. And Telemachus, as abruptly, had a father of whom he had no memory. Now, Telemachus desired nothing more than to come full circle and return to rule, just as his father, grandfather, and great grandfather before him had ruled, just as he had been raised and educated to do.

The Heraclides wanted Oxylus to be general of their infantry. He had fought among the best of his time and could recount tales of men at their most excellent and most wicked...for such is the power of warfare and battles, allowing men to discover the substance of their souls. He had tasted the bitter ire of Ares and Apollo, and he felt that mortal man was far better off when these vengeful gods remained ensconced in their palaces in heaven.

"Furl the sail, the gods be dammed," the captain shouted. "We circle about ourselves as a cur after its own tail. The windy brothers are contrary and difficult today. May they suffer in Tartarus as their forebears."

The eternal groaning sounds of the sea drawing back forever lament the lack of a father. For Pontus the sea was born of Gaia without the aid of a father. Sailors called Pontus "the large-wide" and believed its endless waters protected them and provided for them. In ancient times, they prayed to Pontus. Since the earth was flat and circular, with Hellas at the center, the sea sheltered mortals from the treacherous currents of Oceanus flowing round the world. Pontus dominated all life, purveyor of rain and fog and breezes.

But Zeus and his siblings rebelled and sent their ancestors, the Titans, to Tartarus, where they remain to this day. With the Titans cast out, the sea became the domain of Poseidon, the brother of Zeus. Poseidon brings food and sustenance to all mortals, allows passage and travel, mitigates the harsh winters, and endows the earth with magnificent vistas and endless motion as a cradle rocks a baby. Poseidon is the most powerful of all immortals, save his brother Zeus. The large-wide sea reflects the two faces of Poseidon: on the one hand, a loving father providing assistance and sustenance to his children, and, on the other, an untrustworthy, vengeful immortal sending mortals into the depths of Hades, never to return.

Pontus and Gaia became lovers, and their descendants, Astraios and Eos, gave birth to the mighty-hearted Anemoi, the living winds. They continue to oversee the large-wide sea under Poseidon's dominion. The two dominant windy brothers forever clash: cruel Boreas frosts the earth from the cold climes, while wet and foggy Notus gusts from the land of the Ethiopians favored by the gods. Their lesser brothers, clear-blowing Zephyrus from the Elysian Plain and sweet jasmine-scented Apeliotes from the summer sunrise, blow steady without pretension; mariners love these lesser brothers, for they are gentle and helpful.*

Two deck sailors ran to the mast and raised the sail, securing it to the *epikrion*, or yard arm, freeing the ship from the breaths of the conflicting winds. Without the sail, the sailors had to put their backs into rowing, but they were used to it, and free of the shifting winds,

---

* The ancient Greeks did not think of the directions of north or south, but rather headings were given by the Anemoi, or personified winds. Boreas is the wind coming from the direction of Macedonia (north), and Notus is the wind coming from the direction of Ethiopia (south). See the wind rose on the map of Ancient Greece.

they could plot a course as the sea crow flies directly toward the distant island, barely visible in the mist.

Merchant vessels were built broad in the beam, allowing space for cargo. In most ships, officers and passengers occupied two narrow decks, one on the prow and the other at the stern. Both prow and stern rose high above these small decks. The prow sported figureheads or painted insignias and was often covered in bronze metal for protection against rocks. On the lower deck, the sailors sat on two longitudinal benches on either side of the cargo space, their long ash oars reaching well beyond the hull. A normal complement of twenty rowers could pull a ship at a slow pace. A single, large, square rigged sail on a yard suspended from halyards, extending beyond the sides of the ship, could move the ship in a good wind. In following or running winds, the ship could sail slowly or utilize a combination of rowers and sail. In contrary winds or frontal gales, these ships could barely keep afloat, tacking was impossible, and in such conditions they had to furl or haul the sail and quickly seek shelter under the might of the rowers. Merchant vessels were useless in battle, slow moving and unable to jibe rapidly. A helmsman steered with two giant paddles lashed to the stern deck and commanded the starboard and port rowers. The *keulestes* controlled the tempo of the rowers by the frequency of his drumbeat. As in all times, the captain ruled his ship.

"Now, we are making progress," the captain shouted to his passengers. "We were fast headed to the Doghouse."

"I doubted ever seeing land again," Oxylus admitted.

"You have to accept the will of the gods," Telemachus bantered, knowing well Oxylus' aversion to the gods.

"I have seen too many men shuttled off in Charon's boat across the dread waters of the Styx. The interests of gods and men rarely align. Military men know that the gods are a crutch for weak-minded farmers."

"You who pray to ivy-haired Dionysus and laughter-loving Aphrodite," Telemachus admonished.

Oxylus ignored Telamachus. "I have encountered many men such as Cresphontes. They take the fates of men in their hands willingly and then ignore any sense of duty or consequence. They make excuses for themselves and find fault in others." Like many close friends, their conversation could jump days or even weeks without loss of a beat.

"You left good cheer in Elis," Telemachus said.

"Good cheer requires terra firma, warmth, and dryness."

"Cresphontes is not as wily as he believes," Telemachus continued. "The Athenians are reticent to support him, though they would rejoice his victory over the Pelopides. But I am convinced the Heraclides do not stand a chance of winning this contest."

"That is why we are invited to the dinner party."

"I am not sure we can make a difference," Telemachus replied.

"Once again, you underestimate yourself, my friend."

"I am only being truthful."

"That is your problem. Devious Cresphontes suffers no such scruple."

"Then why, Oxylus, my brother, are we attending this assembly?"

"We have much to gain: you, Ithaca; and I, Elis."

"We must consider the words of Heracles: 'Never forgive your adversaries, nor trust your allies.'"

"A miserable adage for someone intent on living peacefully," Oxylus replied.

The two friends looked at each other, as miserable as two dogs tied to a post in a winter downpour.

"My wife believes we are being taken in by these Heraclides."

"Women believe they can see into the depths of men's souls," Oxylus replied.

"You have never known the joys and tribulations of a strong woman."

"I prefer the agreeable wiles of harlots."

"Polycasté is against this venture," Telemachus continued. "She fears for our sons. She fears for the rule of her family. And she fears for herself."

The cold and damp halted the conversation. Telemachus knew he could never trust the Heraclides. He had traded horses at their palace in Marathon, and he recognized their hunger. Twice before, the Heraclides had taken armies into the Peloponnese to fight the ruling Pelopides. And twice, they had been defeated and humiliated. Thousands of men had died. King Orestes of Mycenae and Argos, son of Agamemnon and head of the Pelopide family, now ruled most of the Peloponnese, having consolidated many of the countries, including Laconia, Arcadia, and Achaea. Now he and his son, Tisamenus, were eyeing Messenia, ruled by King Nestor and his family – the family of soft-eyed Polycasté, Telemachus' wife.

The Heraclides had offered Telemachus an opportunity. In return for his services to them in their latest (and last, according to the prodigies) attempt to return to the Peloponnese, Cresphontes offered Telemachus rule over Ithaca and the offshore islands. They had also offered the throne of Elis to Oxylus. Both regions were small, without resources, under populated, and isolated from the large Aegean cities. They held no attraction to the Heraclides. In this way, they hoped to attract the two counselors-of-war to their cause without any cost to themselves.

But this same bargain placed Telemachus on a direct course in conflict with his wife's family. As a distant relative of the Pelopides, his father-in-law Nestor had ruled in Messenia since before the war in Troy. And if the Heraclides were successful in their return to the Peloponnese, they would most likely continue into Messenia. How could Telemachus enter into an agreement that could very well spell the end of Nestor's long rule of Messenia and the destruction of Nestor's family?

Before Telemachus and Oxylus could come to any agreement with the Heraclides, though, much had to be considered. And, of course, all dramas on earth must be rehearsed in heaven.

IV

As the merchant ship drew near the island of Zacynthus, the immortals initiated a discussion on the summit of Mount Olympus, home of the gods. The long-haired gods were assembled in the great hall of the palace of Zeus, father of immortals and mortals alike. Sunlight fell onto the white marble floors and walls, reflecting dazzling luminosity and warmth into every corner. Zeus sat on the highest throne at the far end of the hall, beneath a giant, arched clerestory, thunderbolts in each hand, the tireless sun lighting him so brightly the immortals could barely glance in his direction. The other gods sat in two rows down either side of the chamber. Each god reclined on a unique throne of marble and gold fashioned by the glorious smith, Hephaestus, the greater gods closer to Zeus and the lesser ones at the far ends.

The newest immortal among them, although he had been resident for more than half a century, sat at the end of the brilliant white hall. Next to him, sat the daughter of Hera, Hebe, his wife, with her beautiful feet and delicate countenance. He looked as godly as the rest of them, a head taller than even Ares, the fearful god of war. Still shy and nervous at his role, he rarely spoke for fear of offending the worthies. This immortal was none other than the hero Heracles, still astounded at his fate. Heracles politely drank his nectar, while the other gods slurped greedily from their golden chalices. The young Trojan boy, Ganymede, ran the hall, constantly refilling their chalices from a dazzling golden ewer.

The war between the Heraclides and the Pelopides weighed on Zeus' mind, for war between families can never have a cheerful outcome. The sire of the gods, his huge head surrounded by a glory of white hair, spoke, at first gently, but growing in urgency:

"The world has fallen into disorder. Mischief abounds. No sooner do the long-haired Hellenes finish one foreign excursion than they begin another. And when they are at home for any time, they battle among themselves. They do this with the counsel of various immortals among us, who take sides and stir up emotions. Who would gainsay such activity? Do you deny, my wife Hera, in your jealousy and spitefulness that you caused no end of suffering to Heracles, who now sits among us? Do you, Apollo my son, deny destroying a large number of Hellenes at Troy because of an argument between two simple mortals over a silly woman? And my brother Poseidon, do you deny destroying the city of Scheria by burying it under a mountain and sending all the Phaecians to Hades – people of great repute and of no evil intentions, your own flesh and blood?

"Now we well know that Cresphontes, one of the descendants of Heracles, seeks to rule the Peloponnese and is supported in this endeavor by some among us. These contests among gods have not ceased since long before that ill-fated war in Troy, where many of our mortal sons and daughters lost their lives. Two generations have passed since this unfortunate affair, and now it begins again.

"Must I remind you, mortals are not like us. They suffer from the knowledge of their short season, and their sorrows are interminable. Mortals know little of life and death and take both lightly. They waste the former and fear the latter, and they fail to appreciate the importance of either. We deathless gods accept this without due consideration. For Time is both the boon and horror of mortals. They must watch their bright-eyed children grow up to accept the boundaries of their lives, then become gray and doddering, while our timeless lives stretch out before us in ever-flowing sunny days.

"Do not mistake the words of Zeus. Forsooth, the nobility of the earth, and of mortals thereon, is born of their short season: the constant changes embedded in their being and the relentless progression of Time. In our dustless domains in the sky, this may seem trifling. But we ask you to consider this. We cannot punish man for trying to be too much like us, while urging him forward in nefarious pride and foolishness of heart. We must help man embrace his earthly existence and find grace in his short season. We cannot offer him immortality, but we can at least offer him hope on earth.

"Now, our children, hear us," Zeus bellowed. "Zeus foresees a time when the oracles will fall mute and when the smells of burning fat of gracious sacrifice will no longer rise to our abodes. We may find ourselves endlessly wandering in the depths of Tartarus, a fate we forced upon our godly parents, the Titans. Mortal man has come from a golden age of perpetual spring and freedom from disease, to a silver age of seasons, to this brazen age of violence and greed. In the future, man will move to an iron age of pestilence and hopelessness, where fathers and sons disagree, where oaths have no value, where strength makes right, and where rule is by envy and evil. Righteous Deucalion and his faithful wife, Pyrrha, cast stones to create the current hardscrabble race of man. Prometheus, aided by our daughter Athene, angered us by giving hopeful fire to these mortals..."

When Zeus hesitated in his speech, Hera, his wife and sister, spoke up.

"Son of Cronos, father of all the gods, why have you called us together? Have I not settled the differences I once had with your son, Heracles, who now sits among us with his wife, Hebe, my own daughter? Does not Ganymede fill our cups? And does not the nemesis of Heracles, Eurystheus, reside in dark Hades? We gods have settled our differences. Aphrodite, Athene, and I are no longer at odds over silly matters. Are not Helen and Menelaus living among the immortals in the Elysian Fields? Priam and the people of Troy, the dearest to your heart, lie buried under the earth at your own instigation. Is that not as you would have it?

I believe that as always," Hera added, "you have something up your sleeve you are not telling us. Some challenge you are setting up. Some mortal offspring you champion."

The father of gods and men grew angry: "Wife, your constant criticism of us we understand and have come to accept. But you are not listening. You of all the gods fail to hear our words. We are saying that we need to withdraw from the affairs of mortals. Zeus may have been an offender in the past, but we are telling you, desist or suffer the consequences." A deafening clash of thunder resonated across the heavens.

At the terrible roar, the immortal gods looked at one another. Their fear of the anger of the sire of gods silenced them. Only the innocent son of Zeus and Hera, Hephaestus, the hard-working god of artisans, ventured to speak.

"Man is wrought a delicate balance, Sire – full mixture of love and evil. Somehow, we must strive to maintain his beautiful alloyed strength without changing his base nature. For even a common metal can be made to reflect the full goodness of the sun and starry skies."

"Man is no mere alloy of metals, my gentle son," Zeus replied mildly. "Man is our creation. We fashioned him, and now we cannot fail him for he is headed in a mistaken direction."

Aphrodite spoke up. "I would remind our father that the end of Odysseus' life is at hand."

Apollo stopped stroking his lyre and joined in. "I think we must remember some of the lies he told and people he betrayed to sack your favored city of Troy. Honesty was never his strength. He inherited this from his grandfather, Autolycus, the cattle thief."

"We are well aware of the life of Odysseus," Zeus said. "And why, in the absence of our daughter Athene is this subject of such paramount importance?"

"Sire," Apollo replied, "Many gods were wounded in that war. Ichor from our bodies spilled on mortal grounds. That cannot be allowed to happen again."

"We are more troubled by continuing discord among the gods, Apollo my son," Zeus said. "There will be many wars in the age of man. This battle between families of the Pelopides and Heraclides cannot serve a good purpose, particularly when the god Heracles is among us today."

Heracles smiled nervously.

Zeus began again: "We would like to await the return of Athene before we seal the fate of Odysseus. As to the war in the Peloponnese, we suggest that we watch this closely. We saw the first generation of Heraclides begin their return before the war in Troy, as they did not understand the message of the gods. The second generation fared no better. What say you, Heracles?"

All the gods turned toward Heracles and his wife.

"Sire," Heracles began hesitantly, "and most honorable of gods, of all men, gods and mortals alike, my father, on earth my anger held too much sway over me. I see that today. But I was born of anger, and I was sorely tested, spilling the blood of countless men. Most deserved their fate, but others may have suffered wrongly. As you are fully aware, my only intent was righteousness, my only weapon, vengeance. I only fought for liberty and justice, which were both withheld from me. Others may have had reasons for me to suffer as I did and perhaps it was just a test as I now understand, but I only want justice for my family and what is rightfully owed to them. By right of birth and by obligation, the Peloponnese is mine, and the death of my son, Hyllus..."

"Thank you, Heracles," Zeus interrupted. "One will learn soon enough the ways of the gods." Zeus paused. "We will once again delay the war in the Peloponnese for there are too many strings that must be knotted before this is allowed to proceed. Apollo, see to it. We are afraid that this may be painful, my son, Heracles, but you must assume your godly mantle and enlarge your view of mortal man. Hermes, off you go to Aeaea to the island of our sister Circe, to initiate the course of Odysseus' fate. And, Hermes, see that you set your mind to this one thing and not become distracted by concerns of mortals – and I am talking about your relentless pursuit of vengeance for the death of your mortal son, Myrtilus, and your quest for the love of Penelope, daughter of Icarius. Better to allow these mortals to suffer their own lives. Hear us well, all you gods, on this account, no mischief, for Odysseus will join us soon enough. And he will be the last mortal ever to do so."

After this, the good cheer returned. The gods feasted on ambrosia and drank nectar poured from an ever-flowing golden ewer and listened to the songs of the Muses accompanied by Apollo's lyre. They conversed cheerfully, late into the pleasant evening on the affairs of heaven and earth.

Meanwhile, nearing the port of Zacynthus, the captain yelled out to his two passengers, "the gods have thrown us under the lee of Mount Elatos, but not free from worry."

"And what does that mean, old man?" Oxylus called back, annoyed with the man and tired of the constant motion and cold dampness.

"For landlubbers, that we are through the channel currents and protected from the blustery winds by the island itself. We may arrive before Helios drives his mares into Oceanus. But it looks as though we are expected...or at least I pray such is the case."

The two old friends looked out from under their soggy cloaks at the sheltered harbor in the distance. The sky had cleared, and the falling sun was lighting the distant mountains. In their discomfort, Telemachus and Oxylus had ignored the approach of the island and the shadowed bay of Zacynthus. They were stunned to see a giant black warship, of some fifty oars churning the seas, riding high above the waves, striking its gold and Aegean blue colors – the flag of the Heraclides – its sail furled for ramming, and its threatening bronze covered battering prow headed directly for them.

V

The Heraclide soldiers waited with great impatience for the contest to begin. They stamped their heavy sandals in the dust, making as much noise as possible and called out to each other about their mothers or sisters. The family remained inside the palace.

Oil lamps ringed the Cyclopean stone walls of the courtyard, casting a fiery yellow luminance into the rising dust. Even the full moon provided scant illumination within the court, as the constellations Pleiades, daughters of Atlas, and strong Orion slipped into the misty sea. The season of fall plowing had begun. About two hundred Heraclide soldiers were assembled in small groups in the open space, holding their ubiquitous blue cloaks about them, even though the evening had set rainless and balmy on Zacynthus. The soldiers ranged around an open space about a half-plethron* in diameter. When the fighters appeared, the soldiers began shouting and wagering whatever their purses contained: nothing valuable, though, for if they had had anything of value, they would have been elsewhere. As the fighters entered the open space, the soldiers began assembling in ranks, leaving room for officers in the front, veterans behind, infantry outside, and then sailors separated from the servants and slaves.

Soon the family leaders of the Heraclides exited the megaron of the palace onto the wood-columned porch above the courtyard. Cresphontes, son of Aristomachus, appeared first. As the great, great grandson of Heracles, Cresphontes was the leader of the Heraclide family. With bald head and aquiline features, he peered assertively above a gray close-cropped beard. Only a slight paunch hinted at his age. A head taller than the other men, he was dressed in a graceful natural colored linen robe and cloak.

---

* One plethron equals one hundred feet. Six plethra equal one stadion. Please see maps for conversion of ancient Greek measures.

Cresphontes' brother, Temenus, followed him onto the porch, elegantly dressed, but shorter and more physically fit than his older brother. Some said that Temenus was the cleverness behind the throne. Deiphontes, son of Antimachus, and a distant nephew of Cresphontes and Temenus, followed. Deiphontes was the leader of the third generation of Heraclides, the so-called third crop, and he was by far the most intelligent and even keeled member of the family. He was stocky and heavy. His marriage to Temenus' daughter signaled his future leadership of the family. The identical twins, Procles and Eurysthenes, sons of Aristodemus, also of the third generation, followed Deiphontes. They were best known for their ruthlessness and their unabashed hatred for each other. Procles and Eurysthenes were short and fair, with long umber hair falling unbraided to their shoulders. Another of the third crop, Aletes, son of Hippotes, followed the twins. Known as Cresphontes' spearman, he was solidly built with black hair, beard, and raptor eyes, framed by heavy eyebrows. If Temenus was the cleverness behind the throne, Aletes was the belligerence. Other family members and officers followed.

As the leaders descended the stairs to the courtyard, the soldiers quieted and opened a path to the front of the ranks. What interested the soldiers was the appearance of two strangers, for they knew that these two men could determine their future as counselors to the family and as their commanders. Telemachus and Oxylus were dressed simply in heavy woolen cloaks, leather jerkins over short riding tunics, with leather belts and heavy sandals. All of the soldiers had heard of Telemachus and knew well the stories of his legendary father. They watched as he moved gracefully down the stairs, his lean body well formed, his golden locks falling to his shoulders. He did not appear a soldier. He looked more like a government official or a wealthy landowner. Could he lead troops? Would he have the guts to dirty his sandals? He was supposed to be the greatest horse tamer in the Peloponnese, but he looked more like a philanderer…a dandy of Apollo or Dionysus.

The other man gave them even more difficulty. He was reputed to be a great warrior, but he was no larger than a small boy. And he was darker than a Cynurian in the month of Metageitnion.* His curly beard and hair encircled his head like a black cloud. What could he teach them? He could not survive in a fight of women. The rumor that he was honored among the Hittites, the greatest fighters of the age, could not be true.

The two boxers moved about in the open space, pumping their arms and stretching their joints. Both men were champions. Troezen, son of Ialmenus, an infantry soldier from Thessaly, was short, heavy-set, with a thick growth of hair covering his entire body. A bull of a man, he had boxed throughout Hellas in games and athletic contests. As a young man he had fought for Cresphontes in the disastrous second invasion and was among the very few who managed to escape with their lives. Now a mature man, he had not seen his grown children and wife for years. As a skilled skirmisher, he specialized in hand-to-hand combat and in the art of killing with sword and dirk. Troezen was not without wiles, for such are the men raised in the direction of cold-blowing Boreas on the hard scale plains of Thessaly. He was surrounded by his Thessalian compatriots.

The second fighter, Zetes the Athenian, son of Demochus, younger and taller was well built, though lighter. He too had won many boxing contests at games and was well liked among the troops. Zetes' father had named him after the legendary Argonaut. His young wife and three children lived in Athens with his parents. Zetes had gained his reputation by demonstrating quickness and agility, both in contests and in battle. His mates from Attica, speaking perfect Greek, looked askance at the sounds of the mangled Greek of the Thessalians.

The two men stripped naked, leaving only their sandals. Their seconds wrapped the *himantes* about their fists. These long leather straps formed the *cestus*, or glove, intended to protect the knuckles and soften the blows. Their seconds rubbed olive oil into the fighters' chests and heads. Both men prayed briefly to Zeus, making a special appeal to the Dioscuri, especially Pollux, the twin who in life had been a boxer and had become the patron deity of boxing.

Cresphontes signaled for silence:

---

* Cynuria is a mountainous region in the Peloponnese, and the month of Metageitnion is equivalent to the Roman mid-Augustus to September.

"We are assembled here on this god-forsaken island in the middle of the godless Ionian Sea to take into our service two counselors: Telemachus, son of Odysseus, and Oxylus, son of Haemon. They are here to assist in our return to our inherited and rightful rule over the Peloponnese. Tonight, we gift them with the contest of two heroes of the Heraclides. Of all games, boxing is dearest to my heart, for it is the contest closest to the struggle of life. The winner tonight will take home a purse of gold to shower upon his family; but should we see the meeting of two cowards then our heroes will soon be high-hanging from the roof beams. Let the battle begin."

With the advantage of reach and youth, Zetes came out quickly, feeling he could win easily, while Troezen, content with his skills and experience, began his battle from a defensive posture. The left-handed Troezen defended himself with his arms, protecting his face, waiting to judge his opponent's speed and strength. Zetes connected with a flurry of jabs to the ribs, propelling Troezen backwards. Zetes' right fist snapped Troezen. Troezen missed with a tentative thrust to the chin and backed away.

Then Zetes surprised his opponent with a clean right, flush on the chin. Troezen hit the ground, skidding backwards in the dust. Some soldiers cheered; while others yelled angrily for the Thessalian to start fighting. Righting himself quickly, Troezen shook his head more from anger and shame than injury. Zetes continued aggressively, though staying at a distance. Moments later, he sank a digging left hook into Troezen's ribs. Troezen backed off, his face stunned. Zetes, feeling lighthearted, danced and continued to score to the head and body of his opponent.

A champion with Troezen's experience does not confound easily. He began to use his size and strength advantage and scored with two straight left hands in the chest, forcing Zetes to give ground. Zetes connected with a solid right hand to the body below the stomach. He then followed with a right to Troezen's face, but in return, tasted a painful right hook to his ribs. Troezen backed, inhaled deeply, wiped the blood and sweat from his face, and rushed Zetes with a stiff right jab to the eye and a follow-up cross. Zetes pushed Troezen back hard and jabbed the shorter man with a left uppercut to his chin. The two men backed away and observed each other. More cautiously now, Zetes connected with another low right hand well below the belly. But this time, he left himself open, and Troezen's left cestus caught him square on his chin. Zetes landed on his backside, regaining his feet after a moment of deliberation.

Telemachus observed the fighters from the front row, not excited, not enjoying the contest. He had never cared for boxing; watching two men attempt to kill each other without cause did not appeal to him. Boxing held no triumph or glory of victory. Rather, he felt only the sadness of defeat. These contests brought out the worst in men, both the fighters and viewers, and usually descended to the ugliest of competitions.

The younger Zetes gathered himself. He resumed slowly, attempting to regain energy, keeping his distance, landing body shots and pushing his opponent away, but his feet no longer moved with the same grace. Each fighter struggled to turn the tempo and the pace of the fight to his advantage. Zetes attempted to keep a distance and avoid entanglement, while Troezen kept low, protecting his head, working on his opponent's body, and grasping the other when he could, rubbing the himantes on his ears.

Zetes scored with a right from the outside. Driving his opponent backwards, Zetes again connected with a flurry of punches to the head. The blood began flowing from Troezen's nose. Zetes began punishing the shorter man from a distance, avoiding his holds, keeping distant, punching and pushing as necessary. The quickness and reach advantage of the younger man seemed telling.

Moments later, Troezen attempted to grab Zetes around the neck and paid dearly when Zetes connected once more below the belly. Although Troezen returned to trapping the taller man, he was now visibly slowed and hulking, wounded. Troezen simply could not get inside to utilize his superior strength. Meanwhile, Zetes dazed Troezen with brutal punches and then squared up the shorter man and connected with blows to the head, followed by a crushing right hand to the chin. Troezen crashed to the ground and came to rest flat on his back, where he remained. The soldiers began shouting madly, a mixture of anger and exhortation from the Thessalians on one side and wild cheering from the Athenians on the other. The other tribes shouted for their favorites, with the Aetolians and Boeotians cheering for Zetes and the various Peloponnesians favoring Troezen, for he was not from Athens, and they hated Athenians more than anything. Slowly rolling over and regaining his knees, Troezen regarded his opponent with a mixture of fear and surprise. Doubt crept into his befuddled mind. He slowly stood, his arms at his sides, sweaty, muddy blood covering his entire chest and belly. He appeared exhausted. His mates yelled encouragement in their own language, forgetting Cresphontes' warning not to speak barbaric languages.

Zetes returned for the kill, landing one blow after the next, driving Troezen back. Again Zetes measured Troezen's chin, and his right barely missed. Troezen began sliding along the edge of the crowd, but the soldiers roughly pushed him back into the circle. Zetes hit him from behind with a weak blow to the kidneys as he moved away.

Cutting off the escape, Zetes connected with a right to the head. In desperation, the hulking Troezen charged the other man, delivering a solid head butt to his opponent's chest, but Zetes was able to connect with a combination to the head. Troezen careened sideways and collapsed. This time the soldiers were quieter, sensing the end of the fight. He lay on the dirt as though gone. But after some time, to the amazement of the crowd, Troezen struggled back to his feet, the features of his face now masked by blood and dirt.

With his hands raised to protect his face, Troezen began to force himself inside, scoring short body blows, while protecting his head and working on his opponent's right eye. Zetes tried to stay outside, pushing the shorter man away, but tasted a hard left uppercut and a head butt to his chin. He stood back for a moment, observing his bullish challenger. Zetes scored with a clean hook, but Troezen was able to land a solid blow to his opponent's ribs. Backing off again, Zetes connected with a weak uppercut to the head, but he too was struggling. Both men exchanged feeble jabs and grabbed and held each other for a moment.

Zetes, wanting the fight to end, attempted to put pressure on Troezen, but once again, to the dismay of the soldiers, Troezen grabbed him in a bear hug. In close quarters, Troezen was able to punish his opponent. Coming out of the clinch, Troezen again caught Zetes' chin with his head. Zetes' legs wobbled and the pain showed in his face, as he daubed at the blood seeping from his right eye.

With the energy rapidly draining from both men, the fight slowed. Both fighters tried to recoup their strength, falling into each others' arms. The soldiers yelled at them. Troezen used his leverage to hurt Zetes with short body blows. Zetes retreated and caught his hulking opponent with a weak combination, but not before a solid left hand struck his chest, stunning him, followed by an uppercut to the chin that buckled his knees. He fell to the ground. Slowly regaining his feet, now it was Zetes' turn to fight defensively. Troezen pushed, butted, and clasped. Zetes connected with a clubbing left hook, but without strength. The two men wrestled for a moment.

Zetes tried in vain to recapture his earlier momentum. Troezen snapped a weak left hook, but was surprised by a flurry of punches and fell to the ground once again. He sat dazed, the soldiers from Attica half crazy. He thought of the boars he had hunted in the mountains of Thessaly. A wounded boar is a dangerous boar. He may lie as though dead, even with a javelin piercing his body, only to strike suddenly and viciously with his sharp tusks. Troezen rose, his feet barely supporting him, and staggered forward with his forearms protecting his head. He received a weak right hand to his face, but he continued forward, staying low. Zetes could not prevent Troezen from grasping him inside. Both men coasted for a while, regaining their breath. Ignoring the taunts of the soldiers, Troezen reverted to keeping his head in the other man's chest, working the inside, punishing his opponent's body and arms. Zetes fought back, but his punches had lost much of their force.

Both men were now moving with effort, drained. They clasped each other. Troezen continued punishing on the inside with his head and himantes. Zetes struggled, flat on his feet, his features swelling, his right eye closed, the blood caked on his face, his chin, and his chest.

Telemachus had seen enough and thought the contest should be ended, but he was in no position to do so. The men were dead on their feet: no fight left in either.

Troezen connected with a right and left to the body. But he was unable to put more than two punches together, before the strength of his arms failed him. He continued to butt with his head. Zetes complained to the soldiers, but they yelled for him to fight. Troezen trapped Zetes and pummeled him with short body blows. Backing off, Troezen landed a solid left uppercut. His fist connected flush on Zetes' chin, who fell back but remained standing.

The fight was halted while Zetes' seconds re-wrapped his left cestus. When the fight commenced again, the frustrated Zetes lunged, realizing his punches lacked power. He knew he would fail if he continued wrestling with his opponent. Troezen continued to punish him methodically from the inside. Both men were flat footed, without energy. Zetes seemed to lack the will to throw punches, and he began holding the shorter man. The crowd became oddly silent.

Rousing himself, Troezen hit Zetes with a right, followed by a left hook to the body that left Zetes gasping for air, but still standing. Both boxers, at the deathly end of their resources, regarded each other. Troezen bravely attacked with a weak combination, while Zetes landed a right but could not follow up. He grabbed Troezen and tied him up. Both men struggled for air and lay their heads on each other. The soldiers groaned. Again, the two men moved apart, arms hanging at their sides. But Troezen saw an opening. He rushed forward and delivered a fierce head butt to the chest. The sound echoed throughout the compound, causing a moan from the quieted audience. Zetes was finished. He did not fall. He held on to Troezen without defense, both eyes shut. Troezen came back with several body blows, but Zetes did not respond. Troezen pushed him away, and Zetes remained upright for a moment longer, until slowly his legs left him. He slumped to the ground.

The soldiers waited for the sign of the index finger from Zetes, signaling his surrender, but he lay in a heap, unmoving. The voices of the soldiers began slowly rising as they realized the fight had ended. Telemachus rushed to Zetes and knelt by his side. There was no movement and no breath. He touched Zetes' bloody, sweaty throat to feel the life blood, but there was no movement. Although Zetes had fought courageously, nothing could be done for the battler now. Zetes would never return to his young wife and children and his parents in Athens.

"You can leave him," dark-eyed Aletes, the young cousin of the third crop said angrily, as he knelt next to Telemachus, forcing him aside bodily. "We can take care of it."

"I am skilled in the healing arts," Telemachus replied awkwardly, not understanding the anger of the man. Aletes ignored him. He turned to Zetes' seconds and signaled for them to remove the body.

Telemachus stood up. "You have much to learn of hospitality, Aletes."

"Save your lessons. I am the son of Hippotes. I am master of my own house, and no man treats me with disrespect." Aletes seethed.

"Respect is earned." But Oxylus intervened and separated the two men.

"Some people take boxing too seriously," Oxylus said and pulled Telemachus away. Deiphontes stepped in front of Aletes. As he did, an immense roar rose from the crowd at the sight of the dead man being carried out. The soldiers separated into groups, arguing over the contest and their bets. The night was young, and they were looking forward to the fiery Zacynthus wine. The leaders returned to the palace to continue their discussion. Telemachus followed Oxylus into the palace, still confused by Aletes' naked animosity. Sometimes, even the briefest encounter can lead in unforeseen directions, and the simplest contest can end in death.

VI

After the boxing match, Cresphontes dismissed the troops with extra rations of wine to await the sacrifice. Since it was common in boxing for one of the opponents to be sent down to the house of Hades, the death of Zetes did not take on significance. There were more important issues to discuss. This was the first meeting of the descendants of Heracles and their advisors. Two prior generations had plotted and battled without success to regain control over the Peloponnese in what was to become known as the War of the Families. This evening, the third generation of Heraclides had assembled at the palace of a noble ally on Zacynthus. They had arrived in five long ships, including the 50-oar warship guarding the harbor that had made a great show of malevolently greeting Telemachus and Oxylus earlier in the evening.

Temenus frequently played the role of conciliator to his brother's harsh pronouncements, but he too had inherited Heracles' short temper and fear of being cheated of his birthright. For before his birth, Zeus had declared to the gods that Heracles would become the greatest King of Mycenae ever. When the other immortals frustrated the oath of the sire of the gods, Heracles struggled his entire life without obtaining the throne of Mycenae. There can be no greater hurt than the sacred pledge of Zeus gone thwarted.

With this as their legacy, the Heraclides had inherited their godly ancestor's aggression and desire for dominion over men. As a legacy of the terrible events over the lifetime of Heracles, the family grew to place self-interest above all else. They were convinced the Peloponnese was rightfully their domain and that its rulers had squandered the resources of the region in the Trojan War and thereafter. They watched as people from other countries immigrated, and they recognized the recent series of plagues, droughts, and damage from earthquakes as signs of the gods' impatience – only the Heraclides could describe the gods as impatient. The Heraclides had waited many years to return to the Peloponnese…and not patiently. Now, Cresphontes felt assured of victory for the oracles foretold success.

The leaders of the Heraclides gathered in the warm megaron, drinking wine mixed with water and sitting on benches and couches around the hearth, with lambskin cushions and carved footstools for comfort. As in most palaces, the megaron was constructed with high ceilings and served as both meeting hall and dining area. The oval hearth in the center of the room stood slightly above the tiled floor. Wood columns surrounding the hearth supported an open clerestory high above to allow the escape of smoke. Low wooden serving tables were scattered among the couches. Large murals enveloped the room on the walls with hunting scenes in muted colors painted with colored plaster, although the quality of painting in this rural palace did not compare with the fine murals of the great palaces of the Peloponnese and Attica.

Telemachus and Oxylus shared a couch and conversed with Deiphontes near the hearth. They glanced at the proceedings, and accepted the food and drink, but they felt like guests at an execution. Telemachus still smarted from his confrontation with Aletes, while Oxylus viewed every action with discomfort and mistrust.

Five slaves led two black oxen into the room from the rear and secured them with ropes on either side of the fire. An official from the town, responsible for such sacrifices, joined the dinner. First, he washed his hands with water from an urn and then sprinkled water on the first bull. After a short, silent prayer to the gods, he threw barleycorn over the bull, into the fire, and around the entire hearth. The combined efforts of several slaves brought the first ox to his knees. A large Ethiopian slave dressed in leather tunic and leggings extinguished the victim's life with a single blow from a two-headed battle axe to the animal's brain at the junction of the neck. The sacrificer quickly slashed the animal's throat with a knife, allowing the blood to flow all around the body and hearth. He cut hair from the gray top notch and threw this into the fire. On the opposite side of the fire, the other ox stood mutely, without comprehension. The sacrificer performed the same ritual, and the slave committed the other animal to the gods.

The official then butchered the animals, first severing the legs and freeing the thigh bones, which formed the foundation upon which the other meats would be burned. Wrapping the thigh bones in stomach fat, he set them directly on the fire to sizzle and smoke. He poured water and wine over the bones, for the essence of the sacrifice was in the smoke and steam, which billowed and blew up to the heavens, where the gods themselves could smell the offerings of burning fat and bones as a sign of devotion. As the thigh bones and fat burned down, the larger cuts of meat were placed to cook over the remaining bones. Smaller pieces were cooked over the fire on bronze spits. Two large bronze tripods stood over the fire to cook the innards in soupy mixtures.

I describe this sacrifice in detail only because the ancients took so much stock in its efficacy. Although the practice has been largely abandoned today, the bards sang of great animal sacrifices of all sorts, and Homer tells of sacrificing hecatombs, or hundreds of animals, dedicated to the various gods. We no longer perform such ceremonies, since we feel we can communicate with our gods through personal prayers, hymns, and offerings. For generations now, new cults have been appearing: the mysteries of Dionysus and Orpheus, the worshipers of the Dioscuri, and even skeptics, such as the mischievous Jewish and Christian sects in our large cities, speaking of one god only. As a result, religious zealotry and uncertainty grow side by side uncomfortably among our young people, particularly among the poorer populace and slaves. We have come to mistrust the very foundation of our existence.

The Sanctuary of Hera is such a cult, where women from Argos gather to worship the Queen of Heaven. Men are not allowed to attend or even enter the premises. Since Hera understands the ways of women, several times a year all the women from the town gather to spend days celebrating and praying to her. What they do at these meetings is secret, although they claim their efforts aid fertility and increase the abundance of crops. I am convinced they gather to bemoan and insult men. At other times, the sanctuary accepts women running away from their husbands, some with children, and helps them find a new life. Obviously, the elders of the town dislike this sanctuary, but it is allowed to exist because of its support from the women of Argos, including the wives of these same archons. The priestesses of the sanctuary are mostly widows. I cannot picture my Alcathöe among these women. But she is strong-willed, and I can only hope she will soon come to recognize the error of her decision.

During the butchery, servants continued to pour wine and water among the Heraclides, who, after a small libation to the gods, drank to their own success and health. Servants moved among the benches with platters of olives, fresh and dried fruits and nuts, flatbreads and steaming barley meal, and morsels of dried fish. Soon, the seared beef was passed around. By the time Cresphontes stood to address the group, the leaders were talking and laughing, eating the meats with enthusiasm. Only then did the servants rush giant platters of meats, barley, and vegetables out into the courtyard for the soldiers.

"Sirs," announced Cresphontes. "If I may have your attention. Tonight, we offer our thanks to Athene, for she is the patron goddess of the Athenians who first welcomed our family to their country and helped Heracles in his battles with Eurystheus. From our fathers, we inherit our strength and our desire for greatness. Every father prays that his sons will be honorable and bear the aegis of his name for future generations.

"We pray also to Heracles, our father and forebear, who as a baby in his crib throttled the evil snakes sent to him in jealousy by Hera, wife of Zeus. We follow the example of his life with our own. In the name of our father, I welcome you and dedicate these meats.

"Finally, we send burnt offerings to all the gods, but especially to Ares, first in war among the immortals. We can gain much from understanding murderous Ares, since he bestows valor on man and fury in battle.

"Let us have our fill of eat and drink. I have great news. We have learned of the death of old King Orestes, son of Agamemnon. It is reported that he was bitten by a poisonous serpent at his palace in Oresteum in Arcadia and there expired. His son, Tisamenus is now head of the Pelopides and King of Mycenae. For this we are grateful, for the gods have given us a weakling king whose rule will be short-lived. We will see to that. Tomorrow is soon enough for business. We pray to the Dioscuri, Leda's sons, the two brothers dedicated to each other in all things and hesitant to leave each other's side. Pollux as the patron of boxers allowed us an exciting boxing competition tonight between two heroes, and I guarantee a full share of the spoils of our victory to the family of the...the Athenian..."

"Zetes," Temenus offered.

"Yes. And of course to the winner. Tomorrow we have much to discuss of our plans for our return to the Peloponnese. The Pelopides, as we all know, were consolidating their control under Orestes. Tributes were at levels unheard of. Now his son, Tisamenus, presents us with an opportunity..."

At that moment, a commotion broke out in the entrance, and a large man strode into the hall, roughly dressed in traveling clothes and light armour. Several uniformed guards halted his progress with the points of their lances.

Temenus looked up. "What say you stranger?"

"I am the herald of Amphimachus, King of Elis. I have a message for Telemachus, son of Odysseus, who I am told is here."

"I am the son of Odysseus," said Telemachus, rising to his feet.

"My message concerns you and you alone."

Telemachus walked over to where the herald stood at the entrance to the hall before the guards. He signaled the guards to lower their lances, which they did.

"State your message," Telemachus told the herald.

"The King of Elis sends his greetings. Yesterday, in the full market hour, Odysseus, son of Laertes, King of Ithaca and Cephallenia, and hero of Ilium, was attacked by an unknown assailant. His condition is uncertain. You are requested to return to your home immediately, where the lady Polycasté, daughter of King Nestor, awaits. May the gods preserve you."

VII

The next morning, when Dawn, golden sandaled Eos, arrived from the home of sweet-smelling Apeliotes, Telemachus and Oxylus once again huddled on the foredeck of the same merchant vessel that had transported them to Zacynthus. Cresphontes had reluctantly agreed to postpone their discussions until Telemachus was able to settle his family affairs. Although the gods offered a warmer and calmer day, the captain ordered the small coastal vessel to beat rapidly across the mouth of the Gulf of Corinth, under both sail and oars, seeking the safety of the Peloponnese coastline as swiftly as possible.

The news of the attack on his father struck Telemachus like an angry bolt from Apollo's bow, for such news does not travel lightly. It opened old wounds and brought to the surface thoughts that had festered for ages.

"What is it to be a son?" Telemachus asked Oxylus. "A good son is loyal, unquestioning, accepting, emulating. But not until his return from Troy did I meet the man, my father. I knew only the legend. And only in the last few years with my own sons approaching manhood did he begin to reveal himself to me." He stopped short.

Telemachus suspected Oxylus had heard the story many times before from the servants or the townspeople of Elis or the songs of the bards.

The Trojan War lasted nine years. At the end of the war, it took Odysseus ten years to return to Ithaca, being blown off course by Poseidon on his voyage home, losing his ships and crew to Hades, being washed up on strange shores, and finally being saved by the people of Scheria and returned to Ithaca. And it took him even more time to heal the wounds of the war, both real and imagined. He returned to Ithaca in the guise of a beggar to better understand the changes that his absence had wrought, and he discovered the sorry state of his palace, its resources nearly depleted, his fair wife

Penelope, his father Laertes, and his son in despair and no longer communicating. His mother was dead. What may have been most disturbing of all was that his position in the household was being expunged like the memory of a long lost relative. His family was struggling from beneath the dominance of the past. They had begun to resume their lives without him. Rather than facing this tragedy, Odysseus chose to address what was easiest to solve. He found many well-born men from Ithaca and the surrounding islands residing in his house, acting with calumny and deceit, sponging off his wealth and servants, all in the pretense of being suitors to Penelope. He took no pity on them. What took him longer to understand, and what he could not fully accept, was the state of his family. While furniture and animals and crops can be counted and weighed, peoples' states of mind are more difficult to measure.

He enlisted the aid of Laertes, Telemachus, Mentor, Telemachus' tutor, and two servants to do battle with the suitors. Telemachus had been trained in the arts of war, but only as a sideline to statecraft taught by Mentor, who was no warrior, though he surprised everyone on that day. Over the last few years, the suitors had allowed Telemachus to join their games and contests, but he was not accustomed to battle and had never before fought a man. After announcing his identity to the suitors, Odysseus began the slaughter. The five men dispatched all of the suitors. Telemachus had never taken a life. Although his father thought little of it and would have considered him a coward for resisting, Telemachus accompanied him most unhappily. To this day, he dreamed of the blood and horror of that battle: the faces on the suitors once they understood – and these men were all well known to Telemachus – and their cries and sorrowful mourning. Of all the suitors, Antinous, son of Eupeithes, was both worst and the best, for he had insinuated himself into the heart of Penelope. He had taken an interest in Telemachus, aiding his training and offering advice as a father might. He had trained Telemachus in wrestling. At the same time, he had also plotted Telemachus' death and had cursed him before father Zeus that he should never become King of Ithaca. Fittingly, Odysseus killed Antinous first off. Telemachus managed to slay some of the suitors, for such his father expected of him: "Do not dishonor your ancestors," Odysseus had warned. Telemachus killed Amphinomus, son of

Nisus, who came from Dulichium and had pleased Penelope with his kind words. Killing the suitors, though, was not as difficult as punishing the twelve female servants who had consorted with the suitors. Telemachus had the servants stretch a ship's cable from the bearing posts, and they hanged all those pitiful wretches: poor girls from local families without resources. Telemachus could never rid himself of the image of the trussed, flightless birds hanging in file. The scoundrel Melanthius, Odysseus' goatherd, who had also aided the suitors, met the most miserable end. They cut off his feet and hands, severed his nose and ears from his head, and pulled his entrails from his body. They threw his remains outside the palace walls to be consumed by feral dogs.

The servants set the bodies of the dead suitors along the walls of the gatehouse, propped against each other. The most promising men of the offshore Ionian islands lay like fish from the nets of fishermen, not treated with contumely, but alone and forgotten.

The following day, the news of the return of Odysseus and the death of the suitors made its way among the relatives. First the parents of the sons of Ithaca came to collect the bodies of their dead. Then they carried the bodies of the suitors from other islands to fishing vessels to be returned to the islands of their births. At the same time, the relatives of the suitors remembered their other dead: those young men who had accompanied Odysseus to the bloody meadows of Troy. Twelve long ships had departed the islands for Troy with three hundred and forty of the finest young men. Neither a single boat nor a single young man returned. In their anger and despair, the relatives rose up against Odysseus and his family and would surely have killed them all. But that day, thanks be to Zeus, the killing stopped.

Odysseus and the bereaved relatives agreed to a covenant of peace. Yet, neither side could abide its pledges. In outrage and indignation, the families of the suitors sought justice for their losses before the court of Neoptolemus, son of Achilles, King of Epirus, and acting authority over the offshore islands.

Now here is a strange story. Years before when the war raged in Troy, well after the death of Achilles, Neoptolemus, Achilles' son – although the son barely knew the father – had come to Troy. His star was on the rise even then. Neoptolemus' actions at Troy, however, showed that he lacked his father's sense of honor and justice, though none of his thirst for blood. In less than a year's time at Troy, Neoptolemus spilled more Trojan blood than most of the veterans of the war had spilled in nine years. Some of the blood was royal. For it was Neoptolemus whose sword dismembered King Priam of Troy at the altar of Apollo, and it was Neoptolemus who tore the babe, Astyanax, son of Hector, from the arms of his mother, Andromache. He threw the babe from the battlements of the city of Troy like a melon at a spring festival and took Andromache for wife and slave. Like most of the Achaean fighters at Troy who had managed to remain on earth, Neoptolemus' return after the war was circuitous. He wandered the Borean climes with his slaves, Andromache and Helenus, son of Priam, a clever seer. Arriving in Epirus, Neoptolemus took to arms, defeating the Molossians and became king by force. Then after the death of Peleus, the father of Achilles, Neoptolemus was crowned King of Phthia as well. Although he had no official authority over the offshore islands – there had been no king since Odysseus left for the war – he was the closest authority for the families to seek justice.

Neoptolemus traveled to Same, the capital of Cephallenia, to hear the complaints of the families. He made judgment without seeking the testimony of Odysseus or his family. He ruled that Odysseus and his entire family were to be banished for life from Ithaca, effective immediately. Neoptolemus allowed Laertes, father of Odysseus, to remain on Ithaca due to his advanced age.

Helenus, son of Priam, had been captured by Odysseus and had told the Achaeans what was required for victory over the Trojans. It was his prophecy that called for the attendance of Neoptolemus at Troy. In seeking to fulfill the words of Helenus, Odysseus had sailed to Scyros to convince Neoptolemus to come to Troy. Odysseus' golden words and arguments were lost on Neoptolemus, even though Achilles, his father, lay buried there. When Odysseus dangled real gold before his eyes, Neoptolemus agreed to join the coalition. At the end of the war, Neoptolemus took Helenus with him as his slave. Many years later at Neoptolemus' death, Helenus married Neoptolemus' mother, Deidamia, and became King of Epirus: from prince to slave to king in a single lifetime.

In one way, Neoptolemus heeded the words of the families of the suitors more than they expected or desired. Although he banished Odysseus, he ruled by the same token that as compensation for injuries done by the suitors to Odysseus' estate, the families of the suitors would pay Odysseus annual recompense consisting of barley, wine, honeycombs, olive oil, salt, and animals for sacrifice for a period of ten years. In addition, he allowed the estate to remain in the hands of the family.

Some said Neoptolemus forever resented that Odysseus had received the godly armour of his father, Achilles, awarded to Odysseus as the bravest of all Achaeans at Troy. Others say that Neoptolemus' ruling against Odysseus was intended to remove Odysseus from the region and thus give Neoptolemus a foothold on the largest of the offshore islands, Cephallenia. Like his father Achilles, Neoptolemus was not one to compromise, and he learned from others reluctantly, if at all. Both Achilles and his son Neoptolemus died as a result of this failing: one on the field of battle, the other at the hands of an adversary, and both in disputes over a woman.

Expelled from Ithaca after only a few months of his return home, Odysseus turned to the advice he had received from Tiresias in Hades, as Homer relates. Tiresias, son of Everes, was a Theban, the son of a shepherd. Zeus and Hera once argued over who enjoyed the pleasures of love more, men or women. Since Tiresias had lived seven years as a woman and in this way knew the secrets of love from both views, he settled the argument: "In matters of love, men enjoy only one part in ten, while women enjoy all parts."

This answer infuriated Hera, and she blinded Tiresias. Although Zeus could not reverse Tiresias' loss of sight, he awarded him the greatest of oracular powers and a long life. Tiresias died an old man before the start of the war in Troy. As Homer relates, Tiresias advised Odysseus of his future:

"Take an oar to a land of people who know nothing of the sea and use no salt in their food. When you meet a man who thinks the oar is a winnowing shovel, plant the oar in the ground as you would a seedling and make sacrifice to Poseidon. After that you are free to seek a new home. You will live a long life, honored among your people. Death will come from the sea, and your life will ebb away gently."

So they had departed Ithaca, Odysseus and Telemachus. Penelope was to join them later. After visiting the Oracle of Dodona and spending a long time searching in the direction of Boreas, Odysseus and Telemachus had planted an oar in the Pindus Mountains, and sacrificed to the gods. They spent many moons in the mountains getting to know each other, at first shyly and then more easily.

It was here that Odysseus first expressed his doubts.

"We cannot depend on the gods," Odysseus had said. "In the forest of faith, silence abounds, for Pan is dead."

"Pan is dead?"

"The one truth of Troy, where the gods committed riots, incest, and rape, is that gods and men have different understandings. All the holy hecatombs ranged on the altars of all the gods could not have changed the outcome of that war. You can depend on only one person in this world: yourself."

"Why Pan?"

"Because Pan is the son of Hermes, who is a liar and thief. The worst of the gods. And Pan is his invention of the sounds of the forests and woodlands to capture women's hearts."

Telemachus had often thought back on these strange statements by his father, but they had never again discussed their meaning.

When they descended the mountains, they stayed with Queen Callidice of Thesprotia, who fell in love with Odysseus, as many women had before, and who offered her kingdom to him. But Odysseus refused.

"Where will we go?" Odysseus asked. "I have thought long on this. Polyxenus, King of Elis, son of Agasthenes, served me well in Troy. His brother-in-arms from Elis, Amphimachus, son of Cteatus, lies buried there, as does Diores, son of Amarynceus, also from Elis. But Polyxenus returned to Elis with his share of the spoils, and he owes both life and wealth to me. He often described Elis and the fertile valley of the river Peneus and the wide expanses of green, where cattle thrive. He cannot refuse us."

And so they had gone to Elis, and King Polyxenus welcomed them and offered them all the land they could desire in the direction of Mount Erymanthus. First Penelope joined them and then Polycasté and soon Telemachus' twin sons. They had labored more than twenty-five years building the estate in Elis. The time had passed rapidly, and the gods had left them to their own devices. And Time is the great Healer.

Even after living with him for almost three decades in Elis, though, Telemachus failed to understand his father. Odysseus claimed that his family was most important to him, and he touted the importance of home and hearth, but his dark silences spoke more loudly than words. Who was this man? It was only when Telemachus began negotiating with Cresphontes and the Heraclides to act as a counselor-at-war that his father seemed to wake from a long sleep. His talks with the Heraclides opened a new conversation with his father. At this late time in life, here suddenly was a common ground that Odysseus knew well, was willing to share with his son, and was of interest to him.

Now the herald's message changed everything. Now Odysseus had suffered an attack and his condition was uncertain – words masking more than they revealed, as words often do. After surviving the war in Troy, the anger of Apollo, the ire of Ares, and the terrible trials of Poseidon, Odysseus, the mortal man, now lay exposed before the gods.

"I believe he loves me," Telemachus said, "though I have never heard these words from his mouth. Only recently, he seemed to awaken to the thought of my return to Ithaca as king. He knows that he will never return to this role, nor will he return to Ithaca. But he wants this for me."

Of late, Odysseus had studied the situation in the Peloponnese and saw an opportunity for Telemachus in counseling the Heraclides in their return to the Peloponnese. He had advised Telemachus to attend this meeting to test the Heraclides, for he realized that Telemachus and Oxylus were essential to the Heraclides' victory. Not only because of the prophecy of the Oracle of Delphi, but because he knew they combined the necessary rudiments for this campaign to be successful. Without their participation, he knew Heraclides would fail once again.

How curious that in a single breath, all can change.

Even the captain of the merchant vessel was quiet and respectful, as the sailors plied the large-wide sea and the *keulestes* sounded their progress. The Heraclides' return to the land of their ancestors would have to wait for their counselors-at-war to regain their sure footing. Although the sun was now high in the cloudless sky above the ship, the helpful winds of Zephyrus chilled Telemachus. Oxylus and he huddled close for warmth, but remained deeply in their own thoughts, waiting for another cold voyage to terminate.

Early one sun-drenched morning on Ithaca when the hopes of Odysseus' return from Troy still remained fertile and before the suitors had begun pursuing Penelope, Telemachus discovered a gift at his door. Telemachus was at an age when the concerns of his tutor, Mentor, were no longer sufficient to keep him satisfied in his studies. The absence of his father had taken root in Telemachus' bouts of gloominess and frustration. Particularly in the long summer days, his resentment boiled over. He was never far from the eyes of the people of Ithaca, who revered him as son of the king and future king and backed and bowed as he passed, even as a small child. Not allowed to play with the other boys of the village, in the afternoons after his studies, he watched bored as Laertes dug in his vegetable garden. He ran among the rocky peaks on Mt. Neritum and Raven's Crag. He left his servants charged with watching over him far behind on the trails above the Gulf of Molo. Or he swam so far out into the sea that the servants stripped off their clothes and fell into a heap of aggravation and fear. Telemachus always looked forward into the future, praying his life would change. He never felt comfortable in the present.

The gift that sunny morning was a nut brown colt standing nervously in the outer courtyard. Ithaca had few horses. Some draught horses worked the island, but never such a fine animal as the one before him. Mentor stood behind Telemachus as they admired the colt: Telemachus and the colt were at one another's eye level. As Telemachus raised his arm to caress the horse, it shied away from his hand. The servant pulled tightly on the halter, to bring it back, but it still refused to allow Telemachus to touch its muzzle.

"We will need to educate ourselves," Mentor said. "Of all animals, the gods love horses most of all for their intelligence and loyalty."

"What shall I call him?" Telemachus demanded.

"First, we must recognize that this is a female colt."

"Her, then," Telemachus replied, annoyed, but accustomed to the ways of his tutor.

"Perhaps, we can name her once she becomes more familiar to us," Mentor suggested.

"We shall call her after the immortal steeds of the chariot of Helios."

"Then," Mentor replied, "you will remember the names of these horses."

"Of course I do. Aethops, Bronte, Eous, and Sterope."

"Well done. And the driver?"

"Phaeton, son of Helios, who is sometimes confused with Apollo."

"And the moral lesson?"

"That one must temper our expectations with understanding. Though, in the case of Phaeton there were extenuating circumstances, that is, he knew not his immortal father and desired to impress him."

"Bravo," Mentor replied, which was a rare exclamation for him. Telemachus looked at his tutor with contempt.

"I shall call her Bronte, after the lead horse on the chariot," Telemachus continued. "And she will be famous in her own right."

That evening at supper, Penelope explained that the horse had come from Pylos, as a gift of wide-seeing King Nestor.

"Who was this King Nestor?" Telemachus thought to himself. Images of the great king of Pylos came to his head. Mentor had discussed the war and the tribes from Hellas in attendance, and he knew that Nestor ruled over a great nation, lived in a magnificent palace above the sea, fought pirates from Notus, and ruled wisely like no man ever before him.

Penelope explained that in Troy Nestor had been as close to Odysseus as a father to his son. Upon his return to Pylos, Nestor had sent the horse to Telemachus as a reminder that his father could not be far behind. Bronte brought hope. Of all the breeds of horses at Troy, the Ainou were among the bravest and the most easily tamed. A horse of this race would be an ideal companion for a young boy. For Nestor knew that taming horses gives great insight into oneself and into the affairs of men. Nestor knew that Telemachus offered great promise. But all that was to come.

VIII

It is paradoxical that in the midst of one story, others must begin, and others must end. All our lives are intertwined, but our beginnings and our ends are separate. This strengthens the whole vine, while at the same time constantly creates the sweet and bitter fruits that are the joy and fate of mortal man.

While today the Roman world is young and vital, the Greek world is unsteady on its feet, unsure of its direction, and too doddering to hazard a new course. We make study of the greatness of our roots, while others borrow our achievements for their own nefarious ends. Just as a father delights in the youth of his children, praying that one day they will achieve greatness, at the same time he must plan his own future. Of course, we know nothing of the gods' own charts, and while the winds bear greatness, they bear evil just as well. It is this misty obscurity that must be piloted, for we can only guess the intentions of the winds.

Alcathöe, my wife, you have oft accused me of having no faith in our daughters' ability to make proper decisions. One is now married with children of her own. We see her only rarely since her husband's family has settled in Knossos on Crete and are involved in trade with countries in the direction of Notus. My youngest child has dedicated herself to the mysteries, and I could not understand that choice, although now of course her mother has followed her. My middle daughter is working with a muralist and seems to have withdrawn from the world of women. Everyday, she works as a man would, often on scaffolding, using paints and plaster and tools, her hair cropped short and her hands always grimy with colors. Gone are the days when a father can control the course that the lives of his children might take, even daughters. Yet I have always attempted to keep relations open with my children. At least my children are all hard workers. As Hesiod says, "whatever your lot, work is best for *you, for both men and gods hate idlers." My digression, though, as it frequently does, has led us back to the gods.*

When like a brisk breeze in autumn stealthy Hermes arrived on Aeaea, Circe's island, he made no attempt at dissimulation. Since immortals recognize one another regardless of their disguise, he was dressed in his finest linen clothes, his long golden locks braided carefully around his bare shoulders, and he carried his sparkling golden rod entwined with carved serpents. He knew Circe well, but both the land and the house had changed since his last visit. For what once had been lush with plant and animal life, enchanting to strangers, was now overgrown without evidence of grounds-keeping or signs of either tame or wild beasts. Where once fruits had grown year-round in profusion, now briars and vines strangled everything in their path, even the tallest trees. Jeweled lakes had turned into swamps and dry pools. The pigsties were empty and torn apart. Careless disorder was everywhere. The interior of the cut stone mansion was the same, with dust and dirt throughout. Broken furniture, filthy, tattered textiles and rugs, and bronze carvings and ceramic shards lay about as though strewn by some fuming monster. It was as though Life had deserted the house, along with Care and Concern, and now Disorder reigned.

Circe, once a great and cunning goddess, daughter of Helios, the sun god, and Perse, was alone in a small, dark room, warmed by an open fireplace, burning splintered pieces of furniture and other debris. She worked attentively on a portable loom without song, the heavy yarn dirty and colorless. She shielded her eyes from the brilliance of the comely god, stealthy Hermes, the giver of good things, who upon entering the room filled it with his heavenly light and warmth and the dulcet tones of his golden words.

"Circe," he said, "what has become of you?"

"Become?" she repeated.

"Yes. The splendid mansion and glorious gardens lie in ruins. You live like an aged harridan, filthy and repellent. You once wove extraordinary fabrics worthy of the gods with scenes of the wild beasts of the forest. Love and lust once ruled here, but both are now departed."

"My servants have deserted me. I am here alone."

"Why that is a fabrication as imaginative as your textiles used to be," Hermes said in disbelief.

"By myself. No visitors. No one cares."

"And what has become of your beloved son?"

"I have no son."

"Listen to me, Circe. Your great uncle, the lord Zeus, has sent me with word for your son, Telegonus, son of Odysseus."

"I have no son by such a man." But when the golden words of the son of Maia washed over her, her head fell, and her hands stopped the shuttle carrying the weft thread between the warp. "There is a boy that lives on the other side of the island, but he never comes to this side. I have no business with him."

Hermes left her to seek out the boy, but not before he touched her with his triple-leafed golden wand to reintroduce her to the lovely goddess Hope.

The boy lived in a neat hut on the shore of the sea. Some of the tame beasts, who had once been men, now lived with him. Great ostriches wandered among lions and wolves. All were gentle and unafraid of men. The godly Hermes approached the young man.

"Are you Telegonus, son of Odysseus?"

"I was once called Telegonus by my mother, but I have never heard this other name."

"You are the son of the great traveler Odysseus."

"I am the son of the goddess Circe, who has bewitched these animals. My father is among them, for they care for me and protect me."

"Your father is named Odysseus, and his wife, Penelope, is the most attractive of mortals. His grandfather, Autolycus, was a favorite of mine, and we once toiled together in the searing sun on the foothills of Mount Parnassus. Odysseus lived on this island for one year. He is a hero of the Hellenes and a man of great renown."

"And why has my mother never told me of this man?"

"You must speak with her, for words come easily when one loves oneself."

"She does not allow me to enter her house and refuses to agree that I am her son."

"That has all changed now. Speak with her."

With that said, Hermes left the young man and the island of Aeaea, having sown the seed that would one day grow into the tree and produce the desired fruit as foreordained by the gods. He had accomplished his one mission, but he did not return immediately to his mansion in the sky.

Hermes was one of the silent gods, a whistler and not a declaimer, for the melodies of time never left his head. Hermes had invented fire. He had taken a turtle and invented a lyre. The sounds of mortal joy and nature obsessed him. Zeus loved his son Hermes and laughed at his jests, but Hermes was also a headache for both gods and men. As the herald of the gods, his missions were often conducted in secrecy and not always at the request of the lord Zeus. He was known as a thief, a dreamer, a traveler, a spokesperson and guide of the gods, and the father of Pan. Long ago, Hermes had fallen in love with mortal life, and though he helped a few people, he cheated an endless number. He loved nothing better than rolling among the pillows, making mortal children.

Meanwhile, Telegonus hurried to his mother's house, where he found her in her upstairs workroom. For the first time in ages, she recognized him, and she was young and beautiful once again, her face bronzed and healthy.

"Telegonus. Where have you been?"

"Mother, I have lived on the other side of the island, where you sent me and all the animals."

"I have been bewitched," she admitted. "I was not myself, for the daughter of the sun cannot live in darkness."

"I was visited by a man who told me about my father."

"Your father?"

"Yes. He called him Odysseus."

"I wanted to tell you myself. I feel as though a great weight has been lifted from my shoulders. Your father was here only a short while. I offered him immortality, for he was intelligent and as striking as a mountain stag, as strong as an ox, and as unyielding in his ways as marble stone. Yet he was always upset and edgy. Like many mortals, he could not accept his good fortune and dwelt in the house of despair. He was a general of the Achaeans, returning home when Poseidon, the saltwater god, blew him off course. He refused to remain here in paradise, preferring to return to Ithaca to his wife and child."

"But why have you not spoken of him before?"

"I let you grow up without the knowledge of him, since I knew that you would leave once you had heard of him."

"I must see him."

"No good will come of it...for you or for him. He will not recognize you, or you him. It will serve no purpose to meet him. You must not."

"I want to know my father. I always suspected you had given him some potion and turned him into one of your animals. I must know my father."

He turned to leave.

"Wait," Circe called. "To find your father, you must be very careful. First, acquaint yourself from afar. Otherwise, you will never know him."

"I do not understand. How can I know him before I find him?"

"Odysseus was most often thoughtful and considered, but at times he was reckless and quick to anger. Ask others. See how he lives. Observe him. But do not force yourself into his life uninvited. That will fail for all."

IX

The island of Ithaca lies in the Ionian Sea at the mouth of the Gulf of Corinth. Low-lying on the horizon, it is sheltered from strong-hearted Zephyrus in the lee of the island of Cephallenia, which rises out of the sea towards the sunset, where the sun hides beneath Oceanus. Not far away are the wooded islands of Zacynthus and wheat growing Dulichium, while other islands lie towards dawn. The highest mountain in Ithaca, Neritum, is covered with all kinds of timber, with corn and olives and grapes growing along its flanks. As Homer describes Ithaca: "the rugged little island is more fit for goats than horses, but no child loves his home more. The water is ample in all seasons for it is a land of bees and honey. Its heroes are counted among those of all of Hellas and certainly the most handsome." Odysseus proved to us that Ithaca is much more than a small island in the Ionian Sea, it is a destination lying deep within our hearts.

On Ithaca, a boy, verging on manhood, walked through the small fishing village on Polis Bay, accosting people aggressively. He was dressed in dirty, tattered clothes, his hair unkempt and filthy, and his manner disrespectful and arrogant. At first, he begged for food, but soon he let it be known that he was looking for Odysseus. People avoided him, fearing he was some mystic or fanatic, since he carried a long bow with a quiver full of arrows on his back and a heavy staff. He stopped people boldly, always asking the same question. They always received his question with dismay and confusion. For although the name of Odysseus was well known, his whereabouts were not. Odysseus had not inhabited Ithaca for decades. People could only point toward the hills, where the palace of Odysseus stood empty under Mount Neion. And then they hurried away.

The boy, Circe's son Telegonus, set out through small farms and olive groves, following a path that led up the hillside. He arrived at a saddleback between two mountain ridges, where a large cut stone building stood. High walls overrun with vines and vegetation surrounded the house. Pine and cypress trees and high grassy weeds produced a barrier around the walls. Large wooden gates barred his entrance, and no one answered when he banged his staff against the thick doors. Certainly, this had once been a wealthy house, a palace. But now, it was strangely unoccupied. The townspeople were poor and lived mainly in small houses of wood and plaster. Why did the villagers not move into this imposing structure? Telegonus could glimpse a double courtyard, two stories, and terraces with balconies and shuttered openings that looked out at both harbors at Polis Bay and Phrikes Bay. Intrigued, the boy walked around the outside wall and noted the wooded hillsides, the terraced olive trees and vineyards overgrown with weeds and native trees. Farther up the path from the house he saw a small farm. Goats and chickens scattered as he approached.

He walked behind a small wooden hut and came upon a larger plot with fruit trees and a small vineyard. As he continued up the hillside, he met a thin farmer coming out of the forest carrying a bundle of firewood on his bare shoulders.

"Stranger," the man addressed Telegonus, "you need not beg another man's hospitality."

"I do not beg any man," Telegonus said, his staff threatening. The farmer observed the boy and thought better than to challenge him.

"I am searching for the owner of that house yonder."

"That would be my master gone these many years."

"And who would be your master?"

"All know that," he replied.

"Dunce. I am a stranger here…to find a man."

"And who would that man be?"

"He is called Odysseus. All seem to know him."

"One and the same," the farmer replied.

"What is your meaning, old man?"

"That Odysseus is my master. He is well known, though less well loved. He was once my father's master, and I suppose he is mine as well, although I have not set eyes upon the man these many years. His father and mother lie buried here, along with my father. This was

Laertes' farm. I barely remember his son, Odysseus, for I was just a boy when he left."

"Then Odysseus is long departed from here?"

"Aye. Gone in all but memory."

"He is dead?"

"I know not, but the people of the village do not disturb his lands, nor mention his name. All I know is that he is the great Odysseus of the songs. More god than man."

"But if you do not know if he lives, then you do not know where he dwells."

"He dwells in our hearts, for as Penelope says, 'he never wronged any man in word or deed and treated all fairly.'" The goatherd quoted the bards.

"You, sir, are an idiot." And with that, Telegonus left, swearing to himself.

He left Ithaca and continued his search, never having difficulty finding knowledge of the man. The problem was that while all people knew of Odysseus, they only knew him from the songs sung by the bards and never thought beyond that, nor considered that this man might still live. For where do Heracles and Ajax and Achilles live? Certainly not on the earth. And undoubtedly Helen and Menelaus have long since departed the scene. And Paris? People looked at Telegonus as though he himself were from some legend beyond man's memory. But the son of Circe had been raised by a goddess and never gave in nor retreated. He continued on his quest and followed the least bit of information. Unfortunately, the people he asked never knew Odysseus' location, and most thought that he was long since gone to Hades or some other destination appropriate to his exploits and station in life.

But as was often the case in things mysterious to man, the gods stepped in. For even Telegonus could not continue to search indefinitely for a man who existed only in people's minds. Stealthy Hermes on winged sandals visited Telegonus for a second time. Had he not, the wishes of the gods might have gone astray. On a dirty street in Athens, full of seamy people, animals, and noise and dust, elegant Hermes grabbed Telegonus by his grimy neck.

"Young man, you appear to be lost."

Telegonus turned quickly to strike with his staff, but when he saw the man holding him and felt the strength of his hold, he restrained himself.

"And what is it to you? Unhand me before you suffer my staff."

"Besides being as filthy as a barrow, you are as feisty as a rooster. Now, allow me to begin once again. You appear to be lost."

Something told Telegonus that he should not question this man dressed in such fine clothes, with a warm, ruddy complexion and muscular grip. "You are right. I am searching for a man, well known among the population, but not well acquainted. His name is Odysseus."

"Odysseus, son of Laertes, King of Ithaca and the offshore islands, whose fame is widely known by his exploits at Ilium?"

"The same."

"And what would a young ne'er-do-well such as you have of this man?"

"He is my father. I have never met him."

"Do not trifle with him," Hermes warned the boy. "He is unlike any man you will ever meet."

"My life cannot be whole until I have found him."

"Then find him you shall. Odysseus lives with his family on a large farm near Elis in the country of Elis in the Peloponnese. In that town, people will know both his reputation and the man himself. In the meantime, my young rooster, clean up, and treat all men with respect or you will come to rue it. For the gods are about."

So Telegonus continued his trek, arriving in Elis mid-day during the festival of the grape harvest, where young men dressed as women paraded through the town with vine branches and clusters of grapes draped about their shoulders, the wine and heat gone to their heads. Helios scorched the earth like the coals of a great sacrifice, and people sought solace inside the shade of their homes, praying for the cooling rains. Even the birds hid in the trees, and the streams contained only rocks and dry earth. The roar of the crickets was deafening.

He had only to ask one man to receive the answer to the question that had been stirring him so long. Once outside the town, Telegonus trudged in the shimmering heat along the road toward breathless Boreas without seeing a single person or cart. He walked through gentle rolling lands, climbing up through gentle hillocks, and then into the foothills of the mountains. He followed the dirt road along a dry stream. Small farms, fields of grain, vineyards, and olive groves simmered in the heat as he walked on. Even under his wide-brimmed *petasos*, the intensity of the light blinded his eyes, and the sweat fell like rain from his head and chest, soaking his soiled garments.

Ahead of him lumbered a herd of massive cattle blocking the road. There must have been over a hundred animals, so big they seemed to roll across the road. A grizzled old man, accompanied by a muscular young man with an immature, golden beard and three dogs, directed the giant aurochs from a meadow across the road into the cooler river basin. The old man stood in the road as the reddish cream colored beasts slowly shambled past, the dogs running around at the back of the herd, barking and nipping at the heels of the stragglers, forcing them to catch up with the rest. The young man stood below the road, holding open a wooden gate. The cattle sluggishly crossed the road, braying, while the younger ones struggled to keep up and avoid the dogs.

"Old man," Telegonus called. "Will you be all day crossing this road?"

The old man replied. "If heaven can await the sacrifice of these animals, you can at least see them across the road."

The old man's words angered the fiery young man. "Some dry old man will not stop my progress."

"I make no effort to stop you. You do not need my permission to pass."

Telegonus waited as the huge beasts continued to block the road. He watched the farmer. The hairy-legged old man, as broad as his beasts, wore a short, dirty tunic, without a cloak, and carried a cane, which he used to harass the cattle, but also to aid his walk. His head was covered by a knitted mariner's cap, barely containing his untamed gray hair and beard.

"You mock me, sir."

"I do not know you, young sirrah."

"And you do not want to know me," the boy replied.

"I think you may be right. But allow me to offer advice as an elder. Beware of judging others," the old man warned, "without first taking the time to understand who they are."

Telegonus raised his staff to threaten the man. But the old man, far from backing off, approached the boy with a quickness that belied his age. The young man crossed his long staff in a quick motion, hoping to surprise the old man. But his staff went flying into the air when, with surprising strength, the cane struck Telegonus' hands.

"Get thee hence," the old man swore. "If I see thee again, I will cut off thy ears and give them to the dogs."

"Grandfather!" The young man came running up to the road.

Telegonus backed away holding a bleeding hand, but the son of Circe did not give ground freely. He continued to move backward, but at the same time drew his bow from his back and pulled an arrow from his quiver. As he pulled the bowstring taut, he saw the old man swing his cane and barely glimpsed the cane flying at him. It struck him full in the face, knocking him off his feet. The arrow left the bow weakly and grazed Odysseus' calf and fell to the ground. Telegonus lay in a ditch alongside the road, not moving, blood covering his forehead. Odysseus walked over to the boy and leaned over, watching the boy's eyes open slowly and hazily. Something in the boy's blinking eyes struck a note of familiarity. He saw surprise and fear and disorientation, no doubt, but he looked deeper, remembering someone he had not seen for many years in the marine blue eyes: if all else changes, the eyes remain the same.

He turned to his grandson: "Autolycus, bring the servants. Quickly."

Autolycus ran off. And Odysseus sat down on the road beside Telegonus. He examined his leg. It was barely bleeding, but his eyes were slowly glazing and his head becoming foggy. By the time, the servants came running, the positions had changed: Odysseus lay in the road, and Telegonus stood over him, groggily wiping the blood from his face with his tunic. Old Philoetius kneeled down over Odysseus, and the other servants surrounded Telegonus.

"Odysseus. Odysseus." He shook him, but Odysseus had lapsed into unconsciousness, his eyes closed.

The name passed through Telegonus' heart like a bolt of lightning. He thought of his mother and her herbs that she fed to wild men to turn them into tame beasts. She had warned him that he needed to know his father before he could find him. He had paid her no mind. How could this wizened old man possibly be his father? He did not know the man who lay before him. If only he had understood who the man was. If only he had known what kind of man he was. If only he had known it was Odysseus. Then it might have happened differently. He watched as the servant failed to wake Odysseus and then scrutinized the wound, where the arrow had sliced the skin on his calf.

"What have you done to him?"

"Nothing. He struck me with his cane."

"And why would he strike you with his cane?" Philoetius looked closely at the filthy young man with blood on his face and dirty tunic. More servants began gathering around Odysseus, and soon he was lifted and carried away to the house. Philoetius and two other servants roughly grabbed the boy by his soiled cape and tied his hands with leather thongs. They forced him to walk along with the others as they carried Odysseus to the house.

Everyone had gathered in the cooler shadows of the front compound as the servants carried Odysseus into the house. Penelope wept at the sight of her husband, and Polycasté directed the servants to take him into a small antechamber and place him on a couch. The servants secured Telegonus to a horse post along the outer wall in the hot sun. They then entered the atrium, now filling rapidly with servants from the house and fields. Old Philoetius went in to join the others in the small side room.

"He is sleeping and will not wake," Polycasté said. "The wound is not serious, but his breathing is shallow and he is not responsive. Get a physician."

One of the servants jumped on a horse and rode rapidly to town to retrieve help. Polycasté turned to Penelope and said in a loud voice: "You must see to your husband." Penelope recovered enough to begin bringing the room to order and making Odysseus comfortable. All the time, the tears rolled from her eyes. She looked down at Odysseus, lying as though asleep, his cap still on his head. He was disheveled, his working clothes covered in dust and dirt from his morning's work. He looked more a servant than a king.

"Come with me," Polycasté ordered Adrastos, son of Eumaeus, one of the larger servants, and she exited to the outer courtyard.

Adrastos hastened to follow her. Telegonus sat in the hot dust, no longer combative, his pride having deserted him. The bow and quiver had been thrown against the wall, and Polycasté carefully examined one of the arrows. Instead of a bronze arrow head, the arrow was tipped with three tiny barbed spines. Polycasté had seen these spines often enough in Pylos, as the fishermen used them for fishing. She was unsure why an arrow would be tipped with such a spine. Fishermen used the poison from the spine of a stingray on bait as a soporific. She was not sure if these minute barbs contained enough of the poison to act as a sedative or worse. She did not question the young man, leaving him to roast in the sun.

When the physician arrived, he closely observed Odysseus, who appeared to be in a deep sleep, breathing calmly without effort. But he could not rouse him. He pried open Odysseus' eyes, but they were without sight. He examined the barbed arrow that Polycasté held forward. Together, they walked into the sunlight to question the boy.

"Where did you get these barbs?" the physician asked harshly.

"They came from the island of my birth," the frightened young man replied, averting his eyes. He acted defenseless and lost. "My mother taught me to use them in hunting wild animals. They are from the white stingrays that inhabit the lagoon on the leeward side of the island. They bring down the largest stag with only a scratch."

"What are you doing here?" Polycasté demanded.

"I came in search of my father." By now Telegonus had left his foolish pride in abeyance and was bitterly contrite and open, aware that he had lost control of his future. "I am the son of Circe, and I was looking for Odysseus, who is my father. I have been traveling for months to find him. I never meant him harm. I never suspected the old man to be my father. I never knew my father."

Polycasté stood back from Telegonus and observed the young man closely. She remembered the stories Telemachus had told her about his father's travels. The stories, in fact, were common knowledge. The tale of the seductress Circe and Odysseus was one of the more common stories told by the bards. Odysseus himself had never spoken of his voyage to her. And the way Telemachus had described it, it seemed like another time and another life and another person...a fantasy. But she too recognized something in the pitiable young man and made no further inquiry.

Back in the house, the doctor explained that he knew this poison well; there was nothing he could do. But the outcome was far from clear. Fishermen were known to wake days after accidentally pricking their finger when using the poison and without ill effect, believing they had just slept the night. The family would have to wait, keep him comfortable, and pray that he wakes soon.

After the physician departed, Polycasté immediately sent a herald under the auspices of the King of Elis to Zacynthus, where Telemachus was meeting with the Heraclides. She then set out to organize the house under new rules, and the servants began moving through the halls with purpose. She dismissed most of the servants for the duration. Before leaving, they battened down the house as for a gathering storm out of respect for the silent battle raging within.

X

For the next two days, Odysseus lay in a profoundly deep sleep. Each breath was regular, not forced, but shallow. He did not drink or take food, although water could be introduced by holding his head in an upright position. His family gathered around him, never leaving him alone. But Odysseus slept like a child, peacefully, without notice of his surroundings. He responded neither to the sounds around him nor to the changes in light as Helios plied his daily flights across the heavens. Brooding clouds began to gather around Mount Erymanthus, struggling against the warmth and sunlight, but no rain fell to cool the earth.

Telemachus galloped into the courtyard on the evening of the third day, his horse near death. He quickly took in the scene. Life in the house had been placed on hold. His mother once again was beyond consolation, and his wife a bundle of focused energy. Each breath of his father was monitored. Everyone walked about in silence or with whispered tones, and Penelope and Polycasté traded off sitting with Odysseus. Amphion and Autolycus, twin sons of Telemachus and Polycasté, watched over their grandfather with concern in their eyes. The few remaining servants prepared soups and cold meats for nourishment, but nothing was as usual.

Telemachus leaned over his father and attempted as the others had to communicate with him. Odysseus appeared relaxed and sleeping, but nothing and no one could wake him. Telemachus finally sat on the couch next to his father. He looked into the rough face and heavy beard. The eyes and nose and mouth were as though chiseled by the sun and wind. So much was unspoken. It had taken Odysseus a generation to recover from the wounds of the war in Troy, and only recently had he begun to take interest in others. His strength of character had never departed him, but he seemed to need to recover from an illness requiring a long healing period during which he could see only his own woes and anguish. Even noble Penelope had failed to reacquaint herself with the man now lying before her. The fact that we live separate lives, no matter how close we are, is easily ignored in the quotidian; it only becomes evident when the gods pay an unexpected visit.

For the first time in his life, Telemachus saw weakness in the face of his father – or was it calm?

That night, Odysseus' breathing slowed. He did not struggle, nor did he evidence pain or distress. It was as though he were gently drifting out to sea. His body peacefully succumbed to the poison from the sea. At the end, his breathing slowed to such an extent that it was barely breath at all; the difference between life and death was almost imperceptible. We assume a wide gulf, when truly only a single breath separates the two.

Penelope, Telemachus, and Polycasté gathered around Odysseus. The twins stayed in the background, while only the closest servants attended. The fire burned down to embers. Hope smoldered. But Odysseus never woke, never recognized anyone, never spoke, and never came back to himself. At a moment not noticed by his family, known only to the gods, his breathing stopped, and he passed into immortality.

In the year of Likymnios in the waning of the Boedromion moon cycle, Lord Hermes, slayer of Argus, guide and guardian for our Father, the whistling god, completed his task, and the accounts were settled. Wily Odysseus slipped lightly into eternity, surrounded by his family, yet far from his island home on Ithaca.

When Athene learned of the death of Odysseus, she rushed to Zeus, so distraught was she with a combination of roaring anger, deep sadness, and a terrible knowledge of the treachery played upon her.

"While I was away, the Titans played a great trick on me. O father, it could not have been these gods. It could not have been my own flesh and blood."

"Take calm, our daughter."

"Tell me that it is not so," she screamed into the empty hall. "If only gods could cry."

"We cannot change a man's fate."

"I am sick to my heart of this battle of words. We change the fate of man every day. It was done for Pelops. It was done for Hector. We can do miracles. It is no trick or slight of hand. It can be done, and it can be undone. We know this."

The voice of Zeus rose. "No." Although he had sympathy for his emotional daughter, not even she could question his authority.

Athene too recognized she had gone too far, and she covered some of her raw emotions with a sincerity of heart.

"The prophecy of Tiresias called for death due to old age, not death by the hand of his son.

Zeus looked at his intelligent daughter and felt a great loss. "The fate of man is sealed; the gods are powerless to change this."

"You never helped him," Athene complained. "You and Poseidon and the others kept him angry, kept him buzzing like a honey bee in a pot, kept him from discovering his true nature. He was a good man and wanted only goodness in his life and the lives of others. And you sent idle Hermes to do your mean business."

"Daughter. He was a good man, and one of the greatest heroes of Hellas. That cannot be gainsaid. He took risks and made mistakes, which is the nature and the boon of mortals. He had the noble loyalty of his wife, the respect of his compatriots, and the love of his family. The years away from his family, the honor to his country, and his ostracism from his reign were not of my choosing but were the price of immortality. At heart, Odysseus was more like his father Laertes than he would ever admit. Unlike his father, his destiny was greatness and his fate immortality. Who can say which is better? Immortal Odysseus now belongs to all of us."

But Pallas Athene, the virgin born of no woman, still hurt and enraged by her fellow immortals and full of sadness, set off to attend the funeral of Odysseus and to make amends. She would not be denied.

XI

Homer loved Odysseus as no other. He described him of whole cloth, multihued and finely woven. I, Antimenes can only admire the manner of his construction, his broadly sketched mortal inconsistencies, much to love and much to doubt in the carefully selected details, so studied among the philosophers. The ancients viewed him from every possible perspective. And Homer, the magician, always retained the last laugh. What high tragedy he brought to people and what abundance of hunger for life. Perhaps the future will be able to delineate Odysseus, to bound him, but we cannot. We are too close to his history and mind. Surely, we know greatness from a distance, but in Odysseus we find greatness living next door to us as our riotous neighbor – always willing to give aid, oftentimes noisy and irritating, always exciting and half-cocked, always slightly beyond our understanding.

Rarely in life does some mortal stand out from all the rest: both imperial and common all at once. Odysseus was full of words and wordless, lying and honest, flawed and perfect, all at the same time. The geography of his mind was "even and coarse," "temperate and chilly," "cheerful and irate," "precipitous and pastoral," "succulent and desiccated," "bursting and vacant," "fair-minded and lascivious." The bards loved him, for he granted sustenance to them and made some wealthy. He was misunderstood by his father and his sons. Can a man of such contrasts be one person, or is he the finest contrivance ever? If it were the latter, then Homer earned his supper.

But of all the sources of Odysseus, it was the bards who took a man and created a legend. Bards depended on the crowds for their livelihood in retelling the stories of the ancients. Some were mere beggars trying to please a few people to earn a drink of wine, repeating oft-told tales without great talent. Other bards showed more faculties, with the accompaniment of a lyre or flute. Still others were high actors, accomplished in the dramatic arts, singing songs of their own concoction, although the tales were well known and passed back and forth among them. Even the best gathered their lines by putting to memory the current tales of others and embellishing and refining them. Entire poems were traded back and forth without changing a single word. And on occasion, should a poet stray too far from the well known text, the crowd would complain loudly to bring him back into fold or, worst of all, just turn on him and deliver the words themselves without providing any recompense. The bard Thamyris was said to have memorized enough lines and stories to continue his presentation for eight days, stopping only for short rests to eat and drink.

The bards were not alone in embellishing and interpreting the lives of mortals. Another group of men earned a living by foretelling the future: the oracles. Oracles were busy at the time of our story and many became rich, seeking gain rather than providing true guidance from the gods. False prophets made their way across the land, spoiling the water in all the wells. Of course, there were official oracles, such as the popular Oracles of Delphi and Dodona, but many people claimed to have prophetic powers. They offered their views of the future, whether personal or god-given, and attempted to weave a tight course between making clear statements that never came about and broad generalizations that could never be disputed. Fortunately, people's memories are short for false statements and long for correct predictions. Calchas, the prophet of the Achaeans at Troy, earned wide renown for telling what would be necessary to bring the war to a close, including capturing Helenus, son of Priam, and a seer in his own right. Calchas died ignominiously when Mopsus, another seer, was able to best him in estimating the number of figs on a wild fig tree and the number and sex of piglets in a pregnant sow. But of all the oracles, the greatest by far was the man-woman Tiresias.

Just as Tiresias' prophecy foretold, Odysseus expired peacefully without regaining consciousness and his death came from the sea. Among mortals, the loss of Odysseus was hardly noticed outside his family. Of his compatriots, many had gone to the house of Hades directly from foreign Trojan soil. Patroclus, Achilles' lover, died fighting a god he could not see. Achilles resided in the house of Hades, "lord of the dead." The greater Ajax, son of Telamon, the best of all the Achaean warriors, killed himself on his own sword.

Tlepolemus, beloved son of Heracles, brought nine ships from Rhodes only to be sent to an early grave by Sarpedon's spear. Antilochus, son of Nestor, a man of great heart and the fastest runner of all the Achaeans, was sent to the underworld by Memnon, king of the Ethiopians. Of those who managed to return, many met their ends shortly thereafter, or left Hellas to settle elsewhere. The lesser Ajax perished in the seas at the behest of Poseidon. Clytemnestra and her lover, Aegisthus, slew Agamemnon upon his return like an ox for sacrifice. Helen, the wife of Menelaus and cause of all the tug and turmoil, now resides in the Elysian Fields with her husband, Menelaus, both made immortal by Hera. Diomedes and Aeneas settled in Italy, each married to a daughter of King Daunus of Apulia. Of those few still on earth, most were too old and too feeble to make the journey or felt the journey too dangerous or just preferred to guard their image of Odysseus as the lively, brash, intelligent leader and proxenos of the Achaeans.

In short, truth be known, in the minds of most people the passing of Odysseus occurred many years before, and the legend of the man had already become immortal. Odysseus' funeral rites were scarcely attended and only by family and locals.

The morning after the death of Odysseus, a saddened Eos, goddess of dawn, departed her island home and rose from the domicile of Apeliotes into the sky in her golden chariot drawn by winged horses. She scattered the dark mists of the night and sprinkled the horizon with rosy dew. But just as she had grieved when her son Memnon was struck down in battle by Achilles, she once again heard the sounds of lament, this time filling the halls of Odysseus' palace. The old women from the town sat around the body of the master to bewail his passing on to the next world.

At first glance, Penelope appeared to have accepted her husband's fate; a closer look revealed behind the charcoal-darkened eyes and forehead, a vacancy that only a son or close servant could perceive.

"I have done my mourning," she claimed staunchly. "He never truly returned to us from that war." Telemachus knew his mother and what rough seas roiled within.

"The man who returned from the war is the only father I ever knew," Telemachus reminded her.

"I knew both men," Penelope replied firmly. "And you were cheated on two accounts: you never knew the first, and the second was not the measure of the first."

"He was changing," Telemachus argued.

"As the mountains change."

Penelope was slight in stature, fair in complexion, but remarkable for her wisdom and knowledge of the families of Hellas. She had been raised in the palace of King Tyndareus of Mycenae as the fair-haired cousin of the king's daughters, Helen and Clytemnestra. As the daughter of Icarius, the king's younger brother, she was close to the throne, but far from its power. She knew the inner workings of the palace, but always from the shadows and never enjoyed the radiance that shined on Helen and Clytemnestra. Penelope was clear-headed and serious in comparison to her flighty cousins and never considered as lovely or precious. But Penelope was gifted by the gods with a firm knowledge of herself, which gave her a solid foundation from which to act, something her suitors discovered to their dismay – and something Penelope believed Odysseus never fully realized. Her quiet dignity and strength gave her self-sufficiency, and she never forgot the lessons of her life.

Penelope assisted in the preparation for the funeral without emotion, trying to help Polycasté and making suggestions, for of all people Penelope knew Odysseus best. She found it difficult to believe her fate: Odysseus had abandoned her once before and now he was gone again, this time beyond recall. Penelope knew well where to find solace for her grief. Just as a turtle withdraws head and feet to withstand a predator, she sought the calm within. In demeanor, she seemed a distant relative, affected by the proceedings, ready to serve, ready to play the widow where necessary. She conducted herself with great pride and aloofness, as beautiful as ever with clear, transparent skin and long, flaxen hair with only a hint of gray. Impeccably dressed, she went about her chores without a show of emotion, attending to the constant stream of Eleans offering their condolences.

Once Telegonus told his story, Telemachus decided that he had suffered his punishment and sent him from Elis to return to Aeaea, his mother Circe's island, never to return to Hellas. No one looked upon him as a murderer. Rather, they pitied him, for he came with nothing and left with even less.

And here, the heavy hand of heaven and the foggy mist of history descended upon both him and his mother; for nowhere do we ever find another account of Telegonus or Circe.

Polycasté prepared a room on the ground floor. The servants removed all the furniture and built a special bed facing the entry that would serve as a bier. Benches were placed against the walls for the town mourners. A single table at the head of the bed contained a small carved statue of Athene and an oil lamp.

Polycasté and Penelope prepared Odysseus' body. They washed him with fragrant soap and anointed him with olive oil and fresh unguents, and for the first time in many moons, trimmed his hair and beard and nails. They inspected his scars and mutilations without surprise. Echoes of past battles pocked and blemished every part of his body. In the end, they could only view him as a warrior. They dressed him in his finest tunic and gathered his prized gold-lined bronze armour and sword, which were never far from his bedside. They strapped on his breastplate, molded to his wide chest. They fastened white-painted, bronze greaves on his calves, hiding the small deadly mark where the poisoned dart had sliced his skin. They girded his scabbard and sword about his shoulders, the very sword, fabricated of bronze with a silver hilt that had been given him by King Alcinous and Queen Arete many years before. They strapped on his heavy sandals. Polycasté arranged his favorite soft wool mariner's cap on his head, for his heart had never journeyed far from Ithaca and the large-wide sea. His bronze helmet with horsehair plumes rested on the bed beside his head. She arranged a light snowy linen cape over his shoulders and beneath his body. And she closed his eyes and tied a scarlet chin strap about his head.

Once the body was prepared, its feet to the doorway, the darkly cloaked mourners entered the room and took up their vigil in earnest, beating their breasts, rending their hair, and crying out to the gods:

"O Zeus, how could you allow this to happen to Odysseus? Your favorite son and hero on earth. Our time is brief, and you would make it briefer yet. Oh, we are all lost."

Their dirges and chants of the death songs filled the house. Only when a king dies do the gods hear such lamentation. His three ragged, unwashed shepherd dogs lay at the foot of the bed, for of all animals Odysseus had loved his dogs the most. The curs rebuffed all attempts to remove them, baring their teeth and growling.

Meanwhile, the servants thoroughly cleaned the entire house and prepared a funeral pyre in the outer courtyard. They hung fresh wreaths of pine and purple crocus, mountain narcissus, and red berried koumaria throughout the house and courtyard. They moved tables into the hall to offer food and drink to the mourners, who began to arrive from the town. King Eleius, the grandson of King Polyxenus who had first welcomed Odysseus to Elis almost three decades before, came to pay his respects to his foremost citizen, along with his son, Dius. Townspeople came who knew Odysseus from trading him fish or crafts in the marketplace. Workers, who had labored next to him in the fields and house and knew him for his diligence and hard work, paid their respects: farmers, metal workers, masons, carpenters, herders, pickers and pruners, and trenchers. People from throughout the region joined the mourners to express their sadness.

The vigil continued for two more nights, with songs and heartfelt lamentations never ceasing. As mourners tired, others replaced them. As people filed in and out of the room, making their way between the rows of mourners, the one constant was the body of Odysseus lying in state with his dogs.

On the dawn of the third day, a small group of family, friends, and people from Elis gathered in the courtyard for the funeral rites. Telemachus presided. First, he poured a libation of wine, which was echoed by others with wine cups. A servant led a honey-colored calf into the courtyard. The calf was a sign of hope sent to the gods. It was the offspring of one of Odysseus' favored cows – one of the breeds he had created, just as his grandfather, Autolycus, had done in Phocis.

The sacrificer from the village sliced the calf's jugular vein with a sharp knife. The blood drained into the fire pit. Once the animal lay still, the sacrificer sprinkled barley corn around the pyre. Two servants lifted the calf onto the pyre and laid it on the platform arranged for Odysseus' body. A stable boy led two of the finest stallions from Telemachus' herd into the courtyard. They reared with apprehension at the crowd and close quarters. The two horses represented strength and rebirth, and many of the people averted their eyes or wept as each of these two magnificent animals was slain in turn and added to the pyre by the servants.

Telemachus then went into the great hall with the pallbearers to retrieve his father's body. Telemachus and King Eleius were at the front of the bier. Behind them in the center were fine-limbed Oxylus and Philoetius, Odysseus' stockman and friend. At the end of the bier were Pisistratus, the son of Nestor, and King Nestor himself. The six men surrounded the bier and lifted it with effort. They filed through the passageway. The twin sons of Telemachus followed directly behind the bier, for never are grandchildren pallbearers, and they in turn were followed by the veiled women of the house and then the servants.

The pallbearers carried the bier to the pyre platform. The surrounding people gasped when they saw the magnificence of Odysseus' finery, the glittering gold and bronze armour and the brilliantly plumed silver-bronze helmet. By his side lay a heavy ash javelin, sized for only the strongest of men. In death as in life, Odysseus, a mild man not naturally bellicose, was recognized for his exploits in war. The servants aided the pallbearers in lifting the heavy bier. Polycasté placed a beautiful lace shroud woven by Penelope over his body.

Telemachus addressed the mourners. "We gather here to lay to rest a man, my father, and the husband of Penelope, my mother. This man, renowned for his sagacity and strategies in war, was long vacant in our lives. I, as his son, welcomed him home as an adult, and he in turn became a father at a late age. My father, vaunted by the bards, is now legend. He never accepted praise easily and was reticent to speak of his past. We had him among us here in Elis for many years, building up his estates, due to the graces of his friend, the great ruler, King Polyxenus, who departed this world years ago.

His grandson, King Eleius, and great grandson, Dius, join us here today.

"Of all Odysseus' accomplishments, building his famous herd of cattle here was one of his greatest. He followed after his father, King Laertes, in this manner, who spent his final years on Ithaca among his vines and fruit trees, having the satisfaction of a capable and celebrated son. But in death as in life, Odysseus, peer of the gods in council, will be remembered for his role in Troy and his commitment to the Achaean cause. No man sacrificed more.

"Although Odysseus achieved a long life, we are grieved that it ended in the way it did, concluding with a singular event, unusual in its provenance, coming from the sea, and late in life, and certainly hinting of some god's unrequited anger. But these are concerns that surpass our understanding. We know that of all the gods, Zeus watches over us, and his understanding outshines all others, and Athene, his daughter, remains vigilant in our defense. May the gods protect us, not only in this our time of sorrow, but at all times."

After Telemachus finished, he yearned to join his wife and sons, but was blocked by the officials and servants surrounding the pyre. He remained among them, watching his soft-eyed Polycasté and his two stoic sons standing with Polycasté's agèd mother Eurydice. He felt lost and alone, fatherless once again. Wise King Nestor struggled forward to address the assembled mourners.

While infirm of body, Nestor spoke with strength and eloquence for his mind was firm: "The greatness of our generation was forged over the coals of Troy. Our hero, whom we come to eulogize, did not exist outside this history. When the time came, and we had to stand together in defense of what we believed in, Odysseus rose to the forefront of our alliance of states. He, like many of us, was reluctant at first. But as a man of his word, for the gods well know there is no worse criminal than an oath-breaker, he sacrificed his life, his family, and ultimately his rule of state and country of birth for a greater good.

"Odysseus understood war far better than any man of his generation. Some people have said that Helen's abduction was a lie or at best only an excuse to go to war. We had seen similar cases before, and they were not cause for war. But regardless, once a decision was made to go forward with the war, it required a vast commitment of individual sacrifice and dedication. War. Man seems unable to live without it. War is a multi-headed monster that wounds us all: those who die on the field of battle, those who return, and those who await its outcome. In war, there is no moral superiority. And even the gods are uncertain of war's outcome. Without Odysseus' brilliance, we would have failed at Troy to the regret of the entire world.

"At Troy, I soon came to understand that Odysseus was much more than a warrior. He was a philosopher. He applied his intelligence, ingenuity, and understanding of people. No leader of the Achaeans understood his own troops and those of the enemy as well. No man communicated his opinion with such potency. King Priam of Troy made the mistake of ignoring Odysseus, for by outward appearances he took Odysseus for a subordinate. But time and again, Odysseus' words wove a compelling tapestry of truth and clarity. It is to Priam's everlasting sorrow that he did not listen more closely.

"Odysseus' family is blessed. Although his sudden departure from life was unexpected and tragic, his legacy remains his family. We knew only of his love and expectations for them. Sage Penelope, a legend in her own right, never faltered in her knowledge of him nor hesitated in her loyalty to him. The excellence of her mind and the strength of her heart aided Odysseus in all things, and Penelope's wisdom will continue unblemished as a model to which we can all aspire. Odysseus' son, my son-in-law, Telemachus, mark my words, determined as he is to act with virtue and respect of others, will become a great king, greater in his way than his own father. Such was the fondest wish of Odysseus. And his grandsons already sparkle in brilliance.

"Odysseus was a compassionate man. He never vaunted over his enemies. He knew well that every man in a battle carries within him memories of his mother and father, his children, his ancestors, and his spirit. Odysseus knew that the differences between men pale in comparison to what men share in common. He was comfortable among kings and beggars, because he considered himself just a man, no better, no worse than any other. And he treated no man as he would not treat himself.

"Odysseus will be long remembered and long honored. His is a dying breed of man that will never again walk the earth. Life consists of a sequence of decisions, most insignificant, some of great import, yet each vital to life's outcome. In the end, each of us must endeavor to ensure that when history is told, the stories will affirm our decisions.

"Just as the seer Theoclymenus presaged of Odysseus, no family will become more powerful and no house more royal than his own.

"O Odysseus, my friend, my master, may the lord of gods, Zeus, guide you and protect you, and may the gods find it in their hearts to welcome you into their house." With tears in his eyes, the old man slowly retreated.

Last to speak was King Eleius of Elis, a short, squat man in golden robes, his son, Dius, by his side.

"When my grandfather welcomed Odysseus to our land, he welcomed a hero of all of Hellas. We have been enriched by this man and his family. We too suffer his loss. And we pray that our families can continue to cooperate for the best interests of all of Elis. May the gods protect you and keep you."

Telemachus dedicated the final offering: "O great Zeus and your children, please accept these rich meats in honor of a great man. May you protect him on his journey and welcome him among you." He signaled for the priest to light the pyre, glancing at Polycasté who stood close to Nestor, holding him. His comments at the death of his friend had drenched him in emotion like a rogue wave. The flames erupted on the pyre in such a rapid fashion that the people had to retreat, even as the chariot of Helios began rising above the earth mostly obscured by the clouds forming around Mt. Erymanthus.

XII

The pyre burned all day and into the evening, the smoke swirling up toward the mountains among the clouds and on to the heavens. The next day, the coals remained too hot to retrieve the ashes. For the first time in many days, the mourners and visitors had departed, and the family was left alone. That evening by the light of several lamps, Telemachus collected the remains and placed them in a ceramic urn, decorated in rose and cream glazes with the scene of Hephaestus assisting the birth of Athene from the head of Zeus. Athene had protected Odysseus in life, and now she protected him in death.

Zeus had cohabited with the goddess Metis and had gotten her with child. But it was prophesied that the child born of Metis would become more powerful than the father, so Zeus swallowed Metis, hoping to prevent the birth...just as his father, Cronos, had done with him. When it came time for the birth, however, Zeus had a headache beyond bearing, and he asked Hephaestus for help. Hephaestus took his sharpest knife and cut open the head of Zeus and pulled from his head the full-grown goddess, Athene. This strange, unnatural birth explains the eternally close relationship between Athene and the lame god, Hephaestus, and the mixture of intense love and heated antagonism between Zeus and his daughter.

Once Telemachus had placed the ashes and fragments of bones in the urn, he collected Odysseus' melted armour, his sword, and the tip of his javelin. The family would hold a final interment during the waning of the moon. Later in the evening, Telemachus, Polycasté, and Penelope sat together in the main hall in the low light from the wall sconces. The servants had long departed, and the quiet had descended.

"Perhaps we should send his remains to Ithaca for burial," Polycasté suggested.

"No." Telemachus said.

"Why?" Polycasté asked.

"Because he never wanted to return," Penelope said. "After so many years of yearning for Ithaca and then being expelled a few days after his homecoming, he had no desire to return. Even when his father died."

"It is still too early for the family to return," Telemachus said.

The newest generation on Ithaca was growing, but memories of the deaths of the suitors remained. The faces of the leaders were changing. Neoptolemus, king of Epirus and Phthia, was dead at the hands of Orestes, son of Agamemnon. Neoptolemus, for all his efforts, never got a foothold in Cephallenia. As Telemachus had learned from the meeting with the Heraclides, Orestes himself no longer dwelt on the earth. The heavy yearly recompense Neoptolemus had ordered the families of the suitors to pay had ended years ago. Still, many families remained bitter.

"There is only one sure way to return to Ithaca – by force."

"My dear, you have been listening to your Heraclides," his mother Penelope commented. "I am sure that you could now return without complaint."

"Perhaps, but not as king," Telemachus said.

"I have been thinking about this," Penelope continued. "I plan to return to my home on Ithaca after I bury my husband."

"Mother?"

"Do not coddle me. I am sure of nothing else. I am a widow now, although a widow once before. And I am soon an old woman. Who would resent an old woman returning to her home? It is time. I am going home." Penelope abruptly left to return to her residence.

"She seems totally accepting of the death," Polycasté said.

"You do not understand my mother, if you believe that."

"That is true. I do not understand your mother. I have given her nothing but my allegiance and perseverance all these years. Always sympathetic. Always offering a strong shoulder. And she has not tossed a single crumb in my direction."

"This is no time to dwell in bitterness. I cannot make my parents different people, though I would have it as you would. You must stop blaming me for their failures."

"What will you do?" Polycasté asked her husband, avoiding a common path of disagreement.

"Continue as I have been," Telemachus replied. "Oxylus and I will meet with the Heraclides again in the spring."

"You know I do not trust these Heraclides," she stated. "And I do not like the direction they are taking you."

"We find them useful."

"You and Oxylus. I do not trust this man either. You have too much faith in others, and none in yourself."

"And you are too quick to judge," he replied, "about others and about me. My father agreed the Heraclides offered me the one way back to Ithaca, and in our last conversation he urged me to explore their offer."

"You fail to consider what is best for our sons."

"That is not true. I have raised them as a father should. I am with them every day. I work with them and teach them to the best of my ability. But also, you must remember they are in line for Odysseus' throne. They have begun training for this role."

"The twins know nothing of Ithaca," Penelope said.

"They are descended from the men who have ruled Ithaca for generations."

"Yes, they are also descended from the rulers of Messenia."

"Your brothers have divided up Pylos and Messenia like ill-gotten spoils."

"My father mentioned that he would like to see you and his grandsons take a greater role in governing Messenia."

"You seem at odds in your loyalties," Telemachus reminded her.

"Not with my sons," Polycasté replied.

"No, with the family of your sons."

"I feel the yoke of a servant."

"You are now sole mistress of the household."

"Strange, I have always felt the foreigner," Polycasté admitted. "This family, so afraid of confidence. So divided. Your father never spoke to me. And your mother only issued orders, although she cared not for most of my duties."

"But where are your gentleness and humor and understanding that once prevailed?" Telemachus asked.

"I cannot be both adamantine and gentle at once. I have tried. Now, I must harden myself against the future."

"You have taken on too much," Telemachus said.

"When we married," Polycasté said, "I worried of just such an eventuality. I expressed myself to my father. I thought I could bring cheer to this family, but now I think the task has swallowed me, and I cannot go on."

"You have to find some comfort for yourself," Telemachus said. "You cannot continue to serve this family looking toward Ithaca and your father's family in Pylos. You cannot heal the wounds between your father and his sons. You are the mother of the future kings of Ithaca. You cannot continue to retract water from an empty well."

"Exactly. I thought I could ignore my feelings. I thought I could store away my resentment and frustration in a secret room. I am dried up," she admitted. "I have given all I can. Too many people have come to depend on me. It is my own fault, I realize this. But I am done. And now the Heraclides..."

"This has nothing to do with the Heraclides."

She hesitated a moment. "As I said, I am depleted."

"We have always worked so hard together, always with a view to the future."

"Telemachus, there is no future. Only today."

"Polycasté, you left my bed."

She quickly scrutinized his face with her soft eyes and saw the hurt and depth of feeling, for this had never been expressed before.

"I did not choose that," he said.

"No? You have accepted it well enough."

"You have no idea."

Telemachus thought of her as a young woman in Pylos years before. She had bathed him, and he remembered his own embarrassment at the time. Her skin had glowed, as her bundled hair had brushed his shoulders. She had smelled of anise and honey and lavender. Her breath was as fresh as Apeliotes' on a placid sea, and her breasts fell free within her loose tunic. She had been so brave, and he so respectful...sometimes he hated himself.

"I have changed. Two children and years of hard work. I am not the same person you married."

"In my eyes..."

"It is too late" Polycasté interrupted. "The storehouse is full. Some things cannot be recaptured."

"Strange, that is what my father said, when he had no tears at the death of his father. It is only an excuse for giving up, for quitting. I will not quit, and I will not allow you to quit. The time is late, and we need to take our rest. Once my mother has departed Elis for Ithaca, and believe me she will leave regardless of our wishes, life here should be quite different. You will see."

And they left together for their chambers. Telemachus worried that his wife was protecting herself against some unforeseen loss, while he was just beginning to find his way forward. For him, the Heraclides offered a means to independence and self-reliance. Much in his life had been served to him on a golden platter. For the first time in his life, Telemachus, "son of the great Odysseus," clearly saw what he had to do. He could now see beyond his frustrating quest to know his father. His task was undeniable: he had to preserve the greatness that came from his father's sacrifice; he had to return to Ithaca.

When the piercing power of the sun and sultry heat abate, Hesiod tells us, the almighty Zeus sends the autumn rains, and men's flesh comes to feel far better. Before the rains, the grape clusters are cut off, and their liquid is drained to produce the joyous gift of Dionysus.

During this short respite between harvest and rain, Telemachus prepared the final resting place for Odysseus. Elis' finest masons had constructed Odysseus' barrow on a small outcrop of land carefully chosen by Telemachus. A good barrow should be naturally impregnable, blend into the hillside, its location known only to the family. They had cleared the site and dug the barrow into the rocky hillside as high as a man stands. From this high, rocky promontory, one could view the entire estate. In the distance on clear days, one could glimpse the large-wide sea.

Once the masons had completed their task, the family and servants gathered on the hillside in the bright, though waning moonlight. Telemachus placed the urn containing the ashes of Odysseus in the tomb built into the side of the hill. The family had brought other items of importance to them, and they threw them into the grave. The twins tossed in two small dirks that Odysseus had given them as youngsters. Each family member then cut a lock of hair from his head and threw it in as well. Penelope entered the site slowly and deposited the melted remains of Odysseus' armour and weapons wrapped in a woven cloth. To this she added a sheet of gold sculpted in the shape of a shield with etched scenes of the sea and land. She placed these against the earthen wall. She remained in the cave for a long while, until Telemachus became uneasy. But she exited eventually, her face unreadable. The masons then sealed the gravesite with a stone wall, covering it with mud and earth to hide it. Water basins were brought around for all to purify themselves. On the small clearing in front, they built a high cairn of tightly-fitted stones to make the gravesite.

The family then made their way down the hillside carefully and quietly.

Strabo called Homer the first geographer. Homer described how Aeolus, the King of the Aeolian Islands and ruler of the winds, gave an ox-hide bag containing the Anemoi, the living winds, his children, to Odysseus. But his ungrateful crew loosed the winds in their greed and as a consequence sent Odysseus in directions unknown to man. When Zeus made Aeolus ruler of the winds, he made him responsible for both rousing and calming the winds, for the immortal winds determine the directions mortals take and bring both joy and pain. When the crew wasted Aeolus' gift, Odysseus begged Aeolus to return the winds to him. Aeolus refused for he was very angry with Odysseus and shouted at him, "You are cursed by the gods. Get thee hence." It lay with the windy children of Aeolus to allow Odysseus to find his way home, which the winds finally did, though not without costs.

Now with Odysseus gone, the riotous winds began blowing in all directions, tuneless and disquieting, and the rain began to fall. Within days of the entombment, Penelope prepared to return to Ithaca. She did not take many possessions with her. She packed her loom and distaff, the same ones that had served her over the years to weave the shrouds of her mother, her father, her mother-in-law, her father-in-law, and now her husband.

On a wet and misty day, her family accompanied her from Elis to Pheia, the small harbor near the mouth of the Peneus. Penelope and Polycasté were driven in a wagon, while the men followed on horseback. Telemachus had hired a small coastal galley with twenty rowers to take his mother and her servants back to Ithaca. The voyage of less than a day would be through coastal waters against the prevailing winds from Boreas, but exposure to the open seas would be limited.

"I pray that we can join you soon," Telemachus said softly to his mother.

"You will when it is possible. But I hope that Amphion and Autolycus can visit me when I get established."

"Yes. We will all visit you soon."

Penelope embraced her son and quoted a common saying between them, "Thick weft on thin warp, my son."

"Yes, mother," he replied, as though still a boy.

Then she embraced the twins, each in his turn. "Amphion, you must continue to learn the ways of men. To treat men with respect and fairness. Look to your father and to King Nestor, for by such men you shall learn of yourself. And you, Autolycus...please do not hug me so hard...the seed of your greatness is within, and only you can guard it and bring it to fruition. Temper your daring and tempestuousness for they can become your strength."

She saved her last embrace for Polycasté.

"My child," Penelope whispered, close to her ear, "all will be well. Only Hera understands women. But you must give credence to the feelings within your heart and welcome the tides of change, for there is nothing more to life."

As the ship rowed out into the channel, the gentle breeze blew directly in their faces, and the sail remained furled. Telemachus watched the ship move off. He felt sadness at the departure, but at the same time he felt liberation, as though a weight had been lifted from his shoulders. He gathered his two young men to his side, comforted by their presence, their strength.

Polycasté stood away from her men. She regarded the large-wide sea, her hand shielding the intensity of the setting sun from her eyes: not as one would watch a sunset, but as one might protect herself against some looming evil. Her life had taken on a direction of its own beyond her control – a direction she feared would result in her destruction. Her life had been one of duty and compliance, and now she saw all that she had attempted to accomplish dissolving like the setting sun leaving only a faint memorial glow on the horizon.

XIII

Polycasté admired Penelope for her strengths, but Polycasté was crafted from a different mold. As the daughter of King Nestor of Messenia, Polycasté knew first hand the power of the throne. As the fruit of his withered loins and the youngest of a family of male siblings, Nestor treasured and protected Polycasté. She grew up under his personal tutelage. By the time she was a young woman, she was administering his faltering regime. Polycasté had soft hazel eyes, an olive complexion, and ample hips. Her size, frankness, and practical nature contrasted with Penelope's firm composure and noble self-possession. Next to Penelope, Polycasté often felt frustrated like a country girl visiting her gracious, royal aunt.

One day not long before Telemachus' meeting with the Heraclides in Zacynthus, Polycasté had sought out Penelope in her workroom.

"My family battles each other," Polycasté said, watching the rapid movement of heddles and shuttle. "They do not listen to reason, and they fail to comprehend forces outside their region."

"My dear," said Penelope, barely looking up from her loom, "sometimes a leader of your father's eminence fails to prepare his heirs, for he is afraid of losing his own power."

"No, it is my brothers who are at fault. My father..."

"First, you must recognize your father can do no wrong," Penelope interrupted. "Such is the relation of daughters to their fathers. But you have two sons entering manhood and a husband set on his own course, which involves aiding these Heraclides."

"But if Telemachus is intent on helping the Heraclides return to the Peloponnese, he is acting against my father and brothers. His actions could result in the loss of their lives and my heritage. Where am I in all this?"

"Your family is here in Elis or wherever Telemachus may choose to go," Penelope stated simply.

"I know that," Polycasté replied sharply.

"Then act like it."

"Perhaps, if you had been more of a mother to your son, Telemachus would be stronger, and I would not have these problems. He is drowning, and he believes the Heraclides can help him."

"Beware, Polycasté, do not enter an inner courtyard without invitation. For I freely admit to failing as a mother, when my husband left me as a widow for almost twenty years. I was absent. I know that. But believe me, I did not fail in my marriage. Do not turn away from your husband, for his needs are great."

"What do you mean?" Polycasté asked.

"What you describe as 'drowning' is merely a man moving in a direction that is both dangerous and full of reward, and he needs your help now more than ever."

"Perhaps, but he is betraying his wife's family."

"For the first time in his life, he is thinking of himself and his own family. As a boy he wanted to please everyone, from his mother to his tutor, from his absent father to the loathsome suitors. A mother can only be proud of the direction his life has lately taken."

"He seeks to overthrow his wife's family?"

"Believe me, at some point in your life, you must take a risk, Polycasté. You have been sheltered. Remember, he is his father's son. Much goes unspoken."

"This family," Polycasté said miserably, "uses silence as a weapon."

"Often, expressing yourself openly leads to ruin, as your ancestor Niobe discovered."

"I feel like a stranger in a foreign land," Polycasté shouted, leaving the room.

Polycasté had explained her forthrightness one day to Telemachus by telling him about her famous great grandmother, Niobe, the daughter of Tantalus. Niobe was a rebel. She tried to convince the people of Thebes that they should devote themselves to the world in which they live and put less emphasis on the world of the immortals. One day, she went so far as to address worshippers in the temple of the goddess Leto. She urged the people to take the laurel wreaths off their heads. She compared herself to the goddess Leto. Niobe had many children, while Leto had only two. And she made fun of the children of Leto, Artemis and Apollo, saying that Artemis dressed as a man and Apollo wore hair as a woman and used women's robes. She told the people of the temple, "Return to your homes and worship your children."

Leto became irate, as did all the gods. Her son, Apollo, came down to earth and killed Niobe's children, all save Chloris, Polycasté's grandmother, and her sister, Amyclas. Chloris and Amyclas had taken it upon themselves to pray at the sanctuary of Leto for forgiveness for their mother. For this, their lives were spared.

Niobe escaped to Sipylus, the home of her father. But she could not escape the wrath of Apollo, who came to Sipylus and turned her into a stone, with tears flowing from its heart day and night.

"At times, I truly think I am Niobe," Polycasté said. "I cannot hold my tongue, even though in the company of men. I am willful and impious. I am my worst enemy, always failing myself."

Telemachus first met Polycasté when he was a young man visiting King Nestor in Pylos seeking word of Odysseus long after the war in Troy had ended. She had bathed him at the request of her father. Being washed by a female servant or slave was commonplace, but never one so lovely, and never the daughter of a king. Telemachus had been so embarrassed that he pretended to be the young prince accustomed to such pampering and once in the bath feigned sleep. Polycasté knew her father well, so she scrubbed the young man as one would a dirty child, but when she anointed him with oils and felt his sinewy back muscles and long arms and delicate chest, she closed her eyes in modesty, feeling emotions she had never felt before. Their eyes met only once as she departed the chamber to allow him to dress in the shirt and mantle she had brought for him. But neither forgot. Telemachus always suspected the great king had planned it all: from his marriage his daughter to the birth of his grandchildren to Telemachus' coronation as king of Messenia.

Nestor had glimpsed an advantage in the union of the son of Odysseus and his daughter. The old king never made a move that did not satisfy both his heart and his head. Polycasté's brothers failed to understand their father's strategy, vying for power in their own right, and were thankful to see her leave the palace in Pylos, for she represented the authority of Nestor. Polycasté was surprised by her hopeless longing to be with Telemachus. Nestor facilitated the marriage of Telemachus and Polycasté. The wedding was the largest in memory in Messenia and attended by people from all over Hellas. For three days, they celebrated these two young people. When the newlyweds departed Pylos, Nestor presented the young couple with a magnificent dowry that doubled the size of Odysseus' estate in Elis.

The first year of their marriage, Telemachus had found his wife loving and accepting well beyond his expectations. She was bright and energetic, and they had occupied their time becoming comfortable with each another. They spent entire days in their rooms in the large bed or on the balcony, talking and laughing together. Polycasté knew how to get along with men; she understood them. She did not require the company of women for her happiness and spent time with Telemachus in great cheer. She was not shy and opened her arms and heart to her husband. For his part, Telemachus had never known such a friendship.

Early in the second year of their marriage, Polycasté gave birth to twin sons. They named the first born Amphion after Polycasté's ancestor, the great King of Thebes. Amphion was the model of Nestor himself, fair-minded, given by the gods at birth a facility to understand others and to guide them. As a babe, he never complained unreasonably. He slept for long periods of time from the start and woke with an instant need to feed his thin body. There was no delaying him, as his loud voice would grow in intensity. Once fed, Amphion would return to his predictable and loving behavior. He wanted to be carried at all times, and fell asleep only in the arms of Telemachus. The young girls who joined the family to help Polycasté loved Amphion and were comfortable with him.

The second born twin was named for his paternal great grandfather, Autolycus. It was said that quicksilver Hermes had given the gift of cunning and thievery to the elder Autolycus and that Hermes himself was the immortal father of the elder Autolycus. Just as Amphion was the replica of one grandfather, young Autolycus seemed to be the replica of the other grandfather, Odysseus. He was strong and sure of himself, daring, a fighter and strategist. From the first day, Autolycus had no patience for pain or deprivation. He was independent, and his parents' caresses and arms were accepted, but not required. He lifted his head moments after birth and with energetic hands grabbed at whatever was offered. He cried often, took his breast milk greedily, and slept lightly. He gained weight rapidly and grew strong and agile. Autolycus was never content, suffering nightmares, waking often during the cold nights, and forever complaining. The young girls who joined the family to help Polycasté would have given their lives for Autolycus, but were slightly afraid of him.

Those who knew the twins, called Amphion the godson of Agamemnon, the peer of Zeus in council, and Autolycus the godson of Heracles, the warrior.

After the birth of her two sons, Polycasté set about the task of managing the estate, which grew to hundreds of servants and slaves in the house and fields, harvesting large crops and preparing all sorts of fresh foods and preserves: oils, wines, grains, dried meats and fruits, and cheeses, for storing, bartering, and paying tribute to the Kings of Elis. After two decades, with the combination of Odysseus' resources and Nestor's dowry, Polycasté administered one of the wealthiest estates in the Peloponnese; the palace and farm in Ithaca paled in comparison. Even Nestor's palace in Pylos was not as fine as their palace in Elis.

During this time, Odysseus and Telemachus had separate ambitions. Odysseus built up the largest herd of cattle in the Peloponnese, and Telemachus the largest horse farm. Father and son worked in their own realms. Polycasté's ability to manage the estate allowed them the freedom to build their respective interests. She raised the twins and built up the estate at the same time, gaining the respect of the women of Elis and becoming a leader among them. Nestor had taught her well.

Polycasté was a frequent visitor to the palace of the King of Elis. She and Telemachus spent many days with King Eleius, who had inherited the throne at a young age. Eleius' wife had given birth to a child, whom they called Dius, at about the same time as Autolycus and Amphion were born. During their childhood, the three boys were inseparable playmates and could be found in the fields riding horses, swimming in the river, or getting into mischief in town. They had their run of the town of Elis and the surrounding hillsides and farms.

As the twin boys grew into young men, Polycasté and Telemachus slowly grew distant from one another. Polycasté could not have pointed to a single event that pushed them apart. All she knew was that a barrier had grown between them. Her nights were long, sleepless, with a sadness she did not understand: her head filled with pointless, anxious prattle.

One of Polycasté's greatest disappointments was that she had not become a daughter to Penelope, even after producing two wonderful heirs. Outwardly the two women were friendly and frequently met to discuss the affairs of the day, but they were not close. Penelope spent long days at her loom, creating colorful fabrics for their home and clothing for the entire family and servants.

By the time the twins were young men, King Nestor had removed himself almost entirely from the governance of Messenia. His sons and grandsons were at each others' throats over the affairs of the large state. Nestor had two sons, Thrasymedes and Pisistratus, and three grandsons, Paeon, son of Antilochus, who had been killed at Troy, Sillus, son of Thrasymedes, and Pisistratus, son of Pisistratus. With Nestor present, the family maintained some order, but as he aged the fighting and backbiting grew bitter and divisive. Telemachus and Polycasté attempted to play the role of mediators, but Nestor's offspring were not open to advice.

"We need not fear the Heraclides," said Thrasymedes. "They simply do not have the resources to mount a campaign against the cities of the Peloponnese."

"You are wrong," Telemachus replied. "They are committed to invading the Peloponnese."

"Their second attempt failed miserably long ago," young Pisistratus said. "They lost all of their army and navy and crawled back to Athens." Pisistratus and Telemachus' had been best friends ever since they rode together as young men to visit Menelaus to seek information on the whereabouts of Odysseus. Pisistratus had become a farmer, but his son, also called Pisistratus, was much more interested in the affairs of state.

"They failed in all their attempts," Paeon said. Although almost the same age as his uncle, Thrasymedes, Paeon's ambitions far exceeded his knowledge.

Polycasté reminded them, "The power of the Heraclides depends on their backers. Athens and the countries of the mainland support them, and several Peloponnesian states, Arcadia and Lacedaemon, would most likely support a third attempt. The leaders of Messenia must be united."

"The Heraclides are led by the older generation," Telemachus added. "Cresphontes and Temenus are aging and have suffered losses. But beware the third generation."

"Do not underestimate them if you love Messenia as I do," Polycasté warned.

"They are far away," Thrasymedes said. "Ever since I was a boy, they have been talking about their invasion and their supposed rights to our Peloponnese."

"After their last failure," Paeon said, "the Heraclides have been very quiet."

"Quiet to you, perhaps," Telemachus replied. "But their family is anything but quiet. And remember, Orestes, son of Agamemnon, has his own eyes set on Messenia."

At about the time of our story, the family of Nestor had moved farther apart. Messenia splintered into four regions, one region ruled by a non-family member. This hurt Polycasté deeply. But the deepest wound was her family's refusal to see the plight of her father and potential for disaster from the Heraclides' invasion.

She turned to Telemachus to try to find an understanding. They had sat together in their suite a few nights before Telemachus was to leave for Zacynthus to meet the Heraclides. The Zephyrian winds blew gently, brushing the dry leaves against the shutters and the walls of the house.

"Are you sure you must go?" Polycasté asked, knowing the answer, but needing an entry to discussion.

"We have talked of this many times before," Telemachus replied, tired from efforts to prepare for the journey, which could keep him away from Elis for several weeks. "Oxylus wants to take his newly forged weapons, which means several servants must accompany us."

"Oxylus. Who is this strange little man? Where is his family? Why has he adopted us so strongly?"

"Polycasté, this is well trodden soil."

"I know. I know," Polycasté admitted. "It is not Oxylus, but what he represents: the unknown mysteries of this venture. These Heraclides could lead you far astray...or worse."

"We do not know where this will lead," Telamachus said. "That is the purpose of the meeting."

"I fear for my family."

"We do not know the intentions of the Heraclides at this point. Perhaps, they have no call on Messenia."

"You know as well as I the greed of these men," she said.

"Yes, I know."

"These men will stop at nothing."

"Perhaps, but they are no worse than Orestes and the other rulers of the Peloponnese." Telemachus paused. "Since your father withdrew, Messenia is disintegrating."

"That can be repaired."

"Not by your brothers."

"By you," she said.

"Me?"

"Yes. You must talk with father."

Telemachus pulled the covers over his shoulders and turned toward the breeze. "I am tired, Polycasté, please. All this may amount to nothing. I need sleep now."

"I am afraid I will lose you," Polycasté whispered.

"You will not lose me. I am here." The gods of sleep entered his mind, and he drifted away.

"You must not leave me," she whispered.

Telemachus did not reply.

Polycasté was left alone once again to consider her own thoughts: her husband, their aging parents, her children, her brothers. No one understood. Her brothers did not understand. Her mother failed to notice, so gone with age. Her own life seemed to be slipping away like dust in a storm. She had spent her life pleasing others. Now she felt parched and empty and confused. Now, she had to save herself. She turned her back to Telemachus, prepared to spend another sleepless night.

XIV

Ten years after the family had settled in Elis, Telemachus watched a horse and rider approach the gates to the estates. As the horse approached, Telemachus observed a small man straddling a monster of a charger, with giant flanks and chest and broad, muscled haunches. The horse was a dappled gray stallion with large fetlocks...an amazing horse, never before seen in the Peloponnese. A servant opened one gate to allow the horse and rider to descend to where Telemachus was working. Telemachus noted that the horse was without his left eye, having only the scar of an empty socket.

"I am called Oxylus, son of Haemon," the fine-limbed man called out. He talked without dismounting, his horse standing quietly his hooves planted to the ground. The man was tiny and sat high upon his horse. "I am newly arrived in Elis and want to board my horse. I heard that you are raising many fine horses, and I know a great deal about breeding and breaking these beasts. In town, there is no space for such an animal as mine, and I want to keep him from prying eyes."

"I can understand that. He is a remarkable creature."

"He comes from Europa. He is called Rhaebus, after the offspring of the mares of Laomedon. I took him from a Celtic warrior in Germania, where no one speaks Greek, and the barbarians are wild and untrustworthy."

"And his eye?"

"He is a wondrous war horse, as willing to enter into furious battle as he is to eat apples in an orchard. In a war in far Illyria, a lance glanced off his muzzle armour and took his eye. Even so, he has never flagged in his courage, and even today he is not bothered by his missing eye. He is pitiless in battle, but, otherwise, as gentle as a kindly serving maid."

"I once had a horse as fine as this," Telemachus said. "Her name was Bronte, but I lost her off the coast of Epirus in angry seas." He ran his hands over the horse, his eyes at wither-level, feeling the strength in the barrel, the flank, the stifle, the stones, the left gaskin, and the fetlock and rear hoof.

"Rhaebus is my heart's desire. He is as trustworthy as a dog to his master and as warm at night as a plump and obliging harlot." Oxylus smiled sincerely.

"You are free to turn him loose in the lower pasture. Although he appears gentle, it will take some time for him to get used to the other stallions. Still, he would be better off in the pasture than isolated in the stables."

The two men became friends almost immediately. It took many months of working closely together for Telemachus to see the darker side of Oxylus' nature, but when he did, it was clear that this man had seen much and had confronted angry men who desired his destruction. At these rare times of blackness, a cruel Oxylus would take Rhaebus out into the fields and ride him wickedly. Gentle Rhaebus would suffer the man and all his indignities. And in the end, Oxylus would return ashamed and contrite.

After their first meeting, Oxylus began spending time at Telemachus' horse farm, working with Telemachus and the servants. Their friendship was based on their knowledge and love of horses, although Telemachus' ideas on training differed greatly from those of Oxylus. Telemachus had grown up with Bronte, his first horse in Ithaca, more a sister than a mount. On many days, he listened to Mentor's abstract ideas on horses. Yet it was Bronte who had taught him to deal with horses. He thought of horses in human terms. The virtues of trust, respect, and mutual understanding were at the core of his taming. His sons had been raised on this treatise, knew it by heart, and as boys both had become adept at taming.

"The first steps of taming must be to recognize that horses are herd animals who seek leadership," Telemachus explained to Oxylus, who listened skeptically.

He went on to summarize his approach. All beings seek leadership, and the tamer must be in the lead position. There are two ways of doing this: by force and domination or by gaining respect. The latter takes more time and is thus avoided by most people. An animal can be dominated by use of ropes and implements throughout its training and may provide a lifetime of hard work and success.

However, there is a world of difference between a horse that acts out of fear versus one that acts voluntarily out of trust and loyalty. The trusting, loyal horse is the superior horse, be it walking down the road, driving cattle, or facing a row of lances. The tamer can only achieve superiority if the horse is not constantly bracing against the possible jab of a spur or pull of a bit.

A foal naturally not only likes men but hankers after them. This is the basis of the relationship. Upon first training, a colt is gentle, tractable, and, unlike men, never holds a grudge. To start a horse, the goal is for the tamer to become the colt's "lead mare." The trainer's job is to make doing the right thing easy for the horse and the wrong thing difficult. Horses have large brains, but most of it is used to keep track of their four feet. They are all about movement, and among horses, the leader is the one who forces movement.

Once the leader is accepted, introducing the bit and saddle pad are not difficult tasks. When the horse accepts and gives to the bit and takes a pad without issue, the tamer must build confidence. Confidence is gained via repeatable prompts and responses. If a horse knows that the response he provides for a given prompt will always be accepted with enthusiasm, he will learn. For this reason, tamers must not allow others to ride a horse in training. A horse should learn to go and follow on a lead rope. He should learn to stand quietly. He must learn to give to pressure, not into it, that is, always move away from pressure of the rein, knee, or foot. A young horse should be ridden to a point, relaxed, and then returned. The horse must not brace against the bit; a finished horse should actually carry it in his mouth with pride. This is lost forever if the horse's mouth is abused. A horse should be able to turn over its front feet for more precise control, turn over its hind feet, and stop on its hind feet. Then the various gaits can be trained of walking, trotting, cantering, loping, and galloping.

The final goal of mutual understanding and trust comes only with time. Communication between rider and a finished horse should not be perceptible to an onlooker. This is a continuous process; the better the horse, the gentler the required prompt.

"But," Telemachus added, "horses are like humans in many ways. You must be patient with them, giving them time to learn.

They must be allowed to come to you; you cannot force them to your will. And the more they trust you, the gentler they become."

Oxylus had trained hundreds of horses for warfare, either carrying a man or pulling a chariot. His taming method had always been by force and domination. But he decided to accept and then came to appreciate Telemachus' taming philosophy. He worked with the twins to build up a group of horses well attuned to military tasks. He found horses started by Telemachus were better prepared to accept the demands of military troopers and for the rigors of battle than those he had trained by force.

Oxylus was not easily impressed. He had traveled widely and had campaigned throughout the world. He had become acquainted with the Celts, with other rat-eating barbarians from the direction of Boreas, with the Persian mounted cavalry, with horse soldiers from Egypt, and with the tribes of the Levant – all excellent horsemen. It took Telemachus several years to pry out of Oxylus the fact that he had lived among the Hittites, spoke their language, understood their ways, and that they had honored him as no Hellene before.

For most of his adult years, Oxylus had led the life of an exile as the result of what he called "an unintended homicide." He told the story in a straightforward fashion:

"I was raised in rocky Calydon on a plain leading to the Gulf of Corinth. My family has lived there for generations, and my grandfather, Thoas, ruled the Aetolians and led their forces in Troy. Like many of the great leaders of his time, Thoas was a suitor of Helen in Sparta and, like your father, had signed the Oath of Tyndareus. As a consequence, he led some forty ships to the war at Troy. Thoas sat with Odysseus and the forty men inside the wooden horse that finally entered Troy to take the city.

"Many times, my grandfather, Thoas, told me the story of the wooden horse. Of the men who entered the horse, the last was Epeus, who had been its designer and master builder. When the others had seated themselves, Epeus climbed up the ladder and pulled it up inside the horse. He closed the trapdoor, bolted it, and sat on the door for fear that one of the men might attempt to escape. For once inside the horse, the hearts of all the men deserted them. And when the Trojans began yelling to them, trying to decide what to do with the horse, calling in various voices, all of the Achaeans sat frozen in fear of being discovered. That is all save one, and his name was Neoptolemus, son of Achilles. Neoptolemus never flinched, but sat in concentration rubbing the golden hilt of his sword, staring at the floorboards. I cannot recall," Oxylus confessed to Telemachus, "if Thoas spoke of how your father reacted.

"But my father, Haemon, son of Thoas, did not travel to Troy and now rules over Aetolia. I, Oxylus should be next in line for the throne, except that my anger got the better of me and would have done me in if not for my quick thinking.

"It happened this way. My younger brother was adopted at a young age, as was I. Haemon married many women but was unable to produce an heir to the throne. He adopted both my brother and me at the Oracle of Delphi, for many people leave children at the oracle. My brother must have come from large people, fair of skin, for he passed me in height when we were yet young boys, and his color never changed with the heat of the sun to become as dark as I was. Like many large boys, he was well adept at games. He could sprint faster than any man in Calydon, and his arm was strong for the javelin, besting all, save Eudoros, known throughout Hellas for his skills. In this contest, my brother and I were competing in quoits. The throwing of the quoit depends on agility as much as on strength. But sure enough, Thermius, for that is how we called my brother after his wild red hair, sent a quoit that surpassed my own, and all others, by far. Thermius would have won the competition if my last throw had not gone astray and struck him hard by the back of his head and killed him. I believe my father would have killed me on the spot. He favored my brother in all things, and I resented Thermius greatly. Although this was many years ago, my grandfather had left the scene by this time, and my father was ruthless. My father considered me the black sheep of his family. As a boy, I was fair of skin and only as time went on did I turn the color of hard-pressed olives and did my hair take on its naturally curly aspect, as you see it now. So when Thermius came about dead, my father was eager to cut me cap-a-pie, and that would have been the end of Oxylus. They would have soon enough forgotten me, you can be sure of that.

"But I had my rebuttal. And there were some among them who listened to my words and believed me. For I really did love my brother, as we were two peas in a pod. And it was not his choosing that he was always the favored one and would have certainly, had he lived, succeeded my father as ruler of all Pleuron and high Calydon even though the younger. In any case, I talked my father out of killing me, claiming that it was an accident that could have happened to anyone. I did not mean to kill my brother. I am sure of that. Furthermore, I was not prepared to be a serving boy. Far better to depart my country and learn from others those skills necessary to lead a military life. So it was decided that I would be exiled from Calydon for the remainder of my life. That was my judgment. As the gods will attest, although I am not well versed in their ways, I am innocent in my heart. And I rue the day that my excellent brother died at my hands.

"After this, I began my travels by trekking by land toward the bitter climes of Boreas into various countries of Europa, where I learned much about the martial arts. Barbarians have much to offer, for other countries are not as backwards as the Hellenes would have us believe. Many of these barbarians have learned the skills of conducting themselves in their hurly-burly worlds, and they are quite dangerous, believe me, even though they speak not a word of Greek. And, furthermore, they have knowledge of warfare that the Hellenes only dream of in their worst nightmares.

"As I have stated, though, I learned much and barely escaped with my life on several occasions. More than I care to remember. Returning after many battles accompanied by my warhorse, Rhaebus, I had experienced the wide scale of mankind from goodness to depravity. For such is the life of man. Although we are all born of mothers, most well loved at the time, we soon enough depart in separate directions – some sooner than others. Some seek knowledge and righteousness, and some seek pleasure and self-gratification without concern for others. It is my fortune to have known evil and goodness, sometimes combined in a single man. And I have come to believe that the gods have little to say on all this.

"And after these times and trials, I realize that my brother had been a good man and that I was in the other camp…at least at that time. For man has been given the ability to learn and to change himself. And that is the saving grace of all humanity. But what bothers me greatly is that I see time and again people repeating errors of the past and learning only reluctantly in many cases.

"At the least, I feel I am a better man today than I was before. Although I cannot return to the country of my upbringing, and I know not who from my family will rule at my father's death, I feel that my time is yet to come. It is my destiny to rule and so I have been told. And so it will be. Just as it is your destiny to rule."

Telemachus and Oxylus became as close as the Dioscuri, Castor and Pollux, the brothers of Helen, and embarked on an enterprise to trade and breed horses from throughout the Peloponnese. It was Oxylus' vision that in the future warhorses would be much sought after, particularly horses that were trained for service. They were soon forced to seek horses outside the Peloponnese, as Telemachus had already selected over most of the Peloponnesian stock for breeding. They began looking for horses for military uses on trips to Attica and Boeotia and then to foreign shores of Ionia and Crete.

During one of these trips to Attica, Telemachus and Oxylus chanced to encounter Temenus, the brother of Cresphontes, the powerful leader of the Heraclides. After the defeat of the second invasion of the Peloponnese by the Heraclides, Temenus had sought guidance from the Oracle of Delphi. The Delphinium priestess again advised the Heraclides "to wait for the third crop." And by "crop" she meant "generation." "When the third crop comes to maturity," the oracle advised the Heraclides "you must hire as a guide, the three-eyed one. And you will be successful, only if this comes about."

By the time Temenus met Telemachus and Oxylus, he had waited until his own sons were men. Now, Cresphontes and his brother were straining at the bit to return to their ambition of recapturing the Peloponnese. When Temenus came upon Telemachus and Oxylus riding their horses and leading many other horses in the mountains near Marathon, he could barely believe his good fortune. For here were the very words of the oracle. Temenus knew immediately that here indeed was the "three-eyed one" that the oracle demanded. For as Oxylus approached on Rhaebus, Temenus observed a small man with two dark, wary eyes, surveying him, while one gentle third eye, the eye of his gigantic mount, regarded him quite openly.

"I have seen the three-eyed one," Temenus later told his brother.

"The three-eyed one?" Cresphontes replied vacantly.

"Yes, the very one mentioned by the Oracle of Delphi."

"Do you honestly believe these quacks? How can you be sure?" Cresphontes asked belligerently.

"I saw this man mounted on a magnificent charger. And the horse had only one eye."

"It is not uncommon for horses to have one eye."

"No," Temenus agreed, "but when I questioned the man, he turned out to be skilled in the military arts. Also, he was accompanied by Telemachus, son of Odysseus. One man was skilled in the ways of war and knew all the strategies and armaments of foreign nations and his own. And next to him was a princely fellow, the son of wise Odysseus, a horse tamer, recognized in the great palaces of the Peloponnese. Telemachus is an expert in horses and knows the Peloponnese as the back of his hand. He is also the son-in-law of King Nestor."

"We have no need of such men," Cresphontes replied.

"Brother, you must listen to the words of the oracle. Then you must use your common sense. These two men were brought to us by some god. I am convinced of it."

"You are dreaming."

"I only dream of returning to the Peloponnese," Temenus said. "These two men are the counselors named by the oracle. I know this. I have invited them to join us for discussions."

"This will come to no good."

"It cannot hurt and may be exactly what we need. For the third crop is not qualified to lead a dancing contest of women."

"I suppose that we could talk with them, but we must be careful. This may be some trick by the Pelopides, for Nestor is in the thick of them."

Temenus immediately set out to invite Telemachus and Oxylus to meet with Cresphontes. This chance encounter eventually led to the first meeting on the island of Zacynthus – the meeting that began our history. This first encounter was frustrated, as you know, when the gods interrupted to carry out the fate of Odysseus. The second meeting finally took place a year after the first.

XV

The wretched days of winter arrived on the estate in Elis. As Hesiod tells us, days not fit to skin an ox, and the frosts of cruel Boreas blew over the earth. The woods roar, and the beasts shudder, their tails between their legs, even those whose hide is covered in fur. Helios drives his horses distantly over the race of man. It is in these times, as Penelope often said that you must weave thick weft on thin warp for warmth and protection and on your head wear a heavy cap of felt.

The death of Odysseus had struck a wound deeper than they expected. And the departure of Penelope made it worse. Their absence slowly was felt, not immediately, not hastily, but as rain seeps into the cracks of a roof tile to water a beam.

Everyone held to his own responsibilities. Telemachus spent more time working the farm and less on his horses, while Polycasté managed the house and servants. She often met with the women of Elis. Oxylus continued to train horses for war. The twins aided as the need arose, but they spent more time away in town with their friends. The cattle herd had been greatly reduced, keeping only Odysseus' favorite animals for reproduction and milk and cheese. Telemachus and Polycasté lived under terms of truce, but without laughter and without merriment. The megaron became a place for eating and discussion of what needed to be done the next day. Amphion and Autolycus became as silent as their grandfather had been and no longer invited the elders into their lives. After a while, even Oxylus refrained from trying to bring cheer into the household and spent his off hours at the wine shops in town.

As winter waned into spring, the swallows reappeared and the pruning of the vines began. It was also during this period that King Eleius of Elis began to distance himself from his old friend, Telemachus. The death of Odysseus seemed to signal the end of hospitality. Eleius began to look on the palace of Odysseus as a ruler might and not as a family friend. He saw the wealth and resources of the estate, which now dwarfed the town's coffers. He resented the power and influence of this household, holding sway far beyond the borders of Elis, and in fact beyond the Peloponnese itself. Eleius saw the large herds of horses, cattle, sheep, and goats, the large production of wine and olive oil, and the visitors to the estates. He set out to exert his influence. He did not deny the rights of Telemachus to the estates, though he did not feel the same allegiance as his father and grandfather had. Memories are short in some cases, particularly when there are advantages to be gained.

After discussions with Telemachus, it was decided that the share of resources given to the King of Elis would be increased and that further land expansion would happen only at the approval of the throne. Telemachus was by far the largest land owner in all of Elis. Eleius set the new agreement at a level that raised a flag in Telemachus' mind: not enough to force changes in operations of the estates, but enough to question the long-term commitment of the royal family of Elis to the family of Telemachus.

This slight uncertainty reinforced Telemachus' thoughts of returning to Ithaca, and he discussed it with Polycasté late one night when the evenings had turned warmer, and they could sit out on the veranda and enjoy the gentle breeze and odors of the blooming fruit trees.

"Penelope reports that she has been welcomed back by the people of Ithaca," Telemachus told Polycasté. "I am confident that we can follow her at some point in the near future. By all accounts, the palace and estates are making their way back to health. The residents of the island are happy with the changes that a fully functioning palace has brought to the island. Penelope's return has brought new life."

"Why do you need to return to Ithaca?" Polycasté asked.

"How can you ask that?"

"I need to understand."

"It is my home and the home of my family. I was forced to leave. Now I must return."

"We have a home here. I have never been to Ithaca. The twins have never been there. And you left generations ago with the rancor of the people."

"Polycasté, our home here is not truly our own. The King of Elis resents our success and tightens the lead rope with every passing season. At some point, we will no longer be free to live here."

"But you ignore Pylos."

"Pylos, where your brothers rule, though they are destined to be replaced if they cannot work together. Nestor is the only mortar keeping the family together."

"My father offered you a role in the governing of Messenia," Polycasté replied. "But he is waiting for your interest."

"Your brothers would kill me if I entered into their affairs. And in any case, you do not listen. Ithaca is my home and the home of my sons."

"And where is my home?" Polycasté asked.

"With me."

"I do not feel it. You have your horses and Oxylus and the farm. And, yes, you have your sons. I am left with managing the servants and meeting with the women of Elis. I need more than that."

"What more?" Telemachus replied with frustration. "By the gods, what more do you need?"

"I am not sure." That was all that Polycasté would say. But she thought she knew exactly what she needed, and to be forced to express it to her husband meant she would never obtain it. Without it, she might survive; asking for it would surely mean death.

Once again, they went to their bed chamber without cheer and divided, lacking understanding.

Following the funeral of Odysseus, Athene returned to her palace in the sky. During the proceedings, she had watched with great sadness and listened carefully to the eulogies and taken in the smoke and burnt offerings. For her, Odysseus had been the ideal mortal, gentle and wise, yet strong, and although Zeus had made him immortal and placed him forever in the skies, she felt a great loss. For few men walk the earth with the authority and command of Odysseus. She met with Zeus in a private audience.

"I have come from the funeral of Odysseus," she told Zeus. "For the greatest man on earth, he had a simple and quiet ceremony."

"We have made him immortal," Zeus replied to his truculent daughter, "even though this mortal expressed his doubts. 'Pan is dead,' he often said. Nonsense. What more can we do?"

"Some god compassed his end."

"Ah, and for that you seek your father's aid."

"I seek only justice."

"And what would you have of us?" Zeus asked, the fatigue growing in his voice.

"Justice."

"Daughter, I have heard you."

"Justice," she repeated.

"Daughter, it is not so easy. Odysseus has been honored as no man before...or ever after. Now, we must move on."

"And his family, once again, is suffering at no cause of their own. His wife, Penelope, has returned to Ithaca. Odysseus' son and his wife are at odds. The grandchildren are being drawn into the dispute. And as you know, soon enough, the blood will begin to flow again across the Peloponnese with the war between the Heraclides and the ruling Pelopides."

"Daughter, be aware that the generosity and goodness of our rule has its limits. I swear we will bury you in Tartarus along the elder gods whose dominions were transferred to us. So, daughter, do not test our patience."

"I plan to support the family's desire to reunite in Ithaca."

"Let us remind Athene once again. We immortals can become antiquated or sent wandering in the cold and darkness, buried under rocks, or forced to reside in the depths of Hades. We forbade all intercourse with mortals. We, our self, have followed this dictum. You too will follow it. We are growing weary..."

"Hera agrees with me, Father. The War of the Families is more critical to the Hellenes than Troy ever was. The two greatest families of Hellas, the Pelopides and Heraclides, cannot long abide together. And it is the people who will suffer. The outcome will be an age as dark as any before, with the loss of all gains."

"We cannot change that," Zeus said.

"We must."

"We cannot. Now, get thee hence. And do not remind us of our quarrelsome wife. You two are like gnats. But listen to us and listen well. We will crush you as Dionysus crushes his grapes and turn you into a seasonal runnel if you continue in your pursuits."

"Then Apollo and Hermes and Ares must leave off as well," Athene said.

"At last we agree." But Zeus was fatigued with the bickering of mortals and immortals alike and could only shake his enormous head in dismay. "Sometimes, we believe that we are all lost." He made this last comment to himself alone.

Strong-willed Athene was not about to give over to Zeus' warnings. This was not the end of the discussion. His thunder claps and bolts of lightening might frighten some, but of all the gods, Athene understood him best. She was born of his head, not of his loins.

Michael Barnes Selvin

XVI

"If you are going to Marathon to meet with the Heraclides, then I am returning to Pylos to be with my family," Polycasté said firmly. "I cannot continue here in Elis and allow my family to perish. I intend to take the twins with me."

Polycasté and Telemachus sat in their sleeping room one evening during the season of wearisome heat. The shutters were open with a gentle breeze from Apeliotes. Neither faced the other. Telemachus and Oxylus had made plans to meet with the Heraclides for the second time, this time at their palace in Marathon. Polycasté's statement shocked Telemachus, less for its intent than for its certainty.

"Your father, Nestor, is not a Pelopide," Telemachus said. "The Pelopides care nothing for him. He owes his office to Heracles."

"The very man that killed his brothers and sisters."

"And you believe those stories?"

"I will not aid the enemies of my father."

"Your father no longer rules in Pylos. Your brothers battle each other to gain control of the kingdom, which is now splintered into four countries. No matter what the Heraclides are planning, King Tisamenus, son of Orestes, will soon overrun Messenia. Your brothers' dissention only aids him."

"Cresphontes and Temenus are using you, my husband."

"No," Telemachus disagreed. "You insult me. They do not even know me. Without them, though, I will never regain my father's rule. I must be strong in this, for another chance will not come along. Hear me, Polycasté. With the Heraclides ruling the Peloponnese, I will have the authority and support to return to my home to rule. There will be nothing the people of Ithaca and the offshore islands can say."

Telemachus glanced at his wife who sat on the side of the bed with her head down. "Our home is not in Elis, and the rulers are making that abundantly clear. I am a foreigner here and only count the days till I must leave. This is not your home any more than it is mine. Your home is with your family, our sons and me."

"I am sorry, Telemachus. You know I serve you in all ways; you and our sons are my family and my life. But when you make a choice that hurts so many, I cannot go along." She paused to think, the tears flowing down her cheeks. "No. Allow me to be honest. I have always been honest with you, though even that is leaving me. No, it is not the fact of the Heraclides alone. I am tired. I am exhausted. I am a shell from which all the vitality has been sucked out. I am no longer attractive or desirable. I have always been dutiful. I have dedicated myself to you at all times. I took care of your father and mother. I washed your father's body in preparation for his funeral. I have not evaded my duties towards your family. But I cannot continue to do this. I cannot stand by to see my father and my brothers destroyed."

"We go around in circles."

"I cannot see them thrown from their home and rule. I cannot be party to that."

"What do you expect of me?" Telemachus asked. "The Heraclides are returning to the Peloponnese, whether I join them or not. And if they do not overrun Messenia, Tisamenus, leader of the Pelopides, will, just as his father Orestes was about to do. Elis too will come under their leadership, as will all the cities of the Peloponnese. This may be a good thing, for the palaces are ignoring too much. The people are suffering. The ruling families are feasting beyond all need…and your brothers are no exception. What would you have me do?"

"I no longer know what is best for you. I am returning to Pylos. My father is old now, and he needs my help. The twins are young men; they can choose. But I am returning to Pylos."

"My sons will come with me. They are of age."

"If they are hurt, I will never forgive you."

Telemachus knew better than to argue with Polycasté for long. She was headstrong and compromised with difficulty. He could not ask for a better wife, but she had always been her own master. Gently, he tried one last time.

"Perhaps, there is another way."

"What would that be?"

"Perhaps the problem lies elsewhere."

"Elsewhere?" She turned to face him for the first time.

"Yes," he said, holding back.

"What do you mean?" she asked again.

"You know, you have not lost your attractiveness. You are as beautiful as you ever were. And we have two fine sons, healthy and strong. We are blessed. Only, you no longer trust me."

"It is not that. I am torn within myself. I understand you need the Heraclides, but I only see them leading you astray. We could all return to Pylos…"

"No," he shouted, "What is Pylos to me?" Telemachus paused. "Polycasté, I only ask that you trust me in this. No harm will come to your father and brothers. I am asking you to help me. I need your trust." He moved closer to her to touch her.

"You do not need me," she said, withdrawing. "You are asking too much and risking too much. My family, my sons, my home, my life. You ask me to follow after you like one of your foals?"

"Believe me, Polycasté. I have to do this. You will come or not, as you see fit."

Telemachus felt that he had already pushed too far. In a discussion such as this one, between people that know each other so intimately, words can be used to harm, and words once expressed, can never be withdrawn. His father had said, "words in council, weapons in war." Polycasté was spoiled as any daughter of a king, the favorite female child and last born in a large family of boys. Telemachus never did well in arguments with her. But he would never harm her with words or impatiently force a decision. So, he ended the dispute, hoping beyond reason as he had every night that another night of sleep and dreams might soften her resolution.

When Eos rose from Oceanus with her golden hues, Polycasté had not softened in her decision. She prepared to return to Pylos. About that, Telemachus was not surprised. What did surprise him was that Amphion would not hear of leaving his mother. And so the twins would be divided for the first time in their lives. Daring

Autolycus would remain with Telemachus, and fair-minded Amphion would return to Pylos with Polycasté.

The family rode their horses to the coast the following morning, mostly in silence, for no one was comfortable with the directions their lives were taking. The horses sweated in the warm morning air, and the riders threw back their riding cloaks. At the harbor at Pheia, a small ship was prepared to sail down the coast to Nestor's palace in Pylos. For a moment, the family stood together fearful of the significance of this parting, but unwilling to express what emotions lay beneath their words.

"I am hopeful that this will be of short duration," Telemachus said awkwardly.

"It depends on father," Polycasté replied enigmatically.

"I hope you find him well," Telemachus said. "Amphion, you must continue your lessons." Father and son regarded each other.

"I shall miss you," Autolycus said, grabbing his brother into a bear hug. He was always the first to touch, the first to feel.

"You can visit," Amphion replied.

"I will. You can bet on that."

And Autolycus moved quickly to his mother and wrapped his arms around her, standing off a bit so as not to do her harm with the strength of his emotions. She held him tightly, for she had never been a reticent mother.

Telemachus embraced Amphion and backed away. He then went to his soft-eyed wife and held her in his arms for a long while, feeling the confusion within her body.

"I am sorry," she said, the tears flowing down her cheeks.

"No, never. I am here. Never doubt that for an instant." They backed apart.

Telemachus and Autolycus stood together as Amphion helped Polycasté into the ship on the gangplank. The captain shouted, and the *keulestes* began a slow beat, as the sailors pushed the ship off the sand and the oars dipped into the sea. They watched the ship slowly beat its way out into the channel protected by distant Zacynthus and jibe to port, the sail filling with the Borean streams.

Telemachus and Autolycus watched a long while as the ship departed, Amphion waving from the prow deck, as the oars dug into the waves, and as the sail billowed and reflected the sun on the large-wide sea. Welcome or not, Time continues his incessant movement.

"How long, O lord?" Telemachus asked himself. "I have lived many lives, but never my own."

Agamemnon and Achilles had struggled over a slave woman at Troy, beautiful Briseis, and perhaps the war in Troy might have been avoided or at least diminished if one or the other had retreated, but neither did. And this clash did not end in Troy, but was revived by their offspring. Just as their fathers had fought over a woman, so their sons, Orestes and Neoptolemus, fought over Hermione, the daughter of Helen and Menelaus. As told by Euripides, after the Trojan War Menelaus gave Hermione to Orestes to wife, but Menelaus forgot he had promised her to Neoptolemus during the war. When Neoptolemus became King of Epirus and Phthia, he reminded Menelaus of his promise and forced Menelaus to change his mind. Always the weakling, Menelaus took Hermione from his nephew, Orestes, and gave her to Neoptolemus. Orestes, like his father, Agamemnon, was not a man to be trifled with. He took a large armed force from Mycenae and met Neoptolemus in battle at the Oracle of Delphi. He killed Neoptolemus and took Hermione back to wife. Hermione and Orestes had a child, and they called him Tisamenus, born of double rage.

A child of great privilege, Tisamenus, grew up in the shadows of his father, Orestes, and the reputation of his grandfather, Agamemnon. After Orestes' death, Tisamenus became King of Mycenae; some say he was the greatest king of the Peloponnese ever, for he ruled over more of the near-island of the Peloponnese than had any other man. He had great intelligence, but, unfortunately, he lacked, as many privileged sons do, the shrewdness of his father and grandfather. He used his intelligence to belittle others. He took enjoyment in exerting his inherited power to pointlessly brutal ends. His considerable charm, which he could start and stop as one opens and closes a gate, contrasted with his enjoyment of seeing fear in the eyes of men confronted with his position and intellect. Tisamenus was greedy and surrounded himself with sycophants. Tributes rose. Wars between neighbors became common. With his control of Sparta, he began harassing Messenia, playing on the weakness in Nestor's kingdom. Even the leaders of Attica felt threatened by Tisamenus, for he had the largest standing army in all of Hellas, and they saw hunger in his eyes.

During the reign of King Tisamenus, the invasion of the third crop of Heraclides began in earnest, and the final phase of the War of the Families reached its conclusion. This war, like most wars, was a war between two men: Cresphontes, archon of the Heraclides, and Tisamenus, archon of the Pelopides. The reason for their enmity went far beyond their personal animosity. It went far beyond their desire to wrest land and dominion from one other. It originated from the deadly rivalry between their two powerful families. A rivalry based like so many before on a contest for a woman: Hippodamia, daughter of King Oenomaus of Elis. And as in all mortal activities, whether noble or evil, the gods stirred the cauldron of ire between the Pelopides and the Heraclides for generations without reprieve.

XVII

A year after their aborted meeting with the Heraclides on the island of Zacynthus, and several moon cycles after the departure of Polycasté, Telemachus and Oxylus finally agreed to a second meeting with Cresphontes and the Heraclides. After the long trek from Athens, their horses breathing heavily, Telemachus, Oxylus, and Autolycus stopped to rest their mounts at the low hills along the coast leading into the plain of Marathon. In the clear autumn day, they could see a great plain spread out before them, sloping into a saltwater marsh and bay. The large palace of the Heraclides was visible in the foothills above the Charadra River at the Borean reaches of the plain, with mountains rising behind. The army of the Heraclides occupied the valley, their encampments spotted between open space, cultivated areas of barley and wheat, small farms, and natural copses. Visitors to the palace could not approach without notice of the troops, and soon enough a mounted contingent of armed soldiers in bronze armour rode up.

"You must be the counselors," a gray-bearded officer shouted, not dismounting. He was surrounded by ten or so troopers with short, light-weight lances. "We expected you, but thought better to nip it in the bud, so to speak. Quite a horse," he said to Oxylus, noting Rhaebus. "That was the giveaway."

"And you are riding the noble daughter of my very mount, Sterope," Telemachus said to the officer, recognizing a horse he had tamed and traded to the Heraclides a few years before.

"I recognize you, sir, from your last visit. I call her Podargus, after one of Heracles' mounts."

Telemachus caught the eye of Podargus and slowly pointed his finger at her. She reacted immediately, bowing her head with a snort. She stamped the ground with her front hoof. She began backing slowly away, forcing the horses behind her to move out of her way, her ears and eyes fixed on Telemachus. The rider frantically pulled the reins but could do nothing with her. Telemachus then lifted both arms high above his head, and the horse followed him, immediately rearing up on her hind legs, pawing the air, the trooper holding on for dear life.

"Please sir, you are making me most uncomfortable," the officer begged, his hands buried in her mane. "How do you do that?" he asked once the horse settled on all four feet. "She was always so manageable, this one."

"Just a tamer's trick," Telemachus laughed. "A horse never forgets."

"Aye, sir. Now, if you be so kind, we will escort you to the godly Cresphontes."

Telemachus and Oxylus followed the soldiers along the trail. As they descended onto the plain, they realized the extent of the Heraclide soldiers. Large groups of soldiers practiced in the fields. Many of the encampments were empty of soldiers, though clearly occupied. Other camps buzzed with activity. Surprisingly, several two-horse chariots made their way along the wide paths. Chariots were nearly useless in most regions of the Peloponnese due to the difficult terrain and poor roads. Soldiers practiced fighting with wooden swords and lances. While others rested or just talked in groups or walked slowly along the trails.

"They seem well occupied, though not productively," Oxylus noted to Telemachus. "Must be three battalions* or better."

The soldiers moved off the road as the escort and the counselors trotted past. They gawked at the enormous war horse and tiny rider, so dark and bright-eyed, and they looked closely at golden-haired Telemachus, who rode effortlessly. They knew him by reputation only, the son of the hero Odysseus. They had no idea who the third man was, just a boy. What roles would these counselors play among the Heraclides? What were the merits of these new and unknown leaders? Did they have anything to offer or were they just other officers ordering them about. No one waved or expressed emotion of any kind, except the soldiers stared with enormous interest in these two strangers, who might have as much to say of their futures as the gods themselves.

---

* A battalion equals one hundred soldiers.

I cannot continue without recognizing that seven hundred years later (the palace long destroyed; the Heraclides a myth) one of the most the famous battles of all time would take place on this very plain of Marathon. The army of Darius, King of Persia, met the Athenians, led by Miltiades, the great general. They had once been great drinking partners and allies. The Athenians triumphed over a much large force, killing over six thousand Persians, while losing only (only) one hundred and ninety-two Athenians and Plataeans. Darius is quoted as saying, "What serves a cavalry without horses?" For, in fact, the Athenians waited until the Persian horses had been loaded on the ships to begin their charge. Callimachus the Polemarch, commander of the right wing of the Athenian, led the charge, won the battle, and lost his life. Aeschylus, the dramatist, was seriously wounded in the fight; his brother died after his hand was severed by an ax at the Persian ships on the bay. What happens in war in an instant lasts a lifetime. Aeschylus never forgot this battle, which gave him a rare insight and knowledge of human nature, particularly the importance of the affairs of family to men and women. You might remember, my dear Alcathöe, the words he gave Apollo:

"Is Aphrodite to be cast aside dishonorably, she who gave rapture unto mortal man? For man and woman the sanctity of the marriage bed, when justly kept, is far stronger than any oath that could be sworn."*

The much anticipated meeting began with a demonstration by Telemachus and Oxylus of the new implements of war. This display was for the benefit of the Heraclide leaders, but also for the dubious soldiers whose allegiance would be crucial. Telemachus stood next to Sterope, in the palace inner courtyard. He faced the leaders of the Heraclides on the stairs, watching him suspiciously, and several

---

* Aeschylus, "The Eumenides," one of the dramas in the Oresteia, which tells the history of the house of Atreus. Of the ninety plays written by Aeschylus, only seven survive in full. We can assume that among the lost plays was the story of King Tisamenus, son of Orestes.

hundred of their troops filled the courtyard behind him. Oxylus stood somewhat apart, without Rhaebus.

Telemachus attempted to fill the courtyard with his voice, but those men at a distance could barely make out his words, and pushed forward to better hear him. All side-conversations were quickly hushed. He began by describing the weaknesses of the states of the Peloponnese: unprepared to defend themselves, ancient weapons and unprofessional militias, bankrupt treasuries, angry and skeptical citizens, and, most importantly, antagonism between each other, ranging from distrust to hatred.

"Whereas some of the cities toward Boreas may be able to produce an infantry, or, combined, they may be able to mount a plausible defensive force, they are totally unprepared to defend themselves against a rapidly moving offensive force, such as we are proposing: mounted horse troops and trained light troops. These states have not come against the strategies of the armies of the Asiatics or the great militias of the Levant, as my brother-at-arms has. They know nothing of the new armaments that we propose and do not have the skills and knowledge to defend against them. Even the heroes of Troy would not have been able to defend against such a force.

"Here are the changes that can shift the direction of war," continued Telemachus. "This is Sterope, daughter of Eous, daughter of Bronte. Sterope has produced many fine colts, some among you today."

"First the bridle." He held up what looked like a normal bridle with the exception that no reins were attached. "The bridle is special in several ways. First there is an iron snaffle, or mouth piece. This is loose in the center of the horse's mouth and gives her more freedom, but at the same time can put pressure on the horse with a small motion by the rider. The bridle attaches over the ears and under the jaws."

Sterope took the snaffle in her mouth, and Telemachus pulled the bridle over her ears and attached the straps under her jaws. He threw over her head a larger continuous strap of leather.

"This single piece of leather serves as the reins. This broad band rides on the horse's neck and can be used as one would use reins. The rider can take the band in his hands to direct the horse. But here is the important part. When not in the rider's hands, the band rides on the neck, still keeping the horse's head down. This leaves both hands of the rider free, so he can guide a trained horse with his knees."

Telemachus then held up a leather saddle pad and threw it over Sterope's back. "Here is a saddle that rides on the horse and does not move." He attached it by a girth under the horse's barrel and another strap around the chest below the throttle. "It provides a fixed platform that gives the rider a comfortable seat, while allowing him a secure bond to the horse at all gaits: a bond for throwing, slashing, and launching bolts."

"Finally, a leather lead attaches from the bit to the neck girth, further restricting the movement of the horse's head and allowing the rider additional control without the use of his hands."

After this, he backed several steps away from the horse and then took two quick steps and leapt onto the horse's back. She remained fixed in place. The soldiers surrounding the horse quickly backed away as the large horse stamped forward. Telemachus approached Oxylus, who handed him a small bow and a quiver that attached to the saddle pad. With the bow in one hand and his other hand at his side, he spun the horse in a quick circle, moving the soldiers farther back. Then the horse broke into a trot, moved smartly to the edge of the courtyard wall, and turned quickly. Telemachus signaled for the soldiers to back toward the stairs. Without any visible command from Telemachus, the horse surged forward, galloping from one side of the courtyard to the other and then wheeling rapidly to return. This time Telemachus had an arrow in the bow and fired at the gate, again causing soldiers to scatter when the unexpected projectile embedded in the post. He wheeled Sterope again, both hands free, fitting another arrow onto the bowstring as the horse galloped. This time, he came closer to the soldiers along the stairs and loosed a second arrow at the door of the entrance to the palace above the heads of the family members. He then wheeled the horse again, charging directly at the men, who were becoming extremely nervous. He halted a few steps before the stairs with dust flying, and the men again moving to distance themselves without appearing frightened.

"Sirs," Telemachus called from the heavily breathing horse, "you can see the authority of a horse and the ability to do mischief to a foe. Imagine a thousand horses and a thousand skilled riders.

"Now, my brother-at-arms, the son of King Haemon, will show you some of these new armaments and describe some of the skills he has learned. He has fought on numerous fields of battle throughout the Known World and is honored by the Hittites. He has trained us, and together we can train you. Follow us, and we can sweep over the Peloponnese as easily as a hawk flies over grassy fields searching for quarry."

He tossed the bow to Oxylus and dismounted, holding Sterope by the strap reins. The two leaders of the Heraclides, Temenus and Cresphontes, came forward somewhat tentatively.

"That was very impressive," Cresphontes said, "But we do not have a thousand skilled riders, nor do we have a thousand horses."

"We do," Oxylus said smiling. "We have more than a thousand horses today and can easily have twice that number. Also, we can train soldiers to ride. For what you have just observed is no mystery, but simply good horsemanship. We can get trained cavalry troops from Thessaly and Macedonia. But allow us to continue with our demonstration."

Two servants pulled a wooden cart into the center of the courtyard. All sorts of weapons and armaments lay piled on it. The soldiers began pressing forward to see what was contained.

"Deiphontes," Oxylus requested, "please retrieve your best sword from the palace."

But before Deiphontes could get a sword, Procles, one of the twins of the third crop, walked forward aggressively toward Oxylus and drew his sword.

"Ah, a volunteer," Oxylus said. "The code of a soldier: never volunteer; never show fear. You may approach." Procles walked forward with his sword held at his side. Although not a large man, he stood a full head above Oxylus.

"So, are you prepared to fight?" Oxylus pulled a long sword from the cart and rapidly approached Procles. He pushed his black beard and broad chest at the young Procles. The two men looked at each other as the surrounding men gave ground.

"No more tricks," Procles said.

"Tricks. I own none." Oxylus swung his sword quickly, giving Procles only an instant to raise his own sword in defense. But to the amazement of the bystanders, Procles' sword failed to stop Oxylus' sword. Instead, Oxylus' sword slashed the blade into two pieces, leaving Procles with a remnant of the sword in his hand.

"If my aim had not been true, you would be standing in two pieces, not your sword."

Fortunately for Procles, Oxylus' aim was true. But the young man stood dumbfounded, observing his bronze hilt and stub. A note of shock and surprise rose among the troops, as they discussed what they had seen.

"Cresphontes," Oxylus said, "we are not magicians. And what we are showing you is only what you have always demanded. It is what you need. If you are to take on the armies of the Peloponnese, you must do so with some forethought. Not like some cockerel among his hens." He stopped for a moment to assess the effect of his words, as some of the soldiers snickered.

"Now, you may wish to attack the Peloponnese as you did before and again lose many men, only to return defeated once more. Or you can listen and learn. You have two skilled men before you, and your success will depend on understanding what we have to say. I understand your forebear Heracles had a similar temperament, taking umbrage and action before consideration." Cresphontes stepped forward, but Temenus held him back.

"Let him continue," Temenus said to Cresphontes, stepping between the two men. Cresphontes and Procles retreated, allowing Oxylus to continue.

Slowly, Oxylus pulled out swords, shields, and armour, breastplates and greaves, javelins, lances, fittings, and tools from the cart. He separated the weapons and armament from the farm tools. For like some itinerant trader, Oxylus carried many samples, including short hoes, scythes, digging implements, and saws, both large and small, that a farmer might find useful. Demonstrating the weapons, he described each one and passed them one at a time for all to heft and view. The soldiers were surprised by the strength and lightness of the swords and javelins. Although the cutting strength of the new metal had already been demonstrated, Oxylus had one further test. He took a shield made of the new metal and laid it next to a bronze shield. He hacked at the iron shield with an iron sword. He could dent the metal, but not cut it. With the bronze shield, he had no trouble slicing it with large gashes.

He took a short javelin with an iron tip. It was shorter than the common javelin and somewhat thicker. He threw it. It flew across the courtyard and stuck in the doorpost, not far from Telemachus' arrow.

"This javelin," he continued, "was derived from a hunting javelin. It is called a wolf-destroyer by the Thessalians due to its weight and strength. It is made of ash and has a tanged, elliptical iron head. Easy to enter and retract. But its shape causes much damage." He passed another javelin around for all to see. "It can pierce the strongest shield or bronze armour and can bring down a man who believes himself immune. And we have hunters from the chilly climes who have used these all their lives.

"But the last weapon is the best. It is a bow of a new design, made of several different woods joined together. It is both smaller and stronger and has a range farther than any bow in Hellas. You just saw Telemachus use it on horseback. It is light and easy to carry, and it is effective from a long distance."

He strung an arrow and shot it far over the walls. Again the soldiers were surprised at the distance, and above all when they hefted the bow and pulled the string back.

"Unlike Odysseus' legendary bow, it can be strung by a small boy, but it will outshoot any long bow the Pelopides have in their arsenal."

"So you have seen our tools for building a capable offensive force to take the Peloponnese. This evening after dinner, I would like to summarize our ideas and how we would suggest that these weapons be used in battle. The tools of war are critical for victory, as is knowledge of the theater of war. But most important of all is the soldier."

With that, the soldiers departed with a new respect for these two strangers, while the leaders had gained insight to their counselors beyond what they had expected.

Bronze was the metal of the Trojan War. Both Achaeans and Trojans fought with bronze armaments. Some time before the Hellenes sacked Troy, the secret guild of metal workers among the

Hittites made a chance discovery. The guild discovered a process to make iron stronger and lighter than any other metal. The Hellenes smelted iron, but it was soft and malleable and not useful for armaments. The production of iron was not difficult, but to produce a hard, weapons-grade iron alloy took a major leap in known processes.

All iron workers prayed to Hephaestus, god of blacksmiths, the true and loving son of Zeus and Hera. When the boy Hephaestus defended his mother Hera against the lord of gods, Zeus became so enraged that he hurled his son from the heavens, where he fell for an entire day and finally landed in Lemnos, becoming lame as a result of his fall. Or so Apollodorus tells us. Others felt that Hephaestus was lame at birth and thrown from heaven on account of this by his spiteful mother. I prefer the former explanation. What mother would throw her child, lame or not, from a great height? In any case, Hephaestus was raised by the goddess Thetis and became the greatest artisan of all time. He fashioned much of Olympus. But it was in metal work that he excelled. He wrought the wonderful armour of Achilles at Thetis' request. He made Diomedes' breastplate and Heracles' greaves. And he produced many of the finest silver and golden bowls and ewers described by Homer. Although lame in his feet, the skills of his hands were beyond compare. His work forced greatness upon all.

Metal workers combined religious sensibility with the secrecy and mysteries of their craft. Secret societies and mysterious rites protected the processes of working metals, allowing the training and induction of new smiths into the craft, while carefully controlling the potential migration of their knowledge and skills. And of course, at the base of the mystery of the metal workers was the professed feat, although never accomplished so far as we know, of creating gold from base metals. The fact that iron has magnetic properties not well understood at the time made the mystery even greater among superstitious people, helping the metal worker further the secrecy and command of their enterprise. When certain workers were able to create a stronger and lighter metal, a metal that could cut through bronze without itself showing any impact, the aura of metal working was raised to a new plateau.

Iron's rise was due to the introduction of charcoal as the fuel of choice for smelting. No one understood why, but allowing the raw slab to heat in contact with charcoal produced a better iron. Gold, silver, copper, tin, and lead or their admixtures were not enhanced by this contact. The iron workers developed new furnaces in secret to produce only iron products. The final step was to discover that quenching the hot metal could further increase its strength. And quenching was even more mystical. Different quenching solutions and recipes were soon put forth as the ultimate: spring water, mud, oils, emollients, and even living flesh. This final step of quenching set the way for metal workers to produce a purified iron alloy, and the first and most seductive use of this new metal was in armaments. The Hittites produced swords that kept a sharper edge and were at the same time lighter, stronger, and more durable. Most importantly, these weapons cut through bronze swords. Being lighter, swords could be made that were longer and thicker, with hilts formed as part of the blade. The first true slashing sword resulted, with a center of gravity farther down the blade, allowing a sword to be used both to thrust and slash. Soldiers could use these swords from horseback.

The Hittites went on to make better javelin and lance points, arrowheads, daggers, armour and shields, horse tack, and many other implements of war. Wars and the way wars were conducted changed forever, giving a new edge literally to those with purified iron at their call. Sadly, it was some time before iron was used for peaceful purposes.

XVIII

Telemachus, Oxylus, and Autolycus met in the banquet hall with the leaders of the Heraclides. The megaron was dark and needed repairs and painting, though the fire burned strongly and warmly, and the servants rushed the sizzling meats to the diners and kept the goblets full. The brothers, Cresphontes and Temenus, were the senior leaders and worked closely together. Both had been involved in the failure of the return of the second crop. Cresphontes, the older, took charge by habit and nature. Where he was quick to take affront and to judge and had a tendency to hear only what he wanted to hear, Temenus was more thoughtful and differential, softening his brother's impact. In the end, though, Temenus always deferred to his older brother. Their distant nephews, Deiphontes, and the twins, Procles and Eurysthenes, were the leaders of the third generation of Heraclides, the so-called third crop. They were respectful and quick to retire when challenged by one of their uncles. Phalces and Cerynes, the oldest sons of Temenus (for Temenus had nine children), stayed close to their father. Dusky Aletes, son of Hippolytus, another distant cousin, short and heavy set, attended with interest on Cresphontes but remained silent and reserved, his dark eyes and brows surveying and measuring. The younger leaders were often at odds with one another and could agree on almost nothing.

Autolycus sat beside his father. His beard was still light, but he was strong and barrel-chested like his grandfather and growing rapidly into a man – only a few years younger than the youngest of the third crop. Telemachus opened the conversation by describing his knowledge of the Peloponnese and its rulers. In the half-light of the oil lamps and central fire pit, it was difficult to see expressions, but it was clear that the Heraclides shared little consensus. Their dialogue often veered off in unexpected directions.

"The Peloponnese is at a low point today," Telemachus explained. "The Pelopide rulers are corrupt and squeezing the people to maintain their palaces. In the last decades, people from the direction of Boreas have been moving in, looking for more fertile soil and better lives. But good soil is scarce, so there is much disagreement and fighting. No one is happy with the situation."

The Peloponnese was divided into five separate regions of power that existed at the time of the Trojan War and still exist today, though not as clearly defined. The most powerful region – Argolis – was found toward the wind Kaikias. This was the home of Pelops, the kingdom of Agamemnon and his son Orestes, the great states of Mycenae and Corinth. Tisamenus, the son of Orestes, now ruled this region. Orestes had been a strong ruler and in the end took control of Argos as well, and then finally of Laconia and Sparta. But for all his success, King Orestes allowed his rule to grow thin and unpopular. He attempted to annex Messenia, but failed, leaving the sons of Nestor still ruling, but divided and weak. At his death, he was annexing mountainous Arcadia.

His son Tisamenus inherited a large kingdom, but a weak one due to its size and lack of allegiance to his rule. He was consolidating his rule and employed the sons of Aegimius, Pamphylus and Dymas, as his generals. Pamphylus was married to Deiphontes' daughter. These generals had owed their allegiance to Orestes.

"The key to the Peloponnese is Corinth," Telemachus continued. "This city is well fortified, nearly impregnable, with two ports and control of the isthmus. Corinth must be taken first off."

Athens had recently threatened Corinth, and the current drought was causing great distress in the area. The region was wealthy and growing, controlling much of the trade of the Apeliotean and Zephyrian seas. Since Corinth was constantly on the defensive with Attica, there was a strong standing army. Tisamenus controlled Corinth, but it exerted its independence from Mycenae by its geographical situation. The kings, Doridas and Hyanthidas, sons of Propodas, jointly ruled, but owed their throne to Tisamenus and could be expected to put up a fight. They had combined armed forces with Mycenae.

Argos and Tiryns, the land of the hero Diomedes, were also controlled by Tisamenus, but this was never a region open to outside rule. The Argives always favored self-rule and freedom and placed limits on the power of their rulers. Local archons governed, and although in the past they had considerable military power, they had suffered internally from the migrations and were unprepared to defend themselves and hesitant to send troops to aid Tisamenus.

The Peloponnese lying in the path of Notus was primarily Laconia, with Sparta as the center of power. Menelaus had ruled there for many years following the war, but now the region owed allegiance to Tisamenus. The people of Sparta were chafing under Tisamenus' control as they had under Orestes. Although they had a significant military force, it was defensive in nature like a hornet when attacked that will sting repeatedly. Sparta would not wholeheartedly support Tisamenus.

The kingdom of Nestor at Pylos was now split among his children, and Nestor was old and no longer ruled. The four regions were ruled separately by three of his descendants. One region was ruled independently of Nestor's family. The regions were constantly at each other's throats and had neither the resources, nor the equipment, nor trained soldiers capable of putting up resistance. In his day, Nestor ruled over a gentle people, a people removed from the rest of the Peloponnese, and he had done so with concern for his subjects and the well-being of his kingdom.

The final countries, Elis and Achaea, were rural and remote. Achaea was the location of the invasion of the second crop of Heraclides, but had few resources and held little sway over the affairs of the Peloponnese. Elis was healthy with good crops and rainfall, but it was isolated and under populated. King Eleius had no defenses and knew nothing of warfare. His treasury was bankrupt, and many of the people that had settled recently in Elis from the direction of Boreas were escaping their own problems and did not want new ones.

"The one thing Peloponnesians hate more than outsiders is each other," Telemachus said. "In a war, the individual countries will stand back to observe and then side with the opponent that offers them the most, regardless of what this does to their neighbor. The true battle will be to convince them that the Heraclides will be victorious. How will you do this? Not by battle and arms, since it is a return to power you seek and not an invasion. The Heraclides must have no intention of plundering or razing the cities of the Peloponnese. Payment to the soldiers cannot be made by booty and loot. You must protect the local people and treat them with respect. If the locals are convinced of this, they will help the forces of return, by providing food and drink and by staying out of the way. Ambassadors must always be sent in advance of the troops. And, finally, the Heraclides must prove to the populace that improvements will come under their leadership."

"What is all this?" Cresphontes said loudly, interrupting. "The Peloponnese belongs to us. Do not venture to tell us how to manage our dealings."

Surprised, Telemachus turned to Oxylus, who stood and turned to Cresphontes and bowed.

"May the gods grant us the gift of understanding and through thought, word, and deed help us achieve our goals in a manner prescribed by heaven and bring joy to ourselves and our friends and grief to our rivals and foes." He smiled with good nature at the stern family facing him.

Oxylus discussed their proposed strategy. He pointed out that where once the Hellenes could field the strongest and bravest army in the world, today they were still fighting battles as their grandfathers had fought. The armies of the Levantine, of Egypt, of the Hittites, and of the barbarians had moved forward in their understanding of warfare, both in military strategies and in materiel.

He suggested a force of about three thousand men, equally split between light infantry and cavalry, professional fighters, highly trained in their expertise. Hellas was full of such men, who would be willing to fight to get established in the Peloponnese. This force would not be a militia or conscripted group, as the Pelopides would marshal, but an army dedicated to the goals of self-interest. The army would be made up of experienced men: Boeotians, Enienes, Paeonians, Thessalians, the greatest horsemen the world knows, and Thracians, Turshans, and Lycians from Asia Minor, Shekelesh, Shardana, and Peleset from along the Adriatic Sea. These men all spoke some form of Greek, and all were ready to fight. The Peloponnese offered them the possibility of a new and better life for their families. They have heard the stories of the wealth and fertility of the Peloponnese, where one had only to thrust a stick into the ground to have it grow into a tree offering fruit.

Oxylus also suggested that a naval force of about forty long ships would be required. The navy would blockade both sides of the Gulf of Corinth, while land forces were applying pressure. But more importantly, the naval force would transport the land forces to the Peloponnese, avoiding the isthmus and Megara, for any force passing by Megara would immediately place the Corinthians on alert.

"Corinth is like seven-gated Thebes and must be handled carefully," Oxylus explained.

Tisamenus controlled many troops at the isthmus, with backup forces at Mycenae and Arcadia. Corinth was well fortified, and an army could defend itself all winter there. The defenses across the isthmus made entry nearly impossible, as the Athenians well knew. The Heraclides were not prepared for a war of slow destruction and would not be able to win such a battle.

"But a man does not win a race by staying at home. We will never confront Tisamenus directly. We will attack like wasps and devour like lions. The ancients say that if you see a lion, he has decided not to attack: you will never see the lion that kills you. No Peloponnesian force is prepared for a well-equipped, mobile army. Beware though, face to face in a conventional war, Tisamenus will take us apart like a cat playing with a bird."

He continued to describe a march across the Peloponnese with the states falling one after the other. The defeat of Tisamenus was the main requirement. All the countries owed allegiance to Tisamenus, for better of worse, and his departure would facilitate the others' decision to agree to a truce. He made it clear that every city or town would receive gifts for the archons, laurel branches, and a conciliatory tone. The Heraclides would be liberators, not occupiers. This war would be the rightful return of the descendants of Heracles and Perseus, founder of Mycenae.

Cresphontes rose. "I thank you for your thoughts, though lacking specificity and veering dangerously into the realm of the family. We look forward to completing our agreement tomorrow. The time of day is growing late. Now our thoughts turn to other climes and restful peace. We will gather together tomorrow following a family meeting."

That night, Telemachus and Autolycus did not enjoy the restful peace of sleep, but waited with wide eyes for the brush of Eos to paint the sky in her golden tones, for much was on their minds beyond the affairs of the Heraclides. Oxylus had sought the boon of sleep immediately after Dionysius' fill.

"After we better understand the Heraclides' plans for returning to the Peloponnese," Telemachus said to Autolycus, "we are going to Pylos to visit your mother and brother and grandfather."

"What will grandfather do?" Autolycus asked.

"He no longer rules. He will remain in Pylos."

"But what if the Heraclides desire to take Messenia?"

"Very likely they will. Then your uncles will have to unite."

"It does not seem fair that the Heraclides remove them from office."

"No, you are right. It is not fair. But it will happen, if not tomorrow, then the next day. If not the Heraclides, then Tisamenus. Whether we are involved or not. We have to consider what is best for us, for our family, for you and Amphion."

"I cannot wait to start training for war," Autolycus said later.

"No one looks forward to fighting."

"I want to be like my grandfather."

"You are like your grandfathers. But you must understand that neither one was a warrior. They both abhorred war, and both tried to prevent war from occurring. But there are always some who have much to gain by it. The tragedy is that it is most often those with little to gain who pay the price."

The next morning, a heavy mist covered the Charadra River valley and the lowlands on the Bay of Marathon, hiding rosy-fingered dawn and obscuring the sun and heavens. But no mortal man can long escape the attention of the gods. For the gods are all-knowing, and what occurs on earth is no surprise to them. Telemachus returned from checking the horses and ate his morning meal with Oxylus in their common room. Autolycus remained asleep.

"We will be returning to Pylos," Telemachus told Oxylus. "It has been many months since I have seen my family."

"I am glad I have no wife. Loneliness is preferable to pain."

"With pain," said Telemachus, "you know exactly where it is, but often not why it is calling your name."

Oxylus smiled. "There are families that love and struggle for each other, as your own; and there are families that do not bother. The Heraclides are among the latter. Temenus and his nephew, Deiphontes, have combined forces against Cresphontes, though undeclared. The twin nephews are constantly at odds, without loyalty to Cresphontes or Temenus. Aletes and Cresphontes have formed an alliance. The others are silent stalkers, as was Heracles."

"Temenus appears truthful," Telemachus said, "but I do not trust any of them. We need to be vigilant and mindful of their deceits. They cannot see beyond their own ignorance."

"Even so, we must not lose sight of our importance to them and our worth. I am sure they are moaning and groaning about our plan and believe, just as Heracles did, that they can strike at the heart of the Peloponnese with impunity. They have tried before without success. They started this when we were still at our mothers' breasts."

"People have long memories," Telemachus said, "and it is these memories we must overcome."

A servant clapped at the door to the room and brushed aside the curtain.

"Excuse me. The family is ready to meet with you."

When they entered the meeting room, the light fell without strength onto the floor. The room was cold and inhospitable, for the fire of the night before had been allowed to die. And the gods were forgotten. The family of Heraclides sat silently and unhappily behind Cresphontes, who welcomed the two strangers.

"Please," he showed them to a couch facing the family. "I pray that you have had a good night's rest. Now, we can complete our arrangements."

Telemachus and Oxylus nodded slightly.

"We were very impressed with your knowledge and suggestions. Your counsel is greatly appreciated, and you have demonstrated a grasp of the military arts and the clime in the Peloponnese. This morning, the family discussed the various strategies that you described and agree to a large extent with your findings. But consider this. We, too, are not without our sources in the Peloponnese. We have all done our time in preparation for military service, although we have never ventured outside of Hellas to mull over what other nations are doing. What we have difficulty accepting is the extent of your plan and the need for such weapons and such a large number of soldiers. Allow me to describe to you our plan, which takes into account..."

"Halt." Telemachus spoke loudly, interrupting Cresphontes and coming to his feet. Temenus had to physically restrain Cresphontes at Telemachus' action. "Listen to me well, for I will not repeat myself. I can only assume that the fault lies with us...that we did not make ourselves clear. We are here by your invitation. We did not solicit this meeting, and we are prepared to return to our homes with nothing gained and nothing lost. We are not negotiating the barter of a horse or bull. You have need of our assistance. And we are prepared to give it to you. But do not treat us as lackeys or hired help. You have heard our counsel, and we will accept no amendment.

"These are our terms of service. You, Cresphontes, will manage the affairs of the family and participate in strategy decisions. Temenus will lead the naval forces. All infantry troops will report to Oxylus, and all cavalry to me. We alone will select the troops and train them. As to the third generation of Heraclides, this is their battle. They will learn to lead the troops, for now they are like suckling babes. Deiphontes, Procles, Eurysthenes, Phalces, Cerynes, and Aletes will lead infantry or cavalry divisions, each to the task that he may best perform. This assumes that the twins can leave off their rivalries.

"What will this cost you? Do not be miserly. The cost of mobilization, training, and battle is nothing compared to the reward of returning to rule in the Peloponnese. Success will reward you beyond measure. We all know this. Of course, the rewards of success disregard the cost in lost lives. Families of all soldiers will be compensated according to their share of the victory...and not the spoils. What is it to a king to help a family find land to cultivate or work to perform? Do not be stingy in matters that have little import. I should point out that if you fail again this time, there will be no return at all, for so the gods have spoken.

"And what do we get? This question has been present like an uninvited guest. Here is the answer freely given. Oxylus will become King of Elis and rule this region independently of all other regions. And I will rule Ithaca, Cephallenia, and Zacynthus, just as my father before me. We will accept no less and do no less. And believe me when I say we are convinced that victory will be ours.

"And the timing? It should align with the moon before the harvest, giving us sufficient time before the rains and cold, for no army can move through the mud across the Peloponnese. We are not prepared to implement a lengthy battle and will lose one. If we are still fighting when the freezing winds of Boreas bear down on us, then we will have failed.

"Our success will be dependent on the benevolence of the gods. We will share with them in all things and respect their wishes. For what army is victorious without intercession of the immortals, and what man is successful without the aid of his personal protectors?"

Cresphontes was breathing heavily. Temenus rose, without looking at his brother.

"These are difficult terms, for what you are asking is total control. I understand you are offering both your oaths and lives in this matter. But you have entered an area that is reserved to family members. I cannot speak for all of us, but we have heard you, and what I would like is some time to reflect on this and then send a delegation with our final offer to you. Please accept our thanks. We agree entirely that this undertaking will be embarked upon only with the understanding that we mortals have nothing that we do not owe to the gods."

When Telemachus and Oxylus returned to their rooms, Autolycus was just waking up.

"Why did you not wake me?"

"If you had wanted to come," Telemachus said, "you would have gotten up with us and joined us. As it turned out, we did not decide anything, but will have to wait until they ponder this and conclude what should be apparent to anyone with a crumb of sense."

"You would have been proud of your father," Oxylus said. "If he liked Cresphontes any less, we could have driven an even harder bargain. When you are perceived as having no need of a thing, your bargaining strength is elevated to its highest. We are leaving. This Attica reminds me too much of my home in Aetolia – full of family duty, obeisance, and intrigue. I long for the freedom of the green hills of Elis."

"Are you coming with us to Pylos?" Telemachus asked Oxylus.

"I think that this trip to Pylos is for the two of you. But you should not tarry in Pylos, for we have much to accomplish in Elis and little time."

Before leaving the palace, Telemachus went to the entry hall to view an impressive fresco he had glimpsed on the first day of their visit. The painter had set the remarkable image entirely within the dome of the atrium to the palace. Here was a large image of Phaeton, son of Helios. Young Phaeton discovered he was the son of the sun god Helios and desired to reconcile with his immortal father, begging him to be allowed to drive the chariot of the sun across the skies for a single day. His father reluctantly agreed, driven by guilt at his absence in the life of his son. Unfortunately, Phaeton was unfamiliar with the route and could not manage the four wild horses pulling the chariot. He lost control, and the chariot veered dangerously toward the earth, burning the lands and throwing sunlight for the first time ever into the dark depths of Hades and even Tartarus, frightening the king and queen of shadows. Zeus, alarmed that the chariot would destroy the earth, reluctantly hurled a thunderbolt to save the earth, but in so doing destroyed Phaeton.

Telemachus wondered if his desire to counsel the Heraclides was similar to what Phaeton had attempted. Would the results be the same?

I, Antimenes believe that few sons truly reconcile with their fathers. For to a small child the father appears a hero. However, with the movement of time and circumstances, the continuous contrary changes between father and son make reconciliation almost unattainable. Much remains forever unspoken.

My father Clinias was a mystery to me, for his business kept him away from home. And when he returned, he was not able to interest himself in his two sons, but wanted time to prepare for the following day. I understand that. But the gift of life a father gives his son is heaven-borne, and my failure to meet this man was a great loss. A loss that I mourn. I did much for my daughters, interesting myself in their studies and problems. I sought no gain save what it brought to my family. True enough, I may have been withdrawn in my studies of the ancients. My scholars may have appeared more important to me than they were. I made every effort for the welfare of our children, Alcathöe. Can a man do more? I struggle with this question, so bear with me.

XIX

Meanwhile on Mount Olympus, Pallas Athene stood before her great and loving father, Olympian Zeus, who sat on his throne in silence, his face furrowed in concern. The far-darter Apollo, and Hermes, the prince of cattle thieves, stood on his other side. At that moment, there was no love in this family. For when anyone, mortal or immortal alike, cares deeply for something and refuses to compromise, there is bound to be strife and struggle. Today was no exception.

"Father, son of Cronos, beloved of all kings, you cannot allow this to continue," Athene demanded. "The family of the Heraclides is prideful and hateful. They are no better than the family they propose to replace. Telemachus has presented his case to the family for the best interests of the people of the Peloponnese, but the Heraclides listen not. They are too full of themselves. And this god, Heracles, the newest among us, is like a wolf in a den of lions. He speaks not and bides his time. His profile is of one who has no shadow and seeks to dissolve like a clod of dirt in water.

"Telemachus is taking on the trappings of a man like his father," Athene persisted. "He considers and does not act in haste or without thought. Cresphontes believes his own knowledge is superior to all mortals and ignores the immortals. Let us bring Cresphontes to the well. His family is divided, and all suffer this same disease. Maybe we should let the third crop of Heraclides fail for the last time. That would solve one problem, but the consequence of this would be to continue the growth of the evil seed of the sons of Atreus – all following their ancestors, Tantalus and Pelops. This family of Pelopides continues in this vein without honor or respect. Let me convince the family of the Heraclides of the right actions and the right measures. They are a godless sort and need educating."

Then fair Apollo looked at Athene with steely eyes, but spoke to his father. "Sire, as you have stated previously, we must allow mortals to act in their own best interests. We cannot intervene in all things. Mortal man learns lessons that encourage his fear and respect for the lord of gods. King Tisamenus, head of the Pelopides, is attempting to unify the Peloponnese. Are we to judge his actions even before he has completed them? You have frequently reminded us that we cannot change the fate of man. This struggle must be allowed to follow its natural course."

Hermes boldly laughed at Apollo. "What do you know of nature? You who would interrupt the life of a mortal to get with his wife. The Pelopides are as evil as man ever becomes."

And even-handed Zeus spoke angrily, his long gold-laced braids whipping about his massive head. "Our wife and children constantly annoy us. We swear, we are most disturbed by your bickering and deceit and will take action. Beware.

"Now, listen well," Zeus repeated. "We will not intervene, for we all know the outcome. However, Athene will appear before Temenus and set him on the right path, for he is so disposed in any case. This may reduce the potential for unintended consequences. We cannot prevent man from struggling, for this is a good thing. We cannot prevent man from killing others in rage or deceit. That is their lot. This will continue until they grow to understand and accept their shared circumstances. We are not some vengeful djinns. What we can do is help mortals overcome their fear of what they do not understand and help them along the road toward righteousness.

"We will bear no defiance on these points. We cannot correct the character of a man. Hear me on this.

"And Hermes...you will remain on Olympus...where I can keep an eye on you."

Ah, Pylos! Sparkling jewel, reflecting the glory of the setting sun. The magnificent palace of Nestor sat high above the coast of the Ionian Sea on a steep escarpment. Neleus, the father of Nestor, build the city as a carefully selected refuge from marauding tribes and pirates. Due to the location of Pylos, no defensive walls were ever built, since access from the coast was gained only by a roundabout means. The palace itself was constructed of giant white stones, glimmering of quartz crystals in the sun's rays. Cleverly built into the hillside, garden terraces stepped down the cliffs to the rocky reefs, with every level open to a brilliant view of the sea and sun. Fishermen used its brilliance to guide their crafts after a long day at sea. But from land the palace was not secure. In the war between the Eleans and the Pylians, Heracles led the Eleans to capture Pylos, killing Nestor's father and all of Nestor's brothers and sisters. Nestor escaped death as he was away at school in Gerenia. Heracles brought the boy Nestor back and bestowed the region upon him as regent, and when he grew to manhood he became the greatest King of Messenia ever.

Upon arriving in Pylos, Telemachus and Autolycus were soon reunited with their family at the palace of Nestor. The twin sons of Telemachus looked at each other at first as though strangers, for although they had only been separated only a few months, they saw differences that had not been apparent before. Soon enough, they were in each other's arms, leaving their parents alone.

Polycasté greeted Telemachus tentatively. She was dressed in a simple gray chiton, with her long braided hair arranged on her head. Her complexion was pale; she was without powder or perfume or ornament. They sat for a moment observing each other in an uncomfortable silence.

"The trip here was rough. We sought shelter in the Gulf of Laconia for a few days, but we had a large ship and made good progress. Oxylus continued on to Elis."

"Do you know these people better now?" Polycasté asked.

"They are a family at odds with themselves. Yet, they are strangely connected by the spirit of their ancestor."

"So they do not want power in Messenia?"

"They are governed by greed. Cresphontes believes so strongly in his mission that his vision is obscured and he cannot hear his own advisors."

"And what will become of my family?"

"I will never sacrifice your family for my own ends. You must believe me."

She looked at her husband of many years, the father of her two children, and wondered if she knew this man. "So much has changed. My mother, kind Eurydice, is now departed. I came to care for my father, and it was my mother who needed my help.

"I am truly sorry," Telemachus said. "Penelope will take the news hard. They shared much in common."

"The one grace is that my mother will not see further dissolution of her family," Polycasté continued. "Now Nestor is weak, and only I sustain him. His sons are not helpful to me or to him; they are occupied with their own families and regions and have grown to hate one another. The palace of Nestor is nearly empty and lifeless. Even the servants have deserted us. You will see tonight when we dine with Nestor. His mind is still lively, and his memory is good, but his body has deserted him."

Telemachus saw that his wife had thinned and her face was drawn and colorless. He took her hand, which she allowed him to retain. "I missed you...and Amphion."

"He is very well and has learned much during his stay here. He and Nestor pass long afternoons together, talking about everything. Amphion is the son my father never had. My father forces knowledge into him like one would fatten a goose. As for myself, I am worn out like an old pillow, without any down remaining. It has been very difficult. It is not as I thought when I left Elis. All has changed here."

They sat together for a moment with much left unspoken. He placed his arm about her shoulder and felt her body against his...and he smelled her hair and body. For a moment, he thought she was about to come to him. He turned his head slightly toward her, but with a start she backed away and excused herself, embarrassed.

That evening Telemachus and Polycasté had an informal dinner in Nestor's suites, for he almost never left his quarters now. He had difficulty getting around with a painful hip joint, and the smaller rooms kept him warm. The rest of the palace was closed. Polycasté occupied a room on the top floor, and Amphion was next to her. The servants had been reduced to a minimum; many of them were quite aged with nowhere else to go, having spent their entire lives serving the family of Nestor.

When Telemachus entered Nestor's suite, Polycasté was staring out the window opening into the evening sky. A servant was helping Nestor to his chair. Telemachus saw Nestor's familiar dark eyes and light shining from them.

"Ah, young man," Nestor said, "you chose to visit at a most inauspicious time."

"It is good to see you, sire," Telemachus replied.

"It is good to be seen," said Nestor as he sat with difficulty. "The gods have rewarded me with a long life for the short lives they gave my ancestors. I have been forced to remain on this earth for a time well beyond my due. Last time I saw you, you were inquiring about your father, the wily Odysseus. How could I ever forget him?"

"He is with the gods."

"I know. I know. Everyone has gone to the other world. Your father is legend and lives on, however. It always will be so. This is the true gift of immortality." He shook his head. "I can give nothing to my family, for they will say of Nestor that he strove, but the forces surrounding him were too strong. Now my sons cannot take a meal together because this Pelopide, Tisamenus, has forced our kingdom to feed upon itself, just as his great grandfather, Atreus fed his own nephews to their father for supper. What can we expect of Tisamenus when he springs from such a family? It will be good to see them leave this earth. They insult the gods."

Nestor paused, his head held low. "I am an old man, and I have seen too much. The great god Zeus has given innocence to the youth, and although they are often impulsive, light-headed, and mistaken in their notions, they can look into the future without being hindered by the past. Your Amphion will become a great ruler. He has the gift of fairness and understanding. I see your father in him. My own family...I have poisoned my family by some means."

"Father," Polycasté said, coming to the table, "please. We should have something to eat."

Nestor turned back to Telemachus. "She thinks that food matters to me. I assure you that it does not. When I was a young man in Gerenia, we ate fried squid and drank dark wine until we could barely walk to piss in the ocean, and we never thought twice of it.

You know, god gave man a short memory for pain and the illusion that time does not move. That was a stroke of genius, for mortals are weak; but we pay for it at a later time in our lives. I have paid many times over. But I would have it no other way. The gods are great." He took a few halfhearted bites at his food.

"Telemachus. They tell me that you are working with these Heraclides. This family is as bad as the descendants of Pelops. But I cannot censure you for this, nor find this strange at all. My daughter fails to understand. The people of the Peloponnese cannot bear up under all these leaders, milking them as you would a sick goat. Orestes killed his mother and her lover and then set out to kill the Peloponnese, just as his father Agamemnon had. It never surprised me what happened to this man upon his return from Troy, for it was nothing that he did not earn.

"You know, here is a secret. When we first went to Troy in delegation to talk with King Priam...this was before the call to arms for all Achaeans...Priam was a reasonable man. And your father and he got along well once beyond the formalities. We could see immediately that Priam had no pride in this son, Paris or Alexander, whatever they called him. Priam agreed to all our requests. There was no hesitation. But it was his family and his son...my memory has long since departed...not Aeneas, Aeneas was a good man...but Hector...yes, Hector. To Hector honor was everything. The Hellenes rank honor above most things, but these Asiatics hold it even higher. Priam did not. He was ready to settle, until Hector stepped in. That is what was remarkable about this man. Hector gave all to protect the honor of a coward and weakling. And he refused to listen to the counsel of his own father. What kind of people are these? You and I will never understand them.

"Sometimes a man must listen to his own mind. That is the mark of a great man. But be prepared to accept the consequences. And young man, do so with a clear mind and conscience and do not let others get in the way of seeing what is right."

"Father, you cannot eat and talk at the same time."

"I do not hold back my mind, such as it is, once it is loosed. And I have a further subject, for my daughter means more to me than the stars in the sky. More than my other children. More than my poor wife. I understand that she is here because you have allowed her the freedom to live with me these days. But I know that a man and his wife must be together, and I never meant to come between you two. So let me say this. You are both strong headed as is the wont of your families and which is a good thing at most times. But you have a singleness of heart. I see this, and we say this singleness is a gift from the gods. You have two fine boys, although I do not know the other of recent. But I have come to love fair-minded Amphion as my own; he holds great promise in my mind to become one of the wise men. An old man sees more than you think. Is your mother yet living?"

"Yes, she lives on the farm in Ithaca."

"Of all the Hellenes, Penelope was the most intelligent, and I do not say this lightly. She saw far beyond all of us. Even wily Odysseus. Many criticized her ways, but what the suitors could not tear down nor understand was her pride in herself and her principles. Is some relative caring for her? For she must be nearing that age."

"She is being cared for by her servants of old. She is alone once again, but she is at home. I am making every effort to return to care for her and to bring my family together on Ithaca."

"I understand," said Nestor. "Sometimes, the will of Poseidon and his emissaries, the winds, send us in strange directions. But the will of Zeus unites us. Your mother is a remarkable woman. If all women were like her, there would be no problem on earth. You hear me, Polycasté? I am not speaking of her refusal to the suitors. I am speaking of her wisdom and strength. Eurydice learned much from her. We all did...your father as well. He could have turned out a scoundrel like his grandfather, Hermes' son, the cattle thief, had he not listened to her."

Nestor paused in thought for a moment.

"And you, young man, the gods wait upon you. You will rule, if not in Ithaca then elsewhere."

And Telemachus felt the compassion of Nestor, and he felt only love for the man. Why could his own father not have been as open and loving...and wise?

Later in Polycasté's room, there was a great awkwardness. The singleness of heart that Nestor had described was sorely lacking.

"Husband, I know that I have failed you and have split the family. I know my duty to you and our sons, but my father is desperately alone and requires my attention. I cannot leave him. At the same time, you are away from home, and your thoughts are not with your family. The words of my father are without frame or reference, but they ring of the truth. And I find myself agreeing with him. But I am powerless at this point. We are both consumed by our families and our histories. It is as though we were never allowed to lead our own lives, and now it is too late. We are caught up in a strong current and neither of us can resist it."

"It is never too late."

Telemachus watched his wife. He had forgotten the clearness of her skin and the pure olive tone of her neck, even without oils. He longed for her. Polycasté and he had lived their lives together, always under the watchful eyes of their parents, even as adults. Now, when their own lives appeared before them, they had become separate and detached.

"I cannot say what will happen," Telemachus said, "but I know that the Heraclides' decision will come soon. I must do this for myself. I agree that I am selfish in this matter. I was not absent in the lives of my children. I tried to give them the tools to become adults by aiding and teaching them, by listening to them, and by respecting them. I can do no more, since I was so aware of what I lacked in my own childhood. Now they are men and choose their own directions. A choice opened to me only recently. And I must take this path or never have one of my own.

"I was raised by Penelope in her absent way. But even then she is the strongest influence in my life. I recognize that, and she is not an easy person, for her greatest strength is also her greatest weakness. Her greatest strength is not her loyalty and devotion to her husband. Her greatest strength is her knowledge of herself. Even though she had little energy left for her child, her commitment to my father and to the family was such a strong part of my childhood that it marked me forever."

"I am not Penelope," Polycasté lamented loudly.

"I know. I know." Telemachus repeated. "I am not asking that."

"You are blaming me for running away."

"No. I just do not understand it."

"I thought I was strong like Penelope, but I am not."

"Penelope's strength kept her from reaching out to me in the absence of my father. All that is history. I understand your dedication to your father. But have you no responsibility to me?"

"I have failed you."

"No."

"Yes, I have. I can command a thousand servants, but I am a slave to my own foolishness." She began gently sobbing. "I know I have failed you."

"Polycasté, please."

"I am a rudderless ship. I know the direction I must take, but I am unable to steer a course. I am so sorry."

Telemachus waited to allow her emotions to subside. "What I know is we cannot continue in this fashion. Tomorrow, I am leaving for Elis, and I will return to Ithaca, whether gods and mortals will it. I expect you to come with me."

"I cannot," she said firmly. "Not yet."

"No? Then when? You are my wife." Telemachus stood to leave the room. "I once said that I could not survive without you, but I have found this to be untrue. Of all things in my life, though, I long to be with you again as we once were."

"It is my fault," Polycasté admitted. "I know that."

"Then, you will return with me?" Telemachus asked gently.

"I think it better if I remain with my father for the while."

"Than you are announcing the end of our marriage?"

"No. Only that I must regain myself. Before I can be a wife, I must be a person."

"I do not understand."

"Perhaps, you are better off without me."

"Who are you to make that decision? I know I am not free from blame. But do not suggest that you are doing this for me."

"Please, allow me the grace of time."

"My life is changing. I need you now."

"Then at least allow me to care for an aged man, who is alone."

"I can only beg so long," Telemachus said, becoming frustrated.

"I cannot see anything else."

"You must do what you feel is right," Telemachus replied.

"I no longer know right from wrong."

"No."

"The columns that support my soul are collapsed. I am so afraid."

"Listen to Nestor," Telemachus said softly.

"This is not about my father," Polycasté replied sharply. "I watch others and cannot fathom how they function. I seek shelter...peace...safety."

"Ithaca will be different."

"No. Pylos. Elis. Ithaca. It makes no difference."

"I must return to Ithaca."

They were silent for a moment.

"When I return to Pylos again," Telemachus finally said, "it will be as a hawk and not as a dove." And he left.

As happens sometimes in the depths of initiate spring, Eos soared over Mount Mathia, carrying her golden weapons, scattering night and enveloping heaven and earth in her warm misty glow. Telemachus rose early and went to the room of his sons. He had barely spoken to Amphion since he arrived in Pylos. He woke them gently. The two young men regarded their father with sleepy suspicion.

"I am leaving to return to Elis. We will be moving the horses out and clearing the house, for we will not be returning to Elis after my business is completed. It is time to return to Ithaca. Your mother will be here with Nestor for awhile. I am sorry I cannot stay longer."

"I must care for mother," Amphion replied.

"Why?" Telemachus asked, surprised by his son's response.

"She is not herself. After grandmother's death, and even before, she has not been herself."

"She needs to remove herself from all these concerns: her brothers' battles, her father's health, and the coming war in the Peloponnese."

"She used to be the strongest woman in Elis," Amphion admitted, "and now she barely leaves the palace."

"I know," Telemachus said, "but I am not certain how to fix this. Maybe you can convince her to leave Pylos for her own good. That would be a first step. By the way, Nestor speaks well of you, and I am very proud of you...proud of you both."

"I will be joining you in a few days' time, father," Autolycus said.

"And you, Amphion?"

"I am learning much here," Amphion said. "I want to stay with mother and help her. Grandfather needs us."

"You may stay for a while. But I expect you in Elis before the new moon." He kissed each as he departed.

Telemachus went to Nestor's stables to borrow a chariot for the trip to Elis. Sterope had returned to Elis with Oxylus. All the fine horses that had once occupied the stables were gone, and no chariots remained. So Telemachus found two older horses that might possibly make the journey to Elis and enough tack to ride one horse, while leading the other. A journey that ordinarily might take two days on a fast horse, took four on these nags. But his arrival in Elis was not a moment too soon, for the heavy hand of heaven had been laid upon Oxylus.

XX

Of all the immortals, Hades is most hated by men. At this time, the only sanctuary for his worship was found in Elis. This sanctuary and its temple were open only one day during the year: the very day of Telemachus' return from Pylos. The townspeople had gathered and filled the street outside the sanctuary in silent prayer, huddling under their cloaks and shawls against a light spring shower. The temple of Hades was poorly built of sun-dried mud bricks, reinforced with wood beams. Barely large enough for one man to enter, it contained a single cella, or inner sanctum. Only the priest was allowed to enter the cella, and no others had ever seen the icon within that represented Hades. Whether it was a wood sculpture or reliquary or some artifact of Hades himself was not known. The priest never spoke of it. No common man could enter, for to enter the sanctuary was to enter Hades, and men go down to Hades only once, never to return.

The basis for the Eleans' worship of Hades was thornier and more difficult to understand. At this time, people believed that the afterlife was an endless darkness in the depths of the earth. Though some believed the spirit flew up to the heavens to await rebirth. Not until recently have the mysteries put forth the idea of an afterlife and immortality of the soul for all believers – something that only the immortals might know.

The Eleans gathered to pray to Hades on account of both history and religion. The truth is that in the time of the great King Augeas of Elis, Heracles came back to avenge himself, for Augeas had not paid him for cleaning his stables. As we know, Heracles had a long memory for slights, and so he marshaled an army from Arcadia, Achaea, and Argolis and went to war against Augeas. During the battle, Heracles killed Augeas and ambushed and killed the conjoined Molionides twins. He gave the throne to the son of Augeas, Phyleus. But after capturing Elis, Heracles continued to ravage the Peloponnese, attacking Pylos.

During the battle for Pylos, Athene stood at the side of Heracles. Remarkably, Hades made a rare appearance on earth aiding the Pylians. Why Hades, the most retiring and isolated of all the gods, referred to as the "unseen one," would take an active role in this fight is not known. In the battle with Heracles, the Pylians fought bravely. Hera and Ares also aided the Pylians. Although Hades was an elder among the immortals and had survived many battles, he was not a great warrior, nor was he courageous in combat. And none of the gods could compete with Heracles. Heracles smote Hera in the right breast, wounded Ares in the thigh, and injured Hades, although the nature of his wound was not reported. All three immortals were forced to quit the battle and retire to Olympus, there to cure their wounds. Needless to say, the Pylians lost the war.

All this in a roundabout fashion explains why the Eleans worshiped Hades. For here their devotion appears to be based mainly on their hatred of Heracles and love of those who opposed him. Heracles aroused such passions. Even today, festivals are held in many parts of Greece, where people gather to insult and yell obscenities at Heracles, even though he is considered a god and is worshiped by many people.

The people of Elis took this veneration of those who opposed Heracles a step further by building a sanctuary and temple to Hades. I find this entire history hard to negotiate. Whatever truth there may be to it, the day of Telemachus' return coincided with the one day of the year for the commemoration of Hades. The townspeople watched mutely as the priest unlocked the gate and entered the sanctuary and then opened the door of the small temple and disappeared within. They waited unhappily, for this was not a joyous ceremony. This was a rite of loss and regret. Whereas in most ceremonies throughout Hellas, songs and dancing commonly took center stage, here there was none. Rather, it was a ceremony in memory of those who dwell in Hades never to return to the land of the living. And when mortals think of Hades, it brings to mind their own final journey in Charon's boat across the dreaded marsh and River Styx to the Plain of Judgment – a journey no one likes to be reminded of.

Telemachus slowly rode past the silent crowd on one of Nestor's elderly horses. Both of his nags were exhausted by the long trip and wanted nothing more than to rest nibbling the grass along the side of the road. He had to drag and kick them constantly during the last few stadia.* Along the main street, people huddled in their cloaks against the sunless day. Telemachus was cold and tired and dirty.

When he arrived at his estates, a squad of soldiers blocked the main road, refusing to allow him entry or even to talk with his servants. And at the same time, they spoke of a minor battle with Oxylus, who a fortnight before had attempted to cross their line. Oxylus' good nature had been sorely tested, and he had rebelled when told that he could not stable his beloved horse, Rhaebus, and Telemachus' mount, Sterope. Although the soldiers were merely country youths serving the king, they learned that size alone does not make the man. They had only been able to disarm Oxylus due to their number, but several rue the day they met the fine-limbed man. The horses were given to a servant, and Oxylus was taken, tied up like a feral cat, to the palace of King Dius, son of Eleius. The soldiers explained to Telemachus that King Eleius had been killed a few weeks before in a hunting accident. Because of Eleius' unfortunate death, his son had been elevated to the throne of Elis. Dius, a young man, no older than Telemachus' sons, had a lot to learn.

Telemachus felt like sending a few additional people to Hades this very day as he returned to town on his nag, leaving the more fatigued horse with the soldiers.

Where once Odysseus and Telemachus had been welcomed to the palace with great respect, today Telemachus was made to wait, without information about the whereabouts of Oxylus. He sat on a bench in an ante-room as servants and officials came and went. He

---

* The stadion is a measure of distance; one stadion equals 600 feet; nine stadia approximate a mile.

had once been close to King Eleius, but he knew little of the son except that Dius, as a boy, had often visited his own sons.

After waiting for some time, Telemachus was admitted to an audience with King Dius. As he entered the small meeting room, he saw Oxylus sitting unhappily with his left arm wrapped in cloth. Oxylus made no effort to greet Telemachus; his good humor had long since departed. In addition to Oxylus, Dius sat with a man that Telemachus recognized from his youth as an advisor to the new king's grandfather. Several youths armed with swords and uncomfortably dressed as soldiers stood at attention at the edges of the room.

"Have you taken leave of your senses?" Telemachus said immediately before seating himself. "You are preventing me from returning to my home? For the sake of the gods, there had better be a good explanation for this. This was not necessary. I am not difficult to find nor hesitant to come at your request. I know you only as a child, Dius, but you seem to be still in your infancy. I knew your father well and his father before him. Your great grandfather, Polyxenus owed his life to my father, for they were together at Troy. By that reasoning, you owe your own life to my father. Perhaps, you would be kind enough to explain your actions?"

Dius glanced at his advisor and then addressed Telemachus directly.

"Please sit down," he said, indicating a space on the bench next to Oxylus, on which Telemachus sat reluctantly.

"It has come to our attention that you are aiding the family of the Heraclides, who, as is commonly known, have been attempting to take over control of the Peloponnese for several generations. You cannot both accept our hospitality and gift of a safe haven and at the same time plan the overthrow of our family. As you are well aware, we have ruled Elis for countless generations. When my ancestor, sleepless Endymion, founded the city, having led the Aeolians from Thessaly long ago, his son, Epeius won the throne in a footrace at Olympia. Great King Augeas, counted among the Argonauts, ruled Elis until Heracles first took notice of the Peloponnese."

"Your studies of history have been rewarded. But of what import is this today?"

"You are plotting evil," Dius replied with force. "You are plotting evil in the very house that offered you sanctuary and protection."

"And on what grounds do you base this information?"

"It is well known."

"Well known? Then you know the plans of the Heraclides?"

"I know what I am told," Dius replied.

"You have discussed this with Cresphontes and Temenus?"

"I know not these men. But nevertheless…"

"Telemachus," the advisor interrupted Dius. "Do not attempt to turn this into unprofitable word-play."

"And who might you be."

"I am Actor, descendant of the Molionides, and advisor to the young king."

"If I am not mistaken, you were advisor to Polyxenus."

"Yes, I have served four generations of the rulers of Elis. And I continue..."

"And further," Telemachus added, "you were there in the chamber with my father and Polyxenus and his son, Amphimachus, when Polyxenus offered hospitality to Odysseus, which gave us land in perpetuity. He set no time limit on this land. We built what is today, and has been for some time, the largest estate in the country of Elis and perhaps in the Peloponnese, providing goods and animals to the palace in great abundance. My father is buried in the hills behind our house, and Dius' father was a pallbearer at his funeral. So we are not lightly of this soil. But let me speak frankly for I believe I understand the direction of your apprehension."

He turned to Oxylus. "And you, my friend, why are you so silent?"

Oxylus shook his head without meeting Telemachus' eyes, but he knew Oxylus well enough to recognize that the man was in a fever pitch of anger.

"As I said, let me explain some details to you." Telemachus turned back to the young king and his advisor. "It is true that we spoke with the Heraclides a few weeks previously, and we are well aware of their thinking. It is also true that we have met with Orestes, King of Mycenae, Doridas, King of Corinth, and Nestor, King of Messenia. As for the Heraclides, we are as well aware of their plans as any non-family member can be, and that is very little. I am willing to describe to you their plans, at least my understanding of them. Allow me first to explain our situation. I have just returned from meeting with the King of Messenia, the great Nestor, and my father-in-law. I explained to him that we are leaving Elis to return to my homeland in Ithaca. We have appreciated and enjoyed your hospitality all these years, but now must leave. We will make every effort to depart in a timely manner. And once we have left, the estates that we have built up will become the property of the king." Telemachus could see that this produced the desired effect in the eyes of Dius.

"And I will state further," he continued, "that we have nothing to do with the Heraclides. They are planning to return to Mycenae in Argolis and have no appetite for anything further as far as I know. I gave my word to King Nestor a few days ago, and I give it to you today. Of course, as descendants of Heracles, these men are not easily contained nor satisfied. And as you know, it is their nature to dissimulate their true ambitions. So I would advise you to build a strong defense here in Elis or to make arrangements with the Pylians. I have a large storehouse of weapons collected by my father that I will leave in place at your disposal. We would now like to return to our home, so that we can carry on with our departure. We have been away for some time."

"You are free to go," Dius said, "but the soldiers will remain. And you will be required to report at your departure."

"And Telemachus," Actor said, "we will hold you to your word."

"I swear to the oath maker Zeus that all I have said is true. We have no desire for your destruction and wish you well, just as you do for us."

They left the palace and mounted the old horse, Oxylus seated before Telemachus. The people of the village watched respectfully, as the two well-known men rode slowly and awkwardly toward Boreas on their old nag, followed by several soldiers.

"What happened to you?" Telemachus asked, once they were out of the town.

"I will kill Dius with my own hands. That is all I have to say."

"You seem to harbor some antagonism."

"I will speak no further."

When they arrived at the estates, the soldiers allowed them entrance. Telemachus and Oxylus walked the horse the final distance and dropped the reins at the house. They entered the courtyard, where the servants welcomed them with a warm fire, fresh clothes, and food. The wound on Oxylus' arm was not deep, but they covered it with herbs and rebound it tightly. Neither man spoke, and each soon went to his room to sleep, seeking the refreshing palliative of the dream world.

The golden hues of Eos, child of morning, fell upon the heavens and the earth, waking immortals and mortals alike. Telemachus rose with great appetite and desire to begin making arrangements to leave the estates.

He remembered his father's description of his trip to the uninhabited island of Lemnos with young Neoptolemus, son of Achilles. Together, they had to convince Philoctetes, son of Poas, to come to the war in Troy, for the bow of Hercules was prophesied as necessary to defeat the Trojans. This was the same bow that Poas had earned by lighting Heracles' funeral pyre. Odysseus and Neoptolemus had disputed during the voyage to Lemnos. Impulsive youth and practiced age discussed how one man persuades another to his own ideas. What devices should one use, and how far should one go with artful designs or even frauds to convince another?

"It is not the powerful arm, but rather the soft enchanting tongue that governs all," Odysseus said. "I will never descend to fraud," Neoptolemus replied, "but would rather fall by virtue than rise by guilt to certain victory." So relates Sophocles.

After his own oath to the young king, walking a fine line between truth and dishonesty, Telemachus had to laugh to himself. Surely, a man is remembered more for his actions than his words, just as a government of men is judged by its accomplishments and not the great monologues of its archons. Today, if King Neoptolemus, who bloodied the waters of Troy and sent the family of Odysseus into exile, had not been killed by Orestes, he would have had no clear footing in any discussion of virtue.

When Telemachus entered the megaron for his morning meal, Oxylus was waiting for him.

"I do not believe that Dius had any knowledge of the Heraclides," Oxylus said, "other than common rumors." He had calmed and ate fresh bread, dried fish, and goat cheese with gusto. "Some spy saw the long ship in the harbor at Pheia and, unaccustomed to seeing ships of this size, made inquiries and discovered the owners of the ship, and then began to add together various pieces of information, until Dius had what he thought was a solid case. They arrested me shortly after arriving here and kept me locked up. I will not soon forgive nor forget. They will come to regret their actions." He sucked on a dried fig.

"By the way, I enjoyed your description of the Heraclides and their return: very effective and pointed," said Oxylus. "Whereas the leader of the Pelopides, Tisamenus, may have some ability to defend himself, these louts in Elis will fall without incident. I will have my kingdom."

"I was not proud of my words," Telemachus said. "They seemed to come out of their own of necessity. They were not lies, though they were not entire truths either. Dius has no need to understand our actions. He must consider his own."

"Your father would be proud," Oxylus observed.

"The actions of Dius had no connection with the Heraclides. This was a slow simmering soup of greed and jealousy."

"Good and evil do not exist, only man." But the twinkle had returned to Oxylus' two eyes.

"There is much to accomplish in the next days, but we must have information from the Heraclides immediately. I will send a herald to give them the time for decision. What I said about Ithaca was truthful. I will be going there either sooner or later depending again on the Heraclides. Autolycus will be here in a few days, and he will be coming with me. You are welcome to join us in Ithaca."

"What about the horses?" Oxylus asked. "The number of cattle has been reduced, but the horses number almost eleven hundred head at this point."

"Ithaca is no place for horses," Telemachus replied. "The entire island could not support more than a few horses, and those would have to be as nimble as goats to survive the rocky slopes. It will depend on the Heraclides. If the Heraclides decline our offer and I go directly to Ithaca, the horses will remain here to be bartered. Although there is no breeder in all of the Peloponnese who would be able to provide for such a quantity of horses. I am afraid that many would end up in the fire honoring some god. I do not think this will happen. My guess is that we will be transporting horses to Attica to train them for battle, for what is a cavalry without horses?"

"And the house?"

"The first order of things will be to clear the house and ship everything to Ithaca. My father was very secretive and hid a great store of things: wine, oil, weapons, and family treasures. I have truly not taken inventory. And Penelope took nothing with her. All the valuables will be packaged and transported to Ithaca. We will leave the old weapons for Dius, for they have no use to us. The rest of the household goods can be distributed to the servants. As for the estate itself, I can only say that it has great value, but I cannot take it with me."

They walked down to the river to view the horses. Across the river, all the hillsides in the direction of Boreas, as far as the eye could see, were spotted with horses of all hues, many of them running wild, never having given to the bit or accepted a rider. These would require extensive training if the intent was to use them for war. The two men came to a large open pasture between the stables and the river, which contained the horses used on the estates. Both Rhaebus and Sterope came running up together. They presented quite a pair: the giant, peaceful stallion Rhaebus and the smaller, emotional and agile mare, Sterope, who ruled her partner mercilessly. We can learn much from horses.

XXI

Over the next few days, activity increased ten-fold, both inside the house and in the fields. Telemachus announced the move to the servants, and all were fearful of what was to come without him in residence, since they depended on the estate for their livelihood. Telemachus assured them that he would help as much as he could. An inventory of the animals was taken. Perhaps only a hundred of the cattle raised by Odysseus remained, but there were large herds of sheep and goats. These were brought down from the hills and sheltered closer to the house in temporary enclosures. The gardens, orchards, and vineyards were dormant, and an inventory was taken of the plants, for Telemachus wanted to be able to communicate the entire value of his holdings.

Underneath the house, the storerooms were opened. Some of these rooms had not been opened since well before Odysseus' death, and they provided insight into the man, for they were filled to the gunwales. The storerooms had been excavated below ground level, and within these rooms great holes had been dug. Large amphorae of oil and wine were buried deeply. The first meager harvest of wine was more than two decades old, and each container was carefully marked for each subsequent pressing. As the harvest grew, so did the amount of wine in storage The wine alone could have filled a lake, to say nothing of the store of oil, grain, dried meat, and other preserved foodstuffs. And Odysseus also had stores of wine and oil and produce from Ithaca.

But the most secret of the storerooms was reserved for entry by Telemachus alone, for this was the store of Odysseus' wealth. Before Telemachus' marriage to Polycasté when they were building the house, he remembered Odysseus spending many mornings in the storeroom, always reserving the key to himself. But as he aged, Odysseus spent less and less time in the storerooms, giving control over to the servants. In his last years, it appeared that he had totally forgotten the rooms and never went there. But he always kept the large key to his personal storeroom on his belt loop. At his death, Telemachus had taken the keys to all the storerooms, but he had not investigated at that time. Now for the first time, Telemachus unlocked the door and entered by himself. He lit the candles on the wall sconces with his oil lamp and waited for his eyes to adjust to the light, but even from the first moments in the room he could see the glints of metal. For here were Odysseus' wealth and armaments.

Cluttered around the walls were javelins, shields, swords, bows and arrows, knives, battle axes, bronze weapon heads of all sizes and types, and piles of armour. The damp room smelled of decay and dried leather. On shelves or hanging from pegs or just piled against the walls, the sheer quantity was impressive. The armaments were functional for the most part and not ceremonial or greatly valuable. Telemachus saw nothing remarkable save the enormous quantity of bronze arms that might have been the collection of some division of an army.

In the center of the room, covered by more armaments, he noticed what looked like a large wooden wheel, lying flat on the floor. He searched the set of keys in his hand, looking for one to fit into a large portable lock on the dusty bolt that was affixed to a large beam set in the floor. Key after key failed to move the lock, finally he found one with a bone handle that fit the lock, but was fragile. Telemachus feared that it would break in the mechanism. The lock was rusty and had not been used in some time. Gently inserting the key back and forth in the lock, feeling for some movement without putting too much stress on the key, Telemachus finally was able to turn the mechanism. He pulled the bolt free of the bronze door ring and lifted the circular door with great effort. A cut stone spiral staircase led farther below floor level into a room about a quarter the size of the storeroom itself. Telemachus took his lamp and descended the stairs. He again lit several sconces on a huge center bearing post, supporting large beams radiating from the center. Slowly the small room came to light with a dazzling reflection.

There was barely enough space for a man to move. All nature of dazzling golden metalwork hung from the walls: masks, diadems, large etched gold plates, ceremonial golden armour, frames, and other common household items, all made of gold. A wine strainer hung next to several hearth spoons and ladles…all in gold. Around the walls on the floor were statues and figurines, large golden urns, ewers, mixing bowls, and all manner of vases and containers, all piled and nested. Telemachus guessed that some of these golden objects were the magnificent and generous gifts from the people of Phaecia, from King Alcinous and Queen Arete, which Odysseus had brought back from his voyages.

In the center of the floor was a buried amphora. He opened the wax seal and saw that the amphora was filled with all sorts of small golden objects: jewelry, carved animals, small religious icons, sculptures and figurines, small seals, and a host of other miniature objects. Scattered among the gold were brilliantly colored stones of all sizes and colors. For many of the objects, the craftsmanship was rough and without character, with the primary purpose being as a store of value. But among these objects were truly exquisite artifacts, the work of skilled craftsmen fulfilling a legacy.

Telemachus had great difficulty believing that his father had accumulated such wealth. Penelope had left to return to Ithaca without even thinking of these wondrous items, for she must have known of their existence – or maybe not. He then saw Odysseus' bow case and quiver hanging from the center post. It was easily recognizable, for it was the very bow that mighty Iphitus, son of Eurytus, had given the boy Odysseus years before in Messenia, when Odysseus was sent to retrieve some stolen sheep. The same Iphitus that Heracles had killed soon thereafter, even though a guest at Heracles' table. It was the very bow that Telemachus had almost strung before the suitors, stopping only when his father warned him off. He could see where the fire had scorched the bone tips, when Eurymachus had heated the bow and waxed it to make it more flexible for stringing. But to no avail. For none of the suitors could string this bow. It was the very bow that Odysseus had finally strung, sending an arrow through the twelve axe heads set up by Penelope in the contest for her hand in marriage. He remembered vividly how Odysseus had then revealed himself, throwing off his beggar clothes and beginning the attack on the suitors. Telemachus slowly pulled the bow out of the case and examined it.

Tears came to his eyes as he held the bow. Telemachus remembered well his fear the morning of this attack, for he had never been to war before, nor had he killed a man. He replaced the bow in its case, feeling the sorrow of the loss of so much time. They had been banished from their home, and the morning of their departure from Ithaca was as clear in his mind as if it had occurred yesterday.

That morning, Telemachus had found his family arguing in the megaron of the palace. As he approached, all eyes turned on him. Telemachus stopped next to his tutor, Mentor. Mentor was a gentle soul and an introspective man. He had never been bellicose and in fact, as he would say, always believed in the supremacy of the intellect in matters of dispute. He had tutored the young Telemachus in statecraft and governing, but according to criticism from Odysseus had neglected the boy's studies on war and its strategies. Mentor was stooped and a head shorter than Telemachus.

"Now, Odysseus," Penelope had said, challenging her husband, "you explain it to him, your very son, for he stands before us. How Neoptolemus has sent us from our home." There was a pause as all held their breaths.

Odysseus finally replied, as though the energy of the thought had to come to a slow heat like molten magna.

"Have you no shame, woman? What do you expect of me? Have I not suffered enough for your delicate nature? I did no more than kill some common criminals. These men had no right to expect otherwise. Dare you compare me with the cuckold, Menelaus? Let me count the nights I had to sit through his circumlocutions at the ships, shoring up his brother Agamemnon's reputation and his own pride. And now Neoptolemus, this son of Achilles – all righteous and full of himself, just as his father was before him, believing himself more honorable and virtuous than Apollo himself – would rob me of my birthright. I do not shrink from Neoptolemus." For a moment, his eyes focused on Telemachus standing behind the servants.

"And look at my godly son. A father could ask no greater gift. He is no longer a boy, but not yet a man. It is time for him to meet his father. I was king at his age, for my father Laertes so hated the weight of office. I had traveled throughout Hellas at his age. I was familiar with the secrets of my grandfather in raising cattle and knew my way around the whorehouses of Athens. I had signed the Oath of Tyndareus at his age. And what is more, if this escapes you woman, I was married to you at his age."

"Yes," Penelope agreed, "I recall. Though, I was never sure that our marriage was not just another way for you to further your ambitions."

Odysseus ignored his wife and turned to the servants. "Are all things prepared?"

"Yes, master," Eumaeus said. "Just as you requested. My son Adrastos is waiting outside. The vessel is in the harbor. All is ready."

"Then we will be on our way. Telemachus, are you prepared?"

"Yes, sire."

"Now," Odysseus said, rising to his feet, "I will take my leave. Penelope, I see no problem in your obstinate refusal to leave with us, for you will be joining us once we have settled. You will take care of her, Euryclea. Just as you cared for me and my son. We will be a family again soon enough. That is my fondest wish. Eumaeus, since my father refuses to see me off, you will ensure his welfare and the security of the estates as you have for these many years in my absence."

He moved to where Penelope was seated and held out his hands to her. "My wife, I may not be the man your father wished for you, but I have loved you well."

"And for that I thank you," Penelope replied, "for your love has given me character." She stood up and embraced her husband. "Now I can watch as you take the last remaining jewel from me...my son. You had better understand the importance of Telemachus to my wellbeing, for a lioness will not brook maltreatment of her brood." She released her husband quickly and took Telemachus in her arms and held him for a long while.

Odysseus pulled his mariner's cap down over his graying hair and strode out of the hall in his hulking walk, the result of a leg injury by a wild boar when a young man, but now exaggerated due to his bulk, age, and war injuries.

Telemachus could barely speak. Penelope clung to him as though she would never see him again. He then embraced Euryclea, his wet nurse and surrogate mother, who had cared for him during Penelope's frequent absences. He touched the shoulders of the servants, all save Eumaeus, who embraced him as a father might. He shook hands respectfully with Mentor.

"Thank you for your patience," Telemachus said to him. "I should have been better at my studies."

Mentor looked at him puzzled. "You were excellent. Perhaps I should have made that more clear. Once you discover yourself and your strengths, you will come to agree with me, of that I am certain."

Telemachus then slowly followed his father out to the portico, feeling that he was being led blindly on an uncertain voyage. He followed his stranger-father like a kid following its nanny, silently bleating out his heart.

In the inner courtyard, Telemachus saw four horses ready with packs. He had raised all of these horses from colts. Ithaca was a steep, rocky and dry landscape, not suited to horses. There was no question of using chariots in Ithaca, but a few of the larger estates kept horses for transportation and farm work. Telemachus had spent much of his youth working with his horses and found solace in their pride and bearing and energy. He had tamed them to take a rider, kept the stallions from hurting the mares in mating, stood watch over the mares during foaling, and cared for them from the first day of their birth. He knew each one intimately. His horses, when he was a boy, had offered him a shelter from the all-consuming concerns of his household. He understood them perhaps better than he understood human beings. Telemachus was riding Abraxas, a large black stallion, and Odysseus rode Abraxas' mare, his beautiful Bronte, the first of the horses on Ithaca. Two other horses carried packs with supplies for their journey. All would be lost at sea; none would set foot on the rolling, grassy meadows of Elis.

As Telemachus walked toward his horses, he noticed the whiteness of the foggy morning light reflecting from the walls and the waxen blue skies slowly emerging from the mist. He turned and saw his mother standing with the servants at the entrance watching their departure. She was the smallest figure, respectfully bordered by the servants, but prominent due to her bearing and bright yellow shawl covering her white *peplos,* or wrapper. Odysseus was already mounted and waiting. Telemachus joined him. As Telemachus mounted, his father unceremoniously threw him a woolen cloak, woven from the wool of the darker sheep and left natural and unwashed to shed the rain and maintain the body heat. He could only assume that his own linen cloak, made by Penelope, was not acceptable for this journey. He exchanged cloaks, handing the linen one to a servant.

Odysseus also handed him two sheathed knives, a larger dagger and a thin dirk, both used in close combat for cutting and gutting.

"A man can have nothing finer than a heavy cloak and two knives," Odysseus said. "Never be without them for unlike a woman, wool keeps you warm every night, and one knife is useless without a spare."

Telemachus was unsure what to do with both, but he put the dagger in his belt loop under his cloak and for the while stowed the other knife in the leather bags behind the saddle pad. He forcefully rubbed Abraxas' mane line where the horse loved to be touched. Odysseus signaled for the gate to open and rode out into the outer courtyard without looking back. Telemachus turned and waved as they rode from the courtyard. The pack horses, tied to Abraxas, followed reluctantly. And so they had left Ithaca.

All that had passed decades before: before he had married, before he had become a father, before his own father had left the earth, before he was being forced off his land in Elis. Now standing in the treasury of Odysseus, Telemachus could only recall the past like a dream. He replaced Odysseus' bow on the wall and was attracted by a brilliant shield hanging next to the quiver. Immediately he recognized the shield and armour of Achilles, surely the work of Hephaestus, the lame god and his inextinguishable forge. He had heard the stories, but he thought the armour lost. Odysseus had described to him how he had been awarded the armour of Achilles as the bravest of all the Achaeans at Troy.

As Homer tells us, Achilles had loaned his armour to his beloved Patroclus, who, wearing it in battle, had been killed by the Trojan, Hector. Hector stripped Achilles' armour off the dead body. Achilles' mother, the goddess Thetis, had then sought the aid of Hephaestus for a new suit of armour to protect her son. Hephaestus had wrought it, for he and his mother both favored the Greeks. Thetis presented the new armour to Achilles as a mother will with all her lioness love to protect him from harm, but as a goddess, she already knew his fate. Achilles avenged the death of Patroclus, only to follow him soon thereafter to Hades. At Achilles' death, the Greeks had collected his godly armour. After victory, Agamemnon awarded

Achilles' armour to the greatest fighter of all the Achaeans before the assembled armies. Surprisingly, the leaders selected Odysseus. The troops moaned and groaned at the selection of Odysseus, for little did they know of his back stage contributions to the victory over the Trojans. Greater Ajax, son of Telamon, heard their complaints and took them to heart. Rather than accept that he was not chosen the greatest fighter at Troy, he fell on his sword before the armies and descended to Hades to his eternal shame.

Telemachus closely observed the elaborate engraving in the gold-lined shield. The flickering lights danced and glimmered across the scenes carved in gold. Telemachus remembered the songs of the bards who had visited Ithaca after the war. They had described the shield "as brilliant as Orion's Hound, the brightest constellation in the harvest skies, warning all mortals for the hound brings fire and fever in his train. And even so did Achilles bring fire and fever."

Telemachus lifted the breastplate to his chest. How can a man measure up to a hero? Yet when he placed the breastplate against himself, he found that Achilles was not a giant of a man, but one of moderate size. Though his size must have been influenced by his intemperate nature, at least in the eyes of his foes, in truth his chest was no larger than Telemachus'. Telemachus stood for a moment, thinking of his father and the legends of Troy. How the godly men had fought and died alongside their brothers-at-arms, and how the gods had struggled and fought one another. His father had discussed his time in Troy only briefly and his voyages, almost never. Telemachus had only the questionable visions of the bards to go by, no much more than we do to this very day.

He replaced the breastplate and retraced his steps. His mind reeled from the discovery of the treasure, but also from his proximity to his father's life and legend. The armour of Achilles was variously reported to be lost in the seas off Troy or given mistakenly to Achilles' son, Neoptolemus, before Odysseus knew his true character. How could Odysseus have recaptured the armour through all his travels?

Odysseus had said that of all the events at Troy, the suicide of the greater Ajax had disturbed him the most. The award must have meant more to Odysseus than Telemachus had ever suspected. For although Odysseus would never admit it, and now could not, to be chosen as foremost among the Achaeans must have been his life's greatest achievement.

Exiting, Telemachus locked the door on the floor of the storeroom and then locked the storeroom door. He kept the keys, as even the most trusted servant would not have understood these riches. He could not trust Oxylus with this knowledge, and young King Dius had no idea of what the house contained. Telemachus was ill-prepared for the stored riches, and he could not grasp their magnitude. But for all their value, they were as dross in comparison to the memories of his father.

XXII

A fortnight later, daring Autolycus arrived at Elis to help with the departure, but, surprisingly, his twin brother, fair-minded Amphion, accompanied him. The sight of the two strong young men riding up to the house on their mounts, so full of godly youth and pride, gave Telemachus a start. Never had he seen such beauty. He ran out to the front courtyard, where the young men were surrounded by servants welcoming them.

"Welcome home," Telemachus said. "You two look capable of eating a wild boar all by yourselves."

"We are happy to be here," Autolycus said. "We would gladly share the meat of this wondrous pig."

"But your mother?" Telemachus asked.

"She was not happy," Amphion explained. "Indeed, she did not stomach well my departure. Her change of mind took me by storm. Nestor gave us both great hugs and heavy slaps on our backs. For he was joyous that we should take up arms, so that one day we could reunite Messenia and bring the family colors back to rule. Mother said that I had nothing more to learn at Pylos, and all the intrigue among the sons of Nestor served ill. She said that I must go with my brother and father."

"I have missed both of you," Telemachus said joyously. "You can help us enormously." He pulled each of his sons off his horse and wrapped his arms around each one in turn. "Tonight, we will sacrifice to the gods in thanks for your attendance and celebrate our final time in Elis. There is much work to do, so come and rest awhile, and then tomorrow we will begin our labors in earnest."

That evening they celebrated. Although no wild boar was forthcoming, a small domestic shoat served the purpose, sending up billowing clouds of smoke from its layers of fat as it was spitted over the coals. Oxylus' humorous side had resurfaced, and he joined along with the servants in celebrating the return of the young men of the house. They tasted the first harvest of wine on the estates of Elis with little water. Its strong, dusky flavor of earth and wild vine berries delighted them, but soon they moved on to better harvests. Fresh baked bread, steaming barley porridge, black olives, fresh goat cheese, and salt from Egypt were served with the dripping meat.

The burnt offerings pleased the gods, as did the homecoming. For the gods always welcomed good smells and joyous attendance at any celebration. There was nothing more pleasing to the immortals than reverence mixed with happiness in a mortal family.

After they had eaten, they relaxed on their couches, enjoying the heat from the glowing embers. They turned to sweet wine flavored with pine resin, a specialty of the region.

Somewhat in his cups, Oxylus spoke to the family: "I am pleased to share with you such happiness. For it is only after hard work that one can experience the gratification of resting. I see before me a strong family, one of the great families of Hellas, not striving toward power and control. A family whose ambitions do not include the harm of others for their own gain. This was not true of my family. My brother, Thermius, strove to rule all of Aetolia, just as our forebear, Thoas, who fought alongside your grandfather at Troy, had ruled over the region. My father, Haemon, failed to give his sons the proper grounding, but instead chose to frequent wine houses and harlots, so lost he was with himself."

"And how did you avoid the same fate?" Amphion asked, knowing the answer.

"Ah, you have not heard my tale and the reason I am here in Elis, though I love its rich earth and lush growth. I was accused of a crime that I committed by unreasoned chance and was exiled. Simple to say, but difficult to live with, though many years and great distances have been traveled since that time. Oh, I spent my time in wine houses and know well the tragic directions and diversions of the ivy-headed god Dionysus. But somewhere along the way I discovered what had most value to me, and wine and harlots were not among these."

"You fought with the tribes in the cold climes of Boreas?" Autolycus asked prompting him, for they all had heard the stories before.

"Yes," Oxylus replied, "I traveled widely and used my skills in battle to allow me to see how others live, indeed, to continue with my own life. For there have been many close calls in the region of Europa, where the Gauls live in mud huts and eat sticks and roots, and where ships sail on an endless sea full of beasts unlike any we know. And toward Boreas across the straights, where the sun fails to shine, the natives' skins are as pink as a goat's scrotum. But of all the tribes, the Hittites are the strangest. These Asiatics do not honor man. For to them life is nothing. Their warriors would kill their masters if they thought they could do so with impunity. And in return, their masters use the lash to motivate them in war. That is why the Hellenes can best them. There is no love between these men; your back is always at risk from the unseen. But the Asiatic craftsmen create marvels, making miracles from the basest of metals. Regard this knife." He pulled out his dagger. It was a two-sided stabbing blade with a diamond cross section made of hardened iron. He took a bronze sword from a servant, and cut entirely through the blade with his knife. He threw the two bronze pieces into the coals.

He handed the dagger to Autolycus, who handled it gingerly, testing its weight.

"I can see you admire it. Keep it. You never can tell when it will come into use," and he smiled. "I have more of these. Just as your father, I always carry two."

"Tomorrow," Telemachus interrupted, "we have to begin bringing the horses down from the hills into the lower pasture. For there is a time to talk and a time to sleep. I will see you early tomorrow." And he rose to leave, but Oxylus and the two young men stayed behind.

"I remember once..." Oxylus began, signaling for more wine all around. "We were crossing the Alpines with snow as deep as a man's head. Three companies of about three hundred freebooters, a few Hellenes, but mostly Gauls and Germanics, with orders to attack..."

But we will leave them and join Telemachus, for he had much on his mind and had fore-suffered Oxylus' stories on many occasions. He lay in his bed, beneath the bedstead with the carved scene of the Pylos shoreline that he had made for Polycasté when she had complained of the fine bed Odysseus had built for Penelope. The comfort of sleep would not close in on him, and his mind reviewed the day's events and surprises, but he continued returning to Amphion's description of Polycasté and wondering what had caused this reversal. Few wives left their husbands. It was not a practice condoned by any family. Sometimes, a woman's family forced her to return to her husband, which was a great insult to him and pleased no one. Sometimes, a woman left in fear of her husband, but was welcomed back by her family only reluctantly. And sometimes, a woman was not welcomed back at all. Some women left their husbands and just disappeared.

Telemachus had come to depend on Polycasté. He had known few women in his life and none well. Penelope had provided little instruction to him about the opposite sex. During his upbringing, she had allowed Odysseus' absence to dominate her life, and Telemachus observed her mainly with her father-in-law, Laertes, or later with the suitors.

Telemachus had never lived with Polycasté alone. Early in their marriage, Polycasté had been preoccupied with their sons, with building their home, and later managing the estates. But Time, father of the *Horae*, forces change on all men. Polycasté was not prepared when the boys sought their independence, and Telemachus had seen her suffering. Further, he knew her efforts to care for Penelope and Odysseus had drained her. When first Odysseus and then Penelope had departed, she seemed to have already passed a point of no return. Something irretrievable had been lost. Although his attention had shifted to his own affairs, the only place where Polycasté felt needed was with her own father, Nestor. Telemachus understood that, but he could not help himself from being aggravated at her disloyalty. What would happen if he went to Ithaca or continued with the Heraclides? Would any of that make an impression on his wife?

Other women? Telemachus had had his chances, but he had never really wanted to deceive Polycasté. She had been such a gift to him at first, and perhaps he had ignored the passage of time. She had given him two sons. Perhaps he expected that she would always remain the same. And now, she resented him and refused to be his wife. He was angry. But more than anything he felt mournful. It was as if all that had preceded had no meaning. He lived well enough on his own, but nothing took on great importance without her. Even the return of his sons was lacking. If only she had come with them. He missed the scent of her bitter-sweet lavender and honey-scented balm. He missed her warmth. He missed her; if only…

Telemachus awoke early the next day, before golden-sandaled Eos extinguished the darkness of night. He gathered up several servants and rode into the hills where the horses ran free within the confines of the walled estate. Odysseus' dogs followed, baying and barking, glad to be occupied. In the hills, the wild horses arranged themselves in bands, each controlled by a stallion. The strongest stallions had the largest bands of mares and their foals and colts. Each lead stallion protected his harem from the younger stallions, which congregated in bachelor bands. The bachelor stallions bided their time in taking a mare to establish their own bands. Contests were common among the lead stallions and bachelors, but since there were many more mares than would naturally occur, the contests were not life threatening. Further, since the bands were held closely together within the estate, there was less competition than in an open space. Once the horses were compelled into an even smaller space, the stallions grew more docile and less combative.

Telemachus rode Sterope for the first time since his visit to Attica. She was ready to run. He kept her in control as they made their way along the Peneus river, a rivulet at this point, with Odysseus' dogs running ahead of them. Slowly, they began to spread out and collect horses. Occasionally, the dogs would take off in a brief sprint necessary to turn a horse. In general, as is the nature of horses, they fell in together and felt comfortable within the growing herd. With horses, the distance separating them from others is vital to their being; proximity to their bands produces contentment; proximity to their enemies, rage.

As she ran alongside the other horses, Telemachus gave Sterope her lead. She had a pride about her, as if she knew that she carried the master and that she was the first among equals. She kept her head high and pranced at times next to the other horses, moving together with their eyes wide and their ears moving forward and backward at the men and dogs, keeping their heads at attention. Sterope knew she could outrun any of these others and had earned her position with the rider on her back.

When he had first begun training her as a colt, the daughter of Eous had been stubborn and resistant. He had to overcome her resistance. He introduced her unhurriedly to the lead, then to the halter, and finally to the bridle and bit. He rewarded her each time. He allowed her to make all the right choices. He patiently touched her, making her feel comfortable with a rope on her back or neck, and allowed her to become accustomed to his smell, his touch, his weight. His hands moved all over her body, until she felt totally comfortable with him. Eventually, he gained her entire trust and her allegiance. And horses, unlike men, maintain their allegiances. By the time he rode her, she had become responsive and loyal, following his every lead. His father had never understood horses; they frustrated him. He preferred his massive rolling cattle and his herding dogs.

After collecting about a thirty horses, Telemachus drove them to the lower pasture. The servants threw them white barley and spelt, the first feed many of the horses had ever eaten. He went for a meal before returning for more horses, and by that time, his sons were ready to accompany him. Oxylus had departed for Elis. They ate quickly and began gathering the horses in the hills. By late afternoon, they had driven about a hundred head into the lower pasture. It would be some time before they would have all of the horses contained in the lower pasture. Rain had not fallen for several days, and the pasture had dried out, but the heavy hooves of the growing number of horses were rapidly turning the grass to mud. They would not be able to keep them for long in this pasture. In the end, the horses established the schedule for their final days in Elis.

The weather shifted, as the earth began to maintain its warmth once the sun sank, and the coldness of the night lost its bite. It would soon be the time of year for the wife of Hades, Persephone, daughter of Demeter, to reappear on earth and to bring with her the long growing season. Hades himself would remain below and would have to wait another six months before Persephone would return to warm his chilly hearth with the tenderness of the earth. Hades had agreed to this arrangement, and he would have to live with it. None of the gods was pleased with the understanding, but mortals were the beneficiaries: if not of the seasons, then at least of the fact that Hades no longer appeared on earth. Instead, he was content to wait in his own abode under the earth for his wife's return. And the comings and goings of Persephone satisfied mortals, for who wants Hades wandering the earth with the other gods.

And now that I think about it, my dear Alcathöe, this may be the real reason the people of Elis gather at his sanctuary one day a year: to thank Hades for remaining forever below, leaving the earth to the hurly burly mischief of the other gods.

XXIII

The plans of gods and men go astray for many reasons. To rely on a single vision without variance or questioning is to compass failure. A ship tucks into a gentle harbor in inclement weather or reefs the sail in high winds. All plans must entertain amendments to redirect progress when events take us in unexpected directions. Without such alternatives, we are doomed to failure.

This brings to mind the question of the infallibility of the gods. The omniscient gods, who can foresee events well into the future, implausibly find themselves at a loss due to some "unexpected" turn in the road. This failure may be due to a hesitation among the gods to look the future squarely in the eye and accept its consequences. What is a greater boon to man than his ignorance of the future? What is finer in life than waking to a new day with endless possibilities?

Aphrodite in her attempt to protect the Trojan hero, Aeneas, suffered a deep wound from the sword of the Greek Diomedes in his frenzy. The weakling goddess was forced to seek assistance to stem the flow of ichor from her wrist. Are we to believe that she had not foreseen this wound to herself? Aphrodite was no more prepared to avoid injury or to protect her son, Aeneas, than she was to foresee the eventual outcome of the Apple of Discord. Had she asked herself the question, however, she would have known the result. We Greeks believe our gods are fallible, and for this we are glad.

Now, the Heraclides were full of pride in their ancestor, the great Heracles. That pride led them to believe they knew the answers to all questions and knew what was best for others. This arrogance was evident in Heracles himself and may have been a family trait. It took a god to remind them that mortals have but a limited view of the world and that those who do not recognize this often come to sorry ends.

In undertaking her mission, Athene appeared as a well-appointed wise man with bald head and gray, owlish eyes in a long robe, carrying a tall carved staff. She found the reasonable brother of Cresphontes, Temenus, on a side street in Athens.

"Temenus," Athene told him, striking her staff on the ground for emphasis, "your family will never return to the Peloponnese if you do not listen to the oracles."

"Sir," Temenus replied, "do I know you?" He looked into the sparking sea-gray eyes.

"You know me well," the wise man said convincingly.

"The oracles were not clear," Temenus explained.

"The oracles were unambiguous," the owl-eyed man replied. "You misunderstood the original prodigy that you would be successful only after "three crops." You thought the crops were mere growing seasons, when they were actually crops of men – your own generations. This failure to comprehend the oracle led to many deaths and two aborted attempts to return to the Peloponnese. Now, you must understand the words, for you have one last attempt. Take for your guide the Three-Eyed One and his companion."

"We cannot," Temenus said. "These advisors went outside all conventions. They refused to compromise and required all sorts of materiel and equipment beyond our means."

"Let me counsel you in the affairs of men," smiled the wise man, his colorless eyes shining with wisdom. "Agamemnon did not go to Troy worrying about the cost of doing battle. He paid for this war with a daughter, a wife, his kingdom, and his life. Would he have gone to Troy knowing this? Do not address costs. For the costs of war are beyond foreseeing. This is feeble thinking."

"My brother feels that he can win under his own guidance," Temenus replied weakly, hearing the desperation in his own words.

"My son," the wise man said, "Cresphontes is mistaken. Listen to the oracle. Without the counselors-at-war, you will lose. You do not need a philosopher to tell you that. You have to pull the wool from Cresphontes' ears and remove the blinders from his eyes. And let me remind you that you must make offerings to the gods or they will forsake you. For the gods will not brook an impious man, nor reimburse unrighteous behavior."

Athene sowed these words deep within Temenus, as one would plant a row crop. When Temenus returned to Marathon to the palace of the Heraclides, he met with his brother.

"We must hire these counselors," Temenus told his brother. "They present us with our only opportunity."

"We do not know these men," Cresphontes argued, "and they could surprise us. How can we give over direction of the campaign to them? Why not invite a stranger to your wife's bed?"

"Telemachus can be trusted, since his only desire is to return to Ithaca. Oxylus is less trustworthy, and we know little of his background. What we do know is cloudy and suspect. Yet, he too has a limited agenda."

"They have little to lose and much to gain," said Cresphontes. "Not a combination for trustworthiness."

"We cannot fail again, my brother. These men are expert where we are lacking. They have ideas that we have not entertained. They know the Pelopides and their states far better than we. We have nothing new to offer," Temenus paused, as if to gather power. "And you know, as our previous failures indicate, we are not warriors as Heracles was. The third crop even less so. We will lose without these counselors." Although Temenus' words had little appeal to Cresphontes, the power of Temenus' arguments, buttressed perhaps by Athene herself, did finally win him over and reverse the direction of his thoughts.

"You may be right," Cresphontes agreed. "We must not fail. We need to put ourselves in the position to have them fail and not us. We will give them rope but not relinquish the ends."

And so it was decided that Temenus and Deiphontes would travel to Elis to discuss the final arrangements with Telemachus and Oxylus. However, although Cresphontes' mind dealt well with ideas and concepts, he was a practical man, one accustomed to getting his way like a spoiled child. He allowed one plan to go forward and kept further plans to himself. Another plan was soon enough put into effect without the awareness of Temenus or Deiphontes, but like all things not without the knowledge of the gods.

The packing and collecting of the animals continued for an entire moon-cycle. With his twin sons and Oxylus in the hills directing the round-up of the horses, Telemachus began packing the household goods. The servants arranged the goods in four giant wooden crates, lined up inside the courtyard waiting for transport by wagons to the harbor at Pheia. The final crate stood empty by the stairs to the entrance hall. Telemachus packed the treasure of Odysseus himself. Of the five crates to be sent to Ithaca, only one would contain priceless objects.

Adrastos, son of Eumaeus, aided Telemachus. Laertes had purchased the baby Eumaeus, and Odysseus' mother, Anticlia, had raised him as a family member, since he was a charming boy and sibling to Odysseus, though servant. Eumaeus had served Odysseus his entire life and had aided him in the battle with the suitors. With the death of Odysseus, Telemachus had given all the slaves their freedom. Eumaeus' son, Adrastos, had continued his service at Elis. Adrastos shared his father's excellent character and love for the family. Eumaeus yet lived in Ithaca, an old man, working the farm of Laertes, and helping Penelope as a free man.

The much-trusted Adrastos would accompany the goods to Ithaca and remain there until Telemachus' return. Together, they packed the treasure. Telemachus worked in the lower storeroom, wrapping the golden objects in large swaths of coarse cloth and tying them with binding cord. He then handed the objects to Adrastos, who carried them to the crate and carefully packed them. They worked the entire day, slowly filling the crate with fine objects, the value of which if Adrastos knew, he never said. Telemachus waited until the last to wrap the famous bow and arrows of Odysseus and Achilles' suit of armour in multiple layers of cloth. He carried these priceless objects himself to the crate and placed them well within, hidden among the other precious objects. They finished filling the crate with ordinary objects, wrapped in a similar fashion, and then closed it, securing it with large bronze nails. The five crates were so heavy that each required a separate wagon and four horses to pull. All the servants gathered to help lever the crates onto the wagons and tie them down.

As the number of horses in the hills declined, it became increasingly difficult to capture the remaining ones. A week after the packing was completed, Oxylus and the twins returned from the hills at crepuscule with the final herd of horses. Helios, god of the sun, drove his own horses into Oceanus in a crimson blaze, and darkness descended on heaven and earth. Now over eleven hundred head of horses champed in the lower pasture. Telemachus stood next to Oxylus and his sons, astonished at the magnificent collection of horses in the waning light. Nowhere in the Peloponnese, or in all of Hellas for that matter, was there a like collection of fine animals. The horses gathered together in the pasture, stallions, mares, and colts – the bands breaking down due to the proximity of the many horses and the feed provided. The servants had set up many feeding troughs for grain within the enclosure. The fresh grass in the pasture had disappeared due to the appetites of the horses and the weight of their hooves on the moist soil.

"We have nearly completed our task," Telemachus said. "We must separate the pregnant mares, the brood mares, their foals and colts, and the yearlings. They will be remaining here. Once we have completed this, we can leave any day."

"We still have wine remaining," Oxylus added, "from many vintages. It will be drunk by others, if we do not enjoy it ourselves."

As the final work on the estates neared completion, Telemachus saw the apprehension in the eyes of the servants. He ordered a feast be prepared for all. A steer and a lamb were sacrificed to the gods and spitted over a large fire in the banquet room. Cauldrons of steamed barley were prepared, with tripods filled with a steaming soup of the inner organs and pungent coriander seeds and cumin. They paid homage to the gods with waves of fresh smoke from the fats and meats broiling over the smoldering coals. After praising the gods, everyone enjoyed the meal: the servants in the courtyard, while the family lounged comfortably around the warmth of the hearth.

"We need to begin thinking in a different manner," Oxylus said finally. "We can no longer depend on the Eleans as friends. Therefore, we need to arm the servants who will be leaving with us. This will require some training, which should begin tomorrow, as the time of our departure approaches. And, of course, we need to be under arms ourselves. There is much of value here for the taking. We are not yet prepared to defend ourselves. Tomorrow," Oxylus said, "I will distribute the new swords that I brought with me."

"We cannot wait much longer for the decision of the Heraclides," Telemachus said. "The herald has returned from presenting our message to the family. King Dius is impatient for our departure from Elis."

"There is a bachelor stallion I would like to ride," Autolycus said, changing the subject. "We found him in the hills yesterday. He is as white as fresh snow and as fast as the wind."

"You are welcome to ride any horse," Telemachus said. "Both of you. But I know the horse. He is wild and magnificent. He comes from the mountains of Boeotia and will not tame easily."

"He is young, though ready to be ridden," Autolycus replied.

"We can isolate him tomorrow," Telemachus said, "and see if he takes to man. Horse taming cannot be done in haste. Horses can see into your soul, and although you can break the horse, you can never replace what you have stolen from him. Do not rush, Autolycus. Amphion, you may want to choose a horse for yourself. We will be riding for many days."

The wine soon went to their heads, and they were close to sleep before the embers, when a commotion arose from the courtyard. They all went outside to see the cause. Oxylus carried his sword. There were several horses and men surrounded by the servants.

Telemachus recognized two of the men, the Heraclides Temenus and Deiphontes, but the two other men were not known to him.

"Welcome," he said stepping into the courtyard and approaching the Heraclides. "Is there a problem?"

"Only that these men want high payment for directing us here," Temenus replied.

Telemachus approached the two men he now recognized from the town. "And what service did you provide that requires such payment?" he asked them.

"Sir, we know you and trust that you will see the fairness of our request. We rode with these strangers to your farm and directed them, taking us far out of our way. We only ask for just compensation."

"Is not hospitality a gift from the gods?" Telemachus asked.

"Right," the man answered, "but that will not place barley on the table."

"Maybe," Oxylus added, "your payment will be to return with your lives."

"No," Telemachus said quickly. "Give them that large barrow that has been bothering the other swine." Four servants ran off to rope the giant pig and bring him to the courtyard. The townsmen were happy to have this for they had anticipated less.

An enormous barrow dragged the servants into the courtyard, and others had to help hold the ropes to keep the pig in check. He was as heavy as five men easily and as strong and ornery as any boar. The two men mounted their horses and took the ropes, dragging the pig with them, but the horses were not comfortable. Between the flighty horses and the bellowing pig, pulling men and horses in one direction and then the other, they would have some time getting him back to town. But off they went to a variety of hoots and mocking laughter.

"Come in," Telemachus said, placing his arm over Temenus' shoulders. "You must be hungry."

"We arrived at the port this morning and had a difficult day getting here. These Eleans are not a friendly people. And we met many louts along the road, until we got to town, where no one wanted to direct us, for there seem to be ill-feelings about this estate. These last two would only help us under duress and then wanted great payment. I am not used to this behavior."

"We have become anathema in the town, for the king, Dius by name, has made it known that we are no longer welcome here. We have paid more than our share of the town levy for years, and many of the townspeople are employed here. But they have no thanks, because we are foreigners here…after twenty-five years."

They entered the meeting hall, where servants had added some logs to the coals and were reheating some of the remaining meat and soup.

Temenus took a place near the fire, throwing off his cloak. "The reason for our delay in arriving in Elis…"

"There will be no talk of business this evening," Telemachus interrupted, holding up his hand. "You are cold and tired from your trip. First, you must warm up, eat, and refresh yourselves. Then you must enjoy the slumber of the gods. There will be time enough to talk tomorrow. In the meantime, please make yourselves at home and enjoy the warmth and good cheer."

Servants filled the guests' goblets with the aged wine of the estate and quickly served steaming meats and soup. The two Heraclides relaxed, enjoying the warmth of the surroundings after a long journey. Telemachus and Oxylus then spoke of their efforts over the last month to prepare to leave the region. They also described their relations with the new King Dius. Oxylus told of his rough treatment by the soldiers, which he had not related to Telemachus before.

From their first encounter, Deiphontes and Amphion realized that they shared much in common, though not in age, for Deiphontes was a mature man with a wife and children. They sat together and quickly began to form a bond of friendship. Deiphontes remembered himself on the verge of manhood. They were both the sons of famous men, both raised in prominent families, and both knew they were destined to rule just as their fathers had. It was as though each man was looking in a mirror and liking what he saw. Truly, it was a godsend to find another person with whom one can be open and share personal thoughts. Deiphontes ate ravenously, while Amphion posed many questions.

"Do you think that the people of the Peloponnese will welcome you back? What about all the new migrants in our lands today, speaking different varieties of Greek? There are so many people without means, barely surviving, while others are well off and enjoying life. And there is the constant threat of the sea people, whose only goal is to sack towns that cannot protect themselves. How can anyone rule such disparate states? Each state has its own traditions, and the people are not welcoming. We are considered foreigners in Elis, though I was born and raised here. And what about the growing numbers of slaves who seek their freedom?

"You know," Deiphontes finally said, "I was born in Athens as was my father and grandfather, but I too am considered a foreigner. My family was granted the right to stay in Attica by the king generations ago. Yet we cannot be involved in the affairs of state and will be always suspected of conducting some deception or mischief. Peoples' memories are long when it come to cataloguing others, and short when it involves their own failings or behavior. You talk of slaves. We were born of slaves, for Heracles was a slave to

Eurystheus. There must be rules for slaves just as for free men. A man cannot live his life in slavery without hope for redemption."

After dining, Telemachus rose to address the Heraclides. "The gods are pleased that you have joined our celebration this evening. And we are pleased to welcome you to our home. We have met before, but never as friends must, over a goodly fire and with excellent foods and drink. Tomorrow morning we will present you with gifts. Tonight, we pray for your health and long life. I feel my mortality this evening for some reason. Perhaps the gods are close by. We mortals must cleave together, for what is more important than human joy, and that can only be accomplished in concert with others. So much of what is blamed on the gods is yet the work of man. The lot of man is difficult enough. Yet we are all intent on making it more difficult for each other. I am reminded of a line of donkeys struggling down the slopes of a rocky hillside under heavy loads of wood, feeling the crop of their master, and at the same time biting at each other's backside. I suggest that we all seek the comforts of sleep, and tomorrow at dawn I will show you some animals that understand this notion of cooperation better than donkey or man."

The next morning, the goddesses Eos and Persephone combined to warm the earth with fresh, strong-hearted sea breezes, the lovely light of the golden glows of dawn and scent of spring. The aroma of fresh turned soil and the decay of humus were the first signs of Persephone coming from the depths of endless night to join her mother, Demeter, in the brilliant heavens. This morning, the air was redolent with the humid odors of renewal. The men ate a hearty meal of dried fish, preserved fruit, and fresh cheese on bread, warm from the oven, sweetened with honey.

Telemachus, Oxylus, Temenus, Deiphontes, and the twins walked down to the pasture. Horses packed the lower field, some grazing, some dozing on their feet, and a few stretched out on the grass asleep. The colts kept close to their mothers, while the stallions stood separately throughout the herd, blustering and blowing with concern. Telemachus had collected horses of every hue, from all the countries of Hellas, Asia Minor, and the Levantine: solid blacks, sorrels, and bays; duns and hinds; pure grays, roans, and light silvers and whites; and mixed and splotchy paints of all colors.

As they approached the stone wall separating the pasture from the house, Sterope trotted forward, followed by the giant one-eyed Rhaebus. Both horses came up to the men and accepted their praise and fondling. Standing near Rhaebus always produced an amazing feeling in men, for his withers were above a man's head, and his head easily surmounted the wall. Rhaebus calmly accepted some dried apples, with Sterope jealously pushing him aside.

Telemachus signaled to one of the servants to rope two young mares. One was a large buckskin from Cephallenia, perhaps five years old. She had a patch of white across her withers and back, spots of white on her neck, and white stockings. The other mare he selected was a bay from Thessaly, smaller, but strongly built. She held her head high with an attitude of conceit, reminding him of Bronte. He had tamed both himself.

"There is no finer gift than life itself. One day, these mares will produce many foals. Temenus, I present you with a tame horse from my country, Cephallenia. She is surefooted and gentle and was born to please. Deiphontes, I think you need a tougher horse, though tame as well, one from the mountains of Thessaly, with the rich color of heartwood and the love of forests and dales."

"Can we test the white?" Autolycus asked impatiently.

"If he will accept a halter, you can begin to tame him," Telemachus answered.

The servants went back into the pasture and found the large white stallion, who reacted to the men with ropes by scraping the ground with his front hooves, and then when they approached he reared up to warn the intruders, his hooves in the air. He neatly avoided a rope and took off across the pasture, charging through the other horses and complaining the entire way.

"He has not seen man up close," Telemachus said. "We will have to wait to mount him." But daring Autolycus would not be put off, and he went after the stallion with a rope and sweets.

Deiphontes and Amphion walked off toward the river. The three elders, left to themselves, walked through the farm, surveying the gardens, orchards, and vineyards. They walked up the hill to the site of Odysseus' grave. Telemachus had not consciously directed them there, but the landscape naturally attracted the men to higher levels to see the Peneus Valley, the town at a distance, and finally at a sufficient elevation to see the distant wide Aegean Sea. When they arrived at Odysseus' gravesite, Telemachus realized that with all his preparation to leave, he had given no thought to leaving his father's grave in the hands of others. Once the crafty Odysseus had ruled the world, but today he lay buried in an unmarked grave. The site was growing up; the natural vegetation had returned. The mound and cairn no longer appeared foreign to their surroundings.

"This is my father's grave," Telemachus stated.

"He must have been a great man," Temenus said. "As wise as Heracles was strong."

"Yes, but I knew him only later in his life. By that time, he had attempted to cool too many tempers, been blown off course too many times, and was growing tired of the constant struggle. My mother, Penelope, called this farm his greatest accomplishment. But I am sure that he would not have agreed with her. The memories of Troy and the call of the seas never left his head.

"Once a man has achieved greatness...or infamy," Oxylus added, "it is not easy to return to a common existence."

XXIV

That evening the men gathered in the great hall for dinner, all save Autolycus. A white lamb was sacrificed on the hearth, and the fatty meats were burned to the gods. After a day of rest, the men gathered in a light mood. Autolycus joined the men after they had completed their meal.

"You look as though you lost a boxing match," Telemachus greeted his son.

"Not only did he come to halter, but bit and bridle, and I was able to mount him as well."

"Not for long," Telemachus said.

"By the end, I stayed with him for more than a few moments. He is full of life and pride and will be an excellent mount. I have named him Boreas after the icy god. Tomorrow, I will ride him."

When the coals burned softly and the wine flowed gently, Temenus addressed himself to the men: "I would like to thank you for your hospitality, Telemachus. You have opened your heart to us and welcomed us as you would kith and kin. I know you today and trust you as I would a member of my own family. I pour a libation to the gods in the spirit of hospitality." He allowed a few drops of wine to fall to the floor.

"I believe our thoughts and goals align and the gods smile upon us. I bring you the words of our family." Temenus paused. "My brother, Cresphontes, is not an easy man. He seeks honor and greatness. He is blinded by ambition and cannot accept that others may be trusted to help achieve his goals. I met a wise man who made me to see the heart of the matter. He said that the gods will not brook an impious man nor reimburse unrighteous behavior. I think our previous attempts to return to the Peloponnese, although we certainly have more claim on this territory than the Pelopides, were made in error. We have to consider the reasons we want to return and not to limit them to our own gains. For this is impiety in all eyes. And further we must return based on truthfulness and with honorable intentions. I say this to give you insight into our family. This is a family born of anger and vengeance. Hyllus, son of Heracles, and my great grandfather, was born of Deianira. This same warm-breasted woman poisoned her husband, Heracles, in her jealousy. Her son thirsted for the blood of Eurystheus, the tormentor of Heracles. When Hyllus killed Eurystheus, he presented his decapitated head to Heracles' mother, Alcmena, who cut out its eyes. Hyllus was the first Heraclide to attempt to return to his home in the Peloponnese, long before the Trojan War. He failed and lost his life. He was killed by King Echemus of Arcadia in hand-to-hand combat.

"Forgive me for dwelling in the past. This does not bear on your roles. But it gives you some insight into my family and the effort required to turn us towards the light. After all, I convinced my brother Cresphontes that we cannot successfully return to our home in the Peloponnese without your guidance. That has been stated clearly by the oracle, and Cresphontes now accepts it. The family has agreed to your terms as you charted them. We are prepared to give you total control of the military. The third crop of Heraclides will report directly to you, and Cresphontes and I will remain in the background, as you requested.

"We are prepared to help you, Oxylus, obtain the throne of an independent Elis and to sustain you in such a position. It would be our hope that, at some time in the future, Elis will become a member of a confederacy of Peloponnesian states. And you, Telemachus, it will be our goal to see you installed on the throne of Ithaca, Cephallenia, and Zacynthus and the islands off the shores of Elis. The success of our mission and your roles would merit these rewards.

"We also recognize and accept your suggestions that this is a return to authority and not an invasion; that we will respect the rights of the peoples of the Peloponnese; that we will not take plunder or loot of any kind; that should we require resources we will establish a market for such; and that we will seek peaceful solutions at all times. I think those were your chief concerns and good ones as well.

"It is our intention that these young people sitting here today may enjoy the sacrifices we are making, and that this undertaking will improve the lot of all people throughout the Peloponnese. For all men desire to live in peace and security in the comfort of their own homes. Just as the gods live in heaven in eternal bliss."

Oxylus glanced at Telemachus and then spoke. "Your words comfort us and provide us with the knowledge of your intentions. I have two fears. This agreement has been slow in the making, and now we have barely seven moons to prepare for a major offensive before the next rainy season. But perhaps more importantly, we have seen the struggle and adversity within your family. I am the last to disparage a family, my own being rift with adventure and mischief. It concerns me that this family of Heraclides is so divided it could impinge on the success of any venture. We must be convinced that your family will stand with us in all climes and under all circumstances."

Temenus took a moment to reflect before replying. "You are correct. The divisions within our family are obvious to all. The sons of Heracles, the first crop, were a bickering and contentious group, for they shared only a father and were, thus, all half-brothers with far-flung mothers. Only two of them, Hyllus and Ctesippus, shared a mother in common, Deianira, the last wife of Heracles. And the offspring of these two full-brothers are the primary proponents of the family today. Cresphontes and I are descended from Hyllus, and Deiphontes from Ctesippus.

"But allow me to be more direct, so that you can come to trust me. First, I am the father of nine children. Of these children, there is one especially that I believe has the potential and desire to lead the third crop. This is my daughter, Hyrnetho. She is a brilliant shining light. There is another person whom I would trust with my life, and he sits before you, Deiphontes. He is the son of Antimachus, a distant cousin, and my daughter is married to him. We form a solid and trustworthy grouping within the family. You can rely on us in all things.

"Now, the twins, sons of Aristodemus, our older brother who was killed in the second attempt, young Procles and Eurysthenes, are like wolves. They will hunt with the pack and eat with the pack, but when winter comes they will be for themselves alone. Understanding this is important, since we can always trust they will never be unified in their pursuits. We cannot fathom the twists and turns of their minds, but we know they pray to the god of self-interest.

"Another member of the third crop, Aletes, is less known to me, but he is a dark, hungry wolf as well. His brooding and darkness often disturb me. And he is as impetuous as his father, Hippotes, who was banished after the second attempt failed because he speared a priest of Apollo. Aletes and Cresphontes are close and must be watched.

"If I were our adversary, King Tisamenus, my best offense would be to somehow throw a bone to this pack of wolves and wait while they destroy each other.

"I cannot swear an oath for Cresphontes. My own wife and children will have nothing to do with the man. He is an uncle in name only. But I can swear that Deiphontes and I will do all we can within the family to assist you and to stand by our agreement with you: the Oath of Temenus."

"I believe you," Telemachus replied, "but I have inherited a weakness from my mother and must always be shown. I tend to take people at their word and am greatly disappointed on occasions. However, I am willing to accept the Oath of Temenus. And you Oxylus?"

"Since as an orphan I was raised to trust no one, my only defense is vigilance. I believe that the Oath of Temenus is acceptable and will drink on it. We have some time to test its merits before we commit our lives on the field of battle, and I will reserve final acceptance of all the terms of the oath until the very day we begin the offensive."

He raised his goblet, and they all drank together.

Late into the night, they worked out and agreed to all the practical arrangements. Temenus would return to the mainland the next day to the port of Naupactus, where the family had a large fleet of ships. He would see to the mobilization of the ships to meet the horses in Dyme, a small port at the mouth of the Gulf of Corinth. Then he would travel to Marathon to muster the family and troops. Deiphontes would remain with Telemachus and Oxylus and the twins to help them move the horses to Dyme. This gave Telemachus additional confidence in the Heraclides, at least this branch. The long ships of the Heraclides would meet them at Dyme and would transport them across the gulf. The family had a large palace and park in Locris in the mountains that could be used for training and preparation. The invasion would preferably begin at harvest time. Failing that, they would have to wait until late spring of the following year.

Day is born of night, and so Eos, the goddess of dawn, cleared away the misty darkness. Then Helios, her fiery brother, began the heavy work of driving the sun through the heavens. The men slept until the light of day fell into their rooms and bade them rise. Their final meal before Temenus' departure was taken on the terrace overlooking the courtyard. And none was surprised to see Autolycus enter the courtyard mounted on a subdued and tired white stallion, covered in the sweat and foam of confrontation. Boreas by name, the stallion was still full of spirit. Not everyone had slept until mid-day.

Meanwhile, when Pallas Athene returned to the glorious heights of heaven, she sought a private audience with the lord god. Instead she found Zeus' marble-lined meeting hall filled with the gods, for some disaster or conflict must have happened on earth or was about to transpire. The brilliant light of Helios fell on the floor and was reflected by the milky white walls, gently warming the large chamber. Zeus sat above the other immortals on his throne with his immense head held in his hands, foggy gloom dimming his brilliance. Along the walls sat the other gods on their thrones. They were all speaking at the same time, with the result that no one could hear or understand the other. Even the newest god was declaiming his intentions with Hebe at his side. The beautiful Trojan boy, Ganymede, ran to refill the golden goblets of the gods.

Apollo raised his hand high to signal for the other gods to quiet down, for he was respected by all. "How can we expect mortals to behave, if we cannot even speak among ourselves? It seems to me that events are moving rapidly now and that once again the Hellenes are falling into a state of warfare. This time it is between them. This is not uncommon, for they have a history of such belligerences. I suppose this is better than plagues or massive inundations or earthquakes or other calamities, yet it is hardly the state of affairs that we would wish upon mortal man.

"Now," he continued, "I believe that some gods are involved once again in the affairs of man." His bright eyes followed Athene as she took her seat. "As we all know, this godly involvement was repudiated by the lord of us all. We confuse man. We cannot hope to fatten swine while withholding feed. I suggest that we listen to our father, the father of all immortals and mortals alike."

He paused, but Zeus remained in his pained position.

Instead, Hera made reply. "You ask an excellent question of my husband and brother. How can mortals follow a path toward righteousness and honor, if we are whispering in their ears various distractions? How can a great god such as your father, exhort mortals to appropriate behavior and then himself act like a dog surrounded by bitches in heat. We must clean our own house..."

But the almighty thunder of Zeus stopped her, and all the gods froze at his fury. "Woman, we have thrown you from the heavens once before and will not hesitate to do so again. Can you not see that we are weary to the bones? But we do strangely agree with your sentiment though not your manner of expression. Today, a serious situation exists on earth that could spell the end of life on the peninsula of Hellas for years to come. Further, it could spell the end of our stewardship. My frustration is deep, as deep as all Tartarus. We rage at you. But you listen not. You are children who refuse to grow up. And now you must. There is still time before events are initiated, but in an instant time passes and eternity is reached. Believe us, beloved children. It is our fault perhaps for spoiling you. By feeding you nectar and ambrosia. By healing your wounds. By not allowing you to suffer pain or illness. By banishing tears. We have failed you, but it is you who will come to regret it."

For the first time, he lifted his mighty head and, parting his long braided hair, looked with his rain clear eyes around the marvelous chamber. "Only Apollo and Athene are to remain. All the rest of you may return to your mansions."

The gods and goddesses rose and began filing out, but not quietly. Their voices filled the air with indecipherable sounds like the screams of angry gulls circling higher and higher on the strong coastal breezes in the failing light of evening. Immortal Zeus waited for the cacophony to diminish. When all were gone save

Apollo and Athene, the two strongest and most vocal of the gods, he signaled them forward.

When they alone stood before his high throne, he spoke to them: "Daughter, you have just returned from earth, where you planted the seeds of compliance in the ears of Temenus, which grew into fruit within the heart of his brother, Cresphontes. And you, my glorious son and the son of our beloved and gentle Leto..." His head shook back and forth. "A woman who never tortured us with her jealousy. You have set Cresphontes on a separate track against Oxylus and Telemachus, who have been appointed by the gods to bring the Heraclides success on the field of battle. Once again, we find ourselves unable to do more than influence the course of events, for the fate of these mortals is set, as is the outcome of the War of the Families. What we fear is the gods fighting among themselves. We see Hera and our son, the smith, Hephaestus, supporting the Heraclides with Athene. Aphrodite and Ares favor the Pelopides with you, Apollo. Your sister Artemis remains unresolved. Hermes is so set on avenging the death of his son, Myrtilus, that I lost track of him mortal generations ago, though certainly he is at work punishing the Pelopides. Recently, we have heard glimmerings that Poseidon is planning on helping the Pelopides, for of all Hellenes they are the only ones to offer him hecatombs.

"Now, we suggest that you agree that no gods will fight directly in these battles. Gone are the days when our own immortal children were involved in these affairs. Of course, some reconnaissance and morale boosting would not be out of order. As long as the other gods are not involved."

Apollo spoke: "My father and lord, you have always tried your best for your children. This was true as well with your son, Tantalus, but he went too far by feeding his son, Pelops, to the gods..."

"Are you making a point here?" Zeus interrupted. "Tantalus...my son, as you call him...is being punished as we speak."

"We restored Pelops to life, and his descendants deserve our protection."

"No."

"There are no clear lines here," Athene interjected. "Heracles was also a Pelopide through his mother, Alcmena, who was the granddaughter of Pelops."

"No," Zeus repeated.

Both Apollo and Athene regarded each other with antipathy.

"No. No. No," Zeus continued to repeat. "Get out. If we find either of you directly involved in this affair, we will cast you both into the depths of Tartarus. And sunlight will be lost to you forever."

Zeus remained on his throne after their exit, and although Ganymede, the serving boy, attempted to cheer him up, it would not be so. Zeus knew gifted Tisamenus, leader of the Pelopides, and he knew optimistic Cresphontes, leader of the Heraclides: this war, he also knew, would not be without its casualties, and all of Hellas would be its victim.

XXV

For every story in Greece, an assortment of bards relates the tale, each in his own way. Often they change the design and consequence to fit their own purpose or audience. For every hero, there are often several manners of death and different burial sites. And for every religious doctrine, there are others that contradict it. This contrariness points out a basic element within our nature as Greeks: we are never satisfied. One rendition of a telling cannot endure without being tidied up and elaborated upon, often to the point of inventing another story altogether. This inventiveness, resulting from the oral tradition, created the richest tapestry of legends of all time, as rich and varied as our people themselves at the crossroads of the world. In later years, as the scribes began to document these accounts, some of the wealth and diversity of the legends disappeared. But just as King Midas of Phrygia expected a few golden coins to fall into the pockets of his advisors, wealth can afford charity. In this manner, a selection took place that ladled the cream from the top of the milk and discarded the watery remainders.

When Rhea gave birth to Poseidon, chief of the watery deities, his father, Cronos, swallowed him. Cronos' father, Uranus, had predicted that Cronos would be overthrown by one of his progeny, so he swallowed all of them at their birth. By the time Zeus was born, though, Rhea had grown tired of Cronos devouring her offspring. She deceived her husband by wrapping a stone in clothing and presenting it to Cronos, who swallowed it, thinking it his new born son. He believed her as is the wont of men, often to their detriment. When Zeus grew up, he administered a powerful draft to his father, and Cronos disgorged all of his other offspring, namely Poseidon, Hestia, Hera, Hades, and Demeter. When the siblings gained their freedom, they did not hesitate to rebel against their tyrant of a father and banished him to Tartarus – just as the prophecy had foretold.

But the Arcadians tell a slightly different story. When Poseidon was born, Rhea tricked Cronos. Rhea told Cronos that she had given birth to a horse. She presented him with a new born foal, which he promptly swallowed. Rhea gave Poseidon to the daughter of Oceanus, Caphira, and the Telchines to raise on the island of Crete. Caphira taught Poseidon all she knew of the seas and oceans that bound the earth and the flowing waters. But Poseidon never forgot the foal that had taken his place in his father's belly. After Zeus forced Cronos to cough up the rest of his children and the foal, Poseidon took special interest in horses. He became god of horses and the first horse-tamer, for prior to this, horses were free to wander the earth, providing no service to mankind. Poseidon tamed the first horse and used his horses with brazen hooves and golden manes to transport him in his chariot. Thus, horse-tamers always pay homage to Poseidon, and this was the case when Telemachus and Oxylus set off with their horses from Elis.

Truth may be lost in the many renderings. But then I ask myself the importance of truth, if such a thing exists, since on the spectrum of truth, myths and legends are by far the more interesting aspects. Read Herodotus, if you find this unusual for an historian.

"May Poseidon, father of Pegasus," Telemachus said, "guide us and protect us on our way. For of all god's creatures, the horse, whose harmonious nature is a model of excellence for man, is the most beautiful in form and function and the most noble in character. And may the indomitable twins of Zeus, the Dioscuri, riders of swift horses, light our way to victory."

They were mounted on their horses in the courtyard of the estate in Elis. Oxylus rode his giant, one-eyed horse, Rhaebus. Telemachus rode his proud lady, Sterope. Autolycus barely held the white stallion, Boreas, under control, while Amphion had a well-behaved black mare, Arion, named after one of the horse offspring of Poseidon. Deiphontes was mounted on the sturdy, young bay with white splotches from Thessaly. He called her Tempe, after the river god in Thessaly near Mount Olympus.

They were joined by fifteen servants on horseback and five driving huge wagons with the household goods, each pulled by four horses. Adrastos drove the lead wagon. All the men were dressed in heavy woolen cloaks, covering light armour, consisting of ordinary bronze breastplates, greaves, and Achaean bronze helmets taken from Odysseus' collection. At the insistence of Oxylus, all wore the new cut-and-thrust iron swords at their sides, concealed in scabbards. Telemachus did not want to give the impression of an armed force, but rather a large cavalcade moving his animals and goods out of Elis, and for that reason they carried no shields or lances. Surrounding the men and horses were dogs of various races, some trained for herding goats and sheep. The cattle dogs of Odysseus followed, wooly monsters with curly hair, large heads with beards, and potent jaws.

It had taken fifteen more days after the departure of Temenus to complete the preparation, and spring was making her appearance. Telemachus had distributed all the remaining household goods among the servants staying in Elis. He had traded most of the animals. He had given away the stored wine and oil and other foodstuffs. The house was empty, but the estates were in excellent shape. Glorious white clusters bloomed on the almond trees. Several servants remained to care for the house and garden.

Now that the horses had been enclosed in the lower pasture, they had formed a larger herd that would stay together over the long distance they would travel. The horses would stretch out along the route for about four stadia. Since they had to pass through the center of Elis, the last horses, with Telemachus in the rear, would leave the estates at about the same time that the lead horses passed through the town. The cavalcade of horses would be the greatest ever seen in the Peloponnese.

Oxylus led the horses on proud Rhaebus, with the help of Autolycus on edgy, snow-colored Boreas. The dogs began barking and racing about as the horses bunched at the wide-open gates, and the servants began pushing them out. Telemachus watched calmly as the first horses began walking up the entrance road over the small bridge to the main road. The others followed closely. It was a long time before the wagons joined the cavalcade at about the halfway point, struggling to keep pace with the front of the cavalcade.

Telemachus, Amphion, and Deiphontes waited as the horses continued to file past. When the last of the horses had left the paddock, the men began moving slowly and reached the entrance to the estates. Telemachus turned Sterope and looked back at the green rolling hills and the large stone-walled buildings, the terraced foothills with the quiescent vines, the fruit orchard in first blossom, the forested hills and mountains beyond, where he could imagine the barrow of his father. The close-cropped grass was just beginning to show hints of new green in the large pasture areas in the hills, now empty of animals. He watched as a few servants moved about the grounds or stood watching the departure.

History is made by the compilation of small moments in people's lives: small efforts and small victories and defeats. Nothing is extraneous. Nothing is unimportant. All events count. You must know that. The family of Odysseus had lived in Elis for many years, raised children, grown older, and even died here. But a strong connection was never established. There never was a major campaign or victory. Odysseus came here wounded. Although those wounds healed slowly over time, the scars of the past remained. Ancient injuries boiled to the surface and proved fatal. And in the forested hills lay the remains of the man, his renown independent of history, and his life inscribed in the memories of those who loved him.

Telemachus nudged his heels into Sterope; she blustered in surprise and lifted her head, turning toward the road, trotting gracefully after the others.

By the time the end of the cavalcade came to the outskirts of town, townspeople were crowded along both sides of the road, laughing and pointing as the horses passed. Children waved as Telemachus rode into the town. He could see the amazement on peoples' faces at the continuing flood of horses. He saw a few soldiers standing in the streets, but the horses passed without encumbrance. At the center of town, a large throng on both sides talked and called to each other in good nature across the constantly moving herd. Never had they seen such a spectacle.

Telemachus turned Sterope when he glimpsed Dius watching from the portico of his palace with his aging counselors. Telemachus rode up to Dius. Amphion and Deiphontes turned their horses to follow him. The horses' breaths steamed in the cool morning air. They moved nervously about, frustrated at being held in check by the slow movement of the herd and now being forced to remain in place.

"Dius, may the gods protect you and your family," Telemachus shouted, as Sterope turned anxiously in a circle.

"And you too. May the gods protect the righteous."

"Thanks to your family, we have been honored here."

"I hope that we meet again," Dius said.

"I am sure we will."

"Remember," Dius said, "there is no greater gift than hospitality and asylum."

"And for that I am grateful, and may the gods reward you." Telemachus spoke, reining in Sterope. "My father is buried in these hills. My sons are leaving their birthplace and only home they have ever known." He noticed the old advisor, Actor, standing off behind Dius. "Dius, remember the lesson of your forebear, the Argonaut, the great King Augeas. You must treat all people with respect."

"And you remember, son of Odysseus, that the gods hate a treasonous man."

"I am returning to my homeland, Ithaca, where I am a faithful citizen."

"You are as deceitful as your ancestors."

Telemachus touched the hilt of his sword, but Sterope quick-stepped to the side. He reined her in again tightly. "You are young, Dius. You have much to learn. Look to your ancestors for guidance."

"Go, before I change my mind. But do not return."

"I shall return, and you will learn the lesson of humility. Act with god."

Sterope heard the tone of his voice and wheeled around in the road, cantering off rapidly, with the others following. They hurried to catch up with the end of the cavalcade, which was now barely moving at the outskirts of town due to the narrow bridge crossing the Peneus several stadia ahead. The crossroads lay outside the town, one direction toward Boreas taking them across the Peneus toward Cyllene and Achaea and the mainland, and the other in the direction of Notus toward the harbor at Pheia and to Messenia, the land of King Nestor.

The road to Dyme descended from Elis to a wide river plain, draining the foothills of Mount Erymanthus. This was a well-watered region, with gentle hills thickly covered with trees of all sorts, sprinkled with small plantings of panic grass, millet, barley, and wheat. The mountains rose steeply, the lofty peaks white capped in snow. They expected the trip to Dyme to take two days at a slow pace, with plenty of time to graze and water the horses on the way. It was about one hundred and twenty-five stadia to Cyllene, a small coastal village on the Ionian Sea. And the small port of Dyme was about seventy-five stadia farther.

As the valley spread out before them, the horses began to walk at a faster gait, and the mid-morning dust began to rise in a great cloud blowing toward the Ionian Sea. Farmers halted their work to watch the long line of horses approach and then crawl through the countryside like an egg snake moving slowly through the green grass. There were no flags or unnatural colors of allegiance, no reflections from shields, and no dull, metallic clang of armour on the march. No lances rose from the hands of the men. No eyes searched for plunder. So the farmers stood in their fields with amazement rather than fear. This cavalcade was peaceful and boded no ill, for the men guiding the horses almost disappeared among the large number of horses.

Although this road was an uncommon route for the armies of the Peloponnese, the farmers and fishermen had seen their share of warriors file past, and the people had not remained along the roadside to smile in wonder, but had evacuated into the hills and suffered from a distance as their fields were devastated, their animals slaughtered, and their crops taken by the troops. As often as not, their houses were razed. Just as storms overran the Ionian Sea, though never welcome, destructive waves of troops from time to time marched across their lands.

The cool, winter-ending weather was perfect for the horses. They continued all day, wending their way along the trail, for calling it a road would be an overstatement. In many places, the trail was flooded and muddy, and they forded slow flowing and shallow streams. The cavalcade moved well and approached the coastline near Cyllene before dusk. They settled in a clearing just outside the village in close proximity to a small freshwater lake with plenty of grass and space for the horses to graze.

As the brilliant red sky marked the descent of Helios and the return of the earth to darkness, the men warmed themselves with the flames from a hastily prepared fire. Adrastos led in a goat and staked it near the fire. But before everyone became too comfortable, Telemachus asked three of the men to retrace their path to ensure that no forces of Dius were following them. The wagons stood nearby, and wine and water were passed around, and soon the tired men were sitting comfortably on camp stools, and the dogs were settled around them, waiting patiently for their due.

Oxylus slaughtered the goat and thanked the gods for their good fortune. He quickly butchered the animal, throwing the coat into the center of the fire, and piling the long bones and fatty meats on the edge of the coals, sending waves of good smelling smoke into the heavens. A servant set up a tripod and dug a spit into the ground, loading it with fresh meat. Dried fruits and nuts, barley cakes, and olives were passed around, and soon the smell of roasted meat filled the entire camp. Wine and water slaked everyone's thirst.

"Dius was not happy to see us leave," Oxylus said.

"He had no options," Telemachus answered. "Whether we stayed or departed."

"No. He has no army and is not prepared to defend himself."

"Men three times his age and more surround him, acting as counselors. They want only to enrich themselves and protect their positions. In truth, Elis is no more than a rural village, ruled by a family that has lost its imagination. I am sure that Dius has no appetite to rule, and this region will not long remain so constituted."

"Though it is a region of abundant resources," Oxylus said, "and can be made to excel. I look forward to my return. Autolycus, how was your horse? Boreas, is that his name?"

"He is strong-willed and independent," Autolycus responded. "I feel as though I am his guest. He never gives in entirely, always testing. It will be some time before he is trustworthy."

"You must show him that you are master." Oxylus said. "Though herd animals, all horses are independent of mind, constantly aware of a hierarchy and where they fit it. But they always respect the leaders of the herd. You must punish him brutally, if need be."

"He is young," Autolycus responded.

"Just so," replied Oxylus.

"Spoken like a man without children…and without understanding of horses," Telemachus added.

"I understand horses. They are beasts of burden that can lighten our loads. I have had my share."

"Horses are gifts of the gods," Telemachus replied. "Of all animals, man included, horses are nearest to perfection in form and function."

"My mount," Amphion said, interrupting the two friends, "was a campaigner. She is sure of foot and always responsive to my commands. She is as good a horse as ever I have ridden. What about yours, Deiphontes?"

"Tempe is young and needs experience, but she did very well. She is strong and smart, and she is yet growing and will put on more weight."

After the meal, the men settled in. They were glad to be finally moving, since the days had been full of preparation and planning for some time. The peacefulness of accomplishment settled over them, aided by the food and drink.

"We are well over half-way," Telemachus said. "We will be in Dyme tomorrow afternoon. The long ships of the Heraclides should be on the beach. Another day of riding will do all our mounts well. The horses are comfortable. No sentries will be necessary. We are off the road, and no one is following us. I think we can relax this evening."

The night was uneventful. All slept peacefully. But the next morning, as golden-sandaled Eos rose in the sky to sweep away the mist of darkness, the rains began to fall steadily. Although they added dry wood to the fire, they could not start it again. Their covers and wool cloaks became soaked. So their meal consisted of damp bread and soft goat cheese, eaten under the wet shelter of their cloaks. They mounted and began once again pushing the horses into the weepy Borean winds and rain.

Their path led slightly off the coast straight through the village of Cyllene. Much of the coastline was marshy, but by the time they reached the village the rocky coast line was covered in mist, and the village was dark and wet. The rains continued to fall steadily. It was the early market hour as they passed through, interrupting the entire village for some time, while the horses dominated Cyllene's narrow road. The villagers waited in the rain for the horses to pass.

In the final stage, the sole route leading toward Boreas from Cyllene became nothing more than a low swale, inundated and washed out from the rainfall. Progress slowed to a snail's pace. The wagons sank into the mud, requiring the men to push and pull to free them. By late afternoon, halfway to Dyme, they had to ford the Larisus, a large river full of mud flowing rapidly to the sea. Telemachus sent scouts in both directions to discover a safe crossing, but the Larisus was swollen by the rains. It was too dangerous to attempt to cross. They moved off the trail, and camped in a forested area nearby. Scouts retraced their path and encountered no forces behind them. The village had regained its peace and quiet.

Since they had anticipated a short trip, they had not brought tents or enclosures to escape the rain. The men protected themselves as best they could against the drizzle and freezing night air under trees. They ate a cold meal and settled down to endure a bitter and soggy night that seemed interminable.

The next morning the golden glow of Eos greeted them among high clouds. The rain had abated during the night. As the sun appeared over the hills, the horsemen attempted to dry off without great success. Scouts returned with news of shallows toward jasmine-scented Apeliotes, rocky and with rapidly moving water, yet fordable. They managed to get the horses moving by mid-morning and began crossing the river. There was little danger of being swept away in the low stream, but the course across it proved treacherous, with large and small boulders and the flowing waters creating eddies and blind spots. Horses are much surer of foot than man. They made their way slowly and carefully across the river, packed together for safety. If one horse stumbled there was always another close by whose body helped the other to maintain its footing. The men watched closely as the horses slowly made their way through the water and gathered on the other side. It took some time for all the horses to cross. While a dozen or so horses lost their footing and fell, none was injured seriously.

After this, the road to Dyme continued in a flat plain, muddy and swampy. Both horses and men welcomed the warm sunlight, and slowly the dampness from the rain began to dry out and depart.

Progress was slow, and it took great effort to move the wagons forward. They did not reach Dyme until late in the evening. Searching for a good spot to camp and secure the horses, they discovered a grassy expanse with a small creek not far from the shore and close to the village. The meadow was protected by forest on three sides, and a rope barrier was strung to make the horses aware of their confines. Still damp, the men built a great fire and set the last of the meats to roast and waited for their clothes to dry and bodies to warm.

The next morning, Telemachus and Oxylus investigated the village. Dyme was a tiny village, situated on a wide expanse of beach, with fishing boats and a few commercial ships either hauled up on the shore, lying on their sides, or laying off the coast, secured by stone sea anchors. No one was awaiting their arrival in Dyme, and no ship of the Heraclides was anchored offshore. The villagers knew nothing of any fleet of ships. The main street had several wine houses and places for sailors to be put up, but more buildings were deserted than occupied. In general, the town was destitute and barely surviving. Although Dyme lay along an active sea route with ships coming from all directions, they rarely stopped, and when they did it was not out of choice.

Telemachus and Oxylus managed to obtain some fresh bread and then returned to the camp to a warm fire and better spirits. But after several days, their spirits began to sag once again, for there was no sign of the Heraclides' ships, they had run out of fresh meat, and the horses constantly ran out of forage and they had to change locations every day. At least, the sun remained out, and the days warmed.

Meanwhile, Telemachus and Adrastos arranged for a commercial ship to transport the household goods to Ithaca. Adrastos was to accompany the shipment, along with three other servants, all of whom would remain on Ithaca, helping Penelope and working to return the palace to its former greatness, anticipating the arrival of Telemachus. Telemachus identified a ship owner, Clearchus, who captained his own ship and plied the islands off Elis, Aetolia, and Acarnania. Clearchus was a trustworthy man, and his twenty-five-oar ship was seaworthy and appeared to be in good shape. Although Clearchus lived in Dyme and was raising a large family, he spent most of his time onboard. His crew was composed of locals who depended on Clearchus for their livelihood. Telemachus felt confident that he would be able to trust them. The distance was not great. A ship could visit Ithaca, leaving early one morning and, with helpful winds, return before sunset the next day. Telemachus thought of accompanying the goods himself, but he felt it would be better to put off his homecoming. By all accounts, Penelope was thriving on Ithaca, and Telemachus felt certain that he would return soon enough. When he did return, it would be as king of the islands – and not a beggar.

XXVI

Two days later, the servants stowed the first of the crates aboard Clearchus' vessel. The ship rode low in the water, but without concern as long as the calm weather held. The morning of the third day, long before sunrise, the ship departed with four servants, both visibly and secretly armed. Telemachus, with Adrastos' help, had chosen three of his servants, who had shown their loyalty to him many times over, and whose families depended on them in all ways. With a great hug, Adrastos left Telemachus, boarded the ship, and departed. Adrastos had no idea of the value of the cargo, although he would protect it as though it were his own.

As planned, Adrastos and Clearchus returned the evening of the following day, and they loaded another crate. On Ithaca, Adrastos had taken the crate to the palace himself and had stored it unopened in a large barn area within the palace walls. Penelope was well and sent her best wishes and hoped the family would return soon. The next day the second shipment left Dyme.

Telemachus and Oxylus continued to watch for any sign of the Heraclides, but without success. The final shipment left Dyme seven days after the first, and Adrastos bid adieu to Telemachus until sometime in the future and wished him god speed. Once again, the treasure of Odysseus was back in Ithaca without incident. In this final shipment, Telemachus sent what Odysseus had treasured most: his three big, curly cattle dogs.

Clearchus returned the next evening with nary a word to report after delivering the final shipment. The cargo had been delivered and lifted ashore at Polis Bay, the main harbor on Ithaca. Adrastos and the other servants had taken the final crate to the palace. This good news was accompanied by bad, which is often the case. Supplies at the camp were near an end, and the men were beginning to lose their tempers at the frustration of waiting. There is nothing that tries the soul of man more than waiting for a battle to begin or a voyage to commence; and both were the cause of this disorder.

At the same time, the horses had to be frequently moved for lack of forage, each time farther distant from the village. This was not of such concern to Telemachus, because of the following: one of the servants, a Thracian, Perses, by name, had gotten himself into trouble. This stout, quiet man had been with Telemachus' family for some time, coming from the cold climes, speaking a tortured Greek. He made wonderful wood carvings for Amphion and Autolycus when they were young. One late night in Dyme, he met some sailors – all of them drunk, as sailors shore-bound often are. They had treated him without respect, mocking his accent. Drunk himself, he had been obliged to defend his honor and himself. Unfortunately, the short bronze cutlass of the sailor who challenged him had been no match for Perses' long iron sword, and Perses had wounded the man fatally.

"I want only peace in our village," the archon, a very fat and very old man, told Telemachus. "This large herd of horses and these armed strangers bother us. What possibly can be their purpose, for never have we seen the like?"

"We are shipping these horses to Thessaly," Telemachus explained.

"And I am Zeus' son," the fat man replied.

"I know nothing of your heritage."

"Yet," the archon continued, "I recall long ago the invasion of the Heraclides at Patrae, just up the coast. Many people lost their lives, and not just the Achaeans. Cresphontes and his troops razed all the villages about and destroyed all their stores. Then when winter snows trapped them, they left about a thousand soldiers trapped without provisions. He and his brothers departed secretly late one night, leaving their soldiers to starve. People have long memories for atrocities."

"I am not sure why you mention this," Telemachus said, surprised. "We are merely trying to transport these horses. That is all."

"By my faith, you take me for the village idiot."

"No, sir. But allow me. Perhaps, we can help the village, since our horses are chomping the surroundings and our men are causing havoc." He held out his hand, which contained a large gold seal. "Athene will provide."

"Yes," the archon agreed, taking the seal. "This man must leave and never return."

Perses was freed. Oxylus was all for flogging Perses and cutting off his ears for his errant ways, but Telemachus won the day, arguing that although this might be acceptable in a military situation, Perses was still a family servant under his purview, and flogging was not one of the features of his employ.

After many more days, a small twenty-man long ship arrived under the Aegean blue and gold royal colors of the Heraclides. Telemachus stormed aboard and demanded the flag be lowered. Word of the Heraclides' arrival would soon enough find an outlet and would add fuel to a fire of curiosity. Upon boarding, Telemachus discovered that no Heraclides were in attendance. The captain had been hired in the port of Naupactus to transport some cargo – he knew not what – back from Dyme; only a day's sail over and back. When informed the cargo was live horses, the captain was not pleased.

"I cannot take horses," he complained.

Telemachus settled his complaints with gold as well.

"I am going with them," Telemachus told Oxylus.

"One of us must go to Naupactus, but I think it better me," Oxylus replied. "Deiphontes can join me. You need to remain with the herd. We need to see if something is truly happening on the other side. I have my fears."

"The captain has reluctantly agreed to carry only a few horses. We need large cargo ships."

"Yes, I will see to it."

"You know, Oxylus," Telemachus regarded his friend, "I cannot return to Elis."

"I know that. I will be back in a few days' time. You have to trust someone, some time."

"I do not trust these Heraclides."

"Nor I," Oxylus admitted, "but you trust me?"

"Yes, I do."

When the child of morning, Dawn, appeared the next day, Oxylus departed with twenty-five horses for the port of Naupactus.

That was all the captain allowed on board. The horses were closely packed and calm. The sun fell brightly on choppy seas, and this was aided by a brisk breeze from the direction of Zephyrus, allowing them to sail downwind directly up the gulf. Telemachus sent Perses and one other servant with the horses, to remain with them at the Heraclides palace in the state of Locris, a ride of about one and fifty stadia from the port.

At midday, Telemachus returned to camp. He found the horses without forage, and they were forced to relocate once again to a new pasture in the foothills in the direction of Notus. Once the horses were settled, Telemachus, Amphion, and Autolycus rode into the village. They were no longer an oddity to the villagers, who treated them as they would the many sailors who spent a few days in their village, friendly enough, but as transients. After bargaining for fish and fresh vegetables from the last few vendors in the marketplace, they settled into a dreary wine shop and drank the local barley beer.

"We are as close to Ithaca as we have been since your birth," Telemachus told his sons.

"What does Ithaca hold for us?" Autolycus asked.

"It is our home, the land of your grandfather and his father."

"But it is a quiet place without great activity," Autolycus said. "Even less than Elis."

"Perhaps you have to be older to appreciate its value. To value Ithaca, you must get to know it, then leave it. Only when you return will you truly appreciate it. I remember evenings that seemed to last forever, warm and balmy. The seas are transparent, as blue as the sky. And the people are friendly and honest and hard-working."

"The people will not rejoice to see you return," Amphion said.

"Perhaps. The suitors of Penelope went to Hades long ago, but families never forget a murder, for such is how they saw the deaths of their relatives. But Time works quietly to lift sorrow and open hearts to acceptance, as sad as it may be."

"We will need to return by force of arms," Autolycus said.

"No. Not by force, but forcefully," Telemachus responded. "Ithaca is our home. The tears of Troy watered the terraces of Ithaca, just as they did the Peloponnese and all of Hellas. When our leaders take us down a path that leads to disaster, we have only ourselves to blame."

Oxylus returned to Dyme five days later on a much larger merchant vessel. He had no good news to report.

"Very little has been accomplished," he said. "The Heraclide family has yet to arrive in Locris, and the park and house are deserted. I am not hopeful. The captain of the ship that took us to Naupactus was hired, not by the family, but by an agent, who lives in Locris and has much to gain by the mobilization. He allowed us access to the house and to the park for our horses. After consideration, all we can do is transport the remainder of the horses to Naupactus, move them to Locris, and then wait to see if the family is serious. We cannot coerce them."

"You had no word from the Heraclides?" Telemachus asked.

"Deiphontes left for Attica," Oxylus said. "He will return rapidly."

"And if they choose to drag their feet?"

"Then we must postpone our activities. I did some inquiring about hiring experienced troops." He explained that the countries of Aetolia, Locris, Phocis, and Boeotia were being overrun with migrants. Great numbers of families from the direction of Boreas were pouring down toward Notus escaping the constant warfare: Thessalians, Macedonians, Illyrians, Thracians, Mysians, Lydians, and peoples from Asia Minor. In the cold Borean mountains Greek-speaking peoples were struggling with the drought and poor prospects for cultivation. They sought warmer climes. Many experienced fighters would be willing to join the Heraclides in return for settlement privileges. The only remaining unsettled cultivatable land in Hellas was in the Peloponnese. Many of these men had fought among the barbarians and were experienced horse riders and peltasts*. Many knew the short javelin and were great archers. The Peloponnese offered them hope for finding land for their families. With the assistance of the kingdoms of the Peloponnese, thousands of people could be resettled without forcing out the current occupants. Since these peoples were trapped on the mainland until the war resolved itself, the Heraclides offered them a way out of their predicament.

---

* An infantry soldier with a light shield for hand-to-hand combat; a skirmisher.

"The fighters are ready to go," Oxylus said. "Now, all depends on the Heraclides."

"Then I suppose we have no alternative," Telemachus replied, "but to move the horses on our own to Locris. Cresphontes is up to something, and Temenus may not be able to handle his brother."

Before the completion of the moon, they were able to transport a good percentage of the horses. When the winds cooperated, they loaded the horses in a single day, walking them up the gangplank from the shore and arranging them tightly in the center of the ship on the rowing deck. However, rain and wind were variable at this time of the year, and when the fog lay heavy in the gulf, there was no wind. This made slow going for the ship with such a heavy load. Soon the days warmed. The rains lessened or fell only during the nighttime, and the last of the herd mounted the gangplank.

The final load of horses coming on board included Sterope, Rhaebus, Boreas, and Arion. Telemachus and Oxylus joined the captain on the top deck. Amphion and Autolycus sat together in the stern along with a few remaining servants and saw to the horses. The day was clear with a soft wind; the gulf was calm, and the damask sea sparkled in the morning light. They set off late in the morning, with a day of sailing before them. With the initial voyages, the rowers had been bothered by the horses: the sounds of their neighing, nickering, and stamping of hooves; their size and bulk; and their smells and offal. Now, though, the sailors were used to their live cargo. They pounded the waves with their long ash oars in time to the drum of the *keulestes*, moving the low-lying ship out slowly into the channel to capture the helpful wind. As the light wind took hold of the large sail, the rowers eased on their task.

On this morning, the channel was clear of vessels. They looked back at the village of Dyme and noted the old archon and several of his friends watching the ship jibe, as the Zephyrian wind took hold.

"He knew all about us," Telemachus commented.

"We must be mindful of that," Oxylus agreed.

"What will be our sailing time?" Telemachus asked the captain.

"It should be about a half day," the captain replied. He was a short man, heavy set with a braided beard falling to his ample belly and what remained of the hair on his head tied by a leather thong. His name was Nisos, and he rolled his long beard constantly with his fingers. He had grown accustomed to these men and their horses. "With a good breeze, we can make the journey in somewhat less time. I can make this crossing in my sleep. But today, we are heavy laden, and the wind is meager."

They relaxed into the journey. The voyage slowed the progress of Time. The winds and currents determined their progress rather than the strength of a courser's legs or one's own clout. They made their way slowly along the coast of the Peloponnese, passing the town of Patrae. Patrae had been rebuilt since it was razed in the invasion of the second crop of Heraclides, but it looked no more prosperous than Dyme.

As they approached the narrows in the gulf, between Aetolia and Achaea, they noted a ship moving off the shore of Cape Drepanum, the point of land on the Peloponnese closest to the mainland. The captain ignored the ship, which was behind them, and began guiding his own vessel to the side of the channel facing Boreas, preparing to come ashore at Naupactus. But the ship behind them was approaching rapidly, and soon they all turned to watch its progress. It was a large ship with an enormous white sail billowed in the breeze and some thirty rowers plowing the sea. It caught them as though they were becalmed. As it came alongside, Telemachus looked and what he saw came as a shock. It was a warship with the vermilion colors of Corinth flying on the mast and soldiers occupying the deck in full armour with weapons visible.

As the warship came close enough to smell, riding high in the water, the captain of the small merchant vessel signaled for the other to lay off to starboard, for the warship was preventing the smaller vessel from making its turn toward Naupactus. The warship did not respond. Instead, it rode alongside the smaller vessel, with the oars of the two ships touching. The warship was longer and larger, and rode higher in the water than the loaded cargo vessel, and its high bronze-wrapped prow menaced the other, smaller vessel. With more rowers and a shallower draft and higher prow, it was faster and quicker in its turns and comings about. There was a large red eye painted just above the waterline on the bow. They watched as the larger ship ominously reefed its sail to slow its progress.

"Identify yourself and move from our path," Nisos called nervously.

But the captain of the larger ship gave no indication of hearing him. Telemachus watched as the man gave orders to his crew and seemed to be waiting for the sail to be completely furled.

The captain of the warship then shouted: "Take your oars from the water."

"I cannot," the merchant captain yelled, "We are heavy laden and need calmer waters to slow our progress."

"Take your oars from the water or I will sink you."

Nisos shook his head with agony and despair. He looked desperately at Oxylus and Telemachus. On the stern deck, Autolycus and Amphion stood at attention.

"Halt rowing," Nisos ordered, which was repeated below deck, and the oars came out of the water. "Raise the sail," he shouted. Three sailors began raising the sail. The horses groaned and snorted at the change in the pitch of the ship, as it began sloppily rising and falling rather than rolling.

Furiously twisting his beard, Nisos turned to Telemachus and Oxylus and whimpered: "This ship is all I have. It is my only livelihood, and my wife and children depend on me. Our parents are dead, and we must work for our living. You have recompensed me for these trips, but what good will this do if I lose my ship or if I am to enter the house of Hades?"

"Quiet," Oxylus said. He turned to the warship and shouted, "Who are you, and by what right do you stop us?"

"Identify yourselves," the captain of the warship replied.

"We are a private vessel," Nisos replied. "Our cargo is horses. We are headed to Naupactus."

"We believe you are carrying contraband. Come alongside, so we may board you to ensure you are a commercial vessel."

"By what authority do you demand this?" Oxylus shouted again.

"By the authority of Tisamenus, King of Corinth and Mycenae, and the gods themselves."

"We need time," Telemachus whispered to Oxylus. "Let them come aboard."

"That might be dangerous," Oxylus warned.

"They can easily sink us." Telemachus said. "We have no contraband, nothing of value. Let them come if they so desire."

"No," the captain wailed. "They will confiscate my ship."

"You may come aboard," Oxylus yelled, "but only one man. Any more will taste the salty water."

Ropes were thrown fore and aft, and the two ships were pulled close enough to allow a wooden plank to be set up between the ships, connecting the foredeck of the smaller vessel with the lower deck of the warship. Even then the plank was not level, and crossing was not made easily. One of the soldiers on the warship made his way across rapidly, using the plank only momentarily, holding on to a rope and almost jumping the distance.

"I am Tellis, son of King Tisamenus of Mycenae." He was a tall young man with a sparse growth of beard. Dressed in a bronze cuirass and greaves, with a short sword in the scabbard at his side, he wore a bronze helmet and horsehair plume. His vermilion cloak was pulled back from his arms on both sides.

"I am Nisos, captain and owner of this ship. You are free to observe our cargo."

"I can smell your cargo," Tellis replied. "And who are you?" he asked turning to Oxylus and Telemachus.

"We are horse traders, making our way to Boeotia to sell our horses," Oxylus replied.

"And by name?"

"I am Oxylus, son of Haemon. And this is my partner, a Thracian horse-tamer by the name of Alexander. He is more accustomed to speaking to horses than to men."

"You will follow us to Corinth," Tellis said.

"We cannot make Corinth," Nisos said. "Our cargo prevents this."

"Then rid yourselves of this smelly cargo."

"Please, officer. Accompany us to Naupactus. That would be preferred."

"We will throw you a rope tow," Tellis said, ignoring the captain.

"Why do you want to take us to Corinth?" Telemachus asked.

"He speaks well enough," the officer said. "If your rowers help, we can arrive at the harbor of Corinth early tomorrow. We will have to position some soldiers aboard."

"You can tow us by our anchor cable," Telemachus offered. "We do not have the space for soldiers aboard. And in these seas you cannot trust rope tows."

"He even thinks," Tellis said. "Let me see the anchor cable."

Nisos, like all coastal commuters, had a large anchor cable for foul-weather nights spent among the rocks. Telemachus had noticed the heavy bronze cable when the ship sat offshore.

"Surely, a bronze cable will be secure," Telemachus said.

The officer walked forward and observed the metal cable with links that were fabricated to withstand the full weight of the ship even in heavy seas. It was securely attached to a flat windlass. He leaned over and caught the forward rope from a sailor on the warship and carefully tied it to the cable.

"We will talk again tomorrow morning."

He signaled for the two ships to come together again and quickly crossed over. The warship moved forward under oar, until its stern was opposite the merchant ship's prow. The sailors on the warship pulled the rope followed by the anchor cable onto their deck. They attached the cable to an aft towing cleat and allowed the cable to play out like a hawser between the two ships. The cable became taut as the forward ship took up the slack. The sail descended on the warship and was secured, and the cargo ship gave a shuddering start as the tow took force under the strength of the wind and oars.

"Lower the sail quickly," the captain shouted hurriedly, "and begin rowing. They will tear the deck to pieces." As the smaller ship took to sail and the oars began to pull at the sea, the shuddering halted. As long as the rowers maintained the pace, the aft ship was able to keep up. The beat of the *keulestes* slowed as the warship relied mainly on sail, for the afternoon winds had strengthened. The horses quieted when the ship took on a constant motion. But the seas washed across the lower deck of the merchant vessel when they encountered larger swells.

"Why did you offer the anchor cable?" Oxylus said, once they were underway.

"Tonight there is no moon," Telemachus replied, "and the dusk will be complete. We can cut the cable and lose them in the darkness."

"How would you ever cut through such a bronze cable?" Oxylus demanded.

"We will test your new iron tools."

"Ach," he said, shaking his head, "that will be a good test, my friend."

They followed the warship for some time as Helios sank behind them, and misty darkness enveloped the earth. The devastated captain, Nisos, could barely contain his anguish, for he knew his ship would be confiscated and his life lost in Corinth, a country he disliked intensely and never visited.

"The Corinthians smell of anchovies and whores," Nisos spat.

"Now," Telemachus told Nisos, "it is crucial that we keep as little pressure as possible on the anchor cable. We have to keep up with the warship, or this will not work. They must not feel the drag of our ship."

Oxylus and Telemachus went below to investigate the tools that were packed away. Telemachus remembered an iron rip saw intended for felling trees. They pulled it from the unpretentious wooden case that followed Oxylus everywhere he went. They brought the hefty saw up to the deck. Telemachus chose a bronze link close to the windlass. They began running the saw blade over it. Oxylus grabbed the wooded handle at the opposite end of the saw to aid Telemachus. The noise of the waves and oars covered the sound of the cutting. At times, they could catch a glimpse of the flickering of some oil lamps on the mast of the leading ship, but they had set no such lamps.

Sure enough, the iron blade slowly and methodically cut through the bronze. Progress was remarkable, though not immediate. Trading off, between the men, they soon cut through one half of a chain link.

"When the cable is cut," Telemachus told the captain, "very slowly reduce our speed. If we can move off course, they will never find us in this darkness."

When the second half of the link was breached, the anchor cable fell on the deck, secured by rope. "Half-speed," the captain whispered to a sailor, who ran to relay his command to the rowing deck. "Leave the sail fully extended. Prepare to turn to port." Oxylus untied the rope and allowed the anchor cable to play out across the deck and fall into the sea.

The merchant ship slowed, and the flickering lights disappeared almost immediately as the warship pulled ahead. They did not breathe as the smaller ship fell back. They waited.

"Full to port," the captain ordered the deck crew, who relayed it to the lower deck. The port oars rose out of the water, while the rudder oars and starboard oars turned the vessel, and the sail luffed. Slowly, the ship came about into the breeze, which had died down to a large extent. Nisos ordered the sail furled. The oars on both sides of the ship began to beat in unison. "Full speed," the captain shouted. "Silence the *keulestes*." And the small ship moved off, this time hugging the coastline of Locris.

It took some time to arrive at the harbor of Naupactus. They tied up along the shore of the harbor and rapidly offloaded the horses. Nisos was not happy. When Telemachus recompensed him, he was slightly mollified, since this unexpected windfall would allow him to maintain a low profile for some time, perhaps at one of the offshore islands. Telemachus suggested Ithaca, since it was off the beaten path and offered an excellent anchorage. Nisos set off immediately.

As they drove their horses out of Naupactus toward the Heraclides' palace in Locris, the first golden glimmers of Eos' began warming the heavens and earth alike.

There was no warmth in the palace of King Tisamenus of Corinth and Mycenae when the following morning his son Tellis reported the adventure. Tisamenus lashed out at the stupidity of his son. He was attended by men who lacked all imagination. Now he feared this included his son. He had his spies, though, and he thought he knew exactly what was happening. The Heraclides were on the move. Cresphontes had held meetings with the King of Athens and his archons. Tisamenus also knew that Telemachus and Oxylus were counseling the Heraclides and had left Elis with a herd of horses. He had no trouble connecting these events.

"I am surrounded by lovely people," King Tisamenus said, "including those of my own family, but not one of them is competent. What profits a man if he rules the entire world, but has a useless family?"

XXVII

I think I can safely say that Athens at the time of our history resembled the Athens of today only in outlook. Even in that day Athens was multihued, attracting peoples from throughout the Known World and offering asylum to people seeking justice. The great architectural feats were yet to come. Athens was spread out and well fortified, with a huge citadel on the summit of the Acropolis, long before the great temple to Athene Parthenos, the virgin, was constructed. The central agora* below the citadel served as the hub of many surrounding villages. Ships arrived at the beach at Phalerum. Here, Menestheus marshaled fifty ships for the war in Troy. And here, returning from Crete, Theseus landed his ship under a black sail, forgetting his promise to his father, King Aegeus. The king, seeing a black sail rather than white, jumped from the walls of the citadel to his death, knowing from the color that his son had preceded him in death.

In the great palace, King Thymoetes, son of Oxyntes, grandson of Demophon, and great grandson of Theseus, listened to the leader of the Heraclides, Cresphontes. Standing before the king and his assembled archons, Cresphontes was drumming up support for the coming invasion of the Peloponnese, and he addressed the assembly as a foreign guest in their country, but one born and raised there, well known, from a family that could take its place at the head of any procession of worthies. His reception was warm and appreciative, but not overwhelmingly compliant to his ideas. Attica had never smiled on the states of the Peloponnese. The Athenians called the Peloponnesians, "acorn eaters," and they had recently been at loggerheads over trade. They had marched against each other on numerous occasions over the years.

---

* Open marketplace and town meeting area.

Cresphontes had spoken to the assembly before several times, and each time they had rebuffed him. Under current conditions, with a bankrupt treasury, trade at low ebb, poor crops, the town full of new migrants, and a weakling king, their support was doubtful. This time, Cresphontes prepared his arguments in such a way he felt surely would result in Athenian aid to the cause of the Heraclides.

Cresphontes spoke: "Today, we must decide whether the risks of action outweigh the risks of inaction: whether the tide of events in the Peloponnese is of such magnitude as to warrant your concern here in Athens and the mobilization of your resources or whether your ignorance and woolgathering can continue indefinitely. We have entered upon a world where the forces of destruction are dramatically different from those of our fathers. An unprecedented capacity for devastation exists today. Barbarians from without possess weapons that could bring low the greatest heroes of times past. Let there be no doubt about it. War is coming. And war should never be an easy decision. It is the last thing any rational man wants. But there are times when it becomes clear that we must choose a path of righteousness. A time when each of us has a responsibility to do all within his power to ensure that when history is written, we will not be found to have been out of the room, while others suffered.

"Our intelligence tells us that the time is right. Delay and inaction will only allow King Tisamenus of Mycenae to gather together these new weapons. When a bone in the body of a man is broken, we must set it immediately or it will undo us. Therefore, I say to you strike we must and soon.

"The danger is clear; the threat imminent. Tisamenus seeks to unite the Peloponnese and is gathering his forces. He has demonstrated his intent within his own empire against his own people, who suffer with only mallow and asphodel* at the dining table. When he grows tired of ruling his own estates, he will come across the isthmus like a ravenous lion in search of prey. If we do not stop him now, we will suffer the mortal consequences. There is no greater plague on this earth than an ungirt neighbor. Well I knew Orestes. And this man, Tisamenus, the son of Orestes, is like his father and grandfather before him. He considers only his own

---

* Foods eaten by the poorest people; weeds.

advancement. He will not be stopped until we bury his head far from his body and send all his sons and daughters into the realm of darkness never to walk the earth again. His father, Orestes, murdered his own mother. We cannot sleep until Tisamenus, the son, is stopped for good, or there will be no help for evil. Theirs is an evil family.

"We see marauding sea peoples and raiders seeking to attack our coasts and sack our towns. We see migrations of peoples from the directions of Boreas and Apeliotes coming into Attica, bringing with them their foreign customs and languages to despoil our own. We see plagues, drought, and famine affecting our outlying cities and our cultivators. Now we must pay the heavy toll to defend our borders. Peace in the Peloponnese will allow us to live in harmony with our neighbors.

"To preserve ourselves and our way of life, we must stop Tisamenus, for his greed knows no bounds nor respect for his neighbors. Take full measure of the man or you will rue the day he marches into the great agora of Athens, while you peep and pitter in your courts. Do not suffer pain as well as shame. Join us now. Do not put off, for the sluggard does not fill his barn."

So spoke Cresphontes before the king and his assembly. The assembly's response was as day-old milk. Attica's leaders were not prepared to assist the Heraclides in any invasion of the Peloponnese.

Long ago, Heracles went down to Hades to bring back to earth Cerberus, the monstrous hound that guarded the gates of Hades. While there, he found Theseus chained to the Chair of Forgetfulness with his friend, Pirithous. Theseus and Pirithous were comrades much in the way that Achilles and Patroclus or Orestes and Pylades were comrades. They fought together, drank together, and chased women together. But in one case, they seemed to have gone too far, for they, the heady sons of gods, listened with relish to the tales of a beautiful young girl, Helen, the daughter of King Tyndareus. This was long before the events leading up to the Trojan War, and Paris was still an innocent boy tending sheep in the mountains of Ida. Helen was barely ten years old at the time. Theseus and Pirithous abducted her from her home in Lacedaemon by force. Further, Theseus and Pirithous were not young men at the time; Theseus was king of Athens, and both were married with children no younger than Helen. But sometimes, the reasons for the actions of men are as mysterious as those motivating the gods – but usually inspired by the male organ.

The two comrades cast lots on who would marry Helen, for even as a ten-year old she wrung the hearts of men. Theseus won, although here many different versions of the legend emerge and many different retellings. Some say that Theseus fathered a child by Helen, Iphigenia by name, who was then given to Helen's older sister, Clytemnestra, to be raised. Of course, Iphigenia was sacrificed at Aulis by Agamemnon. It is perhaps somewhat easier for a man to sacrifice another man's daughter than his own. Others say that Theseus respected the child Helen and left her to be raised by his mother, Aethra, in the village of Aphidna. One would have to question this; if he put such energy into taking the child, why would he place her with his mother?

Whatever the cause, Zeus was outraged at the abduction of his daughter Helen, and he placed false thoughts in the minds of Theseus and Pirithous, making them believe that they could steal Persephone from Hades. While they were away on this false and mad inspiration, the Dioscuri, the brothers of Helen, rescued her, took his mother, Aethra, as a slave, and placed Menestheus, son of Peteos, on the throne of Athens. This entire story is full of holes, since it is treated in so many different ways. Of course, Homer mentions that Helen was in Troy with her slave, Aethra, and who else could this Aethra be than the mother of Theseus?

Once in Hades, though, Theseus and Pirithous failed miserably, ending up in the Chair of Forgetfulness. If Heracles had not come along in one of his labors demanded by Eurystheus, the two men would have been seated in Hades to this day. But when Heracles saw Theseus and Pirithous seated with their minds empty, freed from all memories, he unchained them and brought them back to earth, along with Cerberus, the frightful hound of Hades. Although Heracles returned Cerberus to Hades, as promised, it was some time before Theseus and Pirithous returned to Hades, although return they did.

Theseus' son, Demophon, became King of Athens. He gave the children of Heracles asylum and aided them in their war with Eurystheus. After Cresphontes' address, Thymoetes, Demophon's grandson, stopped far short of giving Cresphontes material support. Though, perhaps because of this history recounted above, he offered

Cresphontes free passage over Attica soil for the movement of troops and materiel, the right to recruit soldiers within Attica, and recompense should the invasion be successful and the two countries begin cooperation. King Thymoetes failed to support the Heraclides and, at the same time, failed to condemn Cresphontes' ideas. He chose a middling path. In so doing, King Thymoetes sealed his own fate, for he would be the last king of Athens in the line of Theseus. Sometimes the easiest and safest decisions, my dear Alcathöe, can have momentous consequences.

Cresphontes and Temenus returned to their estate in Marathon, feeling greatly disappointed in the Atticans. They were on their own against Tisamenus. But they could see the carrot held out in front of them. As Cresphontes expressed it:

"Heracles was tested furiously by the gods. He succeeded time and again, alone and at his own instigation. So too will we prevail in what is right. And then all will seek our patronage."

Meanwhile at the Heraclides' estates in Locris, Telemachus and Oxylus waited impatiently for the arrival of the family. A host of tasks had to be accomplished before any reasonable force could be marshaled against the Peloponnese. For the time being, the counselors had full reign of the house, and the horses were secure in the enormous enclosed park.

Late at night, the men sat alone in the meeting room, having taken their evening meal. They rested tranquilly, watching the glowing coals of the fire diminish.

"Maybe we should return to Pylos," Amphion said. "I am worried that Mother may need our help."

"What use are we in Pylos?" Autolycus said roughly. "Grandfather says these things, but nothing comes of them."

"Nestor would welcome our aid."

"What do you suggest, brother?" Autolycus replied. "Do we attack our uncles? Do we fight the Spartans? You always have these notions of doing what is right, but, in reality, we can do nothing. We must continue training the horses for combat. Many have never been ridden."

"Then I will go alone," Amphion said. "Our presence alone could be beneficial. Mother feels abandoned."

"How do you know this, Amphion?" Telemachus asked.

"I know," he replied.

"You dream," Autolycus added meanly.

"At least I care," Amphion said angrily.

"We all care," Telemachus responded quickly. "What do you think?"

"I think we are off on some rabbit hunt with these Heraclides," Amphion said. "They promise us everything and deliver nothing. And what means more to our family than Mother and Grandfather? What importance is Ithaca? Why would I risk a hair on my head for this family of Heraclides?"

"Brother, what you say is true. But consider. We have to take this step by step. We are not jumping from the ramparts. We are not discarding our family. We need to think and act with intelligence and foresight. Can you see that?"

"Yes, of course. But if we all went to Pylos…"

"And fought Tisamenus," Autolycus interrupted, "or fought Cresphontes ourselves. What kind of sense does that make? How would that protect Mother or Grandfather?"

"Enough," Telemachus spoke emphatically. "Polycasté may need our help in the future, and she shall have it. But not at this time. We are not deserting her or your grandfather. Listen, you two, we are in this together. We are deserting no one."

"They will come." Oxylus said simply, taking a long draft of his wine. "This family of Heraclides is determined to return to the Peloponnese and will do anything to accomplish it. They will not be hurried by us or by the gods."

"Yes, and will they attack Messenia and Pylos?" Amphion shouted. "And will we aid them in this wickedness? Have you considered this? Have you?"

"Yes," Telemachus replied. "I have."

XXVIII

Meanwhile, Tisamenus, King of Mycenae, called a meeting of his archons in Corinth to discuss the threat of the Heraclides. He had returned from Arcadia to his fortified palace in Corinth to collect his defenses. Word had reached him of Cresphontes' speech before King Thymoetes and the assembly in Athens. Tisamenus ruled over more than half of the Peloponnese, only lacking the coastal regions toward Zephyrus. Tribute came from far and wide. He was king of the greatest cities of the Peloponnese. His archons and generals came from all over the near-island: Corinth, Sicyon, Mycenae, Epidaurus, Argos, Tiryns, Tegea, Lacedaemon, and lesser cities in Laconia and Arcadia. And he was no one's fool.

Early one fair morning after the solstice, the archons and generals gathered nervously in the palace to suffer Tisamenus, for they knew that in any meeting with this man, their lives hung in the balance. Tisamenus stood before them bleakly, dressed as he always was in white linen robe and cloak that offered no contrast to his long gray hair and beard and waxen complexion.

The Kings Doridas and Hyanthidas, sons of Propodas, held the floor. They jointly ruled over Corinth, owing their throne to Tisamenus. They were direct descendants of Sisyphus, the first king of Corinth, who is best known for his punishment in the underworld. Sisyphus confessed to the river god Asopus, father of Aegina, that Zeus had abducted his daughter. For this, Zeus punished him forever, forcing him to roll a massive stone up a hill, only to have it roll back to the bottom, never surmounting the summit. Of Sisyphus' statesmanship of Corinth, nothing is known.

King Doridas spoke hurriedly with passion: "This is not to say that we should not take their threat seriously, for it is real and looming. But we are well fortified, and the isthmus is impossible to cross without large numbers and great loss of life. Our harbor at Lechaeum is well protected, and our navy is prepared. We must place the first wall of resistance at the boundary between Megara and Corinth. Here, Echemus killed Hyllus, son of Heracles, in hand-to-hand combat in the first invasion. We can fall back if necessary to Cenchreae..."

"Fall back?" Tisamenus asked. "What are you talking about? You are already preparing retreat?"

"No, Sire. I misspoke. What I meant was that the isthmus is protected by Poseidon, while Apollo rules the heights..."

"And now you propose the gods in our defense?"

"Sire, that is a saying here in Corinth," Doridas replied weakly. The sweat poured from his forehead. "To approach Corinth from the Lechaeum would be impossible without overcoming our navy. The fortifications of the city make it impossible to attack directly. We are not Trojans, easily deceived. We are protected by the heights of the Acrocorinthus, and the road from Sicyon will be protected by Lacestades at the head of the Sicyonians."

"And what of Lacestades?" Tisamenus demanded. "He is descended from the Heraclides, is he not?"

King Hyanthidas, the brother of Doridas, seeing his brother's distress, addressed Tisamenus. "Lacestades is the fourth generation to rule Sicyon. He was born there, and his family resides there. He is well known to all of us."

"And so was Palamedes among the Achaeans," Tisamenus interrupted. "And he was stoned to death for his treasonous behavior. I give not a fig for his roots. Do you not see the importance of Sicyon to our defenses? Am I surrounded by numbskulls?"

"Indeed, you can depend on Sicyon, Sire," Hyanthidas said in reply. "Doridas, my brother, and I will visit with Lacestades and report back. Could someone open a shutter? It is very hot in here. Meanwhile, we will need your help in securing the isthmus."

"My help? Help is what you are here for. Do not come crawling to me like a dog seeking a ragbone or some female afraid of the dark. Are you not well taken care of? Do you not live in a fine palace and have mistresses to your heart's content? Is your belly not full of meat?" He paused long enough for his thoughts to sink it. His greatest delight was to watch men squirm like worms. "Lacestades is no friend of the Pelopides, nor was he friend of the sons of Atreus, my grandfather and great uncle," Tisamenus said, "and, if this were not true, then he should have put in an appearance today. For, as you say, he knows us well. Now, you will ensure his allegiance. Is that understood?

"We are your servants in defending your rule of the Peloponnese," Hyanthidas replied. "I meant only that we must plan our defense of Corinth, for our city will not stand alone."

Tisamenus looked at the man as if to throttle him, and then turned to his generals, Pamphylus and Dymas. "You will see to it that these kings of Corinth fulfill their obligations or else." Pamphylus and his brother, Dymas, were the two generals responsible for Tisamenus' troops in Argolis, and by extension and scope, accountable for the defense of the Peloponnese.

Pamphylus spoke: "I am married to the daughter of Deiphontes and Hyrnetho. I know this family of Heraclides well. They are headstrong. Cresphontes believes that the legacy of his forebear gives him the gods' wisdom and everlasting praise. Time and again, he has failed by underestimating the forces against him, and the gods have turned against the family for its pride. They have been punished by plague, by antagonistic climes, by heavy seas, and by failure in combat. They always bite off more than they can swallow."

General Dymas added: "Lacestades is with us, or he will no longer rule Sicyon. A traitor is soon discovered by his own vanity and ambition. My brother and I will join Doridas and Hyanthidas, who rule in Corinth at your behest and who owe you their livelihood and position."

A well-dressed man in the rear of the room stood. "Beware your friends do not drown you with unspoken truths."

"And who are you?" Tisamenus asked sharply.

"I am your regent in Arcadia, new to this group."

"Yes, with excellent advice," said Tisamenus. "Now, allow me to explain the situation to all of you, sirs. The Peloponnese is a fortress with a single entrance. If the entrance is breached, we have lost our greatest defense. The Heraclides claim title to the Peloponnese because a looter razed our cities and took our people into slavery. They have no more right to this land than the barbarians who seek asylum here." He took a long leather thong and folded it in half and then in half again. He then tied each end and held it before the assembly.

"We are only as strong as each of us. If we cleave together, we are stronger yet." He pulled on the thong to indicate its strength. "If we fight individually, we are weak and will be defeated. And when I say defeated, I mean we will be sent to the depths of darkness never to return." He unknotted the leather thong and pulled it into a single strand. Tisamenus easily broke the single strand into short pieces, which he then threw at the men before him. "At this point, we are single strands of leather, hoping for the best. Do not let this happen, or I will see to it personally that each of you, and your wives and children, will hang from the columns in the central agora of Corinth."

Later in the meeting, General Pamphylus described the state of the defenses of the Peloponnese: "We have troops numbering more than one hundred thousand throughout the Peloponnese. Of these, a certain number will be required to defend their individual cities and towns. Others still require training and education. Generations have grown up since the Trojan War. They have not been called to arms and have little experience in warfare, and their children even less. They will need new armaments and battle dress, for much of what they have is outdated and useless."

"What am I," Tisamenus roared, "a sutler from whom you order supplies?"

"No, no, Sire," Pamphylus said quickly. "What I was getting to was that we can marshal close to fifty thousand battle-ready troops today. I can have ten thousand men at the isthmus tomorrow or at least next week."

"Then, see to it," Tisamenus said in a slightly friendlier tone.

"We have five thousand men stationed in Arcadia. They can be here in two weeks," Pamphylus continued. "Argos and Lacedaemon will offer us as many as twenty thousand soldiers."

"We must be prepared," Tisamenus replied, feeling somewhat better, "for this is a real threat. Cresphontes and his family have long sought to invade the Peloponnese, and they have the necessary resources to do so. We cannot sit back and think we are ready to repel this determined family without taking extraordinary measures. We know they are not alone. Attica is behind this as usual. And they have Oxylus, a military man from Aetolia, and Telemachus, son of Odysseus and son-in-law to Nestor, aiding them. This crop of Heraclides will not be as innocent and naïve as the last two crops.

They will come prepared for victory, and I fail to see that we have a similar resolve.

"Go back to your regions and draw up your plans. Recruit every able-bodied man and put him under arms. Every farmer, every trader, every slave, every son and his father must take up arms or we will all bite the dust together. You will report back to me in two months. At that time, if you are still unprepared, then I will take action. Either you are primed to keep your seats or you will be unseated. Our honor is at stake and the honor of a great family, the sons of Pelops, the House of Atreus. We cannot fail."

And so the kings, generals, and archons returned to their communities and began the process of calling their subjects to order. Planting would not begin for some time, so the men came forward, and each of the regions began preparing its defense, assembling its arms, and training for war. But war was not foremost in the minds of the people of the Peloponnese. As the drought continued even in lands in the face of Zephyrus, there were fewer crops to set aside and more mouths to feed. Sickness was about, and children suffered.

Apollo sat alone before his father in the glorious meeting hall of the gods. He was in a furious passion against the other immortals.

"I disciplined the second crop of Heraclides for their irreverence. When Hippotes killed my priest, Carnus of Acarnania, for merely telling the truth, I struck down their leader, Aristodemus, brother to Cresphontes and Temenus, and I will do it again. Athene unites the Heraclides, while the forces of Tisamenus are divided and muddled."

"Perhaps, this is of Tisamenus' own making?" the lord of the gods replied.

"Surely, you see the outcome?"

"Yes, I do," Zeus said. "But as long as these mortals ignore their gods, they will suffer the consequences. Is this struggle based on anything other than pride and avarice? Mortals are their own worst enemies. You would think they would learn, but they do not.

The Heraclides are intent only on mastering the Peloponnese. Tisamenus' only interest is in feathering his nest. I see no difference."

"The Heraclides have no claim on the region," Apollo interjected. "For the descendants of Pelops have ruled for many generations."

"Our son," said Zeus, sire of gods, "these mortals appear like leaves on a tree in the rapid growing season, and then in autumn they dry and fall to earth. They act as though they are immortal. This godly feeling may be important for them, but they fail to recognize that all men share this feeling. They treat each other with contumely and then go to the house of Hades. We are always starting over again with them."

But Apollo would not listen. "As a ruler of men, Tisamenus is no prize. But Cresphontes is worse and of evil intent. Cresphontes would bring much misery to the people of the Peloponnese."

"Since when are you so concerned with the lives of mortals? We have seen you counsel the heroes, Apollo, our son, and not with concern for the outcome. Now we have a battle at hand between two strong families. There can be no greater acrimony than between families. We cannot continue to look upon these men as our children, applauding and rooting for them as we would our own offspring. They are grown now and must accept responsibility. They must discover what is best for them."

"As long as Athene shores up the Heraclides, then I will take action to assist the Pelopides."

"Is this the justice that you represent? Is this measure and rationality? No, this is some personal ill will you bear against your sister."

"I believe in fairness."

"Fairness? Ah, then, our son, let them fear Dionysus and love Apollo. For Dionysus would feed them wine and passion, while Apollo gives them clarity of mind and order."

Apollo halted. He reconsidered for a moment, for his father's words had touched him. The voices of the other gods had distracted him, but now the voice within his own head was clearer. He thanked his father and left the palace to attend to his own thoughts, and with gods thoughts and deeds are not far separated.

XXIX

In Locris, the star Arcturus rose from Oceanus, the Holy Stream, and became visible at dusk. Then, the family of the Heraclides arrived with great fanfare at their palace in Locris like the garrulous Philomela, daughter of Pandion, making her appearance in a swarm of swallows. They came by ship to Naupactus and reached their destination on elegant horses, golden chariots, and stylish wagons. Everywhere, flags of the golden baby Heracles on a field of Aegean blue flapped in the wind. Cresphontes and Temenus led the family on magnificent war chargers in the finest of armour. Behind them rode Hippotes, who, because he had killed a priest of Apollo, had been blamed for the defeat of the second crop. He had returned from banishment and was now dressed in full battle regalia.

Following Hippotes, and in no less finery, was the third crop: his son, black-eyed Aletes, Procles and Eurysthenes, the twin sons of Aristodemus, in golden chariots, Deiphontes and his wife, Hyrnetho, both on horseback, and the many sons of Temenus, including Phalces and Cisus, all in similar show and ceremonial dress. Wives and families followed in wooden wagons draped in gold and blue, with flags flying. Behind them came hundreds of armed troops, and behind the troops came the servants, slaves, and countless animals for slaughter and sacrifice. The Heraclides had moved out of their palace in Attica and were now committed to going home to the Peloponnese. Telemachus, Oxylus, and the twins watched with amazement mixed with bemusement at the show of greatness. Telemachus could only shake his head in disgust at the display.

That evening Cresphontes ordered a great celebration and sacrifice to the gods. For in the interim and after many warnings by the oracles, the family now counted respect for the gods among their daily rituals. They tallied their blessings like children anticipating gifts with the odors of sizzling fats and meats over the open fiery pit. Tonight was no exception. The dark smoke reached high into the sky as the men ate their fill, surrounded by women and children. The servants hurried through the large group with plates of fresh-baked breads and early spring vegetables. Of course, the wine flowed from giant ewers into the golden goblets raised many times in libation and thanks.

"As this is our first night in Locris," Cresphontes announced, "I offer thanks to Apollo and all the gods who support our efforts, for they know the righteousness of our quest. The King of Attica, Thymoetes, has given us his approbation. Attica is allied with us in our return to the Peloponnese. What could be a stronger alliance? Aetolia is behind us as well and Elis and the offshore islands. All of Hellas is standing at our sides as they did once before to help us rout the tyrants and drain the swamps. For we believe in ourselves and the honor of the House of Perseus. We stand on the eve of a new era of change and growth. For we believe in the promise of the Peloponnese, a land blessed by the lord of gods, Zeus, and a country that exists by the grace of the gods and that we are proud to call our home. For of all things, a man needs a homeland for his comfort and security.

"Now we are engaged in a great battle, but we are assured of victory. I commit to you tonight that our children will grow up in their own homeland. The forces that would prevent us from returning to our hearths will be defeated. The gods are with us."

Telemachus leaned over to Temenus. "He seems converted."

"Yes," Temenus agreed, missing the irony, having listened to his brother too often. "We delayed our return on account of Attica. Although we did not achieve all our objectives at the meetings with the archons, we did receive their tacit approval. For like all politicians and gamblers, they are masters at preserving their options and withholding their thoughts. They will clasp us to their breasts in victory and shun us in defeat."

"At least Attica protects our backs," Telemachus said.

"Yes," continued Temenus, "they have guaranteed that. But tomorrow, we will begin to make our arrangements. I would like to take you and Oxylus to Naupactus to visit one of the ships that brought us here. I think this will be another factor in our favor. I, myself, was instrumental in its construction."

Later that night, Telemachus and Oxylus sat alone in their small room, for they had been moved to another area of the palace. Cresphontes had ordered a dormitory set up for the third crop, and Amphion and Autolycus had been relegated there.

"We are not prepared," Telemachus said, "nor have we come up with a strategy, yet they display their colors as though they were already victors."

"This is the way of Cresphontes," Oxylus said. "He relies on the outward trappings to convince others of his greatness."

"As you well know, without the element of surprise, we are lost."

"Yes," Oxylus agreed. "The surprise will not be our forces or intent. It will be our strategy and armament. It will also be the makeup of the troops."

"Nevertheless, we need to keep our plans secret for as long as possible," Telemachus said. "I do not intend to communicate it to the Heraclides until the last possible moment. And even then, I will not lay it out before them in its entirety."

"Herding this family will not be easy," Oxylus said.

"It will require all our skills and then the providence of Athene."

The next morning, the rosy fingers of Eos, goddess of dawn, stretched over the horizon, but failed to wake the sleeping household, for the celebration had lasted late into the night. Telemachus and Oxylus woke late and hurried to the stables to prepare their horses. Temenus was already there. The three men mounted and left the palace before the house awoke.

As they rode, Oxylus announced a trip in the direction of Boreas, to visit Aetolia (avoiding his home), Phocis, Boeotia, Attica, the home of brave Achilles in Phthia, and into Thessaly, the land of horses. He foresaw experienced soldiers at all places: horsemen, men skilled with the short javelin and with the bow and arrow, men accustomed to taking down a wild boar or birds in flight. These would not be farm boys, but fighters and hunters tried and true. The occupation of war had gone wanting over the last decades, and men yearned for honor on the field of battle. Theirs would be an army of veterans, professionals, skilled freebooters, ready and willing to fight.

Soon they arrived at the port of Naupactus. This was an important port, where commerce moved in all directions. Here ships arrived from the islands in the direction of Zephyrus, from the coast of Epirus and the Peloponnese, and from far-away Italia and Europa. Goods were transferred across the gulf to the Peloponnese or toward Apeliotes by road to Attica and Argolis. The ships lay in the sand. As they viewed the harbor, they noted one remarkable ship. The extraordinary vessel stood out like a laurel among the vines. It was easily three times the size of the largest ship in the port. On its mast, the blue flag of the Heraclides bearing the golden baby Heracles flapped in the warming breath of Notus.

Oxylus and Telemachus had never seen the like.

"It is the largest and fastest ship in the Known World," Temenus explained proudly, "with seventy oarsmen at two different levels and a broad beam that can accommodate hundreds of troops and their equipment. Only a few of such size have been built, and those lie beneath the seas off the shores of Troy. This one was designed and built by the Phoenician, Xenodamas, who has built many seaworthy ships. Its prow is reinforced by heart of holm-oak and covered in thick bronze that can break ships into pieces with no damage to itself. It is quicker and more maneuverable than any craft plying these waters, with the largest sail ever. Three others are now under construction."

"I hope that this is not well known," Telemachus said. "We do not want Tisamenus to be made aware of these ships."

"They are being constructed at the shipyards at Cirrha, the port of the town of Crisa on the Crisaean Gulf. This is not a well-traveled site, but I agree with you. There is no need to fly the flag and make others aware of our activities."

"And this will only become more important," Telemachus added. "This ship will allow us to move rapidly into the Peloponnese."

"Tomorrow, I leave to begin recruiting," said Oxylus. "We will send heralds to the town centers toward cold Boreas and invite professional fighters to join us. And from that time on, the reports will begin making their way across the isthmus, long before any troops appear. Nothing is a secret for long among the Hellenes, particularly plans for war."

XXX

At this juncture with Oxylus off recruiting, Telemachus felt the need to remove himself from the Heraclides for a few days. The third crop was beginning the process of taming the horses, but this could only be accomplished with the arrival of many experienced horsemen. The existing troops of the Heraclides trained halfheartedly, awaiting the arrival of the new recruits. The leaders of the Heraclides, when in residence, discussed plans for the return to the Peloponnese. Telemachus listened, but he carefully reserved his ideas or judgment. Heralds arrived daily at Locris with information from Corinth. King Tisamenus appeared to be making little preparation for war, with no major troop movements or preparations.

Telemachus and his sons rode up into the mountains to visit the Oracle of Delphi and to spend a few days alone.

The Oracle of Delphi existed long before it was called by such a name, and long before Apollo became its patron. Its strange odorous vapors emanated from a cleft in the earth and an endless supply of clear water gurgled up from the rocks. It was sacred to the Titans long before Zeus made his appearance. From times immemorial, pilgrims from throughout Hellas considered Delphi the center of the world. In ancient times, a gigantic monster settled there, a snake many times the size of man by the name of Python. Legends tell us that although this snake monster could foretell the future, he was consumed by evil intent. Only the most desperate of mortals sought his counsel as many of them ended their days in his belly.

Long after the disappearance of the Titans, Hera, Queen of the Heavens, driven by venomous jealousy, caused the downfall of Python. This time, she sought to punish Leto for transgressions with her husband, Zeus, lord of immortals and mortals alike. Leto, normally the gentlest and kindest of all the immortals, lay with Zeus and got with child by him. Pregnant with twins and escaping from the jealousy of Hera, she traveled throughout the world searching for a place to give birth. Hera sent Python after her to destroy her before she could give birth. No one would aid Leto, and many obstructed her. Finally, she came to the rocky shores of Delos, one of the Cyclades in the Aegean Sea. There she gave birth to the immortal twins, first Artemis, and then aided by Artemis' divine midwifery, Apollo. Leto's twins immediately punished all who had refused aid to their mother. Four days after his birth, the baby Apollo sought to destroy Python. Apollo took on the appearance of a dolphin and swam from the island of Delos. Observing a Cretan ship sailing from Knossos, he directed the ship to the port of Cirrha. From there, Apollo journeyed up the slopes of Mt. Parnassus in the body of a mortal. When Apollo found the cave, he slaughtered Python with a single shot from his godly bow. As soon as he had removed Python from the site, he took over the oracle and designated the Cretan sailors who had accompanied him on the journey as his first priests of the sanctuary. The Cretan sailors then established an oracle to Apollo Delphinius, after the divine dolphin that had guided them to the location. They called it the Oracle of Delphi.

From the Heraclides' palace, Delphi was less than a day's ride on horseback, in the mountains in the direction of Apeliotes, passing through the town of Crisa. Telemachus and his sons rode through the sacred plain of the Pleistus River valley, with terraced vineyards on both sides of the valley. Ascending the mountains, they could see the Gulf of Corinth, the isthmus, and the Peloponnese in the distance. They continued to ride along the well traveled route, entering Delphi through a narrow pass guarded by two large cliffs forming the gates to the oracle. On one side stood Mt. Cirphis, and on the other side Mt. Parnassus. Once inside the sanctuary, they hobbled their horses in the foothills behind the pilgrims' camp and made ablutions in the Castalian waters. The source flowed from a natural spring in the hillside, emptying into a pool that fed an eternal stream.

The temple of Apollo was a crude building made of mud bricks, located in the center of the settlement. Other temporary buildings surrounded the small temple. They were called treasuries, for they contained the official votive offerings and religious objects of the neighboring states and communities. Despite its remoteness, suppliants flocked to the oracle in all seasons with their ills and concerns. For people believed they could only communicate with the gods through such oracles. This day, only a few suppliants were camped by the pool.

Telemachus and his sons approached an old priest outside the temple. He welcomed them and inquired of their interest.

"We have come with a question for the gods," said Telemachus.

"Then you have come to the right place," the toothless priest replied sourly. "Whoever wishes to consult the oracle is obliged to pay the "*teleno*," a tax that gives you the right to approach the great altar of Apollo Delphinius to offer sacrifice. The priestess is tired today. Perhaps you would like to return at another time."

"Are the gods unavailable?" Telemachus asked.

"No, as you might surmise, the gods are always available. It is man who is often unavailable. But you must approach the gods with the proper attitude. I see you have doubts."

"No doubts, only the desire to know the truth. Our journey was long, and business takes us elsewhere."

"Then I suggest you return at some other time." But the priest hesitated when Telemachus opened his hand to reveal a small gold medallion: a likeness of Apollo himself. The priest's eyes were startled. "Ah, allow me to address the priestess." He entered the small temple and closed the drape behind him.

Telemachus smiled, for the priest soon reappeared.

"Is it just the three of you?"

"Yes."

"Have you formulated an appropriate question, for this is of the utmost importance?"

"Yes."

"Then the priestess would be willing to see you. Please enter." He held open the drape as they entered, and Telemachus placed the small medallion in his extended hand.

Inside the mud hut, hazy smoke rose from a small tripod, sitting over well-tended coals. A bulky old woman with stone-white hair and skin as dark and as dirty as the brazier sat encircled by the smoke and the filth of countless sacrifices, her enormous breasts resting comfortably on her lap. This was the Pythian Priestess. She did not look up as light momentarily filled the room. The priest seated the men against one wall. It took some time for their eyes to adjust to the darkness. The priest sat down on a low stool opposite them next to the priestess.

"Pythia speaks with the gods," the old man said by way of introduction. The old priestess began ceremonially washing herself in a ewer below the tripod, for her hands were filthy and would not clean up without heavy scrubbing. When she had completed washing her hands, she flicked the water into the tripods, which sputtered and smoked. She then mixed some leaves and blue flowers together and began stuffing the mixture into her mouth, throwing larger branches with green leaves into the tripod, filling the small room with pungent smoke. She scooped up what appeared to be pieces of fat from the dirt floor and threw them into the burning kindling. Flames jumped from the coals, and the entire room filled with acrid smoke, making it nearly impossible to breathe. She then spat her chewed mouthful into the fire. At this point, the priestess fell into a trance, her hair draped loosely around her shoulders and her meaty arms hanging at her sides.

"Please whisper your question to me," the priest told them.

Telemachus leaned closer to the priest. "We are exiled from our native land and wish to return. We desire to know if we will be successful in achieving our goal." Although whispered, all could hear the question, but no one could hear the words of the priest as he whispered into the ear of the priestess.

The priestess began mumbling and moaning, speaking in some barbarian tongue. As she reached before her and threw additional objects and herbs onto the coals, her voice reached a feverish pitch, cooing and burbling in high tones that were far from Greek. Her body shook. And then silence. The priest remained quiet for a while, and then began to speak slowly. At one point, he misspoke, and the priestess corrected him in proper Greek:

"The sanction of Apollo garlands your heads,
And the light of Helios guides your horses.
The son of Ethiops leads you to the shores of eternal seas,
Though you must surrender what you cherish most.
Broach casks on holy days and believe in yourself.
I whisper your name and see your face."

As they walked from the hut, Telemachus noticed a road below leading to what was called the Sanctuary of Athene, an open area with a roughly carved wooden statue of the goddess Pallas Athene looking out over the valley below and the surrounding mountains. He left his sons and walked down to observe the statue and to think about the oracle. Had he glimpsed the future? He was not sure, but the prophecy had struck him far beyond what he had expected. The hazy mountains in the distance merged with the sky. He watched as a white-tailed hawk, gliding on the gentle breezes from the valley below, suddenly stopped in mid-air, flapping its wings to remain fixed in place, having caught site of prey.

Later that night, Telemachus, Autolycus, and Amphion sat around a small fire of twigs in the field behind the Oracle. They had eaten a few cold foods, and the hobbled horses were occupied with fresh grasses in the field. The father and his two sons settled in their heavy cloaks against the cool evening air, facing the warmth of the coals.

"I once traveled with my father into the Pindus Mountains," Telemachus said, "and I have never forgotten that trip. For it was there I first glimpsed my father. I was about your age."

"Never fear, father, we know you well," Amphion said. "But what have we learned here?"

"Nothing," Autolycus said quickly. "Nothing at all."

"Do not dismiss the words of the oracle so rapidly," Telemachus said.

"Why? How could you believe anything?" Autolycus asked. "We could ask a beggar on the streets of Elis and receive similar advice."

"The priest knew who we were," Amphion said.

"How would he know?" Telemachus asked. "We never told him where we were from or who our ancestors were."

Autolycus poked at the fire with a stick. "It is no more than a magician's trick. It plays on people's superstitions and only has to touch a few notes or even just one to make believers out of skeptics."

"You must admit that the priestess made more than a few points," Amphion said. "By chance? Not entirely, certainly. "

"Perhaps," Telemachus agreed. "But it is well we think about things, for we are beginning a voyage that may take us to unexpected ports. That is the only reason I gave ear to the words of the oracle. Can we win this war? How shall we protect Polycasté and Nestor? Can we trust the Heraclides or even Oxylus for that matter? What of our lives? This could go terribly wrong."

"I think I made a mistake leaving Pylos." Amphion said. "There I could do whatsoever is necessary to protect Polycasté and Nestor. If they are hurt or worse, then this would all be futile...even returning to Ithaca."

"My father," Telemachus said, "set out reluctantly for a campaign that was to last a summer and returned two decades later. Many never returned." For a while, there was only the gurgling of the creek.

"Mother will never leave Grandfather," Amphion said. "And Grandfather is too old to leave his home."

"We are taking this too seriously," Autolycus complained. "Who are these people to know anything?"

"If we were to trust the oracle," Amphion said, "It seems to say we will be successful, but that any victory will be costly. We need to be mindful of that. What do we cherish most? Our lives? The lives of others?"

"What you cherish most could be something other than life," Autolycus said.

"It places too much reliance on the gods," Amphion replied. "We must depend on ourselves for our success."

"These may be the words of the gods," said Telemachus.

But Autolycus was not convinced. "That woman...did you see her? And the greed in that man's eyes. And we are to believe they foresee our future?"

But Amphion's mind was elsewhere. "You see, I am no use here as a soldier or leader of troops. Leave that to our passionate hosts with much to gain. I know the family of our grandfather, and I can be of greater use there."

"You may be right," Telemachus admitted. "But we have time to consider this further. Decisions arrived at in haste are often flawed.

Sleep may be the greatest boon to mankind and to his powers of judgment...and to the understanding of prophecies. I suggest we proceed in that direction for this evening, at least. We have a long ride tomorrow."

But Telemachus did not sleep well that night. He went over the words of the oracle time and again. He wondered what he "cherished most" that he would be willing to surrender to return to Ithaca. His father had surrendered the love of a family and his kingdom to win victory in Troy. Would that be the price for him as well?

"I whisper your name and see your face," the priestess had said.

The simple line repeated in his head like a wood thrush:

"I whisper your name and see your face."

He listened to the rhythmic repetition of the words...

And he whispered, "Polycasté."

He resented the fact that she had deserted him. Yet, he had allowed her to leave. Other men might have stopped their wives, but he had always respected her. She had always ruled herself, and he loved her fiery independence and outspokenness, although he recognized that even those had retreated recently. What could he have done? Had he removed himself from her...even faintly? Had he assumed to much...assumed her devotion? Had he failed to honor her? You cannot have it both ways: a strong woman and a submissive one. He would never attempt to extinguish her spirit. That would be like breaking a fine mare. Had he failed to notice a fissure in her independent spirit? What did he cherish most: his life, the return to Ithaca, the lives of his sons, Penelope? He listened again and again until the soft nickering of the horses and the gentle murmuring of the Castalian waters finally lulled him to sleep, just before golden robed Eos began her preparations for leaving the warm bed of her forever dear and aging husband Tithonos.

XXXI

Antagonism and resentment lie at the core of all mortal endeavors. This may come from some self-protective trait inherited from the gods, or it may result from the sweat and strain of our daily lives. Antagonism and resentment may be important aspects of our natures: a defensive contrivance like a mother bear that will attack without fail if approached too closely or a competitive spirit of bettering our peers. I, Antimenes have three daughters. We still celebrate them, and I would do all within my powers to guard them from harm. That is natural among men, just as it is with beasts, the only difference being that the gods have given us the capacity to judge our actions individually. Within broader groupings of men, families, tribes or countries, this instinct of defense is cumulative and can be destructive. Fear, insecurity, and isolation feed this instinct, making it grow into hatred and belligerence against others. And what is the greatest fear, but that of the unknown, the unfamiliar, the barbarian. We fear what is different, and our politicians play upon these fears just as the sure hand of Apollo plays upon his lyre.

All this continues over the generations. I do not believe it gets worse nor that it improves, for it is based on our natural makeup. I would give anything if people would come to know one another. Fear can be tempered with understanding. We are all the beloved sons and daughters of noble mothers and fathers. Here I am, a man feeling his age, considering ancient tales of mortals and immortals alike. My wife has left me to discover something missing within her life. What is the importance of these tales? What we can learn from them?

Homer tells us of King Priam of Troy, grieving at the death of his son, Hector, seeking out Achilles, the murderer of his son, to recover the body of his most beloved child. Stealthy Hermes, the cunning slayer of Argus, led Priam to Achilles, who agreed to return the body of the son to the father. And the two men agreed to halt the fighting for eleven days in honor of the fallen Hector. The two enemies ate together, conversed, and slept, and discovered they shared much in common. The lot of all men is full of both joy and sorrow. Sadly, only sorrow led Priam and Achilles to their mutual conclusion – too often, sorrow is the motivator and not joy.

Democritis of Abdera had much to say on the subject of joy and man's relations with others. Socrates and Democritis debated in the great agora of Athens before thousands of their fellow philosophers, scholars, and followers. At the end of the evening, it was Democritis who bested Socrates, not for his oratorical skills, but for his humanness. He was a man who understood men. From that time on, Socrates sought to silence him and burned all of Democritis' books he could get his hands on. Socrates, an ugly, fat bear of a man, unwashed and unkempt, shuffled through life without truly understanding man, only his lofty ideals of what man can endeavor to become. Democritis knew what it was to be human. He followed the Pythagoreans, and his writings were saved by them. His thoughts found great resonance in the lands toward Apeliotes. Plato, who spent so much time explaining his teacher, Socrates, makes no mention of Democritis, although he listed all of the other great philosophers. It required Aristotle to deal with Democritis. But Aristotle, as well, attempted to cast Democritis' theories into the garbage heap of history.

Democritis, a flower that bloomed out of season, lived to be one hundred and nine years old. He always subsisted simply and modestly. He stated that all things are made of atoms and that nothing is ever created nor destroyed, but borne about in endless revolutions. Not being a mathematician, I believe his greatest treatise is "On Cheerfulness." In this work, he ascribes the chief good of all men to be cheerfulness. Cheerfulness is not what at first blush one might suspect. Cheerfulness is not the same as pleasure. Nor is cheerfulness a light and airy feeling without content. Democritis understood cheerfulness to be a condition according to which the soul lives calmly and steadily, respectful of oneself and others, undisturbed by fear, superstition, or other passions. He called this state, euthymia and considered it the chief goal of mankind. Such a simple concept: cheerfulness. But we all know the great effort required to achieve this feeling, to say nothing of prolonging and sustaining it. Some people never achieve it, and many others never *even think to try. Cheerfulness means avoiding violence and disturbance, understanding that life offers mysteries that we can never understand, and that, while we must strive to achieve the most we can, we must recognize our limits. It assumes that we are all of the same maker and that we all must face the same state of affairs. We call Democritis the laughing philosopher, and I love him dearly and sit with him late at night, as you know Alcathöe, by the fire rereading his thoughts and wishing we could all live in such a way.*

By the time of the bloom of the artichoke and the piercing song of the cicada, the park of the Heraclides in Locris had taken on a new aspect. The entire hillside was covered with tents, and late into the night, fires lit the branches of the oaks and filled the air with misty smoke. Over four thousand men had joined the campaign. Many of these men came from Hellas, with Greek, if not their mother tongue, at least their second language. But half the men were *xenoi*, or so-called barbarians, and spoke Greek only awkwardly. Cresphontes feared a coalition made up of tribes of the barbarian nations, and he ordered Greek speaking at a basic level the first requirement of joining the forces. Each man had been tested in Greek, and many had failed and had been sent away. By mid-summer, though, most of the remaining men were comfortable if not entirely fluent in Greek.

When walking among the tents with the soldiers at leisure, though, one could hear conversations in many barbaric tongues, at whose origins one could only hazard a guess. In short, Oxylus had sought professional soldiers in all the directions of the godly winds, and men had flocked to this venture like ants to honey. For earning a living and feeding a family had become nearly impossible in many areas of the world. Some men join military ventures to tide them over the slow growing seasons or to cover the cost of another mouth to feed. Other men spend their lives tramping from one adventure to the next. One of the greatest evils of war is that men come to enjoy its trials, and those are the men that must be commanded with attention. For to enjoy war is to have no respect for yourself or others and little fear of Hades. This is a recipe for acts that reach well beyond those of civilized men. For the most part, though, men recognize that war is only a means to a full stomach and to obtain plunder to take home, should one be so skilled or lucky enough to return.

Both Xenophon and Herodotus, the greatest war historians, describe mercenary troops moving into a country and leaving a swath of blood and destruction in their path. Troops would enter an alien country, living off the land and the villagers, and leave behind nothing living. As an army marched, it expanded like a giant snake, growing larger depending on its success in finding prey. Each village entered and exited added booty and pillage to the lengthening caravan, with growing numbers of wagons and slaves following behind the army. The growing beast of a war machine usually expanded only to a point, and then, due to a lost battle or a geographic area that could not support the number of men, horses, animals, and captured loot, human and otherwise, it tended to decline in size. For when there is nothing to feed the belly, the troops will no longer look with such pride on their plunder. Slowly or rapidly, depending on the circumstances, the snake will slough off the excess skin, until it is able once again to return to the comfort of a full belly and begin the process of growing all over again. Their ambition was to return home the largest snake possible.

The greatest enticement for men to join the Heraclides' campaign was the offer of land in the Peloponnese in return for military services. This was not a common practice. Oxylus made it clear from the start, and Cresphontes and Temenus agreed, although they were somewhat less vocal perhaps, that if the warriors were to become occupants of the countries they were conquering, they must take unusual measures not to be seen by the populace as marauders and looters. The offer of land to cultivate for raising a family in ground where every seed germinated, not one in ten, and where every grape was rich and full of sugar, was a boon. If the soldiers were to set ablaze all that was left behind them, they would have nothing to return to. To say nothing of the people who might escape their claws, and then at some time in the future return full of hatred and desire for retribution. How could that be described as a return of the rightful leaders of the Peloponnese? Although all could easily agree to that basic principal before the commencement of the campaign and understand its wisdom, in practice Oxylus knew it would be difficult to achieve. As a result, it became one of the primary goals in the selection of troops, their officers, their training, and their discipline.

On the other hand, experienced veterans of past campaigns were highly sought after. Although few veterans of seven-gated Thebes or majestic Ilium were still living at this time, for two generations and more had passed since these cities had been captured. The men that gathered on the hillside in Locris were the sons and grandsons of the victorious Epigoni at Thebes and of the Achaean heroes of Troy. These men had fought in battles and knew the ways of war among the great kingdoms. They had fought skirmishes with the Thracians against the Hittites, following the Treaty of Kadesh. They had been freebooters from Lycia and Europa and attacked the city of Ugarit from the sea and plundered and pillaged its inhabitants. They had razed the Halys River valley with the barbarous Kaskans, living along the Pontic range, and put the torch to Hattusas and other cities – the scribes called this the attack of the hordes. They had followed the Pharaoh Rameses III and fought at Megiddo and in the streets of Palestine's greatest cities. They had been skirmishers with Meryre, son of Did, and attacked the Delta and were defeated by the largest chariot force in the world fighting in support of Merneptah.

Yet, the veterans shared a desire to settle down and leave warfare to the younger men, and for that very reason they were manageable and cooperative. Also, they had no illusions as to the honor and glory of war. They were happy to have their stomachs full on a regular basis and a warm cot at night. Of course, in all large gatherings of men problems arise and sickness was common, and this camp was no exception. Physicians aided as best they could the aches, pains, and health of the men. However, fights were frequent, and every night somebody would be hurt or killed. A large security force had been appointed to manage the troops and to preserve peace as much as possible. Heavy arms were kept in the palace in a secure location, but small arms and natural weapons were ubiquitous. The best remedy was hard work and fatigue after a long day of intense training and small rations of wine.

The men were divided into four divisions of ten battalions. (A battalion consisted of ten companies of ten men each.) Each division was commanded by a general. Oxylus managed two divisions of infantry: one division was commanded by dark-eyed Aletes aided by Phalces and Autolycus; and the other by the twins, Procles and Eurysthenes, aided by Cisus. The infantry battalions were made up of archers, skirmishers, light infantry, armed with swords and short javelins, and *shardana*, or specialists in hand-to-hand combat, armed with short javelins and close order implements, such as swords, maces, and axes.

In this campaign, the Heraclides wanted to make a point, and so for the first time in the history of Hellas, they outfitted the troops in standard uniforms.

At this time, freebooters among the Greeks supplied all their own armaments and armour. Not until Alexander the Great did troops have standard issue. Professional soldiers carried their armour and weapons with them from war to war. Often their attire and tools of the trade were gained in spoil, for outfitting was very expensive and beyond the reach of a simple farmer or hunter. These tools were passed from father to son. Armament and armour were so valuable that they were rarely buried with a soldier. Homer describes great fights over the armour and armament of fallen heroes. They fought over the armour not only to vaunt, but for quite practical reasons. Soldiers needed the equipment and arms. New weapons were rare. Broken weapons were retooled in the smithy. Only in a few cases of wealthy rulers or generals were weapons or armour added to a barrow, and this was done at risk for the first thing that grave robbers looked for were weapons, even before gold.

The standard Heraclide outfit was a short-sleeved tunic made of wool with fringed skirt or kilt and a leather jerkin. Over this, they wore a brazen bell-shaped cuirass or corselet with leather attachments at the sides, white-painted bronze greaves to protect their ankles, and heavy sandals. Each man was issued a standard Heraclide bronze helmet, with a low metal crest resembling feathers running from forehead to nape of the neck, adding strength to the helmet. Heavy woolen cloaks, dyed a light indigo, served for the cold, rain, sun, wind, and sleeping. The men trained with long cut-and-thrust swords, hilted and double edged, made of iron rather than bronze. And the infantry sported small, light, circular bronze-lined shields. These did not require a neck strap and two hands to carry, but fastened to the wrist so that they could be used offensively in hand-to-hand combat. They provided less protection than the large shields in use throughout Hellas against aerial assaults. But the Heraclides assumed their composite bows would allow them to mass out of range of enemy archers, and the lighter shield would give them far greater mobility and freedom of movement up close.

The strength of the Heraclide infantry, however, was its archers. They were skilled fighters supplied with composite bows. These bows were constructed by bowyers who used strips of horn threaded into grooves running the length of a wooden bow-stave and then wrapped in sinew. They could decimate an army at a distance that left their own men outside the range of the enemy. The archers practiced day and night and when not training were employed in constructing arrows. Bronze arrowheads were used, but additional supplies of the iron arrowheads, lighter and giving a longer flight, continued to arrive. Each archer carried more than a hundred arrows in a shoulder quiver.

Oxylus planned no heavy infantry, that is, men sporting long lances and heavy shields. He knew that the Heraclides could not field the numbers of troops that Tisamenus could bring to bear. The Heraclides were not prepared to confront the enemy with slow moving ground forces. The offensive structure of the Heraclides was based upon rapid movement across all terrains with light infantry, supported by rapidly mobilized archers and cavalry. The only chariotry used would be in the land forces moving through the isthmus, but these were limited to the commanders, who needed to move quickly.

Companies within the battalions were primarily divided among fighters with similar backgrounds and from common tribes. Many of the archers came from Thrace or from the directions of Boreas and Kaikias. The *shardana* came from the directions of Notus and Euros, from Egypt and the Levantine, where they had gained experience in close quarter fighting. During exercises, Oxylus and his officers scrutinized and graded the fighters in the infantry in their abilities and specialties. Each man was tested under a variety of conditions for a variety of skills and then assigned to a company that could best utilize his skills. The two divisions were named the "Reds" and the "Greens," and they were soon conducting exercises against each other. It became clear soon enough that the "Reds" were the superior force, made up of the top recruits.

Telemachus commanded the single division of cavalry, along with Deiphontes and Amphion. The horse troops were carefully selected from among the soldiers. Some of the men came as foot soldiers without experience in riding. But among the soldiers were many fine horsemen, many from the broad expanses of Thessaly and Thrace, but others from throughout Hellas, and the direction of Notus as well. Each horseman carried two short javelins and a long cut-and-thrust sword at his side. But the horse riders were trained primarily as archers, with a shoulder quiver for arrows and a small composite bow. Archers from the infantry were tested on horseback, but for the most part experienced horsemen were trained in archery while riding. Telemachus' special bridles and leather saddles had been prepared and were completely distributed among the riders. Telemachus gave each rider his own mount, so that horse and rider could become accustomed to each other. Each rider was responsible for taming, grooming, caring for, and feeding his mount. The cavalry troops, called troopers, were separated from the infantry to be close to their horses. Soon, camaraderie became established among the troopers, and exercises took them far from the palace into the hills of Locris.

Temenus took charge of the navy, which consisted of a single division. The naval forces had been relocated to Cirrha, the port of the town of Crisa. By mid-summer, the three Phoenician long ships were nearing completion and the fourth had been relocated to Cirrha from Naupactus. These ships were outfitted for transporting troops, horses, and supplies. The rest of the fleet, some forty ships located in Attica, was slowly moved to Cirrha to avoid suspicion as much as possible. Many of the ships were outfitted for blockading and sea battles, with the masts removed and the prows reinforced and covered with sheet bronze.

As the days lengthened, the Heraclide troops made great progress in their preparations under the guidance of Oxylus and Telemachus. The two leaders worked with the troops every day, all day into the night, and often nights as well. They soon built up strong feelings of trust and loyalty among the troops. Telemachus and Oxylus became identified with their specialty because of their knowledge and willingness to teach. The troops looked to them for guidance in both military matters and in other areas of their lives. They identified with these two strangers, whose goals seemed to align with their own. They caught glimpses of Cresphontes and Temenus, but they did not trust them and knew their lives depended on their two commanders.

Cresphontes called a meeting one moon after the summer solstice. That evening, the Kneeler stood out clearly from the sparkling Via Lactea – the milk of Hera, which had flowed from her breasts when she discovered the trick played by the whistling Hermes and tore the suckling baby Heracles from her breast. The Kneeler constellation shows Heracles slaying a dragon. When Zeus and Hera married, Gaia gave them the gift of a golden apple. Hera asked the Hesperides to plant the apple and care for the trees in her garden on the slopes of Mount Atlas. To protect the apples, Hera chose a giant dragon, Ladon, who furiously guarded the orchard and prevented anyone from stealing the apples. When Eurystheus ordered Heracles to retrieve a golden apple from Hera's trees, he slew the dragon and brought an apple back to Eurystheus. The constellation immortalizes Heracles' success, although Hera resented it greatly. Proof of the gods filled the starry skies.

All the leaders joined the assembly. Cresphontes returned from Athens. Temenus came from Crisa and the naval yards. The twins, Procles and Eurysthenes, returned from their palace in Marathon. Aletes and Autolycus had become the hardworking generals of the infantry and had agreed to take a night off with Oxylus. Amphion and Deiphontes spent their time with Telemachus training the horse troops, and they came with the scent of their occupation.

After sacrificing a lamb and sending burnt offerings to the gods, and after they had taken their fill of good things to eat and drink, Cresphontes stood before the family, his sparkling linen robes falling to the floor. He began a description of the progress they had made and related information on developments in the Peloponnese according to his sources.

"My family and sirs, since our discussion with Thymoetes, King of Athens, and his assembly, we have journeyed a great distance. I look out at the park and see the fruits of our labors, and I think that the leaders of this effort can be proud of our progress. In the mornings, I see the mountains of Achaea in the distance, and I think of the generations of Heraclides that have waited for this moment, for I truly believe we are on the threshold of our return. As foretold by the gods, we have fulfilled all that is required of us. We are ready to mount the final return to the land of our ancestors. The third crop will be victorious."

He looked down at the table before him, piled with goblets and plates and dishes, some unused and others with half eaten foods and drinks. Large silver bowls of fruits and nuts took up the remainder of the space. He reached down and pulled out a dried clay tablet from under one of the bowls. Notations had been etched in the tablet.

He had requested an inventory of the current state of affairs. "I do this to remind you that we are now committed to our return. Our treasure is dedicated to this effort." He read an accounting of the accomplishments:

Thirty-five hundred troops in residence at Locris, making up
    three divisions
One naval division of one thousand sailors located in Crisa
Forty-five ships, including four designed by Xenodamas of Crete,
    the largest long ships ever constructed, now completed
Fifteen hundred horses, including over thirteen hundred chargers
Horse tack, saddles, and armour for over one thousand horses
Twenty chariots
Battlefield dress and armour for the troops
Armament for three divisions, including lances and javelins,
    bronze shields, small arms, and backup supplies
Iron weapons from the Hittites, including new style swords and
    weapon heads for javelins, spears, lances, arrows, and other
    missiles
Two thousand composite bows, both large and cavalry-mounted
    sizes
Two hundred wagons for transportation of armament, armour,
    and other supplies

Special sutler wagons for victuals, medical kits and other supplies for physicians, and for sacrificers and priests

Portable forges for metal workers, including raw supplies of all sorts

Colors, flags, and banners bearing the gold and blue

Cooking wagons with pots and pans and braziers and tripods

Dried provisions for several months, including grains, barley cake, nuts, cheeses, honey and fig cakes, fruit, dried fish and meat, and maza

Oil and olive pots and wine amphorae

Pack and sacrificial animals, including horses, oxen, mules, donkeys, sheep, and goats

A large stockpile of foodstuffs in Locris, including live animals, for additional supplies

"We have enough provisions and inventory to last at least five months on campaign. This does not take into account what we will obtain at the villages and towns as we pass through, at a market price, mind you."

Cresphontes had traded the family property, or so he said: the estate in Marathon, the large family residence in Thebes, and committed to transfer this palace in Locris as well. All slaves associated with these properties were to be sold. Those slaves entering into military service were offered their freedom. In addition, the treasury in Marathon had been depleted of all save the important artifacts of great Heracles and his gold hoardings, which would never leave the family coffers.

He went on to describe how Tisamenus had relocated to Corinth and taken up residence in the palace of the kings there. Although he was rallying his forces, the states and cities under his control were not cooperating, or at least begrudgingly. His informants estimated Tisamenus' standing troops at about ten thousand, but they were spread thinly across Argolis, Laconia, and Arcadia. They were not well supplied or well armed and had no battle experience. Recruits were arriving slowly and were farm boys and itinerants with nothing better to do with their time.

The kings of Corinth, the brothers Doridas and Hyanthidas, sons of Propodas, jointly ruled and sought only to preserve their rule.

They were older men of the generation of Orestes, the father of Tisamenus, and felt less allegiance to the son than to the father. Cresphontes felt they would not play all the stops to win victory. On the other hand, Tisamenus' generals in Corinth, also brothers, Pamphylus and Dymas, were committed to him. But they too were appointed by Orestes. They had no background in the military arts, for truth be known they were chosen for their ability to anticipate and fulfill the whims of Orestes and grovel at his every wish. Orestes chose them not for their greatness but rather due to his own weakness. The archons surrounding Tisamenus were selected for their ability to stomach him. They did not think on their own nor did he encourage them to do so.

"We know one of his generals," Cresphontes said. "Pamphylus is married to Orsobia, the daughter of Deiphontes and Hyrnetho. Believe me this union was not met with great approval among our family."

"Sometimes," Temenus interrupted, "children are headstrong to a degree that refutes reason. But Pamphylus is a reasonable, though limited, man and finds himself in a difficult position."

"Yes," Deiphontes said, "Pamphylus, son of Aegimius, finds himself in a prickly place, far from Athens, where he sought scholarship, and where he met my daughter Orsobia, and yet owes allegiance to the Pelopides. Pamphylus came from Boeotia and helped Orestes solidify his rule. Where Orestes was bright and capricious, Tisamenus is brilliant, tempestuous, and sadistic. And these are the words of my daughter."

"Right," Cresphontes replied, "you are most charitable, Deiphontes. In reality, Pamphylus is a fool, and Tisamenus a prideful scoundrel who acts like a woman."

"Perhaps," Temenus agreed.

"However, there is one among them whom we do not know," Cresphontes continued. "Lacestades, King of Sicyon, is a descendant of Heracles. This branch of the family took the throne in Sicyon when Heracles first conquered the Peloponnese. They lost touch with our family over the generations since Heracles left the Peloponnese."

"We know," Deiphontes said, "that Lacestades is no lover of Tisamenus, just as he was no lover of Orestes, or Agamemnon, for that matter."

"How is it we know this?" Cresphontes asked with suspicion.

"Sicyon has remained independent of Corinth," Deiphontes replied, "and its peoples have limited the powers of their rulers. Sicyon has always been a thorn in the side of Corinth, and certainly in Orestes' side."

"What we do not know," Cresphontes said, "is if any legacy of Heracles remains with this man."

"We must talk with him," Telemachus spoke up quickly. "We need to know our friends. I suggest that Deiphontes and Amphion visit him secretly as ambassadors to unearth his intentions."

"What good can come of this?" Cresphontes asked.

"It answers a question we are facing," Telemachus replied.

"And what would that be?" Cresphontes demanded sharply.

Before Telemachus could reply, Temenus interrupted. "Do we all agree?" he asked quickly. He waited, and no one disagreed. "Then, I suggest that this be carried out immediately."

"We will see if this allows us any advantage," Cresphontes continued. "Now, we need to plan the commencement of our move, for the harvest season will soon be hard upon us, with the rains to follow."

"I am no farmer," Oxylus replied, glancing at Telemachus, "though I am a wine-bibber and am forever grateful for the gifts of joyful Dionysus. I know that the time of harvest is critical to the crop: too soon and one has unripe fruit and undistinguished and weak wine; too late and the wine is heavy and cloying and full of ash. We must time carefully our initial foray. I suggest that this discussion would be better closed to the four seniors here."

"Why is that?" Cresphontes demanded angrily. "We need this information for all. Do you think that the family is not trustworthy?"

"I have no doubts on that score," Oxylus said smiling. "But those who have experienced battle understand military decisions are best made by a few and not a large group. This is an army and not a family gathering, or Telemachus and I would be elsewhere. In an army, decisions must be made that cannot reflect all opinions and all attitudes like some debate. And once made, decisions must be followed."

"Agreed," said Temenus. "We can meet separately after the return of Deiphontes and Amphion."

"But," Cresphontes added, "I would like to remind all of you that to postpone the campaign is to incur further costs to our treasury and hoards. We must move forward."

"We are close," Oxylus replied with good nature. "Every day, we must sample the grapes."

XXXII

Meanwhile in Corinth, the god Apollo, son of Leto, attended the meeting with King Tisamenus and his generals and advisors in the palace. He appeared as a priest and soothsayer, disguising his glorious body and beautiful face as a three-legged man with white hair and stooped demeanor, leaning on his well polished staff. His invitation came as the result of a prophecy of success by one of his priests that had been relayed to Tisamenus.

Dymas, son of Aegimius, and general of the Pelopides spoke: "We are prepared across Argolis to confront the enemy. Our sources tell us that their numbers are few, only about three thousand troops, and that they listen to the counsel of two. Telemachus, son of Odysseus, without any military training or experience, is aiding them, although it is difficult to see how. He raised horses while in Elis and has moved them to Locris, but how can they be effective against heavy infantry? It is believed that he is assisting the Heraclides in his desire to return to Ithaca to rule as his father once did. The other is Oxylus, son of Haemon, from Aetolia and a knockabout who killed his own brother to take control of the kingdom of Aetolia. He was judged guilty and exiled. Rumor has it that he is the bastard son of King Memnon by a Trojan woman. Memnon led the Ethiopians at Troy and was killed by the sword of Achilles. When Memnon died on the battlefield, as the bards tell us, his warriors from Ethiopia all turned into sparrows and flew away..."

"Get on with it, Dymas," Tisamenus interrupted. "The bards will not help us here."

"My point was that this family seeks others to do their dirty work," Dymas continued. "And their counselors are not qualified. This is a great failing in my opinion. Another failing is that the Heraclides do not share a harmonious life. They are bickerers and dissenters. They work harder against each other than they do against their enemies. Is this not right, Lacestades?"

245

All eyes in the room turned to Lacestades, King of Sicyon, who was not at all surprised to be put on the spot by such a question.

"I can only assume, Dymas, you call me out because I share ancestry with the Heraclides, since my great grandfather, Phaestus, was one of the four-score sons of Heracles. I have never met these people and do not know them. I was born and raised in Sicyon as were my father and grandfather before me, long before your ancestor Sisyphus betrayed the trust of Zeus. We are leaders of the Sicyonians first and foremost. Sicyon has always supported the rulers of Corinth, your father, Tisamenus, and the sons of Atreus, and the rest of the Pelopides. I only add that we are prepared to defend Sicyon and to assist Corinth in any assault."

"Thank you, Lacestades," Tisamenus replied, "We never doubted this. Dymas, continue."

"Our line of defense will be the isthmus," said Dymas. "Although we have word that the Heraclides are preparing a fleet of ships, we believe they will come across the land with infantry and cavalry. They will meet the battlements across the isthmus at the Sanctuary of Poseidon and a force of some ten thousand troops. We have reinforced the great trench, closing the approach, and can withstand any force for an extended period. They will lose many men if they attempt to cross the ditch*. And Corinth remains well fortified should they cross the line."

"And why would they come at us at our strongest point?" Tisamenus asked.

"We are observing their naval force, currently congregated in Naupactus," Dymas replied. "Should they attempt to move across the Gulf of Corinth, we will be well aware. At this time, they have no ships outside the gulf. We, on the other hand, have over one hundred vessels. Several of our long ships ported at Patrae monitor all ship movements into and out of the gulf. The remainder of the fleet is at the Corinthian harbors of Lechaeum and Cenchreae on the Saronic Gulf, both well protected."

"Then why do they have a naval force at all?" Tisamenus asked.

---

* The ditch was a natural and man-made barrier constructed entirely across the isthmus to control entrance to the Peloponnese. It had existed since ancient times.

"We believe that they hope to use it for supplying the land forces. They have less than fifty ships, and they cannot hide in the waters of the gulf. Once they begin hostilities, we will attack the fleet and cut their supply lines."

"Perhaps we should not wait," Tisamenus suggested.

Dymas glanced at Pamphylus, but did not reply.

"What about Argos and Laconia?" Tisamenus demanded. "Are they prepared to assist us?"

"As we know," Dymas continued, "they have sent troops to assist us, who are now located at the ditch. In addition, they have strong defenses..."

"What do I care of their defenses?" Tisamenus yelled. "If the Heraclides traverse Corinth, we will all be lost, including Argos. Get them to send more troops."

"Yes, Sire."

"And what of Messenia with all this?"

"They are divided into four kingdoms and are in no position to assist us or even defend themselves. In fact, once we have taken care of the Heraclides, we might have reason to move in that direction to consolidate our control of the Peloponnese; for we believe the Pylians are supporting the Heraclides. Time is on our side. Once the weather turns, they will not be able to move on land or sea. The longer they hesitate, the more difficult their task."

"And this new king in Elis? Have we talked with him?" Tisamenus asked.

"This is a rustic state without importance," Dymas said. "Elis is not involved."

"Really?" Tisamenus asked in disbelief.

"Yes, Sire."

"What of all these horses?" Tisamenus asked.

"They are useless at the ditch," replied Dymas.

"Once again," Tisamenus said bitterly, "am I here on my own? Dymas, you may be a good general, but you lack all imagination. Find out the purpose of thousands of horses."

Tisamenus turned to the priest and soothsayer sitting somewhat separate from the rest. "What say you, grandfather? For you have been silent heretofore, and all men must sing for their supper."

"We must never judge other men using ourselves as measure," the soothsayer replied. "We do not know our enemies as we know ourselves. We must seek another measure. We must understand our enemy's conceits. To be successful is to see through deceptions."

"That is all good and well, but will we be victorious?" Tisamenus demanded. "Are you not the soothsayer who predicted our victory?"

"I have spoken: victory will come if you do not misjudge your enemy."

"And wise man, how would we misjudge our enemy?" Tisamenus asked.

"By believing that you are cleverer than they."

"Ah, but we are cleverer. And this contest will be determined by strength and advantage."

"This contest will be determined by the grace of the gods," the old man replied.

"And have I not sacrificed hecatombs to the gods? Have I not furnished my share of burnt offerings?"

"Just as your forebears did before you. All feasted to the gods, and all met sorry ends. The Pelopides must learn that sacrificing an animal and eating its flesh have no significance to the gods without devotion and belief."

"Who is this man?" Tisamenus shouted. "Do you have any idea of what it is to rule men?"

"I rule the multitudes."

"Yes, you and the other swindlers. You trade lies for gold."

"A deaf man hears only himself."

"Get him away from me," Tisamenus ordered his guards.

But when the old man struggled to his feet before the assembly, the guards halted, and no one dared approach. He flexed the muscles in his arms as though he were a young man, and his chest expanded and his backbone strengthened with each of his words: "Tisamenus, surely you of all men must know that there is a limit to the grace of the lord of gods. A family sorely tested as yours must recognize that honor must be earned. Do we not learn from adversity? Did the fates of Orestes and Agamemnon teach you nothing? What of Atreus? And what of Pelops, himself. Surely some god has it in for you."

"How dare you speak of my ancestors?"

"I only remind you that a family born of blood cannot sustain itself without remorse."

"Remove him," Tisamenus shouted.

"Tisamenus, hark my words," the soothsayer said softly. "Be wary. When foes become friends and ships sail across the land, you will meet a watery grave."

"How dare this stinky old man speak thusly? Who got him here? Guards. Guards. Take him away and throw him into the dungeon."

But still none would approach him.

"The voyage may be set, the vessel fit, the sailors resolute, but only the gods can determine the outcome."

So spoke Apollo, and he left the room under his own volition, without the use of his staff.

Telemachus and Oxylus saw Amphion and Deiphontes off from Locris the very evening of the Heraclide assembly. The two men departed on their mounts to the port of Crisa. Against the advice of Telemachus, but at the insistence of Cresphontes, both men were dressed in the uniform of the Heraclides. They would spend the night aboard a small warship and dock at the mouth of the river Sythas at Aristonautae in Achaea. Cresphontes had sent his herald with word to Lacestades, asking to meet with him in confidence. Aristonautae was about ninety stadia from Sicyon toward Zephyrus, not much farther than a running contest might entail. Amphion and Deiphontes hoped to spend no more than a day in Achaea and then return to Locris the following day with word from Lacestades.

Telemachus embraced his son, Amphion. "Be careful, for we do not know this man Lacestades."

"Yes, father. You need not worry."

"I know, but I cannot help myself."

After this, both Telemachus and Oxylus returned to their chambers at the palace. The evening had not gone well. As with all meetings with the family, constant bickering and useless discussion ruled. Of all the Heraclides, the twins were the most quarrelsome.

They never missed an opportunity to best one another and had no shame in their own behavior. And everyone grew tired of the constant scuffle between Temenus' voice of reason and Cresphontes' dictums and refusal to agree to anything.

For Telemachus and Oxylus, the spring had been intense with recruiting and training. For there is nothing more challenging than working with diverse peoples and attempting to wed them to a common effort and a common ideal. Much of what they were attempting to instill in the soldiers was contrary to past campaigns. In battles in history, including at Troy, tribes had come together to fight alongside one another, but not as a combined force and never as a mixed force.

Telemachus and Oxylus were using troops from throughout the world and assigning them to battalions based on their skills and propensities. This had never happened before. The great armies of Persia, the Levantine, and Egypt were made up mostly of conscripts who came from small villages of the regions, full of resentment and trepidation. Although unified in their backgrounds, they often lacked resolution, had little respect for their leaders, and would never see the benefits of success. In tight situations, it took only a disciplined and determined opponent to create panic (a word after the riotous god, Pan) among their ranks and to force a thoughtless retreat, where slaughter soon transpired. The Heraclide army turned out to be a tripod of mixed meats, and the unifying force was the possibility of tasting a new life of freedom in a rich and fertile environment. Much of the training consisted of getting different men to work together, to recognize each others' skills, and to learn to depend on each other. Telemachus and Oxylus were determined to coalesce the fighters into a unified force. Selection of the officers for their abilities and skills was vital. They both knew that the success of the army would depend on these men and their ability to gain the respect of their troops. They had made progress, particularly in the cavalry, but further progress was necessary, although time was running out rapidly as Cresphontes demanded action and the lights of Orion grew stronger in the night skies.*

---

* August-September.

Telemachus had not talked with Oxylus for some time, and they sat opposite one another as two old friends who recognize they have gone through much together and remember what their lives were like before. Perhaps not oddly, they did not speak of the coming campaign.

"I have lost my humor," Oxylus said. "I have lost my cheer and good nature. My gentle horse rues my temper."

"First, we must get over this complicated obstacle. And, in any case, Rhaebus always rued your temper."

"I dream of the future," Oxylus said. "In my dreams, I am no longer without a home. I have a wife and children prattling about the house. My respect is returned to me, at least by my horse. And Rhaebus is surrounded by his foals."

"That is a prayer, not a dream," Telemachus commented.

"I have traveled great distances in my life. Much greater than you may suspect. I have trekked both geographically and spiritually. I am far from my home and far from the person that I was. My father died when I was still in swaddling cloth, so I always lacked an underpinning."

"I thought you were raised in Aetolia by your father."

"Haemon, my step-father, adopted me as a small child. I am not Greek, but I have adopted Hellas as my country."

"How so?"

"I was born in Phrygia."

"Why are you telling me this now, after so much time?"

"I suppose it is like any soldier, a pre-battle confession. But it will do me no good. It is just that we both have much to gain from the success of this venture…and much to lose."

"I too have grave misgivings," Telemachus admitted. "I am unsure how vital this campaign is to my return to Ithaca, so I question risking my life and the lives of my sons for this family without virtue."

"Our success will ensure your return to leadership of Ithaca and Cephallenia."

"Possibly. I have been thinking that perhaps that goal is less important than I believed. My wife is estranged," Telemachus said. "In fact, I may not have a wife at this point."

"She will return when Nestor completes his god-given lives."

"I think not. We have raised two children and laid two parents to rest. We have two parents remaining. I have been running away from my duties for the last year, escaping into a world of men who only talk of their families as an excuse for punishing their adversaries. What is really important in our lives? How many of these men will ever see their families again? I have no desire to see my sons on the battlefield, for I do not believe as my father did that war is man's business or that honor and excellence on the field of battle will earn renown. I do not want to see them die on the battlefield. I lead my troopers as though each were my son – probably not a smart thing to do. Unlike you, I do not foresee my grandchildren prattling about my knees before the hearth."

"You are not a soldier by trade," Oxylus said. "Soldiers require myths to survive."

Apollo returned to the heavens in a rage. His anger so often led to massacre and mayhem and the flight of arrows more numerous than summer quail. But this day, he only sought an audience with the father of the gods. His fury accompanied him.

"The son of this family that eats their own children deserves to be swept away from the earth. The grandson of the pillager of Troy. The scion of a mother murderer. Why do I attempt to protect this family, the produce of your seed?"

"Our son," Zeus replied, "we need to leave our anger at the gates of heaven. We must sit in judgment of these mortals and not occupy ourselves in their short lives."

"They listened not to my counsel."

"And would this be the first time that mortals failed to hear their gods?"

"They esteem no one." Apollo shouted "They lie to themselves. They tell great stories that are intended only to advance their cause. They are sycophants and lack all candors. They are blind men in a room of mutes."

"Is this just cause to punish them eternally?"

"Yes."

"No," Zeus said. "A rock hangs over the head of Tantalus, our own mortal son. And neither food nor drink passes his lips, though he is surrounded at all times by fruit and fresh water. Tantalus murdered his own son, Pelops, and served him to the gods. We restored Pelops: the only mortal ever to be returned to earth after death. And then Pelops, great charioteer and lasher of horses, cursed his own children, Atreus and Thyestes. The whistling god Hermes saw to that. And Atreus served his brother Thyestes' children to their father for supper, just as Tantalus had served Pelops to the gods. And the children of Atreus, Agamemnon and Menelaus, were cursed and their children in turn. Mortals cannot learn. Our own mortal offspring fail to comprehend no matter how loudly we shout our message. What more can we do than to permit them to suffer themselves?"

Why do we Greeks love Apollo? Apollo is not the most consistent of the gods. Too often, he allows his emotions to rule. Sometimes, he finds himself on the wrong side of events, as indicated by his unjust actions helping Hector kill Patroclus, or in allowing Paris, who had demonstrated no ability to shoot a bow, to kill Achilles. Perhaps we love him for this inconsistency. He loves his lyre and his bow, both. He loves truth and fairness. His prophecies show us the way in an uncertain world. He loves mortal man. He sees the world with optimism and hopes for mankind and can accept no less. He appreciates the finest that man can offer: his paeans, his faience, his theater. But with people who refuse his aid, he loses all patience.

As I age and come to a greater understanding of the spectrum of life, I also come to comprehend Apollo and to forgive him his lapses. I find myself becoming angry for the most menial of errors, my own mostly, for accidentally hitting my head on a beam or for failures in my memory – really angry. Something that would have not had significance a few years ago now takes on additional meanings. I reprove myself mercilessly, just as Oxylus punished Rhaebus. Why? At heart, I rant and rave as Apollo. Angry that I wake up in the *mornings, my joints full of pain. Angry that my children no longer have need of me. Angry that my friends have departed this world. Angry that I can no longer do what I once found commonplace. Angry that I am alone, my wife having forsaken me. Angry that the large part of my life is now well behind me. Angry that I live in a house whose many doors are no longer open to me.*

XXXIII

Now I must retreat to history for you to understand this Heraclide family. Forgive me this long interruption to our narrative, but the Heraclides deserve our attention.

Long before the Heraclides and Pelopides massed on the isthmus, Zeus held a dalliance with beautiful Alcmena. This did not go unnoticed on Olympus. Hera, the wife of Zeus, a goddess known for her jealousy and lack of forgiveness, took it upon herself to get even with her deceitful husband. When Alcmena was about to give birth, Zeus announced great tidings to the assembled gods that a descendant of Perseus was to be born in the Peloponnese:

"This child shall be the greatest king ever of Mycenae and the savior of his people."

Zeus' ruse did not fool Hera. She knew exactly what he was referring to. In her anger and desire to get even with her ever-unfaithful husband, she sought to trick him, of which she was quite capable and had oft done in the past. She visited Ilithyia, the goddess of childbirth. At Hera's request, the goddess retarded Alcmena's pregnancy and hurried the birth of another child in the Peloponnese, also a descendant of Perseus. Eurystheus, son of Sthenelus, son of Perseus, was born a seven-month child to Nicippe, daughter of Pelops. A few months later, Alcaeus, the son of Zeus, was born of Alcmena, for so she named him after his paternal grandfather.

Of all things, a god's oath is most precious. According to the pledge of Zeus, Eurystheus inherited the throne of Mycenae. This was the real inauguration of the war that would spill throughout Hellas: the War of the Families. Although Eurystheus was a descendant of Perseus, he felt more strongly a Pelopide. And Alcaeus felt strongly a Perseid: which would be called "Heraclide" in the future.

It was all Zeus could do to fend off his hateful wife, Hera, throughout Alcaeus' life. At this time, the gods were more active among mortals and took pleasure in making appearances and stirring the caldron of passion among these unfortunates. Hera began immediately at the birth of Alcaeus to make his life as difficult as she could. At eight months, she sent two huge venomous snakes to his crib. Even as a babe, Alcaeus, the son of Zeus, demonstrated amazing virtues. He rose up in his crib and with his small hands strangled both snakes.

With the vindictiveness of Hera, or perhaps because of it, Alcaeus grew up in the likeness of his father. It was plain to anyone with knowledge of the way the gods work that he was the son of Zeus, as the fires of heaven gleamed from his eyes and he never missed with bow or javelin. According to the historian Herodorus, he was a giant of a man, measuring four cubits and one foot* in height, and he was as fair as the heavens, from his curly locks to his heavenly feet; he was beloved among women and worshiped by men. So beautiful was Alcaeus, in truth, that he would sire over one hundred children. Paintings and sculptures do him no justice.

But Zeus had no time for his son. Since even as a boy Alcaeus was too much for his mortal step-father, Amphitryon, to handle, Alcaeus was raised on a cattle farm in the woodlands of Thebes and taught to drive a chariot, wrestle, shoot a bow, fence, and throw missiles. His education was undertaken secretly by the god Hermes and the centaur Chiron, half man and half horse. His mother Alcmena, although she loved her son as much as any mother can, never revealed to him or anyone else his true birthright. And Hera continued to persecute Alcaeus. Apollodorus describes Hera in her own craziness eventually driving Alcaeus mad. He flung his own small children by his wife, Megara, and two children of Iphicles, into the fire and killed them all. Some assert that he killed only his own children. But when he was about to throw his father, innocent and well-meaning Amphitryon, into the fire as well, Athene intervened and threw a stone at him to render him unconscious. Why Athene? Athene saw the injustice of the battle between Zeus and Hera. She pitied the good natured, though cuckolded, Amphitryon. And she loved Alcaeus' potency and pride. From that day on she supported Alcaeus and his family.

---

* Five feet nine inches.

When Alcaeus recovered his reason, his remorse was great, and he condemned himself to exile. He set off for the oracle of Apollo at Delphi to consult the Pythian priestess on where he could find peace from his madness. She told him that he must dwell in Tiryns in Argolis and that for twelve years he must serve Eurystheus, King of Mycenae. This was the same Eurystheus whom Hera had made king through her mischief accelerating his birth. Here we see the workings of the gods, ironic, spiteful, and seemingly not always with the best interests of mortals in mind. The Pythian priestess said that if he accomplished all tasks assigned to him, he would achieve greatness. Finally, she suggested that he change his name.

Alcaeus was reborn Heracles, the glory of Hera: ironically named after his immortal pursuer, Hera, who fought with all her might to send him to the darkest depths of Tartarus rather than to the marbled halls of lord Zeus. The Pythian priestess named the young man appropriately, and here we may see the intelligence and foresight of Apollo, for what challenges us gives us strength. And when tested by the daughter of Cronos and wife of Zeus, one cannot take a middling path. Heracles, forever assaulted and forever attempting to prove his worth to his father, could find no sanctuary from his pursuers. There was no proffered shoulder to rest on, no breast to assuage the hurt, no port of wellbeing in his stormy life. He became the averter of evil and the kallinikos, or glorious conqueror, taking on injustice and dishonor, but often overzealous and fanatical or lion-hearted, as he was called. Heracles lived a life of frustration and anger, never recognized for his greatness in his own time, always contrary, most frequently resorting to violence, and covered from pate to toe with the blood of his enemies.

But as you are well aware, the life and trials of Heracles are considerable and documented in legend and history, in choruses and tragedies, by poets and historians. The verity of his life encompassed great exploits and great madness as befits the mortal son of god. I must refrain from digressing here and allowing myself to be carried away by these legends though they offer us great insight. Let it be said that of all the Greek heroes, he is the greatest, and his life and temperament bear thorough study.

In short, Heracles began his labors in service to Eurystheus, the man whose very life was fabricated of lies and jealousy, and whose very existence was measured unfavorably every day of his life against Heracles, his adversary. And as we know, although the bondsman Heracles became immortal and his legend walks among us to this day, we have little knowledge of the life or achievements of his master Eurystheus. What stronger statement can the gods make? But what concerns us here is that although Heracles performed all the impossible tasks and more given to him by Eurystheus, he was never able to satisfy this man nor win the smallest degree of respect or a moment of respite, just like Sisyphus and his rock.

At Heracles' death, he was promoted to immortality by his father, Zeus. Heracles now resides in heaven and is reconciled with Hera, his namesake and queen of the gods. He lives in eternal happiness, although truly this is difficult to believe in his case. Today, throughout Hellas, people have shrines to pray to lord Heracles. They name their sons after him, so they may bear the mantle of Heracles.

All Hail Heracles, zealous lord of the underprivileged, purveyor of justice and virtue, whose only fault was his passionate pursuit of virtue – at all costs.

But as legend and history converged at the demise of Heracles, Eurystheus was not satisfied and began to battle the children of Heracles. Thus continued the war between the family of the Heraclides and that of the Pelopides. Homer talks of Tlepolemus, the son of Heracles and brother of Hyllus. But he makes no further mention of the Heraclides, except to explain the apotheosis of Heracles, whom Odysseus encounters in the House of Hades.

Aeschylus, Euripides, and Pindar tell tales of Eurystheus' persecution of the children of Heracles following his death. At first, the children hoped to be allowed to live in peace in their home in Tiryns, but they did not reckon on the extreme hatred Eurystheus bore their father. As the King of Mycenae, Eurystheus ordered the execution of Heracles' entire family. Escaping the Peloponnese, Heracles' children first fled to Trachis toward Boreas on the mainland and sought the aid of Ceyx, King of Trachis, who had been a close friend of Heracles and had previously given him shelter and hospitality. But Eurystheus demanded the king return the children and threatened war between the two countries. Trachis was a poor and remote area, and the king had no desire to enter into battle with the most powerful nation in all Hellas and could not offer protection to the children. As a last resort, the children took refuge at the altar of Mercy in Athens, or so Aristophanes tells us. In fact, my research tells me that the suppliant Heraclides were offered asylum and assistance by Demophon, son of Theseus, and king of Athens. Demophon had fought at Troy and was counted among the Greeks in the wooden horse.

Why the Athenians supported the Heraclides is not agreed by all. Heracles had saved his father, Theseus, and there were family ties. But according to the account of several authors, the Athenians shared a distrust of Eurystheus and had a long running battle with Mycenae. They chose to offer the Heraclides protection for their own security, if not for the injustice of the situation as well. Eurystheus marched his army across the Isthmus of Corinth into the heart of Attica and met the army of Athens, which was led by Iolaus, the agèd Athenian general assigned to assist the family, since he was the nephew of Heracles.

As Euripides tells us in his tragedy, prior to the battle the oracles, both public and secret (for the family sought several different oracular opinions), agreed on one sentiment: to win the war the Heraclides must sacrifice a noble maiden to Demeter, daughter of the Titans, Cronos and Ops, and sister of mighty Zeus. Now, I would hazard that much of this story is creative conjecture, for human sacrifice was not condoned at this time nor do we have evidence that it was widespread. Homer makes no mention of it. We do know that the dramatists used it as a dramatic convention. Euripides used it in his drama, Iphigenia at Aulis, where the daughter of Agamemnon, Iphigenia, was sacrificed at Aulis for the benefit of the Achaean ships trapped in the doldrums on their way to Troy. Whatever the case may be, the legends tell of Heracles' lovely daughter, Macaria, who volunteered to meet the death god and by dying save her brothers, family, and country. Eurystheus did not believe the oracle, trusting Hera over Athene, for such was the thinking at that time: namely that Hera was still settled against the Heraclides, while Athene was their only hope. Even in our time, people speak so, but the truth is quite different. Brave Macaria was sacrificed voluntarily and entered the house of Hades with great honor and pride.

The battle between the Athenians and Eurystheus was fought near Marathon, in the gap between the mountains of Pentelicus and Humettus, forming the gateway to the plain of Athens. The strength, armour, armaments, and numbers of the Athenians overwhelmed Eurystheus. The Athenians killed all of his sons: Alexander, Iphimedon, Eurybius, Mentor, and Perimedes, for anger always reaches out to others. The death of Eurystheus, himself, has been reported in various ways. I am particularly attracted by the version of Euripides, who tells of the valor of the agèd Iolaus, the Athenian general. Iolaus prayed to Zeus and Hebe, the daughter of Hera, for one day of youth to battle Eurystheus. His prayer granted, he fought Eurystheus in one-on-one combat and captured and returned him in chains to be executed.

Later versions, perhaps skeptical of this miracle of the return of youth, follow in general the version maintained by the family of Heracles and later attested to by Apollodorus. In this version, the coward Eurystheus refused single combat. The Athenians were victorious on the battlefield and destroyed the army from Argolis. But Eurystheus fled in his chariot. The son of Heracles, Hyllus, pursued him in his chariot and shot him from behind with an arrow, jumping on the body with his dirk to complete the chore. He cut off his head and buried the body in an unmarked grave near the foot of Pentelicus in Attica at Gargettus, on the side of the gap facing the winds of Notus. Hyllus brought Eurystheus' head back to his grandmother, Alcmena, the mother of Heracles, who gouged out the eyes with knitting needles. He then buried the head at the village of Tricorythus, close to the palace of the Heraclides, on the high road beyond the spring of Macaria, so-named after the Heraclide heroine who gave her life for the victory, and the place was henceforth referred to as the "Head of Eurystheus."

And so as was commonly said, "Eurystheus was never king of Mycenae or Argos, since he was never king of himself." And the fate of Eurystheus was to be forever the loathsome master of a great man, and this became known as the "Labor of Eurystheus." The Labors of Heracles and the Labor of Eurystheus, two tests initiated by the gods, were in reality the consequences of the choices two men made during their lives, something we must all consider.

The victory over the Pelopide Eurystheus was only the first of a long struggle of the generations of offspring of Heracles against those of Pelops to return to the Peloponnese over a fifty-year period.

After the death of Eurystheus, the descendants of Heracles argued that they had rightful power in the Peloponnese for three reasons. Their ancestor, Perseus, had founded Mycenae, the largest and most powerful city in the Peloponnese. They had defeated and killed Eurystheus, King of Mycenae. And finally, Heracles himself had conquered the Peloponnese. He restored King Tyndareus, Helen's father and Penelope's uncle, as the ruler of the Lacedaemonians, whose major town was Sparta, also called Lacedaemon. He placed the boy Nestor on the throne of Pylos and Phyleus, son of Augeas, on the throne of Elis. Heracles believed he had created these kingdoms in trust.

Hyllus, son of Heracles, after killing Eurystheus, led the first attempt to return to rule over the Peloponnese. This took place before the war in Troy, as described by Diodorus Siculus, although the history of the first return is sketchy at best. What we know is that the Heraclides successfully captured all of the cities of the Peloponnese. But Hyllus never sat on the throne of Mycenae. Why? Because shortly after their victory, a terrible blackness enveloped the entire region; plague, drought, and earthquakes visited such devastation throughout the whole of the Peloponnese that survival of the region was in doubt. Seeing that they could not rule under such circumstances and believing that the gods were sending a bitter message, the Heraclides retreated to Athens. Hyllus later visited the oracle at Delphi to inquire the cause of the darkness and to see if there was a solution. The oracle declared that the Heraclides had caused the troubles and that the people of the Peloponnese were the victims, all this because the return was too soon after the death of their father, Heracles.

The words of the oracle did not become clear until many generations later. Temenus, the brother of Cresphontes, approached the Oracle of Delphi to seek elucidation. The oracle gave him exactly the same answer that Hyllus had received generations before. Temenus became upset and exhorted against the oracle, for the Heraclides had trusted in the reliability of the prophecy and had followed their instructions to a tee. In an unusual response, but due perhaps to the importance of the matter at hand, the oracle answered that the Heraclides were to blame for not understanding the prophecy. Apollo Delphinius had represented that the Heraclides must delay their return for three crops. These crops were not as crops from the earth, but as generations of men. The prophecy had said that to win they must travel the narrows, which the Heraclides had assumed to be the isthmus, but in point of fact were the narrows in the Bay of Corinth.

Temenus realized that Hyllus was the first generation after the death of Heracles, or the first crop using the terminology of the oracle. He, Temenus, the great great grandson of Heracles, and his brother Cresphontes represented the second crop. Their sons and nephews were the third crop. He felt confident that this third crop would be successful, as all the prophecies pointed in that direction. Temenus and his brother, Cresphontes, would lead the final effort by the third crop of Heraclides to return to rule the Peloponnese. It was this return that sought the aid of Telemachus and Oxylus as counselors-at-war. But now my good wife, Alcathöe, god willing, we must return from history to our story, for Lacestades, King of Sicyon, naive member of the Heraclide family, held sway to his family's future.

XXXIV

In the Peloponnese, Boreas blew kindly across the waters of the gulf. The Heraclides' small, anonymous warship beached on a sandy spit after a night voyage from Crisa. Twenty-five Heraclide sailors immediately surrounded the vessel. Some helped the two horses debark onto the beach, while others acted as guards to protect the vessel, although no one was in evidence. Cresphontes' herald was awaiting their arrival and told them that King Lacestades had agreed to meet them at the crossing of the coast route and the Helisson River, just outside of Sicyon.

Amphion and Deiphontes rode their horses slowly along the coast route in the direction of Apeliotes. Their mounts, the black Arion and the bay Tempe, walked comfortably along the trail, although the horses were caparisoned with bronze head, chest, and thigh pieces. The men carried long cut-and-thrust swords sheathed at their sides, with no bows or javelins. Initially, their blue woolen cloaks covered their shoulders and arms, hiding their upper bodies, but as the golden light of Eos spread across the sky and the warmth of the day began to mount, they pulled the cloth back, exposing their bronze cuirasses and bare arms, with the cloaks falling over the croups of their horses. The rising sun reflected gold off their polished bronze helmets.

As they met farmers bringing their produce into the village, the farmers moved aside to allow the two strangers to pass. They stopped twice to wait as herders moved goats and sheep across the road to new pasturage. As they approached the river crossing, the trail became more traveled with farmers and herders walking in the direction of Sicyon, who mostly ignored the riders or gave them furtive glances. When they came to the river crossing, the riders dismounted, led their mounts off the trail toward the sea, hobbled them, and waited alongside the shallow stream beneath willows and tamarisks. Beyond the closed marsh, calm waves broke along the shore, and far across the gulf they glimpsed the mountains of Boeotia and Mount Helicon. Drinking dilute wine and eating dried cheese and bread, they waited. They waited long into the afternoon, their apprehension slowly rising.

Finally, a large group of riders arrived from the direction of Sicyon at a rapid trot, raising dust and scattering people on the trail. They halted at the crossing. About twenty horsemen in the vermilion uniform of Corinth and an officer looked about, their horses breathing heavily and stamping their hooves. Amphion and Deiphontes watched anxiously as the soldiers sighted them and dismounted. The Corinthian officer and an older, well-built man, dressed in dark robes and a mariner's cap, turned their horses to ride down toward them.

"We may not get the dialogue we anticipated," Amphion whispered to Deiphontes.

The officer and the older man approached cautiously, dismounted, and led their horses by the reins. Deiphontes looked startled. He bounded to his feet and strode up to them rapidly. He embraced the officer.

"Amphion, this is my son-in-law, married to my daughter, Orsobia: Pamphylus, son of Aegimius." And then he turned to the other man. "I am Deiphontes, son of Antimachus, son of Thrasyanor, son of Ctesippus, son of Heracles."

"I am Lacestades, King of Sicyon, son of King Hippolytus, son of King Rhopalus, son of King Phaestus, son of the indomitable Heracles." Lacestades' close-cropped beard was still dark and heavy.

"And how is my daughter?" Deiphontes asked of Pamphylus.

"She is well," Pamphylus replied hesitantly. "Our third child is on the way. The boys are off in Lacedaemon. They are growing up rapidly. I regret that we have not visited Attica. We have been occupied." He stopped as Amphion walked up to where the others stood and greeted them both.

"I am Amphion, son of Telemachus. Come join us in our meager rations."

The four men seated themselves uncomfortably among the rocks overlooking the marsh. The unexpected appearance of Pamphylus added a shrill note of uncertainty. Amphion glanced up to the road where the other horsemen waited next to their chargers. They were well armed with lances and swords.

Deiphontes began speaking rapidly to Lacestades. "We bring greetings from Cresphontes and Temenus, sons of Aristomachus and leaders of the Heraclides in Attica."

"I have never had the opportunity of meeting these men. I have heard of them of course," Lacestades said.

"We have a message for you," Deiphontes continued. "As you know, the Heraclides are intent on returning to their rightful home and to reinstate the family into positions of leadership within the Peloponnese. They choose to do this without evil intent and with the least amount of damage or injury to the people."

"What makes you think," Pamphylus said, "you can dance like Terpsichore into the Peloponnese as women do at the festival of Thesmophoria and claim rightful proprietorship?"

"Forgive me," Deiphontes said, turning to Pamphylus, "but I have lost contact with my daughter. What is your role?"

"I am general of the guard and defender of Tisamenus, King of Mycenae and Argos. I was chief of the palace guard for Orestes, son of Agamemnon."

Amphion and Deiphontes glanced at each other, arriving at the same conclusion.

"You must have failed your original role," Amphion said, "for Orestes lies buried in Tegea in Arcadia."

"He died unfortunately of a snake bite in Oresteum," Pamphylus replied defensively. "Otherwise, we would now rule all the Peloponnese, and we would not be having this conversation."

"The works of the gods are indeed mysterious," Amphion said.

"You must take after your grandfather," Pamphylus said, "whose smooth words won fame in Troy, while all of his countrymen went straight to Hades."

"And now you serve Tisamenus, a mere shadow of his father, Orestes," Amphion replied.

"Tisamenus learned from his father and is a statesman as Agamemnon was. But there was no greater man than Orestes, who overcame great adversity to rule over a larger empire than any man before him."

"But," Deiphontes said, "you are not from this region."

"No, I came from Boeotia to Athens and then to Corinth, where I joined the guard. But I am still uncertain as to what exactly your message is."

"We want to send a message to King Tisamenus," Amphion replied. "We are willing to offer him safe passage to the country of his choice, as long as he leaves the Peloponnese peaceably."

"What? Who are you to make such an offer?" Pamphylus asked arrogantly. "What has he to gain from such an offer?"

"His life," Amphion replied.

"Ah, you come into the hornet's nest to seek their submission. I think not. Tisamenus would have my stones if we took you to see him with that message...or allowed you to leave for that matter, my young friend." He looked directly at Amphion.

"We have come as ambassadors," Deiphontes said, "seeking a peaceful conclusion before many innocent people lose their lives. You are married to my daughter. I am grandfather to your children."

"You may be surprised," Pamphylus replied, ignoring Deiphontes and confronting Amphion, "who will be the first innocents to lose their lives."

All the men arose simultaneously, backing away from each other.

"We came here freely, seeking discussion," Amphion said. "We will not surrender without making it difficult for you." And his hand strayed to the hilt of his sword.

"You came here," said Pamphylus, "with your fancy swords and costumes, like two jackdaws, hoping that we would welcome you. We are not the idiots you take us for."

Lacestades held up his arms. "Friends, before we go too far along this road of no return, allow me to set you right. You are guests in Sicyon and not Corinth. I am the king of this region. First, Tisamenus will not welcome any discussion of his capitulation. That will not sit well for any of us. He sees himself in an unassailable position. He also is prepared to defend and repulse anyone who would seek to attack his reign over the Peloponnese. Secondly, it is not our intention to keep you here as our prisoners. That would not be right, and I am sure that Pamphylus would agree with this once he calms down. Finally, I am an ancestor of Heracles, although I have never thought of myself as a Heraclide, for no such term was employed within our family.

"But let me tell you a story of our family that might shed some light on our position here in Sicyon. Bear with us a moment, Pamphylus. All his life, Heracles, the son of Zeus, was deeply persecuted by Athene and Hera, and as a result he became quite mad and killed his wife, Megara, and all their children. Once he regained his senses, though, he went to Delphi to seek information from the oracle on how to recover his sanity and life. The priestess advised him to retire to Tiryns and there to serve Eurystheus, King of Mycenae, which he did."

"What is this about?" Pamphylus demanded angrily.

"Pamphylus," Lacestades replied, "you may join your fellow soldiers if this bores you. Or you may remain quiet for a moment and allow me to speak. Do you believe history has no import?"

Pamphylus stared at Lacestades with mistrust, but did not reply.

"Now, once Heracles met King Eurystheus of Mycenae, he knew that to defy the king would mean a return to madness and most likely death. So he committed to perform ten labors for Eurystheus. As we all know, he performed all his labors successfully, and these labors were of such a magnitude that even one of them would have been more than any mortal could hope to accomplish. And he completed all ten...and more, for Eurystheus demanded additional labors of him.

"During the final labor, number twelve, he went into Hades to bring Cerberus, the hound of Hades, back to earth. And this may have been the most difficult labor, for he had to face the lord of death himself and then take his ferocious dog from his domain. But he did so. And what happened when he returned to Eurystheus? He gave the dog to the king? No, the king shrank from the horrifying dog as any man would. Heracles recognized that the king had never wanted him to achieve any of his labors and this last one least of all. Heracles realized that he had accomplished all his tasks. There was nothing more to do. So he returned Cerberus to Hades, left the service of the king, and was given forgiveness by Athene and Hera and peace of mind.

"But King Eurystheus' unreasonable hatred of Heracles continued to fester. After the death of Heracles, Eurystheus threatened the children of Heracles, and he led an army to kill them. The Heraclides and Athenians prepared to defend themselves, and the two armies met on the isthmus to do battle. Hyllus, the brother to my ancestor, Phaestus, challenged Eurystheus in single combat to avoid bloodshed, and Eurystheus agreed. The contest was imbalanced from the start. Hyllus killed Eurystheus easily and became King of Mycenae. All of this occurred because Hera deserted Eurystheus. Hera, who had protected Eurystheus since his birth, left him to fight his own battle. She reconciled with Heracles, and as we know, Heracles is the immortal son-in-law of Hera.

"Now, my point is this. King Tisamenus will never allow the return of the Heraclides. That will not happen. Our final message is to Cresphontes. Tell him my words: Cresphontes must follow the will of Zeus. Now go and do not turn back, or you will come to regret it."

Pamphylus said nothing, but watched with irritation as Amphion and Deiphontes mounted their horses and rode slowly up to the road, turning in the direction of Aristonautae. The horses nickered at the unfamiliar smell of the horses of the Corinthian soldiers, who watched the two men spitefully. When they had moved out of sight and sound, they kicked their horses into a gallop, hoping to gain time before Pamphylus changed his mind.

They sprinted to the beached warship at full gallop. They did not stop to listen for the sound of hooves. When they arrived at the warship, they roused the sailors from their slumber in the declining afternoon sun. The horses were loaded, steaming and panting, and the oars dug into the waves as the ship moved rapidly off the coast. They did not relax until they were far offshore, although the captain was concerned with the possibility of Corinthian warships once they were out in the channel.

"Well, that did not go well," Amphion said to Deiphontes.

"No." Deiphontes agreed. "I met this man, Pamphylus, only once before at the wedding, so I did not get to know him, but I feel great sorrow for my daughter. He asked for a very small dowry, and they both were too young in my opinion. Athens is like a love goddess that seduces all within her confines. Well, Orsobia has made her bed. Yet, my friend, we did receive our message from Lacestades."

"How is that?"

"Lacestades is a Heraclide, and I liked this man. His message to Cresphontes was in his story of the labors of Heracles. As Lacestades knew, Pamphylus has no knowledge of this family and its history. In fact, just like the guard he is, he closed his ears to the tale. But even if he had listened, he would not have understood nor seen all the holes in its rendering."

"I am no expert, but I listened."

"And you did not hear anything?"

"I heard many names, but I did not hear a message."

"I will be quick," Deiphontes smiled. "And I will test my thoughts with my uncles. Though there are many versions of the stories of Heracles, the family has but one. First, the two armies did not meet on the isthmus, but in Marathon. The coward Eurystheus refused single combat with Hyllus. The army of the Athenians emerged victorious against the forces of Eurystheus. Everyone knows that, but perhaps not Pamphylus. Eurystheus attempted to flee after the battle, and Hyllus killed him escaping. That is a famous story. Hyllus presented Eurystheus' head to Heracles' mother, who poked out his eyes. Hyllus never became King of Mycenae, for the Heraclides were never able to consolidate their rule.

"Pamphylus might have known this if he had thought about it, but his mind was occupied with thoughts of killing you. After the death of Eurystheus, the throne was taken by Atreus, the son of Pelops and uncle of Eurystheus, and the throne remains in the family of Pelops. Zeus always intended the throne of Mycenae for Heracles, from the day of his conception to the day of his death. Lacestades knows it and is retelling us that fact. Finally, Hera never deserted Eurystheus. In Lacestades' tale, replace the name Eurystheus by Tisamenus. Tisamenus will battle on the isthmus, lose his life, and the throne of Mycenae will pass to a Heraclide."

"If you are right, then Lacestades is a willing ally," Amphion replied excitedly. "I saw it in his eyes."

Such was the uncertain conclusion to a noteworthy day.

In the darkness of night, the warship beached safely at Cirrha, without encountering a Corinthian long ship. Amphion and Deiphontes returned to the palace early the next morning. The waters of the gulf had been rough on the return, for a storm was impending, and they had secured little rest as the thunderbolts of Zeus lit the sky. As a result, once in their own beds, they slept well into the afternoon of the next day. It was not until evening that they were summoned to join the senior Heraclides.

Cresphontes, Temenus, Telemachus, and Oxylus sat at a single couch, their faces exhibiting great displeasure. They had reached the time when the soul is uncovered, and each man is naked before the others. The air was thick with rancor. No one was cheerful or content. The table before them was empty, save a few chalices for water, and the hearth was cold. The doors were barred, and the servants were out of sight. Barely recognizing the entrance of Amphion and Deiphontes, Cresphontes asked immediately for a report of the meeting with Lacestades. Deiphontes described the entire incident, the unexpected attendance of Pamphylus, and carefully repeated in detail the words of Lacestades. Here the members of the family had the advantage, for it was their history.

"These are not the words of someone who is against us," Temenus said. "Under the eye of Pamphylus, Lacestades could only give a coded message. I think Deiphontes has correctly interpreted the words. Otherwise, why would he repeat so many simple falsehoods of a commonly known family history?"

"We know nothing of this man, Lacestades," Cresphontes said. "For all we know, he may be leading us into a trap, intentionally or ignorantly, just as happened before with the second crop in Patrae. We cannot trust this garbled message. The only route into the Peloponnese is via the isthmus."

"We are not prepared for a direct assault on Corinth," Oxylus said. "We have not trained for such an eventuality. All this has been discussed before."

"Wait," Telemachus said. "We must make this message of Lacestades clear. There can be no doubt." He turned to address Amphion and Deiphontes, who continued to stand before the others. "Did Sicyon appear to be on the defensive? Were soldiers in evidence? Were there any fortifications?"

Deiphontes replied: "We did not enter the city of Sicyon, but were close by on the outskirts. There were no preparations or soldiers on the route to Aristonautae. The ship lay at the shore without attracting any undue notice. The people barely recognized our presence as we rode along the route. And the only soldiers we saw were the Corinthians with Pamphylus; Lacestades appeared to be on his own, without attendants. We waited a long time for Lacestades to arrive, perhaps meaning that he was coming from Corinth, not Sicyon."

"That would agree with the herald," Telemachus said, "who said he found King Lacestades in Corinth in the company of others. Now, most importantly, you must interpret the message."

Deiphontes spoke carefully: "Lacestades final words were, 'Cresphontes must follow the will of Zeus.' Zeus always planned for Heracles to take the throne of Mycenae. Zeus never wanted Eurystheus in power. I think that is our answer."

Cresphontes dismissed the two men. "You may leave. Now, we need to come up with our strategy. We are in a smaller group that can make decisions as you required. It is time."

"What of the message?" Telemachus demanded.

"It is safe to say that Lacestades is on our side," Temenus replied.

"That seems possible," Cresphontes admitted without enthusiasm.

"Then we have discovered the back door to the Peloponnese...by the narrows."

"What are you talking about?" Cresphontes demanded with a tone of irritation.

"I am talking about victory over the Peloponnese," Telemachus said.

Telemachus and Oxylus then described a plan they had discussed based on the outcome of the visit to the Peloponnese. Part of the first infantry division composed of the "Greens" under the command of the twins, Procles and Eurysthenes, would march on the isthmus through the town of Megara in full colors. This short division would appear to be a conventional army, with heavy infantry, lances, and large shields. They would not engage the enemy. They would scatter the people off the roads and make a nuisance of themselves, positioning themselves before the ditch on the isthmus. They would make plenty of noise. They would be slow and take no action save defensive if needs be, and even then they would back off.

The Red division, under the command of Oxylus and the direction of Aletes, Phalces, and Autolycus, and the full cavalry, under the command of Telemachus, Amphion, and Deiphontes, would be transported to Aristonautae by night. The two divisions and their horses and supplies could be transported across the gulf in three nights of constant work. This naval action would be critical, for without the element of surprise, the plan would fail. Temenus would direct this naval effort and afterwards blockade the entrance of Corinth by sea.

The show of force along the isthmus should occupy Tisamenus, while the main body would strike unexpectedly from the back door in the direction of Zephyrus. The success of this line of attack would depend on the Green fighters on the isthmus...and their leaders.

"This is the strategy?" Cresphontes groaned in disbelief.

"Yes," Oxylus replied.

"We will take the isthmus," Cresphontes shouted. "We will be home free. Tisamenus has placed the better part of his defenses there."

Here Telemachus interrupted. "My father once described to me the state of the men in the Wooden Horse..."

"I cannot see the relevance..." Cresphontes began, but was interrupted by Temenus.

"Allow him to speak."

Telemachus continued: "Fifty men sat enclosed in a tiny space at the mercy of the Trojans, listening to insults from without and their own devious voices from within their heads. Death was at hand. Their hearts deserted them. They sniveled and their bodies quaked with fear. We are these men now. This is the point. If we are to take on Tisamenus directly, we will be defeated, and many soldiers will lose their lives. We have one chance, but we must work together, and we must not lose heart or we will all be lost."

"Brother, we have come this far," Temenus said. "We must listen to our counselors."

"May you rue your blindness," Cresphontes shot back fiercely.

"Then perhaps we should postpone our invasion," Temenus replied.

"Yes, you would like that."

"We have come this far." Temenus said angrily. "We must listen to our advisors. The gods know this. Surely, you can see. Never have I undermined you, my brother. Always the dutiful younger brother. Our father spoiled you. I spoiled you. I stood by while our brother Aristodemus was killed in the second attempt. I am older now. My own child died for you. My wife will not speak to me. I deserted our troops in Patrae at your insistence to my everlasting shame. Now, I say to you, listen to our counselors. We will do as they say. Or, all this will be ended here and now..."

"What I do see," Cresphontes screamed at the counselors, "is that should this plan fail, I will hold you all responsible for its failure. You will wish that you had never met Cresphontes or any Heraclide for that matter. You will view the statues of Heracles worshiped throughout Hellas, and you will weep."

Cresphontes stormed out of the room, turning only to say: "We will begin mobilization tomorrow."

But the morrow broke rainy and stormy, with Eos out of sight and the angry winds stirring up the seas across the gulf and battering the trees on the hillsides, where the soldiers hunkered in their tents and the horses dug their hooves into the muddy soil. No one was prepared to mobilize.

XXXV

Meanwhile in the palace in Corinth, Tisamenus and his advisors met with his generals, Pamphylus and his brother, Dymas. The powerless kings of Corinth, Doridas and Hyanthidas, were not in attendance, as Tisamenus did not cherish their counsel, and they were not integral to his defense.

"I do not trust Lacestades," Pamphylus was saying. "The Sicyonians are too independent, and Lacestades has a history with the Heraclides. They seemed to have much in common in their conversation."

"How so?" Tisamenus asked. "Are you saying that they are acting together? What was the purpose of this meeting?"

"Amphion, son of Telemachus, said they wanted to send you a message."

"A message?"

"Yes, Sire. They wanted to offer you safe passage from Argolis."

"And what was your response?" Tisamenus asked, amused.

"I said their suggestion was out of the question and you would not meet with them."

"That was the end of it?"

"No. They went on with this legend of Heracles and his labors and clash with Eurystheus and the war with Athens…"

"What exactly did they say?" Tisamenus asked.

Pamphylus hesitated, for in truth he could not recall the story. "Lacestades described the labors of Heracles just as the bards do and went on and on. He told of the killing of Eurystheus by some ancestor…Hyllus…and Hera and Zeus. He said they should stay in Attica."

"Were you there? Or are you making this up?" Tisamenus demanded angrily.

"I was there…"

"And then you let them depart? Did you not think that they might provide useful information to us? Are we so proud that we allow our enemies to come into our midst and then walk away? You are my general in charge of the defense of my rule. What were you thinking?"

"Lacestades…"

"Lacestades. Who is he? He is my subject. He has no importance."

"I saw no threat from them…"

"No threat? And for this my father Orestes selected you and placed his life in your hands? Do you not perceive the importance of Sicyon to our defenses? I am surrounded by morons. I want Sicyon buttoned up as tight as your wife's reticule."

When the earth was born from chaos, some god – it is not known which – separated the land from the sea and the air. He distributed the mountains, woods, rivers, and plains. He took especial care in forming the Peloponnese. For here is a blessèd land; as Hesiod says, "a land where you must strip to sow, strip to plough, and strip to reap." It is a land of contrasts: high mountains divide the regions, acting as rugged barriers, separating wide stretches of coastline and creating broad swaths of fertile valleys. The Peloponnese is what is called a near-island. The ancients likened it to a mulberry leaf, both because of its shape and its numerous mulberry trees. The thin petiole of the leaf is a narrow neck of land, the isthmus, separating the waters of the Gulf of Corinth and the Saronic Gulf and attaching the leaf to the mainland of Greece. But more notably, the isthmus separates the power and influence of mainland Hellas, Thebes and Athens, from our Peloponnesian states: Corinth, Mycenae, Argos, Lacedaemon, and Pylos.

The isthmus has never been a happy crossing. This narrow strip of land serves as an entrance to the Peloponnese, but also a barrier. During times of war, it is built up to prevent entry; in times of peace it is a thoroughfare for trade and commerce and the movement of peoples. But because of this same narrow, perilous entry, the glorious Peloponnesian landscape was preserved, and the cradle of our civilization flourished.

The stormy weather ended as quickly as it had arrived. It lasted barely two days. When gold-sandaled Eos arose the following morning, her warm light fell upon calm waters and a clear sky, and the heat of day ascended to dry the grapes on the vine that were rapidly maturing. Word was passed down to all the troops that they should prepare to evacuate the camp. The infantry battalions made ready to march out. The cavalry prepared their horses.

Seven battalions of foot soldiers, the "Greens," moved out for the march through Boeotia to Megara and the Isthmus of Corinth. The distance was some six hundred stadia* and would take four or five days. They intentionally set a slow pace to allow ample time for the naval forces to transport the cavalry and infantry across the gulf. Also, their pace would allow time for information on their movement to flow across the isthmus to the palace in Corinth. Information of the movement of the rest of the infantry and the cavalry by the naval forces would be held in check by a blockade of the harbor of Cirrha and movement only by night.

The twins, Procles and Eurysthenes, were in foul moods, for their assignment was not at all to their liking. They blamed the counselors for this, and they faulted their uncles for acquiescing to this travesty. They also were upset by the selection of battalions, since all among them could see that they were left with the rag-tag tail-ends of the fighters. And after all their training with swords and javelins and bows and arrows, the fighters were issued heavy lances and large shields as though they were headed off to fight the Persians. Of course, they were told only that they were to go to the trench across the isthmus and there to wait for further orders.

The cavalry was prepared to ride by mid-afternoon. The skilled "Red" infantry battalions departed on foot. The cavalry followed them

---

* 70 miles.

directly to Crisa, through the small town to the harbor. People along the way and in the town had long known that an offensive was being prepared, but once they saw the fighters and horsemen moving across the landscape in uniform, they were shocked at the level of the effort. They had seen armies gather and march across the land. They had sent off their own husbands, sons, cousins, and neighbors to fight in distant battles. But they had never been at the center of a conflagration and seen all the faces and heard all the noises and smelled all the stench of men and animals as they moved through. No one cheered or smiled as the men passed. It was not known what this effort was for, and in any case as everyone knew, none of them ever gained from war. War brought only hardship and sorrow. So as the soldiers moved through, the people prayed to the gods that the battle occur somewhere distant.

Telemachus and Oxylus wished each other god speed in their sleeping chamber as they prepared to depart early in the morning.

"Well, this has been a long time coming," Oxylus said.

"Have we decided to do this?"

"I suppose we have, although I have gained no more trust in these Heraclides."

"Some decisions at best left to the gods."

"Perhaps. Victory will be its own reward."

"May the gods go with you," Telemachus said.

"And with you as well, my friend."

"I embraced my sons this morning," Telemachus said. "I was sorry to see them so full of energy rather than dread and trepidation. This is a job for young men, who do not respect yet the full value of what they are hazarding. We have lived too long, my friend. I would give anything to have them at home minding the sheep. And should anything happen to them, Polycasté will blame me, and rightfully so. Pray that I am the one chosen and not them."

"On the day of battle, the Hittites always said, 'The gods willing, I will die for the honor of my family today.' I have no similar feeling. My only family, Telemachus, is your own. I have learned from you more than you realize. I owe my life to you. I hope you understand. I will never pray for myself, but I pray for you and your sons."

"Thank you, Oxylus, my brother."

"It is foretold," Oxylus declared, "we will be drinking wine from our own vineyards soon enough."

And, with that, the two men embraced, kissed, and left to join their troops.

And what were the gods doing at this time as mortals initiated the largest conflict Hellas had ever known? Since the gods have seen wars many times before and can see far into the future, they ignored the mortals as they set out. The gods joyously shared their ambrosia and nectar in the glorious palace of their father. Although the gods will willingly take sides on occasion, as we have seen, on this day they were at peace.

Zeus, lord of mortals and immortals alike, was content to have his children with him, enjoying themselves rather than confronting one another on the field of battle, all save Hermes, who as always was away on some stealthy mission known only to him. Zeus' thoughts were far from the mortals traipsing across the muddy shores of Boeotia or making a cold watery landing in Aristonautae. He knew full well the troubles and sorrows they would face, but then that was the fate of mortals.

XXXVI

Pamphylus went immediately to Sicyon, following another regrettable interview with King Tisamenus based on the news of the approaching Heraclides on the isthmus. He had fortified himself with sufficient troops and enough wine to have no worries about achieving his task, which was to bring Lacestades back to Corinth. King Lacestades eyed Pamphylus without respect or warmth. They were both slaves to the king, certainly, and both desirous of continuing along the path of life, enjoying their status and families. However, Lacestades, king of Sicyon, was born and raised a Sicyonian, a descendant of Heracles to boot, and a subterranean flow of independence surged through his veins: so far from god, so close to Corinth and Mycenae.

When Pamphylus first ordered him in no uncertain terms to join him in a conversation with Tisamenus, the first thought in Lacestades' mind was how to postpone this unpleasant visit. Pamphylus would have none of it. The doltish Corinthian guards accompanying Pamphylus reminded Lacestades that Corinth was not a force to be trifled with in terms of resolution or military strength. Sicyon had troops that could be numbered on no more than several hands, and these troops were farm boys who served mainly to preserve order during markets or festivals and to settle occasional arguments among neighbors.

"You know," said Lacestades, hoping to shape the simple mind of Pamphylus, "Tisamenus is not the man that Orestes was. The son has never tasted the acrid flavor of struggle and adversity as his father did. He has frittered his life on tope and young boys. And now we are expected to follow him on this slippery, asphodel-lined path to Hades. I cannot just leave the affairs of state to join him, particularly at a time like this.

"Even during the time of the Trojan War, when the Sicyonians were subject to the whims of King Agamemnon," Lacestades continued, "most of us were not warlike. We prefer to stay at home rather than go to war. Our city is notorious for its independence from the rulers of Argolis. We did not enjoy our proximity to the rule of Agamemnon, for we saw him as a tyrant, taking as much as he could and never returning anything to the people. The people of Sicyon are convinced that Tisamenus is determined to place Sicyon under his thumb, as he has many of the other states of the Peloponnese. A bad neighbor is a great plague. Let me tell you a story, my friend Pamphylus, since you are a Boeotian, if I am not mistaken."

Pamphylus said nothing, but his eyes rolled above his flat nose.

"Echepolus, son of Anchises, was a wealthy trader conducting business in Sicyon. His family had lived here for many generations, and he had a reputation as a man who had made his own success by diligence and hard work and by knowing who his friends were and giving and receiving gifts as a natural part of his business. If a man would stoop to help him in his affairs, he would send him a great golden ewer or some godly statue, but in return he would look for assistance at some time in the future. Agamemnon came to the house of Echepolus one day and suggested that he participate in the war in Troy. Echepolus offered to give Agamemnon the gift of his finest and fleetest mare, Aethe by name, on the condition that he would be relieved of any duty to go to Troy. Agamemnon eyed the horse and pictured himself seated upon this beautiful animal before his army. He gladly accepted the offer. Echepolus did not go to Troy, but lived his life in ease during the Trojan War and continued to amass his wealth, until he strangled on a mouthful of mutton and went straightaway to Hades.

"In Echepolus' place at Troy, though, Leonteus, of the race of Ares, joined the coalition. He is said to have contributed nineteen ships to the allied fleet. And who should ride the mare Aethe in Troy, but Menelaus himself."

"You will come with me," Pamphylus replied.

Evidently, Tisamenus had allowed no discretion in Pamphylus' assignment. This guard of guards, and now a general, would brook no deviation from the command of his senior officer. If there was one attribute of Pamphylus that could be admired, if that is the appropriate word, it was his capacity to follow through on a specific command. This may have been the one characteristic that facilitated his career as the personal bodyguard of Orestes. There is no other way for such an imperfect man to move so far within the ranks. Lacestades had hoped at best he might delay the meeting. He had lived many lives before this day and had some remaining.

"I will leave tomorrow morning, as I have scheduled an assembly with my council this afternoon. For as you know, there are rumors of an invasion from the direction of Skiron. And we have to prepare our defenses."

"Now," said Pamphylus.

So Lacestades found himself rudely interrupted and without recourse. Since Pamphylus had not brought an extra mount, the King of Sicyon had to ride his faithful mule into Corinth accompanied by a heavily-armed contingent of King Tisamenus' guard. As they rode, he considered his situation and formulated various tactics within his mind, but as King of Sicyon, he had successfully navigated similar shoals before with Agamemnon and Orestes, and he felt he could do it again. Only, this time he was less sure how his fortune would come out.

When they arrived at the palace in Corinth, circumstances had changed. People were rushing about, both civilian and military, for it seemed that the invasion had begun. They were ushered immediately into the king's throne room, which was buzzing with activity. Tisamenus was in a state of agitation. He gave out immediate decisions and instructions like fig cakes at a festival. People streamed into the room, priorities were established, and then they waited patiently for their brief encounter with the king. Doridas and Hyanthidas, the titular rulers of Corinth stood beside Tisamenus, but they were not a part of the decision-making queue.

"At last," Tisamenus said to Lacestades and Pamphylus. "We are getting many reports of movements of the Heraclides and their numbers, but we know that they are at the Sanctuary of Poseidon on the isthmus. They have massed heavy infantry troops along the great trench. Your brother is at the front at this moment. I do not know how long this face-off will last, but I am going myself to view the scene before the sun sets this evening. In the meantime, we must assure ourselves of our defenses as Zephyrus blows. We must have the enemy in sight. No surprises." He stopped, expecting a reply, but when none was forthcoming, he continued with irritation.

"I am reluctant to conclude that the Heraclides expect to best us across the isthmus, for we have over five thousand of our best troops there at this moment, with more to come. We have sufficient armament. And we have the ability to fall back if needs be behind the gates of the city. Further, we have a large contingent from Arcadia joining us. We have heard rumors of troops crossing the narrows at night, although our black ships have seen nothing. What progress have you two made as to your defense of Sicyon?"

Lacestades waited for Pamphylus to speak, but the man made no such effort. Undoubtedly, Pamphylus had fulfilled his command, bringing Lacestades before the king, and was now awaiting further orders. He may also have felt that silence offered him the best chance for surviving the wrath of Tisamenus.

Lacestades began to speak slowly. "The defenses of Sicyon are in place. We are not a large town, as you are aware, but we have taken some measures. As of this morning, we had no reports of any movements of any kind, other than it being market day obviously. Everything is in order." He looked at Pamphylus for an instant, who remained rigid and did not return his glance. "We were interrupted from an assembly this afternoon to discuss ways to further strengthen our forces."

"What measures have you taken?"

"We have set out a blockade of the road from Aristonautae, and several vessels under our control are monitoring ship movements along the coast."

"Have you seen anything? Do you feel you can halt a secondary invasion of the Heraclides?"

"I cannot foresee the strength of their army, but we can surely stop a small force and delay a larger one until reinforcements arrive from Corinth." He hesitated and then continued. "But as you would expect of him, Pamphylus has thoroughly reviewed our defenses when he met with the Heraclides and again this morning. And we have discussed his approach to improving our defenses. You can depend on his knowledge of coastal defenses and effective barricades. We Sicyonians are simple farmers and fishermen and have only limited knowledge of these things."

"Yes, you are a simple man, I am sure." But his head turned quickly to his general. "What say you, Pamphylus?"

"Sicyon. Yes, Sicyon is prepared. You can depend on that."

"You seem uncertain. I need no uncertainty today of all days. Do not amuse yourself thinking that you can pull the blinders over my eyes, while your brother, Dymas, is in the thick of things on the isthmus."

"The defenses of Sicyon will be in place this afternoon."

"Are you certain?"

"Yes, sire."

"Then once again, and I am growing tired of this, allow me to assist you, for you two are like roasted Asian pheasants stuffed with horse manure. I want one thousand troops blockading the Sicyon road. In addition, send a large contingent to Aristonautae. Take all the palace guards and five battalions from Dymas. That will leave us short at the palace, but I will be joining Dymas on the isthmus with my personal guard. No movement takes place from that direction. Do you hear me? Not a farmer. Not a hind. Not a hare. And I want messengers to bring me news of any sightings or encounters there immediately. If a bird chirps, I want to be notified. You may go, but make sure the soldiers are in place this day. Your life depends on it. Both of your lives."

"Thank you," Pamphylus replied weakly.

The two men left the king, as others began instantly competing for his attention, but they heard him shout at one of the soldiers around him:

"But what of the horses? Why would a heavy infantry need thousands of horses?"

Pamphylus did not stay with Lacestades, but left him rudely with a simple remark: "Return to Sicyon immediately and make sure that what you told Tisamenus is true for the sake of your life and the lives of your family. I will be there shortly."

Lacestades rode by himself through the streets of Corinth, his mule familiar with the route. At the agora, the vendors had departed. The stalls were deserted, and the shops had been closed and boarded. A few people scurried past paying close attention to their errands, but for the most part the streets were empty. Initially, the route to Sicyon was crowded with people leaving Corinth, heading for their home towns, family residences, or just moving off into the hills. By the half-way mark at the lagoon, Lacestades saw no one; an unnatural silence prevailed along the tree-lined trail. As he came to the outskirts of Sicyon, he was met by a large contingent of heavily armed soldiers wearing Aegean blue cloaks. They waited for him to approach and signaled for him to dismount. A short, broad-built man approached him, his dark eyes flashing and a sword in his right hand.

"I am Aletes, son of Hippotes, commander of the Heraclides. Who might you be?"

"I am Lacestades, King of Sicyon."

"Come with me. We have been expecting you."

Lacestades noticed that there were even larger numbers of mounted troops along the route as they entered the city. The troopers cantered by quickly, moving in the direction of Corinth. Large contingents of infantry marched by and were camped on the streets. As they entered the town square, Lacestades saw a large campaign tent with soldiers coming and going. The square itself was filled with soldiers, and the villagers were not in evidence. Aletes led him into the tent.

"Sirs," Aletes announced, "I would like to introduce Lacestades, the great King of Sicyon." Everyone turned in his direction. "Our officers: Deiphontes, son of Antimachus, whom I believe you know, and Phalces, son of Temenus. These others are our advisors, Oxylus, son of Haemon, and Telemachus, son of Odysseus."

Oxylus approached Lacestades. "Please excuse the manners of our young friend, Aletes. I am Oxylus, general of the infantry, and this is Telemachus, hipparch. Let me explain to you the situation. We are in control of Sicyon. We have encircled the town. And the people have been very cooperative. In return, we have treated everyone with deference. No one has been harmed. But you now must make a choice. You can cooperate and become a partner to the kingdom, or you can wait and see the outcome. If we fail, you may preserve your position of power, although I would be highly surprised if Tisamenus allowed you to continue living. But if we succeed, and you have not joined us, you will be forced to leave or worse. We were uncertain of your message to Deiphontes, but some saw it as an offer of assistance or alliance. Excuse me. Phalces return to administer the road block toward Apeliotes."

"I thought my message would be understandable to any Heraclide," Lacestades said. "Obviously, the newer generation does not know these legends. Anyway, I have no great love for Tisamenus, and he is no friend of Sicyon. I welcome the offer of joining your coalition, assuming that I will retain my throne in Sicyon."

"Yes," Aletes replied. "We can assure you of that, although you will become allied with the King of Corinth."

"The choice is not a difficult one," Lacestades said. "I believe my message was that I support the return of the Heraclides and will gladly join forces. But allow me to warn you: Pamphylus, general of the Corinthians, is close by with a contingent of palace guards, about a thousand soldiers, lightly armed. Pamphylus is a moron and will not be a worthy opponent."

"Aletes," Oxylus interrupted, "move two battalions forward to support Phalces. Move quickly. We must intercept Pamphylus. Not a single soldier must be allowed to escape back to Corinth."

"Better that I remain here," Aletes responded.

"Perhaps you did not hear me," Oxylus replied strongly, facing Aletes. Everyone waited.

Finally, Aletes left the tent, though reluctantly and in a state of rage.

"Deiphontes and Amphion," Oxylus continued, "take Dardanos' tribe* of cavalry into the hills of Corinth, allow Pamphylus to pass unhindered along the way, and then follow him from the rear, blocking any retreat." The troopers left quickly. "Anything further you can tell us?" Oxylus asked.

"Yes, Tisamenus is visiting the troops on the isthmus as we speak. He has positioned five thousand troops along the trench across the isthmus, and he believes that the direction of Sicyon is protected. Also, he is expecting a large contingent from Arcadia to reinforce the isthmus. I would hazard that they could double his forces. One other thought. The city of Corinth is deserted and offers no defenses at this moment. Tisamenus is depending on using the fortifications of the city as a fallback position."

"Very good," Oxylus replied. "Very good."

---

* A tribe is made up of one hundred troopers (mounted cavalry), ten files of ten troopers each. A tribe is led by a phylarch, and a file is led by a decadarch. The decadarch is responsible for relaying orders, keeping his file under control, and knowing his troopers. That is why it is said the cleverness of a cavalry lies at the spurs of the decadarch and the reins of the phylarch.

After Lacestades and the others departed the tent, Oxylus turned to Telemachus:

"It looks as though our efforts have paid off. Tisamenus has no idea the greater part of the Heraclides are at his back."

"We can thank Temenus, his long ships, and his crews," Telemachus replied. "Three nights of determined labor: twenty-five hundred men, nearly fifteen hundred horses, equipment, and supplies. And we have preserved the element of surprise."

"Now, we must prove ourselves," Oxylus said. "And who knows what surprises Tisamenus has up his sleeves...or the gods for that matter."

XXXVII

Immediately after their dismissal, Deiphontes and Amphion departed Sicyon with one of the top tribes under the command of Dardanos, son of Belos. Corinth is about a hundred stadia from Sicyon. A man can walk from Sicyon at the early-market hour and arrive in Corinth before the close of market in the much larger agora there. The cavalry rode in a lose formation of files of four abreast into the hillside to avoid the main route. They encountered the Heraclide infantry encircling the town, but no one else. They kept about four to five stadia off the coastal route in the foothills, riding parallel to it. In the afternoon light, they could easily see the land sloping into the gulf with occasional glimpses of the road through the trees. They rode as rapidly as possible, given the obstacles of brush and trees, occasionally interrupted by a farm or vineyard or orchard, and made as little noise as possible. They could see the main roadblock set up by the Heraclides on the empty road and saw the preparations spreading across the plain. The Corinthians had not yet arrived. The troopers continued in the direction of Apeliotes.

At first Deiphontes and Amphion thought they had come to the gates of Corinth. They soon discovered they were viewing the fortifications of the citadel of the Acrocorinthus, a sprawling fort used defensively in ancient times to defend the city of Corinth. They had gone too far. They retraced their steps and approached the city. Hidden in the hills above the city, they could now see the large stone buildings in the center of the city, the open Agora, the palace and government buildings, and the temple of Apollo in the direction of Sicyon. They could smell the unpleasant odors of a large city: hearth fires, sewage, offal, and rotting garbage. The comings and goings within the city could be easily observed, but Corinth was deserted. A gentle breeze wafted off the gulf, keeping the sounds and odors of their horses away from Corinth. Deiphontes and Amphion split the tribe into two groups: Amphion remained with five files, and

Deiphontes and Dardanos left with the other five, retreating ten stadia toward Sicyon to observe the road from another vantage point. The fifty troopers with Amphion waited in the warm afternoon air, long enough to begin worrying that something was amiss.

The calm was broken by the sound of heavily armed men marching and talking, their bronze armour clanging against their large shields. Soon the front of the ranks appeared. The thought of being observed by an adversary was far removed from their minds. The men marched without order; they carried their lances loosely on their shoulders, the bronze tips pointing in all directions. As they walked, they talked and joked. Perhaps they were thankful to be marching away from the isthmus. There appeared to be seven or eight battalions, or perhaps eight hundred men. Amphion immediately sent two troopers to warn Deiphontes.

When the last of the soldiers had passed the sanctuary of Apollo, Amphion signaled the troopers to backtrack a few stadia and then descend to the road. He ordered a file to remain above the road to watch for any further troop movements toward Sicyon. The rest of the files kept pace, but remained well behind the Corinthians, having no trouble knowing their exact location from the loud talking and noisy armour.

Soon, Deiphontes caught sight of the Corinthians and sent two troopers to warn Phalces at the roadblock. On horseback, they would have more than enough time to give notice to the troops. Although if all failed, the infantry would certainly hear the approach of the Corinthians from several stadia away. They watched as Corinthian soldiers broke rank to urinate on the side of the road, and then hurried to catch up, dragging their shields in some cases. Deiphontes waited for the other files led by Amphion to join him. By the time the two groups met, the Corinthians had passed in no particular hurry. Amphion and Deiphontes discussed the possibilities.

The mounted Heraclides formed a line three files deep and spread out across the landscape, with one group on the road itself, another along the coast, and the other three remaining in the foothills. All were at the ready, with their bows strung and the notches of the arrows gently inserted in the twisted linen bowstrings. They rode with both hands free, guiding the horses with their knees, just as they had drilled over and over again in Locris. They would not make a move without word from the infantry blockade, however. They did not have long to wait.

At the same time, news of the Corinthian guards on the march arrived at the Heraclide command tent in the center of Sicyon. Both Telemachus and Oxylus left immediately to ensure the success of their first meeting with this opponent. Telemachus led another tribe out of town to provide backup, and Oxylus led three more battalions of foot soldiers to shore up the infantry at the roadblock. These additional reinforcements were not necessary, for the Heraclides had a large numerical advantage, and there was limited space within the clearing of the barricade. As the troopers galloped out of town, dust blew across the empty streets. Sicyon had not seen such activity since Antiope married Epopeus, son of Poseidon, for the town was small, and the people were used to going to Corinth for large festivals and ceremonies.

At some point in their march, the Corinthian guards began to realize something was wrong. The route to Sicyon was deserted. Not a single farmer or herdsman appeared along the way. The sounds of the forest were diminished, with no birds in evidence. The good nature and boisterousness of the Corinthians departed like a god displeased. Quiet fell across the troops, the only sound being the ringing echo of metal on metal as they moved slowly along the trail. Instinctively, the men closed rank and began marching in earnest, their lances now all pointing in the same direction, toward heaven.

Pamphylus, riding his horse at the head of the soldiers, was not concerned. He had been in the town that morning and had noticed nothing and could not conceive that any force now occupied the town. But he too became aware of the change in the environs. The afternoon light played out across the trail with long shadows from the high trees and flickering glimpses of the shiny waters of the gulf in the distance. He led the column, but was not the first to notice the blockade. Soon enough, though, as the Corinthians entered an open area of the forest, he observed a massed contingent of soldiers dressed in Aegean blue cloaks, with mounted riders on both flanks, and gold and blue flags flapping in the breeze. It was impossible to assess the number of Heraclide troops; they were stretched across the road, extending to the shore and into the foothills. And the depth of the soldiers was hidden by the brush and trees. The soldiers did not appear to be in formation; they were lightly armed with short javelins. Archers could be seen among the infantry.

Pamphylus halted the guards. For a while, Heraclides and Corinthians eyed each other. Word made its way up the column to Pamphylus that they were being followed by hundreds of blue-clad cavalry. Now there was almost complete silence within the hollow: no Persian doves or cawing crows, no metallic clanging, and no joking, only the occasional nickering of a horse. All appeared calm like the stillness before mighty Zephyrus reaches into his robes to send the strongest of his progeny against man.

Pamphylus ordered his guards to form a wall facing the Heraclide blockade. The Corinthian soldiers hurried to reassemble into formations eight deep, packed along the road, with lances at the ready, but as they did so, the mounted Heraclides behind them closed in. Pamphylus began to realize his problems when he saw additional Heraclide forces in the hills and along the shore, both mounted and infantry.

At this point, Aletes came forward on the road stepping out from the Heraclide troops and shouted: "Pamphylus, order your men to surrender."

Pamphylus had been in many actions, but never in a large massing of troops such as one might encounter in Armina or the Levantine. His father had been too young to have been at Troy, but he had listened to the bloody stories from the veterans and had seen the scars. He was unsure of the number of men he was facing, but could easily see that he was out-numbered and surrounded. His training was not in field tactics, and his troops were mainly composed of day fighters: men who returned each night to their families in Corinth or the surrounding communities. Some were farmers, looking for a better living; others were unskilled men from Corinth. Although all were proud of being Corinthian soldiers and of the respect this gave them, they had meager training and had never seen action on the field of battle.

Pamphylus ordered the lances in forward and closed position, massing the troops as closely together as possible. As the bronze tips were lowered toward the troops in the blockade, their large shields forming a near-wall with the lances jutting out from the barrier. Pamphylus sat on his horse with three phalanxes before him and the remainder behind. The Corinthians were no more than a plethron* distant from the blockade. The Heraclides made no movement to form ranks. They just watched as the Corinthians prepared to attack. Pamphylus stood behind his guards, eyeing the Heraclides closely.

Aletes tried again to mediate, calling out: "Pamphylus, do not test our might. You will rue the day. Lay down your arms, and you are free to sit out this war."

Pamphylus did not respond. Instead in a low voice he ordered his guards forward. Slowly, the guards advanced, step by step. Before they had taken ten steps, they heard the sounds of horses' hooves beating down on them from the rear. Four files of cavalry came straight up the road. As they drew near, the files separated directions, one cantering up the hillside and the other toward the shore. As they separated, each horseman sent an arrow into the rows of the guards, wheeled, and returned to the road in formation.

The configuration of the Corinthians crumbled and the front rows halted, as most of the arrows hit their marks. A high moan came from their midst, as men found themselves shot through by an arrow, and their fellows surrounding them began picturing the same for themselves. With lances held forward and their large shields before them, it was difficult for the guards to defend their backsides. Although their cuirasses provided some protection, an arrow hitting directly could easily puncture the bronze to such a degree as to be a fatal strike. The forward progress of the guards halted. They all looked about to assess the damage. Within their ranks, several of the guards were no longer on their feet.

Pamphylus yelled for the troops to reform. The guards were disciplined enough to attempt to form again in close order, but when a man and his shield are lying on the ground, it is difficult to close up rank. For a second time, Pamphylus commanded his soldiers forward. They were brave men and had paid attention when the more experienced of them had talked of finding honor on the field of battle, but their hearts were not in this fight.

Once again, the terrible sound of hooves on dry-packed dirt came from behind them. This time, six files of troopers cantered forward, waiting until they were hard upon the backs of the guards

---

* About 100 feet.

before flanking their horses. The arrows flew into the guards at close range and continued until all the horses had passed. The success of this assault could be heard instantly by all and echoed throughout the clearing, as the wounded guards fell to the ground, some moaning while others dropped without a sound. The Heraclide horses were breathing heavily as the files of cavalry reformed on the road. The Corinthians dropped their lances and shields and stood in a posture of defeat. And this time, there was no one urging them forward. Pamphylus' horse stood alone among the soldiers. Pamphylus himself lay in the dirt along with many others. Pamphylus, son of Aegimius, married to the pregnant Orsobia, daughter of Deiphontes, with sons training in Lacedaemon for the military, lay among his guards with the life draining out of him, far from his family home on the slopes of Mount Hypatus in Boeotia.

The Heraclide soldiers moved forward, led by Aletes. They came up to the guards, and stripped them of all their arms and armour, tossing the armament into a growing pile. The Corinthians complied willingly. Soon they stood together in only their cloth corselets and sandals. Everything else was taken from them.

The Heraclides descended into the opening from the hills and shore, filling it entirely. The Corinthian soldiers stared in amazement at the number of troops and horses surrounding them. When Oxylus rode into the center of the glade on his giant charger, Rhaebus, sitting high above the men, the Corinthians looked at one another as though they were in the presence of some diminutive god.

"Take our prisoners back to Sicyon. We have some celebrating to do this evening. Excellent job."

So the first encounter with the Pelopides ended auspiciously. There had not been a single casualty among the Heraclides. Not a single Corinthian soldier had escaped to warn of the Heraclides on their backside. Thirty Corinthian guards were dead, and many more suffered with arrow wounds. Some of these, though, might survive to see another godly sunrise.

XXXVIII

Telemachus, his sons, and Oxylus never made a conscious decision to join the Heraclides. I believe it came about based primarily on their relations with the soldiers themselves, for a bond grew up during training. The leaders felt as deeply as the soldiers that they were connected, responsible for one another, willing to come to each other's aid. Loyalty of troops, as General Xenophon tells us, is earned – and not by coercion. "Authority without consent" exercised by a ruler will fail; while a "legitimate and positively desirable ruler" with a "seeing law" will ultimately succeed. History teaches us this. Through training, the counselors became involved in the lives of their soldiers and by so doing became committed to each phylarch, to each decadarch, and to each trooper or soldier, all of which implied commitment to the cause of the Heraclides. There was not a particular time when this occurred, because it is the natural order. When the command to mobilize came, there was never any question. It had nothing to do with their possible recompense; it had to do with their task, duties, and relations with the other men involved, though strangers, barbarians in many cases, and certainly not the kinds of men they would normally associate with. But both soldiers and their leaders were dedicated to the principal goal of returning to the Peloponnese with respect for the local populace, so contrary to the campaigns of times gone by.

High above Sicyon that evening, the waning moon rested squarely in the mansion of Capricorn, the sea goat. To the people of the region, this meant that the time of fall sowing was nearing. In the town square, the Heraclide soldiers lit fires to share sacrificial offerings with the gods. They set up tripods, spits, and braziers before the fires. They led sheep and goats into the square, and the priests sacrificed them before the fires, praising the compassion of the gods. Soon the burning meats and fats gave off good rich smoke and smells, rising into the night air to share the good tidings with the gods.

People from the town contributed an ox to the sacrifice, for word of the victory against Tisamenus' guards had spread, and Sicyonians were no followers of the King of Mycenae. Most welcome of all, though, farmers brought several large amphorae of wine and poured for all who joined the troops in the agora, while the priests tipped libations in thanks to the gods for the successful encounter. After this, several flute players joined the celebration, and the townspeople listened to the music. The soldiers from Macedonian even danced.

As the celebration continued and servants distributed steaming meats and bread, the officers met in their tent to plan for the following day. Lacestades, King of Sicyon, joined them.

The emotion of the fight had washed over dark-eyed Aletes. He was now quite drunk and walked among the officers in the tent, slapping them on their backs and praising the god Heracles. For he had awarded himself credit for the entire battle. Phalces and Autolycus remained sober, slowly tasting their wine and water. They would wait another day for their time to arrive.

Telemachus thanked Deiphontes and Amphion for their excellent work, tracking the enemy, warning the troops, and then attacking in a restrained yet effective manner. The cavalry had won the day, that was evident, and Telemachus was very proud of his troopers.

Oxylus, too, happily drank his thanks, pouring as much wine on the ground in libation as into his mouth. He addressed the officers: "Let us be unambiguous. This day will not come again. From this point on, we will be tested by real adversity. First, we need to get a messenger to the isthmus to talk with Procles and Eurysthenes. God knows what they are up to. They need to know that Sicyon is secured and that we are moving out tomorrow early. Lacestades, can you name a trusted soul to make his way into Corinth to assess the situation? I would not expect that anyone could slip through the battle line along the isthmus, but maybe he could garner information in the town or harbor."

"I can do better than that," Lacestades said. "We can send a small fishing vessel to the isthmus to come ashore on the Heraclide side."

"Excellent," Oxylus replied. "Temenus should be blockading the harbor at Lechaeum, and you may be able to contact him directly. Give it a try."

"I would do this myself," Lacestades said, "but I am too well known in this region. Polyphontes, though, would be a natural. He is trained in boat building and is very sly, knows his way around Corinth, its harbors, and the isthmus, has the energy to do this, and is a Heraclide, for he is my only son. Leave it to me."

"We will need him back tomorrow morning early," Telemachus said.

"You will have him." And Lacestades departed.

"Now tomorrow," Oxylus continued, "the next step: Corinth. From our intelligence, we know that Corinth is not well defended and even less so after today. Send a tribe of cavalry to the outskirts to relieve the troopers that are there now. We need to shut down all entrance to the city from the direction of Sicyon. Also, we need to know what is happening in the city from the direction of the isthmus. Most importantly, we must prevent anyone from giving information on today's battle to Tisamenus. We will keep Sicyon closed for the rest of the evening with our perimeter guard in place. Tomorrow, we all move up to Corinth...before sunrise."

"Dardanos, son of Belos," Telemachus said, "has proved his worth today. He can lead a tribe to Corinth. He is the best phylarch we have, and he can choose from the best decadarchs."

"He is a good man," Oxylus replied. "Sardine, they call him, no? For ourselves, we must greet Eos tomorrow morning at the entrance to the city. We need to strike like the thunder of Zeus. Gods forbid us, but now we must douse the fires and resort to the dream world. Tonight, we sleep with the peace of knowing we have accomplished much, but also with the challenge that we have yet to begin our contest."

History often reports a kernel of truth, but fails to record the tasty meats surrounding. As reported by the historians, Aletes, son of Hippotes, son of Phylas, son of Antiochus, son of Heracles by Meda,

and the general in charge of the Heraclides, surprised Sicyon by night. Aletes spared Lacestades, because he too was a Heraclide, being the son of Hippolytus. In return for his cooperation, Lacestades became a partner in the kingdom. From this time on, it is said that the Sicyonians became Dorians. (For such was the name the historians gave the Heraclides. In fact, as we know, the Heraclide soldiers were from all parts of the world, Greek and barbarian alike.) Spacious Sicyon became a part of the Argive territory, as it had been under the rule of King Adrastos, but not since that time.

XXXIX

The next morning, while Dawn Eos and her husband Tithonos snuggled in their cozy comfort, the troops of the Heraclides departed the town of Sicyon, cold and damp, many suffering the ill-effects of over-imbibing. Messengers from the cavalry tribe under the command of Dardanos reported that all remained quiet in Corinth and that only a few soldiers appeared to be guarding the city. The citizens of the city were not about, and roads leading into the city were empty. It was as though the gods had warned everyone not to venture forth and to remain at home before fire and hearth. More importantly, the messengers reported rumors of a harsh battle on the isthmus, though no evidence of this could be observed in Corinth.

The cavalry led the march along the coast road, not straying far from the infantry. Scouts had scoured the entire distance and had discovered no obstacle to their advance. The victorious horse files from the day before, the pick and flower of the troops, led the march. Their helmets glittered in the moonlight, and they pulled their blue cloaks tightly around them against the cool matinal air. Other than the muted sounds of the horses' hooves and the tintinnabulation of the armour, the shore and groves of trees were silent: still too early for the muted cooing of the turtle-doves. The soldiers kept to themselves after the evening of celebration, no joking or talking.

At this time, the terms "city" and "town" must be used loosely, for the larger cities were not as we know them today. A city such as Corinth was mainly a grouping of small surrounding villages under the patronage of a king or great palace, which provided protection and community. Most people lived on small cultivated plots or in fishing villages around Corinth and were mostly self-supporting, depending on the climate. And the populations were small, not as we know them today, since that came later with the migrations.

Due to its location connecting the Peloponnese to the mainland of Hellas and its two ports on either side of the isthmus, Corinth was important as both a sentinel and a customs agent to the flows of peoples, armies, and goods across the isthmus and between the gulfs. Corinth was not the wealthiest city in the Peloponnese. That distinction belonged to Mycenae, though that was changing rapidly. Nor was Corinth the most populous, that being Argos, stretched out in a wide fertile valley. Corinth suffered not as the first born, nor last, but as a hardworking and diligent middle child of a large family, hoping to please his father through his assiduous efforts, though often overlooked in contrast to his more flamboyant and vocal siblings: Mycenae, Lacedaemon, Argos, Tiryns, and even fair-minded Pylos.

Long ago, Ephyra, an amazing beauty and noted member of this particularly promiscuous sorority known as the Oceanids,* dwelt in the city of Corinth. The city was first named after her. But when Phoebus Apollo and Poseidon began a terrible dispute over the city of Ephyra, all of heaven's forces became aware of this backwater. Zeus chose the Hecatoncheires (hundred-handed ones), the most horrifying sons of Uranus, father of Cronos, to arbitrate between the two gods: Poseidon's potent nephew Apollo and Apollo's disaffected uncle Poseidon. The Hecatoncheires awarded the isthmus and the neighboring lands to Poseidon, and this award included the land where the city now sits. To Apollo, they granted the hills above the city and the surrounding region, including the high outcropping above the city that later became the Acrocorinthus. The Acrocorinthus served as an acropolis, the citadel of defense and refuge for the Ephyrians against the frenzied nations storming into the Peloponnese through the isthmus and then retreating, just as the sea rants and raves against a narrow inlet.

The first great king, Epopeus, son of Poseidon, came to Ephyra from Thessaly. After Epopeus died, his gentle son, Marathon, ruled judiciously for many years, and the people were content. In his wisdom, when he departed from this earth, he divided his kingdom among his sons Corinthus and Sicyon. Thus, the two kingdoms were separated, each named after a son, but forever linked happily and unhappily as is the custom within families.

---

* Any of the ocean nymphs believed to be the daughters of Oceanus and Tethys.

Telemachus, Deiphontes, and Amphion followed the first two files. The cavalry stretched out behind them. Oxylus, Aletes, Phalces, and Autolycus led the infantry more than four stadia behind the lead troopers. The entire army extended over ten stadia, with the wagons finally departing Sicyon long after the leaders had left. Lacestades remained in Sicyon with several companies, with orders to hold the Corinthian prisoners until hostilities came to an end. His son, Polyphontes, had not returned from the isthmus at the time of the departure, but when he did, a messenger would be sent immediately to Corinth.

By the time the golden glow of Eos began to suffuse the gulf, the first contingent of cavalry met up with Dardanos and his troopers on the outskirts of Corinth. They were scattered across a hillside above the road with a view of the city. Telemachus dismounted Sterope. From this vantage point, he could see the outlines of the city in the morning glow. Ordinarily, at this time of day the farmers and shopkeepers would be trudging along the route into the agora to set up for the twice-weekly morning market. Today, the trail was empty of all save a few curs scuttling along the drainage channels. He motioned to the troopers to direct the flow of horse files into the hillside above the city. Deiphontes and Amphion joined him.

"What say you, Dardanos?"

"Nothing to count, sir. Nary a bird on wing. The city sleeps like a babe after its fill." Dardanos was a thin, nervous man, with a close-cropped beard and bald head. He had been raised in Pylos in a family of fishermen, a saltwater man – thus, his nickname, Sardine – but as a young man he had trained in the military and had become a freebooter, which was not common among Hellenes at that time. Where he learned to ride a horse was anyone's guess, but he did so with great enthusiasm.

"Can you account for the guards within the city?" asked Telemachus.

"Only scattered ones. No formations, no reinforcements. All seem to have gone to the ditch."

"And none reporting back?"

"No, sir. We watched the agora and the palace, but none returned last night."

Telemachus turned to his lieutenants. "Deiphontes, take a tribe and set up a roadblock to secure the entrance to the city from the direction of Apeliotes, but avoid any contact. Flee if necessary. No engagements. We must attend the arrival of the infantry in force. Send word if you see troop movements. Do not allow any citizens to enter the city; instead, send them home. Amphion, organize a tribe to enter the city, only the most worthy files, and send a scout with word back to Oxylus to press forward quickly and to hold at the edge of the city, for we are entering nothing loath. Go with the gods."

Both Deiphontes and Amphion mounted quickly and rode back to their troopers. Moments later, Telemachus could see Deiphontes lead a large contingent off along the road toward the isthmus.

"Well done, Dardanos." said Telemachus. "You can take your troopers to rest now along the hillside."

"Aye, sir. But far better for my men to enter Corinth along with the others. For this is the fish we have in our net."

"Granted, if your troopers are up to it, join Amphion and his troopers. We can take two tribes into the city, but we cannot be stumbling all over each other."

"Thank you, sir."

Telemachus waited as the two tribes gathered into formation. He had spent a restless night after seeking solitude from the festivities. Too many thoughts prevented his sleep. He had refused to allow himself to think of Polycasté, but her image troubled him. What was she doing at this moment: washing her hair, dining with her father, thinking of her sons?

Amphion led the first tribe with Dardanos' tribe following, or about two hundred mounted troopers in all. Riding at a canter, four abreast, with slashing swords drawn by the outside troopers, such a squadron was enough to place Panic, the brother of Fear and Flight, in the minds of all observers. The troopers had drilled to perform various configurations according to the situation or terrain, all based on the unit of the file. They could rapidly fan out to fill a square or courtyard or form a straight wall five horses deep in an expanse. Telemachus mounted Sterope, drawing his cut-and-thrust sword, and followed the last troopers.

The horses and their riders sprinted down the hillside onto the road that led into the city from the direction of Sicyon, with Notus blowing in their faces and their cloaks flying behind them. They filled the entire roadbed, with dust swirling about their hooves, rising into the air on all sides. On the outskirts, they passed mud huts and shanty wooden structures. Dogs scampered out of the way. If there were people about, they remained ensconced within the huts and shanties. As they entered the city proper, the troopers rapidly passed a small temple, veered to the left down a street of small shops and buildings, and then turned sharply into the agora and circled the open space, slowing to a walk. The agora was a large open space without vegetation, swept clean of debris, with a small basilica and separate entrance at one end. In the middle, stood a row of makeshift enclosures, and on the side of Notus a long *stoa** fronted shops, taverns, and government buildings in stone. All were closed up, and not a single soul was in evidence. Before the basilica stood a large wooden statue of Artemis and an open cistern of water for public drinking and washing. Telemachus ordered a file to remain in the courtyard, while the rest left to secure the palace.

The palace of the king was located on the opposite side of the *stoa* and was a long stone building, rising two stories, with views of the Acrocorinthus on the one side and the agora on the other, and in the distance the port of Lechaeum and the Gulf of Corinth. The horses wheeled out of the agora and picked up speed as they circled the rear of the stoa and approached the palace, which was surrounded by a high wall with a heavy wooden entrance gate. The gate was closed and bolted. After some effort, two troopers were able to gain leverage over the bronze hinges using a battle axe. With the aid of ropes and their horses, the troopers pulled the left hand door off its hinges, dragging the door backward into the road, and the other gate swung open.

The opening revealed about twenty people: men, including several soldiers, and a few women as well. Frightened, they quickly ran onto the colonnade at the entrance of the palace to avoid the horses and riders that began pouring into the courtyard below them. The colonnade placed them about five steps above the courtyard and ran the entire length of the stone palace. At the center, the high

---

* Raised porch running the length of a structure, usually covered with an overhanging roof supported by wooden columns.

entrance doors of the palace were shut. The small group huddled together in fear in front of these doors.

Telemachus held up his hand for the troopers to take formation. Dardanos' tribe formed a line of horses four deep facing the Corinthians, with the other tribe behind. The horses entirely filled the courtyard. Of the few uniformed soldiers among the people, none attempted to interfere or brandished a weapon.

Telemachus twisted on his saddle pad and called: "Amphion, take your tribe and secure the rest of the city. Set up in the agora for holding prisoners and as a base of operations."

He then turned to address the small, huddled group: "We are the soldiers of the Heraclides, and we come in peace. We would like you to depart. You soldiers will remain here." He signaled for the troopers to open a way out of the courtyard, and the people began to make their way tentatively through the sea of blue cloaks and snorting, stamping horses. As they passed, their faces were full of anxiety and their head lowered.

"Go to your homes and stay there. If you go outside your houses today, you may find yourself in jeopardy. We have thousands of troops surrounding the city. Soon even more troops will be joining us."

When the Corinthians had departed, five Corinthian soldiers remained. They were quickly relieved of their weapons and taken away to the agora. Dardanos dismounted. He walked up to the doors of the palace and knocked with the butt of his sword.

"Open up, or we burn you down."

He waited. The doors slowly opened, and several servants peered from the entrance.

"Everyone out of the building," Dardanos shouted. "You can choose to walk out, or we will carry you out on our shields."

Soon the colonnade began filling with people, mostly servants and slaves, but also some well dressed archons and ranking soldiers.

"Who will act as spokesman here?" Telemachus shouted.

The crowd remained quiet, until a tall man stepped forward, dressed in elegant robes of natural umber linen.

"I am Deioneus, son of Ixion, and a Corinthian by birth and preference. I am advisor to the Kings of Corinth, Doridas and Hyanthidas, and a counselor to the people. You have no right to be…"

Telemachus interrupted him. "I am Telemachus, son of Odysseus, and general of the Heraclides. You will listen carefully. All citizens are free to retire to their places of abode. I want the palace vacated in the next moments, because when we enter no one else will exit alive. You there," he pointed at several servants, "bring out any who remain within."

Several servants ran back inside the building.

"Your father is well known among us," Deioneus said, "but I wonder..."

"Silence," Telemachus shouted. "I want everyone to leave now. If you have nowhere to go, then you will find sanctuary in the agora, which is protected by our troops. Anywhere else will place you in peril for your life. Soon this city will be filled with soldiers, and I would prefer that they had no excuse for harming the citizens. Quickly now."

The people filed out apprehensively between the horses.

"Sir," Telemachus addressed Deioneus, "would you please stay with us for a while. But I would suggest you remain silent."

After a short while, all that remained in the palace courtyard were about ninety mounted troopers facing Dardanos and the Corinthian archon, Deioneus, on the terrace. The last servants had exited the palace and departed.

"Dardanos, take a file and secure the palace."

Dardanos signaled for his personal file to dismount and follow him into the palace. They quickly disappeared into the building.

At this point, Aletes and Oxylus galloped into the courtyard and came to a halt next to Telemachus.

"Any problems?" Oxylus asked Telemachus.

"None. The city is under our command," said Telemachus. "I want the infantry to remain outside for the time being."

"Too late," Aletes replied, his black eyes shining in the morning light. "They are right behind us."

"Not too late," Telemachus shouted. "Keep them out. Do you hear me?"

"No," Aletes said, "they are following my command."

Telemachus glanced at Oxylus and spoke: "The city is secure. The infantry is needed with the main body of troopers along the road to the isthmus. Not here. Deiphontes is there. He needs your help. Is that clear, Aletes?"

"Aletes," Oxylus said, "send Phalces to support Deiphontes with a division of infantry. Autolycus can hold at the Sicyon road with the rest of the cavalry. After they are set up, bring Deiphontes back to the palace so that we can reconnoiter."

Aletes looked from one man to the other, kicked his horse maliciously to back up, then wrenching the horse's head, turned him viciously in a tight circle and sped out of the courtyard.

Telemachus shook his head.

Oxylus grinned without joy.

"All clear," Dardanos shouted, coming out of the palace. "Only one slight problem, but we took care of it." They noted the blood on his sword.

"Deioneus," Telemachus said, "would you like to escort us through the palace." He dismounted. Oxylus jumped down from Rhaebus' high back. They joined Deioneus and Dardanos on the terrace. "Please, sirs, lead the way."

The men entered into a gigantic atrium with a ceiling two stories high with bright mosaic murals on the walls. Inside, a wide central staircase gently spiraled to the second floor. On either side of the staircase were entrances leading to the back end of the lower floor. They surveyed the first floor: several meeting rooms, the central dining and megaron with hearth, various offices, storage rooms, and a food preparation area, connected to an enclosed rear yard with massive clay storage vessels, penned animals, and poultry. On the side of the rear yard was a large washroom with tiled murals, tubs, and sitting areas. They climbed the spiral staircase to the second floor, where they found additional offices, storage rooms, and a large number of sleeping spaces along the main corridor, some quite small with only enough space for a bed, while others spacious, with dressing rooms adorned with beautiful textiles and painted scenes on the walls. Although the clear openings with wooden shutters faced Boreas, the diffused morning light lit the rooms. At the end of the hall, the men entered the largest bedroom, where they found two Heraclide troopers standing over the body of a Corinthian guard lying in a pool of blood. His right arm, severed from his body, lay on the floor, still clasping a bronze sword. Behind the troopers, sat a woman on the bed, her head in her hands, crying softly. Two small children, one a tow-headed boy of perhaps three or four years old and his sister, slightly older, stood next to her staring at the body on the floor.

"And who would this be?" Telemachus asked Deioneus.

"The wife of King Tisamenus and his children."

The young woman glanced up at the soldiers, but her tearful eyes swiftly lowered. She pulled her shawl over her head to obscure her face. She was very young and exceptionally beautiful, in white silk robes, now spotted with blood. The children did not move.

"Where is your husband?" Telemachus asked roughly.

"I do not know."

"Where is your husband? I will not repeat this question."

She glanced at the stern face of Telemachus. "He left yesterday. He said he would return last night. But he did not."

"Where are your servants?"

"They departed when the soldiers came."

"Dardanos, send one of your men to the agora, to retrieve her servants. She can remain here for the time being."

"Aye, sir."

"And get rid of the body." Telemachus turned to Deioneus: "Now, have we seen the entire palace?"

"Yes…"

"Well, have we or not?"

"There is more…below the first level."

"Lead on. Oxylus, we should set up in the meeting room."

"Yes. We will."

They left the bedroom and descended to the first floor. Deioneus led them to a spiral stairwell passage on the side of the building, behind the atrium. As they descended, the natural light gave way to a single oil flame, and then a series of sconces lighting a long corridor, smelling of decay and sewage. As they entered, they heard the low moans of human voices. They had entered a confinement of some sort, for along the length of the corridor they could see a series of wooden doors. Telemachus halted, for he suspected what they might see.

"We can hold off visiting this area until later." The three men turned and ascended to the first floor.

In the atrium, they discovered Aletes, Amphion, and Deiphontes, directing a number of soldiers coming and going. Telemachus stepped outside onto the terrace for a moment to get some fresh air, but the courtyard was filled with both troopers and infantry soldiers. He reentered the palace angrily.

"Would you please join me in the central meeting room," Telemachus said, directing the officers to the left entrance. "Deioneus, would you mind waiting for us for a moment? Dardanos, see to the lower floor, take its occupants to the agora for interview, and clean up here. Set up for a meeting this afternoon. I suspect we will not be here long."

When they were together in the large meeting room, Telemachus ignored Aletes and turned to Deiphontes.

"So what have you found on the isthmus?"

"We set up a barricade on the entrance to the city toward the isthmus at the river crossing, but very few people were about, and we encountered no Corinthian troops. We sent scouts to get a view of the isthmus, and they returned with several captured Corinthian solders. The soldiers told of a great battle yesterday...a great rout of the Heraclides that led almost to Megara. They saw many wounded Corinthians retreating to the harbor of Cenchreae, but we did not enter the village. We also sent scouts to the opposite side of the isthmus at Lechaeum and found that Temenus now owns the harbor. When Phalces and Autolycus arrived with the infantry at the barricade, I felt I could return to relay this information."

"We searched Corinth," Amphion offered. "There is no resistance and no troops. The people are either in hiding or have left the city. We have posted guards, but the main body of troopers remains on the Sicyon road outside of town."

Telemachus stepped toward Aletes: "There is a large group of infantry in the courtyard. What are they doing here?"

"They are protecting the city, as I instructed them," Aletes replied with strength, not backing away from Telemachus.

"I thought we agreed to keep the infantry outside of the city." Telemachus moved forward again, until he was almost touching the man.

"I did not."

"Allow me, Aletes," Telemachus cursed as though talking to a child, "I give thee two mistakes, because I am older and know far more. Thou made one. Now, thou hast made another: thy last. Do not test my resolve with a third. Take all infantry from the city. Is that clear?"

Aletes glared at Telemachus and then Oxylus, but he chose to remain mute, the anger jetting from his darkly malevolent eyes.

"Take all infantry from the city," Telemachus repeated in a softer tone. "Do not fail me. Go now. They are needed at the barricade toward the isthmus."

"I do not take orders from you," Aletes said. "Cresphontes will hear of this."

"Cresphontes is not in charge," Telemachus stated without emotion, his head shaking in disbelief, but carefully watching Aletes' hand move to the hilt of his dirk.

But before Aletes could withdraw his knife, Deiphontes had his sword drawn and faced his distant cousin. For a moment, Aletes hesitated, but only a moment, and then he stormed out of the hall.

"He cannot be trusted," Deiphontes said, replacing his sword.

"We must secure the harbor of Lechaeum from the land side," said Telemachus, moving on, "and then get into contact with Temenus. I am sure that the twins and Cresphontes are in big trouble. There is no way that a short division of Heraclides, especially that one, can stop the combined forces of Tisamenus."

Oxylus pitched in. "Amphion can take two tribes of cavalry to secure the port at Lechaeum and contact Temenus. Will that be enough troops, Deiphontes?"

"More than enough," Deiphontes replied. "All the Corinthians appear to be at the ditch."

"In the meantime," Oxylus continued, "we need to move up at closer hand to understand the events occurring on the isthmus. The reason Tisamenus did not return last night to the palace may have been the success of the battle. We can meet back here after sunset."

"Deiphontes," Telemachus said in a friendlier tone. "Mobilize the troopers that remain on the road to Sicyon. Let the infantry maintain a small roadblock. Move the remainder in support of the infantry on the route to Cenchreae on the Saronic Gulf. All our forces should move up to the barricade at the river crossing. What say you, Oxylus?"

"Right," Oxylus agreed. "We only need a small force on the Sicyon road and a few files of troopers in the city."

After Deiphontes and Amphion had departed, Telemachus and Oxylus sat for a moment together.

"Aletes is treacherous," Telemachus said. "We must be wary."

"It has just begun," Oxylus replied. "They are in a deadly contest against us and each other. Only the gods can imagine what deviousness Cresphontes is contriving. And I say this believing that man is the lone navigator of his soul."

"My only desire is to find a way out with our lives and limbs intact and those of my sons as well. Do I ask too much?"

"You ask more than the gods can assure."

"'Embrace your enemies; death comes at the point of an ally's knife.' My father's words."

XL

On the way to the isthmus, the main road from Corinth led through a lush river valley and then to a low range of hills, descending after perhaps twenty-five stadia to the port of Cenchreae on the Saronic Gulf, in all about sixty stadia from Corinth. From the port, the road turned in the direction of the mainland to cross the isthmus. The ditch was fifteen stadia from the harbor. The Heraclides had set up a barricade along the main road at a river crossing about ten stadia from Corinth. Almost all the Heraclide infantry troops and cavalry had moved up to camp along the river awaiting orders. For most of the soldiers, the day had been uneventful. They recovered from the festivities of the night before in the warm midday sun, near the cool flowing stream. But such is war: solid boredom interspersed with instants of intense distress.

Telemachus and Oxylus left the palace well guarded by Dardanos and his troopers, and rode off in the direction of the isthmus. When they arrived at the river crossing, they found the hills covered with troops and horses spread out along the slow moving stream. Deiphontes, Aletes, Autolycus, and Phalces were at the river crossing. Telemachus and Oxylus halted to confer with the officers.

"We know that there is fighting on the isthmus," Oxylus said, "but we do not want to walk into a hornets' nest. Give us until the sun is halfway in its descent to Oceanus. If we have not returned, then release the cavalry to take Cenchreae, with the infantry following as rapidly as possible. In the meantime, move the troopers away from the road and do not congregate like some town meeting. We will return shortly. Are there any scouts on the other side of the hill?"

No reply.

"Then send some troopers. Can we use our heads?"

Instead of heading along the main route, Telemachus and Oxylus led three files of cavalry along the river toward the Gulf of Corinth and the small port of Lechaeum. One of the files with

Telemachus was his personal file, his so-called tablemates. This file was dedicated to protecting Telemachus as the hipparch, or general of the cavalry, and they never left his presence. Every phylarch, or leader of a tribe, had his own personal file. The Heraclides rode rapidly along the river and approached Lechaeum from Apeliotes along the shore. The port consisted of a number of ramshackle structures and a wide rocky beach. As they approached, they noted the remains of partially submerged ships in the harbor. Bodies of soldiers lay in the sand. They rode on to the center of the beach, where they found Heraclide soldiers and sailors standing around a large ship with the flag of Heracles whipping in the breeze. In the center stood Temenus talking to Amphion. They rode up and dismounted, handing off Sterope and Rhaebus.

Temenus welcomed them: "Congratulations on your success in Sicyon and Corinth. But, we need help. The army of Tisamenus attacked us in the isthmus. We have lost many men and are now being pushed back in the direction of Attica."

Telemachus interrupted. "You mean Tisamenus forded the ditch?"

"Yes."

"Why would he do that?" Telemachus asked.

"Well, Cresphontes took it into his mind that he should attack to test the will of Tisamenus."

"This was not the plan."

"As you like," Temenus said without rancor. "We both know my brother. They attempted to cross the ditch yesterday to fight, but were quickly driven back last night. The ditch is full of our troops. The Corinthians learned of the Heraclides' troop strength and saw they faced a meager and ill-prepared army. As a result, this morning, Tisamenus himself crossed the ditch, and now a heated battle is going on. If you can call it that. Our troops are fighting valorously, but they are far out-numbered and are retreating rapidly."

"Allow me to put it a different way," Telemachus said. "Cresphontes, caring not for the lives of his troops, wanted to see if his theory of pushing through the isthmus was sound. By doing this, he gave Tisamenus a clear indication of the number of his troops and their strength. As a result, Tisamenus seeing that he was far superior in numbers felt he could end the affair at that point. But the question is if Cresphontes and the twins can keep their troops from being routed back to Megara."

"They are several stadia from the ditch," Temenus replied, "where some natural barriers offer protection, and the Heraclides are holding for the time being. But I am not sure how long this will continue."

"There may be a benefit here," Oxylus said. "We now command the ditch."

"You are absolutely correct," Telemachus agreed. "But at what price? We must act immediately. We must take Cenchreae now, and then we must move our infantry up to the ditch as rapidly as possible. If we can do that before nightfall, we will have Tisamenus surrounded, without water or supplies."

"Cresphontes in his inimitable way chanced upon a strategy that flushed the lion from his den," Oxylus said. "We must not allow Tisamenus' return."

"Where is our navy in all this?" Telemachus asked.

"We destroyed many vessels outside the harbor that now lie on the bottom of the gulf," Temenus replied. "We lost only one ship. Tisamenus no longer has any ships on this side. We command the gulf."

"Good," Telemachus said. "First, we need to give Cresphontes additional infantry, archers and skirmishers, and troopers. Can we get ships to transport six hundred troops to the Heraclides on the isthmus, equally divided among cavalry and skirmishers?"

"Yes, the ships are just off the isthmus. They can be here well before the sun sets, and we can reinforce Cresphontes after nightfall."

"We need to return to our troops immediately," Telemachus said. "And move the entire force to the isthmus. Amphion, take your troopers quickly back along the river to join the others at the river crossing. Send two tribes in this direction and four infantry battalions...the best of both, particularly the archers. They will meet Temenus here to move by ship up the coast to reinforce Cresphontes. This may take all night. Then you and Deiphontes will immediately attack Cenchreae with all remaining tribes. The infantry will move up as fast as possible. No need to keep a guard at the river crossing. Our immediate goal is to seal off Cenchreae. The infantry must run as never before behind the horses. Either they will be needed at

Cenchreae, or best of all they will pass the port and secure the ditch from this side before Helios disappears into Oceanus."

Telemachus, Oxylus, and Temenus waited as Amphion mounted Arion and shouted to his troopers. They galloped back toward the river crossing. The three men watched them depart.

"This is not the battle we foresaw," Oxylus said. "We must be careful not to allow this to change our strategy. Our horses will not be effective at the ditch. And we do not want to be sucked into a battle of heavy infantry or a standoff."

"No," Telemachus agreed, "but we did not anticipate that Cresphontes would disregard all we agreed. We still have the element of surprise. Tisamenus has at best only a sketchy idea of the forces on this side. Without water, there can be no standoff. Oxylus, you need to go with the troops. I want to return to Corinth to ensure there are no problems there and to begin the movement of our supplies forward. I suspect that Aletes may be up to something. I will take my tablemates and join you later."

"Yes," Oxylus agreed. "We will meet at the isthmus this evening."

At this point, Oxylus on Rhaebus and two files of troopers rode off toward the main force, leaving Telemachus and Temenus on the beach, with a single file and a few sailors.

Temenus shook his head. "Once again my brother allows his faith to direct him without considering the circumstances."

"Well, it was costly in terms of lives, but perhaps not disastrous in effect. Temenus, I know we cannot control your brother. Remember, though, all we need do is hold the Pelopides on the isthmus. We can strangle them from this direction: no food, no water, no supplies. No need to counterattack with the reinforcements. No heroes. Just hold tight, and leave the rest to us. We must avoid hand-to-hand combat."

Suddenly, Telemachus felt the pain of doubt. He looked at Temenus, a tall white-bearded stranger. A man with much to gain from this affair. He could barely contain his animosity for Temenus' brother, Cresphontes, who showed over and over again his overweening hubris. This family had a grand view of their mission and dogged determination to fulfill their ancestor's destiny. Did they honestly believe that their decisions had no impact on others or that their family was of such consequence that the lives of others had no import? He thought back on animated arguments he had had with others. He could recall heated reactions to some question or another, the matter itself long forgotten, and he had fought with intensity for what he thought was right. Afterwards, the person he had fought had departed or gone on to the underworld, never to return. And what good had these arguments and discussions served? We all fight and bruise and kill one other to achieve some goal, and then we all disappear. The only legacy is hatred, for people have short memories for kindness, but never forget an insult.

And here they stood on the edge of the gulf in the sunlight with a cooling breeze blowing across the waters, hearing the gentle sounds of the horses and looking out at the isthmus. What was his life worth? The lives of his sons? The lives of his troopers? Was the return of the Heraclides…or his own return to Ithaca for that matter…worth these lives? Was he trapped in this same greed…had he gone too far? And what would be the cost?

"…you must surrender what you cherish most."

XLI

Telemachus left Temenus rudely. His personal file of troopers jumped on their horses to catch up with him. Temenus returned to his fleet to muster the transport for the reinforcements, while Telemachus raced into Corinth, passing several Heraclide guards on the outskirts, and came to a halt in the agora. The agora was deserted, except for the last supply wagons and a few Heraclide guards. He left the guards and sent the wagons on toward Cenchreae and the isthmus. The palace too was abandoned. There were a few troopers at the entrance gate, but no one else was about. His file dismounted behind him and watered the exhausted horses. Dardanos welcomed him as he entered the large atrium.

"Sir. Come, I have something to show you."

"We cannot delay. We are on to Cenchreae."

Dardanos looked at him as he might a small boy. "You have a moment, sir, believe me."

"How is that?" Telemachus slowed himself and smiled at the thin fisherman.

"If I told you, you would not believe me."

Telemachus followed him as he opened the door that led down into the darkness of the lower floor.

"We took all the prisoners to the agora," Dardanos explained. "Most are men who stood against Tisamenus and some petty criminals. All were as innocent as the doves. Happy to see us, they were. We sent them all toward Sicyon."

"Where is Deioneus?"

"We allowed him to return home, but told him to rest close at hand." Dardanos stopped to light the lamp in his hand with the wall sconce. They walked down the corridor with the doors of the empty prison cells now open. There must have been forty cells, obscure without candlelight, and barely wide enough for a man to lie down. They smelled of desperation: a small house of Hades on earth.

At the end of the corridor, a heavy timber door encased in bronze halted their progress, but in the candlelight, Dardanos stuck a large bent rod through a hole in the door and managed to release the bolt. The door pivoted on bronze sockets in the lintel, very slowly; Dardanos had to apply his full weight. Telemachus felt he had been here before.

Dardanos disappeared into the total darkness, but the light from the lamp reflected on the low vaulted ceiling and stone walls. Cold humid air rushed out from the interior. He lit several oil sconces, and slowly the room began to appear out of obscurity.

"Deioneus was not cooperative in giving us access. But we changed his mind."

The treasury of Corinth presented itself. Of course, gold in all its manifestations can be easily imagined. And the treasury of Odysseus came to Telemachus' mind. But this one differed greatly in both extent and kind. The room was cavernous, scores of times larger than Odysseus' store, stretching far back into the earth. This was an official depot, and row upon row of objects appeared, carefully arranged in size and type. Wooden shelves around the walls held larger objects, statues, figurines, large vessels, and carvings. The largest objects stood on the dirt floor against the shelves around the room. There were life size statues of gods in solid gold, immovable. Gold containers on wooden tables spanning the entire length of the room were filled with various objects of value: necklaces, rings, bracelets, earrings, pendants, pins, death masks, pectorals, wreaths, cups, vessels, seals, precious stones, and ivory carvings. But this paled against what they found underneath the tables; carefully stacked on the floor were rows upon rows upon rows of massive bricks of cast electrum.[*]

Telemachus picked up a small statuette of Hera seated on her throne in a long flowing gown, falling naturally to her sandaled feet. In her lap, she held a flowering branch of an apple tree, just as she had done in the gardens of the Hesperides, where her golden apples grew. The statue was beautifully crafted and by its weight solid gold.

---

[*] Electrum is a naturally occurring mixture of gold and silver. It was the foundation of gold metalworking, and further refinement, i.e., separation of gold and silver, was not possible at that time.

He examined the delicate carving and exquisite folds of Hera's gown and the diadem on her head. He replaced it on the table.

Dardanos remained at the door, as Telemachus walked around the room, occasionally stopping to touch a particularly elegant piece of jewelry or a carving. The storehouse of value here was beyond imagining. This could only have been Agamemnon's hoard, so often figuring in the songs of the bards, but never believed: Agamemnon's share, the largest share of all, of the wealth taken from Priam's treasury. Here too must have been the electrum taken from Palamedes, who was accused of treason, but actually was storing the gold his father had earned by supplying the Achaean army while they were beached at Troy for nine long years. Here was the gold garnered from razing countless cities in Asia Minor and Thrace during the war. He looked to identify pieces from Troy, but could not easily tell the origin of the objects. The richest houses and largest properties with hundreds of slaves in the center of Athens could not exhaust the wealth in this room in thousands of lifetimes. A farmer could struggle his entire life to feed his family and raise his children and not come close to expending the value of the smallest, single object in this room. And there were objects beyond count. But what good is gold to a man who cannot feed his children when rain is scarce and the earth burned to a crisp? What possible use could this storehouse serve, when the kings of Argos and all the other states continued to require tribute from the people? When others were starving? When every morning in every city beggars were found dead in their wraps? Telemachus stood stricken with awe; a feeling of sickness swept through his stomach. All this wealth had not aided Priam, Agamemnon, and Orestes, and now it would not help Tisamenus. Born naked; I go naked to my grave.

"Cresphontes can go to the underworld a happy man," Telemachus said to himself. "This storehouse must remain a secret," he said to Dardanos. "Take a memento for your wife, and then close this vault tightly. Seal the staircase and do not mention the existence of this room to anyone."

He waited patiently as the thin saltwater man walked about the room with new found respect. He chose a necklace of solid gold beads; a very practical selection as it could be stowed away in the pocket of his tunic and never be glimpsed to arouse suspicion. Telemachus put a gold signet ring into his own pocket.

"Pray to Poseidon that I return to the shores of Ithaca," was all he said. "And you to the fishes of the seas of Pylos."

"Aye, sir."

They quenched the oil lamps and closed the heavy doors. At the top of the stairs, Dardanos shut the door and sealed it with several bronze spikes. Telemachus suspected that he would never return here. Perhaps this storehouse was fueling Cresphontes' aspirations, beyond his family's desire to return to their home and rule. Men rarely reveal their base motivations. All had heard of Agamemnon's hoard, but few believed it. Priam's gold was more likely buried with Troy or lay at the bottom of the large-wide or was imaginary from the beginning. As they walked out into the last remaining light of the day in the palace courtyard, Telemachus welcomed the fresh sea air and golden glow of the sun sinking into the mountains. As he mounted Sterope, he felt her strength and readiness to move at his direction. But for a moment, he felt like a small boy taking his first ride, reluctant, shy of the world, forcing himself to act like a man. He prayed to Athene to give him fortitude.

Dardanos mounted his horse and signed his troopers to mount up.

Telemachus took off without waiting and called to Dardanos: "Come with me, Son of Belos, and stay with me. We will return together to your home in the kingdom of the great and wise Nestor and the welcoming ruby-red seas off Messenia, the gods willing."

They galloped through the deserted streets of Corinth in the ruddy half-light, Telemachus and the two finest files of troopers among the Heraclides.

Whenever the smell of the blood of men mounts to the heavens, the gods become ill at ease, and the battle of the isthmus was no different. For many men lay dead and dying in the ditch and along the sands of the seashores and on the route through the isthmus. Men like dry leaves continuously plummet from the branches of trees, but the gods take notice when the shores of Styx become overcrowded beyond the ability of Charon to transport the souls to the Asphodel Fields. The pitch and dust and acrid smoke of bitter battle rose to the heavens from Hellas once again like a whisper for help.

Phoebus Apollo, the far-shooter, descended to earth in the guise of a son of Pelops and wounded warrior for the Pelopides. In the darkness of night, he stood before King Tisamenus, appearing as a large man, dressed as a common soldier, in a filthy uniform splattered from the bloody give and take of war, one thigh wrapped in dirty linen. He held his tarnished helmet in his hands, his long golden locks falling to his shoulders.

"My king, we must remove ourselves from the isthmus," he said to Tisamenus, wiping the mud from his face with his vermilion cloak.

"And who are you?" demanded Tisamenus, for he was surrounded by his officers, bringing him information on the state of the battle. Their forces were camped about 10 stadia from the ditch in the direction of Megara. Tisamenus was shocked that an ordinary soldier would dare speak directly to him, but he allowed the man to continue.

"I am a faithful fighter for your greatness and honor," Apollo replied. "I have insight into the will of the gods. Our greed has taken us far from the ditch and far from our enemies."

"What are you saying, sirrah?" Tisamenus demanded. "We have them in our grasp. They cannot escape. I counted five hundred of them dead in the ditch this very morning."

"The darkness can save us from defeat," the soldier told King Tisamenus. "But return we must...and now."

Tisamenus stared at the man, yet his anger remained in check, and he replied: "We are in short notice of sending Cresphontes and his Dorians to an early grave. Tomorrow, they will be finished. The gods are with us."

"No, no, you are mistaken," the soldier stuttered. "Corinth has fallen."

"Nonsense. This is treasonous. How do you know this?"

"Believe me," Apollo said.

"Believe you? If I believed every quack who would seek to advise me, I would not be standing here lord of all I see."

"Open your eyes, for they serve you naught."

"Get back to your troops, man. Take him away," Tisamenus ordered his lieutenants. But Apollo turned away and limped off without aid. No one challenged the wounded soldier, and he disappeared among the fighters of the Pelopides.

"Tomorrow, we will mount a final offensive to complete our rout of the enemy," Tisamenus said. "They are finished. Do we have evidence to the contrary?"

His lieutenants looked at each other. Finally, Dymas, his general in charge, spoke up. "We have no news from my brother, Pamphylus, in Sicyon."

"That is a good thing," Tisamenus replied.

"Perhaps, but I expected him to return with news."

"No, I sent him there to stay, but to report on the slightest provocation."

The Kings of Corinth stood beside the group of warriors, and Doridas commented without enthusiasm, for he was at this point used to being ignored as a counselor to Tisamenus. "We left the city unguarded with the soldiers sent to secure Sicyon. We should send a squad back this evening to assess the situation."

"Yes," Tellis, son of Tisamenus, said. "The supplies for this evening have yet to arrive. I will send three squads back to the port."

"Send as many as you like," Tisamenus replied, annoyed. "But we will be settled on our own couches before they return."

Meanwhile, outside of Corinth an old priestess sat along the roadside leading from Corinth to the port of Cenchreae, begging for alms from passers-by. The road was deserted. The people normally using the road were nowhere in sight. All day long, the only travelers were soldiers, passing rapidly on fine horses or marching in formation, with their blue *chlaina* billowing behind them and their bronze helmets shining in the sun.

When Telemachus spied the woman from a distance, he signaled for his troopers to halt. He pulled Sterope up close, and she wheeled about.

"Why are you sitting in the road, grandmother? Everyone is in their homes, for there is a war in progress."

"I fear no war. My husband left me and our children for the glory of war and never returned. He must have found a younger wife. My children left me as well and now occupy the soil of various countries unbeknownst to me. I am alone and live off the kindness of strangers."

"You look familiar to me," Telemachus said, for he noticed her sea gray eyes. "Are you from Lacedaemon, for I once visited there?"

"I have been there many times and my husband carried the crimson-colored shield of Sparta against Argos, but I am a citizen of no country. I am a mouthpiece for the gods and have a message for you."

"Do you know who we are?"

"I once knew the boy that you were; now I see the man you have become. Victory will be yours, but you must sail from one gulf to the other."

"Why would we want to do that?" Telemachus laughed.

"The gulfs are united."

"But the isthmus?" Telemachus asked, surprised. He looked more closely into the stony gray eyes, seeing rocky crags and seaweed lying on empty beaches.

"Like all things," she replied quickly, "the will of the gods and the intelligence of man can connect mighty gulfs." She raised her hand in benediction, indicating the end of the conversation.

Telemachus reached into the pocket of his tunic and pulled out the golden signet ring. He flung it into the old woman's lap.

"Bless you, grandmother."

He kicked Sterope, who jumped at the unexpected and unnecessary blow. The two files sprinted off toward Cenchreae. When they were gone, Pallas Athene, driver of the spoil, rose to her beautiful golden feet and returned to her abode in the brilliant heavens, but she had not completed her task.

XLII

Although Cenchreae is a larger port than Lechaeum, both were in fact poor coastal villages that became crowded only at rare times like these. The battle for Cenchreae did not amount to much. The troopers, led by Deiphontes, about two hundred strong, swooped into the small village, full of warehouses and storage facilities for goods coming from the direction of jasmine-scented Apeliotes. The Heraclides found a few active Pelopide soldiers and quite a few wounded ones. At seeing the massive swarm of horse riders, the active ones threw down their weapons. Those who resisted quickly came to the end of their lives with flashing iron swords.

Tisamenus was using Cenchreae as a supply area, and the Corinthian sutlers, butchers, and provisioners quickly acceded to the instructions of the Heraclide horse soldiers. The village was full of the walking wounded from the battle up on the isthmus. They rested in the waning sunlight, spitefully eyeing the horse soldiers, although they were content to remain where they were. The Heraclides soon secured the port, with all weapons, armaments, and armour piled in the street. All ships, both beached and at anchor, were secured. The Corinthians, both hardy and wounded, were herded into an area where they could be watched. As with most soldiers, when the end of the fight is apparent, the appetite for further hostilities evaporates.

The Heraclide infantry division marched in later in the darkness, spending only enough time to water and eat dried barley cakes and green olives, before they departed along the isthmus road. Led by Phalces and Autolycus, the elite foot soldiers' only complaint was the constant tramping on their way to battle, while the cavalry troopers, having taken Sicyon, Corinth, and now Cenchreae, received all the glory.

Telemachus arrived in the port later in the darkness of night with Dardanos and the two files of troopers.

"The infantry now owns the ditch," Oxylus explained. He and Telemachus munched dried figs and cheese with hard bread, washed down with wine and water in equal parts. They sat on the sloped beach, looking out into the openness of the Saronic Gulf. "There was only one Pelopide division guarding the ditch, with their backs to us. They were not eager to make a battle of it, and most are now here in Cenchreae. We have about two thousand troops along the ditch, including all the horse troopers."

"What about the reinforcements for Cresphontes?"

"We sent four companies with a large contingent of wolf stabbers from Thessaly, the finest archers from the Levantine, and slingers from Rhodes with metal bolts. They will quickly put an end to Tisamenus' heavy infantry."

"And the troopers?" Telemachus asked.

"We sent two horse tribes to help out. Combined, they are an excellent mixture of infantry and troopers, just what Cresphontes needs to contain Tisamenus," Oxylus said quietly. "I personally sent Aletes to command the infantry reinforcements on the isthmus, much to his dismay."

"Aletes. Can we trust him?" Telemachus asked.

"Yes, in this case only. I thought it might serve him to work with his cousins and uncle and to keep him away from us for the while."

"Who is leading the troopers?"

Oxylus shuddered, for he knew the consequence of his reply. "Amphion." That was all he could say.

"Amphion? Amphion? You sent Amphion?" His son's name echoed in his head like the reverberations of a bronze bell. His heart sank. His entire being froze. He pictured his young, idealistic son: at all times careful, never wanting to insult another, always acting correctly. Telemachus remembered the words of Nestor: "More hateful than the gates of heaven is a man who hides one thing in his mind and speaks another."

"How could you send Amphion with Aletes?"

"When it came time to select the leader of the troopers, Amphion refused to send anyone else. I tried to dissuade him."

"On his own? With Aletes, Eurysthenes and Procles, and Cresphontes?"

"He refused to send his best troopers and not accompany them himself. There was never any question. He is a strong leader. He will be fine."

"He will trust what these men say..."

"He is a grown man," Oxylus said defensively. "He will make his own decisions."

"I have failed," Telemachus repeated to himself. "I have failed."

The isthmus connecting the Peloponnese with mainland Hellas is about one hundred and seventy stadia in length, from Cenchreae to Megara. At its narrowest point near the Sanctuary of Poseidon, it is only thirty stadia wide. Here in ancient times, long before peoples' memories, the Corinthians constructed what they called "the ditch" or "the trench," stretching across the width of the isthmus from the Gulf of Corinth to the Saronic Gulf.

When the Heraclide army arrived, even under the most euphemistic of visions, the ditch was no more than an uncertain and hesitant shallow channel. It consisted of a dug-out trough, at places deep cuts in the earth and at other places natural pits, full of dirty water in the rainy season mixed with saltwater seeping from the gulf. At each end of the ditch littoral marshes met the gulfs, and the ancients had piled Cyclopean boulders to prevent passage along the shoreline. But it was more than a deeply excavated trough. For all along the ditch man-made barriers had been built over the ages to improve upon the ditch, consisting of walls of rock, huge piles of detritus, stones, mud, and gigantic timber walls. All were in varying states of decay and disrepair; some barricades dating from the time of the ancients were dissolving into dust, while others were newly constructed and impenetrable.

Barriers to separate men are doomed from the first brick, and the variety and state of these barriers lying along the ditch gave ample evidence to this. Barriers serve no more than as a useless symbol of man's fear of his neighbor and inability to understand his fellow man. Hesiod says, "call your friends to feast, especially your neighbors, for when mischief happens neighbors arrive ungirt, while friends and kinsmen must girt themselves." In this world, we are all the guests of Zeus.

Along the isthmus, all trees and vegetation had been denuded for centuries, save accidental weeds and grasses. Wild flowers bloomed in the spring when moisture was sufficient, but for most of the seasons the isthmus was a narrow desert with little life present in any form. Mortal man did not linger. Only the marsh rats enjoyed immunity.

The road to and from Attica passed over the isthmus on the Saronic Gulf side. Although the road was normally well traveled, it was rough, with many spots where a wagon might bog down. During the rainy season, it was often impassable. In the hot summer months, the road dried to hardpan, dusty and dirty, but passable. When mortals closed the road by digging out the trench and building barricades, only armies might attempt to use it and only with care, particularly in the face of antagonists. The junction of the road and the ditch had been filled in and dug up uncountable times over the eons to allow or prevent crossing the isthmus.

At the time of our story, the road ended at the ditch with a deep precipice on both sides. The newly dug dirt was piled high on the Peloponnesian side in great mounds, further blocking the road. Soldiers could cross only by climbing down one steep side and then clambering up the other. With shields and armour and weapons, this was difficult. With lances in your face, to attempt to cross was a mortal error. The Heraclide troops under the command of Cresphontes had discovered this to their everlasting sorrow. And the troops of Tisamenus had gained confidence of their superiority at war and their numerical advantage when they saw the Heraclide bodies piled in the ditch. Forgetting the lesson of the ditch, the Pelopides left the comfort and security of the Corinthian side and crossed over in pursuit of the Heraclides.

But the ditch was not simply a construction of man used for war and defense. Just as deadly poisons can be transformed into remedies for life saving, the ditch had another existence; the ditch was an idea for improving the lot of man. For centuries, the sages had dreamed of uniting the trade routes of the Gulf of Corinth with those of the Saronic Gulf. Rather than a voyage to circumnavigate the Peloponnese in capricious seas, requiring entire moon cycles, one could sail straight across the isthmus in no more time than it takes to enjoy a chalice of wine and with no greater risk. All that was required was to dig a deep trench, opening a waterway between the two gulfs.

Even a thousand years later, though, the ditch amounted to not much more than an obstacle and a filthy reminder of the failed dreams of mankind. The imaginings of men well up like bubbles in a spring, effervescent and full of spirit, bursting at the surface and leaving nothing behind. As Democritis reminds us, though, cheerfulness can only be found in the memories of achievements for the good of others. Of course, many wars have been fought for what was believed to be the goodness of others, but I am convinced that men learn from the errors of their past and from those of their ancestors. No doubt, the way is narrow and steep, and progress is slow, but eventually advancement is made. Certainly, the ditch represented a nexus, where the voiceless reminder of the power of the destructive forces of man met in harsh contrast with his imaginative and creative undertakings.

The ancients and all who came after attempted to excavate such a waterway, what the Corinthians came to call "the Corinthian Channel." All failed. But man never shuns the goddess Hope. One day it may come about. I am convinced, though not in the lives of my grandchildren. But I too, Alcathöe, as all mortals do, sleep with the comforting warmth of the goddess Hope by my side.

"You sent Amphion?" Telemachus continued to question Oxylus.

"I did not send him." Seated Oxylus could not stamp his foot, yet he too was becoming frustrated.

"You sent him with those evil men? He has Cresphontes, Aletes, Procles, and Eurysthenes as his champions, and he faces the best of Temenus' troops? You should have sent me. Or Deiphontes. Amphion cannot control those men, and his defense will be the last in their thoughts. How could you possibly allow that? I cannot understand."

"I love Amphion as my own son," Oxylus replied feebly.

"You have no sons, and you were never a son yourself. You have no idea. That is how you could do it." Telemachus closed his eyes and only half-listened as Oxylus attempted to move Telemachus from thoughts of his son.

"The reinforcements should arrive tomorrow morning, after a short rest on the ships during the voyage. We have to turn Tisamenus back toward the ditch for this to work out. That is the command that Aletes contains within his corselet. We will know soon enough tomorrow. The infantry captured three squads of Corinthian guards coming from the isthmus earlier this evening. They had been dispatched to survey their backs. Only they did not foresee an army in their path. They have been detained and were not displeased to speak openly of their fellow troops on the isthmus. Tisamenus is driving his troops hard, and there have been many casualties on the Corinthian side. He is convinced that victory will be theirs tomorrow. But his troops are less certain. No one is telling Tisamenus the truth, for all can see that they lack the equipment and the training of their opponent.

"Our infantry and troopers have now taken up positions along the ditch on the Corinthian side. They won this position without problem, killing and capturing the small number of Corinthian troops left to guard the ditch. Though clearing the ditch of bodies was another matter. It took hours, and now hundreds of bodies, mostly Heraclides, lie piled on this side of the ditch. But I am certain that tonight, for the first time, the bitterness of the situation Tisamenus finds himself in is beginning to expand to fill his mouth: no food, no water, and on the wrong side of the ditch."

Telemachus closed his mind to thoughts of his son for the moment and began considering a solution. "I am thinking that we must capture our enemy's attention and make him even more aware of his situation."

"What would that take?" Oxylus asked, glancing at his friend, knowing that he had failed him, the person most important in his life...just as he had failed his step-brother, Thermius.

"Tisamenus and his army must be made aware of our presence and believe they are battling the harried demons of Hades. We must put the fear of god in their stomachs. We must make them believe we are a vast number. That we are invincible. That we are aided by the gods. It will force his army to think on its own, which is always dangerous in war."

"And how will we accomplish this?"

"We will light the ditch. Just as Prometheus proved to Zeus that mortals hold greatness, turning their lives from a curse to a blessing, we will give fire to the Corinthians."

"Dardanos," Telemachus called. Dardanos walked over from where he had been eating and drinking with his troopers. "Carry these orders to Phalces and Autolycus at the ditch. I want to light up the sky across the isthmus for the entire night. Burn everything that can burn in the ditch and throw anything else into the fires. Then enlist the troopers to help out. You have my permission to take down every building here in Cenchreae and drag the timbers to the ditch. We want to wake up the gods and send them burnt offerings."

"Aye, sir. I will go myself."

The skinny man turned, ran to his mount, leapt onto the back of his grazing horse, and set off at a gallop. The distance was barely ten stadia. The other troopers calmly continued their meal.

"We found the treasury of Corinth in the palace," Telemachus mentioned to Oxylus after a few moments.

"Well?"

"Beyond belief. So much gold and valuables that it was beyond imagination. It must be the hoard of Agamemnon, the wealth of Priam in our own midst. Of all shares, Agamemnon's must have been by far the largest."

"I wonder if Cresphontes knows of its existence."

"Of course he does"

"If we have learned one thing, it is this," Oxylus said. "Man's greed is beyond measure and never diminishes. Greed for wealth, for power, for women, for greatness, for honor, for immortality. It both drives us and kills us."

Later, a large contingent of troopers arrived in the port and began dismantling the Cenchreae warehouses and dragging the wood back to the ditch. Soon, the yellow glow of many bonfires stretching across the isthmus began to light the sky. The ditch was full of rotting timbers of various barriers. When the dry beams and wood from the town were thrown on top of this kindling, the fires began in earnest. From Cenchreae, they could see a steady glow in a wide defile across the horizon. The glow began to light the smoke, billowing straight up into the cloudless evening. Even in the darkness, the filth and blackness of the smoke could be observed in the blaze.

The winds were breathless, and the columns of white and black clouds rose high above. As the conflagration grew, flames erupted from the ditch, soaring into the night sky. The fires were visible from all over Attica and Boeotia and the mountains of Argolis. Later generations would call it the "Fires of the Isthmus." The bards would whisper its significance, for fire brings transformation and destruction, but also creation. As Prometheus learned, fire can bring hope and dash hope, just as a two-sided sword cuts in either direction. To the Heraclides, the fires brought good tidings, while the Pelopides viewed them with trepidation.

For Telemachus, the fires took on a frightening aspect. Others might view the fires as just another battle, one opponent against another. But to Telemachus, it became a revelation of a greater conflagration, an energy of alteration, happening at this very moment. An alteration that he felt helpless to control, just as one feels during an earthquake or a volcanic eruption. And he had initiated this one. He had been foolish enough to believe that he could control the direction of battle. Nothing is ever created, and nothing is ever destroyed. All things are made up of infinite combinations of atoms, which swirl about in endless revolutions. The motion is constant. The soul and the mind are one. All else exists only as thoughts. Waves of change constantly wash up on the beach without our consent or foreknowledge or ability to manage. Only the gods can help us understand.

The fires continued burning throughout the night, while Telemachus' mind surveyed endless possibilities.

XLIII

Eos, the child of morning, fell in love with Tithonos, son of Laomedon and brother of King Priam of Troy, and she eloped with him to her home in far Ethiopia. She loved him so much that she asked Zeus to make him immortal. Zeus gave Tithonos his immortality, but in his unfathomable way did not free Tithonos from aging. Every day of his immortality, he grew older, while his goddess wife remained forever young. As time went on, she never stopped loving him in his hoary presence and always lay with him.

The morning after the great conflagration, the golden tones of Eos were obscured by a heavy, dirty mist of smoke slowly rising along the breadth of the isthmus. The previous evening, the Heraclides had moved into position. Almost two full divisions were arranged along the ditch, with the majority of the soldiers at the junction of the isthmus route and the ditch, facing chilly Boreas.

By mid-morning, the heavy smoke from the fires had nearly dissipated, but the old timbers continued to smolder along the ditch, and smoke and spouts of steam rose across the isthmus. Occasionally, small hotspots spurted into flame and then died back.

For the Heraclides formed up along the ditch and watching the isthmus before them, the first sign of battle was the sight of wounded Pelopides making their way to the other side of the ditch. Some walked under their own will power; others were carried along by mates; while a few were dragged on litters. In those days, an entry wound of any sort was most often fatal. And soldiers were well aware of this, having observed their comrades succumb to similar wounds. Telemachus and Oxylus stood behind the lines at the edge of the lacuna where the road had crossed the ditch. The wounded soldiers did not appear shocked as they first noticed the blue-draped troops on the opposite side of the ditch. The sight only verified their fears produced by the fires the night before. They simply followed directions as the Heraclides signaled them to move to the Gulf of

Corinth side of the isthmus between the marsh and the seashore, where the giant boulders sat. There, the number of men grew, as more and more wounded soldiers filed in to collapse on the rocky shore.

"If the Corinthians' main force does not return to the ditch," Telemachus said, "we will have to build a crossing for our horses to reach them."

But by late morning, Telemachus and Oxylus began to see evidence of the effectiveness of their reinforcements. A large Corinthian force came up to the ditch; some of the men had slight wounds, but most appeared hale and hearty. They were warned back, and they retreated outside of the range of the archers. They had discovered a new respect for the range of the Heraclide archers, though, for they settled far beyond what they would have done normally. They were joined by others. Soon enough, infantry companies in formation began appearing, and the Heraclides could see the dismay on the faces of the soldiers as they realized that gaining the other side of the ditch would not be painless.

The sun sat high now, and the heat was becoming intense. Sweat poured off the sun-scorched men in their armour on both sides of the ditch, and they sought shade. They hid under their cloaks and shields. Any shade gave a modicum of relief. Outside the direct rays of the sun, a gentle breeze cooled them. They loosened corselets and greaves and stuffed their wool undercaps into the pockets of the tunics. But those in the full sun suffered, and only the side toward Notus had any possible shade. A further difference between the two sides was that the Heraclides had plenty of fresh water brought to them from the rear in giant leather bladders. They watched as some of the Pelopides went into the sea to cool off, but on that side there was no drinking water.

At this point, word came that Temenus was on the shore on the Gulf of Corinth side of the isthmus with news from Cresphontes. Both Telemachus and Oxylus rode rapidly across the isthmus, where they could see the ship pulled onto the sand, the "babe" Heraclide flag, flapping in the breeze. A group of sailors stood on the shore with a large rope securing the ship. Telemachus and Oxylus cantered down onto the beach, and Temenus walked away from his sailors to join the two riders, who remained mounted, occasionally toeing their mounts to calm them as they moved with nervous energy.

"We spent all night moving the reinforcements, but they made all the difference," Temenus said. "The enemy was demoralized by the accuracy of the archers and slingers, and their thrusts against our positions were thwarted by the javelin throwers. We were no match for fighting in close quarters in the open, but from positions of protection, they were devastated. There were many casualties, and they lost heart for battle. But we have also lost many men. On the first day alone, Cresphontes estimates that we lost a fourth of our company, perhaps two hundred dead, and many wounded. We took an equal number of the Pelopides. Today we made up for it. They took many times more than that in casualties, and their wounds put those still standing at the run. Their main force is now headed in your direction."

"Can you transport more horse troops?" Telemachus asked.

"Two of our large Phoenician ships are just off the coast. We could bring them here in no time, and they could carry a few hundred horses and men."

"We will be back with the cavalry as soon as possible. Bring both of the ships."

When they returned to the intersection of the ditch and road, they found heavy fighting. Telemachus set off immediately to order two tribes to the ships. Horses were useless at the ditch. The horses were herded together, while the troopers used their bows from behind the Heraclide lines. Telemachus found Deiphontes.

"Take two tribes of troopers to meet Temenus and the ships and from there join Amphion and Aletes to force the tail end of the enemy into the ditch. You need only to press from behind to prevent their escape and not attack them directly. The horses will be perfect...like herding cattle. We must disrupt the frontal assault and instill fear and uncertainty in the men at the edge of the contest."

Deiphontes saluted as he mounted his horse.

"Deiphontes, can you look out for Amphion for his father's sake."

"Yes, but you need not worry. No man is a better rider nor wiser in his actions than Amphion."

"Act with god," was all Amphion's father could choke out.

In any battle, a warrior must place his god-given terror of death in another compartment far beneath his skin. He must retire all personal and sentimental thoughts. He cannot survive if his thoughts turn to wife and children or parents at home or his own loss of life. He must temporarily inter these thoughts beyond recall, leaving only hatred and desire to overcome others. Even his own instinct to survive must be quarried away. The future does not exist, and the past is a black mist hiding all from view.

Antagonists understand this way of thinking and in combat attempt to dredge up these buried emotions and transport them back to the surface. This can be done in many ways, by the give and take of the goddess Victory, by stealing confidence, by massive charges with all the dint and din of war, by singing and shouting, or by absolute silence, which the Spartans used to perturb an enemy. In battle, victory feeds upon itself. By forcing an enemy to admit his weaknesses and to see defeat in his future, we place the heart back into the man and, by so doing, extinguish his ability to function as a soldier. For when we say, "take the heart out of the man," we really mean "place his heart back in command," which spells the end for a warrior.

In the words of Homer, it took a god to bring Achilles to his senses and reintroduce him to his feelings of sorrow and pity and by doing so to bring him to his senses, then to his knees, and finally to the dust.

The battle of the Heraclides and Pelopides boiled and raged in the ditch, for the Pelopides knew they had no choice but to attempt to cross. Wave after wave of Pelopide heavy infantry pushing their long lances and heavy shields before them sought to gain a foothold on the other side of the ditch. The Pelopides fought with intensity and died quickly, for the climb onto the slope of the ditch put them in the face of the Heraclide infantry and made it almost impossible to protect themselves. They used their long lances to keep the Heraclides away, but they had to drag their shields up the incline, exposing their bodies to the deadly wolf-killing javelins at close range. As one fell, another came from behind. In the insanity of war, the soldiers used the bodies and shields of their fallen comrades as stepping stones up the incline of the ditch. They slowly constructed the pilings of a bridge across the ditch with the bodies and shields of their comrades.

Oxylus went along the line urging and exhorting his men to prevent the Corinthians from mounting the ditch. Archers and javelin throwers fired from distances normally associated with lances. But as more men fell in the pit, the closer those that followed came to the level of the road. The death of one man provided another stepping stone toward victory, as though Hades were directing the assault.

Phalces and Autolycus worked their infantry troops at the edges of the pit, substituting one company at a time, pulling another back to rest, for there is nothing more exhausting than the give and take of murder. The fronts of the battle on the ditch were miniscule. No more than one company at a time could effectively battle the oncoming soldiers, but there were only three established hotspots. The Pelopides paid dearly to establish a hotspot, climbing the slope of the ditch, being forced from behind by their own troops. One man pushed on the back of the next. Men behind used their comrades as shields, hiding at the back of a living body, thrusting their lances at the defenders.

The Heraclide troops formed up at the edge of the ditch, four deep, using their own lances or ones taken from the Corinthians to punish the invaders, at times falling back to allow the archers and javelin throwers space, and then forming up again into a deadly wall. They clutched at the bronze-tipped lances of the Pelopides that appeared above the road level, pulling the man behind the lance into the open and sending their destructive missiles down into the pit. But the enemy continued to slog through the blood and guts of his own dead to climb up to certain death at the level of the isthmus. Gradually, more heads appeared at the surface, but those soon disappeared into the abyss.

Time slowed to a halt. The sun above the battling men seared the earth, but failed to move in the sky. Helios seemed more interested in the battle than in driving his horses and chariot across the heavens. Phalces had formed a solid rank of skirmishers ready for hand-to-hand combat with their cut-and-thrust swords. Behind this formation stood the dismounted troopers with their bows and arrows at the ready. And behind them, Telemachus had set up detachments of mounted troopers at the ready in a semicircle around the battles. If the enemy managed to gain a foothold on the Corinth side of the ditch, he would then confront the heavy skirmishers, followed by the pointblank punishment of bronze-tipped arrows, followed by the full force of the armoured horses flying at him with swords flashing.

At one point, a Pelopide soldier with his lance ahead of him broke free of the Heraclide line of defense into the open on the Heraclide side of the ditch. Before the archers could fire on the man and put an end to him, Oxylus turned Rhaebus in a tight circle, and man and horse descended upon the soldier, who had managed to gain the farthest foothold against the enemy of all his compatriots. The archers held their arrows in abeyance when they saw their diminutive general on his giant charger spring forward. The Corinthian soldier could only attempt to set his lance in the earth at the oncoming horse and wonder at the monster falling on him, surely the ill-deserved wrath of some god. The lance shattered harmlessly on the Rhaebus' bronze breast plate. The sword of the rider and horse flashed by him. The helmeted head of the Corinthian skidded back to the ditch, falling among the human pilings of the bridge, as his body sank to the earth. Never again would he see the old men of Argos or the fabled walls of Tiryns or the vineyard lands of Epidaurus. The Heraclide soldiers and archers cheered in honor of their general and began fighting all the harder to the dismay of the oncoming Pelopides.

Across the ditch, Telemachus caught glimpses of the Pelopide generals, for by now the main forces had gathered on the other side. Just as the preponderance of the Heraclides stood at the ready, so too did the Pelopides, as though they were observers to the event. The effort on the part of the Pelopides was to bridge the ditch in any way possible, and they continued to send waves of men into the backs of their fellows to keep up the pressure points against the Heraclides. Slowly, the ditch filled with human detritus.

Telemachus caught up with Oxylus.

"We must rekindle fires in the pit to stop the advance."

"They are taking tremendous casualties and cannot continue this for long," Oxylus replied.

"They will continue until they have filled the ditch with bodies."

"They are losing forty men to one of our own, or more."

"But when they break through…"

"We can stop them."

"No. We must stop them now," Telemachus argued. "We will bring up wagons with loads of tallow and olive oil, fire them, and send them into the pit."

A small group of troopers returned to Cenchreae to collect wagons and to fill them with oil in large ceramic containers from the sutler wagons and dry tallow wax used by mariners in ship building. Soon, they returned with the first of the old wooden wagons. The rear was filled with oil containers and large blocks of tallow. The troopers had added bundles of dry rattan used in chariot, furniture, and container making, which they had confiscated from one of the shipping warehouses. The soldiers lined up the wagons at each of the hotspots in the direction of the ditch behind the archers. They rapidly unharnessed the horses and disconnected the draw poles and whiffletrees that connected to the horse harnesses. To keep the front wheels in line, they hurriedly tied ropes to the axle. By the time they had completed all this; fires were already burning in the wagons. They decapitated the oil containers. The wax, bundles of rattan, and wooden sides of the wagon began flaming strongly.

Oxylus ordered the archers and skirmishers back from the ditch to open passages among the infantry solders. They backed off only long enough for the wagons to be pushed up to the edge and then over into the ditch. The wagons tumbled into the ditch, one after the other, knocking men aside, throwing their contents onto the men below, and then falling on top of the heap of men, both living and dead. It did not take long to begin burning in earnest, as the oil covered the piles of bodies and the reeds and rattan began blazing. What most likely set the blazes apace were the hot embers of the logs at the base of the ditch, which had burned all night and had turned into smoldering coals.

Forgive me, but the human body is not easy to set on fire, but once it begins to burn it acts like a candle turned inside out, with the fat on the inside and the wick on the outside. The heat from the reeds and wax set the bodies, clothes, wooden-framed shields, and logs on fire, which in turn melted the fat from the bodies and blocks of tallow and began a general conflagration. By the time the Pelopides could react to the wagons falling onto them and attempt to scramble to safety, the pit was burning rapidly, evolving into an inferno. The flames began licking the sides of the ditch, forcing both armies back from the hotspots. The Heraclides stood back and cheered in approval, as the flames shot up above the ground level of the isthmus, sending smoke high into the sky, wafting toward the Peloponnese.

Now, people have asked me of the smell of this fire. I, Antimenes must say that the smell of a human body burning cannot be too different from that of a sacrificial animal. But certainly the gods know the difference. I can only describe the smell as acrid and the smoke as dirty and sullied. The smoke rising to the abodes of the gods from this fire was, undoubtedly, not appealing. This offering did not please the gods and, in fact, affronted their senses. If this were not true, all our traditions and beliefs would be backwards.

The heat from the fire forced the soldiers farther back from the ditch. The two sides eyed each other through the smoke and flames with a newly-gained hatred: the Heraclides held Victory to their hearts, while the Pelopides were frustrated and disheartened. Finally, Helios dipped in the sky, perhaps disturbed by the direction the fighting had taken. Twilight began to fall. Without the heat from the conflagration, the afternoon sea breeze might have been comforting to the soldiers. The fighting, though, had come to an end for this day. Both sides retired to lick their wounds and consider their circumstances as the conflagration continued strongly. The smoke continued to rise in the sky and was received by the gods not as a burnt offering of joy and thanks for their goodness and understanding, but rather as a sign of rancor and acrimony.

Before any food was served, the troops were dispatched to bring additional timbers, to feed the hotspots across the isthmus to light the night skies. They dismantled additional buildings in the port village and transported whatever would burn back to the ditch. Soon piles of timber posts and columns rose along the road, for they had more combustibles than the fire could consume. As darkness fell, the fires blazed in earnest. Sentries were set across the isthmus to ensure that the Pelopides remained on their side and to observe any development.

The Heraclides started a final bonfire on the road well back from the ditch, but close enough to be in full view of the Pelopide troops. They brought twenty sheep and twenty goats up to the fire, and the priests sacrificed them to send burnt offerings to Zeus and Athene. Soon, the sweet smells of broiling meat overcame the acrid smoke of the remnants of the human bodies and trash being incinerated. Limited rations of wine and plenty of water were passed among the Heraclides, and the soldiers splashed the dry earth with libations to their personal preferred gods.

At the same time across the ditch, the Pelopide army settled down to another night without water or food, warily watching the Heraclides celebrate their day's victory. Peerless King Tisamenus of the Pelopides could not think up a way to combat the Heraclides, and he was accustomed to getting his way. Tisamenus had even prayed to Poseidon to save the Pelopides by some extraordinary means, since Poseidon was known to dislike foreign adventurers on his soil. Tisamenus would have liked to sacrifice some hecatomb to the gods, but he knew that messages were received even from petitioners who could not afford such offerings. Strangely enough, for the gods work in mysterious ways, Poseidon answered his prayers.

XLIV

The Pelopide leaders gathered in a campaign tent on the Borean side of the ditch. After much rancor, his voice hoarse from yelling, King Tisamenus eyed his officers with resentment and anger, listening in silence. A single lamp flickered, and the men's faces were drawn and haggard.

Doridas and Hyanthidas, the Kings of Corinth, watched without enthusiasm. They were the descendants of Ornytion, in the line of Atlas. These men discussing the future of Corinth were mainly from Mycenae, Argos, or elsewhere in the Peloponnese, or even from outside. Not so long ago, these men were enemies of Corinth, and, most likely, they would be again.

Doridas spoke: "my brother and I have ruled in Corinth since the time of your grandfather, Agamemnon. Corinth is the jewel of the gulf. We wonder if there might be some agreement with the Heraclides, the Dorians, as you call them. Both sides have lost many men, and the city itself may be in danger."

"No wonder that no one seeks your advice," Dymas, the general in charge and brother of Pamphylus, shouted. "The difference between a fool and a wise man is that the fool believes he is wise. The Dorians will offer us nothing, not even our lives."

"Perhaps," Doridas continued, "a sharing proposal could be put forth."

"We are not ready to concede," said Tellis, son of Tisamenus.

"You must be blind," Hyanthidas yelled.

"I see you," Tellis replied angrily, "you weakling…at the end of my knife."

"Blame must be accepted by all," Dymas said firmly. "Our troops failed to break the lines of the Dorians in either direction. But we must not lose our will to fight. Victory will come if we persevere."

"We can possibly survive another day without water," Tellis said, "but certainly not two more days. No substantial food remains, and our supplies of water were exhausted by mid-afternoon. The troops are now parched beyond belief. We must choose a direction to turn. We must push through the Dorians at all costs."

"The strength of the forces at our fronts and backs can only be guessed at," Dymas continued. "Though it appears the greater force of the Heraclides is in our faces. We must move toward Corinth and break their hold on the ditch."

Tellis, son of Tisamenus, spoke. "What a mistake it was to trust Lacestades and Pamphylus. Certainly, some treasonous arrangement was brokered that facilitated the entry of the Dorians in such numbers into our own backyard. And what of our wives and children? Certainly the soldiers razed all in their path and put the people to the sword. Is there anything to return to at this point? Why has our navy not supported us? Where are the reinforcements promised by the archons in Arcadia? What about the Spartans, famed for their fighting skills? They provided a handful of troops to the effort and stand by watching as the defense of the Peloponnese falls on Corinth and Argos."

The talk continued into the night with accusations and indictments traded back and forth like children's knucklebones,* but without resolution.

Finally, Tisamenus rose and spoke in a low voice, barely audible: "We must ask ourselves the penalty of failure. What are these Dorians but a horde of barbarians who will settle for nothing short of the end of our civilization as we know it? We believe in ourselves and the dignity of our home. My grandfather, the hero Agamemnon, fought for our freedom and our values. Now, we are tested by barbarians. Either we strike or we die. They will not spare us. I want a plan before sunrise. Do not fail me in this." He rose and walked out of the tent.

With Tisamenus departed, the officers began fighting like dogs over gnawed gristle.

Outside the tent, Tisamenus called to one of his bodyguards to bring Glaucus, son of Tros, to him. He then walked down to the sea. Although a young man, Glaucus was one of his best fighters and a native of Epidaurus.

---

* A children's game played with the bones of small rodents.

When Glaucus arrived, Tisamenus looked at the man. He was as beautiful as young men can be, strong, lithe, innocent, and bright-eyed. He stood before his king with a mixture of pride and trepidation. He was younger than Tellis, Tisamenus' son by his first wife, and far older than his only other son, now barely four years of age. He signaled for Glaucus to approach and sent his guards off.

"My young friend. Tonight, Argos and Corinth depend on you. Are you prepared to sacrifice for your country?"

Glaucus nodded his head. "Yes, Sire."

"You must swim around the troops in the direction of Boreas, avoiding the enemy, and then take to land. You will come to the small fishing village, Cromyon, on the isthmus road. There, I have a ship of state. You will talk to the captain and then return with the ship tomorrow to the Sanctuary of Poseidon."

"Yes, Sire."

"Your father served my family well. Now, it is your turn. And you will be rewarded handsomely."

The sea was still warm from the day's sun. Without hesitating, Glaucus disrobed. Swiftly, he dove into the dark sea, shimmering in the moonlight, and surfaced with strong strokes, swimming directly out into the Saronic Gulf. He swam powerfully and well. In a short while, the reflections of his wake could no longer be seen.

Meanwhile, on the other side of the ditch Telemachus and Oxylus ate sparingly. Their appetites had departed them. But they too prayed to the gods and with every drink poured a libationary offering. They assumed that tomorrow would be the major battle, for the Pelopides could not survive another night on the isthmus. The strategy of the Heraclides had worked well to this point, and save for the troops under the command of Cresphontes, they had not suffered heavy losses.

"Tomorrow," Oxylus said to Telemachus, "we must spread the infantry across the isthmus. Deiphontes, Aletes, and Amphion will attack at dawn with the horse troops on the opposite side, and we must be prepared for a desperate move on the part of the Pelopides.

Your troopers will be our line of communication as Tisamenus' plans develop."

"When a wild beast is surrounded," Telemachus said, "his defense become offense. He will strike out in some direction. If he chooses to charge in the direction of Boreas, we will have to cross the ditch with our horses to chase him down; otherwise he may well break out. But frankly, I think he will come in our direction. And I am sure Tisamenus will not hesitate to send many more men into the ditch."

"At least our troops will be fed and watered," Oxylus said. He paused a moment to consider an unasked question on both of their minds. "I am sure that Amphion is well. He is a good boy and a strong rider. Would that I had such sons as yours. Both are showing their mettle on the battlefield. Without Autolycus, we would have suffered greater losses at the pit. He fought his heart out, and the soldiers respect him. Phalces, too, fought well."

"I would much prefer to see them in the vineyards among their children, as they once played among the vines with me...and Polycasté."

Telemachus strolled out to the shore of the Saronic Gulf. The night was clear, with only the coiling tails of residual smoke rising from the remaining hotspots. The warm windless night air embraced him. He remembered one such night on Ithaca as a young man – about the same age as his sons were now – when he had been invited to join the suitors. Mentor had always advised him to stay clear of the suitors, but several of them had befriended him. They offered him a seat at the couch as the wine flowed and the suitors told their stories. Some described great battles and hunts and travels. They told of liaisons with goddesses. A few talked of their plans for Odysseus' kingdom if successful, always careful to include Telemachus. Even now, his life seemed commonplace in comparison. What was important to him? As a young man he had wanted to be like these men, these suitors: not doing what they were doing to another man's estate, but to live as they had. He thought of the tales he could tell as a mature man. Yet, he knew exactly what he wanted, and it did not entail oath-breaking, theft, or murder. It involved setting a course without harm to others and navigating the shoals and winds to arrive at a destination, pride intact. It involved accepting no less in others than he would in himself. Yet somewhere, he had gotten off course. He had placed Polycasté, Amphion, and Autolycus at risk, and it was not their fight. He had not meant to do that. If only the gods would grant him the grace to hold them from harm.

At dawn, the blustery sons of rosy-fingered Eos, the windy *Anemoi*, remained quiet and still. The Heraclides were spread across the isthmus. Additional piles of timbers had been collected during the night, and more incendiary wagons had been set up ready for use. As the first glows of Eos filtered through the mist, the sounds of battle could be heard from across the ditch. The troops moved up to the edge, watching for some sign of the enemy. The first word of attack came from the Gulf of Corinth side. The Pelopides had built ladders and wooden bridges and were attempting to cross the ditch. Word soon followed that they were doing the same at other points along the ditch. The Heraclides rapidly responded, building formations at each potential crossing point. The archers gathered at each crossing. The Pelopide soldiers on the ladders made easy targets, long before the javelins were in range to strike. Arrows flew across the ditch, punishing the Pelopides on the opposite edge, until the troops were forced to stay well back from the edge where their brethren were attempting to gain a foothold.

Telemachus rode back and forth at each of the hotspots. At the same time, he was watching the other side of the ditch in the distance, for he was hoping that the Pelopides were fighting on two fronts. For a while, the ditch continued to fill rapidly with the bodies of the enemy, but this time the bodies were spaced across the ditch and did not build as quickly into bridges. For every man that made it across a bridge to face the Heraclide skirmishers, five or ten fell into the ditch. But when one Pelopide did cross and made it into the front, it forced the Heraclides to reform to repulse him. The javelin throwers came up from behind the wall to use their javelins as missiles and short lances, pushing the points at the heavy shields of the Pelopides. At such close range, the archers could not loose their missiles, since their aim was blocked by their own troops. Slowly, the Pelopides gained footholds on the opposite side of the ditch, but at a tremendous cost.

The Heraclides fell back from two of the entry points across the ditch. The others held. At these two points, Oxylus ordered the archers back to get a better view of the enemy. Since the ladders could accommodate only a few men at a time, they began sending volleys of arrows at the troops massed on the other side of the ditch. The arrows darkened the skies like locusts over barley fields. At the same time, he sent in reinforcements of infantry with their cut-and-thrust swords to meet the heavy infantry of the Pelopides. Hand to hand combat began in earnest. The archers made it very difficult for the Pelopides, but they began jumping down into the ditch and climbing up the sides. Since the Heraclides had backed off, where yesterday the Pelopides had been unsuccessful, today they managed to gain access to the Heraclide side of the ditch. But for every man who managed to come to his feet on the Heraclide side of the ditch, many more men fell. And of those who crossed, many soon returned to the bottom of the ditch to join their fellows in the depths.

The hand-to-hand combat continued to force the Heraclides to spread their forces. The sword fighting was an exhausting process. Each stroke, whether striking an opponent or not, took its toll on the fighter. Exhaustion came quickly, and it required that one man spell another rapidly. The companies cycled hurriedly to replace the exhausted men at the front of the ranks. As men fell, others took their places as well. The iron cut-and-thrust swords proved their worth. They cut the bronze tips off the ash lances of the Pelopides, leaving them to resort to fighting with their short bronze swords and heavy shields. The iron swords cut through the shields, leaving the soldiers without defense and often without limbs to hold their shields. The shorter bronze swords could not withstand the force of a slashing iron sword.

Telemachus watched in amazement as Autolycus managed one hotspot, keeping his soldiers rotating at the ditch, allowing the skirmishers to finish off those Pelopides who managed to gain a foothold. He watched as his own son entered into the battle. Autolycus confronted a large Pelopide with his sword, ducking and slashing under the man's large shield, taking him down with a wound to his legs, to be sent down to Hades by a pig sticker from a large Heraclide skirmisher protecting Autolycus. Autolycus stepped back, continuing to order his troops. Telemachus could not bear to watch any longer. The babe who had slept in his arms had grown into a man, and Telemachus could do nothing to help him or save him, and his help was not being sought. He turned Sterope and rode off rapidly with his tablemates following him.

For a long while in the morning, the troops of the Pelopides frantically fought their way across the ditch, losing many men in the process, but the few who gained access to fight on the opposite bank began to take a toll on the Heraclides. Those who crossed the ditch allowed others to follow. They, however, had short lifetimes, but as they fell into the dust of the isthmus, they took with them a Heraclide or two. The odds clearly were against the Pelopides; they could not field enough soldiers to continue sacrificing them at this rate. Yet, they continued to cross the ditch, driven by their bravery, willingness to die, or mindlessness. Behind each man who crossed the ditch was another pushing him forward.

Under these circumstances, the fighting continued. But by mid-day with the sun at its height, it became clear that crossing the ditch was not the only problem facing the Pelopides. On the far side of the ditch, formations of fighters with their backs to the ditch began to appear. Among these fighters, blue cloaks of the Heraclide infantry could be glimpsed. No longer Aegean blue, their cloaks were covered in blood, grime, and the dirt of battle. They were a welcome sight to the defenders along the ditch. On both sides, the dry dust of the isthmus itself was turning to mud and gore. The dead and dying covered the earth like fresh-turned soil. It made fighting difficult, the footing uncertain, and, even in places where there were no bodies, blood ran like streams of water in a downpour. The Pelopides continued pressing their way across the ditch. They now had no other direction to turn, with forces at their backs. The sounds of the battle changed. Where the Pelopide soldiers had begun the battle with cries and martial verses, now the sounds were of the striking of armaments, shouts of warning, cries of pain and anger, and the moans of the wounded. The soldiers no longer wasted energy but concentrated on their horrifying job.

Telemachus rode from one side of the isthmus to the other. His troopers were either off their horses as archers or backing the fighting. A few remained mounted, prepared as the final line of defense, but no Pelopide had managed to survive to this line. On the horizon across the ditch, he could see more and more blue of the Heraclide troopers. The Pelopides had to turn and form rank against the rapidly moving formations of troopers, peppering them with arrows. At the same time, the troopers prevented the Pelopides from supporting their compatriots at the ditch. The horses galloped rapidly along the Pelopide line laterally, taking aim at the closely ordered soldiers, protected only by their shields. Every horse file that crossed in front of the formation took a deadly toll on the Pelopides.

As Telemachus approached the fighting on the Saronic Gulf side, he saw a ship bearing no colors sitting off the coast. He asked several troopers to remain there and send him information on its movements.

On the Gulf of Corinth side, Temenus had pulled one of the large Phoenician ships up on shore. He brought word of what Telemachus already knew that Cresphontes and the twins were driving the Pelopides back to the ditch. The horse troops and javelin throwers had turned the tide against the Pelopides, who were retreating toward the ditch. With Temenus was Polyphontes, the son of King Lacestades of Sicyon, who had been sent the first night to assess Cresphontes' situation. Telemachus described the progress being made on their side of the ditch.

Although the melee continued on both sides, it was clear that the Pelopides were surrounded and fighting on two fronts and losing on both. The Heraclides were pressing from the direction of Boreas and defending from Notus. Slowly, the pinchers of the crab closed about its prey. A scent of victory was evident among the Heraclides, and there is no better tonic than this for revitalizing one side against the other. The Heraclides were occupied with killing, but they saw the end. Both sides saw the end, but somehow this fact had to make itself known. How long can a soldier watch his peers fall in the dust, knowing that it is only a matter of time before he will follow?

Oxylus sensed the opening. At one of the hotspots, he ordered his troops to stop fighting and to back off from the ditch. It took some time to implement his command along the entire length of the ditch. And it is true that the Pelopides continued to cross the ditch, but when they arrived on the other side they were confronted by the piles of dead and the formation of the Heraclides facing them, with four ranks of archers at the fore. The Pelopides digested this shift in strategy. For a moment, both sides faced each other head-on. Soon, the Heraclides on the Borean bank began to fall back, for they saw their fellows on the Notus side and so took the same measure.

The two armies faced each other. As they did so, perhaps Zeus decided that the time had come, that too many of his sons lay on the battlefield never to return to their families. Or perhaps it was the decision of a single fighter whose heart had been returned to him. A Pelopide soldier threw his sword onto the ground and made his way forward through the bodies and mud into the no-man's land between the two armies and sank exhausted to the ground. He was followed by a second and then a third man. The Heraclide troops watched respectfully and began rubbing the hilts of their swords against the basin of their round shields. A wail arose, somewhere between the sound of cats screeching in the night and a high drumbeat. The Heraclides made the sound as a sign of victory, while the Pelopides heard it as a threat that the opposing fighters were dedicated to continuing the battle without relent. The sound rose across the isthmus as though a giant flock of geese were flying in close order over the land on their way to Egypt and Ethiopia and the lands of Notus so beloved of the gods. The sound continued until an order went down the line from the Heraclides. The Heraclides raised their voices to yell at the Pelopides, repeating over and over again:

"Return to the other side of the isthmus, and you will live. Return to the other side of the ditch to live. Return and live. Return and your life is yours."

The Pelopides threw down their weapons and dropped to the ground. Some stood on the edge of the hateful ditch and threw their swords and shields down into its murky depths.

The sun was now low in the sky, and the mountains in the distance were covered in long shadows. The Pelopides began returning to the other side of the ditch, which was not easy. Oxylus was signaling to the horse troops on the other side in the distance to back up to give them plenty of space. He could now see Heraclide infantry and cavalry formations behind the Pelopides. The Pelopide officers began yelling at their men, but the storm of war had becalmed, and the skies were clearing. The officers knew it as well as their men. The soldiers climbed back toward Boreas, leaving their weapons behind, and sat down along the ditch. A Heraclide solder advanced to the ditch with a bladder of water and handed it to one of the last remaining Pelopides, who took it with him across the ditch and when he surfaced at the other side took a long draft and then handed it off to another.

What followed was not remarkable. A man often clings to his opponent after a deadly combat where both survive. The tides of rage mount rapidly, but withdraw at an even faster rate. It is strange that deadly enemies can shift their emotions so quickly. Perhaps it is a final recognition at the lowest point of our emotions that we all suffer in similar ways and that we all meet in Hades, sooner or later.

Heraclide soldiers began to cross the ditch to distribute water among the Pelopides and at the same time gathered their weapons into piles. The formations of Heraclide infantry and cavalry came down to the ditch from the far bank, and a cheer arose as they waved across the ditch at their fellow soldiers.

It was at this moment that a rider galloped up to Telemachus.

"Come quickly."

XLV

Telemachus followed the trooper. They galloped along the ditch to the Saronic Gulf side of the isthmus and came to a halt along the shore at the end of the ditch where the great boulders prevented passage. On the far side of the barrier, Telemachus saw a small jolly boat and two rowers making their way to shore from a long ship waiting in the calm waters, its sail hanging loosely, as it faced the bright sun now low in the sky. He could make out a few Pelopide soldiers in vermilion along the shore facing the oncoming boat. Among them he could see a tall man with a white beard and white robes.

"Who else can that be but Tisamenus?" Telemachus asked himself. "We cannot allow him to escape."

Telemachus galloped back to where Oxylus stood, with Rhaebus at his side. Oxylus was beginning the process of preparing for peace: bringing the Heraclides to one side, collecting the Pelopide armaments, feeding the soldiers, and setting up for the next few days.

"Tisamenus is escaping," Telemachus yelled.

"We cannot allow him to escape...all would be lost."

"We must be sure," Telemachus replied. He wondered who could identify Tisamenus. He remembered that Polyphontes was with Temenus on the Gulf of Corinth side of the isthmus.

"Get Polyphontes," he ordered two of his tablemates, "and bring him to us at the Sanctuary of Poseidon."

Oxylus mounted Rhaebus, and they galloped off toward the Saronic Gulf. After a short while, a blue-clad trooper rode up with the young son of Lacestades riding behind him, holding on to the trooper's cuirass.

"Do you know Tisamenus?"

"Of course," answered Polyphontes.

The jolly boat was now pulled up on the sand. In the distance, it was difficult to make out distinct figures, and the Corinthians surrounded the boat and individuals

"I thought you were lost," Oxylus said to Polyphontes. "Your father was waiting, but you did not return."

"I was with Cresphontes, and this man kept me prisoner. He accused me of being a spy and threatened my life." His anger began mounting in his voice. "He treated me as one would treat a slave or even worse. He was in the process of hanging me, when Temenus arrived and told him who I was. I had a rope tied around my neck. I thought I was dead. Never in all my life have I been treated with such contumely. He insulted my family and knew nothing of my father..."

"Look," Telemachus reminded him, and he glanced at the boat.

"Wait. Now I can see," Polyphontes said, tearing himself from his deadly anger, shielding his eyes from the sun.

The soldiers surrounding the jolly boat moved back up the beach, leaving the boat and several sailors exposed to view. Two sailors steadied the boat as the man in robes stepped in and sat down. Several sailors pushed the boat into the gentle waves and jumped in to begin rowing. The boat moved slowing. There was no breeze.

"Is that him?" Oxylus asked.

"Yes," Polyphontes replied, still visibly angry. "That is the King of Mycenae, Argos, Corinth, and Arcadia and the Prince of the Peloponnese. And I would choose him to rule a thousand times over this Heraclide, Cresphontes, whom one day I will repay for his treachery to me." He paused for a moment to gulp down his fury. "And that is his son, Tellis, with him."

"If Tisamenus escapes," Oxylus said, "we will have gained nothing. We will have lost."

They sat motionlessly on their horses, watching the jolly boat slowly row out into the sea toward the long ship.

"All is lost," Oxylus declared.

History has a way of repeating itself. Long before the war in Troy and the War of the Families, Laomedon, King of Troas, Phrygia,

and Mysia, of the family of Dardanus, was one of the great kings of Persia. Laomedon tracked his family roots back to the immortals, the lord of gods himself and Electra, the daughter of a Titan. But to the gods, all mortals must prove themselves regardless of rank or position.

Here then, Apollo and Poseidon chose to put Laomedon to the test. The nature of the test hints at wider participation among the gods. The two immortals disguised themselves as common laborers and hired themselves out for wages to design and construct at Troy the greatest fortification the world has ever known. This occupation lasted more than a year, and the complications of two immortals on earth for such an extended period can only be guessed at. They completed the impregnable walls and ramparts and battlements, which served many generations until the Greeks came to retrieve Helen and razed the entire city and its population.

Apollo and Poseidon worked as hard as any mortals, and when they had completed their magnificent architectural defense (for surely gods cannot build a common structure), they went to the king for payment. Laomedon in his hauteur and disdain failed to see the urgency in paying these two common laborers and refused the advice of his counselors. As we have seen, gods make appearances in the most unexpected places and in the most unexpected guises. The Greeks treat all people with respect, since you never know when you may be in the presence of a god. Or said another way, the gods reside within all of us.

The gods became incensed at Laomedon's refusal to pay, and just as mortals feel injustice, so too do gods, but gods are not without resort, even to a great king. Apollo chose to send plague and pestilence, and Poseidon sent a great sea monster with numerous legs and arms. Unfortunately, as we so often see in these dealings, it was the people who suffered for the errors and outrages of their leader. So fear and panic descended upon the people of Troy.

Now King Laomedon was immune and far removed from these events, but his counselors did inform him of the suffering of his subjects. They related to him the dark and evil mood of his people, the closed buildings and shops, the empty streets, and the hopelessness and ominous fear running rampant in his realm. Laomedon decided that this state of affairs should not be allowed to continue and sent for the most prominent seer of his day, the very man who had foreseen the greatness of his rule. The oracle explained that the king had insulted the gods and must expose his golden haired daughter to the sea monster. By so doing, he would appease the gods. Desperately and with great sorrow, the king had his young daughter chained to a rock on the edge of the sea in hopes that she might be devoured by the monster and that this might propitiate the gods.

At this same time, Heracles was traveling in the lands of Apeliotes and came upon the child chained to the rocks with the waves pounding about her. He went for an audience with King Laomedon and promised to save his daughter and to slay the sea monster. In return, he would be given the mares of Ganymede. These magnificent and immortal mares had been traded by Zeus for the beautiful serving boy, Ganymede, who relieved Hebe in the mansions of the gods. Laomedon agreed to this arrangement, and Heracles dispatched the sea monster and freed the child from her chains. When he took the child and the head of the monster to the king, once again Laomedon refused to honor his bargain.

Slighted, Heracles attacked Troy. He brought his fleet of eighteen long ships to the shore and besieged the city. Heracles knew that his argument was with King Laomedon alone. He went into the city with Telamon, father of the greater Ajax. This same Ajax who would later return to Troy with the Achaeans and shame Odysseus at the awards ceremony. Heracles vanquished Troy even with its great fortifications, although he did not destroy the city or its occupants.

But King Laomedon slipped thorough his fingers and snuck off in his ships into the Aegean Sea along with his entire family. Since there could be no justice without the death of Laomedon, the fleet of Heracles set out after the Trojan ships. They met off the coast of Lemnos, and there Heracles rammed the ships of Laomedon. Laomedon and all his sons and daughters perished in the seas – even the daughter that Heracles had just rescued – all save his son Podarces, whom Heracles took pity on, for Heracles was a curious admixture of fury and compassion. Heracles pardoned the boy-child and took him back to Troy. With Laomedon gone and the sea monster destroyed, the gods lifted the dusky clouds that had *obscured the skies over Troy, and prosperity and goodwill descended upon the city.*

When Podarces grew up, Heracles appointed him to take the throne of Troy. Podarces accepted his appointment, but chose to rule under a different name. From that day on, he was known by the name of Priam, son of Laomedon, and he became the greatest and most just of all the kings of Troy, father of ninety children, and forever grateful to Heracles for his life and rule.

"All is not lost," Telemachus said, "but we will have to move rapidly."

Oxylus, Polyphontes, and the several troopers all turned from the sea to look at Telemachus.

"Polyphontes, what kind of ship is that?" Telemachus asked.

"That is a coastal trader ship, twenty oars, built wide in the beam for cargo and not for speed."

"We can catch them," Telemachus said.

"How?" Oxylus asked. "All our ships are on the other side of the isthmus."

"We will bring over the seventy-oared Phoenician."

"Telemachus, how do you plan to do that?"

"We will sail it. Have you never seen a boat sail on land?"

No one spoke.

"I have," Polyphontes suddenly replied. "I worked at boat building and have moved many boats several stadia on land. But never across the entire isthmus."

"We must capture Tisamenus, and we can do it," Telemachus said. "We have the timbers. We have the men and horses. A beggar on the road to Corinth showed me the way."

XLVI

Back at the road crossing on the ditch, Telemachus explained the situation to Phalces and Autolycus: "We are going to pull the Phoenician ship from one side of the isthmus to the other. And we must do it before the sun sets.

"Phalces, the job of the soldiers has just begun. Will you take charge of disarming the Pelopides? Give them food and water. Set up tents for the physicians, and gather the wounded. I am sure that Cresphontes and the twins will want to cross the ditch soon, so set some men about rebuilding the road across the ditch. After that, begin collecting and identifying the dead. We will bury everyone here in a mass grave – blues and vermilion both – for we now must become one. And we will raise a high barrow for all to know that in all families there are disputes, and here was one of the largest. Post guards, for everyone will remain on the isthmus tonight. But first, we must not allow Tisamenus to slip through our fingers.

"Oxylus, we will need about two hundred infantry soldiers at the ship on the Gulf of Corinth side as soon as possible. Two battalions must collect all the timbers and columns we can find that will roll. Autolycus, can you command the infantry in collecting the timbers and work with Polyphontes in laying out the route, beginning at the Phoenician ship and continuing all the way across to the shore of the Saronic Gulf?"

"And the timbers must be carefully spaced to allow free roll of the ship," Polyphontes added. "The Phoenician galley is unusually large and has a broad beam with a flat bottom and will roll well. I know the isthmus and will see to the path across."

"Has anyone seen Dardanos, son of Belos?" Telemachus asked.

There was no reply.

"Alexandros, son of Pelius, will have to do it. Oxylus, can you find Alexandros and place him in charge of four files of troopers and get them to the ship as soon as possible. Other files can support the infantry in dragging the timbers to the route. Everything must be done immediately." Alexandros was one of the best young phylarchs.

With that, Telemachus took off toward the Phoenician ship. The others rapidly began their tasks: Autolycus to command the infantry and distribute the timbers, Polyphontes to lay out the route, Oxylus to organize the troopers, and Phalces to begin the process of tidying up after the war.

Upon arriving at the ship, Telemachus began immediately organizing the sailors. Temenus was unbelieving.

"We will need all the rope you have on board," Telemachus yelled to the sailors. "We must jettison everything that is not absolutely necessary to sailing. The ship must weigh as little as possible. We need four heavy-duty lines of three plethra* in length to support the weight of the ship. So we may have to double up on the ropes."

The sailors at first laughed at the entire scheme, but soon enough they were working rapidly. A large store of heavy rope was on board, but in the case of the pull ropes, Temenus thought they would need to weave three ropes together for increased strength. The sailors attached the two primary pull ropes to the fore cleats and stretched them out for more than three plethra or a half a stadion. They attached two shorter heavy ropes at the side cleats, extending out from either side. They emptied the ship of all stores, armament, and extra sailing supplies and masts. Sailors cleared the decks. The ship was ready.

Meanwhile, the infantry arrived and was split into two groups, one for each pull rope. Telemachus explained the job, and they began immediately to disrobe, shedding their armour and greaves and tunics. By the time the young phylarch, Alexandros, arrived with the troopers, the naked infantry pullers were in place. Telemachus sent two horse files to either side to provide lateral support to keep the ship upright, while the main motive force would be the men pulling the two tow ropes, about a hundred men on each rope. On the isthmus, soldiers and troopers were placing timbers collected from the piles of unused tinder, creating a rolling bed for the ship.

---

* One plethron equals about one hundred feet.

At this location, the isthmus was about thirty stadia wide, shaped like a flat table about two plethra above sea level, with steep slopes into the water at either side. Polyphontes knew the isthmus well, and he selected a route unencumbered by depressions or holes. The route paralleled the ditch, about a stadion closer to Corinth, running in dry grass and hard pan. The infantry hastily policed the route, clearing it of obstacles and dry brush, and placing timbers.

"We are ready for a test," Telemachus shouted. "Level the ship." The sailors scrambled to raise the sail, but Telemachus was adamant: the sail should remain extended, though free to swing with the breeze.

The horse troopers on the starboard side began to pull, and the mast slowly rose to a vertical position. When the mast righted, the two lines of infantry soldiers began pulling the ship forward. In the soft sand, the ship came out of the water and began making slow progress up the wet shore. The entire ship now rested out of the water. Two soldiers stood at the edge of the isthmus, marking where Polyphontes had set the beginning of the route.

Telemachus rode Sterope up to the bronze-sheathed prow of the ship between the two pull ropes and faced her directly at the ship. He began backing her up the hill, not an easy exercise for a horse, contrary to her instinct and training. But she was an excellent horse, well tamed, and she slowly backed up the sandy slope of the hill, trusting her master. As she backed, she gave the pullers a moving target to aim the bow of the ship. Telemachus slowly backed Sterope to mount the hillside laterally, directing her toward the two soldiers at the top of the hill and signaling the pullers with his arms. The ship followed. The incline was fairly steep, and it was all the pullers could manage. There was always the possibility of ripping the hull apart. The ship slowly advanced up the hillside. The infantry pullers occasionally stumbled or fell, but there was a constant pressure on the pull ropes, and the ship slowly moved, sometimes in fits and starts. On the sides, the troopers moved forward to give additional pull, while keeping the ship upright. Like a giant turtle leaving the sea, the ship left a furrow in the sand, even where the placid waves began to cover the track.

Everyone seemed to understand that they were facing the most difficult pull of the voyage across the isthmus. As the ship came up to the steepest angle of the hillside, it became harder for the men to pull, and progress ground to a halt. The men left off their pressure and the ship settled back slightly. A call went out, and soon more soldiers and sailors were on the lines, which now could not take any more pullers, as men extended the full length of the ropes. The direction of the ship was adjusted to cut more laterally across the slope of the hill. For a moment, Telemachus thought all might fail. But the soldiers and troopers kept pulling. Save for a rope or cleat breaking or ripping a hole in the bottom of the ship, they should be able to bring the ship up to the top of the isthmus.

Slowly the ship rose up the hillside. As it approached the top, the prow of the ship rose into the air. The pullers were now extended on the summit of the isthmus, pulling in a direction off the direction of the movement of the ship. For a moment, it appeared that the prow would never descend, but other soldiers and sailors, seeing the problem, gathered at the stern of the ship and lifted just enough so that the belly of the ship continued up the hill at a point mid-way along its length. The prow suddenly dipped and the weight of the ship shifted off the slope of the hill onto the surface of the isthmus. This shift in weight sent many of the men sprawling. They quickly jumped up to regain their feet, but the ship had mounted the isthmus and now rested firmly on level ground.

Telemachus then turned Sterope from the prow to face the Saronic Gulf. Before him, a row of carefully spaced timbers extended into the distance, where soldiers continued to add additional timbers. The ship rested at the first timber, which was touching the bow. For a moment, everyone regained their breath and readjusted their leverage.

The men and horses began again to pull. This time, the ship came more easily. There was a large crunch as the bronze-sheeted bow bit into the first timber, but it held, and the ship rose up and began rolling the timber and mounting the next one. Polyphontes' spacing was excellent. At all times, there were either four or five timbers supporting the weight of the ship. It rolled smoothly, even when a timber dug into the earth and hit a subsurface rock or obstacle or when a timber disintegrated entirely. The ship moved forward along the line of timbers, not at the rate of a forced march, but at the pace of an older man walking comfortably after dinner for his digestion. Although it now appeared that they might actually move the ship from one side of the isthmus to the other, the state of the hull at the end of the land voyage was in question.

As the ship moved, Telemachus spurred Sterope forward ahead of the ship along the track. Oxylus rode Rhaebus at the side of the infantry pullers. At about ten stadia, a third of the way, they ran out of timbers. Polyphontes stood exasperated.

"We will have to use the ones that are behind the ship." Telemachus said.

He rode back to the shore where they had begun the voyage, waving for several files of troopers to follow him. The troopers tied lengths of rope to those timbers that remained useful. They dragged them forward quickly beyond the ship, laying them at the feet of the soldiers working to extend the line. The progress of the row of timbers recommenced as did the progress of the ship. The soldiers and troopers were able to stay ahead, adding timbers at about the same pace as the ship itself.

By the time the ship was halfway across the isthmus, everyone was exhausted. From the Heraclide line along the ditch, the soldiers watched the progress of the ship. As they watched their comrades struggling, they ran to assist. On the other side of the ditch, the view was different, for the Corinthians could only see the decks and sail of the ship above the isthmus. They watched in amazement as a ship sailed across the isthmus in a direction only dreamed of by the sages, its mast high in the sky against the mountains of the Peloponnese. The Pelopides showed as much interest in its progress as the Heraclides. They had no idea of the use of the ship or that Tisamenus had escaped. But they were joyful that the fighting had ended and a new task was being undertaken. The image of a ship sailing across the isthmus was no stranger than other events of the last three days.

The second half of the voyage went faster, as the men understood their tasks and managed the movement of the ship, avoiding some of the problems they had encountered at the beginning. Telemachus rode ahead to the opposite shore. He sat on Sterope looking out into the Saronic Gulf. Oxylus joined him. The sun had dipped beneath the mountains of Argolis, but the gulf waters still reflected its last rays. In the distance, they could see a vague outline of the islands of Aegina and Piraeus and the coast of Attica. More importantly, the bright white sail of the trader ship could still be seen, slowly rowing out into the gulf without a hint of wind.

When the Phoenician ship arrived at the edge of the slope down to the sea, they had to reconfigure the ropes, moving the pull ropes fore and aft: one rope pulled the ship down the slope, while the other kept it from sliding too rapidly onto the shore. By this time, the soldiers and sailors were a team well acquainted with the give and take of their task, and they succeeded in lowering the ship onto the sand with grace. With a great shout, the sailors, soldiers, and troopers gathered around the ship and celebrated their success, some dancing in the sand. It was all Telemachus could do to quiet the men. There must have been a thousand men standing on the beach, some in armour, some in sailor's garb, and many naked men among them, all happily congratulating each other. How good it is to complete a task that is not destructive in its nature.

"I want to thank all of you and the gods as well," Telemachus shouted over the men, who slowly quieted. "We have one further task, and we will return soon enough. Please hold the celebration until then." The men groaned. "I promise a great festival upon our return. But today, we must return to the work of war. I want the five best archers, five best javelin throwers, and five best skirmishers with us. That is all. Sailors make ready. We are leaving."

The sailors, who had almost forgotten their role, ran to make ready, grabbing the long oars they had carried separately across the isthmus. With that, Oxylus and Telemachus gave their horses to their troopers, and everyone pushed the ship out into the water. Oars, boarding hooks, and ropes were thrown on board. The soldiers on shore held the ship, while the sailors scrambled into position and the captain, the helmsman, the *keulestes*, and the deck crew assembled aboard. Temenus joined Telemachus, Oxylus, and the fifteen soldiers on the foredeck, as the oars dipped into the tepid waters and the ship began moving out into the gulf. The Phoenician builder had designed a sturdy hull, for no leaks were noted. The only damage was to the pitch and paint on the surface of the ship, but that could be easily repaired. In the distance, the sail of the trader was clearly observable in the waning light and would continue to be visible until the final rays of light left the earth.

"All you masters of the ash," the wiry captain shouted, "there is a time to beat and a time to rest. Today, we row. You can rest in your graves." He was a short man, whose face mapped his life on the deck of some sailing ship or another. The *keulestes* set up a rapid beat.

"We should have checked the bottom for problems," Telemachus said.

"No signs of leaks," the captain said, "and we will not entertain a storm."

"If we sink, pray that it be close to shore," Oxylus said.

"I never thought you would make it," Temenus said.

"We still have a long way to go," Oxylus replied.

"Yes, but we have come a long way," Temenus added. "We have been successful, not by force but by imagination and conception."

"They have us by about a hundred stadia," the captain said. "Without godly winds, we can better their speed by three or four times. We are the fastest of the Phoenician galleys. We will pull upon them before the Pleiades are high in the sky. That will put them in the lee of Aegina, unless they put in."

The sailors bent their backs and legs into their work. The evening air was still warm, and the sweat began pouring off the men. The sailors passed water bladders around frequently and handed out thick bread and cheese. A single oar out of the water for a few strokes was acceptable, but more than one was not. The sailors had built up massive shoulders, arms, and backs, and they could row over long distances. In some ships, rowers were slaves, but in the fastest and best of the coastal vessels, the crews were free men or foreigners, earning a modest amount, better than fishing or farming. And it was a full-time occupation, since ships constantly skirted the shores of Hellas. Ships normally carried extra sailors to relieve the rowers, but every rower was expected to put in his time, one watch on, one watch off. And a watch could last half the day or night. The Phoenician ship carried only one set of sailors; there would be no relief for these sailors.

As the ship glided rapidly through the calm water, they could no longer make out figures on the beach. The light left the earth entirely, and the stars filled the skies. The ship ahead of them ran without lanterns, but even in the dark they could make out the sail black against the starlit horizon. The Phoenician galley too did not light the port or starboard lanterns, but had several marine candles on the rowing deck. In the darkness, the men on deck listened to the sounds of the oars beating the water, the constant drumming, and the occasional cough or swearing of a man.

"You might want to catch a nod," the captain said. "I will wake you as we close in on Aegina. They cannot hide at that point."

The soldiers lay on the deck, with the wind from the ship's progress blowing over them. They wrapped themselves in their cloaks and settled down to consider the long journey they had taken over the last few days. A few of the men actually slept.

XLVII

The slowing of the *keulestes'* beat startled everyone. The island appeared ahead, a large dark mass in the night sky. They could even see oil lamps or fires from the town on the side of the island facing Notus.

"We are on them," the captain called. He pointed ahead, and sure enough there was a shape darker than the horizon headed directly for the port. "No change in their beat. They must think we present no threat."

"Can we catch them?" Oxylus asked.

"Oh, yes," the captain replied. "No warship, she. We can easily take her from behind with our prow. We can use the grappling hooks abreast. Or we can come about and alter their course. Depends."

"We want to ensure we have captured Tisamenus," Telemachus said. "Come abreast and change their course, and we can talk to them. What do you think?"

"Yes," Oxylus said, "But they may be armed."

"At best, they are lightly armed," Telemachus replied. "We can stand off at first."

The captain ordered the beat to speed up, and he shifted the stern oars to the starboard side to better steer the ship. The sailors furled the sail, for the wind had died down to almost nothing, and the sail would only slow an attack. The soldiers gathered their weapons and stood at the ready. The Phoenician gained rapidly on the smaller merchant ship. At this point, the other ship took notice of the warship on its stern and increased its beat, attempting to make landfall. On the deck of the trader, men were visible, but no weapons could be observed.

As they came alongside, Oxylus called out: "In the name of the Heraclides, come to a halt or prepare for battle."

They waited, but the other ship continued rowing as rapidly as possible.

"Halt or you will be sunk," Oxylus called again. When the other ship ignored the warning, he turned to his troops. "Put some arrows across the deck, but do not harm anyone." The archers sent five arrows straight across the vessel at a height slightly above a man's head, several embedding in the mast.

"Halt. Final warning," Oxylus yelled.

This time, the captain of the trader called out. "Who are you?"

"We are a warship of the Heraclides," Oxylus shouted. "Bring your oars out of the water, or you will be scuttled."

At this, there appeared to be some discussion aboard the merchant. The merchant was only five or six stadia off the island of Aegina. They could smell the night fires. The beat of the warship had slowed to keep apace the other vessel, and they were now running abeam of each other with the warship high on the merchant's port side against the island. Oil lamps at the entrance to the port on Aegina could now clearly be seen.

"You have no right to stop us," someone finally shouted.

Oxylus' face turned serious, and he turned to his archers. "Take one on the deck out. The figure forward at the prow."

Again, the archers let loose. This time, they hit a target that fell with a thump to the deck. Clearly, most if not all the arrows achieved their aim. They waited.

After a few moments, the captain of the trader vessel ordered his oars out of the water. Both vessels slowed to a crawl. Without wind to speak of, the two ships drifted off the island with the water lapping at their sides.

"What do we do with Tisamenus?" Telemachus asked.

"He might be useful as a prisoner," Oxylus argued, "for a while."

"Better dead," said one of the skirmishers with a lance in his hand.

Everyone turned to observe the speaker: a tall soldier, an Ethiopian by his complexion, his pig-sticker in his hand regarding them. He was remarkable for his godly looks and long, braided hair.

"What say you?" Telemachus asked. He had noticed the man during the night, who was constantly whistling some tune to himself.

"Sorry, sire, to interrupt. My passion got the best of me, and I spoke out of turn. But the man is no good."

"Go ahead," Telemachus invited him.

"Sire, only to say, the man is hateful to the gods. His family has caused great pain. They treat others without respect. They pay no reverence to the gods. Keeping such a beast alive would only bring further suffering. Allow Hades to care for him."

"I agree with the man," Temenus said. "His death will mark the end of the Pelopides."

"His son is with him," Telemachus noted.

"All the better," Temenus replied.

"Tow them into the open sea," Telemachus said. "Await the sunrise."

"Right. We can decide in the clear light of day," Oxylus said. He turned to the other vessel and shouted: "Throw us a tow rope."

It took several throws, but finally a light lead line with a weight was thrown across to the warship. A sailor amidships, pulled the lead line until a heavy tow line came across. The larger vessel attached the tow line at the stern and under oar moved forward, slowly coming about toward the coast of the Peloponnese, slowly moving ahead until the rope took weight and began dragging the smaller vessel about in line with the larger.

"We have to watch that they do not escape," Telemachus noted.

"The jolly boat is on the lower deck in the stern," the captain said. "You can see it if you look with care. And we will be far from the island."

"We can put his eye out, if anyone touches it," Oxylus said. The archers saw the dark object the captain pointed out.

Slowly, the island receded, as the larger ship continued turning, until the prow was facing the isthmus as if to return to the point of origin.

"That captain should be placed in charge of goats," the captain swore, as the other ship failed to dip its oars.

The joint speed was not hopeful. Pulling such a dead weight was not in the design of the warship, which wallowed with the burden. They were in the dead of night, and with the moon low in the sky, there was little light.

"We should drop a sea anchor," the captain said. "This is too much work. The men will never last."

"How can we assure that they do not use the jollyboat?" Telemachus asked.

"We can put our own out to their stern with some of the soldiers." The captain pointed to his stern, where a six-man jolly sat.

"Good," Oxylus said. "Take a few sailors and two archers. At worst, you can warn us if anyone should attempt to jump ship."

After this, the small boat was lowered into the water and moved off toward the stern of the following vessel. The small boat was not visible in the black water, but any voice could serve as a warning. With that accomplished, the soldiers on the deck settled down for a night on guard, while the sailors slept next to their galley benches. Quiet descended on both ships. The only sound was the gentle lap-lapping of the water against the sides of the ships.

In the darkness, both ships waited. On the warship, the soldiers snacked and stared at the darkness. No one slept. And the eyes of the archers remained on the dark object on the stern deck. On the merchant, like a snake in a bird's talons high above the land, they had to consider when to strike.

The night passed slowly. As the golden hues of Eos began to lighten the sky, just before Helios began his climb, there was a loud splash and a warning shout from the stern of the merchant trader. The sailors on the warship moved quickly into action. They dropped the tow line into the sea. The large ship quickly came about along the port side of the trader. When the warship cleared the other vessel, in the half-light they could see a single jollyboat in the water. Several men were swimming in the water as well. Ignoring the men in the water, the warship made straight for the jollyboat. This was no contest. There were only four rowers, but in the rear of the boat sat Tisamenus in white robes, accompanied by Tellis, his son, in a vermilion cloak.

"There is your Tisamenus," Oxylus shouted.

The warship passed the small boat and then turned directly into its path. The oars were lifted. And the large ship drifted toward the jollyboat. In a game of cat and mouse, the smaller vessel was easily the more maneuverable, but it was no match in speed. It could turn and avoid the other, and move off in a new direction, but the other would then recover and catch up rapidly.

Oxylus leaned over the side of the warship. "Halt or we will fire." He was annoyed with the game.

When the boat did not stop rowing, he nodded to the archers. The three men on deck calmly took aim and loosed their missiles. One arrow hit a sailor in his shoulder, knocking him out of the boat. Another arrow hit the side of the boat. The last arrow hit Tisamenus in the calf. He writhed in pain in the rear of the boat. The Heraclides watched as the remaining sailors jumped overboard, leaving Tisamenus and his son alone in the boat. Tisamenus was in too much pain to notice their departure, and Tellis was attempting to help his father. The sailors began swimming toward the island about ten stadia off. They could probably make the island before mid-morning if left alone.

"Sink that boat," Temenus cried.

The captain, used to the senior Heraclide's orders, commanded the ship forward at full speed. The heartbeat of the *keulestes* hammered rapidly. They ran directly over one of the swimmers and then turned to come into line with the stern of the jollyboat. The beat increased, and the oars dug deeply into the water like claws. The reinforced bronze prow came directly upon the small jollyboat. No impact was felt on the warship. There was only a muffled sound of wood shattering, as the prow of the warship demolished the small boat. The captain shouted for the oars to halt. In the dawn half-light, they saw nothing to the stern: no boat, no swimmer, only shards of wood. One sailor remained, desperately swimming toward the island, but the warship moved swiftly over his path, and he disappeared as well. They waited for signs of motion in the calm water, but the surface remained unbroken. They made a wide circle of the area, but the crimson surface lay oily and flat in the morning light without even a sea crow breaking its surface.

Tisamenus, son of Orestes, son of Agamemnon, son of Atreus, and King of Mycenae and Argos, who had extended his rule beyond his ancestral dominion to Sparta, Corinth and the greater part of Arcadia, was sent down to the house of Hades, along with his son.

After this, the men on the warship noticed that the trader had moved off quite a distance during the confrontation. It was sailing under wind and oar in the morning breeze, running down wind toward Aegina. For some reason, Aegina seemed to offer sanctuary, although it was a difficult landing, surrounded by low rocks and outcroppings. Before the warship could pursue the other, they pulled several of their own drenched sailors out of the water. Of the men sent to guard the trader during the night, two of the archers and a sailor had been killed. They had been surprised and overwhelmed by several sailors from the merchant swimming in the darkness. Their boat had been scuttled, allowing the jollyboat from the trader to be lowered into the water with Tisamenus and his son on board. The Pelopide sailors had now gone down to the underworld, along with the three Heraclides. None would return to the arms of their loved ones.

Here in the early morning light, once all hands were accounted for and the sea judged free of any more swimmers, the warship began chasing the smaller trader. The larger ship quickly caught up and violently smashed the other with its prow, opening a giant hole in the stern of the trader. The ship sank immediately. Only a few men were able to swim free from the sinking wreck. Many others sank with the ship. Of the survivors, they counted no more than ten men. No women or children were seen. All were sailors, used to the wickedness of the seas and sinking ships.

"Leave off," Telemachus shouted, when the captain turned to Temenus for orders. "Those sailors who can swim to Aegina will survive."

The warship came about into the wind, made a further inspection of the waters around the fight and discovered no additional survivors.

After that, they plotted a course in the direction of the isthmus and arrived in the afternoon at a sheltered beach a few stadia from Cenchreae, toward Notus. As they approached the rocky shore, Telemachus could see several troopers waiting for them, among them Autolycus and Deiphontes. First off the ship, Telemachus hurried up to the troopers, who looked at him expectantly.

"Tisamenus is dead," Telemachus announced in response to their hungry looks, but he had misread their faces. The news made no impression on them. His heart beat unsteadily in his chest. He looked directly at Autolycus, standing among the men and their horses. "Well?"

"Amphion is missing," Autolycus said, meeting his father's eyes. "His black mare, Arion, returned last night, but not Amphion."

Deiphontes spoke more ominously: "He has not got far. We shall find him."

And back in heaven, sly Hermes, slayer of Argus and bringer of good luck, silently rejoiced at the death of the Pelopides with a blissful tune. Even Apollo could not construct pity in his heart for the end of Tisamenus, but thought that maybe it should not be as easy or painless for the Heraclides as Athene would have it.

XLVIII

On the evening of the return of the Phoenician galley and death of Tisamenus, the Heraclide priests sacrificed a true hecatomb of animals over a large open fire on the side of the ditch facing the warm airs of Notus. From the early evening, sweet smells of roasting meats rose into the air surrounding the isthmus and climbed into the sky to the mansions of the gods, bringing renewed hope and cheer.

The Heraclides had rebuilt the road across the ditch, and Cresphontes had crossed victoriously with his troops in a festive mood and had taken command. The day had been devoted to celebration; the cleanup had yet to begin. The vermilion and Aegean blue uniforms mixed comfortably on both sides of the ditch. The foreign flavor of the Heraclides added spice to the gallimaufry: songs of far-flung Lydia and Thrace; dances from wide Thessaly and Macedonia; tales in Greek from the Levantine; and Egyptian prayers for the dead. Cresphontes had posted armed guards, but most of the soldiers were too happy and had toped too much wine to be of any use or concern. At the same time, even after the fires were lit and the sun had left the sky, wounded soldiers, both red and blue, continued to wander into the brightly lit camp. The physicians and their helpers worked constantly to care for the wounded and comfort the dying, while the hale and hearty celebrated.

Upon his return, Telemachus set out to interview the men of the mounted file that supported Amphion, and Autolycus joined him in this effort. The job of Amphion's tablemates was to defend him, as both phylarch and decadarch, at all times. One of his tablemates, Leukon, son of Dias, gave a moving account. This curly headed young man, not much older than Amphion, originated from a large combined family of fifteen children on the plains of Thessaly. For as long as he had memory, he had tamed wild horses along the Tempe and was an exceptional rider. When Leukon left home, his father had wished him well, but both realized that one less mouth to feed was a gift of the gods. Leukon told his story shyly, as a boy might report a successful hunt to his father, holding the rabbit high.

"We came ashore at the marshes. Two tribes strong, fresh as the morning dew, along with the pig-stickers and bowers. We made our way toward Notus, with Boreas biting at our backs. When we joined the main pack, Procles and Eurysthenes appeared happy enough to see us. The Pelopides had them on their backsides. We were a surprise to all. But more to the "Reds," for they thought the fight over. That morning we sent them running. The pig-stickers dropped them in their tracks. And the archers had their way, like shooting finches. And the troopers rode freely across their formations. And nothing they could do. Soon, we had them on the run.

"Our squad stayed with Amphion. He was the greatest...or is. We would not let him come to harm, and he directed the attack, but he never shied from battle. We all took part. But it was not until the afternoon that we ran into the main forces of the Pelopides. For we did not know they had so many men. That was when we began taking losses. Our infantry was moving up, but they had been pretty badly beat up before we arrived. The pig-stickers and slingers were fresh, but the rest were weary, all except the archers who, thank the gods, kept up a mighty rain. When they came at us, we faded away like a phantom, giving them nothing to wrestle down to the ground. But the infantry was overrun and took losses. We returned to help, and managed to avoid a rout. Now, the horses were being battered pretty good. And we were losing horses and troopers, both. We are not good battlers. We want the open spaces. We do best when moving rapidly. But not when our horses are being taken out from under us.

"Amphion pulled back distant from the Pelopide formations, but Procles wanted us forward. That is not our battle way. We cannot attack heavy infantry in their faces, but that is what the twins were demanding of us. You know. Like wolves on attack. Keep distant and then move in for the kill. Keep to the sides. If the archers and pig-stickers had not been there, the "Reds" would have overrun us.

"Amphion refused to give in to the twins, keeping pressure on the "Reds" from their sides. We were punishing them. But there were many of them and few of us, and they kept moving forward, and our infantry kept retreating for the heavy "Reds" could not be stopped.

We troopers fell back and then came like a hornet and stung where least expected. Every time they thought they had us, we came back and routed them. It was a deadly game for both sides. But we were giving more than we got.

"That was when the "Reds" decided to stop the hide-hide game. We collected and, then, came at them. This was along the road, so there was no concealing. We drove at the lancers, but they presented a wall and the horses turned back. Our infantry pushed but could not move them. We were making it hard on ourselves. We all knew that. Finally, Amphion changed the direction of battle. The horse troops pulled out and made a wide circle, coming back along the beach. There must have been ten or twelve files. We rode down the shore and came up behind them. Put the fear of god into them, we did. Taking them from behind. First with the bows and then with our swords. They could choose the pig-stickers or us. And they chose to run, and we cut them down pretty good.

"Dymas, one of their generals, was in his chariot, protected by a group of heavy infantry. We knew him by all his fine garments and shiny armour. But we caught them unawares and mowed them like summer barley. They ran like snakes from a nest toward all the godly winds. We took them from every bearing. Dymas was hit by an arrow in his side and would have escaped if Amphion had not caught him with his slasher. About took his arm off. And that was when things got confused.

"With Fear and his brother Panic driving the "Reds," and us going after them, we lost our file formations. All going our separate ways. And the worst, we lost Amphion. On my faith, I failed to see it. But the "Reds" took off, and we took off, and we were all running after them at every turn. Cutting them down like so many dogs in a pack. Even the infantry began working. The best the "Reds" could do was hold their shields over their heads and run toward the ditch, for they thought that they would find protection there.

"By the time some of our file got back together, Amphion was nowhere to be seen. We had to push forward. Procles and Eurysthenes kept after us to move. We looked for Amphion, but could not find him. We were told that the Pelopides were reforming at the ditch, and we had to keep thrusting forward."

"But your duty was to your commander," Telemachus interrupted. "You should have been with him. How many wounded in your squad?"

"Oh, Sire, that is not easy…"

"Why? You do not know your comrades in your file?"

"Yes, sir. I mean things were moving so fast. Now I know that we lost Pharius and Hippalmus and Menoetes. And Catreus and Ligyron were deathly wounded and will probably not make it. And Xuthus lost an arm, but they say he may yet live…I have not seen or heard of the others. But I kept expecting to see Amphion. Kept waiting in the back of my mind. That was when his mount came up to us, and we knew he was on his feet…or worse."

Telemachus looked at the boy. One of the top young troopers. At any other time, a golden boy. "Leukon, forgive me, you have done well."

"No, sir. I failed my duty. I failed noble Amphion."

"Listen, Leukon." Telemachus interrupted. "I need your help. Tomorrow, early, we will ride back to the battle scene and look for Amphion."

"I will do anything for him. He was my master."

"We will find him," Telemachus replied softly, any anger having dissipated. "We will find him."

The night was long and harsh. Telemachus sought isolation in his tent, but the sounds of the celebrating men filled the air. He had spoken with Cresphontes briefly, and Oxylus had begun the arduous task of cleaning up. For after any battle, there is another struggle: to count the bodies of the dead and identify them if possible and to prepare the burial. So many young men would never return to their homes. The Pelopides had the same duty to their wounded and dead, but they had no guidance. After the fighting stopped, the Pelopide officers had deserted toward Boreas to hide in the back-street retreats of Athens or Thebes, in hopes that one day they could return secretly to their families in the Peloponnese. Honor be damned.

That night Telemachus suffered as never before: worse than when Odysseus returned to Ithaca and they had to face the suitors the next morning, worse than when his mother left the family in Elis, worse than when the herald brought the news of his father's attack, worse than when Polycasté announced the end of their marriage. Sometimes, you believe it cannot get worse, and then the gods show the error of your thinking.

Amphion, the grandson of the Kings Nestor and Odysseus, was wise beyond his years. He was temperate with his fellows, yet strong of will, and never failed to live up to his father's expectations. He surpassed what can be expected of a child. He was caring and sensitive, a born leader of men, like his grandfathers. He acted as a youthful sage, a person in charge with respect for his followers, and a commander who would not ask something of others that he would not ask of himself. He felt concern for his troopers' wives and children and parents, though they be twice his age, about their fears and dreams, about their stomachaches and headaches and bruised behinds and aching backs. He gave out liniment balm as a man gives out honey to his children, like a father to his sons.

And the father's mind, swirling with fear and hope...waiting...expecting...praying. What can anyone do? But every question led back to Polycasté and blame. For every married couple at odds with each other seeks blame and exoneration at once. What would she think? He knew well the answer. Why had he involved his sons in this war? She would hold him darkly responsible. He knew that. But she had deserted the family to return to her father. This was not done. Never. Women belonged with their husbands. That was the way. Penelope waited nineteen years for her husband to return. And even when he did, she continued to wait. Even Nestor thought it wrong when his daughter returned to Pylos. He urged her to return to her family. He apologized to her family and to Telemachus. But Nestor's age argued against him. And the difficulties of his kingdom and his antagonistic and greedy sons caused him grief. Polycasté knew him better than anyone else, even his own wife. And Polycasté brought small moments of joy back into Nestor's life. Who would refuse an old man? And at the same time, who can censure her? But if her cubs came to harm, she would blame Telemachus with all the ferocity of an enraged lioness. He knew that. And the worst of all was the realization that she would be correct.

Sleep, so akin to death itself, took over at some time during the night. It is believed that the gods converse with mortals while they sleep and visit clear images upon them, useful and remedial images, for the god of Sleep seeks elucidation and clarity. Yet even in sleep, Telemachus' thoughts never strayed far from the outlines of his search for his son, just as the bards described his father's visit the depths of Hades, consulting with the shades for a way home. Telemachus' search for Amphion expanded into a pursuit of understanding: why had he failed to protect his godly son, why had Polycasté deserted him, why had his absent father sought repute above family, why had his wise mother withdrawn from her offices, and why, beyond all, had he himself, a man by all accounts, never found his proper mooring?

Long before gentle Eos rose in the sky, they rode off from the camp in darkness: Telemachus, Autolycus, Deiphontes, and the young trooper, Leukon. While the Heraclides and Pelopides slept off the night's celebration, they crossed the freshly piled earth now filling the ditch, reconnecting the road across the isthmus. Sleeping bodies were everywhere. Men lay wrapped in their cloaks like so many autumn leaves on the land. The "Blues" and the "Reds" as far as the eyes could see, on both sides of the ditch. Only a few guards stood watch, nodding as the horsemen passed.

The riders made their way toward Boreas, for the cold blowing wind leads one there. In heaven, Helios, god of sight and healing, strapped on his cuirass and grieves, mounted his four-horse chariot, and prepared to commence his diurnal journey. As the horsemen progressed into the isthmus, they saw the bodies of soldiers who lay impervious to merriment. They threw rocks at the feral dogs and vultures to no avail. They rode for many stadia along the road and then, following the directions of Amphion's file mate, Leukon, crossed into the dry plain of the isthmus.

It was obvious when they arrived at the battlefield. For here, the bodies lay together like rotten fruit fallen from some prolific tree. But there were no trees. Here the pell-mell of mad confusion could be seen. For bodies were scattered everywhere, such as one might only imagine upon entering the house of Hades: each body mute with a terrible story to tell; bodies of both men and beasts; bodies piled together, but separate in their resting forms. And throughout lay the implements of their destruction: swords, javelins, lances, shields, axes, metal weights, arrows and bows, broken shafts, weights, rocks, and knives. And common to all were the bloodied surroundings of dirt and filth.

Telemachus dismounted, ignoring Sterope, leaving her to nibble at the sparse grasses, shying from the lifeless forms. He took several containers from his pack and went off by himself, away from the others. Just as Odysseus had once done, Telemachus set out to pray to the gods to help him on his mission.

First, he cut a square libation pit, poured a mixture of milk and honey onto the fresh earth – a drink offering. Onto this mixture, he poured a second offering of wine and then water. Finally, he sprinkled white barley meal where the liquids had been absorbed by the earth. He threw his blue cloak on the ground over the dampness and waited, praying:

"O immortal Zeus, father of us all, of all the ghosts in your house, return my son to me. I have suffered more than most and made no complaints to you. My father and grandfather, both beloved of you, and both righteous men, have gone down to the house of Hades. Do not take my son. I would go down gladly in his place among the lost souls. I can only offer you myself and my submission. Return my son to me, and we shall burn the finest hecatomb in your honor at home on the shores of low-lying Ithaca. Return my son, and I shall give up my desire to rule. I shall take dominion over no man, except myself. The throne of Ithaca, Cephallenia, and Zacynthus shall pass on. If I never see Ithaca again, then so be it. I will dedicate myself to what is important in life: love for myself and for others and for the gods. I can only believe that these aims align with your desires. I only ask for the time allotted to my son, for him to taste the wonder of your opulence. Lord of immortals and mortals alike, ruler of heaven and earth, our protector and destroyer, I beg of you."

And on this plain, in a world of death and destruction, offering neither hope nor understanding nor freedom from pain, Telemachus set out looking for his lost son. He began moving from one body to the next like a honey bee visiting the small blue clusters on rosemary, looking into the faces, young and old, bloody and clean, eyes open and shut. But none with joy. Those bodies lying on their stomachs or sides, he rolled over, exposing the faces. Each face unique. Each face known and loved. Each the son of a father and the heart of a lioness. Each face human, though not the face he sought.

And the bodies of horses, mules, and asses lay about. Living animals, some still on their feet with open wounds, wandered lost among the soldiers' bodies or stood above their senseless masters. And gore, for the smell of death was everywhere. Bodies lay in pools of blood, often flowing together into a shared puddle. And limbs scattered about and helmeted heads. It was a secret, self-contained world, and a certain horrible unity of color and scent existed, as one might find in a forest dell of high trees and grasses and ferns or after a wild forest fire. The sun had departed, the stars had left the sky, and genesis was disrupted. Living man, wanting to rescue its dwellers, intruded in this hideous world. Vague rumbling sounds of phantoms and creatures come to the end of their time, rose from the earth: "As you are, I once was. And as I am, you shall soon become."

And when pathetic light appeared above the mountains, Telemachus continued trudging through the fields...ignoring the crimson leaves and concentrating on the blue. Rational though it was, it felt wrong. At some point, Telemachus began turning all bodies toward the insipid glow, regardless of uniform. Some still breathed, though barely. And to those, he offered fresh water, but he did not dally.

As he worked, his horse moved off after better grasses, though carefully, nervous at the trundled bodies on the ground. He fanned out from the center, the bodies growing less frequent and wider apart. The meager sun declined toward the mountains of the Peloponnese, and Telemachus continued into the murky afternoon, turning and lifting and viewing. The blue and the vermilion: All had become sons of the soil.

The ancients believed in the Sons of the Soil and called them "autochthonous," the aboriginal occupants of the land. With neither father nor mother, they arise from the earth as a plant does, growing toward the sun. Only during disruptive periods in history do they make their appearance, and only when the revolution of the universe is reversed. Even the gods are wary of this occurrence, where Helios moves from Zephyrus to Apeliotes. For normally, progression of the universe proceeds in a divine and immutable forward direction. But when the gods withdraw in response to man's fate, the universe can, under its own volition, reverse direction and turn backwards upon itself. And the parentless children are left to themselves.

The ancients believed the autochthonous children played an important role: half punishment, half renewal. We all need to be aware of the possibility of backward progression; such awareness gives us wisdom and forbearance. Pray that the gods do not withdraw and we do not return to this misery.

Telemachus felt as though he had voyaged to the depths of the earth, each dead soldier a cobblestone on the narrow path, each face a world of its own. He had turned countless bodies. Surely the ferry of Charon was overcome with transporting souls. Had he seen the devolution of the earth? Had he seen what the gods withhold from mortal man?

By the time the light of day had dimmed, the men returned to where they had begun the search. They had failed to find any evidence of Amphion. They built a fire, realizing that they had not considered the time for the search nor thought to bring anything to eat. Yet, no one wanted to return to camp. So they settled down to pass the night on empty stomachs. Autolycus went to hobble the horses, but reported that he could not find Sterope, Telemachus' mare. Telemachus knew that she would graze her way back, for she knew where they were. Horses can smell the scent of men from many stadia away.

There was no conversation as they lay around the fire, for despair reigned. The blackness covered them all and kept them warm.

Later that night, with the moon high in the sky, Telemachus was awakened from his restlessness by the neighing of a horse in the distance. As though in a dream, he vaguely recalled that Sterope had not been with them earlier in the evening. But the neighing was followed by a distant whinny. He rose and went to where the other horses were hobbled. They welcomed him, but Sterope was still missing. He listened to the night air. Again, he could hear the neighing, and so could the other horses, turning their ears from him toward the sound.

He walked along the flat isthmus. Like a pharos, the sounds directed him onwards. The moonlight provided sufficient illumination to avoid the obstacles. Finally, almost at the neck of the isthmus on the Gulf of Corinth side, he made out the figure of a horse in the distance against the stars in the skies and the lightness of the horizon of the bay. He whistled, and she raised her head and nickered and blustered. She shook her head and then rapidly nodded up and down, her ears trained on him. But she did not move from where she stood.

Sterope stood resolutely, and at her feet was the fallen leaf of a man. The moonlight shining in his open eyes. Telemachus broke into a run. He came to the figure, and he knew it instantly.

"Amphion. Amphion."

Telemachus knelt down. The eyes blinked. The mouth attempted to make a sound, but nothing issued forth. Amphion's lips were dry and parched, his face gaunt in the moonlight, but his lips moved toward a smile and then collapsed. Telemachus had brought no water. He examined the young man quickly. There was a bruise on the right side of his face, but not serious. His helmet was missing, but his cuirass was in good shape, and no blood was visible. He noticed the unnatural angle of the right leg, which must have been broken, though lifting the tunic no blood or bone was visible. Telemachus pulled the cloak from beneath his son's body and enfolded him and laid his own filthy cloak over him.

"I will return shortly."

He mounted Sterope, who gladly broke into a trot across the isthmus. At the campfire, he woke the men, told them what Sterope had found, and gathered a bladder of water. He rode back to Amphion. He knelt down and slowly administered water as a physician might apply precious medicine. The others arrived soon enough. The four men crouched around the reclining figure and listened to a barely audible voice.

"I fell from Arion. Is she all right?"

"Quiet. Rest." Telemachus tipped more water into Amphion's mouth. They attempted to get him into a more comfortable position, but when they moved his right leg, he groaned in pain and lost consciousness.

By morning, though, Amphion was talking and sitting up, although not moving his leg. They carefully cut his greaves off, and immobilized his leg with broken javelins, which were lying about the field, wrapping it tightly with cloth, which they tore from his cloak. They fashioned a travois out of two intact lances. The travois was tied between Sterope and the large white stallion, Boreas. Autolycus and Deiphontes lifted Amphion and carefully placed him onto the sling. The tears began flowing freely from Telemachus' eyes as he thanked the gods. The riders slowly and carefully made their way back to camp. But when they arrived at the ditch, they found the leaders in an angry dispute.

XLIX

An old man in filthy raiment sat on the earth in the center of the field facing Temenus, Cresphontes, and Oxylus, all on their feet. He was a big-boned, corpulent man, well-fed and bald, but most notable, both ears had been severed from his head. An unkempt white beard covered his chest. Behind the three leaders stood many officers, and the entire group was surrounded by soldiers. The sun was high in the sky; it was hot and humid. The leaders were arguing, and the soldiers were attempting to follow the dispute.

When the horses trotted in, several troopers came forward to help with the litter. Telemachus allowed the soldiers to carry Amphion to the healing tent. The physicians had been working there for two days straight. They were in no mood to argue over various treatments or coddle the wounded man or discuss procedures with his father. They moved quickly and decisively and, in so doing saved many men to fight again, but would not discuss with any man their remedies. They did not brook the interference of father and brother and sent them away immediately.

In the tent, the physicians had a variety of instruments. Hot coals burned in one corner for heating the various cautery irons. Large basins of water were nearby. Since most of the wounds they saw were caused by sharp implements entering the flesh, they were surrounded by poultices and thin sutures of gut. On tables behind them were piles of various herbs and linen for wrapping. Puncture wounds were cleaned, cauterized, stuffed with poultice, and then tightly wrapped. The physicians were expert at these types of wounds. They also had metal inserts, which they called pigs, of different sizes for deep wounds or wide punctures. These they heated to a cauterizing temperature and inserted directly into the wounds. They would remove the pigs at a later time, once the oozing and exudations lessened. The physicians were also expert at severed and broken limbs.

When they inspected Amphion, they realized the problem immediately. His femur was broken, possibly in several places, but more immediately serious was the separation of the bone from the hip joint and possibly a fractured hip. They were able to treat most fractured arms, legs, and shoulders with great success. But with the fracture of internal bones, they prayed to Apollo, god of the cure. With separated joints, they were equally skilled at returning the bones to the correct alignment, although not without impact on the patient.

They raised Amphion onto the table and administered an infusion of powdered mandragora root, which eventually put him into a stupor. After testing the alignment of his leg, they built a strong splint on his leg and immobilized it with linen wrappings, leaving space at the hip joint. When he was breathing comfortably, they surrounded him. Two giant soldiers held his shoulders firmly in place on the table. Two others held his midsection. With a sign to each other, they began applying pressure to hold him fast, while two physicians manipulated his leg as though it were a wooden post being twisted out of dry ground. One pulled the leg by the splint, while the other took hold of the top of the femur, pulled, twisted the leg, and with great vigor wrenched the bone by dint of strength back into its socket. With a scream, Amphion came out of his stupor momentarily and then sank back into stony sleep. They inspected the joint and the leg to ensure that the fracture had not worsened, then wrapped the entire leg, and the two giants carried Amphion out to another tent to recuperate. They prayed that Apollo might heal any internal breakage or bleeding.

During this treatment, Telemachus and Autolycus had joined the heated discussion with the beggar. The evil smelling man had come to the isthmus in search of his son. As he expressed it, he had come all the way from Caria, where the conflict was known. His own interest though was predicated on two facts. His son, as a resident of Aetolia, had volunteered as a soldier for the Heraclides and was deeply involved in the fighting, or so the man avowed, although no one had been able to identify his son. The second fact was that the gods had shown him a sign. He was a seer in his home and could find divine significance in common things, such as the flight of birds or their intestinal deposits. At this point, Cresphontes had assumed the man was a crackpot and had insulted him. The old man took umbrage and sought the help of the gods, and it was then that he admitted to being a priest of Apollo.

The soldiers gave access to Telemachus to enter the circle. He listened to the rising banter back and forth on both sides, but mainly between Cresphontes and the old man. He saw nothing being gained and made a suggestion.

"Perhaps," Telemachus offered, "we should not forget our hospitality and remove this discussion from the heat and sun of mid-day and take refreshments in a shady tent. There is much to accomplish, and this discussion is leading nowhere." He also had seen a glimmer of truth in the old man.

"Excellent idea," Temenus said before Cresphontes could continue the argument. "We can retire to the meeting tent, which was set up this morning."

Telemachus addressed the surrounding officers and soldiers. "In the meantime, I suggest that we muster and begin the collection of the bodies across the ditch, for the isthmus is full of them, both colors. We need to gather them and identify all that we can and take care of them as if they were our family, for truly they are. Then, we must make dedication and offerings to the gods in a serious manner. There is still work to be done, believe me, and important work. And a final conflagration will honor the fallen."

With a groan, the soldiers realized dirty work awaited them and the festivities were at an end. They retired unhurriedly and without enthusiasm.

When the officers reassembled in the tent, Cresphontes, Temenus, Oxylus, and Telemachus were together for the first time since their victory.

"I understand that Amphion was hurt," Temenus said.

"We found him and brought him back for treatment of a broken leg," Telemachus replied.

"They say that he killed Dymas," Temenus said.

"So I heard," Telemachus replied. "More importantly, his troops broke the back of the Pelopides."

"We will not forget him," Cresphontes said. "Nor you as well. We owe you and Oxylus much."

"Now," Telemachus said, "we must reply to this man here." They all turned to the miserable old man who sat at one side of the tent. "Would you like food or drink?"

The old man looked at him quizzically.

"Would you like food or drink?" Telemachus repeated.

He shook his head in the negative.

"Bring some fresh water and honey cakes," Telemachus ordered one of the soldiers. "There is a stranger in our midst." He turned to the old man and addressed him in a louder voice.

"I am Telemachus, son of Odysseus, and hipparch of the Heraclides." He pointed out the other men. "Before you is Oxylus, son of Haemon, general of the infantry, Cresphontes and Temenus, sons of Aristomachus, and heads of the family of Heraclides, and future rulers of the Peloponnese. We are at your service, sir."

Cresphontes began to say something, but Telemachus stopped him. "We understand that you are from Halicarnassus."

The old man looked around at the ranking men surrounding him. "I am a poor man, but I am wise in my ways. My wife departed this earth early last year. We were joined for fifty-six years, and I have but one son, whom I have not seen these many years, but good word was brought to me that he is a fighter among you. I am a priest of the son of Leto, the healer. They call me Lykeios. And I was born in Delos like my god and brought to the Oracle of Apollo at Delphi as a young man and dedicated to this god. I have served him with great sacrifice and dedication ever since. My son, Apollonius is his name, was born in our small village in Caria, a true son of Hellas. After his birth, we journeyed to the oracle, and there, to my everlasting shame, we gave our beloved first and only child to the greatest of all the gods. And yet my pride in the boy grew apace, as I returned to the oracle many times in my occupation, and each time, the priestess told me of the progress of my son, since it had been prophesied that he would become king of the Aetolians of all Pleuron and high Calydon. He was raised by the great king Thoas and adopted into his family."

"Here we must all recuse ourselves," Telemachus interrupted, "and drink to the gods, for without them we are nothing. Your words of old have dried out your mouth, and you need to replenish your liquids." He mixed some wine in a ewer of water and poured a nearly clear drink for the old man.

"And how old would your son be today?" Oxylus asked. "For we do not recognize the name of Apollonius of Caria among our troops."

"My son?" The old man took a long draft of the water-wine and thought a moment. "He was born while we were still living in Iasus. He would be fifty years of age, no older surely."

"And did your son have flaming red hair?" Oxylus asked.

"Red hair?"

Oxylus nodded.

"Ah, he had the color of his mother's temperament...fiery."

"And were his ancestors all large as you are?"

"Why, they say we come from Cyclopean stock at some distant time. And my brothers, who are all gone now, excelled in sports and contests. Your questions bespeak some hidden knowledge that you may have."

"Perhaps, but this is long ago," Oxylus admitted. "If this be one and the same, your son is not a fighter for the Heraclides and is not among us this day on earth."

"How so? I have excellent information that he is one of the leaders of the Heraclides."

"There must be some confusion. But let us hold this conversation until this evening, for this story bears on my own. And you must be tired and in want of fresh clothing and rest. And this story is not for all ears."

"Yes, you glimpsed into my soul," the old man admitted.

"Come," Oxylus said. "We will adjourn for the while and give you some time to refresh yourself. You are welcome to my tent and to my valets, who will look after your needs. You will be my guest at supper this evening. In the meanwhile, let me show you the way."

Oxylus led the old man out of the tent. The others stood in amazement as they departed.

"Have you visited Corinth?" Telemachus asked.

"Not yet," Cresphontes said. "But with Tisamenus and his family defeated, we intend to do so this afternoon. We have posted guards throughout."

"It seems as though many moons have waxed and waned since we entered Sicyon. King Lacestades proved to be extremely helpful and his son, Polyphontes, as well. They will be good allies. But now it is time to reopen the city and to allow free commerce and trade to begin again."

"Yes," Cresphontes agreed. "We will do so. But now you speak of this man Lacestades and his son and bring evil memories to my mind, for I am convinced that they were up to no good."

"How so?"

"This young man came among us demanding information, and this was right after we had taken a beating from the Pelopides in our first encounter."

"But I sent him to bring us word, for we knew naught of your situation."

"And so he told us," Cresphontes replied. "But I was not about to give him free run of our troops. And he became belligerent and intemperate. We had to restrain him. Not until Temenus arrived did we hear his story."

"We owe this victory in large part to the aid we received from Lacestades of Sicyon. And his son was the only person we trusted to find his way to you. They are both of your family, and we promised Lacestades, and you can ask Aletes for he was there, that the kingdom would remain in his family, which means Polyphontes. Both are Heraclides."

"Telemachus," Cresphontes replied angrily. "You overstep your bounds. Do not dare to tell me who is or who is not a Heraclide. This young man is lucky to be alive today. And he can thank me for that favor. But these concerns are not your own. In answer to your question, for so I took it, Aletes is leading a delegation to meet with the town archons this afternoon, and we will join them. We have made an offer to the Pelopide troops you see before us, those who want to continue as an infantry division of our own under the command of Procles and Eurysthenes. Many have expressed interest. But we cannot stay in the isthmus much longer and must move on."

"We have moved several other ships across the isthmus to Cenchreae," Temenus added, "using the timber track we created for the Phoenician ship. So we will soon have naval fleets on both sides. We must prepare to take Laconia and Messenia."

"We have surmounted the greatest obstacle with the demise of Tisamenus," Telemachus said, "but I agree we must be prepared for further antagonism. The one obstacle we must overcome is arrogance. And we will not enter Messenia without my command."

Cresphontes stared at Telemachus, but remained silent.

After this, Telemachus left the tent and entered the sunlight. He went to check on Amphion and found Autolycus and Deiphontes with him in a small tent. Amphion still slept, although his color had improved and his breathing was regular and not forced. He looked better.

"How goes it?" Telemachus asked the two men.

"He is comfortable," Autolycus replied. "Perhaps, he is lucky, for he is out of the fighting for a while."

"What are you thinking?" Telemachus asked Autolycus.

"This life of soldiering is not without its pain," Autolycus replied.

"Yes," Deiphontes agreed. "To listen to Cresphontes, this is just one step in a long march. But to live through it is appalling. We lost many of our best fighters. We lost your decadarch, you know?"

"Dardanos?"

"Yes. And many of your tablemates."

"No!" Telemachus replied in shock.

"Dardanos took a lance in the neck."

"We dreamed of returning to the fishing shoals off Pylos," Telemachus whispered. "He is gone? He has wife and children about. A saltwater man…"

"And the death accounting is just beginning," Deiphontes continued.

"The worst is," Autolycus said, "the very enemies we were battling yesterday are now offering their services in aid of the Heraclides. The enemy of yesterday is the friend of today."

"Aletes took a battalion into Corinth before the battle at the ditch," Deiphontes added. "They took the palace and sent the trooper guards back to their tribes. They put Tisamenus' wife and his two young children to the sword and in so doing ended the line of Agamemnon and the House of Atreus."

"What are you saying?" Telemachus asked in disbelief. "By the gods, Aletes was fighting on the other side of the ditch."

"No. He was in Corinth during the battle," Deiphontes replied.

"Aletes did not go with the reinforcements?"

"No," Deiphontes replied, "he was in Corinth."

Telemachus shook his head in despair and white-hot fury. His own son had volunteered to aid his brothers-at-arms, while Aletes had remained behind, disobeying Oxylus' command.

Deiphontes continued. "There are rumors that they have discovered Priam's gold hidden in the palace, which Agamemnon brought back to Hellas from Troy. A vast store of wealth."

"It will only bring sorrow," Autolycus added, "as it did for Priam, and as it did for Agamemnon."

"Neither of you is fit for the military life...nor I," Telemachus said vacantly, still astounded by the news of Aletes. "I am going in search of Oxylus. Let me know when Amphion wakens." He wandered out of the tent dazed.

Along the ditch, the soldiers were struggling with the dead bodies, which were being gathered into two large piles: one vermilion and one blue, but sharing a common color of dried blood mixed with earth. Both Heraclide and Pelopide soldiers transported bodies from the far side of the ditch in wagons. The armaments were stripped off the bodies. Clothing and sandals and armour that might still be useful were thrown into another pile. Due to the numbers, the soldiers could not clean and anoint the bodies as would have been done with a loved one, but they wrapped the bodies in shrouds of thin cloth, which was one of the supplies kept in abundance, and then placed them respectfully in position for cremation.

Telemachus found Oxylus in an agitated state. They walked down to the shore of the Saronic Gulf and sat together on the rocks, looking out into the calm water, shading themselves with their Heraclide cloaks.

Oxylus shook his head: "Just when you think your past is buried, it returns to haunt you."

"What do you make of this man?"

"It is very difficult to tell," Oxylus admitted. "But without doubt, there is more to him than meets the eye. My brother has been dead for decades, and I am sure that the son he seeks is my brother. I had not dreamed those unhappy days might return."

"And your brother was adopted just as you were?"

"Yes. I have lived with that fact my entire life. Not contentedly. We all want to take pride in our parents. Some of us cannot. I know who my parents were, but that does not give me solace. People look at me, and they know."

"How is that?"

"They know I am not Hellene."

"So?"

"I am Hellene by intrigue and design. But Trojan and Ethiopian by birth. For my real father was Memnon, King of the Ethiopians, who brought his troops to assist the Trojans at Ilium and was touted as the most handsome man at Troy. And my mother was the daughter of Priam, Philomela, and the most beautiful of all his daughters. Both of my parents were killed in the war, and, like many of the orphans that survived the razing of Troy (and due to the thoroughness of the Achaeans there were not many of us), I was given to the priestess of Delphi. I lived at the oracle for several years, and the priestess told me of my parentage and foresaw great tidings for me. When Thoas, King of Aetolia, visited Delphi in hopes for an issue for his son, Haemon, the priestess divined that Haemon would never produce a natural heir to stand in line to the throne, and she told Thoas of my background. Together, they compassed my future as the son of his son, though not with any special accuracy, as you are now well aware.

"My father, Memnon, was a great warrior. He killed many men at Troy, including the runner Antilochus, son of Nestor. When Memnon fought raging Achilles over the body and armour of Antilochus, he was stabbed in his breastbone by Achilles. My father died on the plains of Troy. It was told that Memnon was the son of the goddess Eos and Tithonos. Tithonos was the son of King Laomedon of Troy and one of the brothers of Priam. Memnon came from a long line of rulers descended from Zeus. And when Memnon bit the dust at Troy, Eos' tears at the death of her son fell without respite. Now, every morning when Eos rises in the air her tears for her son, Memnon, color the leaves of plants and grasses.

"But before the Trojan War, Memnon ruled over the huge and divided kingdom of Ethiopia, for it lay at both margins of Oceanus, far larger than all the lands and isles of Hellas. Memnon was described as dark as ebony and the handsomest man alive. That you know just by observing me. Haemon, though, was never pleased by my complexion, as pleasant as it is. And for this reason, he finally exiled me. For I have come to believe the killing of my brother was most assuredly an accident and not my intention."

"All this history serves naught today," Telemachus said.

"I am only telling you this to make you understand. I have no family. I consider your family my own, if that is not presumptuous. I would never choose to harm you or your family. I have never had a friend such as you, and I will kill to retain your friendship. I give you this story to understand me and my failings. That is all I have to give to you...my honesty."

"Thank you, Oxylus," Telemachus replied, but he had not the heart for the man this day. "We must deal with the old man, Lykeios, and another matter."

"You know, it is too much to believe. Why would he appear just now? And for what reason? Only the gods know. We must send him on his way."

"How will we do that?" Telemachus asked.

"I do not know." The cheer had departed Oxylus once again.

"Then allow me to add one more note of discord to your day," Telemachus said. "You told me you ordered Aletes to command the reinforcements sent to aid Procles and Eurysthenes."

"Yes."

"Well, he did not go with the reinforcements," Telemachus said bitterly. "No, he went back to Corinth, and took an infantry battalion with him. He killed the wife and children of Tisamenus. And he discovered the Treasury of Corinth."

"Are you sure of this?" Oxylus demanded.

"In his place, Amphion led the troops."

"That move," Oxylus said, "could have spelled our defeat."

"It certainly put Amphion's life at risk."

"We will not long forget this," Oxylus said. "I have been in many campaigns, and this behavior is called treason. And in war, traitors live short lives."

L

When Telemachus returned to the tent where Amphion was recuperating, he found him awake and talking with his brother.

"How are you feeling?" Telemachus asked.

"As though my body was used to till a field of stone."

"From what I hear, you did well."

"I remember very little. My horse?"

"Arion suffered no wound and is waiting for you," Telemachus replied. "But it will be some time before you ride again. I think your days as a trooper are at an end. When you are able, you will go to Ithaca to recover. We are marching out tomorrow, and perhaps you can stay with Lacestades for a while. You have earned your wages for the Heraclides."

"But when I recover…"

"No. You are finished. The gods do not grant third lives."

That evening, Oxylus and Telemachus joined Lykeios, the seer from Halicarnassus, at supper. They gathered in Oxylus' tent, and the old man was now cleaned and properly attired. In his new manifestation, he had lost a few of his many years and appeared more reasonable and rational. He began asking questions far afield from his initial concerns for his son.

"And Tisamenus? What has become of him?"

"He dwells in the house of Hades, along with all his family," Oxylus replied.

"And will Cresphontes rule well?"

"He can be no worse."

"And this family of Heraclides?"

"We hope for the best, but you never know."

"My son would have been a great leader," Lykeios said. "It takes a man who, although full of himself, respects others and listens to others' views."

"I believe that your son was raised as my brother," Oxylus confessed. "He excelled at all things and was beloved of the king. For at this time, Thoas had fled the scene, and Haemon was King of Aetolia, although not the man his father was. We called your son Thermius, and he was as large as any man in all Pleuron and high Calydon and bested all in the javelin, all save Eudoros, known throughout Hellas for his skills. He had fiery red hair and a desire to compete."

"And you say that he is not here in Corinth?"

"He was killed in the games by accident, when we were young men."

"How so?"

"He was hit by a quoit, which was misdirected. So well did he throw the quoit that in competition all struggled to surpass his mark."

"Yes," the old man agreed. "When one does not measure up and is afraid to admit it, then things may go wide of the mark."

"I have lived with this my entire life," Oxylus admitted.

"God sows within each of us the seed of greatness," Lykeios said. "And we must be broad in our definition of greatness. Only a few succeed in nurturing the seed of greatness through so much adversity. Many deny the existence of the seed within. Many are afraid to see it germinate. Many men spend their lives spoiling the germination of the seed within others. All in all, the birth of greatness is successfully accomplished by only a few men. We call these the "Chosen." What we must understand is that the seed is there alive within all mortals."

"I failed my brother," Oxylus said, "for I loved him as a true brother. I failed to see him, for I was so wrapped up in myself."

"As father of the son, I forgive you, but I ask a favor of you in return."

"Yes, if I only could fulfill it for you."

"Do you have children?"

"No."

"When you do, I ask that you raise your sons as though my Apollonius, or your brother, Thermius, were before you at all times."

"I swear to the brother I no longer possess," Oxylus said.

"Then you will be successful in all things, both of you. For I feel the presence of the gods with you as well, Telemachus, son of Odysseus. May Apollo love you and care for you as I did for my wife. May he cure your ills. Now I will return to my country, for I have found that which I sought."

With that, Lykeios stood, kissed the hand of Oxylus and then of Telemachus. He departed the camp and the Peloponnese and Hellas, for that matter, and ascended to the heavens.

That evening, a single white bull was sacrificed before the ditch on the isthmus. As he fell to his knees and his blood poured out onto the dirt, the priests prayed for the departed souls of the fighters and dedicated the site to the memory of Poseidon, for these were his lands and soil. Without the shedding of blood, there can be no forgiveness. They flayed the meat and fed the fatty inner meats to the fire. Soon the burnt offerings rose to the mansions of the gods. And the gods smelled the good smells and accepted the offerings and smiled down on these mortals, struggling to live their lives.

With this offering, the priests set fire to the wooden pyre that had been constructed over the bodies of the dead, for the vermilion and blue had been joined together. The sweet smells of the roasting meats were now mingled with the smell of human lives lost. Of the seven hundred Heraclide soldiers of the second infantry coming from Boreas, only two hundred or so remained. Of the five thousand Pelopide soldiers who had initiated the fight on the isthmus, three thousand would never return to their homes and families. In all, well over four thousands souls had departed the earth. The flames and smoke forced the living soldiers far back from the fire. Many went down to the seashore to observe the conflagration from afar and to feel refreshed by the sea breeze and humid marine odors.

This night, a single bonfire burned. In the morning, as golden Eos rose in the sky, her tears for her son, Memnon, still covered the land. The soldiers rolled great rocks onto the cinders and hot ashes and build a great cairn. Soon a cyclopean barrow appeared along the isthmus route and remained there for many generations, in remembrance of the brave warriors.

To this day, there is a sanctuary dedicated to dark-haired Poseidon on the coast at this location. And people come from far and wide to offer thanks to the son of Cronos and sibling of Zeus and to ask his help and support in their lives, for of all the gods, Poseidon loved the Hellenes the most. Only a handful of people today recall the struggle along the isthmus of the Heraclides and Pelopides.

Among the brave men known to us who would never return to their loved ones, both Dardanos, the fisherman from Pylos and Heraclide Phylarch, and Troezen, the boxer from Thessaly, the champion skirmisher, lay buried along the isthmus. I, Antimenes believe that in one way mortals are superior to their gods and that is in the giving of life. No deed by any god has such meaning, however heroic or honorable. The well-meaning gods will never realize the significance of giving one's own mortal life for a belief. For some men it is out of duty or coercion, but for others it is for a worthy idea, and that surpasses the acts of all the gods.

By mid-morning, the Heraclides marched out of the isthmus toward Argos, masters of all they saw. Notus blew agreeably in their faces.

The country of Argos was about two hundred stadia distant from Corinth. The army had to pass through the isthmus and then along the edge of the city of Corinth. The route to Argos led out of the city alongside the Acrocorinthus, passing through forested Cleonae, a small village in the foothills, and then ascending to the pass on Mount Tretus. At the summit, a road led to the great city of Mycenae, set deep in the mountains among the forested trees. Then, the gentle slope from the mountain pass descended into the wide river valley of fertile Argolis. A runner might travel the distance in a morning at a good pace. It would take the Heraclides most of the day to traverse the foothills and the plains. But, if they marched without respite and did not encounter any hostilities at Mycenae, they would arrive in Argos well before Helios disappeared below the mountains.

The victorious second infantry division led the march off the isthmus, although their numbers were greatly diminished. On the march, as in the war, they were joined by the reinforcements, both horse riders and archers and skirmishers led by Deiphontes, who rode in the place of Amphion, leading Amphion's black mare out of respect. Together, they sang the paean of victory to Apollo himself. The generals, Procles and Eurysthenes, followed in their chariots, along with Cresphontes and his bodyguards.

The second division had fought its way along the isthmus, suffering immeasurably, and by dint of their perseverance had been instrumental in forcing the Pelopides to surrender. The first infantry division that had taken Sicyon by night followed, led by Oxylus, Aletes, Phalces, and Autolycus, with the Aegean blue colors held high. The cavalry came after them with the high-strung horses slow-walking nervously and shyly. The new third infantry followed with a mixture of vermilion and blue. This division was formed by the Pelopide fighters who had agreed to join Cresphontes and his Heraclides. At Cenchreae and the outskirts of Corinth, the supply troops with hundreds of wagons merged with the soldiers. The land army, now some five thousand strong, began its march into the heart of the Peloponnese. As the soldiers departed the isthmus, they saluted their fallen comrades and swore to return one day to give proper honors to this battlefield.

Ahead of them lay the armies of Mycenae, Argos, Sparta, and King Nestor's Messenia. But of all the men to confront them in the future, the most dangerous men marched with the Heraclides.

LI

In the early morning hours, Telemachus and his tablemates took fair-minded Amphion to Sicyon to recuperate in the palace of King Lacestades. By the will of heaven, the file that Dardanos, a simple fisherman from Pylos, had once commanded as the personal guard of Telemachus was now under the authority of a young phylarch, Alexandros, son of Pelius. Alexandros was one of the young troopers that Telemachus had come to depend on during the isthmus fighting. He had demonstrated his skills among the troopers, aiding at the ditch, both as a wily fighter and as a clever leader. Born and raised on Zacynthus, he had joined the Heraclides after proving himself a horse tamer and rider of excellence. He had joined Telemachus' table mates and had agreed to accompany him all the way to Ithaca.

Lacestades and his son Polyphontes welcomed the troopers at their simple palace in Sicyon later in the morning, offering them food and wine. The single file had carefully transported Amphion in a wagon. As they made their way through Corinth, the town was just waking to a new day. A few people occupied the agora, but most of the streets remained empty, save the Aegean blue of the Heraclide guards throughout the city. People walked past the guards without fear or anger. The news of the deaths of their kings, Doridas and Hyanthidas, had not particularly bothered anyone, since the lives of the people were far removed, and the two kings had never been greatly loved. Mystery surrounded their deaths. The kings had not entered into the hostilities, although they found themselves on the wrong side of the ditch along the isthmus and in the heat of battle. It was rumored that the Pelopide officers, before escaping from the isthmus, had not wanted the brothers to return to power or to tell tales and had ended their reign themselves.

The news of the death of Tisamenus was received with more sanguinity, although no one would have expressed it as such, for after Agamemnon and Orestes and now Tisamenus, the Peloponnese was like the mesh skeleton of a dry sponge: little goodwill remained. The Corinthians reacted to the news of a new ruler in the vein of what we hear so often, "the gods know, he can be no worse."

The troopers carried Amphion to a ground-floor room in the palace. The quarters opened to a courtyard full of sunshine, giving view to the gulf through the pines, but more importantly, allowing the healing breezes off the gulf to enliven the room. It would be many moons before Amphion would know if he was ever to walk again. He would need exercise and care. Even then the physicians doubted that he would have full use of his right leg due to the disturbance suffered from the break and dislodgment. He suffered fevers, but his complexion was good, the leg was not discolored, and he slept comfortably for much of the day. When he woke in his new environs in Sicyon, servants removed the dressings and rewrapped his leg in herbal compresses to drain the fever.

Telemachus accompanied the troopers to the room and sat on the bed next to Amphion, thanking the goodness of the gods for this admonition. He had bargained the safe return of his son, and the gods had fulfilled their side of the transaction. Now, it remained for Telemachus to discharge his obligations, which he would do willingly, even if it changed the course of his life. Warm air filled the room, and Telemachus felt good that his son was now safe and could recover and return to his life. One son safe for the moment; the other remained endangered and on his way to Argos with Oxylus.

He looked into Amphion's face and saw Polycasté's soft eyes. He recalled her visage full of joy and humor combined with tenderness from his first visits to Pylos before their marriage. These visits had occurred before the second crop of Heraclides had invaded Achaea. Polycasté surprised and amazed him. Once Nestor agreed to their marriage, she no longer stood apart from him in any way. Her shyness and coyness disappeared, and she treated him with loving respect, though never without wit and humor. They could not keep themselves from laughter; the joy of finding each other overflowed like a mountain spring. During their long engagement, they could often be seen in the streets of Pylos, walking or greeting well-wishers, for all Pylians knew of the incipient wedding, or just ambling among the sands and rocks along the shore. And in the long nights, they would name the stars and constellations and think up appropriate names for their children: he wanted girls and she, boys. He remembered a conversation just before the wedding ceremony:

"Elis is far from the shore," Telemachus told her, "but it is balmy and warm in the evenings, and it is temperate in the winters."

"And what of our bed?" Polycasté always surprised him in her candid fashion, having been raised with her coarse brothers.

"Our bed?"

"Yes, our marriage bed."

"I have not thought about that."

"Everyone has heard tales of Penelope and Odysseus' bed. Can you so easily ignore this?"

"As a child, I often slept in this bed of such renown. But there are certain things that I am not at liberty to disclose to you, my bride-to-be. You will have to take heart and have patience." He wondered how he could possibly respond to this challenge.

"You must trim your beard. It is becoming stiff and abrasive."

"And you must promise never to cut your hair."

"My father and mother no longer sleep together, you know," she said.

"How do you know this?"

"I often wake my father for his offices early in the morning. I can tell for my mother's bed is distant. Promise me you will never leave my bed, even when I am old and no longer desirable to you."

"That day will never come."

"Yes it will. And you will throw me from your bed like an old scarf. And then you will take a younger woman."

"Never."

"Yes, I know men. They are fickle."

"Perhaps your brothers, but that is not true of all men. Particularly in my family."

"Ah, but we have heard of your father's travels."

"I was thinking of my grandfather."

"Ah, but you take after your father."

"Only in some ways."

"Then you promise never to cast me off."

"Yes."

"And if you do?"

"I just promised."

"I know and thank you. But just in case."

"There is no just-in-case."

"You never know."

"Some things, you do."

"Really?"

"Really."

Oftentimes, their talks would spiral into the heavens of total nonsense, but they always ended back on earth with their arms around each other, content to hold on against a world of unknowns.

Not only did Telemachus see Polycasté in Amphion's sleeping countenance, he also saw Nestor: a patient and wise man, who had lived longer than any man of his generation. In some ways, Nestor was more of a father to Telemachus than Odysseus had been. Nestor had shown an interest in him as a boy, sending him his first horse, Bronte, had welcomed him to his palace as a young man searching for news of Odysseus, and, while he was courting Polycasté, had always treated him with great warmth and listened to his ideas. Telemachus leaned over the sleeping Amphion and embraced him for a moment.

"When I see you next, we will be walking in Laertes' garden on Ithaca, god willing," he whispered.

Later in the shaded courtyard, he sipped a chalice of wine and water. "Thank you for caring for Amphion," Telemachus said to Lacestades. "I will never forget this."

"I am hopeful that the Heraclides will bring growth and health to the region. So many people are dispirited, particularly in Corinth and particularly the young. We need an extended time of peace. We only need to be left alone to plant our crops and pull our fishes from the large-wide. Whether Cresphontes will be just another tyrant in a long line of tyrants or a true leader is yet to be seen."

"I have my own thoughts, but I remain hopeful as well."

"It is unfortunate that the greatest of the Heraclides are outside the family."

"This is the right place for Amphion. Your hospitality is beyond measure. I hope to return before winter sets in, for we are expected in Ithaca before then."

"May I speak frankly with you?" Lacestades asked.

"Of course."

"You well know that I never thought myself a Heraclide in the current sense of the name. But my son has returned to me a changed man. He has a hatred so deep for Cresphontes and these Heraclides that I cannot fathom his feelings. I only know that it does not bode well for either. I care not for Cresphontes. But somehow it is as if a well has been poisoned deep within my son. I now both fear him and for him."

"Cresphontes has a shameful mind and deceitful nature," Telemachus replied, "but to him his treatment of Polyphontes was not an important matter. He will have no memory of it. You must counsel patience with Polyphontes. He should not lay up these things within his heart. The intensity of the young is frightening."

"He is immature and impetuous."

"Just so," Telemachus said. "Cresphontes for the moment is riding on a wave that may carry him far and make him more powerful than any man in the Peloponnese. But in a young life, there will be many changes. Patience, for the gods humble the proud and raise the obscure."

"Although I concur with you. I am afraid he will have none of it."

"Lacestades, you have navigated the treacherous waters of this region with Agamemnon, Orestes, and Tisamenus. I am sure that you will do equally well with Cresphontes."

"I hope you are right. As Sicyonians, we keep our heads down, our feet flat on the ground, and our backs engaged."

Telemachus took his leave, once again thanking Lacestades, and promising to return in no more that a moon's time when Sirius passes overhead. The troopers rode off through the town of Sicyon, where market day had returned to normal. In the small agora, people offered fresh produce and fish. The villagers greeted each other and talked quietly, while looking for the ingredients for the midday meal. To view Sicyon, it was as though nothing had changed in the lives of the occupants. And perhaps that was the best result. But change is deceptive and may not be visible to those involved until after the fact and sometimes not until many years later. Change is like a storm brewing on the horizon with the living winds blowing from all quadrants, impossible to predict or anticipate in which direction it will fall or with what intensity, until it is upon you.

Telemachus and his tribe hurried back to Corinth, alternating between trotting and walking. The city was now open and coming to life. But here in the light of day, changes were more visible than when they had passed through earlier in the morning. A large Heraclide infantry contingent was stationed at the palace. Two battalions were left in the city under the command of Temenus and his navy. Most of the Heraclide ships were beached now at Lechaeum, with a few at Cenchreae. In the city, wounded Corinthian soldiers could be seen here and there, no longer in uniform, the lucky ones bearing the visible evidence of war in bandages and bound limbs. Of the others, those who ventured out did so only with the help of relatives or with wooden crutches. And above many doors of homes and buildings the black signs of death hung in effigy. The palace had been converted to care for the wounded Heraclides, so the town was full of the walking wounded. But the people went about their affairs, and the large agora was bustling once again. Only the government offices were closed for the interim. The roads were filled with people, animals, wagons, and carts, and cheer seemed to have returned to the city: cheer tempered somewhat by grief and trepidation.

Earlier in the morning, the forced march to Argos took the Heraclides through Corinth. It must have been a sight to the townspeople to observe the forces of the Heraclides marching through the streets, their colors high, their troops full of the piss and ruddy spirit of victory, and their horses raring to run to release their pent-up energy. Now as the small detachment of Heraclide troopers rode through the city and set out on the road toward Argos, few people glanced in their direction.

As with all cities, the history of my home, Argos, is complicated and brimming with the names of its abundant leaders and heroes and goats, but the city of Argos bears heavily on our story. To the historian, names are vital to understanding. To the casual reader of histories, names may offer a challenge of questionable import and are often skipped over or ignored. I, though, urge you to recognize the importance of names. Evil is the man who

refuses to give his mane or would truncate names or bury a body without identity. Names give us a man and his family, for no man stands alone. And when repeated sufficient times, names give us a hero. And when repeated all the more times, names give us a god. It is our name that we are known by, whether we be captain of a ship or gatherer in the fields. And these names, when combined, create history, whether majestic, commonplace, or execrable. Take notice. Names honor us all. Just as I note my Alcathöe.

Forgive me this capsule history, for every word masks a host of events, long forgotten. Bear with me, for surely you will see the repetitive nature of history. As I tell my scholars, you will not be held responsible for the content, only the intent.

Argos is the heart of the Peloponnese and the home of the Heraclides. Argos is known as the cradle of civilization favored by Hera. It sits within the fertile barley and wheat growing plain formed by the confluence of the Inarchus and Charadrus Rivers leading into the Gulf of Argolis.

In Argos we find the challenge of history. The founder of Argos, Phoroneus, son of the river god Inarches, was said to be the first man to set foot on the earth. Phoroneus was the first king of all of the Peloponnese. His daughter, Niobe, should not be confused with the Niobe who was Queen of Thebes, mother of the Niobids, and angry relative of Polycasté. This Niobe, daughter of Phoroneus, was the first mortal woman with whom Zeus ever had intercourse. And as a result, she gave birth to Phoroneus' successor, Argos, who called the state after himself. As happened commonly among the gods, Poseidon disputed patronage of Argos, this time with Hera, and Zeus selected three river gods to arbitrate. They awarded the patronage to Hera. Poseidon, angered at his loss, dissipated all the waters from Argos, so that only when it rained were waters available to the people, and thereafter all the streams and wells dried up.

The history of Argos begins in Egypt. For there, the great King Belus had two sons who could not stand the sight of one another – we have oft heard this. In an attempt to solve this poisonous problem, Belus sent one son, Danaus, to Libya, and his other son, Aegyptus, to Arabia. But even at such a distance, the two brothers continued to bicker, fight, and compete against one another. Both brothers married many women and fathered many children. Fittingly,

Danaus had fifty daughters, and Aegyptus had fifty sons. Now, fearing the treacherous, avenging sons of Aegyptus, Danaus constructed a ship, the first sea-going vessel ever built by man, and fled to Hellas with his fifty daughters. He arrived at Argos in the Peloponnese during the reign of Gelanor, seventh king of this dynasty. Danaus invaded and killed Gelanor. He named the inhabitants of Argos, Danaans, after himself. Thus, we see Homer naming the Hellenes at Troy oftentimes as Danaans – again, names.

But the sons of Aegyptus were not content to see Danaus leave the region with his daughters and relocate elsewhere, particularly successfully, and they pursued him. After much fighting and negotiating a solution, Danaus was forced to consent to the marriages of his daughters to their cousins. At the same time, an evil plan was created by the daughters of Danaus against their grooms, for as with their fathers, there was no love lost between the cousins. On their wedding night, all the daughters, whom we now call the Danaids, maliciously allowed their husbands one final joy and then murdered them all. All except one sister, who for one simple reason did not murder her husband. For this terrible deed, all the Danaids were sent to the house of Hades, where they are found to this day, punished by having to carry water from a source to fill a jar that continues to leak and never fills. The one Danaid who did not kill her husband soon became fat with child and gave birth. She named her son Abas, and she loved both husband and son dearly. When Danaus died, his grandson Abas inherited the throne of Argos.

Abas soon took a wife and had twin sons, Acrisius and Proetus. But somehow the eternal hatred of the sons of the great King Belus passed on to them, and they quarreled while still in their mother's womb, causing her and them no end of pain. After their separation at birth, their enmity continued with no less ferocity. When the time came for them to rule the kingdom of Argos, they could not agree on any way to divide the kingdom to both their satisfactions, so they started a war against one other to settle their differences by sword. Many soldiers lost their lives, and the battle continued for many years. At some time during this war, Acrisius invented the use of shields for his troops, for no one had ever thought of them before. And it was the use of shields that turned out to make all the difference in the battle. Acrisius emerged victorious.

Now after he won, Acrisius banished Proetus from Argos. Since Proetus had married the daughter of the King of Lycia, he sought his father-in-law's help in his struggle against his hated twin. And the king gave him an army of Lycians. Soon enough, Proetus returned to Argos with his army and captured the coastal town of Tiryns. After this, the two brothers divided the Argive territory into two regions: Acrisius reigning over Argos, and Proetus over Tiryns. The two regions have remained at odds ever since.

It was at this time that an oracle announced to Acrisius that if his daughter, Danae, gave birth to a son, he would grow up to assassinate Acrisius. Because of this prophecy, Acrisius built a large room of bronze to isolate his daughter and to keep her from losing her virginity. But she was a clever child and managed to escape one evening and met a man who seduced her and made her with child. Some say this man was Zeus himself in mortal trappings. Enraged by his daughter, Acrisius locked her and her child in a brazen strongbox and took it out into the middle of the Gulf of Argolis and dropped the box and its contents over the side of the vessel. But he outwitted himself, for the box was so well built that it floated on the seas and was not harmed by the waves or rocks. Both mother and child survived. The child's name was Perseus, and he became one of the greatest heroes of all Hellas.

When Perseus grew up, he traveled throughout the world, but one day he returned to the kingdom of Acrisius, his grandfather, in Argos. In the battle that ensued, the leaders knew naught of each other, and Perseus mortally wounded his grandfather, and the oracle was fulfilled. When Perseus discovered what had happened, he preferred not to win the kingdom illegitimately and proposed trading kingdoms with King Megapenthes of Tiryns, son of Proetus. So, gladly agreeing, Megapenthes ruled over Argos, while Perseus reigned over Tiryns. Perseus turned out to be the greater leader, and Tiryns prospered. He founded Mycenae, which became the wealthiest city in all the Peloponnese.

But when Megapenthes discovered that Perseus had killed Acrisius, he pursued Perseus and killed him. After Perseus' death, his son, Electryon, succeeded him to the throne of Tiryns and Mycenae. And at this point, the blood began to flow like a river in spring.

Electryon had a daughter, Alcmena, who married her cousin, Amphitryon, the son of Alcaeus, brother of Electryon. As you may recall, Alcmena was deceived by Zeus and conceived Heracles. But separately from this, Amphitryon accidentally killed his father-in-law, Electryon. The third brother, Sthenelus by name, took the matter into his own hands and judging the death an accidental one, banished Amphitryon and took over the throne of Mycenae and Tiryns himself. Sthenelus married into the family of the Pelopides, as had Electryon. As we have seen, by the instigation of the gods, father Zeus and jealous Hera, Sthenelus was succeeded to the throne by his son, Eurystheus, the tormentor of Heracles, who ruled over all three towns: Argos, Mycenae, and Tiryns. Thus, the families of the Heraclides and Pelopides were not as distant as they would have us believe.

When Eurystheus was killed by Hyllus, son of Heracles, in the beginnings of the War of the Families, the throne became vacant for a time, as the Heraclides were not able to take over rule. But Atreus, son of Pelops, and his brother, Thyestes, fought over the golden lamb given to Atreus by stealthy Hermes, who could not leave well enough alone. Although Thyestes seduced Atreus' wife and with her help tricked him with the golden lamb, Atreus took over the throne when the sun moved backwards. He banished his brother to Lydia. Thyestes sought the oracle, who told him that if he had intercourse with his own daughter, he could recover the throne. The product of this unnatural union was Aegisthus, an evil man. When Aegisthus grew up, he tricked King Atreus and killed him with a sword. Aegisthus gave the throne to his father, Thyestes. As king, Thyestes banished the sons of Atreus, Agamemnon and Menelaus, from Argos.

For a long time, the two sons of Atreus plotted the death of their uncle Thyestes. Finally with the help of King Tyndareus of Sparta, they returned to Argolis and drove Thyestes into exile. Agamemnon took the throne of Argos, Tiryns, and Mycenae, and at the death of Tyndareus, Menelaus took over the throne of Sparta. However, that did not end the affair. During the Trojan War, with the two kings away at war, the son of Thyestes and killer of Atreus, Aegisthus by name, returned to Mycenae and became the evil lover of the wife of Agamemnon and daughter of King Tyndareus, Clytemnestra. Together they killed Agamemnon upon his return from

Troy like an "oxen in his stall." Aegisthus then took the throne of Argos, Tiryns, and Mycenae.

But Orestes, son of Agamemnon, never forgot, and when he grew up he returned to Mycenae and killed both Aegisthus and his mother for wrongfully killing his father. Orestes went mad for a time after this, but was eventually acquitted of this double crime of murder and matricide. With an iron hand, Orestes reunited the kingdom of Argos and expanded it to include Corinth, Arcadia, and Sparta. His son, Tisamenus, followed him on the throne of the enlarged kingdom.

The death of Tisamenus and his family ended the reign of the Pelopides. The history of the Pelopides is a bloody, unnatural stew, full of evil ingredients, stirred by the gods from beginning to end. This unhappy family left the scene, having accomplished nothing more than the untimely deaths of many people, most notably their own family members. Some families are known for their lives, while the Pelopides were known for their deaths.

Thus, I offer a capsule history of Argos and its names, with the full understanding that, if we so desire, we can all learn from and improve upon the lives of our cherished or not-so-cherished ancestors – just as they would have it or, possibly, even against their defective judgment.

Telemachus and his troopers rode rapidly into the foothills of Mount Tretus, passing through the town of Cleonae. As they cantered through, people on the main street waved happily at them, though perhaps warily as well, it was difficult to tell. They continued into the mountains, until at the peak they got their first view of the plain of Argos and the Gulf of Argolis stretching out into the mist in the distance. They rested their horses among the mountain grasses for a short lull, and then began the gentle descent into the fertile river valley.

Entering Mycenae was a shock. For the mighty circuit walls encircling the great palace were garlanded with flowers, and Heraclide guards were posted out front. The people from the surrounding buildings were still celebrating in the streets. It could have been a festival day, with dancing and music and young children running through the crowds. Hawkers of all sorts of foods and sweet meats filled the city with good smells and cries, promising the excellence of their offerings. Harvest grapes were abundant to test the crop, since the grapes were now at their ripest and harvesting and pressing had commenced. To the tongue, the grapes were raisiny, with bittersweet juice – a wine to be appreciated in the future.

Within the battlements stood the magnificent palace of Agamemnon, the greatest leader of the Achaeans. The city had become for the most part a government center, dominated by the royal palace. Beyond the circuit walls, the city was surrounding by wood buildings and mud row houses of the workers who supported the government functionaries and courts. Since Orestes had moved the capital and residence to Arcadia, the city's wealth had fled. With the return of the Heraclides, though, the people were hopeful of a return to the wealthier times under the sons of Atreus when gold from all corners of the earth flowed constantly into the coffers of the king.

Telemachus and his troopers slowed to a walk. They were showered with flowers and good wishes as they rode through, children's hands touched the sweaty flanks of the horses or grabbed gently at the Aegean blue cloaks for good fortune. Argos lay only sixty stadia farther on, so they dismounted and took a moment to eat and rest. The people surrounded Telemachus, offering him various meats and delicacies. In their efforts, they pushed and pulled until his guards were forced to warn them back.

The Heraclides spoke of the "return to the Peloponnese," but the people of the Peloponnese regarded the army as foreign. They had heard the stories from the bards of the Pelopides and Heraclides, but to them the Heraclides were Dorians, foreigners speaking an accented Greek language that was rough on their ears, unlike their own mellifluous tones. Still, depending on their ages, the women pressed about the young troopers as mothers would surround their children or as lovers might stand a little too close to one other. Smiles and good nature appeared on many faces, for most believed that the gods were smiling down from the heavens just as Helios cast sunlight upon the earth. Yet, one could feel a scarcely concealed mixture of antagonism and resentment.

"Welcome, master," a man called out from the crowd, his one remaining eye and one arm raised in salute. His head stood out above the others, and the crowd separated from him fearful of his antics. "You are welcome to the greatest of all the countries of Hellas. Where do you hail from, if I may be so bold?"

"Ithaca," Telemachus replied uncomfortably. The troopers gathered around him to ensure no mischief.

"Aye, sir. I have heard of such a country. Land of the Cyclops, I am sure. Where Odysseus slew cruel Polyphemus, son of Poseidon."

Telemachus stared at the man, but made no reply.

"We just saw the godly Cresphontes, son of Heracles, pass through here with laurel on his head. All these gods to lead us. But they do not put barley on the table nor stave off the barbarians. Mind you, my master, that you Dorians do not repeat the errors of those who came before."

Telemachus mounted Sterope, and the troopers followed suit, sensing the madness of the man.

"Thank you," Telemachus said to the man uncomfortably. "I will consider your advice."

"They do not put barley on the table nor stave off the barbarians," the man said, his voice rising. His one eye flashed with lunacy. "When you return to your country," he shouted as the horsemen retreated, "beware you are not welcomed by deadly gifts."

LII

The troopers rode the remaining distance to Argos in a foggy haze of glory. Soldiers dream of this late at night before a battle. Without praise and honor to warriors, there would be no wars. And without the smiles of young women, the feelings of righteousness and nobility would not accrue. The battle for Corinth had not deteriorated into a morass of indignity and disgrace as so often happens. In this case, the armies were not oppressed into fighting to the last man. The fighting did not include razing the towns and villages. For this, the people were grateful. The Pelopide army was composed of men from the surrounding communities, and over the years they had known many leaders. Their allegiance went only so far for the current ones, until they threw their weapons to the ground. On the Heraclide side, the soldiers stood to gain a foothold in a new region, and they were willing to go further in their commitment and dedication. The limits of their loyalty had yet to be tested.

The troopers continued through the valley, passing vineyards, olive groves, orchards, and large empty fields where barley and wheat grew. The farmers waved from their fields. The grape harvest was at full swing. They crossed the Inarchus and Charadrus Rivers and came into the outskirts of the city of Argos. Unlike Corinth, this was a rural city with its wealth determined by farming, and it was built low to the ground, without large public buildings or fortifications.

When they arrived in Argos, Telemachus and his tablemates found the entire town square filled with Heraclide infantry troops, spilling over onto the side streets. The citizens of Argos walked among the troops, and once again there was a spirit of festivity. Fires had been started in the broad agora, and sheep and goats were waiting to be slaughtered for the evening ceremony, for Cresphontes had ordered another celebration of their victory. With the compliance of the archons of bluegrass Argos and high-walled Tiryns, the Heraclides had now successfully taken nearly all of the territory ruled by Tisamenus, based on his father's acquisitions. Only Sparta remained. Tisamenus had never been a popular leader. He had inherited the animus of his father, Orestes, whom people associated with the greatness of the sons of Atreus and the shame of Orestes' murdering his own mother. This matricide was condemned by all. The perfidy of his mother in killing his father was considered a lesser offense. Now, the blood players had departed the scene. The land and its occupants could return to a more innocent view of itself. For just as spring is born of winter, so too do generations renew the earth.

Telemachus finally found Oxylus outside of town in a tent he shared with Autolycus, who was no longer welcome among the infantry and glad of it. The horse troopers had taken up occupancy in fields providing forage and pasturage far from the city agora. The cavalry had separated from the infantry, now under the mounting control of Cresphontes and remarkably changed with the introduction of the Pelopide fighters. With all resistance dissipated, the Heraclides were becoming arrogant and self-confident.

"They are fighting amongst themselves," Oxylus said. "They have already begun arguing over the spoils."

"Are they backing away from our plans?"

"One day can change all. We are no longer of use to them. They have concluded they owe us nothing," Oxylus replied. "They are discounting the taking of the isthmus and are dividing up the Peloponnese among themselves."

"What about Laconia and Arcadia?"

"Laconia and Arcadia are expected to pledge alliance," Oxylus replied. "It is just a matter of taking them officially. You recall the forces reported to be coming in support of Tisamenus from Arcadia and Sparta? Well, that was just a move by the Arcadians to place their bets on the Heraclides, while hedging with the Pelopides. And the Spartans only sent their worst, keeping their best at home. The

Arcadians won their bet and are now clearly joyous at the collapse of Tisamenus."

"We are about to lose all that we have set out to accomplish. Cresphontes will attempt to hamper our objectives of taking Elis and protecting Messenia. Tonight, I will suggest that we split the forces of the Heraclides. Half will go to Laconia and half to Elis. Then, the two forces will reunite to take Messenia."

"Assuming that we do not become bogged down in Elis, which I cannot foresee, we will move on to Messenia, and there take the last remaining piece of the Peloponnese. This will allow the Heraclides time to come to terms with their success. There is nothing more divisive and disruptive than swift success."

"I must protect my family in Pylos," Telemachus replied.

"Cresphontes owes us today," Oxylus admitted. "But with each passing day, his debt declines. We will do all within our power to see he keeps his bargain."

"That will not be easy."

Later in the evening, the bonfires burned brightly in the agora. Many animals had been sacrificed, and the farmers from the surrounding communities continued to bring animals and foodstuffs to the sacrifice. The priests had been busy in their work of appeasing the gods, and now the good smells of roasted meats wafted from the center of Argos into the skies and entered the mansions of the gods.

Before the meats and other foods were served, Cresphontes stood on a platform, lit by the fires of the square, dressed in his fine white robes. On his head was a laurel wreath. He addressed the assembled soldiers and citizens of Argos.

"I would like to report to you tonight of our success and the valor of our troops. We have seen the courage of our soldiers, and we have seen the endurance of the people of the Peloponnese. Throughout Hellas, people have taken notice of what we have accomplished. We have received heralds of congratulations from far and wide. On behalf of the Heraclides, I recognize the outpouring of support for our goals. We will never forget those who gave up their lives to help us in this fight against tyranny as well as those who stood with us.

"We have known wars before, and we have sacrificed in our fight for freedom. But now in the center of the great city of Argos on a peaceful evening, I say to you we will prevail against our enemy. Our cause is just, and tomorrow will bring a new order. We must ask ourselves on what basis this will come about and how we can continue to protect ourselves against these enemies. The sea peoples from barbarian shores are intent on our destruction. There are thousands of them, and they continue to grow in numbers. And let me make it clear, they do not merely seek to end lives, but they are intent on disrupting our way of life and destroying our traditions.

"We must armour ourselves against them. We have taken the preliminary step, and now the tyrant Tisamenus has been killed on the field of battle. His army has joined us in our fight. Now I ask that you help us in this effort, and together we will combat the forces of evil. I ask that you pray for those who gave their lives and for their families. Tonight, we face a new challenge, and we will join together to promote stability and security of our shores. We will not falter nor tire in our pursuit. In the months and years to come, life will return to normal. But our resolve must never fail.

"Fellow soldiers and citizens, we will meet tyranny with firm justice, assured in the righteousness of our cause. In all that lies before us, may the gods grant us wisdom and may Zeus, lord of all the gods, watch over us."

After the ceremony, the leaders met in the tent of Cresphontes.

"How can you suggest such an idiotic thing?" Cresphontes demanded angrily. "That is out of the question. I should have you both strung up for treason. If we had listened to you, we would still be trapped on the isthmus. Instead, the states of the Peloponnese are all falling into our basket like fresh olives after a good shake of the tree."

"Look," Oxylus explained patiently, "Lacedaemon will fall in line with Argos. No doubt about that. Here, though, we must proceed with caution. Messenia is divided, but still could present a barrier. I only suggest that we strike quickly in two directions and then reunite to complete our goals."

"No. It is out of the question." Cresphontes said.

"You assume too much credit," Procles said. "It was the sacrifices that our division made on the isthmus that broke the back of the Corinthians."

"Yes," Oxylus replied, "sacrifices that were not necessary, unfortunately."

"We won the battle," Eurysthenes said. "Did we not?"

"You failed," Oxylus argued. "Without reinforcements, you would not be here talking."

"We need not fight over credit for our victory," Aletes said, his black eyes veiled. "We need to agree on a strategy for completing our campaign. Our counselors are no longer necessary to this strategy."

"You, my friend, should be the last to speak," Oxylus said. "You avoided duty on the isthmus, while others died in your place. Your deceit placed the entire army at risk."

"There is only one leader here." Aletes replied. He turned to his uncle.

"We are off the subject of our meeting, even so," Cresphontes said.

"Correct," Oxylus agreed. "Tomorrow, we are dividing the troops and going separate directions. We will reunite in Messenia. That is simple. We know what confronts us in Lacedaemon, but we are not sure of Elis. Do not be confused. The people of the Peloponnese accept the donation of our food in celebration, but we are foreigners occupying their soil."

"That is absurd," Cresphontes roared. "We are the rightful heirs of the Peloponnese."

"They look upon us as a Dorian invasion," Oxylus replied. "Just look outside and see who the Heraclides are in fact. Listen to their speech. Observe the gods they pray to. They are from all the countries surrounding the Peloponnese, and almost none from within."

For a moment, the men looked at each other. The one advantage that Oxylus and Telemachus had was that the family remained divided, although they veiled their discordance from view.

"Tomorrow," Oxylus stated, "we are taking the entire cavalry to Elis. You have three infantry divisions remaining. We will strike quickly at Elis, while you enter Sparta. We will advance together on Pylos: you, from the direction of Notus, and we will come from Boreas. Together, but not separately, we will enter Pylos. Temenus will join us in the harbor of Pylos. After that, we will take certain troops and ships to Ithaca. At that point, you will be free of our services, and our agreement will be completed."

"No," Aletes said, "we will need the support of the cavalry at Sparta."

"There is a question of the loyalty of the troops," Telemachus said.

"What are you talking about?" Cresphontes roared.

"You may be surprised at the allegiance of your army," Telemachus stated.

"You are talking treason," Cresphontes railed. "You will see what happens to people that deceive Cresphontes."

"And what of our agreement?" Oxylus asked.

"Our agreement," Cresphontes said, "is not in question. You will receive your compensation."

"What compensation?" Oxylus demanded. "We are talking about our understandings on Elis, Pylos, and Ithaca. Simply that."

"We can discuss that later," Cresphontes replied. "Tonight, I have heard enough to turn my stomach. We will meet again tomorrow. You will not make a move until that time. Is that clear?"

The men finally left the tent in ill-humor and with great dissatisfaction. Telemachus stayed behind for an audience with Cresphontes alone. But Aletes refused to leave, and Cresphontes agreed for him to remain.

"I have dedicated myself and my resources to this effort," Telemachus explained. "My own son lies unable to walk at your sacrifice. I ask now for my payment."

"I said you would receive payment," Cresphontes replied angrily, tired of the demands.

"I speak only of your sincerity in what we agreed to in Locris. I ask simply of your good faith. No more. That is all. That you keep the body of troops outside Pylos before I enter."

"Telemachus," Cresphontes said, "we have not seen eye to eye on many things. But I have respect for your counsel, and I am indebted to you. If I can offer you this, then I do so."

"But we must be wary of Oxylus, who seeks an empire for himself." Aletes said.

"He only seeks what was agreed," Telemachus said, "the rule of Elis."

"You do not know his history," Aletes replied.

"I know him better than any man."

"He attempted to gain the throne of Aetolia by killing his brother."

"He was acquitted of any crime."

"He is full of treasonous thoughts," Aletes added.

"I will keep it simple," Telemachus replied angrily. "As I must with you, Aletes. I trust Oxylus. I fear weak men who do not honor their pledges. But most of all I fear cowards, for like snakes they are unpredictable."

"Watch yourself, Telemachus," Cresphontes counseled. "The gods look askance at a naysayer. You are no longer critical to our mission."

"And there you are wrong. I ask that you honor your pledge as a man before the gods."

Cresphontes grunted enigmatically, signaling the end of the discussion.

After Telemachus' departure, Cresphontes turned to Aletes.

"We cannot continue with these two men."

"I hate Telemachus for his counterfeit righteousness, but Oxylus is treacherous," Aletes added. "He must be stopped."

"You are wrong," Cresphontes stated strongly. "Oxylus may be hungry for power, but he is no threat. Telemachus is the last and greatest threat remaining in the Peloponnese. He is yet to recognize it himself, but believe me when I say this, the son of Odysseus has it within his power to ruin everything. We must rid ourselves of him."

"And how would you suggest that we do this?"

"First, we block their route to Elis, for they will not listen to us. And we will take Messenia without their help or counsel. The family of Nestor must not live."

"And what of the counselors?" Aletes asked.

"You have ears, sirrah. I suggest we change their direction. I would not be unhappy to see them bite the dust."

"But we must be careful," Aletes warned his uncle. "For the troops, particularly the horsemen, pay allegiance to them."

"The Pelopides now have aligned with us, and the infantry will follow Procles and Eurysthenes. And the navy is ours. That leaves only the mounted troops."

"Yes, but..."

"You need to understand this. We cannot complete our return to the Peloponnese with traitors among us. Is that clear? We cannot give them Elis and Messenia, or even the offshore islands. Who are they? The Peloponnese belongs to us. We have fulfilled the prophecy. This is no time to think small thoughts."

"We will be betting that the troops will follow us without the counselors."

"Do you dare to disobey me?" Cresphontes said spitefully.

"No. But..."

"Then do as I say."

"We must be careful how this is accomplished."

"You question me? So be it," Cresphontes replied angrily. "Your father, Hippotes, shamed us once, and then he refused to join us on the isthmus. He now resides in Lydia. You, too, can be banished for life from Hellas...or worse."

Black-eyed Aletes left the tent angrily. One learned rapidly that Cresphontes did not brook debate. He would listen to the opinions of others, but it was never clear how much entered his mind. It was even less clear how he used this information, if at all. For his ideas seemed to be rigid and fixed in his mind, and there was never a hint of what was behind his thinking. However, one learned that when his eyes lowered and his chin pressed against his chest, further debate led only to misery. He would punish anyone within an inch of his life who dared to drag him beyond a certain point. Aletes had learned this early on, but many, to their sorrow, had never learned it, family members among them. These men were no longer a part of the Heraclides or residing on earth.

In heaven, Athene and Apollo seemed at odds no longer. Zeus was pleased with this. For his gods had managed to remain for the most part outside the brawl in the Peloponnese. The newest god, Heracles, and his wife, the gentle Hebe, daughter of Hera, now enjoyed wider acceptance among the gods. And the other gods were at ease as well, all save Hermes, who was often away. Even the gods knew not where.

"Hermes," the lord of the gods said one day when they were alone together. "What have you been up to? You so often miss our assemblies."

"Sire?"

"Do not lie to your immortal father."

Hermes hesitated. "Believe me father. I have only respect for you. By oath, I am not guilty."

Zeus laughed at his son, who as a newborn had tricked Apollo and stolen his cattle that rolled when they walked.

"I am not accusing you, my son."

"I love you, my father. And you know I am innocent," he whispered.

"Our son, it was long ago they murdered your mortal offspring. You must move on."

"Please, father. I hear songs in my head."

"You must find forgiveness within your heart," Zeus said. But much more serious thoughts weighed upon his mind.

The future itself occupied his intellect. He had managed to be loyal to his wife for an extended period, and she had become even more loving and attendant to him as a consequence. And he was glad of this. But he missed his adventures on earth. He had almost entirely removed himself from the day-by-day aspects of the lives of mortals, believing this approach was better for all concerned. And he had urged his fellow immortals similarly to take such an approach. And they, too, had, in the main, toed the line. But his thoughts had taken on an especially dark aspect lately, and the gods all knew it. Impossible as it may seem, it was as though a curtain had been drawn across the skies, blocking some of the brilliant light and honeyed warmth of heaven.

His thoughts ranged far and wide, but all attended on his vision of the future and the roles of the gods. He agonized over this in his chambers, and Hera could not abide his sagging shoulders and bulky head weighing so heavily upon him. She was helpless to cheer him. Like an old mortal, he dreamed of past heroics and exploits and could not bear to compass the future. He struggled with these black thoughts constantly. The other gods often found him in a dark cloud of ill humor, raging with anger at some plight, but for no reason they could determine or influence. It seemed as though the joy had left his demeanor due to the darkness of his contemplations. Just as on earth, in heaven the tides of change occur slowly and subtly.

Now, here is a story we have hinted at and one that might be mistaken at first blush for its insignificance. Yet, this story moved mountains and kingdoms and the Peloponnese itself. It is Hermes' story: another story of a father and his son.

Pelops was the only mortal ever restored to life after death. His father, Tantalus, son of Zeus, cut him up and served him to the gods in a soup. When the gods discovered Tantalus' sacrilege, they were so outraged that they punished the father in perpetuity. They then replaced all the bones of Pelops – all except his shoulder bone, which had been consumed, and they fashioned one of ivory – and brought him back to life. You would think that Pelops would have been grateful, but he soon forgot his saviors.

Reestablished in life, Pelops left his family home near Mt. Sipylus in Asia Minor and discovered a land endowed by the gods, which one day he would name after himself, the Peloponnese, the land of beautiful women. When he first spied the dancing-eyed Hippodamia, the daughter of Oenomaus, King of Pisa in Elis, he knew he had to have her. Hippodamia did not suffer from lack of suitors. Eighteen of their heads crowned the gates of the city. King Oenomaus had a standing offer that anyone who could best him in a chariot race would win the hand of his daughter in marriage. Unfortunately, all of the suitors had failed and had lost their lives in doing so. Pelops, newly re-given to life, was determined to win the heart of the king's daughter and in so-doing, the kingdom.

The secret of the king's success lay with his chariot driver, Myrtilus. Myrtilus was the son of Hermes by a mortal woman, Theobula. Both were treasured by Hermes. Myrtilus became the greatest driver of the wonderful horses of Oenomaus and had never failed to achieve victory. In all of Hellas, no driver excelled as Myrtilus, and his father reveled in pride of his son. Pelops, though, took a devious route by first seducing the bride before the marriage. He convinced Hippodamia to ask Myrtilus to throw the race. Myrtilus, silently in love with Hippodamia for many years, was in turn seduced by her, for she offered him the one prize he wanted more than anything: herself. Myrtilus inserted waxen linchpins into the wheel hubs of the king's four-horse chariot. The race began with Myrtilus at the reins and the king behind, while Pelops had a young boy as charioteer. Half way to the finish, the wheel of Oenomaus' chariot came loose, and the king was flung out of the car to his death. Myrtilus survived. Pelops won the race, the hand of Hippodamia, and the kingdom.

When Myrtilus innocently sought payment from Hippodamia in loving reward as they had agreed, she refused. She then went to Pelops and lied, claiming that Myrtilus had raped her. Pelops was not angry, for in truth he cared nothing for Hippodamia. He invited Myrtilus to supper, just as his father had invited the gods to feast on a dreadful soup of Pelops himself. Instead of discussing Hippodamia, he vaunted Myrtilus' ability at driving the chariot and offered him half the kingdom in return for throwing the race. He then fed Myrtilus a murderous soup. After this, Pelops carried Myrtilus to the sea at the mouth of the Alpheus, where he threw him off the cliffs. As he fell, Myrtilus called out to his immortal father for help, cursing Pelops, his whole house, and all his descendants.

And even though Pelops built the first temple to Hermes in the Peloponnese, Hermes never forgot or forgave. A harsh lament played within his brain over and over and over again. The curse of Myrtilus fell heavily upon the Pelopides; the blood of revenge flowed for generations.

LIII

During this time, the roads in the Peloponnese were not as they are today – the Romans saw to that. Natural mountain barriers kept the regions separated, and passage from one country to the other was difficult if not impossible during much of the year. And for that reason, the isolated countries of the Peloponnese had developed their independence and self-reliance. Only one route was known from Argos to Elis. It led towards the winds of Lips and the town of Tegea, thence to the coast at Bassae, where it veered in the direction of calm Skiron along the coastal path. This road was not the easiest to pass and often during inclement weather dissolved into mud and rock and became impassable. But at the time of our story, the route was clear and unhindered by nature.

Following the assembly, Telemachus and Oxylus returned to their tent on the outskirts of Argos with the horse troops. They refused sleep. Instead, they considered what they could do to protect themselves from Cresphontes. For they had seen clearly that he desired their destruction.

"We have no choice," Oxylus said. "Either we confront them directly, or we are lost."

"What will a battle with the infantry do for us?" Telemachus asked. "The troopers are outnumbered three to one. And it may show that they have not the will to support us. Even though they dislike Cresphontes, their future is tied to him."

"The infantry will follow us as well."

"That idea, my friend, is one I would not wager my life on."

"I would."

"There is another division now. One that knows us not. But there is an alternative to a battle with the Heraclides."

"What would that be?" Oxylus replied, annoyed that Telemachus always thought up answers beyond the argument.

"Cresphontes is intent on stopping us from going to Elis and likely will fight to prevent us. But I have heard of another route connecting Elis and Argos. This route leads into the forested mountains of Arcadia through small villages, ending at the village of Psophis on the Aroanius River. After that, the road disappears into tracks and paths used by the mountain goats and wild boars on the slopes of high Mount Erymanthus. The River Peneus originates in these mountains and descends directly onto the fertile plains of Elis, both town and region. In my travels, I have followed the route from Elis on the Borean flanks of Erymanthus to the source of the Peneus. We can connect these two points, for they do not lie far distant from one another."

"And have you made this journey...on horseback?"

"No."

"Then how do you know it is feasible?"

"I know two facts, and I am connecting them together. Cresphontes will prevent us from going toward warm-blowing Notus; instead, we will head toward chilly Boreas."

At this moment, Alexandros entered their tent.

"Excuse me, sirs."

"Yes," Telemachus said.

"We just received word the Corinthians are marshalling under the twins, headed for Sparta. And the second division is blockading Argos, with Aletes in charge. They are armed to the teeth."

Telemachus and Oxylus arrived at the same conclusion.

"Thank you, Alexandros," Telemachus said. "Prepare the troops for war. Full battle dress."

As golden-sandaled Eos rose in the sky, her ochre tones filled the valley. Oxylus, Telemachus, and Autolycus led their troopers away from Argos, back in the direction of Corinth. Rather than confront the infantry, they headed off the beaten track toward Psophis and Mt. Erymanthus. About seven hundred horsemen and dozens of spare horses rode out.

Telemachus had met with Deiphontes late in the night. Deiphontes was torn between the rival factions within the Heraclides and was not pleased with Cresphontes' actions. He agreed to keep three tribes with him, knowing full well the loyalty of the troopers to the counselors. He would for all appearances support his uncle and bide his time. At the same time, Deiphontes selected two troopers to leave Argos and return to Corinth to contact his other uncle, Temenus. They would relate the breakup of the army and relay the message from Deiphontes to move the Heraclide navy from the port of Cenchreae to Pylos to provide assistance. Deiphontes was convinced that Temenus would be a voice of reason, and he alone could put a hold on his brother Cresphontes' greed. Telemachus suspected that Cresphontes would not involve Temenus in his plans and was happy to leave him in Corinth. Without Temenus, Cresphontes had the will of the family at his beckoning.

Setting out in a good mood on a beautiful fall day, they made excellent time without hindrance. Only the Heraclide guards on the outskirts noted the horse troops leaving, but saluted their brothers-at-arms as they passed. The troopers intentionally traveled light, without wagons or backup supplies, although the horses were packed with both extra armaments and provisions. They rode slowly out of the city. It would take two days to reach the slopes of Erymanthus. Beyond that, they could only guess at the requirements to surmount Erymanthus and then to find the source of the Peneus to arrive at Odysseus' palace in Elis. They would need to forage or barter for foods along the way. Water would be no problem.

Telemachus knew that their departure would be discovered soon enough, but Cresphontes could never catch up with the horse troops and would lose valuable time if he attempted to do so. Before leaving the camp, Telemachus had sent Alexandros and two of his tablemates to reconnoiter secretly with the Heraclide infantry and then to catch up with the main body of troopers as soon as possible. It took almost all day for Alexandros and his troopers to catch up with the main cavalry force, but they finally did so as the horsemen passed through the town of Mantinea.

"We saw troops posted throughout Argos and a large formation of infantry blocking the road to Sparta," Alexandros said, breathing heavily. "Many of the red-swathed Corinthians were among them. We pastured the horses and ventured to where they were stationed. Probably an entire division. They slept not last night. I saw my Macedonian friend, Dolon, son of Pittheus, and a fellow horseman. He gladly came over to us for he owes me gambling debts from Locris. I pray the gods grant him life to repay me. He said the orders were to stop all traffic on the main road, including any Heraclides or deserters. But was given no further information. We saw Aletes among them, so we took care not to be observed. Dolon said that one division was gone to Lacedaemon under the twins with the goal of taking Messenia as soon as possible. Forced march. No celebrating in Sparta, for emissaries had already returned with the terms of allegiance for the Spartans.

"Dolon is quite a politician and is always free with his thoughts. With no obvious leaders of Lacedaemon and word of the Heraclides' one-sided victory on the isthmus, the city archons were quick to terms." Alexandros paused to draw breath. "Some of their soldiers had been killed in the fight for Corinth, for Sparta had supported Tisamenus to a limited extent. And those who lived were with the third infantry division. The Spartans at home have no desire for another bloody battle. The real battle will be for Messenia, and that will be a battle of time."

"Any reason for this urgency?" Telemachus asked.

"They want to finish this war, sir, and they want the entire Peloponnese. Oh, and the troopers under Deiphontes are grousing that they must remain with the infantry. They are afraid that they will be lance fodder in any fight."

"Excellent, Alexandros. Good job."

When the troopers had returned to their file, Telemachus turned to Oxylus.

"What do you think?"

"Without Temenus," Oxylus offered, "Cresphontes has no restraints. If we are able to get to Elis by this circuitous path of yours, he cannot prevent us from taking the city. But he could take Pylos and make your life difficult. He could also take Nestor hostage and your wife as well...or worse. He may believe that you as the son of Odysseus and son-in-law of Nestor could reunify Messenia and come to the throne yourself. Not impossible to imagine." He smiled broadly. "We could be neighbors."

"We can be neighbors under any circumstances."

"No one has ever ruled over the entire Peloponnese," Oxylus continued. "I am certain this is in Cresphontes' thoughts."

"I would never hazard a guess at what is in his thoughts," responded Telemachus. "But I would never underestimate his appetite. We need to move quickly, though, for we cannot allow him to take Messenia under his own terms. Your plans for a comfortable retirement would be in jeopardy should this occur."

After this, the cavalry quickened its pace.

The troopers reached Psophis in the foothills of Mt. Erymanthus after two long, difficult days on the saddle pad. The horses were famished, and the men had barely eaten. Fresh mountain water ran freely down channels along the main street, even though it had barely rained for many months. The town was clean and smelled fresh, unlike many of the villages they had ridden through, and they bargained for fresh meats and vegetables. They set up camp outside the village, with plenty of forage for the horses and fresh water for the men to drink and bathe in. Bladders were filled with the fresh river water. The village elders loaned them three tripods, and soon the smells of roasted meats and saffron-spiced soup filled the air. The villagers also brought a large cask of fresh wine still bubbly to be shared by the soldiers. And best of all, the villagers gave them directions for crossing through the mountains.

Since leaving Argos, the troopers were relaxed and cheerful. Mixing with the infantry troops had not been to the troopers liking, and neither was the command of Cresphontes and his third crop. They felt their expertise was special and reserved. They had not liked being at the beck and call of the leaders of the infantry forces. Now, they laughed and joked among themselves freely, without fear of being brought up short or held to task. As horsemen, they moved quickly, acted quickly, and resented the infantry's plodding determination – as a spotted eagle would resent being commanded by a winter cormorant, even though both were hunting the very same fish.

After a good evening, the men rested and well-fed set off early next morning with the first golden tones of Eos, skirting the mountainside. It was slow going. At first they followed goat paths and crossed many small streams, always keeping the peak of Erymanthus on their right hand. Soon enough, any sign of man disappeared, and they were left to deer paths or forging their own trail through brush and woods. The treacherous footing and loose soil caused many horses to slip and fall, but only a few had to be killed due to fractured legs. The strain of always fighting the slope made progress slow. Branches of trees became dangerous obstacles, and large rocks offered perilous challenges. They moved slowly in single file, oftentimes walking their horses, but the passage of horses hooves built up a path that their followers could trust. And horses are notoriously sure-footed beasts. Left to their own devices, they rarely stumble or fall due to poor footing. It took all day and many false tracks before they found a stream leading off the mountain in the direction of Zephyrus. Here it became cold with patches of snow and ice remaining from last winter. Due to the tree cover, they could not see their progress from afar, but Telemachus guessed from the slope and the duration of their travel that they must be near the source of the Peneus.

They halted as Helios sank into Oceanus, making further advancement impossible. They settled down for an uncomfortable night. The horses minded somewhat less than the men, but no one was happy. They ate cold foods. They could not hobble the horses, so they erected a rope barrier, allowing the horses to drink from the stream, but without forage. The steep slope prevented sleeping comfortably. Rocks supported a few, but most of the troopers had to sit in the dirt, wrapped in their cloaks, holding their knees, chilled to the bone. A thick mist fell on them, until they became soaked. The freezing night passed interminably.

The next day, they woke feeling miserable and began struggling down the mountain side. This was even more difficult. Most of the way, the troopers were forced to walk their mounts, and the horses often rebelled, sliding down the steep slopes, their rear legs fixed. There were sheer cliffs and steep slides that had to be avoided. But with each step the slope of the mountainside flattened out and their footing improved. The streams began joining, forming deep crevices, and falling rapidly in cascades. Several times, they were forced to retrace their steps, and this was made nearly impossible by the single file many stadia long of horses and men. By the afternoon, they were confronted with a fast moving river, cascading down the hillside, among the pines, oaks, and poplars. After slow progress, they emerged from the forested slopes and came out of the mountain ridges. At lower elevations, Helen's plane trees and wild olives and dense figs became more common. Finally at one point, they obtained their first vista of the plains of Elis spread out before them. They could make out the tiny mountain village of Pylus in the distance. Elis was just beyond the varying tones of the cultivated fields of the valley.

Heartened by the view, they were able to find a path that led out of the hills between two large palisades. The final barrier was a steep ravine along the river with only a narrow path above the rapidly flowing waters, but they could not retrace their path here. For a distance of two stadia, the men led their horses along a slim path where one false step led directly into the river. It took the remainder of the day for the men and horses to pass this barrier, and they lost four horses and a trooper, who they hoped would be able to swim to safety downstream. On the other side of the barrier, they built a camp and set a fire for heat. Telemachus knew the site, which was no more that a hundred and fifty stadia from Elis.

The next day, they approached the estates of Odysseus in mid-afternoon, finally passing through small terraced vineyards and olive groves. Many of the horses began to recognize the land of their birth and its smells.

Telemachus advanced with some apprehension. It had been almost a year since their departure, and he had no idea what had become of the house and lands. As they drew near, they could see that someone had been caring for the property. When they arrived at the road crossing and the entrance, the horses gladly entered the pasture that had not been used all year. The fall grass sprouted from beneath dry summer grasses still lying on the earth. The grounds were well kept, with the vines stripped of their grapes. Inside the house, a fresh-cooked meal lay on the table, and flowers had been arranged in the atrium. The occupants of the house had run for their lives.

By nightfall, they had set up camp in the courtyard and posted guards along the road to town. The troopers started a fire and discovered a store of barley and dried fruit. Telemachus could not envisage what defenses the town might offer. Dius, the King of Elis, was too young and inexperienced and the region too poor to marshal a large defensive force. It was unclear what information if any on the Heraclides' victory might have reached this remote area of the Peloponnese. Had they heard of the fall of Corinth and Argos and now perhaps Sparta?

"Shall we visit the good King Dius?" Telemachus asked Oxylus.

"Yes," Oxylus agreed. "The time is opportune. I saw a hawk take his prey in the air on my right hand. Never a better sign."

Even though the men and horses were exhausted, Telemachus and Oxylus took three files, all well dressed and prepared for battle. They trotted into town in the moonlight along the road the two friends knew so well, passing the farms and vineyards of people also well known to them. This did not appear to be hostile territory, nor were any defenses in place. There was no welcome as they entered town. The townspeople moved hurriedly off the main street and out of the way. No one waved or threw flowers in their path. When they reached King Dius' modest palace, they found a few guards, but no troops. Almost immediately, though, as they rode into the small courtyard, filling it entirely with their horses, several men came out onto the colonnade, followed by Dius.

Dius, son of Eleius, stood on the porch. With him as before was Actor, descendant of the Molionides and advisor to the young king.

"Well, you have changed your uniforms," Dius called out.

"But you have not changed your manners," Oxylus called back.

Actor whispered into Dius' ear. "And for what purpose do you come into our village with such armaments?"

"We come to offer you a laurel branch," Oxylus replied.

"Why? I have done nothing to deserve such an honor."

"This offering is for what you are about to do. For your rule of Elis has come to an end."

"I have made no such agreement."

"Then you are prepared to die in battle?"

"I have no forces. This is a small town. You are not entering Sparta or Athens. But I will make you an offer." Actor reacted quickly, but Dius held him off with his hand. "I am prepared to meet you on the field of battle, but in one-on-one combat. The winner of the contest will decide the outcome of the war, and all will agree to this beforehand."

"Why would we do this," Oxylus laughed. "You treated me with contumely before. And now you expect fairness from me?"

"I expect nothing from you. I expect honor from Telemachus, for he knew my father and the father of my father."

"That is far-fetched," Telemachus replied. "What honor did you show me or my family?"

"We may be disposed to agree to your terms," Oxylus said suddenly, touching Telemachus' shoulder. "Are you suggesting that you and I meet on the field of battle?"

"No," Dius replied. "I am no military person. I am the hereditary King of Elis, with all attendant rights. And you are a foreigner, who would seek to impose your will upon us. I would choose to front Degmenus, a bowman, and a native, born and raised on this soil."

"And we can choose whomever we please? And the loser will then remove himself and his family?"

"Yes," Dius agreed, "or all his troops, for I am informed that you have brought no small contingent."

"We did not come to enter into athletic contests," Oxylus said. "We came with the authority of the rulers of Corinth, Mycenae, Argos, Tiryns, and Sparta. We came prepared for war, not a contest in running or jumping."

"And so you will have your war," Dius replied. "But it will be on a scale that we can all agree to. Are you prepared to set your battle on the shoulders of a single man? And I care not who this person be. We will meet tomorrow morning with good light in the open festival field outside of town."

"I have no need to grant you this opportunity," Oxylus said. "And believe me, I would be granting you a gift, since with these troopers you see behind me alone, we could easily take the town. In the past, you provided no aid to me or to Telemachus. But the gods must be with you today, for given my choice, tomorrow could easily be your last day on this earth. I agree to your terms. We will return tomorrow morning."

As they rode back to the estates, Telemachus expressed his surprise for Oxylus' consent to a one-on-one fight. Although this was a common occurrence among the cities of Hellas, it was usually done when both sides were more or less equal and wished to avoid enormous casualties.

"I hope that you did not agree to this on my account," Telemachus said.

"No such thought. I want this to be a fair match for all the townspeople to see. If we took the town by force and killed its king and archons, what foundation would that be to my rule? This may be a risky course, but at least it has the outward trappings of fairness. At least fairness to an outsider. Have you forgotten that Pyraechmes, son of Antiphus, rides with us?"

"I know this man by name only."

"He is from Thrace and is the most skillful warrior I have ever encountered outside the court of the Hittites. He is equally skilled at the bow or javelin or sword. And he is the finest horse tamer I know."

"Well, perhaps he can tame their champion," Telemachus said. "Your future depends on this man."

"I am well aware."

That evening, when Oxylus explained the agreement to the troopers, they had mixed emotions. Most were as surprised as Telemachus and felt there was no need to risk all, when the village could offer no defenses and was ripe for the taking. Others approved the wisdom in Oxylus seeking to legitimize his rule of the region with little bloodshed. The one-on-one combat would commit both sides to its outcome. The strongest vote of support to Oxylus' commitment came from the man himself, Pyraechmes. He was neither shy about his ideas nor reticent in expressing his emotions.

"I have battled with the full fear of god in my stomach weighing like the ballast of a ship, and I have survived," he explained. "I have killed men in the heat of conflict. No small few. And I have fought in wars throughout the world, from the heathen shores of Europa to the barbarians of Asia Minor and those who worship the far-flung gods of Apeliotes. And I have fought in this acorn-crunching land of the Hellenes. And in all, I have always felt the bitter taste of death in my stomach, my own death. But I have never, never felt the fear of death in one-on-one combat. No, my comrades. I long for the taste of the blood of my opponent. If I were given the choice of a sweet young girl, as beautiful and willing as the whore Helen, or the sweat of one-on-one, there would be no hesitation. Helen be damned. Give me the sticky bath of victory rather than my wife's loving arms and legs. Forgive me god, but I am ready. More than ready."

"Oxylus," he yelled raising his cup, "once again, your wisdom has ruptured your helmet like Athene's birth. God save us and preserve us for tope. Libations for the gods, and when I am victorious, I will settle across the road with my wife and grandchildren."

And the entire cavalry shouted with him and drank with him. But Pyraechmes may have been overestimating his powers. For what appeared in the light of a bonfire, with enough of the fiery local wine, rosy and easy to conquer, in Helios' clear morning light appeared agonizing and tricky.

LIV

The next morning, the troopers slept late and took their time preparing for the fight. They cleaned themselves in the river and ate breakfast from the barley store in the house, stripping the figs remaining on the trees. By the time Helios was on his ascent, the seven tribes formed and began the ride into town. They had dressed for the occasion, with polished helmets and cuirasses, and the horses were curried and their bronzes polished as well. Their champion, Pyraechmes, rode at the front rank, accompanied by his file mates, followed directly by the officers, and then the tribes riding two abreast.

No longer a young man, Pyraechmes' long brown hair was streaked with gray, and his beard nearly obscured his sharp avian eyes and nose. As a freebooter, he had lived his life away from family, traipsing from one war to the next. His sinewy body was covered with drawings from Asia Minor and the orient, describing the entire story of war: horses, ships, javelins, swords, and above his heart his favorite god, Hades. The scars of numerous battles obscured some of the marks. To love death, according to Pyraechmes, is to have no fear on earth. His competitor, Degmenus, had never ventured far from his home in Elis. Standing taller than most men, he had once lifted a bull above his head, and size of his arms and shoulders made clear how this was possible. In contests, he could throw a boulder farther than any man in Elis.

At the field outside of town, they found the king and his archons and some scattered troops of the Eleans, who eyed the troopers nervously. Only a few citizens were in attendance. Either the Eleans were not interested or not encouraged to attend. The forces of the Heraclides outnumbered the townspeople by many times. The field was used for festivals and was hard packed, without grass. It was level and clear of all obstacles. With all the troopers and their horses, an area had to be cleared for the fight to take place. Soon a space as large as a small theater was created, surrounded mostly by the Heraclide troops. The troopers hobbled the horses along the length of the road and posted guards.

Dius walked forward into the central space created by the crowd. The hero of the Eleans, Degmenus, followed him. He was a large, muscular man, who dwarfed Dius, with shaved head, closely cropped beard, and hard blue eyes, his bronze helmet by his side. He held a long javelin in one hand and a wicker shield in the other. A thick bronze sword hung from his belt. Oxylus came forward with Pyraechmes, who held his pig sticker and the standard issue small bronze shield and helmet. He had a long cut-and-thrust sword at the belt of his tunic. Both men had light body armour: a cuirasses and greaves.

"May the gods smile upon us today," Dius announced for all to hear. "We have agreed on single combat to settle our differences. The loser will immediately withdraw from Elis, without further pursuit or condemnation, and the victor will rule over all things Elean. This I covenant and warrant. With me is our champion, Degmenus, son of Triopas, and grandson of Diores, who lies in the meadows of Troy. May Poseidon the earth shaker come to our aid."

"It is my pleasure to accept your terms," Oxylus said. "The champion of the Heraclides is Pyraechmes, son of Antiphus, a Thracian by birth, but a citizen of all the countries of the world by virtue of his repute. May the gods witness what we are about to undertake today, for the gods love nothing better than a fair fight. The fight will end upon the surrender of one of the opponents or his failure to rise.

Oxylus and Dius backed out of the circle, leaving Pyraechmes and Degmenus to confront each other. The combatants backed away to get better aim, for their first line of attack would be the javelin. The soldiers moved back as well to avoid an errant javelin. The two men crouched behind their shields with their javelin arms in the air. They slowly circled, eying each other carefully. The expression on Degmenus' face was a slight sneer, obviously feeling the advantages of age, size, and strength. Pyraechmes' face was a mask, absent all emotion. His eyes bored into his opponent's every move.

Degmenus was the first to throw his javelin with a shout, and it glanced off the shield of Pyraechmes, but its force carried beyond the shield edge and took a nasty slice off Pyraechmes' left shoulder. As the blood began to flow down his arm, he took no notice, continuing to circle with his own javelin still threatening. Degmenus kept hidden as much as possible behind his large shield. The wicker shield provided no protection from a javelin other than to hide the position of his body.

Pyraechmes felt no hurry. He watched the forward foot of the other man, lining it up with his spine and vital organs. He calmly waited for the man to shift his weight forward, preventing him from lateral movement. The moment he saw the weight shift, he let loose. The short javelin tore through the wicker as though it were not there. The javelin would have entered the chest and exited the back of an ordinary man. But Degmenus was not an ordinary man and, besides being huge, was quick on his feet. He moved to the right at the sight of Pyraechmes' lowering arm, and the heavy javelin passed through the shield without contacting the man. The javelin almost hit one of the Eleans, skidding to a halt outside the circle, with the crowd animated by their own surprise and fear, yelling and shouting.

Both opponents reached for their swords. The cut-and-thrust sword was longer by a forearm than the other sword, but again Degmenus was no ordinary fighter, nor was his sword ordinary. It was made to cut shields, several times thicker than a common sword and heavier by half. Only a giant could wield such a weapon. The two men approached each other, and the voices of the crowd, particularly the troopers rose in support. The first stroke of the cut-and-thrust sword completely decimated the wicker shield, making it useless. Degmenus threw it off. Pyraechmes came forward for a second sweep of his sword, but instead received the full force of an overhead blow on his shield, which he raised to avoid decapitation. The bronze sword smashed the shield with a great racket, and the Eleans cheered wildly. Although it did not cut through the small shield, it was of such force as to damage the muscles of Pyraechmes' shield arm, which was already covered in blood from the shoulder cut.

Pyraechmes backed up with some distrust in his eyes but not an obol of fear. He had fought many men. And many of these men had been stronger and quicker than he, but they had not walked away from the field of battle. One almost never wins at war by strength alone. For what is snatched thief-fashion by cunning and stealth from the enemy is difficult to combat: just as small boys hide twigs in their fist to guess at the longest one, so fighters must hide their true strength until the right moment.

They began trading blows along the lengths of their swords. The bronze sword was too thick to be easily cut by the stronger iron sword. Their swords clashed, and the shouting continued as the sweat and dirt began coloring the faces of both men. Degmenus' beard was now nearing the color of Pyraechmes' hair and beard, a reddish gray. They moved against each other, neither man with an advantage. The longer length of the cut-and-thrust sword annulled the reach advantage of Degmenus. They continued struggling, with each blow taking its toll, not only on the man it was intended for, but also on the man delivering the blow. Each blow was a step toward the dangerous time of exhaustion, when blunders result in fatal wounds.

By this point, Pyraechmes realized he could not outlast this younger and stronger man. He had to do something quickly or risk being worn down to such an extent that he could no longer defend himself. At the same time, he thought he had discovered a weakness. Degmenus liked nothing better than to come down from overhead with a punishing blow, since his height and the weight of the bronze sword created havoc from such leverage. Pyraechmes knew that this would be the death blow. He could picture the man with his arms extended with the weight of the sword and the full leverage of his arms descending onto Pyraechmes' skull.

The two men continued to fence with their heavy swords, their feet no longer moving with lightness. Fatigue filled their muscles, and their arms and legs began slowing. Pyraechmes took on a defensive posture, allowing Degmenus to come at him with blow after blow, fending each one off, but always with effort. He gave his opponent the offensive, permitting him the idea that the zeal for fight was rapidly departing the older man, but also allowing him to tire himself. He countered each blow, but began slowly to move closer to the other man, reducing the leverage and thus the force of the blows from the heavy bronze sword.

The crowd quieted as they observed both men struggling. The fighters closed in on one another. Pyraechmes was using his sword to ward off the blows of the other man's sword. His shield arm was almost useless. The troopers feared for their champion…and their general.

As soon as Pyraechmes sword began to fall lower in defense, Degmenus was on him with blows from the side. The two men were close, and the points of the swords were useless at this distance. They were connecting at the midway point of both swords and even closer to the tangs. The cut-and-thrust sword is not designed with this in mind.

Here Pyraechmes dropped his sword arm slightly, and Degmenus sword struck him full on the side of his helmet, producing a metallic clang, shocking everyone. The blow was strong enough to knock Pyraechmes off his feet onto his back, with his sword swept from his grasp clunking to the ground. His helmet skittered off from his head, and his ears rang with the intensity of the blow. He lay at the feet of the other man, and with his left arm he moved his battered shield over his chest as the last defense to protect himself from the inevitable. As he did this, Degmenus moved over the prone man, brought his sword back for the overhead stroke that would end the fight. When his arms were extended over his head, and the forward and downward motion of Degmenus' sword just commencing, Pyraechmes sat up, extracting a dirk from behind his shield and extending it before him. In the instant that Degmenus saw the man sit up, it was too late to stop the downward motion of the heavy blade. Degmenus attempted to change the trajectory of the cutting edge, bringing it closer to his body, but the weight of the blade made him overshoot his target, with the tip of the blade hitting the dirt beyond Pyraechmes. The hilt of the sword, though, connected squarely with Pyraechmes' head in a solid blow, its force reduced by the angle and the impact of the blade of the sword on the ground behind Pyraechmes. Simultaneously, the follow through from his stroke brought Degmenus' chest almost to other man's head, and Pyraechmes stuck the length of his razor sharp dirk into Degmenus' intestines, just between his cuirass and belt, and sliced horizontally. That was the last Pyraechmes remembered, and Degmenus stumbled and fell directly on top of him.

It took some time to disengage the two men. At first, Degmenus ignored his wound, and he struggled to free himself, getting to his feet with the help of several of his fellow Elean soldiers. He turned toward the Eleans, feeling the intoxicating joy of victory from such a contest. But when he rose, he felt his intestines give way and blood and tissue spurt forth. Instinctively, he grabbed his stomach with his hands, but the blood continued to pour from the wound into his hands along with his intestines. He took several steps and then could walk no farther and sat down hard. He was soon surrounded by Eleans.

The troopers surrounded Pyraechmes as well. He was breathing, but barely, and he was covered in blood, with additional blood flowing slowly from his head wound. Water was brought to both men. Their armour was peeled off and the wounds cleansed. Pyraechmes gradually returned to a state of semi-consciousness. Across from him, the life of Degmenus slowly oozed away. Pyraechmes sat up dazed and senseless and would not have recognized his wife or closest friend. He stared blankly at the faces of the troopers around him. In fact, it would be many moons before Pyraechmes regained his senses about him. And when people told him of his victory over the Eleans, he could remember nothing of the actual fight. He came to understand his victory, but always as a tale told by others.

Degmenus did not walk away from the field that morning; Pyraechmes did, with the help of his comrades.

After the fight and the death of Degmenus, Oxylus and Dius conversed confidentially for a short while, embraced, and then separated. The troopers returned immediately to the estates of Odysseus. They filled their water bladders and stuffed dry food into their packs, taking everything edible and transportable.

There was no time for the Heraclides to celebrate their victory, for the race to take Pylos had commenced. Although Pylos was about twice as far from Elis as from Sparta as a bird might fly, the Taygetus mountain range forced Cresphontes to march the entire distance along the coasts of Laconia and Messenia. Cresphontes had one or two days' advantage on the troopers, depending on how much time the Heraclides had spent in Sparta. But there was no telling what extraordinary means Cresphontes might institute to secure his goals. He had three hundred horse troops and more than two thousand infantry troops under his command, and he could select a contingent to send forward at a pace that the entire army could not maintain. Another unknown factor was the response of the Messenians. The four regions of the Messenians had fought against each other for some time, brothers against brothers, and they had men under arms. They could not withstand a concerted attack by the Heraclides, but they might be able to slow the advance.

What may have been a factor in Cresphontes' thinking was a fact of history itself, although buttressed by a recent discovery: the treasury of Agamemnon.

Sated with the blood of the Trojans, the Hellenes chose their slaves from among the royal family of Priam and divided his gold and wealth. Such was the temper of the Greeks that they violated all places, both hallowed and wicked, enslaved the populous, those that remained on earth, and reduced the once great city to rubble and burned it to its foundations. For this sacrilege, the gods finally united in their view of the war and took umbrage at the behavior of the victorious Greeks. They sent emissaries of Athene and Poseidon to survey the scene at Troy. What the gods saw shocked even them, though gods have no misunderstanding of the low levels that mortals can sink to. They returned to father Zeus, who had loved Troy as his own creation and the Trojans as his own children. They related the horror and infamy of the Greeks, and Zeus decided to punish the Greeks with a return that would not be a return and a victory that would not be a victory.

He set Poseidon and the forces of nature against the Greeks as never before as they filled their ships with their shares of the booty. For that reason, much of the plunder found its way only to the bottom of the seas. Of all those who returned to Hellas, the so-called Nostoi, only a handful arrived unscathed by the elements. Most of the Achaean leaders at Troy lost their share of the booty to the wind-whipped seas and Poseidon's angry minions. Agamemnon was one of the few to return unscathed. But when he did return to his home in Mycenae, he was greeted with infamy: murdered by his deceitful wife, Clytemnestra, and her lover, Aegisthus. The extent of his share of the gold of Priam was not known until the Heraclides killed his grandson, Tisamenus, and discovered his hoard. His was the largest share, and all others scaled down from there rapidly.

One other Hellene returned unscathed: Nestor. The booty that Nestor was able to bring with him to Pylos may not have been as large as Agamemnon's, but it must have been larger than all other shares, save perhaps Menelaus'. Nestor, the wisest of the Greeks, was not consumed with greed as some of the others had been. He was more concerned with keeping some pretense of civility to the proceedings. And he would have agreed with the view that he failed miserably in this objective. But the gods for some reason did not avenge the acts of his brethren on him directly, and Nestor escaped their vengeance to return to his home and wife and children. Although he left one son, Antilochus, buried in the meadows of Troy.

Cresphontes was well aware of this history. With his discovery of the treasury of Corinth, he may have suspected that similar riches might be found in Pylos. That may have been one of the motivations for his intense desire to take the city of Pylos before the arrival of Telemachus, in addition to his personal animus for his counselors-at-war and his desire not to share power in the Peloponnese with anyone. The motivations of men are often difficult to discern and may be complex in their makeup, but with Cresphontes it was clear that he would not be happy to see any wealth that Nestor may have accumulated disappear into someone else's coffers, particularly those of his counselors-at-war.

While the troopers were preparing for their journey to Pylos, Telemachus rode up into the hills to the barrow of his father. In the afternoon sun, the light obscured the distant view. After two years untended, weeds and wild berries had grown up onto the stone cairn. Where once it had been a foreign presence, now the mound of stones had been accepted and unified with the landscape in all aspects. Telemachus felt a sense of relief and contentment.

"Father," Telemachus said aloud, "for so long, I stood in awe of you, of all the stories and songs, of your reputation, of the reactions of others to your name, and of your mind and intellect. Your greatness was without compare. You gave so much of yourself to the world and for that I am proud and grateful. Though I was never able to talk with you of things of significance, what I inherited from you was enough and has served me well. You set me on this course. And I thank you for that. I feel as though I am returning from Troy as you once did with a hard-earned appreciation of what in life is important and a battle for homecoming. So much time is spent on efforts that serve no purpose or are destructive in their nature. Now, I must return to Ithaca as you did. I thank you for your gifts to me and seek to repay you by living the life you granted me in a way that is a tribute to your sacrifice. You moved heaven and earth and paid dearly, but I think it was worth the candle."

Oxylus was a whirl of activity, ordering the troopers, securing the house, setting up an interim administration of the town, and leaving a small squadron at the house to observe the movements of Dius and his family. He left Melas, son of Ion, in charge of a small garrison to maintain control of the town until his return. Melas was a young phylarch and a leader of the Heraclide troopers. He had proved himself many times over. He was a fellow Aetolian, who wanted to settle in Elis with his family. So Oxylus felt sure that he would execute his assignment with care and assurance. He also left Pyraechmes, whose days of combat lay behind him, and a well-deserved rest lay ahead.

He mounted Rhaebus, and he and Telemachus led the defile of horse troops through the town, only this time the people lined both sides of the street as the Heraclides passed through. The women and girls smiled. They even threw a few flowers at the troops. Oxylus happily smiled at his new-found home and felt impatient to return.

As for Dius, he knew that any change in his mind or refusal to honor his agreement would result in his death and the death of his family. He made arrangements to settle in Attica, a sanctuary to many political refugees, just as it had been a sanctuary to the sons of Heracles. His old advisor, Actor, retired to his broad estates.

And the race to Pylos and control of the Peloponnese was on.

LV

Telemachus knew every stream crossing, every village, and every mountain col on the road to Pylos. He had traveled it many times over the years: as a friend visiting Nestor's son, Pisistratus, as a suitor of Polycasté, as a joyful bridegroom, as a young father returning with his family to visit his wife's home, as a son-in-law accompanying his wife on her later to her parents, and now as hipparch of the Heraclides leading hundreds of mounted troops. Pylos was six hundred stadia from Elis. Over a good road, a chariot might travel perhaps five hundred stadia in a day; a gritty force of troopers might travel somewhat less. From Elis, the road led over low hills to the town of Letrini, near the harbor of Pheia. From Letrini, the road mounted into the coastal ranges, passing through Olympia, near the summit of Mount Typaeus, through forested mountain villages, and finally returning to the coast at the village of Samia. From that point, the road hugged the coast, crossing many rivers and marshy areas and several mountain passes, leading to Nestor's palace in Pylos.

The horse troops did not expect to encounter any resistance along the road. But Telemachus constantly sent small squadrons ahead to scout the coming landscape and villages. No hostilities were discovered. As they passed farms and small communities, the large size of the mounted force in their blue uniforms and shining helmets surprised the local people. When they recognized that the army was not hostile, some of the farmers offered fresh and dried fruits and nuts and water.

After a long day of alternating between walking and trotting, the troopers were fatigued. They set up camp on the outskirts of Cyparissiae, a small town inside Messenia. The horses grazed in a wide pasture next to a fresh water lake. Troopers stood guard, and a squad scouted the road ahead and set up a barricade. In the camp, the troopers started a fire and roasted three large rams slaughtered at the estate in Elis. The warm evening air was soon filled with the smells of roasted meats. Very little wine was available, only a few bladders, but there was enough for a libation to the gods for their success in Elis and for a prayer for their success in Pylos the next day. They ate, knowing that this might be their last meal for days.

Telemachus, Oxylus, and Autolycus ate together.

"Young Dius was relieved to lose," Oxylus commented between chewing crusty mutton loaded with fat globules. "He seemed satisfied with our agreement and not at all disturbed at the loss. I plan to honor him."

"Why would you do that?" Telemachus asked.

"I learned from my grandfather, King Thoas. He always said, 'Honor your enemies as you would your friends.' I always liked the man. I admired his ability to lead people. His son, Haemon, fell far from the tree. In any case, I want to remain in Elis for a long time. When I have a son, I will want him to inherit the throne. Today, people are uncomfortable with the powers of the kings, particularly since they cannot provide as before. People want more say in their lives. The great palaces cannot continue to take without giving in return."

"In one way," Telemachus said, "people are willing to hand over control to a single individual. It makes life simpler...seemingly more secure. But it can be a deadly bargain."

"The great palaces can no longer ensure that everyone is fed. And there is a large question of trust. So many of the kings have sucked their regions dry. Why should one person live in luxury while others starve?"

"So you intend to be a better leader?" Telemachus asked.

"Yes."

"And what will you do differently?"

"What I can say is that I am not greedy."

"That is a start."

"It is about fairness and holding contempt in abeyance."

"Not many leaders have fared as grandfather has," Autolycus added.

"True," Telemachus said. "The gods blessed him with wisdom. We will meet with Nestor, perhaps tomorrow."

"The gods are given too much credit," Oxylus said.

"I pray to return to Ithaca," Telemachus replied. "That is all I can do. Ithaca is a small island, dependent on fishing and small farmers. Ithaca will not make you rich. I only ask to live in peace…with my family."

At that moment, a commotion arose in the center of the camp. Telemachus and Oxylus arose to investigate. They found two guards holding a man dressed in the uniform of a Heraclide trooper. His mount was behind him.

"This man is a spy," one of the guards explained. "He was in one of the files that remained in Argos."

"I am no spy," the trooper yelled in frustration. "I am Perius, son of Boeus, and I know you well, sir. I came to warn you."

"How did you know where we were?" Telemachus asked.

"I did not. I stumbled on the guards on my way to Elis. Deiphontes sent me to contact you in advance."

"And what was your purpose?"

"To warn you. Cresphontes is bogged down in Asine. The horse troops arrived in Pylos yesterday."

Telemachus' heart fell, and a dull pain throbbed in his stomach. "Wait. Allow this trooper to eat and drink to his fill. Allow him to rest for a moment."

After this, Oxylus and Telemachus sat down with the man. Perius was one of the few troopers from Messenia, and therefore chosen to ride to Elis to contact the rest of the Heraclide mounted troops. He ate ravenously, since he had not had a full meal for many days.

"Now," Telemachus commenced. "Tell us what has occurred since you left Argos."

"Well, sir, Cresphontes raged after you departed Argos. He failed to anticipate your course, for he had planned to prevent your flight. After that, all changed. No stopping at Sparta. No stopping for anything. No rest for days…and nights as well. The infantry had it worse than the troopers. Many were left behind or deserted. Our horses suffered. And the heat…unbearable. We could not even stop to bathe in the sea.

"At the elbow of Messenia, the cavalry met up with troops from Melanthus, the king of that region. We fought near Asine, a nice village on a point of land surrounded by the large-wide sea, and easily defeated their army or what they took as an army. Melanthus is now captive. But then the Heraclide third infantry arrived, tired and hungry...and angry. They went from one end of Asine to the other. Drank everything in sight. Fired the houses. Took the people prisoner. Many of the townspeople were killed and outraged. It seems the Spartans had some kind of feud with the town. They acted like barbarians sacking the village. Nothing left but smoke." He paused for a moment to allow his emotions to subside.

"Procles and Eurysthenes were there and did nothing. And when Cresphontes arrived, he did not raise a hand. The cavalry was at cross-purposes with the infantry, and fighting broke out between us."

"How many Heraclide soldiers are there?" Oxylus asked.

"Cresphontes stationed soldiers all over: Corinth, Argos, Tiryns, Mycenae, Sparta, and in the smaller towns. Probably about a division and a half remain, or less. Phalces stayed behind with the first division in Argos. The division at Asine is composed of the rotten apples led by the twins. Mainly those from the newly-formed third division, the rotten Corinthian and Spartan soldiers who volunteered on the isthmus. Aletes has what remains of the first and second divisions."

"What is Deiphontes doing?" Telemachus asked.

"After Asine, the troopers met and decided we wanted no more of this war. But we knew that Cresphontes would not honor our efforts. So we sent a delegation to talk with Deiphontes, and he listened to us and then met with Cresphontes. After that, Deiphontes ordered us to Pylos, double time. But when we arrived yesterday, he kept us on the outskirts of Pylos, where we are blockading the road. That was when he sent me out toward Elis, since I know the way, even in night."

"Where is the infantry now?"

"The infantry is in Asine tonight, but they are within a day's march of striking Pylos."

Oxylus looked at the young trooper. "You have lived in Messenia. What do you think we should do?"

"The infantry will sack Pylos. I know it. The Lacedaemons have no love for Messenia, and particularly Pylos. And they are desperate for loot – otherwise they would not have joined the Heraclides. Pylos is a gem that must be preserved."

Banished from Thessaly for killing his stepmother, Nestor's father, Neleus, came to Messenia. He created a new dynasty on a high promontory, looking out as the setting sun sinks into the large-wide sea. He called the citadel Pylos. The location was selected as a refuge from pirates operating along the beaches of Messenia.

But the coastline has changed greatly since Nestor's time. No large bay existed when he ruled. Instead, the shore stretched out in the distance in a long, straight spit of land facing the Ionian Sea, connecting two opposing headlands. Behind the spit of land, which acted as a natural coastal levee, lay a large freshwater marsh and coastal woodland, teeming with wild animals and birds. Nestor often spoke of his days hunting wild boar and roe deer with his javelin in the forested slopes and marsh below Neleus' palace. And on the spit was a small port town of Sphacteria. The high citadel of Pylos offered excellent views of the coast and port, but direct access only by a perilous footpath, mounting the cliffs. To arrive at the sea, one had to descend the entrance road behind the palace and then take the main route on the landside of the marsh to a path leading out to the sea. Many villages along the coast of Messenia offered far better locations for ports and fishing, but not protection from marauders.

The saltwater bay we know today was formed after Nestor trod the earth. A large portion of the isthmus in the direction of Notus was destroyed as a result of a great earthquake that damaged the entire region. When the isthmus was breached, salty water filled the marsh, killing the wetlands and creating the giant bay. Although we do not know the exact time of the destruction of the isthmus, many believe that it was shortly after the return of the Heraclides to the Peloponnese, or at least within a century of their return, for records found within the palace point to that time. The headlands directly opposite the original citadel became the site of modern Pylos, with improved access to the sea, allowing for shipping and the fishing ports. But all that is long after our story.

"I too know Pylos," Telemachus told the young trooper, Perius. Oxylus and Autolycus closely watched Telemachus in the firelight. "And I think I know a way to stop them, but we must arrive before the infantry. Let's move out immediately." He stood up, and the troopers began breaking camp.

In the darkness of night with only a crescent moon, the troops moaning and groaning, the cavalry set out for Pylos in full battle dress. Pylos was some one hundred and fifty stadia off, or, under the circumstances, a ride of about half the short night.

LVI

Racing against Cresphontes, Oxylus and Telemachus led the troopers rapidly through misty Cyparissiae, while the people slept warmly under their bedcovers. The horses trotted quickly through the village, their hooves reverberating between the plastered mud and stick structures. Even in the darkness, they rode nothing loath along the coastal road threading the shore and low-lying mountains. Well before Eos rose to greet a new day, they arrived at the junction of the road to Pylos and the coastal route. Here, they surprised the three tribes of Heraclide troopers blockading the entrance to Nestor's high citadel. They rode up quickly, waking the troopers. Suddenly, the road was filled with horses and men, but there was no doubting the allegiance of the troopers as the men embraced and sought information from one another.

Deiphontes warmly welcomed them: "My greatest fear was that you would arrive too late. My uncle is not far distant and is leading mean and greedy troops."

"So we have heard," Telemachus replied. "Deiphontes, we will talk later today. Now, I want only one file blockading Pylos. Everyone else, follow us. We have no time to lose."

The main body of troopers moved down the coast road about thirty-five stadia beyond Pylos to the junction of the coastal route leading to Asine and the route to the seashore below Pylos. The smaller and narrower route, a path really, led through a heavily wooded forest, alongside the freshwater marsh, eventually arriving at the shoreline and the port of Sphacteria, which was about twenty stadia from the main road. This was the way Nestor would take for hunting or for boarding one of his ships. Once at the shoreline, a long spit of beach extended between high cliffs falling directly into the rocky waters below. The forest path was the sole entrance and exit.

The troopers halted at the crossroads, and the men gathered about. Telemachus began issuing orders.

"Since the Heraclides are unfamiliar with this region, we will offer them a gift," Telemachus told the assembled troops.

First, he sent a file to scout the location of the Heraclide infantry without being observed. He felt sure Cresphontes would be tramping along the road, oblivious to military strategy, and the men would be fatigued and heavy from their days of drinking and carousing.

Next, he ordered the men to find a location far out of sight and sound in which to contain the horses.

Then Telemachus described the strategy. "We want to disguise the main route. So that a traveler would have no choice but to follow the path leading to the shoreline. The main road leading to Pylos shall disappear from sight. In its stead, we will continue the coastal road into the forest and swamp. We will allow the infantry to defeat themselves, forcing their advanced battalions onto the shore, with the remaining troops cramped by the trees and marsh where numbers are of no advantage and, forsooth, a disadvantage."

The soldiers understood immediately. They began designing a natural turn in the road, transplanting trees, bushes, plants, grasses, and detritus along the main route to hide it from view. They widened the route to the sea at its commencement, making it appear as a natural extension of the main road. Soon, no juncture was apparent. The coastal route simply made a turning and continued into the forest, slowly diminishing into a narrow path between wood and swamp. This was accomplished quickly. Most of the troopers had been raised on farms, and they knew the touch and feel of the natural environs. They were familiar with the plant species and were able to create a temporary façade that would have had local inhabitants scratching their heads in disbelief at the disappearance of the coastal route.

As men worked on disguising the road, Oxylus and Autolycus took a large contingent into the forest to begin planning offensive locations that would make it impossible for the Heraclide infantry to retreat. The only exits would be the marsh, the sea, or to return along the forest path. The marsh was impassable due to the dense growth of rushes and galingales. The sea was available only by ship, since the mountains prevented any retreat along the coast. And the forest path would require turning the entire division in the opposite direction.

This direction would be blockaded by its own wagons at the tail end of the troops, since the wagons would be stopped before they left the forest. Archers were positioned in the hills and trees along the path with excellent vantage of the shore, the path, and the marsh below them. It would be a prison for any army, regardless of size or armament. If they attempted to exit the forest path, it would be like shooting rabbits in a hutch.

Telemachus sent Perius and a file into the small port of Sphacteria to evacuate the village. The people were not resistant, and many had departed the day before, fearing hostilities, for word was about. The remainder of the people walked out along the narrow trail and were escorted in the direction of Pylos, where they were allowed entry to the city. The entire region was aware of the presence of troops, although they had yet to discern their intent, and, for the most part, people living outside of Pylos remained in their homes.

By the time the first scout galloped into the midst of the construction, most of the work had been accomplished. The scout announced that the force of Heraclides was approaching slowly in irregular formation and in a state of dissoluteness and inebriation. It would be late afternoon before the first cohorts began straggling in, giving the troopers plenty of time to complete their tasks.

Before long, all construction was concluded and in place. The men had gone so far as to temporarily reroute a stream and create a small lake flooding the hidden main road to Pylos. The final efforts were dedicated to dressing the new route with dry dirt, horse manure, and wagon tracks to make it appear absolutely normal. The main road had disappeared for the moment, only to reappear several stadia distant, far out of view. Telemachus positioned two tribes to protect the road from the direction of Boreas and to ensure that any possible breakthrough of the Heraclides would be met with force. He sent one tribe back to the crossroads of the city to assist the blockade of Pylos, and held two mounted tribes back among the pastured horses prepared to attack. That left about four hundred dismounted troopers to guard the path to the sea. After a final conference, the troopers took their places along the route with their composite bows and cut-and-thrust swords and plenty of arrows. Oxylus and Autolycus remained among them in command. Telemachus waited with two tribes positioned off the main road with a vantage of the juncture.

They waited longer than they had expected. But the first soldiers began arriving, hot and tired and hung-over, straggling in twos and threes, their lances and javelins on their shoulders and their corselets loosened to allow air to reach their bodies. Many of the men had strapped their helmets to their sides and stuffed their undercaps away. The march from Asine had taken much longer than anyone would have conjectured due to the soldiers' fatigue and lack of enthusiasm following their mischief, and their moods ranged from sour to bad-tempered. At the turn in the road, they neither hesitated nor took notice. They continued marching along the route they supposed to be the one leading to Pylos.

The true test of the deception came when Cresphontes and his lieutenants arrived at the crossing. The officers rode horses, following the troops before them, without enthusiasm or interest. Their chariots had been judged useless in these environs and discarded. Cresphontes and the twins, Procles and Eurysthenes, rocked uncomfortably on their saddle pads. Cresphontes seemed oblivious to his surroundings, paying attention neither to his officers nor the soldiers ahead of him. His head nodded sleepily to the gait of the horse. Aletes appeared at least alert, his dark eyes dancing, but he followed the other family members into the forest.

Finally, the supply wagons and feed animals arrived, making the turn and heading into the forest toward the shore. But the column did not end with the wagons: a bedraggled group of women and children followed the wagons. This group was stopped by Telemachus' troopers before they could enter the forest, questioned briefly, and then sent back to their destroyed town.

From the hillside and trees along the forest path, the troopers watched as the leading infantry soldiers became aware that the path was narrowing and leading through a forest on the one side and a low marsh on the other. The high pines, willows, and thick brush cut off the sunlight, but ahead an opening appeared. They came out into full sunlight, open skies, with only a few low-lying clouds on the distant horizon, and an immense open space. They mounted a slight incline onto a raised spit of sand that ran parallel to a wide beach and sandy shore. On their left hand, they noted high cliffs and in the far distance up the spit they saw a promontory and rocky cliffs. The shoreline itself was flat and open to the sea, forty or fifty stadia in length, with gentle surf breaking up the strand. They could see a single sail out in the sea, sailing downwind with Boreas blowing. The small port village of Sphacteria lay in the distance on the spit.

As more soldiers came out of the forest into the open, they began to question where they were. But more and more of them continued to enter the beach, forcing those who were there already to move farther down the shore. Some of the soldiers took the opportunity to step into the surf and cool themselves, while others went to the other side of the spit and drank from the fresh water of the marsh. Others lay on the sand, glad for a respite. The officers dismounted and gathered together, not certain of their location. Soon the one end of the beach was filled with soldiers.

From a distance, Oxylus and Autolycus watched Cresphontes ride onto the spit of land and begin questioning his officers. He rode his edgy horse about, circling his officers. When all the infantry troops had passed, Oxylus gave the order for the troopers to take the wagons. With bows at the ready, the archers came out of hiding and signaled for the wagon drivers and sutlers to descend and move forward. When the drivers saw the troopers, they did not know what to make of it. But they gladly followed orders and were soon walking out onto the beach. The troopers cut the horses and draft animals loose and forced them to follow the drivers, effectively blockading the exit route.

As the drivers and their loosed animals came onto the spit, it became apparent to the leaders of the Heraclides that they had not only taken a wrong turn, but they were being manipulated by an unknown assailant. The officers ordered the soldiers to form up along the beach. The soldiers did so with some reluctance haphazardly. Slowly, it dawned on all of them that they were no longer in control of their own destiny.

Finally, Oxylus and Autolycus came out of the forest into view of the infantry. Behind them stood a contingent of archers. Oxylus waved at the generals, who finally took notice of him. Cresphontes came forward rapidly on his charger. He slowed, seeing the bows raised toward him. He dismounted at a distance, wanting to get to the bottom of this, but not wanting to appear too hostile to avoid going immediately to the house of Hades.

"What do you mean by this?" he said, remaining at a distance.

"We would like to chat," Oxylus said. And he signaled for Cresphontes to come closer.

They watched as Cresphontes, his face flushed with anger tempered by uncertainty, came up to the two men.

"Welcome," Oxylus said. "We have been expecting you."

"Of course. Of course. But I do not understand."

"We asked that you not enter Pylos until Telemachus had time to meet with his family."

"Yes?"

"We were informed that you were headed directly for Pylos."

"Well, we wanted…"

"We also learned that you sacked Asine," Oxylus interrupted. "That was not part of our plans."

"No. That was unfortunate. The soldiers got out of control."

"Yes," Oxylus said calmly. "Now they are back under command."

"Yes."

"You misunderstand, Cresphontes. They are back under *our* command."

"Your command?"

"Yes. We suggest that you camp here for a few days. There is plenty of fresh water, and the men can bathe in the sea. Your provisions are available on the trail. But you may not leave the area."

"You will not succeed. You forget your place. I will have you hanged and your bodies thrown out for the dogs." But he stopped himself as rapidly as he had begun, seeing the futility of his anger. "Some day, Oxylus, you will pay for this. Whether today or in the distant future, you will pay."

"You can rant and rave, if you desire, and threaten me. I am merely explaining to you that if you want to leave here alive, you should not attempt to resist. We will meet again tomorrow, after we have had a chance to talk with the archons of Pylos and Messenia."

Clearly, the soldiers were very interested in this conversation that undoubtedly affected their future. This last division of the Heraclides was an undisciplined group, split evenly between

Heraclides and Corinthians and Lacedaemons. The Corinthian and Lacedaemon regulars had not been trained in Locris and had no allegiance, except to themselves. All the troops knew that they had overstepped the bounds at Asine. But they did not want to be sold down the river by their officers. Oxylus knew the Heraclide soldiers, who had gone through training at Locris, and knew that he could influence them against Cresphontes easily. He felt sure that Cresphontes was aware of this as well.

"Are we agreed?" Oxylus demanded.

"Yes. Yes. Tonight, we will camp here. But tomorrow, we must talk. These are not my only forces, you know," he added unconvincingly. "More are on the way."

"I hold you to your word on this, for what that is worth," Oxylus said, turning rudely and walking away, followed by Autolycus.

Cresphontes rested alone for a long moment and then turned toward the beach and walked his horse back to his officers. The troopers pulled back into the forest, but watched as the Heraclides broke formation and separated into groups: officers, Heraclides, Corinthians, Lacedaemons, and others.

Oxylus left Autolycus in command of the archers. He felt that although the Heraclides might attempt to discover a broader understanding of their circumstances, they would not make a wholesale attempt to battle their way out to the main road this day. That would come at a later date. He walked out of the forest stiffly to join Telemachus, for Rhaebus was with the other horses.

He found Telemachus at the disguised junction of the road to Pylos. After describing the success of their fraud and the surprise of the troops on arriving at the beach, he depicted the consternation of Cresphontes:

"It was wonderful," Oxylus said smiling. "I have never seen him at such a loss, deserted and alone, raging like Poseidon and crying like Aphrodite, all at the same time. Seeing this was worth all the troubles he put us through."

"That, my friend, can only last a short while," Telemachus said, patting Oxylus on the shoulder. "We have one night in Pylos. Tomorrow will be a new day. We can fight his troops, who are not likely to put up great resistance in honor of Cresphontes, or we can come to some agreement. We know with certainty we cannot rely on his word."

"Well, then, it is time to visit Nestor," Telemachus replied, "who is worthy of our trust."

LVII

Three files of the most excellent troopers in full regalia began the ride into Pylos, which lay at a distance of only a few stadia from the blockade on the main road. The road led up a steep hill to the rear of the city. Not knowing what to expect, they approached the city cautiously. When they entered the city, they found it empty of people. The agora was vacant. They saw a man in the distance as they approached, but he disappeared rapidly. The word of the rape of Asine must have spread to the city, and the people were afraid of some similar violence befalling them. Telemachus recalled racing horses through the streets years before at a festival prior to his marriage and walking with Polycasté into the center of town from the palace along this very road. He felt the anxiety in his stomach, not as a Heraclide, but as a man returning to his wife and family after what seemed a long and perilous journey. He led the troopers up a side street toward the magnificent palace of Nestor, which lay above the town, but descended in gardened terraces almost to the sea.

At the palace, Telemachus and Oxylus tied up their horses and left the troopers in the courtyard. They pushed open the doors and came into the large stone atrium at the top level. What once had been as beautiful as any palace in Hellas was now dark, cold, and dirty. The murals were still on the walls, but the polished floors were covered in filth. There were wooden crates along the walls, and a feral cat scampered out of sight at their entrance.

"Is anyone here?" Telemachus shouted, his voice resounding in the hall.

There was no response, and no servants came forward.

"I will go investigate the apartments," Telemachus said.

He descended the stairs slowly, somewhat awkwardly, knowing the palace well, yet feeling an intruder. He walked toward what used to be Nestor's suite. Nothing. The rooms were vacant. The furniture had been removed, and it appeared from the dust and dirt that no one had occupied the rooms for some time. The terraces were covered in filth and dead plants and trees. He found this true of all the other levels. He stopped at what had once been Polycasté's suite in the women's wing and found it equally empty. When he returned to the ground-floor atrium, Oxylus was no longer there. He opened the doors into the sunlight and saw Oxylus talking to a tall, well-dressed man in the courtyard. As he approached, he recognized Pisistratus, the son of Nestor, looking older with gray in his beard, but with the same piercing eyes and upright manner. He did not know how to approach his brother-in-law and friend of his youth, but Pisistratus came quickly forward to fold him in a warm embrace, which he returned with a feeling of gratitude.

"Let me introduce you to my friend and fellow officer, Oxylus. He is commander of the Heraclides." They nodded to one another. "Where is the family?" Telemachus asked.

"Much has changed since you were last here. We moved out of the palace a year ago. Well before that, my brothers and my son relocated to separate kingdoms and began fighting amongst themselves. That you may know. But since that time, Alcmaeon, grandson of my oldest brother, Thrasymedes, whom I blame for much of the problems in Messenia, now rules Messene. Thrasymedes was killed last year in the fighting. His son, Sillus, was also killed in the war. Now, Melanthus, son of Andropompus and not a relative of Nestor, rules in the region on the Gulf of Messenia. Paeon, son of Antilochus, is ruler of Thuria in the direction of Notus. And my son, the younger Pisistratus, is now ruler of Pylos, but resides down the coast. Nestor, along with Polycasté, relocated from the palace to a smaller house in town. He has aged, but he is as wise as ever. His body has deserted him, and he barely walks unassisted."

"We need to talk with the rulers of Messenia," Telemachus said.

"That is easily accomplished, since the family has gathered due to the impending attack of the Heraclides. All the rulers are here, although not happily. All, that is, except Melanthus, who, we have been told, is dead from an attack at Asine. He was never a friend of the family."

"As far as we know, Melanthus is arrested." Telemachus corrected him.

"Even before these Heraclides, Messenia was under hard times: divided and poor. Nestor is destitute and must depend on the kindness of others. We have no defenses. Everyone struggles, and no one is able to fight or even has the desire. We are truly a region of fishermen and farmers and small villages. No more."

"Can we meet with your family?" Telemachus asked, afraid to ask the one question on his mind.

"Certainly. Follow me."

Pisistratus, too, felt constrained to express his emotions. Telemachus had always thought of Pisistratus as a brother. They had traveled together and knew each other well, even before his marriage to Polycasté. He longed to step out of his role as Heraclide and return to a simpler relationship.

They walked from the palace down the road into town. The troopers led their horses. Telemachus noted that the palace stables, which had once been filled with the finest horses from throughout the world, were now deserted. Over the years, Nestor had given Telemachus some of his finest horses, including Aethiops, a beautiful nut-brown mare, several from the Levantine, and, of course, his first horse, Bronte, when he was just a boy. In town, Pisistratus led them to a two-story dwelling of wooden posts, bricks, and whitewashed plastered mud. They entered and found three men seated around a low table in the entry room, which took up most of the space of the lower floor.

Pisistratus introduced Telemachus and Oxylus to the men, who remained seated:

"This is my son, younger Pisistratus, ruler of Pylos. Alcmaeon, my cousin, is ruler of Messene. And another cousin, Paeon, rules in Thuria." The men did not offer their hands or greet Telemachus and Oxylus.

Telemachus looked around the room, but no one else was in attendance. A servant brought goblets for the two strangers and served them wine and water.

"And Nestor?" Telemachus asked.

"He is upstairs. Let me see if he will see you." Pisistratus left the room.

"Sirs," Oxylus began, "allow me to introduce ourselves. We are both commanders of the Heraclides. I command the infantry, and

Telemachus commands the cavalry. But we are not family members. The Heraclides are here in force and well-armed. Their intention is to return to power in the Peloponnese and the only remaining region outside their authority is Messenia. They now control all countries, save Achaea, which is certain to fall under their influence in the future. But allow me to be entirely honest with you. I use the word 'they,' because we are not for sooth of them, but are counselors to their cause, and not contented with their actions.

"We were not at Asine, but believe that certain carnage took place. That was never part of our agreement. Now, it is our job to determine their future, so to speak. Telemachus and I command a large contingent of horse troops here, who are loyal to us alone. We do not come as barbarians seeking lucre and slaves. Telemachus has taken extraordinary measures to protect Nestor and his family." At this, there were some objections from the rulers, but Oxylus held up his hand. "Listen to me. We will provide safe conduct to you and your families, to wherever you wish. But believe me, when I say that the Heraclides are intent on ruling and will do so by force, and they are not afraid to cause casualties, as you are well aware. For the moment, we have their agreement to negotiate a peaceful settlement, but by tomorrow I am not sure we can continue to restrain them." He went on to explain the situation without too much detail and to discuss their tenuous agreement with Cresphontes, but did not reveal the true circumstances of the army.

When Pisistratus returned, he signaled for Telemachus to follow him, leading him into the back, leaving Oxylus talking with the unhappy and angry rulers. Pisistratus led Telemachus up some dilapidated wooden stairs to a tiny hallway. Pisistratus directed him to the room at the end. He brushed past the curtain, and there sat an old man upright in his bed, smiling with bright eyes. The late-afternoon sun fell into the room from open shutters.

Telemachus tucked his helmet under his arm, feeling embarrassed in the small room in his bronze cuirass and blue cloak and long sword. He walked over to the side of the bed, and knelt with his head down next to the old man. He felt a hand rest on his shoulder.

"My son," Nestor said. "You have returned."

For an instant, Telemachus wondered if Nestor knew who he was. The voice was the same, perhaps weaker, but it brought back the many times they had spoken in the past.

"They tell me you have Cresphontes trapped on the shore," Nestor said. "And you now command his army. That all of Pylos awaits your wishes. Would that I had held Agamemnon in similar circumstances."

"The line of Neleus must be allowed to continue," Telemachus replied. "That is my reason for being here."

"The line of Nestor has been violated. But I want to thank you," Nestor said.

"Thank me?"

"Yes. You have given me so much in my final days on earth. You have allowed my daughter, your wife, to stay with me during these hard times. And your son, Amphion, is the light of my life."

Telemachus raised his head. "My wife came of her own volition. She has chosen to be your daughter and not my wife."

"Ah, yes," he said nodding his head. "And for that I am sorry. And Odysseus?"

"He died two years ago."

"Ah, yes. And Penelope?"

"She resides on Ithaca at her home."

"Good. Good. A woman whom many failed to comprehend or took lightly, as men are wont to do with women. But she was remarkable. None like her and certainly not her cousins, Helen and Clytemnestra. Agamemnon never understood your mother; neither did his red-haired brother. Nor did they understand your father. Never understood principles. Your dress brings to mind our trials at Troy."

"Sire, I must ask for your own sake, for Cresphontes, head of the Heraclides, is nearby. Do you have any treasure that we should hide from him?"

"Treasure? My family has squandered my treasure."

"What of your share of the spoils of Troy? The treasure of Priam?"

"Ah, the treasure of Agamemnon. No, Agamemnon took all the gold. And he would have it to this day had he not insulted the gods by treating the Trojans with such brutality."

"You have no treasure here?"

"My son, does it appear as though I am hiding great wealth? Let me tell you a story, and then I need to rest. All my stories are short now. True, Agamemnon bestowed a great share of Priam's gold on me, but I never returned with it. I returned from Troy unscathed, thanks to the gods, while many others died or had god-given difficulties in their return. But my treasure was gone, and here is the reason. When I saw what the Greeks intended for Troy, it surpassed the mind. We threw compassion to the four winds. One Trojan in particular, I had grown to respect, and his name was Aeneas, son of Anchises. For often, along with the healing of the wounds of battle, comes respect for your enemy. Here was a man unlike many of his brethren, who fought honorably. He clashed with Diomedes and Achilles. But in the end, he sought to salvage his people and the house of Dardania. I helped him escape in more than twenty ships with many Trojans, young and old, and with his father. I gave him my share of the gold. I gave him all my ill-gotten earnings. Aeneas survived in Italia, and for that I am thankful. Although I no longer hear of him, I know that he is well.

"Now, my son, I tire easily. I have followed your career. I am as proud of you as any father can be. Odysseus could not have wished for more or better. My own family has deserted me; they squabble like chickens over last night's peas. I would give anything to see you rule Messenia...and your sons. And I will support you in this endeavor. It is yours for the asking."

Telemachus shook his head. "Cresphontes is not alone in this affair, and your own family would hate me."

"No matter. They are full of hate in any case. Such considerations only beg the question. You must think carefully before you bargain away honor and immortality, such as your father knew."

"At the moment, my only goal is to save your family from destruction. Given the Heraclides' wanton behavior and greed, if left to their own devices, they would not allow anyone to escape alive. We are here to offer your family safe passage to anywhere they desire."

"I know the man, Cresphontes, and his father before him, and so on," Nestor said. "I understand what you are saying. Yes, you are right. Even the greatest king must meet his maker."

"Will you speak with your family?"

"Yes, though they do not listen."

"I offer you the hospitality of the palace of Odysseus on Ithaca."

"And I offer you the throne of Messenia."

"Please," Telemachus replied. "I can only think of completing my assignment...to see you removed from harm."

"I am a very old man. Propped up by heaven like a puppet. Ithaca. Your father spoke of nothing else. He made it seem larger than all of Hellas, with wine grapes the size of melons and fountains that never ceased overflowing with fresh water. I will speak to my children, but you, my son, must examine your heart." He sighed, and his eyelids began to fall.

"One day your boys will rule. They are fine boys. You are blessed as your father was by heaven, both as regards wife and offspring. Your father. He was a proud man. But in his mastery of man, Odysseus lost some of his compassion. Innocence is a treasure we must preserve. A good man, though. At the end, who can ask for more?"

His eyes closed, and he seemed to sleep, or his energy failed him. Pisistratus helped Telemachus to his feet, and they left Nestor to his nap.

As they came out into the hallway, Telemachus glimpsed Polycasté in a drab linen robe; her wet dark hair lay on her shoulders. She was entering a room at the opposite end of the hallway. Pisistratus also saw her as well and hurried to descend the stairs. Telemachus stopped in his tracks and stared at his wife. Polycasté turned her head and regarded him with hazel eyes, her lovely face a mask. His heart stopped, but before he could speak she allowed the curtain to close behind her. He stared at the moving curtain, listening, thinking...he realized that he had surrendered what he cherished most of all.

Allow me to append a note on history. We may look askance at Telemachus and fault him for his choices. He had Cresphontes trapped with troops whose allegiance was doubtful. He had only to offer the troops their liberty and some compensation and see who remained to support Cresphontes. Why would he allow Cresphontes to escape? With Nestor's blessing he could have ruled a reunited Messenia. Without Cresphontes, the Heraclides could not have prevented it, and many among them would have favored it. And it was not because of his prayer to the gods for the return of his son Amphion. Telemachus never ruled in Messenia, we know that from history. Alas, history bounds my story. Though, it is constructive to see how decisions in history are made – some excellent, some fraught with terrible consequences, and some personal with motivations of all hues. Let us continue with our story before we judge Telemachus too harshly and begin our own stories. The telemachia will become clear soon enough.

LVIII

Telemachus returned to the first floor, his mind reeling from seeing Polycasté and from the course of his conversation with Nestor. In the front room, the atmosphere had charged like an unexpected thunderstorm from Zeus; the leaders of Messenia had turned against Oxylus. No one was bothering to drink from the cups before them. Pisistratus stood against the wall, watching his family attack the resolute stranger.

Alcmaeon was speaking: "What of our land and homes? You expect us to leave this behind? We were born in this country. We have lived our entire lives here. My father and grandfather are buried here. Thrasymedes, my grandfather, and son of Nestor, led the Pylians to Troy and returned to become King of Messenia. By what right do the Heraclides presume to rule in Messenia? They only want to line their pockets."

And Paeon spoke: "I am the son of Antilochus, who was fleetest of foot of all the men at Troy. Antilochus participated in games throughout Hellas and won many laurel wreaths. But he never returned from Troy and now lies under barbarian earth. He gave his life in favor of the sons of Atreus, the Pelopides. The black-complexioned and wooly-headed Ethiopian, Memnon, fighting for the Trojans, stabbed him in the back. Achilles and Memnon fought over the body and armour of my father, and Achilles killed Memnon. The blood of my ancestors has watered this land. What more right to this land does anyone have than myself and my family?"

And young Pisistratus added: "The great King Nestor lies abed in this house. He has ruled Messenia three generations beyond the age of a normal man. The blood of his ancestors flows through the streams in this land feeding the parched roots and giving sustenance to the soil. When Heracles came to Messenia long ago, he ravaged the kingdoms in the direction of Notus. He came to Messenia to kill Neleus and all his sons, save Nestor. And now his bastards would return to occupy what their father desecrated? And they expect us to retire grateful for our lives?

"And this man before us, this Telemachus, this man whose wife hides in her bedroom full of hatred and bile. A traitor to his own family. He considered gain above all else...even his family. And I can..."

"Enough," his father, the elder Pisistratus, yelled. "You could not understand."

"Halt," Oxylus shouted as he would stop a soldier. "I listen to you and hear the pain in your stories. I too could tell similar tales. For your stories bear strangely upon my own. But I am not here to battle with you on behalf of the Heraclides. We have come in advance of Cresphontes and his forces to offer you your lives. I am here only at the stipulation of Telemachus. Without Telemachus, you would have been treated as the Heraclides treated the Corinthians and the Spartans and the Asinians. No questions asked. Tisamenus lies beneath the waves in the Saronic Gulf. We did not negotiate with him, and he had an army of ten thousand men from all across the Peloponnese. Telemachus and I have made efforts and continue to take measures to protect Pylos and its people. We are offering safe passage to the four leaders of Messenia and their families and protection to the people of Pylos. That is all we can do at this time: delay and temper the invasion of the Heraclides. If you look over the cliff of Pylos, you can see the troops marshaled on the shores below, and the navy will be arriving soon as well. If you do not agree to relocate, by this time tomorrow, Cresphontes will be seated upon this very cushion, and his blue cloak will be splattered by the blood of Pylians and the family of Nestor. You have until tomorrow to make your decision.

"And by the way, Memnon, King of the Ethiopians, never stabbed any man in the back."

With that, Oxylus joined Telemachus, who had been standing next to Pisistratus. They left without farewells, but Pisistratus accompanied them to their horses and the waiting troopers.

"Will you return to the Heraclides' camp this evening?" Pisistratus asked.

"No," Telemachus said. "We have many other matters to consider. We will stay at the palace, if that is acceptable to you."

"Yes. I will bring you some food later this evening. And, Telemachus, forgive this family at odds."

The troopers set up a camp in the hall of the palace on the hard polished stone floors. They started a small fire in the gigantic fire pit, collecting debris from the rooms of the palace. Since there was no spit or tripod, nor any meat for that matter, they chewed on dry bread and fruit to relieve their hunger. In the waning light of day, Telemachus and Oxylus walked out onto the first balcony above the town and sea to be alone and away from the troopers. They sat on the wall, almost at the exact spot where Telemachus had first talked with Polycasté as a young man visiting the family of Nestor.

"You know, I did not like those men," Oxylus told Telemachus.

"They have taken root far from the tree."

"But they will relocate," Oxylus said. "I am sure of that. They are too practical and full of themselves."

"They have no choice," Telemachus added without enthusiasm.

"Telemachus, you see life in two colors only. Life is multi-hued."

"I accept what I have been given."

"Telemachus, listen carefully. Do not refuse to look into the future nor reject outright your fate. We have Cresphontes cornered without recourse. His troops will not fight for him. We know that. With Cresphontes and his cousins out of the way, that is to say, sent to the house of Hades, you could easily rule Messenia. Temenus would make an agreement with us, and you know as well as I that he would not rue the death of his brother. And tell me, who has more authentic rights to the throne of Messenia? The son-in-law of Nestor and son of the hero of the Hellenes and king of the offshore islands. Elis and Pylos have always been enemies. With our combined rules, we could unite to withstand any pressure from the Heraclides in Argos or the Lacedaemons. The Ionian Peloponnese would be ours. And Ithaca would be included in the bargain. Your sons could one day rule a much greater area than any of their forefathers."

Telemachus did not reply.

"What I am saying is that we are in a position to put forward our own agenda," Oxylus finally said, frustrated at Telemachus' silence.

"It was not meant to be," Telemachus said simply.

"How can you say that? It can be any way we desire. The gods are in heaven, and we rule the earth."

"Of all the kingdoms in the entire world," Telemachus said, "I would rather have my family about me. Oxylus, we did not set out to become tyrants of the Peloponnese. We can leave that to our employers. We set out only to save ourselves, as you may recall. Both of us exiled from our homes. Both with something to prove. We have done that.

"But let me be more truthful," Telemachus continued. "I lost my son on the isthmus, as you are well aware. As I searched for him, I had to decide what was valuable to me in my life. I asked the gods for help. They offered it, but in turn they wanted me to understand who I was and what was best for me. They forced a decision on me, and I happily made it. I will never become the King of Ithaca, Cephallenia, and Zacynthus or king of anywhere else. Today, I have both sons about me, and their lives are just beginning. And if I can extricate myself in one piece from this final quandary, I will return to Ithaca almost a cheerful man.

"Besides, Oxylus, is the kingdom of Elis not enough for you? Why add fresh woes to rotten ones before we have drunk to the dregs? You are in a position to have what you desire most. Do not let greed poison the well of your hopes."

"At least I had to try," Oxylus replied. "You always manage to see through deceit, even self-deceit, because you are the grandson of a cattle thief and the son of a wily strategist…"

"All my life I have listened to these charges," Telemachus interrupted without anger. "The bards called my grandfather a cattle thief and my father a wily strategist. The truth lies elsewhere. My maternal great grandfather, Autolycus, was the cleverest man of his day, and some thought him the son of Hermes. Yet today, they call him a cattle thief and magician. His only magic was his intelligence. He was able to change the color of cattle through breeding different races. He created cattle with horns and without horns, black with white spots, white with black spots, and pure white, and cows that produced milk endlessly. People had never before seen cattle like this that resembled the famous rolling cattle of Apollo. He taught his grandson all he knew, but he never revealed what he knew to others.

"As for my father, the wily strategist: he had an imaginative mind and knew the difference between right and wrong...a combination lacking among many of our leaders. He solved Agamemnon's problems through perseverance and originality. He had been raised to mind the roof when the rain leaked through. He knew what it was to work. While the leaders sent others to do their tasks, he set out on his own. He used his head, but he was not afraid of using his back as well."

"I thank you for clearing this up," Oxylus replied. "You come from a rare family. And if the Messenians do not accept our offer?"

"They will."

"But should one of them hesitate..."

"Nestor will talk to them tonight. For all his age, he still rules."

They watched Helios and his horses dive into the Ionian Sea, with the brilliant rose tints and golden-haired goddesses celebrating the end of the journey. They heard Pisistratus approach on foot. Two servants followed him, carrying panniers covered in cloth. He signaled for the servants to enter the palace, while he came over to the balcony to join Telemachus and Oxylus.

"They are discussing their voyage to Athens," Pisistratus said.

"Then they are prepared?" Oxylus asked.

"They should have left years ago. I blame myself. But mostly I blame my brother, Thrasymedes, who wanted only to best his father."

"Pisistratus," Telemachus said, "I offered to take Nestor to Ithaca, and I believe he will accept. I make the same offer to you and your family. Cresphontes will allow no Neleidai to remain in Messenia."

"I know. I would gladly visit Ithaca for the while. And my father as well. And it is time for my sister to return to her home."

"She has always known what is best for her," Telemachus said stiffly.

"You still do not understand my sister," Pisistratus replied. "She is the daughter of one of the greatest kings of all Hellas. She is not used to taking orders, but some decisions are best made by others. I can see into her heart, and she yearns for you. After Amphion left to join you, she became silent. She refuses to speak to any of us. She nurses Nestor as a loving servant would, and that is all. She risks losing herself. But you have to take command. She will not approach willingly. Come, I will eat with you as is proper. We have forgotten much, but we must never fail to remember our hospitality."

They ate silently around the fire along with the troopers. The panniers contained fresh bread, morsels of dried fish, fresh anchovies in oil, black olives, dried cheese, and several earthenware jugs of wine. They had not had such a good meal in many days, not since the invasion began. They appreciated the excellent flavors and strong wine. Pisistratus left them. And the Heraclide troopers settled their cloaks about their bodies for warmth, lying on the hard floor, as the smoke from the dying embers gently curled up to the heavens.

The next morning when saffron-robed Eos rose in the sky, servants brought large ewers of fresh water to the palace. The troopers gladly stripped to wash off the accumulated dust and dirt of the campaign, leaving the courtyard dotted with muddy pools. They ate fresh bread spread with dark honey. As they prepared to leave, they saw a number of ships out on the horizon. Even from this distance, they could tell that these were not normal coastal traders, but were sailing as a fleet. They identified two large Phoenician-type long ships with their giant sails spread in the wind. There must have been twenty ships in all. The smaller, twenty-five-oar warships surrounded the larger ships like young dolphins tagging after their mothers.

The troopers mounted and rode into town to the house of Nestor. They waited out front, as Telemachus and Oxylus entered the building once again. The family was all there, save Nestor and Polycasté, who remained out of sight. Pisistratus senior welcomed them, and for the first time led the discussion.

"First, we want to thank Telemachus and Oxylus for protecting us to the extent possible. I understand the difficulty of this endeavor akin to balancing a two-edged sword. It has not gone unnoticed. And my father thanks you.

"We have discussed your offer and sadly pledge ourselves to its acceptance. The families of Pisistratus, my son, Paeon, and Alcmaeon will relocate to Athens. We have seen the fleet of ships below our cliffs. My family, my wife, and I, will relocate to Ithaca. Nestor and Polycasté will accompany us. We will be prepared to leave in three days, since Pisistratus, Paeon, and Alcmaeon must return to their homes outside Pylos. We would ask that the Heraclides remain in their camp until after our departure. However, we will not depart or agree to anything without the pledge of your leaders that the soldiers will respect the people of this region. There will be no killing and no slave-taking. For several days now, the people have been prevented free movement, and we would request that the roadblocks be removed. The people have resorted to their homes out of fear. This must come to an end.

"In all, we are hopeful that reunification of Messenia will be favorable, for this truly is our homeland, and we look to its best interests. The last years have been hard on everyone, and the people have suffered greatly. This is a poor region. War will not cure what ails us. We are attacked from within and without daily. We hope and pray to the lord Zeus that what we are doing, and what the Heraclides are doing as well, will have beneficial value. "

He crossed the room and embraced both Telemachus and Oxylus.

As they slow-walked their horses from Pylos toward the main road, Telemachus and Oxylus rode ahead of the troopers.

"You know, we have come a long way," Oxylus said. His smile had returned since the battle for Elis. "You must decide on your future. We have Cresphontes snared like a wild boar with a caltrop around his legs. The infantry, even the Spartans, would gladly walk away from him. The troopers would support any move you made, for they have come to respect you greatly. They abide me, but they fight for you."

"Oxylus, we have discussed this."

"I want to be clear. Your sons are in line for the thrones of Messenia and Ithaca and Cephallenia. You have Nestor's praise and approbation. Temenus and Deiphontes would not be disappointed if Cresphontes and his supporters disappeared from the scene."

Telemachus hesitated. "Life is truly not complicated," he thought to himself. "It is man who forges complexity out of simplicity to feather his own nest." Out loud he said, "I have learned much from this experience. I have had my wind-blown adventures of heaven and earth, just as my father before me. I now seek only to return to my home."

On the beach, the Heraclide troops were not able to see the ships until later in the morning. They gathered along the shore and helped the sailors pull the ships up onto the beach and secure them. Temenus came ashore. The family gathered on the beach before Pylos. They sat together on the spit, looking out into the wide sea, as Cresphontes went on and on about the treachery of Oxylus and Telemachus, how they had tricked them by altering the route, and how they had boxed them in. He described how he would rip both of them apart, his counselors. Under the questioning of Temenus, though, a fuller story came out, including the battle with Melanthus, who was here under guard, the desertion of the cavalry under the guidance of Deiphontes, the sacking of Asine, the race to occupy Pylos against the agreement with Telemachus, and the meeting planned this afternoon with the two counselors.

After this, Temenus walked by himself up the beach to the edge of the forest. He continued along the path, discovering the supply wagons stuck in the mud, one after the other, blocking the path. Almost immediately, several archers came out of the forest and asked him to wait while they had an officer join him. A few moments later, Autolycus came forward.

"I understand that you have taken measures to slow the advance of my brother," Temenus said.

"We only forced him to honor his word," Autolycus replied. "After Asine, we no longer trusted him or his troops. Unfortunately, the name of the Heraclides will long be engraved in the memory of that city."

"I understand, and I am sorry for that," Temenus said. "Where are your father and Oxylus?"

"They are meeting with the archons of Messenia and will return soon to let us know the results of these discussions."

"Good. We will await their return. In the meantime, you can call off the guard."

"I apologize, sir, but for the moment our orders are to keep Cresphontes on the beach and not allow him to advance on Pylos. We have many troopers in the forest here with their bows trained on Cresphontes' troops at this moment and more tribes on the road to Pylos. We will remove them all when we have clearly come to an agreement with Cresphontes."

"Thank you, Autolycus. I understand." And Temenus returned to the beach.

On Mount Olympus, Athene approached her father, the lord of mortals and immortals alike.

"My father, of all the gods you are the fairest. You as well as I can see the darkness ahead for these mortals. On the beach of Pylos resides a solution that could spell the end of hostilities in the Peloponnese, and it is not being proposed by the Heraclides, the sons of the newest immortal among us. For we both know that their rule will only hasten the end. All that can be changed. The son of Odysseus believes that he has a bargain with the gods, but this bargain serves no one. Least of all the gods in heaven."

"My daughter, we understand the direction of your words. We can do nothing. For the power of the gods resides in the minds of men. Our influence is in their best interests, but just that. Gone are the days when we could inhabit earth among our children. At some point, a father must allow freedom to his children, regardless of the outcome. This notion is daunting to an immortal, but we too must observe the natural order. The hardest punishment of all is to see a child suffer and to be incapable of doing anything about it. We would give anything if this were not so, but it is our fate, just as it is man's fate. Odysseus is installed forever in the skies among us. His son will suffer the pain of mortal man. We cannot change that.

And yet there is a delicate beauty to this as well. We will it so, and so it shall be."

"But the decision of the fate of Telemachus is near, father," Athene said. "He is not an old man. He is vital and must live to see his grandchildren."

"That too is not up to us."

"What do you mean?" she asked.

"I mean daughter, we cannot change a man's fate as you well know."

"But his son, Amphion? Did you not change his fate?"

"No. That would be impossible."

LIX

As they came to the junction, Telemachus and Oxylus joined Deiphontes. They ordered the blockades removed from both sides of Pylos and the main road cleared of camouflage and opened to travel. They left the troopers in place, though, within the forest leading to the seashore. By the time Telemachus, Oxylus, and Deiphontes arrived on the spit of land along the sea, the infantry soldiers had slept a night, eaten, and were in a better state of mind. When the counselors rode out onto the beach, they were welcomed by Temenus. Cresphontes had to be physically restrained in his anger. It was apparent to all, save Cresphontes himself, that all his grand objectives had been achieved, and that, although he would never forgive his counselors for deceiving him and making him appear powerless before his troops, they had succeeded in securing agreement for the final step in the Heraclides' return to the Peloponnese. The third crop had achieved victory, just as the oracles had foretold – led by their counselors.

Oxylus explained: "The three rulers of Messenia and their families have agreed to relocate out of Messenia. We offered them transport, and they requested Athens. They have also asked for three days to arrange their affairs, which we granted. Nestor and his family will relocate to Ithaca in the final step of the return of the Heraclides. Telemachus and I will lead a small contingent of troopers to secure Ithaca, Cephallenia, and Zacynthus. We will take two tribes and about ten ships, including the two large ones. In three day's time, you will be able to take over the palace in Pylos, and Messenia will be yours."

Cresphontes was first to reply: "You cannot order us about like servants."

"Forgive us," Telemachus responded. "The speaking staff is no longer in your hands. You have no standing at this discussion. If you believe otherwise, then you are free to mount an offensive."

Cresphontes looked at Telemachus with naked hatred, but he made no reply.

"At that point our services will be terminated," Oxylus continued, "but we need to discuss the sharing of the spoils of the capture of the Peloponnese."

"We owe you nothing." Cresphontes said like a dam bursting. "Nothing. The troops under my command took the isthmus. Tisamenus escaped because you failed to secure the road. We took Mycenae and Argos without your help. We took Laconia and most of Messenia without you. And now we are prepared to complete our return to Pylos without your assistance."

"We have suffered you," dark-eyed Aletes added. "Neither of you has earned anything but our future enmity."

Oxylus began to speak softly and distinctly: "You would have failed to set a single foot on the Peloponnese without us. What is up for discussion is your word. I must again remind you that of all things in this life, a man's word is his bond. If you are seriously considering walking from this beach and taking over the rule of the Peloponnese, then we will require a pledge from you. Otherwise, you might consider sailing back to Locris, that is, if your infantry will abide while you abscond for a second time. For they too have accepted your word and are expecting you to fulfill your side of the agreement. And when I speak of just recompense, I am thinking of our promises to the soldiers."

"How dare you threaten me," Cresphontes shouted.

"No threats. A man lives or dies on his word."

Temenus interrupted. "We have journeyed a long way together. We will not desert. We will honor our word. Everyone will receive his share of the victory. Telemachus and Oxylus will receive their shares, for without them we would not be discussing this. We are grateful. I give you my word and the word of the family of Heracles that we will do all within our power to complete our agreement as we promised. I pledge this to you, and my brother pledges this as well. All soldiers will receive their fair shares." He turned to Cresphontes, who gave no sign of agreement. He returned to Oxylus and Telemachus. "You have given us more than we can ever repay. But what we can do is ensure that our agreement is completed with transport to Athens and Ithaca and then on to Elis. We hope that in the future we will be able to govern together for the benefit of all the Peloponnese and for the people who reside here. Tonight, we will celebrate the victory with a hecatomb for the gods and games tomorrow for the men with prizes for all."

Cresphontes glared at the men around him, but remained silent.

We cannot be certain of the events that followed the truce. History tells us that the next evening on the shore, the Heraclides, believing they were masters of the Peloponnese, held a family gathering in the privacy of their tent. They set up three altars, one for each country under their authority, and they dedicated the three altars to father Zeus. A sacrificer cut the throat of a suckling lamb on each altar in honor of the father of the gods and allowed the blood to run freely onto the altars. Three small fires were constructed on the altars, and the lambs were placed whole into the fire to purify them and send an offering to the gods.

After that, the family of Heracles struggled among themselves to discover an equitable way to divide the territories under their dominion. At the suggestion of Temenus, they cast lots for the regions of the Peloponnese under their control. They decided to each choose a colored stone that could be identified with a region: green for Corinth and Argos, vermilion for Lacedaemon, and ochre for Messenia. They dropped the stones into an earthenware pitcher of muddy water. But Cresphontes wanted to rule Messenia from the palace of Nestor, so instead of a rock, he formed an ochre stone of mud with his fist and dropped it into the pitcher. Why he chose Messenia rather than Mycenae is lost to history – although, if a man stares long enough into a mirror, he must come to see himself at some time.

Temenus was first to draw a stone from the water. He reached into the pitcher and withdrew the green stone and, thus, became the ruler of Corinth, Mycenae, and Argos. At the insistence of Cresphontes, he rewarded shadowy Aletes with the throne of Corinth, but he swore to allow Lacestades and his son, Polyphontes, to continue as the rulers of Sicyon, although Corinth and Sicyon would be beholden to him, as King of Mycenae.

Next, Procles and Eurysthenes took their chance. After fighting over who would withdraw the stone, Procles finally reached into the jar. For the sons of Aristodemus, Procles withdrew the red stone. So Procles and Eurysthenes became joint rulers of Lacedaemon.

It was Cresphontes' turn. He lifted the pitcher and poured out the water, announcing that all that remained was the rule of Messenia. So Cresphontes became the ruler of Messenia.

Finally, Temenus succeeded after a heated and bitter argument with his brother to award Deiphontes with the rule of Tiryns.

The next morning, the family awoke to find a prodigy that could only be the work of the gods. Each altar of the awarded regions showed the sign of paternal Zeus. Temenus found a freshwater toad sitting on the altar allocated to Argos. The toad meant that the ruler of Argos should stay within the boundaries of his country and never venture outside, since a toad is unable to travel far from his pond. But it also meant that when one cares about one's abode and takes its improvement to heart, then success will be assured.

Next, unhappily, the twin sons of Aristodemus found a two-headed serpent wrapped around the base of the altar of Lacedaemon. Since they were bitter enemies from the day of their birth and would only become more so as time went on, Lacedaemon would be divided into two royal houses, competing with each other to the detriment of both. Those who found the two-headed serpent would fail in attack, and it took many generations and hardships for Lacedaemon to achieve its greatness, and when it did, it was as a cold, belligerent military power, based on intolerance and tribalism, without compassion for its own people or others.

Sneaking behind the altar of Messenia, Cresphontes discovered a sly fox. A fox is known to be wily and quick to change directions, but never a friend of anyone and always a loner. Cresphontes would rule Messenia alone, capriciously, and without concern for his subjects. As it turned out, Cresphontes misunderstood the sign, as was his wont. The prodigy of a fox meant something entirely different: a fox never forgets where he has buried his ire and will always return to that spot. Cresphontes forgot his misdeeds, and they would return to haunt him.

LX

For the three days before the transport of the rulers of Messenia, the Heraclides celebrated on the beach. The Heraclide soldiers held festivities honoring the gods and made rich sacrifices of goats and rams on the beach and sent burnt offerings in honor of Zeus and Apollo and all the other gods who had aided them in their victory. They held games in wrestling and boxing, running and jumping, throwing javelins and stones, and in archery. And many soldiers won prizes of gold and silver. Even the troopers joined the festivities and held contests in horse riding and racing, although they remained apart from the infantry. Telemachus refused to remove the guards from along the forest path until the departure of the family of Nestor.

On the final evening, Oxylus and Telemachus participated in the celebrations, although without enthusiasm. Telemachus had discarded his Heraclide dress and armour, for he was through with wars. He wore a short riding tunic and leather jerkin, and even Odysseus would have approved of his heavy wool cloak. Oxylus remained in uniform. Both men wanted to put on brave fronts for the soldiers, who sought nothing more than assurances they had accomplished a great victory and would have their compensation. Particularly, the foreign soldiers wanted to be sure their desires for a new homeland would be honored by their officers. Temenus reassured all that the war had come to a successful conclusion and that all would be rewarded for their efforts. But no one trusted the Heraclides.

As they walked among the drunken soldiers, being greeted and jostled by the well-meaning young men, Telemachus and Oxylus felt separate and foreign to the festivities, for they knew too much. Everyone was joyous, dancing and singing the many songs of their homelands. They did not see family members about, but the troops happily gathered around the giant bonfire, drinking and toasting the gods. Everyone was glad to be finished with warring; they were looking forward to being home with their loved ones with something to show for their hard labor. They toasted all and poured libations freely.

"One day the poets will sing of us," a drunken trooper called to Oxylus and Telemachus, raising his chalice. "How can they not?"

Suddenly, black-eyed Aletes appeared before them, accompanied by a spiteful group of soldiers sporting Corinthian cloaks. Aletes had been drinking, but not cheerfully. His dark eyes peered at the two counselors with ill will. He still wore his armour and helmet.

"Ah, our counselors," he said, as though he had been searching for them. "The counselors to the Heraclides. Imagine that you would dare set foot on this beach."

"You are drunk, Aletes," Oxylus warned him.

"Yes, perhaps, but I see deceit and calumny before me. I see two rubes, who should be on their knees before me, the King of Corinth. But my fight is not with this swarthy, wooly-headed one. Get him away from me."

Before Oxylus could resist, several large soldiers surrounded him and incapacitated him, leaving Telemachus facing Aletes. The surrounding soldiers began moving backwards, sensing a confrontation. Aletes drew his sword.

"I have no fight with you, Aletes," Telemachus said. "I have no weapons." The world closed abruptly about him, concentrating time. All else was irrelevant. The end of the war was at hand, and now this man, who had doggedly tracked him from the very beginning, seemed intent on erasing all that he had worked so hard to create and control. A meaningless drunken brawl would determine his fate. Where are the gods in this? Athene had deserted him.

"And what is that at your belt?" Aletes demanded.

"That, my friend, is a knife given to me by my father."

"You are a no-account, Telemachus, just as your father was. Your father could not heft the shield of Heracles in body or mind."

"I did not scuttle from the battle at the ditch like some rodent," Telemachus replied, feeling that he could survive this assault in only one way. "I did not put other people at risk to spare myself, like the coward you are." The surrounding circle in the sand grew larger and wider as more and more soldiers gathered around the two disputing men, leaving space for a fight. The troopers and infantry began eyeing one another, forming two groupings. "My only fear is that you will produce some evil brood that may spill over into the Peloponnese."

An older, grizzled Corinthian veteran stepped out from the soldiers and approached Aletes: "Let this be a fair fight." He held out his hand.

Aletes stared at the man in amazement, but he gave over his sword.

"Now, let the gods decide the matter." And with that, the soldier dissolved into the ranks.

"I am a man of honor," Aletes said, and he withdrew a knife from his belt. "Now we are equal."

"This knife has been with me since I left Ithaca," Telemachus said, drawing it from his belt. "Given to me by my father as we departed my homeland. I will be sorry to see its blade soiled with your blood."

"You are always so neat and tidy," Aletes swore. "You always act finer than others. The vultures and dogs will attend your funeral." Aletes charged Telemachus with his knife.

Telemachus was able to move aside and avoid the thrust, but Aletes was clearly frenzied and fuddled with drink. The younger man turned quickly, this time approaching more slowly with his shoulders down and both arms outstretched for balance. Telemachus pulled his cloak off his shoulders and wrapped it around his left arm to use like a shield. They circled, with Aletes swiping at the wrapped arm several times without striking home. Telemachus remained away, using his knife defensively. The soldiers surrounding the two men began yelling. Soon the entire camp was surrounding the two men. The festivities and good cheer halted. Mortal man never moves far afield from his antagonism and resentment.

"Aletes," Telemachus said, "you need to use your head. If you harm me, you will not survive, believe me. There are a thousand troopers who will not allow you to escape."

"No, Telemachus. For once, you are wrong. I will survive as King of Corinth, and you will taste the asphodels of Hades."

Telemachus recognized that Aletes had gone too far to retreat. Too many men were observing him. He could not accept dishonor and could not withdraw. He also realized that Aletes was not as drunk as he first appeared. One of them would not walk away from this fight.

"Aletes, I will give you one chance," Telemachus said. "Just as Heracles did for Nestor." His mind was racing in search of some advantage, some way to put Aletes off balance.

"What?"

"Throw down your knife. We can box fairly as the Dioscuri admonish, if you need to settle something with me."

"Why would I do that?"

"For your life."

"I do not see it, Telemachus."

"There is much you fail to see. You and your family."

Aletes charged Telemachus again, this time sinking his knife deeply into the wool wrapping and pushing Telemachus backwards.

Telemachus did not feel the blade slice his arm, but he felt the warmth of the blood flowing down his hand. He tightened the cloak, now serving as a tourniquet as well as a defensive weapon. He wondered why Aletes hated him so, but only for an instant, for Aletes was at him again. This time, Aletes came in lower, swiping at Telemachus' bare thigh, but missed. As he backed, Telemachus was able to smash Aletes' helmet with his knife hand without great force, but enough to send Aletes sprawling on the sand.

Aletes quickly regained his feet. The two men observed each other for a moment. With blood flowing from his hand, Telemachus knew this fight could not last long. He felt he had one chance. His father had been a fine wrestler. He remembered his long days as a young man with the suitors. They had often wrestled in the courtyard and had welcomed the young Telemachus into their contests. One of the suitors, Antinous, had worked with Telemachus to improve his skills in wrestling and fighting to the consternation of Mentor, his tutor.

Aletes, younger and quicker, was being carried along by his resentment. He regarded this older man, wounded, but still defiant. He had hated him from the instant of his first sight of him. He had been raised with the stories of wily Odysseus, the greatest of the

Achaeans. And he had resented the son for what he saw as smugness and conceit, when he should have shown respect and gratitude. Now, he had to finish it. He charged Telemachus once again, his knife hand ahead of him. Telemachus took a deep breath, set his legs as if to absorb the full force of the man, and then quickly stepped back, hoping to catch Aletes off balance. Aletes struck at Telemachus and at the same time attempted to shift his weight in line with Telemachus. Aletes' knife swiped Telemachus' right hand, and the knife flew out of Telemachus' hand toward the surrounding soldiers, landing harmlessly at their feet. Telemachus suffered a minor slash along his wrist. Aletes backed away, ready for the final thrust. He hurried to confront Telemachus before he could recover his knife. He quickly moved forward and slashed at Telemachus' mid-section. Telemachus jumped back, narrowly avoiding the blade, but he was able to thrust his cloak-covered left hand into Aletes' helmet, blinding him for an instant. Then he pounded Aletes' shoulder with his fist as hard as he could, forcing Aletes to stumble and fall face first onto the sand. He jumped on top of Aletes with the full force of his body, landing on Aletes' back. Telemachus hoped beyond hope that his body had knocked the wind from Aletes' lungs or his position lying on top of the man would immobilize his knife arm to keep Aletes from striking again. Telemachus lay heavily on the man with all his might and weight, feeling Aletes struggling beneath him to free his right arm. Telemachus did not hesitate. He withdrew the thin-bladed dirk from beneath his tunic – the second knife his father had given him on leaving Ithaca. Without thinking, without remorse or pity, he plunged the long, sharp blade into Aletes' left kidney in the girdle below the cuirass and sliced horizontally, just as a sacrificer might crop the ligaments of the long bone of an ox, powerfully and surely. The struggling ceased almost immediately. The crowd was silent as Telemachus stood up unsteadily, his hand and tunic spattered with gore – no longer his alone. He looked down at Aletes, who remained prone in the sand. Oxylus and Autolycus rushed to Telemachus' side, pulling him away. The soldiers began to scream at each other. Infantry soldiers surrounded Aletes, shouting at the Heraclide troopers, who moved around them, threateningly. Telemachus' tablemates and the other troopers formed a wall around their generals to protect them. Although most weapons had been confiscated before the celebration, soldiers brandished knives, hammers, and a few lances. The entire crowd broke into groups eyeing each other with animosity like water dripping on smooth marble paving. And out of the firelight at the periphery of the soldiers, a wall of troopers stood with fully drawn bows and arrows.

Telemachus gave a great cry: "Wait," he shouted, with a voice so loud that everyone halted in their tracks, as if glorious Zeus himself had threatened. Oxylus and Autolycus continued to support him with his tablemates protecting them all. "Let this fight be the last," he shouted. "We are finished here. Let the bloodshed end."

With that, the red-cloaked infantry soldiers backed off slowly. Several Heraclides carried Aletes away. Telemachus, Oxylus, and Autolycus returned quickly to their camp along with all the troopers, but not before Oxylus ordered the path to the main road closed once again and additional troopers added to those on duty. The knife wounds to Telemachus were not serious. One of the physicians sewed up his left arm and cauterized the cut to his right wrist. He applied an herbal poultice and wrapped both wounds tightly with clean cloth. The scars would always be visible reminders of Telemachus' service to the Heraclides and his good fortune at having survived. The gods had blessed him.

And so as the historians tell us, the War of the Families came to an abrupt and harsh end. The rule of the Pelopides had been terminated along with the family itself. The House of Atreus was no more of this world. The four former rulers of Messenia were banished from the land that bore the names of their ancestors. Namely: Pisistratus, son of Pisistratus; Alcmaeon, son of Sillus, son of Thrasymedes; Melanthus, son of Andropompus; and Paeon, son of Antilochus. The four rulers departed and settled in Athens, where they founded the famous Alcmaeonidae and Paeonidae clans. And further, Melanthus, the non-family member, eventually came to the throne of Athens, deposing Thymoetes, son of Oxyntes, violently, the last King of Athens in the long and ancient line of Theseus. This was the same Thymoetes who had hedged his bet by refusing to give *outright support to Cresphontes and the invasion of the third crop of Heraclides.*

For the first time in history, the vast majority of the Peloponnese was united under the rule of a single family. And the Heraclides took over the great palaces of the Peloponnese. Only Aletes failed to come to the throne of Corinth, and in his stead Deiphontes became the first Heraclide to actually rule over Corinth, obedient to his uncle and father-in-law Temenus in Mycenae. Dark-eyed Aletes was buried in Pylos as a result of his injuries from the knife fight. And as they said, he never became King of Corinth, because he had never become king of himself.

In the heavens, all was strife. Although the gods were content with the close of hostilities in the Peloponnese, Zeus was once again enclosed in a black fog of despair.

For the first time, Apollo and Athene had joined forces and settled their difficulties. This had not been so thorny a problem to solve, for Tisamenus, who now occupied his place in Hades among the shades, had refused all aid. He had been chief architect of his own demise, as most of us are, but at the same time was oblivious to any potential for his own salvation. The gods took no pity on him, for he had turned out to be without redeeming virtues. He had been a limited man, spoiled by his family and raised without understanding or concern for his fellow man. He had buried his own failings so deeply within himself that he no longer saw them, and no one about him had the temerity to suggest differently. He trudged through life believing he knew what was best for others. He used his skin-deep charm, the name of the gods, and the threat of harm as one would hire a thug to put fear into the hearts of his subjects. And while fear is a most effective ruler, it is ultimately self-destructive. The gods mourned his family, but a man's choices affect others. In the view of the gods, the sons of Heracles had been only modestly better, and there was no great outburst of joy at their ascendancy. For there was much to regret about their behavior and devotion. They had prepared hollow sacrifices in form only: burnt offerings without understanding or appreciation of the immortals.

And now the Peloponnese was settled for an instant in time. The father of the gods looked out into the future. His eyes saw darkness descending on Hellas and the coming conflicts from within and without, mass migrations of people searching for better lives, and Poseidon's anger-sent tribulations of drought and fire and earthquakes. Zeus' love and hopes for his mortal children were not extinguished, but his energy for renewal flagged, at least for the moment. He gazed into the shadows of the future and knew that there was little he could do for them. Mortals had a way of escaping the best efforts of the gods to assist them and guide them in directions less destructive and more cheerful.

As always, Zeus, the lord of gods, saw out far into the future. And what he saw distressed him greatly. Although immortals are able to glimpse the future, they prefer to observe what lies closer by and avoid the pain of distant views, for the future is like a trail of tears to come. What could be more horrifying and disparaging than seeing faraway into the future and knowing what was to come...to watch time unfold instantly, not like the gentle seasons, but like flashes of memories in your mind? Zeus looked out, and he observed a bleak and deserted future, bereft of loyalty and responsibility. But he lowered the eyes within his mind to address the near-present.

"My children," he said, his annoyance having departed with his bleak thoughts. "We have weathered the storm of our mortal offspring, and they are once again returning to normalcy. That is the best that we can hope for them until one of us walks among them with the truth."

"We are not yet finished," Hera spoke to her husband. Although she hated his black moods, she had been contented with his loving behavior recently. Her mistrust and suspicions, however, were never far below the surface of her beautiful countenance.

"And how is that, my wife and daughter of my father?"

"Women's work. The toil of loom and distaff."

"You speak in dissembling words. That is unlike you."

"I speak when I am listened to, and I do not think you listen. These affairs concern women. You remember women?"

"Ah yes, women. I have fond memories."

"Then you would do well to relegate yourself to the affairs of men, for Athene and I have come to an agreement, and it bears not upon you."

"Now, once again, woman, you test my wrath. I would suggest that this next venture of yours and our daughter be constructive."

"And so it shall be," Hera replied.

"But allow me to pass on to the business of today," Zeus continued. "I want to attempt something different for the while. Perhaps young Ganymede can hurry with the cups, for the immortals have powerful thirst, as always. Now, I want to suggest a new structure to the heavens, for what has passed is past and what is to become will become.

"I have divided the dominion of the earth into four constituencies, each for a blustery Anemoi, sons of the Titans Astraios and Eos. Let each of you care for a separate region of the blow: the chilly-horned stallion, Boreas, fresh Zephyrus with his spring lyre, fiery Notus, both hot and misty, and Apeliotes, the Persian warrior from the home of Helios. Let the children of Leto, Apollo and Artemis, care for Apeliotes, and remove themselves from the care of other regions. Athene and Hermes will fly over Zephyrus and the barbarian lands."

Stealthy Hermes is not around as usual, Zeus noted to himself.

"Cold Borean climes will be the realm of Aphrodite and Dionysus, both in need of gentle cooling. And my wife and our son, Hephaestus, and angry Ares will preside over Notus. Hades will remain sealed beneath the reach of light. And my dark-haired brother, vengeful Poseidon, will continue as the bane of sailors and the builder of mountains and destroyer of reefs."

At this announcement, the gods set up a great commotion within the glorious hall, for gods do not like to be treated like children. But their rumblings were soon silenced by the terrible thunder of the anger of the father of mortals and immortals alike.

Zeus, father of us all, hoped to prevent fighting among the gods by dividing the realms of the earth. And he hoped that by this means mortals might return to joy and cheerfulness and respect for their gods. Further, he hoped that his immortal children might find a way to administer their regions of the earth for the betterment of all mortals.

But our story does not end here, beloved Alcathöe, for there is no greater story than the tale of two lovers separated in heart and mind.

LXI

The time for cutting wood clear of wormholes was soon to begin,* and the Heraclide fleet set off from Pylos. Many ships turned toward Notus, heading for Sunium and the Saronic Gulf, delivering the leaders of Messenia to Athens. The rest of the fleet, about ten long ships, including two large Phoenician-type warships, sailed in the opposite direction toward low-lying Ithaca.

The sultry heat of Helios had abated. The winds across Hellas increased in intensity, and the weather mounted rapidly, forcing many ships to stow their wings, hang their well-shaped rudders over the smoke to dry, and haul up for the winter. But this day was mild. No storms were foreseen over the next few days, as the skies were clear with only traces of high clouds, the night skies teeming with stars. The firm winds allowed the Ithaca-bound fleet to head into the cooling breath of Boreas, commencing a long tack out to sea under oar and then by force of wind to come under the lee of Zacynthus into the mouth of the Gulf of Corinth, thence to complete the voyage under oar along the lee of Cephallenia in the channel. The sailors would earn their supper this day, dipping their oars into the confused currents. The ships spread out from each other across a wide expanse of sea, always steering the same course.

In the first Phoenician galley, Polycasté sat on the forward deck with her father, King Nestor, in leather deck chairs. Troopers and their horses packed the rowing deck. Nestor was wrapped in a heavy woolen cloth, his nearly bald head covered by a thick felt cap. Together, father and daughter watched as the cliffs of their home receded into the distance. The banging of the drum and slapping of the oars in unison on the large-wide sea marked the beginning of a new life away from Pylos. Nestor accepted this change in his life as calmly as he had all the others. His narrow eyes had seen much in

---

* Winter according to Hesiod.

their time, and he was clear on the one certainty of the movement of the universe. He had counted many generations of men. His contemporaries were gone, most lost to history. Nestor had surpassed their time by three generations. At some point in aging, understanding and wisdom overcome anger in the minds of the greats, and they can observe what others cannot. This god-given capacity for vision is illusive and is only awarded to a few. But for Nestor, it rang in a firm understanding and acceptance of all that life can bring into being. He harbored no illusions. He had seen his brothers and sisters murdered as a young boy. He had buried a wife and outlived two sons. He had lived beyond his usefulness, watching grandchildren grow into tyrants. He had seen his kingdom divided and weakened and then acquired by Cresphontes. The path of Nestor's life was lined with the names and memories of people, good and bad, leaving a range of images, from vague reminiscences to passionate feelings. Now the wind blowing across the bow of the ship bore many of these names and places to his mind, as he watched their progression along the coast. The waves mounted before them; the spray from the oars rose in the air and then fell into the wake, as the ships slowly moved through the soapy seas.

Polycasté did not share her father's equanimity. She sat rigidly against the wind, a shawl wrapped around her upper body and head, with only her eyes open to view. She raged that her life was determined by the actions of men. She felt anger at the fallibility of her position and her inability to shape her own circumstances. She hated that these events had swamped her and forced her and her father from their home. She resented not only the invasion of the armies of men, but the fighting among her own brothers over the spoils of their father. The move from the palace had been a terrible blow to the family, forcing most of the servants and slaves to retire. In her way, she had fought her brothers and nephews tooth and nail for many years, but especially since returning to Pylos. But they had disregarded and ignored her efforts or brushed her aside. In her powerlessness, she had retreated further into her only enduring role, caring for her aging father. But she harbored anger like a dam.

Her own husband had left her without resort. She had struggled to live a life of service and compromise, of clarification and apology, of explaining what others meant. She felt that she had become empty and vacant, like a cracked vessel, and that the very soul of her existence, her sons, had been taken from her: first Autolycus and then Amphion. Telemachus had taken them away from her for his own hazardous purposes. He had introduced them into the appalling life of men, and now their lives had been severed from her own. She felt inert and sure that the death of her father would mark her own. She longed for the warmth of the festival of Thesmophoria and the understanding of women and prayed to Demeter to cover her with warm earth and fallen leaves. Leaving Pylos was like a long funeral march for her, and the banging of the drums and beating of the oars marked the songs and lamentations of the ages.

Pisistratus and his family were on the same ship. They kept to themselves, for it appeared that the younger Pisistratus had created a rift in the family. Although his son had departed with the others to Athens, two grown daughters, still unmarried, accompanied them. His wife seemed at a loss and was in a state of mind that left her mute and dispirited.

Telemachus and Oxylus were on the opposite galley, running parallel, along with Autolycus and Alexandros, the young phylarch and decadarch of the file of tablemates supporting Telemachus. They, too, shared quarters with a ship full of troopers and horses, surrounded by the odors of war: dirty men and horses, damp and rotting leather, and the putrefying grease of armaments. Telemachus had decided to transport two tribes to Ithaca, more as a show of strength than for any other reason. For Ithaca, Samos, and Zacynthus had no defenses of note. Even the sea peoples had long bypassed these poor islands for communities with spoils more worthy of their efforts.

Telemachus had chosen the best of the cavalry, with the most trustworthy phylarchs and decadarchs, and the most skilled men. The troopers were spread among the ships, both large and small. They spent their time on board cleaning, oiling, and polishing their armour and equipment, washing and currying their horses, allowing them to rest and rebuild their lost weight with whole barley corn and wheat, and swabbing the manure from the deck to the consternation of the sailors, who were forced to lift their feet as buckets of sea water washed the offal beneath their seats. When not working, they sat on the decks in small groups talking about their lives, which they now looked on with greater optimism. Fortunately for the sailors, the rowing became light once they came about into a course where the sails filled with wind and the *podes* lines pulled taut as the ships headed back toward the coast.

Later during the night watch, the breezes abated as they reached the lee of Zacynthus. The sailors began to take up the effort, digging deeper into the water, pulling the ships forward. Troopers had passed out dry foods and wine earlier in the evening, and now most of the passengers lay on the decks, wrapped in their cloaks against the cold air. The horses massed together for warmth and stability and slept for the most part, occasionally nickering or blustering into the wind.

LXII

When Eos rose in the sky the next morning, her amber hues outlined the bulk of the mountains of the Peloponnese toward Kaikias and covered the waters of the Gulf of Corinth with misty light. Ahead lay the island of Cephallenia, with low-lying Ithaca now visible on the distant horizon in the crisp winter air. By mid-day, they could see the mountain of Merovigli and the coastline of Ithaca. With the wind dying, they furled the sail and continued under oar along the channel. After some effort, the ships entered Polis Bay on Ithaca, a sheltered cove with a narrow expanse of beach. The clear waters of the bay danced with the surrounding colors of ochre and jade and azure. The crystalline shore was occupied by a few fishing boats, but no other ships were moored or drawn up on the beach. The Heraclide fleet filled the harbor with their azure and gold "babes" flapping in the sun. Slowly, the ships made their way toward land, the sailors jumping out of the vessels to pull them out of the water and onto the beach, forming a line like beached whales.

The troopers carefully led their horses down the gangplanks. By the time all the ships were vacated, many islanders had gathered around in a friendly manner, shyly talking to the sailors and watching as the troopers dressed and outfitted their horses. They wondered at the circumstances leading to this friendly invasion and the people involved. When informed that their king was returned, they recognized Telemachus by name only. Too much time had passed since his days on the island.

A small camp was set up on the beach before the little fishing village. Nestor and Polycasté were made comfortable for the while in a small tent. A contingent of troopers remained on the beach, while the remainder mounted their horses and filed up the hillside through the town. The path from the beach led through the main street of the village, past a sanctuary dedicated to Poseidon, and then up the rocky hillside among the modest residences and buildings built upon the limestone slopes. The narrow path, barely wide enough for two horses abreast, wound its way along the rugged sides of a dry swale formed by a seasonal stream between Mount Neion and Mount Neritum. On either side of the path, small vineyards and olive groves grew on the terraced hillsides. Pear, pomegranate, apple, fig, and nut trees surrounded the small farm huts. Late season grapes lay on cloths, turning into raisins in the declining sun. Small, neat, single-story houses of whitewashed mud, dotted the slopes, their front yards swept clean. Pine, poplar, and alder trees and dense vegetation covered the hillsides. Water was no problem on this island, as it was on many of the islands. When the streams descending from the mountains disappeared during the hot months of summer, numerous springs and wells provided ample sources. People had a saying that the land was so beautiful that birds gave milk.

The line of horse troops made its way slowly through the village, the islanders watching them as they moved up the hillside. In the sunlight, the troopers sweated in their helmets and armour, but soon the villagers were full of stories of the return of the son of Odysseus and his army. They were not sure which of the two leaders was the son, whether it was the slim one with flowing straw-colored locks and beard, or the other tiny, fine-limbed man with darkly toned complexion. And they did not ask, although they freely conversed with the soldiers, for such a question would not have been appropriate.

The palace of Odysseus sat high above the town and shore, but was set back within a col formed by the two mountains, and it could be seen only far out to sea, not from the village or harbor. It was set in the foothills of Neion and stretched out with one building abutting another across the entire hillside, with views in all directions, but particularly of the bays toward Kaikias: Aphales and Phrikes. The palace was built of bright stones, the only stone building of size on the entire island, with the surfaces of the walls reflecting the light. In places, it was two stories high, with open balconies above. Odysseus had carefully constructed a high surrounding wall, entirely encircling the structure for defense. Heavy double-folded doors of fine workmanship in the front of the outer courtyard prevented entry.

Telemachus led the troopers to the palace, with Oxylus and Autolycus following close behind. Autolycus viewed the structure with amazement. He knew every stone and column from the stories of his childhood. The grounds and walls of the palace were clean and cared for, without vines or creepers. The exterior of the building was large and imposing, with the carved front gates closed. But from within, the sounds of a lyre and the smell of roasted meat welcomed them. Telemachus dismounted and knocked on the gates with a giant bronze knocker in the shape of a boar's head. The sharp thump of the knocker echoed in the courtyard, and they heard the sounds of someone hurrying to the gate. First one gate opened and then the next, and before them stood Adrastos, son of Eumaeus.

"Welcome, master." He ran forward to clutch Telemachus' hand, first kissing him on the head, then the shoulders, and finally both of his eyes.

"Adrastos, much time has passed," Telemachus laughed, finally gently pushing the man away. "We have returned."

"So I see," Adrastos admitted, eying the mounted troopers behind Telemachus. "We have known of your coming return for many days. Ever since the day Amphion arrived."

"Amphion is here?"

"Yes. He came in a ship much like the ones that brought you." Then he saw Autolycus still mounted. "Young sir. Come here."

Autolycus jumped from his horse and came into the arms of the son of Eumaeus, who held him as one would hold a son returning from the wars.

"And word came this morning," Adrastos continued, not relinquishing his hold on Autolycus, "that you were returning with many ships. We have set out meats and foods for you." But as he looked farther out into the entrance, he glimpsed the large number of horses and troopers still arriving. "But I had no idea."

"Do you have animals?"

"We have the pigs of my father, the cattle of your father, and more sheep and goats than you can throw a stick at. Come in. Come in. Penelope awaits. No one will starve this day."

Telemachus turned and ordered the troops dismounted, feeling that this show had served little purpose. Who could object to a man returning to his home?

"Oxylus, can you see to a cart and an escort of troopers to bring King Nestor and Polycasté here to honor their arrival? They need their rest, both of them. And I suggest that the remainder of the troopers remove their armour and store their weapons on the side. We appear to have come upon a celebration: the celebration of our return. Autolycus, follow me."

And they, father and son, entered the courtyard together. Everything looked clean and well-kempt. Giant earthenware vases stood along the walls with date palms, papyrus, and flowers growing from them. The grounds were spotless. And when they proceeded into the inner courtyard, a large fire burned with spitted meats around it, and servants rushing about in response to the unexpected large number of mouths to feed. The servants noted the return of the son of Odysseus. Only the oldest had seen him before. They bowed as he passed. Extra meats were being added to the fire to roast. They quickly set up additional tables with all sorts of good things for the troopers to eat. A man walked about playing a pan-flute, with the children of the servants running and dancing behind him. Adrastos led the two men into the shade of the atrium. Stairs on either side of the large room led up to an open second-floor balcony. At the base of the stairs stood Penelope watching her only son. A servant stood next to her, holding her arm. She began slowly walking forward but only managed a few steps before Telemachus was with her, holding her in his arms, carefully examining her as one might scrutinize a precious jewel.

She had aged. She appeared tiny, smaller than before, and light-boned as a bird. The tight translucent skin of her face and her white hair severely pulled back into a bun at her neck gave her a haughty and regal appearance. She was entirely covered in a long flowing tunic of dark violet linen, the color of the kermes worm, with sculptured gold pins at each shoulder. But the smile on her face and in her eyes erased many of the years, and the joy at the sight of her son and grandson gently erupted from her with joyous tears flowing down her cheeks. She too searched the face of her son. Autolycus stood behind Telemachus.

"And look at you, you have become a man," she said, embracing her grandson, who carefully returned the embrace. "The one and only benefit of war is that it takes boys of all ages and, those who return, do so as men."

"Mother, you do not know how good it is to be at home." Telemachus said. "You managed so well in my absence. Everything looks better than when we left. You included. And Amphion is here?"

"Yes," Penelope replied, "and every day he is getting stronger."

"I will go see him," Autolycus said, quickly ascending the rest of the stairs and disappearing down the hallway to the bedroom suites, knowing exactly where he would find his brother, although he had never been in the palace before.

"Yes, dear child. Always in such a hurry." She turned back to Telemachus. "Lacestades, son of Hippolytus, came with him. Such a nice man and so helpful. You must thank him for me. They showed me the great ship that brought him here. Never have I seen such a vessel."

"Mother, we brought guests to stay with us. Nestor, who is far older than you, will be staying here. Polycasté has been taking care of him. Pisistratus, the son of Nestor, and his family will also be staying with us for a while."

"Where is Polycasté? We have much to discuss."

"She will be here shortly."

"You know, I never met Nestor. You think I would have met him after all these years. He is practically a living god, such is his reputation. When Odysseus first arrived home, he spoke of him alone and his stewardship of the Achaeans at Troy. I will welcome him and his family personally this evening."

Telemachus did not contradict her.

"Everyone is welcome here, for as long as they need be," Penelope continued. "The house has been too long vacant. The servants are many, and the house is large. Now I must take care of myself. I no longer have much vigor for long periods, but rather need my rest during the lengthy afternoons, and I am afraid all this excitement has tired me." She signaled for the servant, who had remained at her side during the conversation. "There will be many stories to tell and much to discuss this evening. Send Polycasté to me when she arrives. Until then..." and with the help of the servant, she turned and made her way toward the back of the atrium to her rooms on the ground floor.

Telemachus mounted the stairs in the direction Autolycus had taken to visit Amphion. He found the two brothers deep in conversation.

"So," he said, "Lacestades brought you here. I am very glad." He leaned over the bed to embrace his son. "How is the leg?"

"Stronger, but full of pain when I walk. I am told that the pain is a good thing, because it signals the renewal occurring within."

"It will take time."

"I know," Amphion admitted. "I missed much, so Autolycus tells me."

"You accomplished as much as any man among us. And you avoided the disintegration. And now you have the chance to recuperate in your own home."

"I like it here, almost as much as Elis. Maybe I will return with Autolycus."

"How is that?"

Autolycus looked guiltily at his father. "Oxylus has offered me a position at Elis. And I wish to build up the cattle herds of grandfather on the estates. I am returning to Elis. I planned on telling you."

"So, Oxylus would steal my sons, as well. And you would follow in the path of your ancestor and namesake, the cattle thief. But there is time to discuss this."

LXIII

When Nestor and Polycasté arrived at the palace, servants rushed to welcome them, helped them up the stairs, and showed them to their rooms on the upper floor. Nestor's own servants awkwardly watched in surprise. Penelope's servants had set up a bright and sunny suite of rooms with fresh flowers overflowing their vases, fruits and sweets, shutters open to allow the sun to heat the room, and wide views of Phrikes Bay and the village of Reithron. Nestor's servants then set about to prepare the rooms exactly to Nestor's requirements, and he was soon resting comfortably in his large bed.

Once Polycasté was settled in her large room, she went in search of Penelope. A young servant girl showed her to Penelope's apartments on the ground floor. The girl clapped and pulled aside the woven curtain to allow Polycasté entrance.

The dark hallway suddenly awoke to the bright afternoon light coming from the window openings. Sunlight fell directly into the room and was reflected by the roof overhang and the colored mosaic floor of the bedroom. The shutters in the rear of the room were wide open, allowing Apeliotes' jasmine-scented breezes to warm the room. Penelope was propped up in her bed, with sewing in her lap. At the headboard was a large natural stump of an olive tree, polished and inlaid in gold and silver and ivory, with an awning of crimson leather stretched above the entire bed.

Polycasté sat down next to her mother-in-law on the side of the bed. Penelope took Polycasté's hand gently in her own.

"You are home at last."

"Thank you," Polycasté said. "I had nowhere to go," but she held her head down and did not meet the older woman's caring eyes.

"My dearest, I know what you have suffered. But that is over now. Your father is safe here. And your two beautiful sons are returned and well and within these walls. Your husband is a man.

Now, it is your time. We must never let them rob us of our own time. Never."

Polycasté shyly glanced into Penelope's eyes for the first time, and the tears began to flow. She lowered her head into her hands. Penelope placed her arm around Polycasté. The silent heaving sobs continued for some while.

"Sometimes, we must clear away the cobwebs and start again," Penelope said. "But we are always stronger for it."

"I am so sorry. I did not mean to be so pitiable."

"Nonsense. We have much to discuss…the two of us."

"I feel like a blade of grass, all dried up and blown about by the wind."

"I know exactly, my child. Now, it is your time, which is so important. Dexithea will draw your bath and scent and oil your body. First we clean. Then we seek the boon of rest. Then we make ourselves into the goddesses that exist within all of us. Tonight, you can have your choice of Helen's robes, for many were returned to me from Lacedaemon. She knew her way with garments that enhanced her beauty, as you know from your own beautiful wedding dress given to Telemachus by Helen. But such a silly woman she was. They say she dwells in the Elysian Fields with Menelaus, her cuckold, poor man, but I have my doubts. Now off to bath with you."

Telemachus and Oxylus spent the afternoon preparing camp outside of Odysseus' palace. The horses were pastured on corn lands that now were full of grasses and weeds, the feed corn having been harvested many moons ago. The troopers set up tents in an orderly fashion. But for the next few days, the population of Ithaca would be overturned by the sudden appearance of soldiers and sailors. The wine shop was full of young men, and the bakery soon ran out of bread. The town water supply failed for the first time in memory. When the fishermen returned to the harbor with their early morning catch of rock fish, squid, anchovies, and several large tunny fish, it all disappeared immediately. The sailors and troopers had to be carefully supervised in town and along the trails of the island, so that they did not upset the lives of the residents. As much as possible, they remained in the hills. But with spare time, such separation was difficult to maintain.

Telemachus sent heralds out to Cephallenia, Zacynthus, and Dulichium, announcing his return and ordering a meeting of the archons of the islands. They were told to assemble on Ithaca at the palace in three day's time in the early market hour or suffer the consequences. Telemachus knew they would come. Word was out of the upheaval in the Peloponnese, and the archons feared for their own survival.

Ithaca would not be able to support this large influx of troopers for long, and the ships must begin departing as soon as possible. There was no military reason to keep the entire complement of soldiers on the island, but Telemachus wanted the archons to be greeted by the sight of this army and navy. Once an agreement had been secured, he would release the troopers and sailors to sail to Corinth to seek their recompense from Temenus. It was no use seeking out Cresphontes in Pylos. Telemachus asked a few of his best soldiers to settle on Ithaca permanently, offering to help them build homes and bring their families to live here. The soldiers could serve possibly as a defensive force against outsiders and also provide assistance in case of internal difficulties. Mainly, though, these were men Telemachus respected, who had much to offer to a small island village. The influx of new families would be good for the island, for this was now happening throughout the Peloponnese.

Oxylus was chafing at the bit to return to Elis. He had no business on Ithaca, other than helping Telemachus in the final steps of their arrangement with the Heraclides. He had much to accomplish in Elis and wanted to begin immediately. He had promised Telemachus he would wait until after the meeting of the archons of the offshore islands. He also wanted to understand this island better, and how it came about that such a small landmass had become so important to all of Hellas and, in fact, to the whole world.

Several days after their arrival, both the interior and exterior courtyards were prepared for celebration of the return of the family to Ithaca. The weather was holding, the rains not yet begun, and the sun was still strong. The entire population of the island was invited. As Helios began to duck behind the mountains on Cephallenia, with the final rays falling on the peak of Neion, people dressed in their finest began to gather in the courtyards: women in bright colors with their tresses piled high, and men in their natural linen robes and cloaks. Giant bonfires warmed both courtyards. Strolling entertainers played lyres and flutes, while children from the village performed local dances with bronze cymbals and castanets and sang to the tune of the pipers.

The troopers were on their best behavior, but they too were anxious to begin their new lives. The fighting had ended. They were anxious that the next step should begin. No small few doubted that anything would come of their sacrifice to the Heraclides' cause, so accustomed had they become to the disreputable actions of the Heraclide leadership. Tonight, though, was their night.

Telemachus walked among the guests, greeting and reintroducing himself to people he had grown up with but had not seen since his boyhood. He did not recognize anyone; he greeted all and introduced Autolycus. It had been generations since the family had departed the island; even so, in his heart he knew the memories of the people returned immediately to the controversy of the suitors and their deaths. No one said anything directly, of course, although many asked about his father. As he was introduced to people from the island, he knew exactly to which suitor they were related. Odysseus had killed Antinous, son of Eupeithes, first off. His brothers and sisters still lived on the island, but they were too old to attend. His son, though, listened to the flute player. Telemachus had killed Amphinomus, son of Nisus, with a spear; his nephews sipped wine in the exterior courtyard. Odysseus had killed Eurymachus, son of Polybus, one of the meanest of the suitors in his scandalous actions with the servants, shooting an arrow through his breast. His youngest son, a wealthy man, now broke bread with two troopers. Odysseus had killed Eurynomus, son of Aegyptius, from one of the best families of Ithaca. He was represented by two spinster daughters, standing off from the crowd. The second cousins of indignant Liodes, slain by Odysseus, now welcomed Telemachus. And there were others. And this could be repeated at Zacynthus, Dulichium, and Samos. The generation that had grown up with Laertes had now departed. The generation of Odysseus was agèd, and many had left the earth. The suitors had been younger, but they too were now elderly. No one had forgotten.

The celebration came to a standstill when Penelope and Polycasté appeared on the porch. They stood on the columned façade rising above the inner courtyard. Their personal servants stood behind them. Penelope held Polycasté's arm for support, as they surveyed the courtyard: the fire with spitted meats and smoke rising into the night air, the tables piled with all sorts of foods, and the many guests and soldiers. Both wore long silk tunics, with light cloaks over their gowns, held by large carved gold clasps. Both were draped in gold: Penelope wore a wide necklace of gold shells and long gold earrings; Polycasté had a gold diadem that had belonged to her mother, gold bracelets on both bare arms, and a gold breastplate. A line soon formed to greet them; such was Penelope's reputation. She rarely appeared in public on Ithaca, and many of the townspeople had only glimpsed her in her comings and goings. The soldiers could only stand in awe of these two beautiful women.

Telemachus joined them to help with the introductions. He was dressed in a light gray tunic with a white cloak. He greeted his mother with a buss on each cheek and his wife in a similar fashion, discarding the thought that he had not touched her in several years, but noting the color in her face and her sweet lilac scent. Autolycus came to them as well, and the family stood on the porch receiving the guests one by one.

At his own request, Nestor's servants carried him down on a chair, and he sat for a while receiving people who gathered to greet a living legend. Amphion too was helped down to the celebration and sat next to his grandfather. The sky was clear, and the fire and oil sconces lit the courtyard, and for a moment people paid homage to the living past without rancor. The soldiers lined up to bow before King Nestor, who had traveled to Troy and guided the Achaeans to victory. To them, he was a man of mythic proportions: a living legend.

Shortly after this, everyone gathered in the outer courtyard around the great fire pit, which Odysseus called the altar of Zeus, where the savor of many sacrifices had reached to the gods. A tremendous white ox was led into the outer courtyard. After the two village priests prayed to the gods, one killed the beast with an axe to the brain junction, while the other quickly slit the animal's throat, allowing the blood to flow into the fire pit. With razor-sharp knives, they butchered the animal and piled his leg bones with fatty meats on top of the coals. Almost immediately the odorous smoke rose gently into the sky, and the good smells of roasted meat and barley filled the courtyard. The fire spat and sparked, with flames jumping around the carcass, burning the fatty meats and bones, forcing the crowd backwards. Everyone joined in singing a hymn to the gods, feeling that this was a special evening and seeing peace and good fortune stretching out before them as far as they could imagine. The soldiers combined for a song commonly sung before battle, but they offered it as a paean at a slow, elegiac pace. And at the termination of the song, a flute set a faster pace, and the soldiers broke out into a wild dance from the Borean climes, each man attempting to outdo the others.

After the burnt offerings, meats were served, and everyone ate and drank to their heart's content. The soldiers had not eaten a meal like this since before the war, and even that did not compare. The wine and water flowed, and good cheer was everywhere. For a moment in the inner court, Telemachus spoke to the assembly from the stairs:

"I would like to welcome you all to the palace of Odysseus. I welcome you for my mother and for myself and my family. We are reunited for the first time in many years. We have all traveled on separate, divergent paths, sometimes jointly and sometimes separately, and now the paths have converged at a single location on this sparkling evening. I would like to welcome Nestor, King of all of Messenia and hero of the Trojan War. We are privileged to be in his presence. And my mother and wife of Odysseus, as beautiful as an almond tree with the first blush of white blooms. And my wife, Polycasté, as enchanting as summer lilac, and my two boys, Amphion and Autolycus, both heroes of the Heraclides.

"We are also joined this evening by Oxylus, son of Haemon, and King of Elis. For he compassed the victory of the Heraclides over the Peloponnese. I owe my life to him. He is my brother, and I wish him well in his new duties, for he is taking my son, Autolycus, to be general of the Eleans. They will continue construction of our farm in Elis, where Odysseus found fulfillment in raising the finest cattle in all of the Peloponnese. I, too, found satisfaction there in raising two fine boys and many fine horses with the love and compassion of my wife Polycasté.

"I want to tell you a true story that bears retelling. Once a strange child was born with goat feet, horns, and a long beard, which became pronounced as he grew. His own parents were disgusted by their son and disowned him, exposing him to the elements. But soon enough all the gods and the animals of the forest came to love him and care for him. With an ear for sounds, he became skilled in music and invented all kinds of wonderful musical instruments. He played tunes for the creatures of the forest and meadows and for the godly winds. He became a herder.

"One day, Apollo heard his tunes and came to earth to compete with the herder, for Apollo believed that no mortal, or immortal, for that matter, could play music better than he. Rhadamanthys evaluated the competition. After carefully listening to first Apollo and than the young herder, Rhadamanthys selected the herder as the better musician. Apollo became so angry that he turned Rhadamanthys into an ass and sent him to Hades, but he could not punish the young man, whose beautiful sounds charmed even him. Instead, he turned the herder into a god. And for all eternity, no one is more skilled in music than he, not even Apollo. We can hear his beautiful music played by the winds and streams and birds and insects, for his name is Pan. Pan lives among us. Listen."

For a moment, silence engulfed the guests, and the sounds of the night filled the courtyard.

"The gods are among us. May they protect us and bless us with peace and happiness. And may Ithaca always enjoy the goodness of wisdom and respect."

LXIV

The archons began arriving at Ithaca by ship early on the appointed day. Their first view was of warships patrolling Polis Bay. All ships were stopped and searched, and then accompanied to the port. On shore, soldiers armed and in uniform directed them to the palace. A few troopers patrolled on horseback, but most were on foot. The archons were made to sit in the large meeting hall, until all had arrived. No servants appeared to offer refreshments or food, and no fire was set in the fire pit. The atmosphere was so uncomfortable and harsh that the men refused to talk even to each other. They silently surveyed the halls of the palace and thought they recognized the signs of struggle and death. As their eyes moved around the hall, they also encountered soldiers standing along the walls at attention with lances and swords.

Finally, Telemachus and Oxylus entered the room. About twenty men sat on the couches in the large hall. They were well dressed, older, with only a few young men among them. Most were from the generation of Telemachus – the sons, grandsons, or nephews of the suitors of Penelope. Telemachus opened the discussions:

"Welcome to Ithaca and the palace of Odysseus. Let me first address the past and then describe the present. More than twenty-five years ago, my father, King Odysseus returned to his home from Troy, after an absence of nineteen years. As king of Ithaca, Cephallenia, Zacynthus, and Dulichium, he had led the brave soldiers from this region against the Trojans, and twelve ships departed these coasts. None returned. All the brave men with Odysseus perished. Many times in the voyages of my father, he, himself, came perilously close to entering the house of Hades. And he returned with all the scars of battle, some visible, but most buried deeply within.

"He profoundly regretted the deaths of his brave warriors, but what disturbed him the most was the despicable behavior of the so-called suitors of my mother. We all know the story well of their profligacy with the wealth of another, and the basic injustice of their pose, assuming that Odysseus was dead and that they should somehow inherit the throne by marrying the queen of these lands. After years away, he returned to these circumstances of contumely and outrageous behavior. These men, whom we all knew well at that time, were the finest crop of youth of this region. They had feasted, game-played, and secretly planned atrocities, while others fought mightily to return from this war of Hellas against her neighbors. Ordinarily, Odysseus might have been more understanding, but under the circumstances of his return, he had no patience for these men, who continued even in his presence to act with contempt in the very household that was providing their sustenance.

"I repeat this oft-told tale only to remind us that Odysseus was punished for his behavior, regardless of how much he was wronged and what crimes were perpetrated by the suitors – for suitors was a common word for an uncommon transgression. By the judgment of Neoptolemus, Odysseus was banished from his hereditary post as king of these islands and died without ever returning to his home or regaining his position. And believe me, he punished himself more than anyone. He now lies buried in Elis, far from the land of his fathers. He has received his punishment.

"And he was not the only one who paid for his actions. His family was also punished. His wife was banished with him, and remained away from her home until after his death. And I, his son, was forced to raise a family and make a livelihood outside of these islands and never returned once, even to visit my mother after she resettled here.

"Now, we have completed a military operation that has changed the landscape of all the Peloponnese. Oxylus, son of Haemon and King of Elis, who stands beside me, and I led the forces of the Heraclides against the Pelopides. We have concluded all operations, and Temenus and Cresphontes now rule where Tisamenus, son of Orestes, once held court. The Pelopides, those few who remain on earth, are now exiled, and the Heraclides sit in the seats of power in all the great palaces. As a final step, we have returned to the offshore islands to take over the hereditary position of our family."

At this, the archons began grumbling, but Telemachus signaled for their silence.

"Over the years, I have learned about the interests of my fellow men. I have led men in peace and in war, and I have counseled at the highest levels of state. I stand before you with an open mind and a desire to see our region take its rightful place among the nations of Hellas. We are independent of the Heraclides and owe them nothing. We are allied closely with Elis and hope to work with that nation to strengthen both regions.

"All Hellas is suffering from three directions: migrations from the direction of Boreas and invasions and attacks from Notus. The third direction is from within, for many people are dissatisfied and have no recourse save violence. We need to have a strong defense to protect our towns and villages. But more importantly, we need to be stewards of our future, to see our children grow up healthy and with food on the table. This region cannot continue as a group of independent islands, but must combine forces to compass our future and the future of our children.

"We do not mean to impose our rule by force of arms. We are committed by the rule of the council of archons and plan to work closely with you. But let me be clear, the family has returned, and we intend to continue the traditional rule of the great kings: Odysseus, Laertes, Arcisius, and Cephalus, after whom this region is named."

Again, the archons grew restless and desired to debate the issues. Telemachus raised his hands: "We will not turn this into some kind of negotiation. The basic question is settled and will remain so. But I will listen to one of you as spokesman to address your concerns. I remind you, we do not want to return under force of arms, and when you return to your homes, you must consider what is best for the islands."

A short, fat man rose from the center of the archons. "I am Eurymachus, son of Eurymachus. It grieves me to sit here where my father was killed without fair contest, trapped and then murdered. And now I find that the rule of law is contradicted, and we must deal with the murderers. I would rather be in a den of wolves than sit here and be treated as though I had committed some crime. It is true that the offshore islands have struggled of late, but we are capable of ruling ourselves. And we will continue to do so. I see that nothing has changed on the horizon. I give not a fig for the rulers in Corinth or Sparta. Of what import are they to me? I agree that excesses by the suitors occurred, but the penalty of an unjust death did not fit the nature of the crime. And I know that you, Telemachus, were an instigator and one of the murderers. I can point to people in this room who were raised without a father on your account alone. How can you step forward and suggest that you have any right to rule?"

At this, there was a general note of agreement, and one of the oldest of the archons rose to address the assembly:

"As you all know, I am Antenor, son of Antinous, son of Eupeithes. My family has lived in Ithaca for generations. Not only did I lose a father, but I lost a cousin, Amphimedon, son of Melaneus. We are a generation of fatherless children, raised by resentful mothers. How can we be ruled by a person with blood on his hands, regardless of his good intentions? We came to Penelope when she first returned to Ithaca and suggested that she choose a successor to her husband, but instead she said that the gods would tell us soon enough. I have seen no sign here of divine intervention, and I thus assume that the decision is up to the leaders of the offshore islands and no others. I do not deny your native right to the throne, but I am of the opinion that the ruling of Neoptolemus is still in force. Although I welcome you here to your home, never would we agree to your taking the throne of your ancestors. And I think that this would be a unanimous decision among us." And indeed the others approved his statement with their voices.

Telemachus raised his arm. "Do not be quick to judgment and narrow in your views. I, too, was a fatherless child and suffered a resentful mother. I number myself among your generation. We are an assemblage who will never forget what transpired and will never overcome our feelings. But the forces of change are constant, and although we may be tainted by the excesses of our fathers, we do not want this to continue indefinitely. We cannot allow ourselves to color the destiny of our children and the future of our islands. We have all suffered. One cannot weigh suffering and say that one man has suffered more than another like a butcher at his scales. A man's pain can be felt only by himself, alone.

"But you make one mistake. I am not here to take the throne of my father and his father before him, and I never suggested that. Your anger and emotions have misled your conclusions. And I agree to your judgment, for the blood of your fathers has never been far from my mind. I accept responsibility for these actions and the actions of my father, just as you must accept responsibility for the actions of your fathers. Your judgment is correct. The throne of Ithaca and the offshore islands will never be taken by one with the blood of our citizens on his hands. But just as well, it will not be taken by one whose actions were no better than a thief seeking to loot another man's wealth, to creep ignominiously into another man's bed, and to compass the murder of his son. Enough. Now you will agree to my own judgment." He glanced at Oxylus, as the archons raised their voices in complaint.

"You will return to your homes and send word to us of your allegiance to the family of Odysseus, or we will be forced to take action. I hope that is clear.

"I would like to introduce you to the new king of Ithaca, Cephallenia, Zacynthus, and Dulichium, to whom you will pay allegiance. He is outside this hall and will greet you as you depart. I give you three days to send your words of allegiance, and if I do not receive word, I will assume that you refuse to recognize the king and therefore oppose him. I suggest you consider this carefully. I thank you, sirs, for attending this meeting and look forward to working with you on the governing council."

After this, Telemachus signaled to the soldiers, who moved from the wall and began shepherding the confused archons into the atrium. Telemachus and Oxylus were careful to thank each man and to embrace each one as he left the meeting hall. Slowly, the archons filed past, somewhat sheepishly, attempting to maintain their dignity and poise as they were moved out into the atrium to greet their new king. They knew they would have had to accept Telemachus as king, if he had pushed hard enough, and they were surprised by his concession. They all wanted to continue in their positions of power within their own communities and with the influences of their families. Now, it was merely a question of whom they would have to deal with. Although they expressed thanks to Telemachus and Oxylus, their minds had already entered the next room and their future.

In the center of the atrium in a leather chair sat the next king of Ithaca, Cephallenia, Zacynthus, and Dulichium, with soldiers on either side. As the archons filed past, each one greeted him with some surprise and then was shown out by the soldiers.

Alone in the hall, Telemachus and Oxylus turned to each other.

"You played that very well. I am convinced you will have no problem," Oxylus said, slapping his friend on the back. "Long before three days time, they will send their whole-hearted concurrence and expressions of fealty. For like many things in life, they have little choice."

"I only wanted to allow them their self-respect. I am hopeful that the next generation will do better."

"If your sons are an indication," Oxylus smiled, "tomorrow will be a better day."

Satisfied with themselves, they embraced and walked out into the atrium together to greet the new king, who sat alone. The archons and soldiers had departed.

"Help me out of this chair," fair-minded Amphion called. "No matter my exalted position, I need more time to heal. The hand of heaven has been laid hard upon me."

LXV

"This is not a woman's world," Penelope said, "but it is the world we inhabit between birth and death. We can no more expect it to change, than we can hope that Helios will reverse directions."

Penelope rested in her bed with her son and daughter-in-law sitting on either side facing her. The servants had removed themselves. It was late at night, and Ithaca had returned to its ordinary sleepy humdrum activities in the absence of the Heraclide soldiers. The troopers had returned by ship to Corinth, all except Alexandros, the young trooper from Zacynthus, and several others who had settled on Ithaca with their families. The only horse left on Ithaca, Sterope, daughter of Eous, daughter of Bronte, now shared a pasture with two asses in the foothills of Neritum; many of the other warhorses had been transported back to their home pastures of Elis. Water once again flowed in excess from the fountains of the town. Fishermen now were forced to barter their catch with the local wives at poorer returns, and the wine shop was vacant once again, reduced to filling the occasional cask or drinking cup.

Of those archons who had attended Telemachus' assembly on Ithaca, all swiftly sent heralds expressing congratulations and allegiance to King Amphion of Ithaca and the offshore islands. Even Antenor, son of Antinous, came the next morning with cap in hand to salute the new king and pledge his loyalty.

After this, Oxylus returned to Elis with Autolycus, to begin building up the farm and expanding the herd of cattle with the new breeds created by Odysseus. Pisistratus quickly found life on Ithaca too uneventful and took his family to Athens, where he would have more opportunities to make a life for himself. As for Telemachus, he placed his life on hold for the interregnum, for the official coronation of Amphion would take place next month in Same, and Telemachus would be invested in the assembly. During this period, he began rebuilding the garden of Laertes and caring for the vineyard and olive groves, for whereas Adrastos was an excellent servant and house manager, he was no gardener.

A few days before, a Heraclide long ship had arrived under guard, sent from Temenus in Corinth and containing a large cargo. As the herald explained, it was Telemachus' share of the spoils of the victorious Heraclides for service beyond all expectations. The herald went on to relay the pledge by the Heraclides of everlasting affection and debt to Telemachus. Among the objects, he recognized the heavy gold statuette of Hera, almost too heavy to heft, which he had first seen in the treasury of Corinth. He momentarily fingered the folds of the long gown and the apple blossom branch, but returned the exquisite statue to the crate along with the other objects. He had the box transferred secretly to Odysseus' vaults to remain sight unseen and unpacked along with Odysseus' treasure returned from Elis.

After life in the palace returned to routine, Penelope had requested a meeting with Telemachus and Polycasté, who were distant and casting an unsettled dark cloud of discontent over the entire house. Polycasté and Nestor lived in one wing of the palace on the second floor, and Telemachus had taken to sleeping many nights in his grandfather's hut in the hills. But with the change in climate and rains, he had been forced back into the palace and was staying in a downstairs room. Polycasté shared her time with Nestor, who never left his suite, and with Penelope, who began once again to teach her weaving and dressmaking. Penelope found Polycasté changed from when they had lived together in Elis. A spark had departed. Polycasté went through the motions of her life, but like an injured bird, the flights of joy and humor had departed.

And Penelope told her, "If the gods are to vouchsafe you happier times in your age, you must seek respite from the goddess Misfortune. For misfortune comes from within, and no one was dealt a heavier blow than I or understands misfortune as well."

This evening in her bedroom, Penelope had requested the presence of both of her children: Telemachus and Polycasté. Penelope was elegantly made up for the occasion, her hair tightly trussed, and her eyes darkly highlighted. A beautiful lavender silk shawl covered her shoulders. The servants had carefully arranged the bed cloths about her thin legs. The exquisite bed cover had been woven of rare purple and golden threads on her loom with her own hands.

She began what she told herself was "the final chore in my life, but not a disagreeable one." She had seen many unexpected twists and turns in the path of her life, but she had met each unforeseen alteration head-on to the best of her ability and according to her finest thoughts. She had gladly listened to the advice of others but always returned in the end to her own counsel. She had been strong and resolute in her beliefs, but now as she attempted to navigate the hidden shoals of personal feelings among her children, she felt that adamantine honesty could be her only guide.

Penelope began softly, gently, allowing her head to sink into the cushions at her back, one hand held by Telemachus and the other by Polycasté, her eyes no longer perceiving objects in the room but set on distant visions within her head:

"Beautiful, wide-eyed Hera, second of the children of Cronos, full of resolve and independence, come hither to me and bless me, O Queen of Heaven, and hearken to my words for I sing to you first and foremost. Give me the command of my thoughts and your facility to dispute among the immortals with triumph. Nurture me by the puissance of my words and the resolution of your clear vision and your indomitable spirit in the face of adversity, just as you nurture the entire mortal world."

And then, she continued more forcefully as the sureness of her words and the past took hold.

"It is fitting that I begin with my ancestors, for it is from our inherited past that we grow to our greatest strength and find our reservoir of resources in times of trial or weakness. I come from a family of strong-willed women, whether right or wrong. My mother, as you know, my dear, was also called Polycasté, daughter of Lygaeus. So I have a fondness for this name and for you. My mother taught me weaving and always made me aware that women must develop a handiwork, but cannot depend on that alone, and must take pride in an excellent mind and be ready to call upon strong and resolute nature to deal with the trials that life will bring. Mother always prayed to Athene, the goddess of the warp and the weft, for her independence and bearing. She often said that the strength of the household depends on the heddle rod and sword-beater. A cloth that is not woven tightly cannot endure. It is up to the weaver to join the threads with great strength so they might never be parted. I still hear her voice saying, "the sounds of worthless murmurings do not go unheeded, so keep your tongue in check.'

"My father was called Icarius, son of Oebalus, King of Sparta. He was the brother of Tyndareus, whose famous daughter, Helen, was my cousin and the cause of so many tears and so much heartbreak. Tyndareus' other daughter, Clytemnestra, became famous in her own right when she took revenge on her husband, Agamemnon, brother to Menelaus, for the two brothers married two sisters. But this was many years afterwards, for the wisest among us soon learn that we have only one thing of value in life: time. Time is the most precious gift given by the gods, for it places value and worth on the simplest of activities, yet many people fritter it away like so many borage flowers along a stream.

"Our family was born of Zeus and the Pleiade, Taygete, destined to be a family of two hands, one of intelligence and the other of obligation and labor; to act correctly in all things as though attending an important dinner party, while always being devoted to doing what was considered right and excellent...to our detriment, I might add...for there are times in life when you may desire with all your heart to depart and to do as others would expect, rather than standing up honestly and respectfully for yourself, regardless of the consequences. I pray to Athene that this lesson be schooled among all people.

"Icarius was the younger brother to Tyndareus and always stood in awe of him, who would become King of Sparta at a young age. When Icarius married Polycasté, my mother, he had a stroke of good fortune. Yes, some say that she was more beautiful than Helen herself, with long fair hair and eyes and skin as bright as the fruit of the soft-shelled almond. Her children were Damasippus, Thoas, Aletes, Alyzeus, Perileos, Leucadius, Iphthime, and Imeusimus, and all are now dead and buried and living in the house of Hades. Each of my brothers and sisters had a story — each with lovers and children, each with joy and pain — and I could pass the night relating their travails. We were a loving family, raised as a single family with the children of Tyndareus on a large estate of many slaves in Lacedaemon. Being the youngest, I was treated like a precious fruit and could do nothing for myself, but was encircled by love and care. It was my mother who kept my feet grounded. She said to take aim at great things and never to settle for lesser attainment. For if you attempt the latter, you will certainly never achieve the former.

"My mother's greatest achievement was to separate Icarius from Tyndareus, so that he could become a man in his own right, out from the under the shadow of his older and more famous brother. His father, Oebalus, never envisioned Icarius as king, but only the brother of a king. And as any mother will tell you, all sons must be kings. That is exactly the route that Polycasté, my mother, took with her husband, and here is how she accomplished it.

"At the death of King Oebalus, my uncle Tyndareus became king of Lacedaemon, but only for a short period, for soon after that Hippocoon, son of Oebalus by a different woman, took the throne through deceit and violence and expelled our family. Helen, Clytemnestra, and I were girls at the time, not old enough to note the change in our lives, but not so young as to be without memory of the palace in Lacedaemon and our charmed lives. We went to live in high Pleuron above the Gulf of Corinth, where we lived for the while under the rule of King Thestius, and under circumstances that had little in common with our life in Sparta, and this has always stayed with me and given me an expanded understanding that people are different and their actions can be understood by looking at their families and upbringings. So many people today are raised in unimaginable circumstances of wealth without care and have no respect or understanding of the circumstances of others. I think that both of you are free of this illusion, however.

"My father and uncle fought in many wars against our neighbors in Aetolia and were often gone long from home, but returned with the spoils of their battles, with gold and slaves and dreadful stories, so I, like you, became accustomed to the life of men at an early age. But at this time, dreadful Heracles came to the Peloponnese and killed Hippocoon and his sons and restored the throne to my uncle Tyndareus, who gladly returned to Lacedaemon. And here my mother saw her opportunity and offered my father the choice of returning to Sparta to be the brother of the king or to remain in Pleuron and to be husband to his wife and father to his children. He chose the latter and never regretted it. He continued to be an advisor to King Thestius, and he was given much land in Acarnania, where my fine-looking brothers ruled for many years, and their descendants rule to this day, although regrettably I never see them nor talk with them and do not know them. I remember thinking as a young girl, seeing my playmate cousins return to the wealth and privilege of Lacedaemon, that my father had made a great sacrifice in not returning to the palace. But now I know that he needed my mother's help in making the decision, and that in the end it was the correct one.

"Of my cousins, Helen and Clytemnestra, I can only say that at times, most often when we were young, we were silly and slaves to compliments, believing beyond hope that we were goddesses before swine, and sometimes we did things that we came to regret, and I shiver at those memories as though they occurred yesterday. Those decisions we make with little thought are often beyond our control, but as we mature we come to realize more and more the consequences of our actions on others and we adjust or ameliorate our dealings. I know that Helen always wanted to do what was right, but somehow she always allowed herself to be led down paths of folly. Clytemnestra, too, married a man and had a lovechild by him, but when Agamemnon came and killed both husband and child, she followed him willingly.

"Helen, too, was led astray at a young age by Theseus and Pirithous, and my cousins, brave Castor, tamer of horses, and Pollux, a boxer of repute, saved her – how I miss my gentle cousins, for to me they were as close and protective as any father. They freed silly Helen, though she never complained of her confinement, and returned her to Lacedaemon. They spent many days in efforts to keep their light-hearted sisters and cousin out of trouble and on the correct pathway. By the time Paris came for Helen, they were older and fatigued and could not follow her and rescue her, and they never lived to see the conclusion of the war or her return.

"I cannot say how we three silly girls became so different in this aspect of our close lives, but I left off silliness after my playmates departed Pleuron, and my mother raised me to use my own mind, something that perhaps she came to rue. By the time I married and went to Ithaca with my husband against the judgments of many people, including my mother, I knew in my heart what was right for me, and that was enough. She had succeeded in her efforts to her own dismay.

"Why my mother objected to my marriage and the manner in which it occurred, I am not entirely sure. She felt that Odysseus came from a lesser family and did not have the prospects of other young men. He came from a small island, isolated from the Peloponnese. His olive complexion did him no good with her. But mostly, she objected to the manner of my marriage, in which I had no say, for my uncle Tyndareus made an agreement with Odysseus and Agamemnon. When Helen came of age, so strong were the demands of the suitors from throughout the great houses...for she was several years older than myself and renowned throughout Hellas for her breathtaking beauty...that her father feared the outbreak of war over his daughter – it had happened before and would again. As a result, he was as lost as a blind man in a forest. It was Odysseus that suggested to him the resolution of his dilemma, which went far beyond the tales that you have heard the bards sing on occasion. Well beyond the desires of his daughter, which were of little consequence to him. Tyndareus had to consider the governance of his country, his family, his followers, wars in the future with Mycenae and Messenia, and as always the opinions of others. The Oath of Tyndareus was the two- edged sword that earned me a husband and tore him from my breast at the same time. When the suitors pledged their agreement to that indenture, my future was determined, as though the gods had sent down to earth the plans for the life of Penelope for all to observe. All was pre-determined and fixed at that point...the worst and the best.

"But when I laid my eyes on Odysseus, utter madness was born in my heart. I cannot name it otherwise, for he was a god in my eyes. He was not a large man, although he was strongly built like a bear, but he was as quick as any man and ran faster than all others. His hair was curly and unmanageable, and he cared not. And he was as dark as a crush of ripe olives and spoke Greek in an accent that sang of the seas, and he could weave a whole cloth out of his words alone. After the first sight of your father, I was lost at sea and sightless, so convinced I was of the rightness of the beating of my heart. At that point, I would have died if I had failed to obtain my heart's desire. These emotions could have moved mountains and warmed the breaths of all the *Anemoi*.

"And when Tyndareus came to my father to compass my future, more concerned obviously about his own future and the future of his daughter, he made an agreement with my father, who knew naught of my madness. Together, they agreed to offer me to Odysseus, who had barely looked upon this lowly child, in return for his service and advice to the state. As we all know, Menelaus was given deathless Helen, and I was offered to Odysseus in a secondary transaction of far lesser import. For this, my father received large tracts of land in Acarnania, full of grapes on the vine and fruiting trees and broad forests. And I received my lover, more precious than all the planets and stars, but more painful than all the winters in cold Chalcidice.

"Odysseus was not an easy husband. At first, he cared not a fig for me. His mind constantly resonated with thoughts and never rested long on a single subject. But soon the authority of my love for him and my strength of character convinced him, and I believe he eventually came to love me and care for me, though those words never passed his lips, and his mind roved as a ship beats the seas. Laertes would often come to me full of apologies for the ways of his son, his sudden trips to Achaea, his nights on the prowl, his bouts of dispiritedness and regret, followed by well-argued requests for forgiveness, and his meandering and gadding about. Odysseus could consider all the ways to plant a field of olive trees, making the conception more time-consuming and difficult than the planting itself. It was in his nature to procrastinate and ponder, just as he would take years mulling over the punishment of a man who had mistreated him and then exact his price.

"And in my heart I never considered myself the fairest of all things. Never as lovely to look upon, my features and allurements, as my cousins Helen and Clytemnestra: always judged by this measuring stick. And this was a failing that I came later in life to repent. But my skin was fair and supple as a newborn baby, and my body was as shapely as the curves and valleys of distant Parnon in the early morning light. My fair hair, the gift of my mother, sparkled as brightly as a horse's mane blowing in the wind, and my scent was as sweet as the yellow jonquil in the blush of bloom. I took only firsts in these games, even though our wedding was not attended by all of Hellas and our vows were heard by the gods alone. What we uttered to each other went far beyond the feeble compliments of star-struck Menelaus and the meager blandishments and veiled warnings of his brother, Agamemnon, who never thought his brother deserved such a prize and treated Clytemnestra like a slave. And there were times when these two men desired me far more than other women and would have had me if left to their own evil intentions, for such was the thinking of these men and their lack of respect for others, including for the wife of a man employed in the service of their greatness. But what is honor among men? All I can think of is Priam and Achilles crying pitifully together at the deaths of each of their loves: a son, Hector, and a beloved friend, Patroclus. How careless men are until it is too late.

"But these thoughts of the sons of Atreus, although full of meaning, move me far off my point. Odysseus was surprised by his reward that Eros had endowed, and it took him by ocean storm, for he had not expected to be dominated by an emotion that he barely understood and had never considered. Such are men. He brought me home to Ithaca to dwell within his house, and I, in turn, gave myself to him without reservation and with such resolve that soon I dwelt within his heart, for all that had gone on before and during our nuptials was nothing and of no value afterwards. There were times when I could not utter a single syllable. When my tongue could not form a single word of utterance. My eyes were sightless, and my mind dark and empty and lost of all thought. Fire raced through the pores of my body, and I melted with the heat of his intensity. My soul knew only one thing and my bosom sought unity as full and loving as eternal Aphrodite could bestow. I cannot describe the beauty of giving love and receiving the love of another. I only know that love shaped my inner-being and filled me with its sweet essence. I can only remember the sound of the gentle Zephyrian winds driving the branches of the great oaks against the closed shutters outside our bedroom throughout the night as we lay on cushions as gentle and revealing as my compliance to the beatings of my beloved's heart.

"Two people, living together, with gentle hearts and gentle ways can build a fortress as strong as any palace in Hellas to prevent the entry of discordant ideas or people who would seek to interfere. Separately, they may be weak and lost; while together they are as firm and vast as any rock boulder wall. For marriage is a hard bond created by the warp and weft of weaving two people's lives together, far stronger than individual threads, and proves a boon to their friends, but is as deadly as a poison dart to their enemies. Our life together lasted ten years before the birth of our son. And this time was filled with joy and riotous laughter and exploration and discovery and hard work and gentle play. For my amusement, he could play the fool better than any man.

"If precious time can evaporate in a single breath, then this came about, for to me this period passed like the instant between the inhalation and release of a mouthful of air. And when it had dissolved into history, I was still satisfied, for within that instant my mind was brimming with memories of our young life together and the growth and fruiting of our love. But once that time was completed, it never returned. When he returned from the wars, Odysseus was a different man. Of all the Ithacans and Cephallenians, twelve ships in all, he was the only man to return, and I believe that when he returned, this notion never departed his mind for an instant. In his mind, he had failed as a leader, and he this image accompanied him when he discovered the suitors seeking my hand in his absence, and he attempted to eradicate this image by the bloody punishment of their travesty, when they had done no more then drink his wine and eat his meat. But the memories of men, who have depended on us and whom we have failed, are not so easy to erase and dwell in our own minds like the eggs of a viper underground.

"But again, I race ahead of my story. And if war brings some people to their knees, it was the birth of his son that forced Odysseus to the ground. He was amazed by the miracle of this birth of his son, and it seemed to bode a different direction to this life. I too was ill-prepared for the birth of our son. I thought I had seen beauty. I thought I had seen promise. I thought I had glimpsed all the jewels that one could desire. Yet here in a living being, I glimpsed all of these and more. I saw our love combined and wrapped in a tiny parcel, and I felt the dreadful responsibility of caring for and nurturing a living human being: a baby boy as lovely and delicate as a summer field of yellow birdsrap. I feared that I was not up to the task. Rightfully so. For of all things in my life, the one war I needed to fight, I failed at miserably. A thousand ships might sail to war with a multitude of soldiers in shiny bronze armour and fancy uniforms, but there is no more important battle than that of a baby at the breast. War is the son of a heroic father and a weak mother. No jewel or gold accoutrement, no silken gown or golden sandal, no ruler on earth or lord on high is worth a single nail on a tiny hand. I saw this clearly in my mind, but so consumed was I with the absence of my spouse that I failed to listen to the advancement of my heart.

"Sometimes, we must pray to the gods to release us from the altar of our desires, for our cruel cares obstruct the very progression of our lives. The high cost of our short-lived happiness was the heavy blow of catastrophe when Odysseus left home for two decades of our life together and then never returned truly; at least as my lover he never returned. In one instant, he held you in his arms on the farm among the furrows against the inquiries of treacherous Palamedes, and in the next he was gone to Troy. And in his best manly intentions, he told me to wait until the hairs began to grow on the chin of our son and then if he had not returned that I was to remarry. Such false clarity of view in a graceless man. He had not glimpsed into the depths of my caring and had no idea of the clearness of my vision. He judged me by his own measures, much askew and misaligned, and lacking determination.

"In his absence, my son grew up without a mother or a father. Laertes came to me time and time again, after the death of Anticlia, to rein me in from my despondency, but to no end, for such was the depth I had sunk to. And Mentor, well-meaning man that he was, took me aside and attempted to shake me awake with his lucid arguments. Not the most loyal servant, not friend nor family, not wealthy suitor, not even my cousin once she had returned to Lacedaemon could convince me otherwise, for I was as lost as Odysseus on his voyage home and could not find my bearing.

"For this I apologize to you now and will always bear the scars of my failure. I cherished you above all things, and somehow I lost the way. Oh, I could enumerate the reasons, and perhaps I am more like Helen than I would care to believe, but I confronted my trial as a man might attack an enemy and allowed my judgment to sway my feelings. My mad heart was no ally in the wars of emotions, and I sowed seeds of sorrow to fester and fail to grow from lack of care. My own tears watered the flowers in my bed of grief. My only desire was to extinguish my cares so I could move forward, but instead my sorrows pursued me like an evil shade, and I could not find escape from myself. I knew what I was doing was wrong, but I could not prevent myself from my actions. As I wove and rewove the shroud of Laertes, and waged a war against the suitors, my only wish was that my woven shroud should welcome me in its sweet embrace.

"My greatest fear was that Odysseus should learn to love another more than me. How infantile of me, but how my body shook with anger and my breast with rancor that my beloved could have forgotten me for another. I was surrounded by my fears day in and day out, just as one eats meals and sleeps and wakes. I could find no opening and no outlet for my desire, and I was halted in my tracks. I welcomed slumber as one would take a lover to her bed.

"Sleep is a god, and often Athene visited me in the guise of my sister, Iphthime. But even she could not change the carriage of my soul, nor affect the direction of my life. I placed all in abeyance and became a widow spider waiting for the next fly to come about. But I waited in vain.

"It was at this point that the suitors began their efforts in earnest, after the wounded veterans of Troy struggled back from the wars with tales of courage and cowardice and the sinking of many of the long ships. The words of Amphinomus, a suitor from Dulichium, began to sound reasonable. And the generosity of the suitor Eurymachus began to seem valid and meaningful. And even the pressing arguments of the scoundrel Antinous began to appear believable, for he whistled a beautiful tune in my ear, as beautiful as the melody of the woodlands. You had become a young man at this point and had your own thoughts of the suitors, many of whom attempted in their fashion to befriend you and to replace the father that you lacked. I saw them instructing you in the manly arts, but luckily their actions spoke much louder than their words to you, for this I am grateful, as my mind had became foggy and hazy with Odysseus' absence. The tune Antinous whistled in my bedchamber one night would have completed me if Pan's discordance had not shaken me from my dream.

"Today, I would be hard put to explain how I lived as I did for such an extended period. Some said it was my love for Odysseus and my deep desire to remain faithful to him, and I can only admit that this was certainly not the controlling emotion. I wanted his love, but he was gone, and many days I would have gladly enjoyed the news of his death, but no such relief was ever delivered. And so I locked myself in the cell of my own making and lived there for much of my married life, and for this I am deeply resentful and regretful at the same time. Time is of such value, and I wasted it. Or I should say that Odysseus wasted it for me, for I have heard the tales of his stays with Circe and Calypso, and I have seen the tropical passion in his eyes. Better not to have lived than to create the image of Faithful Penelope waiting at home weaving a sorrowful cloth. What care I for such telltale chitchat? I should have preferred to follow the course of my cousins with their husbands and lovers: to have lived at least and not to have merely abided. For I have had my opportunities. I should have preferred to be a serpent, slipping slyly through the shadowed floors of dusky forests.

"Why then did I do as I did? What reward was there for me? I traded away my life. I lost my only child. My husband never returned to me. And now that my prime is far passed, I can only take responsibility for myself and what resides within me, and I must eschew things that are outside my control, such as my physical body, my property, my reputation, and my command of others. I can only say that I followed my desire and that was enough. I loved madly and was loved in return, if only for an instant. For there is one certainty to life: nothing is greater or more worthwhile in our lives than the love of another.

"And when he finally returned to Ithaca, Athene held back the night. Odysseus' faithful shepherd dog, Argus, the gentle giant, was the first to recognize him, and his wet nurse, dear Euryclea, practically a mother to him, recognized him as well. But he could never fool a wife or mother to his child for an instant in his disguise. Such a man, who would believe that he could conceal himself from his wife. Such a man as well, who would believe that Euryclea would not come directly to me and blabber the news. Only in stories do we achieve such silliness. So I put him to the test: his stories and foolish male pride. Although I loved him for it, I saw through him like gazing into the depths of a clear pond at mid-day. I told him the intimate details of my dream of an eagle swooping down to break the necks of twenty geese. Not even Athene could put him up to such belief that I would reveal these thoughts to a stranger and beggar to boot. I played along, but all the better to see who it was who wanted access to my bed. In some accounts, he acted no better than another suitor. I set up an archery contest knowing full well his penchant for such silly competitions. But it was not until he revealed to me the depths of his care, through the description of our peaceful home and the construction of his bed, as you see it now, that I could make out in his eyes, beggar or king, that he loved me and me alone. It was at that point that I allowed him to expose himself and gave him the gift of thinking that he was making known some great secret. I shared my bed with him after all, but knowing with the certainty of my heart that he was returning to me and to me alone.

"I learned two hard-earned lessons or, more to the point, was forced by my life to accept two truths. You cannot change someone else. Odysseus would not become who I would have him be, regardless of the lengths I would go to force some change within him. I might influence some of his thoughts, but I could not change anything fundamental about him. Nothing. And once I had come to this realization, it was comforting to know, for it implied acceptance of who he was at heart. Secondly, I had to depend on myself to maintain my own cheerfulness. I could not depend on him or anyone else for that matter. For certainly, there were moments when he brought great joys to my life, but in the main I had to accept these as gifts, however frequent or infrequent, and I could not assume that they would always be forthcoming. Instead, I learned that I had only myself to depend on to bring cheer. I could not blame others for my own unhappiness. Again, the comprehension of this brought even greater comfort to me, for once I had it within my command, it brought greater cheer to the both of us. But believe me, this was the hardest, most difficult truth to learn.

"Now as the child of evening descends and we hear the voice of the dove, and as the stars leave the skies and time rushes onward, in the warmth of my rooms I loose my outer garments and draw my robe about my legs with the remembrance of tastes and smells as strong as afternoon sunlight reflected off the gentle sea. I weave no more, though my hands are full of the lifelong skill and expertise. I no longer find solace in the strength of the warp and weft. Under the sinking stars of the Pleiades, daughters of Atlas, and the waning moon, I lie in my bed alone with my memories and thoughts. These thoughts succor me and give me comfort, but I would rather, a thousand times over, have an impassioned man by my side, one who loves me and desires to give me comfort and joy. Unquestionably, I would give all I have to return for only an instant to relive just one memory among those innumerably impressed upon my intellect.

"Now, where does this lead us?

"The life of man is subject to the whims of the gods. For this, we put our lives in the hands of Hera and Athene and her father, lord of all the immortals. I cannot answer unasked questions. I cannot make decisions on a course against the winds of time. I can only provide the truths that I have found in my few years between two eternities. For my child will not live forever, and this is my greatest shortcoming as mother and progenitor. I am helpless. I only know that if you are to live, you must hazard all. We are not like some foal following his mother by instinct alone. If love is to blossom, you must unveil your innermost feelings and bestow the grace of your deepest thoughts. This is no slight matter, for while common acquaintances can do me no wrong; those for whom I care most deeply can do me great injury. My stories are not fables or oracles meant as well-laid plans to be followed carefully. They are the fumbled thoughts of a smart old woman, longing to see that others do not mistake a trap and fail to experience the joys that life has to offer. They are the only gifts remaining that a mother can give to her son and daughter.

"And when I am gone, who will honor me with garlands of woven asphodels and goats rue twined in my hair? We must all dance joyously around the hyacinthia altar at the Thesmophoria festival, weaving tendrils of desire. We must give full measure to the beatings of our hearts. My lover beckons me. I open my arms to him in the delight of his return, and, as a spring bud reverses course, I remain forever a maiden in the arms of my lover, hearing the melodic voices of the epithalamium.* What came before and what will follow are of no significance to me. I remain aloof from care. O Hera, bring on the burnt offerings and fatty meats and raise high your arms and sing another song to celebrate the miracle that is life."

---

* A wedding song performed by the guests and relatives of the newlywed couple at their bedroom door on the wedding night.

When Telemachus returned to his rooms, he fell exhausted to his bed. Over the years, Penelope had always been an extremely private person. Never complaining. Dutiful and resolved, but strong at the same time. The type of person who would be in the final stages of an illness before she would begin to admit to not feeling well. Of course, there were times when her substantial façade would crack and the emotions would erupt with all the anger and rage of a woman restrained. But these times were rare and usually short-lived. This evening had been different. Her honesty and depth of feeling had moved him greatly, and her revelations of her life with his father had gone well beyond what he was comfortable hearing. He could not tell the impact of her words on Polycasté, but the two women had grown very close since they had returned to Ithaca, and he had not had time until recently to consider the state of the household.

He had visited Nestor often over the last months. Nestor seemed to have accepted his situation away from Pylos, but remained in his rooms, never venturing out. His legs could no longer support him, and he had to be carried downstairs if he wanted to enter the meeting hall or leave the palace. He chose instead to spend his days in bed or on the upper balcony in the waning sunlight. Before Pisistratus left with his family for Athens, they had met in Nestor's bedroom suite with Telemachus and Polycasté. Nestor had described his wishes for his departure from this earth in a straightforward manner as one would discuss the market shopping for the next day. But then again, Nestor had always been open and clear-cut in his affairs.

Penelope on the other hand had never been open about her life. Even when the suitors were pressuring her, she had kept up a brave front, and Telemachus was shocked at the intensity of her pain during this period, as she described it tonight. Of course, he had been occupied with his own problems, and his mother had never been very communicative with him. But tonight, she had revealed the might and effort required of her to survive the absence and the loss of

Odysseus. He hoped that Odysseus had understood how much his mother had sacrificed and how much she cared, but he doubted it.

When he finally fell asleep, it was late in the night, and even the owls were silent. He could not have said how long he had slept. At some point, he became vaguely aware of an interruption to the stillness, a sound of the curtains opening, and a movement in his room; he ignored it and continued fitfully in his slumber. Then, he felt movement on the bed and the covers lifted. He turned and saw Polycasté climbing into the bed to lie next to him. Her hair was wrapped, and she wore a full-length night dress. She held her fingers to her mouth to signal silence.

He lay still as she settled under the coverlet next to him. She smelled of bitter-sweet lavender. And she must have run from the warmth of her own bed, as he could hear her breathing and feel the warmth of her body, even her feet. He turned slowly onto his back and could feel her against his side. She moved toward him and buried her face in his shoulder, with her arm over his chest. He raised his head and found the hollow of her neck and shoulder and moved toward her. He inhaled deeply, drawing her essence into his lungs, feeling, smelling, and tasting her all at once. He had waited so long and gently, with all the patience within his soul, as one would for a young and obstinate foal refusing the softest sheepskin bridle. And he whispered to her:

"I love you, Polycasté...my life."

In one moment, she came to him. He dissolved into her body. They were together again in a oneness, as though they had never been apart and would never part again. He felt like a shipwrecked man finally finding the fundament of the farthest shore. Telemachus had finally returned from his voyages on the large-wide sea to his home in Ithaca.

And the immortals in heaven heaved a collective sigh of relief, for such had been their objective all along. When two people are in love with one another, the gods are joyful. They toasted their success with golden chalices full of nectar. The future could be considered tomorrow. Zeus, father of the gods, held his huge head high, his gold-flecked braids falling to his shoulders. He smiled down at his children, feeling the pride and warmth of their presence. He beamed at Hera, his wife and sister, still beautiful and desirable after all these years.

And the evening passed, with the dulcet tones of the gods' voices and the melody of Apollo's lyre. Hermes, in his throne for the first time in many crescent moons, nodded off to nap, his triple-leafed golden wand resting in his lap, his mind freed at last from all those terrible tunes.

Now I, Antimenes must end this story. I find myself at the final chapter. Two of my daughters are busy raising my grandchildren and assisting their husbands, and one works as a man might in the mural arts. I see them at times during the year and enjoy their attention and closeness. As a teacher, I have been blessed beyond my utmost anticipation with riches from my scholars. What can be more rewarding than greeting a confused and eager youth and watching him grow into a rational and confident homo hominis? However, my wife continues with an order of women propagating the Mysteries of Hera here in Argos as though she were a widow, but my anger has subsided – perhaps Heracles' passionate life has taken on more meaning for me. I sit alone at night, just as Penelope did, thinking thoughts of our shared past. This is good and natural and full of life and god-given. This history will perhaps serve as herald to you, Alcathöe: for as Homer says, "There is nothing finer or greater than when a man and a women share a oneness of heart and mind." I have loved you always, Alcathöe, and my heart remains forever open to your return. For at the end of it all, we are the creations of the lord of gods who has given us the only true gift in life: the love of another.

Epitome

I, Antimenes have just completed the year 69 AD, marking the completion of our chronicle in what is being called the Year of the Four Emperors. History begins only yesterday. Vespasian took six months to eliminate his rivals. He entered Rome victoriously, having triumphed over the Jews in Judaea and now over the Emperor Vitellius. The troops accompanying Vespasian included legions from Judaea and Syria, as well as from Moesia and Pannonia in lower Germania, and all have repudiated Vitellius and sworn allegiance to Vespasian. They met the emperor's forces in Bedriacum in the Po valley, where, although outnumbered, they soundly defeated the emperor's legions after many deaths. At this same location, Vitellius had defeated the forces of Otho only eight months before. Otho had taken the place of the womanly Galba, who had lasted even less time.

The story goes that when Vespasian's troops entered Rome, they found Vitellius cowering in a janitor's closet, with a belt of gold pieces strapped about his fat belly and a vicious dog chained to the door outside the closet. The soldiers quickly dispatched the dog and led Vitellius, nearly naked, his clothes in tatters, by a noose around his neck through the streets of Rome to the Forum. Vitellius, whose family descended from a shoe maker, was a tall man, with a great paunch and an alcoholic ruddiness to his nose and face. He had a permanent limp from an accident caused when Emperor Caligula had ridden over him in a chariot race. Vespasian's soldiers exposed Vitellius to the angry crowds, who threw filth and excrement at him, and then they put him to the sword on the Stairs of Mourning and dragged his body by a hook to the Tiber, where they disposed of his remains.

In one year's time, we have had three disastrous emperors: Galba, Otho, and Vitellius, and now Vespasian. Worse than a disaster, they used their powers for their own amusement, degrading, *debasing, debauching, demeaning, and killing senselessly without thought or concern. I could not have written my history of golden Telemachus without these atrocities weighing on my mind? It goes without saying that we are optimistic that Vespasian will be better, but, as we hear so frequently and often inaccurately, he could be no worse. Happily, the emperors remain for most purposes in Rome. If the gods were awarding prizes for leadership, though, Cresphontes, King of Messenia, or Tisamenus, for that matter, in comparison to these Romans would be judged as wondrous, enlightened leaders and moral guides, with the interests of their subjects always close at heart.*

Today, the greatness of Greece is at low ebb. We are subject to the whims of Rome. They have appropriated our greatness, or at least those aspects appealing to them: our science and philosophy, our language and written word, our arts and culture, our system of education, our religion, and, I hate to say it, our tactics in military matters. Though in their thefts, they thoughtlessly overlook much of what we feel are our most valuable contributions. What they cannot expropriate is our history.

Pericles, son of Xanthippus, summarized these feelings in his famous panegyric at the funeral of those who had given their lives in the first year of the more recent Peloponnesian War...so many wars and so many killed before their time over the millennium. It is so difficult to name them all that we are forced to resort to numerals. Pericles said that we must pay homage to our ancestors first and foremost. He went on to describe our form of government, specifically Athens, which favored the many instead of the few, and the fact that our doors were always open to the world of ideas and trade. But most importantly, he said that it is by love of honor and not gain, as some would believe, that age and the helplessness of life are cheered. And, if I might interpret and extrapolate, great will be the glory of not falling short of your natural character. For by all rights, Greece is the school of the world.

Of our friends in Rome, I cannot speak too highly. But as an historian, I must set my sights on the receding horizon, and Rome plays a role of lesser import and appears late on the scene. Of all the Roman emperors, Nero showed the greatest interest in Greece and took our lessons to heart. He once traded the island of Sardinia, which was very prosperous at the time, to the citizens of Rome for all of Greece, allowing Greece full independence. Vespasian, the bureaucrat, cancelled this benefit, and Greece once again began paying tribute to Rome and is now subject to a foreign governor. According to Vespasian, "Greece has forgotten how to be free." Can we assume that Vespasian never studied history?

The Emperor Nero traveled to Greece on many occasions. Most recently, he left Helius, his freedman-secretary in charge of the affairs in Rome and set off for several months in Greece, an act that was to be the final straw in his downfall. He traveled throughout Greece, displaying his dubious artistic abilities of singing and playing the lyre in all the great theatres of Hellas, including Argos and Corinth. He won many prizes for lyre playing, offering Roman citizenship to the judges and other inducements from the state. And those audience members who applauded his performances with vigor were rewarded with interviews with the emperor and gold for their pockets. Those who fell asleep or attempted to leave during his performances were lambasted. At one point, he began barring the gates during his performances. Babies were born and men died during Nero's recitals.

He was the first to initiate music contests in the games at Olympia, and he won these contests as well. But Nero was also a horseman from a young age, and he was fascinated with racing chariots, although his body was not that of an athlete, being rather pustular and malodorus, with protuberant belly and spindly legs. At Olympia, he won a chariot race even though he fell from his car and retired before the end of the race. The judges ruled him the winner on account of his immense effort. He rode a ten-horse chariot at the games as well, something he had criticized King Mithridates for in one of his best-known poems, and he received an Olympic wreath in this contest. He also won at Delphi in the Pythian Games and at Corinth in the Isthmian Games. When he returned to Rome, he held a triumphant procession through the streets, displaying his many laurel wreaths, as though he had conquered another nation for the tax rolls. Nero razed a portion of the city wall of Rome, which was the Greek custom of a victor returning home after a great war of annihilation. He collected many master works of art, which were transported to Rome and never again seen in Greece.

When Nero visited Corinth, he touched upon our own story, as he opened the construction of a canal across the isthmus along the ditch, connecting the Gulf of Corinth with the Saronic Gulf. Of course this was an ancient plan, as we know, which did not take a savant to envisage, but merely a practical mind. Early in the sixth century, the Corinthians had constructed the Dioikos, a paved road along the ditch with limestone blocks and a wheeled vehicle, the olkos, that carried ships from one gulf to the other, but did not entirely solve the problem. Nero applied Roman might to the task of construction of the project, ordering Vespasian to send six thousand forced laborers from Judaea to dig out the canal. The young Jewish men were transported to Corinth, where they were treated as slaves, and forced to camp along the ditch in the high heat of summer, just as the Pelopides and Heraclides had done so many years before. And in a parallel fashion to the original battle, many of them lost their lives along the ditch, and none of them came to love Greece. Several years later, the canal still remains far from complete, not greatly altered from what it was in the time of the Heraclides, more than a thousand years before.

After the victory by the Heraclides and once peace had been established throughout the Peloponnese, and after shadowy Aletes met an early death on the shores of Pylos, Temenus, King of Mycenae and Argos, appointed his son-in-law, Deiphontes, King of Corinth. Success did not preclude further intrigue by the family of Heracles. As we know, Deiphontes was married to Temenus' daughter, Hyrnetho, and had a special relationship with his father-in-law, who valued him for his intelligence and loyalty. Because of Temenus' favoritism, though, his sons, particularly Phalces and Cerynes (the younger, Agraeus, disapproved the plan), plotted to drive a wedge between Deiphontes and Hyrnetho. By doing this, the sons hoped to commence the destruction of Temenus and to take over rule of the most populous cities in Argolis. Intrigue is never replete.

First, the brothers visited the home of Deiphontes and Hyrnetho in Epidaurus and sought an audience with Hyrnetho. When they were granted a meeting, though she suspected some mischief, they produced all the arguments they could think of without resorting to truth as a guide. They attempted to turn wife against husband by proclaiming the stronger bond of brother to sister. Not being married themselves, they had little idea of the strength of the marriage bond, and an argument based on lies ultimately festers. As a result, they did not sway their sister nor could they change her mind in the least about her husband. For in truth, Deiphontes was an excellent husband and father to their three sons and daughter. Further, he was a faithful and loyal son-in-law to Temenus, who in turn loved him as a son.

The strength of their arguments failing, the brothers concluded that they had no other choice but to abduct Hyrnetho from her home against her will. Deiphontes soon learned from the servants of this heinous act and set out immediately after them on his horse. The two brothers rode in separate chariots from Epidaurus toward Corinth, with Hyrnetho being physically restrained by Phalces. Deiphontes quickly caught up with the chariots and shot and killed Cerynes. But he was afraid of harming Hyrnetho and did not attempt a shot at Phalces, following closely after the chariot. Driving and holding Hyrnetho at the same time, made it difficult for Phalces to gauge the violence of his hold on his sister. And his arm encircled her with such force that she could hardly breathe. As he struggled with the wild horses and careening car and frightened woman all at the same time, he mistakenly strangled his sister and killed her. Before Deiphontes was able to discover this, though, Phalces began driving with such abandon that he lost control of the chariot, and it turned over, throwing both of the occupants to the ground. Deiphontes quickly dismounted and ran to the body of his wife and held her in his arms. Being thrown from a chariot was not normally a mortal event, but as he held her he discovered that she took no breath. At the same time, he observed Phalces struggling to right himself from where he had been catapulted by the chariot. Deiphontes carefully replaced the body of his wife on the ground and went to where his brother-in-law lay and drove his sword into the center of his chest. Without a word and without the least feeling of remorse, he sent Phalces down into the house of Hades. After this, he gathered the body of his wife and mother of his children with enormous sorrow and took her back to Corinth for burial.

At the site of her murder, though, the Epidaurians constructed a shrine in honor of Hyrnetho in an olive grove. When branches of the olive trees, or other trees for that matter, fall, they are left on the spot. Each fallen branch serves as a reminder of the life of the fallen Hyrnetho. And the shrine exists to this day.

The death of his daughter was extremely painful for Temenus, made worse by the deaths of his sons, particularly since her death was caused by their calumny. What can be worse to a father? Yet he continued to demonstrate his intelligence and humanity in governing the largest region in the Peloponnese. He made sure that Cresphontes' promises to the soldiers of the Heraclides were carried out. The treasury of Corinth had been depleted with the sharing of the spoils among the leaders of the Heraclides. That enormous store of wealth, when divided by enough shares, had declined greatly. But Temenus made sure that the soldiers had access to land and resources to establish themselves in a new livelihood. The arrival of these men and their families upset the residents, many of whom moved away from the cities into Arcadia and Achaea. And as the families of the soldiers established themselves, other families and fellow countrymen came to the Peloponnese to get their own start. Thus began the influx of the so-called Dorians.

The Dorians were not a single people who spoke a single dialect of Greek. They were made up of many different tribes of Greek-speaking peoples from Boreas. The drought and cold weather made it almost impossible for them to feed a family and forced them off their farms. The Dorians also came from beyond these regions, and many did not speak Greek at all. They brought their own languages and customs, including the new art of iron-making, not just for weapons, but for farm implements and tools and other uses. They brought new traditions to Hellas and new impulses and new ideas.

Many of the new migrants used the Peloponnese as a stepping stone, continuing on to the islands in the Aegean and the Sea of Crete and on to Cyprus. Coming from many different backgrounds, they were an open-minded people and mixed with the Phoenician tradesmen and received an invaluable gift from them: the alphabet.

The Phoenician alphabet resembled the Hebrew letters used in many documents at that time, but the Dorians soon adopted the characters to fit their own needs, and this became the basis of the Greek written word, allowing the greatest thinkers of all time to write down their ideas and to preserve them for all mankind. History began to be documented at this point, and we came to understand our ancestors and could apply their ideas and thoughts as our own and modify them as we saw fit.

And, thus, Homer was able to take the myths and stories of his ancestors and put them to the page to document and preserve them. To this day, we know little of Homer, and it is not clear how much he actually put into the poems himself, for certainly the bards far and wide told the same stories of the Achaeans and the Trojans. Whether Homer was alone responsible for their reproduction as written texts or not, we will never know. But we can thank Homer, either the man or the people responsible under his name, for the foremost stories of all time.

Returning to our own story, Temenus, strangely enough, introduced sacrificial offerings to Augeas, the great king of Elis. It was Augeas who would not pay Heracles for cleaning his stables and who would die on account of this. Augeas as one of the nemeses of the ancestor of Temenus, you would think, would not be an object of admiration by the Heraclides. But he had been an excellent ruler, or so his reputation was years later. The offerings to Augeas continue to this day as a custom in the city of Temenium in Argolis. The city was named after Temenus a few years after his death. Deiphontes came to the throne following the death of his father-in-law, and he had the tomb of Temenus constructed in Temenium. To this day, it is a site of worship for the Dorians from the region.

Cresphontes, the brother of Temenus and leader of the Heraclides, was not as lucky as his brother. History has been parsimonious in the accounts of Cresphontes. We know that Euripides wrote a drama about the man, "Kresphontes." But only fragments remain of this work, not enough to put together the entire story. I have assembled ideas from various sources so that we can see what became of this hubristic leader.

As you recall, the son of Lacestades, King of Sicyon, was called Polyphontes, and he was a Heraclide through his father. Polyphontes nursed a bitter hatred for Cresphontes based on the insults he had suffered during the war. After the war, Polyphontes traveled to Pylos, where Cresphontes was just beginning his rule of a reunited Messenia. Polyphontes came claiming friendship, but had ulterior motives. He rapidly insinuated himself into the heart of the wife of Cresphontes, Merope, daughter of King Cypselus of Arcadia. He began behaving toward her as if he were her husband and not entirely to her satisfaction. For although Cresphontes treated his wife as he would the couch in their meeting hall, she had enough pride in herself not to be taken advantage of. Soon though, she found herself in a plot on the life of her husband from which she could not withdraw. Reluctantly, she accepted the fate that the gods had cast upon her, for she had suffered greatly under her husband's mistreatment.

Polyphontes murdered Cresphontes and all his children, only months after Cresphontes had assumed the throne. No one mourned the loss of Cresphontes, and no one attended his interment. After this, Polyphontes forced Merope to marry him to legitimize his claim to sovereignty over Messenia, although truly he had none. Merope, though, being well aware of his plans, took her youngest child, the son of Cresphontes, named Aepytus, and sent him away before Polyphontes took his revenge. She sent the child to relatives in the mountains of Arcadia. Polyphontes' mind was so consumed by revenge, he barely noted the missing child. When he did, Merope told him the child had been taken away, and she did not know where. Polyphontes did not believe her, so he issued a large reward to anyone who could prove the death of the child, but no one came to claim compensation.

Polyphontes ruled over Messenia for many years, almost forgetting that a child existed. Merope became wife in name only, and Polyphontes took many mistresses to his bed. But Merope never allowed the child in Arcadia to forget his ancestry, for Merope sought her own revenge, not for the death of her loathsome husband, but for the murder of her innocent children.

When Aepytus grew up and became a man, he came to Pylos to complete the circle. For often in the lives of men, what deeds they perpetrate along the path of their life, whether good or evil, come back to revisit them at a later time. The young Aepytus arrived at the palace in Pylos in the guise of the son of the King of Acarnania, and claimed the reward, asserting that he himself had killed the last son of Cresphontes. As proof, he carried the golden profile of Apollo around his neck, which had been given to the child at his birth by Cresphontes and only could have come from the child, since it was one of the pieces from the hoard of Priam. King Polyphontes was unmoved by the story, for too much time had passed, and he was too parsimonious to give out riches to anyone at this late date. But when Merope saw the medallion, she nearly executed the young man herself, believing that he had indeed killed her last son. But quickly, before his mother could strike him down, Aepytus showed her a birth mark on his neck, proving that he was indeed her child. Merope recognized the mark at once and fell into his arms. From that point on, mother and son plotted the final revenge on Polyphontes.

The next day was a festival and sacrifice in the town, and Polyphontes was to attend and lead the festivities. When the sacrificial animal was led to the altar of Apollo, Aepytus stepped forward to sacrifice the beast, but to the surprise of all the townspeople he sacrificed Polyphontes on the altar instead, although human sacrifice had been outlawed for generations. He then turned to his mother, who, he knew, was complicit in the murder of his father and brothers and sisters, and he slew her as well. With blood flowing into the fire pit, Aepytus explained who he was and what had led him back to Pylos. The people, who resented the rule of Polyphontes and his wife, were not displeased to have a new leader, and Aepytus, son of Cresphontes, then became King of Messenia. Of his outcome and the benevolence of the reign of Aepytus, history is mute.

In Laconia, the twin sons of Aristodemus and the generals of the second infantry division of the Heraclides, Procles and Eurysthenes, at first shared the powerful throne of the kingdom of Lacedaemon. These two spiteful brothers, who could not share the same womb, soon split the kingdom of Lacedaemon into two royal houses. The twin thrones of Procles and Eurysthenes turned Sparta into what it became at a much later date. Here is the explanation. The land of Laconia is split into two valleys separated by a high mountain range, impassible during the cold winter months. Toward Apeliotes lies the valley of Lacedaemon and toward Zephyrus, Messenia. When the Heraclide twins first arrived, they forced the residents of the valley of Lacedaemon to become serfs to the *government. But as the Dorian settlers arrived in the two valleys, the Lacedaemon side could not support the needs of the growing populace, and in defense fought a bloody battle and annexed the adjacent valley in Messenia. Generations later, the farmers of Messenia returned to fight for their freedom from the other valley. These struggles were immortalized by the poet Tyrtaeus of Laconia, whose songs were sung in battle: "Youthful warriors are beautiful in battle until the blossom withers. Men gape and women sigh, and death brings no end to their beauty."*

But the leaders of Sparta knew that this situation, created by Procles and Eurysthenes, could not continue. In its stead, they instituted draconian measures through education and public discipline to build a militaristic society, from cradle to grave, and in so doing created the most conservative, authoritarian state known to man. As Thucydides said, "They were bullies at home and bullies abroad, and even their boasted discipline was defective." They produced not a single artist or thinker or writer of note. They were like a scorpion that was forever fearful of his neighbors, hiding in his hole, and stinging if approached too closely. Sparta became a hateful, aggressive country without respect for life.

Unlike the Spartans, and the Heraclides for that matter, Oxylus, as King of Elis, set out to improve the lot of the Eleans. He introduced to the under-populated region many of the Heraclide soldiers and their families and also immigrants from Aetolia, the region of his origin. These immigrants, contrary to what some would have us believe, helped turn Elis into a bountiful and productive region and improved the lives of all the residents. Wisely following the old precedents, Oxylus accorded to Dius, the young king who had lost his throne, the rights of a hero. He wanted the Eleans to continue their lives as they had under Dius and his forebears, who, after all, had not been such terrible leaders. He did this with grace. At the same time, he honored Degmenus, the valiant local fighter, who had fallen in hand-to-hand combat with the champion of the Heraclides, Pyraechmes. A statue of Degmenus was commissioned and installed at the barrow of Degmenus at the site of his death. The last time I traveled to Elis, the statue of Degmenus stood exactly in the same place, and although the town has grown far beyond the site of the fight, and people no longer knew the details behind the statue, you can see them occasionally visiting it and pausing for a moment with their own thoughts.

Oxylus' cheerful eyes and sense of humor, which had been placed in abeyance during the war, returned to him, and there was no greater joy than riding gentle Rhaebus into town to discuss affairs with the people in the small agora. The Eleans gradually looked upon him with respect and warmth as he rode by, and they came to him with their troubles and concerns. Oxylus admitted that he was shocked by the size of his share of the spoils for the return of the Heraclides, but he used it for good purposes. He improved an estate across the river from Odysseus' estates, not as large, but with plenty of pasture for his horses and terraces for his beloved grapes.

For many years afterwards, Oxylus and Telemachus kept in touch. They often traveled on affairs of state or just visited each other and their families. Telemachus and Polycasté often visited Autolycus on Odysseus' estates. And Oxylus visited with fair-minded Amphion and developed strong relations between the two countries. Telemachus and Oxylus passed many evenings together sitting on one of their balconies, whether in Ithaca or Elis, smelling the salt air and fresh summer breezes from Zephyrus, comparing vintages, horses, cattle, or talking of past events. They never discussed the war. Oxylus lived to be a doddering old man, visiting the grave of Odysseus more frequently toward the end. He could often be found at the estates where Autolycus lived and raised his family.

Oxylus' one regret was that he never produced any children. He married a local woman, but she was beyond the age of childbearing. At his death, the throne of Elis passed to the general in charge of the defense of Elis, a job that had never amounted to much. General Autolycus, the daring son of Telemachus, had become like a son to Oxylus. Autolycus inherited the throne and ruled with the vision and the insight of his father, just as his brother did in Ithaca and the offshore islands. For the sons of mothers are all kings.

Over the years, Telemachus and Autolycus attempted to keep the site of Odysseus' grave free of encroaching plants and trees. When I visited Elis, I could find no evidence of a gravesite in the foothills, although I believe that I came close to what must have been Odysseus' estates. Much of the environing hillsides have been cleared for planting vineyards and olive trees, and the dense forests have been pushed far back far from the Peneus. There were many outcroppings with distant views of the Ionian Sea, but I never found any evidence of an ancient gravesite.

As the bards tell us, Nestor had been granted long life for the evil that Apollo had wrought in killing his uncles and aunts, the Niobids. The years that Apollo took from his relatives were given to Nestor. He never left Ithaca once he settled there, although occasionally visitors from far off would call on him for short periods. But eventually, even these rare visitors came no more. He lived long enough after the war in the Peloponnese to see his children and his grandchildren prosper in Athens and his great grandchildren earn honors. When he died at one hundred and seven years of age (almost the age of Democritis), he did so peacefully, without fanfare. If people had thought about it, they would have concluded that he was the greatest statesman of his time and the most worthy compatriot of the heroes: Odysseus, Achilles, Ajax, Agamemnon, and Menelaus.

History is parsimonious on fair-minded Amphion, although it is noted he became famous in the offshore islands as an orator and sage and judicious counsel to the local archons. Beyond that, there is little evidence of his life following his investiture. It is parsimonious further on Telemachus and soft-eyed Polycasté. However, an historian can take certain liberties. Telemachus and Polycasté lived happily together as married couples often do, with renewed joy, sharing a foundation of memories and concerns. Of all Telemachus' accomplishments, the old horse tamer would always say that gentling Polycasté was his greatest and most rewarding. Without trust, life is empty. Certainly, he owed his mother greatly in expanding his outlook on this matter, for unquestionably horse taming is only one means of understanding our fellow mortals. And he thanked Odysseus as well for demonstrating such a thirst for life. Golden Telemachus traded the renown of his father for a measured life of ordinary pleasures, and he found peace. But thirst can be quenched in any number of god-given ways. Hesiod said that his native country was Ithaca, his father, Telemachus, and his mother, the daughter of Nestor.

As an historian, I know both Amphion and Autolycus saw great changes during their lifetimes. For following the return of the Heraclides, there is a gap in the history of the Peloponnese. It is *believed that this gap included earthquakes and volcanic eruptions, invasions of marauding tribes (the so-called sea peoples), continuing battles among the states of the Peloponnese, and massive uprisings against tyrants. This we know for certain: within a century of the end of the War of the Families, all the great palaces of the Peloponnese were razed to their foundations. The great houses were destroyed, their treasuries dispersed, and their heirlooms looted. How? Why? No one knows. Following this was a gap in history termed the "Dark Ages"; it can be called, more appropriately, an undocumented period of transition. People continued to lead their lives, to procreate, and to battle one another. We may never know what exactly caused this "dark age," whether it was man-made or natural in genesis or likely both. We do know with all confidence that the seeds of the flower that became Classical Greece grew during this gap in history from the seeds sown by men and women such as Nestor, Odysseus, Penelope, Telemachus, and Polycasté. Out of any catastrophic conflagration, new plants and trees grow back rapidly in far greater profusion and soon fill the forests of time.*

Act with god.

Antimenes of Argos, 69 AD

List of Characters

Actor
> Descendent of the Molionides, advisor to court of Elis

Adrastos
> Son of Eumaeus, faithful servant of Telemachus in Elis and Ithaca

Alcathöe
> Wife of the author, Antimenes, and mother of his three daughters

Alcmaeon
> Son of Sillus, grandson of Thrasymedes, great grandson of Nestor, ruler of Messene, one of the split regions of Messenia, during invasion of the Heraclides

Aletes
> Son of Hippotes, one of the leaders of the third crop of Heraclides, co-conspirator with Cresphontes

Alexandros
> Son of Pelius, young Heraclide phylarch and tablemate of Telemachus

Amphion
> Son of Telemachus and Polycasté, leader of the Heraclide horse troops, named after the maternal grandfather of Nestor

Antenor
> Son of Antinous (suitor of Penelope), archon in Ithaca

Antimenes
> Son of Clinias, narrator of *The Telemachia*

Aristodemus
> Son of Aristomachus, brother of Cresphontes and Temenus, killed before the return of the second crop of Heraclides

Aristomachus
> Son of Cleodaeus, leader of the return of the second crop of Heraclides, father of Cresphontes, Temenus, and Aristodemus

Autolycus
> Son of Telemachus and Polycasté, leader of the Heraclide horse troops, named after the maternal grandfather of Odysseus

Cisus
Son of Temenus, one of the leaders of the third crop of
Heraclides

Clearchus
Ship owner in Dyme, transported Telemachus' household
goods to Ithaca

Cresphontes
Son of Aristomachus, Heraclide family archon, one of the
leaders of the returns of the second and third crops of
Heraclides

Dardanos
Son of Belos, Heraclide phylarch from Pylos, a saltwater man

Degmenus
Son of Triopas, champion of the Eleans, competed against
Pyraechmes in hand-to-hand combat for control of Elis

Deioneus
Son of Ixion, advisor to the kings of Corinth

Deiphontes
Son of Antimachus, one of the leaders of the third crop of
Heraclides

Dius
Son of Eleius, young King of Elis during the return of the
Heraclides

Dolon
Son of Pittheus, Macedonian infantry soldier of the
Heraclides

Doridas
Joint King of Corinth with his brother, Hyanthidas

Dymas
Son of Aegimius, general of the Pelopides under Tisamenus,
brother of Pamphylus

Eleius
Son of Amphimachus, King of Elis, grandson of Polyxenus,
who welcomed Odysseus to Elis, father of Dius

Eumaeus
Faithful servant and swineherd of Odysseus on Ithaca, father
of Adrastos

Euryclea
Daughter of Ops, faithful nurse to Odysseus and Telemachus

Eurydice

> Wife of Nestor, mother of Polycasté

Eurymachus

> Son of Eurymachus, archon in Ithaca, whose father was one
> of the leaders of the suitors of Penelope

Eurysthenes

> Son of Aristodemus, twin brother of Procles, one of the
> leaders of the third crop of Heraclides

Glaucus

> Son of Tros, Pelopide fighter and swimmer sent to save
> Tisamenus

Hippotes

> Son of Phylas, one of the leaders of the second crop of
> Heraclides, banished for killing a priest of Apollo and blamed
> for defeat of second crop

Hyanthidas

> Joint King of Corinth with his brother, Doridas

Hyrnetho

> Daughter of Temenus, wife of Deiphontes

Lacestades

> Son of Hippolytus, King of Sicyon, relative of Heracles,
> helped with return of third crop of Heraclides

Laertes

> Son of Arcisius, King of Ithaca, father of Odysseus

Lykeios

> Priest of Apollo from Caria, searching for his son in Corinth

Leucon

> Son of Dias, Heraclide trooper in the file supporting
> Amphion

Melas

> Son of Ion, young phylarch left in charge of Elis at the
> departure of Telemachus and Oxylus

Nestor

> Son of Neleus, King of Messenia, father of Polycasté, leader of
> the Achaeans (Greeks) at Troy

Nisos

> Captain of the merchant vessel that transported Telemachus'
> horses to Naupactus

Odysseus
> Son of Laertes, King of Ithaca and the offshore islands, father of Telemachus, leader of the Achaeans at Troy

Oxylus
> Son of Haemon (adopted), counselor of Heraclides and general of the infantry, best friend of Telemachus

Paeon
> Son of Antilochus, grandson of Nestor, ruler of Thuria, split region of Messenia during return of the Heraclides

Pamphylus
> Son of Aegimius, general of the Pelopides under Orestes and Tisamenus, brother of Dymas, married to the daughter of Deiphontes and Hyrnetho

Penelope
> Daughter of Icarius (son of Oebalus, King of Lacedaemon), wife of Odysseus, and cousin of Helen and Clytemnestra

Perius
> Son of Boeus, trooper sent to meet Telemachus and Oxylus on their way to Pylos

Perses
> Thracian servant to Telemachus who got into mischief in Dyme

Phalces
> Son of Temenus, one of the leaders of the third crop of Heraclides

Philoetius
> Servant and stockman for Odysseus on Ithaca and in Elis

Pisistratus
> Son of Nestor, friend of Telemachus

Pisistratus (1)
> Son of Pisistratus, grandson of Nestor, ruler of Pylos, one of the split regions of Messenia during return of the Heraclides

Polycasté
> Daughter of Nestor, wife of Telemachus, mother of Amphion and Autolycus

Polyphontes
> Son of Lacestades, helped the Heraclides and was deathly insulted by Cresphontes

Procles

> Son of Aristodemus, twin brother of Eurysthenes, one of the leaders of the third crop of Heraclides

Pyraechmes

> Son of Antiphus, champion of the Heraclides in battle for Elis, competed against Degmenus in hand-to-hand combat

Sillus

> Son of Thrasymedes, grandson of Nestor

Telegonus

> Son of Odysseus and Circe, searching for his father

Telemachus

> Son of Odysseus, hipparch of Heraclides

Tellis

> Son of Tisamenus, captain of the Corinthian long ship and one of the leaders of the Pelopides

Temenus

> Son of Aristomachus, brother of Cresphontes, one of the leaders of the returns of the second and third crops of Heraclides

Thymoetes

> Son of Oxyntes, King of Athens during the return of the third crop of Heraclides

Tisamenus

> Son of Orestes, King of Mycenae, leader of the Pelopides during the return of the third crop of Heraclides

Troezen

> Son of Ialmenus, champion boxer of the Heraclides, Thessalian fighter, who fought Zetes on the island of Zacynthus

Zetes

> Son of Demochus, champion boxer of the Heraclides, Athenian fighter, who fought Troezen on the island of Zacynthus

Historical Personages

Achilles
> Son of Peleus, most famous of Achaean (Greek) heroes at Troy

Acrisius
> Son of Abas, King of Argos and grandfather of Perseus, who eventually kills him fulfilling a prophecy

Aegeus
> Son of Pandion, King of Athens and father of Theseus

Aegisthus
> Son of Thyestes, deceitful lover of Clytemnestra and killer of Agamemnon

Aeneas
> Son of Anchises and the goddess Aphrodite, Trojan leader

Aepytus
> Son of Cresphontes, only surviving offspring of Cresphontes, later became King of Messenia

Agamemnon
> Son of Atreus, leader of the Achaeans at Troy, King of Mycenae and Argos, most powerful ruler of his time

Agasthenes
> Son of Augeas, King of Elis

Ajax
> Son of Telamon, Achaean hero at Troy, committed suicide at Troy at the award of Achilles' armour to Odysseus (greater Ajax)

Ajax (1)
> Son of Oileus, Achaean hero at Troy (lesser Ajax)

Alcmena
> Daughter of Electryon, wife of Amphitryon, mother of Heracles by Zeus

Alcinous
> Son of Nausithous, king of Phaecia, great friend and savior of Odysseus

Amphimachus
> Son of Cteatus (one of the Molionides), King of Elis and leader of the Eleans at Troy, killed in Troy by Hector

Amphimachus (1)

> Son of Polyxenus, King of Elis and father of Eleius, named after son of Cteatus

Amphinomus

> Son of Nisus, suitor of Penelope killed by Telemachus

Amphitryon

> Son of Alcaeus, mortal father of Heracles, raised the difficult child along with his own son, Iphicles

Amphimedon

> Son of Melaneus, suitor of Penelope

Andromache

> Wife of Hector, slave to Neoptolemus after the Trojan War

Anticlia

> Mother of Odysseus, wife of Laertes

Antilochus

> Son of Nestor, killed in Troy by Memnon

Antinous

> Son of Eupeithes, most vile of the suitors of Penelope and first of suitors killed by Odysseus

Arcisius

> Son of Cephalus, father of Laertes, grandfather of Odysseus

Arete

> Wife of Alcinous, Queen of Phaecia

Astyanax

> Son of Hector, baby thrown from the battlements of Troy by Neoptolemus

Atreus

> Son of Pelops, King of Mycenae, father of Agamemnon and Menelaus

Autolycus (1)

> Possible son of Hermes, grandfather of Odysseus, cattle breeder

Augeas

> Son of Eleius (1), son of Aetolus, ancient King of Elis, an Argonaut, killed by Heracles when he refused to pay Heracles for cleaning his stables

Briseis

> Girl friend of Achilles taken from him by Agamemnon in the *Iliad*

Cephalus
> Son of Deion, founder of Cephallenia, great grandfather of Odysseus

Chloris
> Daughter of King Amphion and Niobe, one of the Niobids who was spared (along with her sister Amyclas) when her mother insulted the gods

Clytemnestra
> Daughter of Tyndareus, wife of Agamemnon

Deianira
> Daughter of Oeneus, last wife of Heracles, her jealousy responsible for his death

Diomedes
> Son of Tydeus, leader of soldiers from Argos and Tiryns at Troy, one of the heroes

Echemus
> Son of Aeropus, King of Tegea, general for the Pelopides in the return of the first crop of Heraclides

Echepolus
> Wealthy Sicyon who avoided conscription in Troy through gift of the mare Aethe

Eurymachus
> Son of Polybus, leader of the suitors of Penelope and liar killed by Odysseus

Eurynomus
> Son of Aegyptius, suitor of Penelope killed by Odysseus

Eurystheus
> Son of Sthenelus, king of Mycenae and nemesis of Heracles

Haemon
> Son of Thoas, King of Aetolia, step-father of Oxylus

Hector
> Son of Priam, Trojan leader at Troy

Helen
> Daughter of Zeus and Leda, mortal step-father, Tyndareus, wife of Menelaus, abducted by Paris

Helenus
> Son of Priam, seer who prophesied what was necessary to win the Trojan War

Heracles (Hercules) (née Alcaeus)
> Son of Zeus and Alcmena, ancestor of the Heraclides, angry fighter and womanizer, bondsman to Eurystheus, King of Mycenae, made immortal by Zeus

Hermione
> Daughter of Menelaus and Helen, married to both Neoptolemus and Orestes, mother of Tisamenus by Orestes

Hippodamia
> Daughter of King Oenomaus of Elis, pursued by many suitors, who became the wife of Pelops

Hyllus
> Son of Heracles, leader of the first crop of Heraclides

Icarius
> Brother of Tyndareus and father of Penelope

Leto
> Goddess mother of Apollo and Artemis by Zeus

Liodes
> Suitor of Penelope killed by Odysseus

Melanthius
> Son of Dolius, goatherd and servant to Odysseus on Ithaca and scoundrel, who was killed at Odysseus' return

Melanthus
> Son of Andropompus, ruler of split region of Messenia, not related to Nestor, became King of Athens after departure from Pylos

Memnon
> Son of Tithonos, King of the Ethiopians, fighter for the Trojans at Troy

Menelaus
> Son of Atreus, brother of Agamemnon, husband of Helen

Menestheus
> Menestheus, son of Peteos, King of Athens, placed on the throne by the Dioscuri, and an Achaean hero at Troy

Mentor
> Son of Alcinous, tutor of Telemachus during his childhood

Molionides
> Conjoined twins (Cteatus and Eurytus), fought Heracles in support of Elis and were killed by him

Myrtilus
> Mortal son of Hermes, famed chariot driver, killed by Pelops

Neleus

> Said to be son of Poseidon, married to Chloris, father of Nestor

Neoptolemus

> Son of Achilles, Greek fighter at Troy toward end of war, became King of Epirus

Niobe

> Daughter of Tantalus, outrageous blasphemer against the gods, great grandmother of Polycasté

Orestes

> Son of Agamemnon, father of Tisamenus, King of Mycenae, Corinth, Argos, and Lacedaemon

Palamedes

> Son of Nauplius, tricked Odysseus into joining the Achaean coalition against Troy and became his deadly enemy

Paris

> Son of Priam, Trojan abductor and lover of Helen

Patroclus

> Son of Menoetius, best friend of Achilles, killed at Troy

Pelops

> Son of Tantalus, only man to be given a second chance at life by the gods due to the infamy of his father

Perseus

> Son of Zeus, Greek hero, founder of Mycenae and King of Tiryns, foremost ancestor of the Heraclides

Phaeton

> Son of Helios, drove father's chariot of the sun for one day

Philoctetes

> Son of Poeas, bowman at Troy with Heracles' bow given to his father

Pirithous

> Son of Ixion (Zeus), with his friend Theseus conceived many hair-brained ideas, especially about women

Poeas

> Son of Thaumacus, shepherd given Heracles' bow as a gift for kindling the funeral pyre of Heracles

Priam

> Son of Laomedon, King of Troy during Trojan War

Sisyphus

        Son of Aeolus, founder of Corinth, famous for his
        punishment due to his betrayal of Zeus

Tantalus

        Son of Zeus and Pluto, cooked his son, Pelops, and fed him to
        the gods

Theseus

        Son of Aegeus, King of Athens, mythic hero of Greece

Thoas

        Son of Andraemon, King of Aetolia, Pleuron and Calydon
        and leader of the Aetolians in Troy, step-grandfather of
        Oxylus

Thrasymedes

        Son of Nestor, leader of the Messenians at Troy, King of
        Messenia briefly

Thyestes

        Son of Pelops, brother of Atreus (father of Agamemnon and
        Menelaus), King of Mycenae, father of Aegisthus

Tiresias

        Son of Everes, blind soothsayer, who lived as both a man and
        woman, advised Odysseus in Hades of his future

Tlepolemus

        Son of Heracles, leader of nine ships from Rhodes at Troy,
        killed by Sarpedon

Tyndareus

        King of Mycenae, father of Helen, instigator of the Oath of
        Tyndareus initiating the Trojan War, uncle of Penelope

The Immortals

Anemoi (the personified winds)

> Sons of Astraios and Eos, the immortal winds: Boreas (N), Kaikias (NE), Apeliotes (E), Euros (SE), Notus (S), Lips (SW), Zephyrus (W), and Skiron (NW)

Aphrodite

> Goddess of love and beauty

Apollo

> Son of Zeus and Leto, god of creativity, healing, and prophecy

Ares

> Son of Zeus, god of war

Artemis

> Daughter of Zeus and Leto, and goddess of the hunt

Athene

> Born from Zeus' head, goddess of wisdom

Chiron

> Son of Cronos, born a Centaur, half-horse half-man, taught several famous disciples, including Achilles and Heracles

Circe

> Daughter of Helios and Perse, goddess living on the island of Aeaea, visited by the Argonauts and Odysseus, mother of Telegonus by Odysseus

Cronos

> Along with Ops, parents of Zeus and children of the Earth and Heaven, sent to Tartarus

Demeter

> Daughter of Cronos, goddess of cultivation, mother of Persephone

Dionysus

> Son of Zeus, god of wine and lover of peace and joy

Dioscuri

> Twin sons of Zeus and mortal Leda, brothers of Helen and Clytemnestra, awarded alternate immortality by Zeus as the morning star and the evening star; Castor, tamer of horses, and Pollux, boxer

Eos
   Goddess of dawn, mother of Memnon by Tithonos

Eros
   God of love and sexuality, seen as a teenage boy

Ganymede
   Son of Laomedon, young herder taken by Zeus to be server on Olympus

Hades
   Son of Cronos, brother of Zeus, ruler of the underworld

Hebe
   Daughter of Zeus and Hera, former server of the gods, who became wife of immortal Heracles

Helios
   God of the sun and driver of the four-horsed chariot bringing light and warmth to immortals and mortals alike

Hephaestus
   Son of Zeus and Hera, and lame god of artisans, creative genius

Hera
   Daughter of Cronos, wife of Zeus and also his sister, goddess of women

Heracles
   Became immortal; see Historical Personages

Hermes
   Son of Zeus and Maia, god of thieves and mischief, messenger of the gods, and noted whistler

Horae
   Goddess daughters of Time, keepers of the gates of heaven

Pan
   Son of Hermes, with goat feet, horns, and long beard, beloved of all gods for his syrinx pipes and beautiful music

Persephone
   Daughter of Demeter, wife of Hades, goddess of the harvest

Poseidon
   Son of Cronos, brother of Zeus, ruler of the seas

Thetis
   Daughter of Nereus, a sea-nymph, married to the mortal, Peleus, mother of Achilles

Zeus
   Son of Cronos, father of the gods, ruler of heaven and earth

Sources Cited by Antimenes

Aeschylus (525-456 BC) – Playwright

Apollodorus (~140 BC) – Historian, *The Library*

Aristophanes (448-385 BC) – Comic playwright

Democritis (460-370 BC) – Philosopher

Diodorus Siculus (90-30 BC) – Historian, *Library of History*

Euripides (485-406 BC) – Playwright

Herodotus (486-420 BC) – Historian, *The Histories*

Hesiod (~700 BC) – Poet, *Works and Days*

Homer (~750 BC) – Poet, *Iliad* and *Odyssey*

Pericles (~495-429 BC) – Statesman and general, "The Funeral Oration"

Pindar (522-438 BC) – Poet, the *Odes*

Plato (427-347 BC) – Philosopher and founder of the Academy, follower of Socrates

Socrates (469-399 BC) – Athenian philosopher and logician

Sophocles (496-406 BC) – Playwright

Strabo (64 BC-24 AD) – Geographer, historian, and Stoic philosopher

Thucydides (~460-399 BC) – Historian, *History of the Peloponnesian War*

Tyrtaeus of Laconia (~650 BC) – Spartan poet, The Spartan Creed

Xenophon (~422-350 BC) – Warrior and writer, follower of Socrates, *Anabasis*, "On Hunting," "How to be a Good Cavalry Commander," "On Horsemanship," "Ways and Means"

Horses

Abraxas
> Telamachus' mount in Ithaca, large black Ainou stallion, son of Bronte

Aethe
> Mare of Echepolus and gift to Agamemnon to avoid conscription to Troy

Aethiops
> Telemachus' mount in Pylos, nut-brown mare given to him by Pisistratus

Arion
> Amphion's mount, black mare

Boreas
> Autolycus' mount, a large white stallion

Bronte
> Nut brown Ainou mare on Ithaca, gift to Telemachus from King Nestor

Eous
> Mare, dark coated offspring of Bronte

Podargus
> Mare, offspring of Eous, ridden by Heraclide trooper in Marathon

Rhaebus
> Oxylus' gentle giant of a mount, dappled gray stallion with large fetlocks, European ancestry

Sterope
> Telemachus' mount, roan mare, offspring of Eous

Tempe
> Deiphontes' mount, bay mare with white splotches from Thessaly

Immortal Horses of Helios
> Aethops, Bronte, Eous, and Sterope; Others: Abraxas, Aethon, Phelgon, Pyrois, Therbeeo

Acknowledgments

Thanks to Johnny Selvin, Fran Furey, Peter Janke, Adam (the horseman) Selvin, Alex Selvin, Joel Selvin, Mike Staples, Annie Beckett, Jerry Immel, Doris Muscatine, Laura Glen Louis, Henry Poppic, and Dan Chao

About the Author

The Telemachia is Michael Barnes Selvin's debut novel. As a vice president in financing services, he published numerous technical works and articles on business and finance. Departing the corporate world, he returned to his abiding passion: historical fiction. He and his wife live in Berkeley and Sea Ranch, California, and on the Mediterranean in Banyuls-sur-Mer, France, where Homer resonates. Just as Telemachus and Polycasté, they feel fortunate to have raised two fine sons.

Back cover image:
The J. Paul Getty Museum, Los Angeles
Jean-Jacques David, The Return of Telemachus and Eucharis, 1818
Oil, 87 x 103 cm